Give Me A Reason

LYN GARDNER

Copyright © 2013 Lyn Gardner

All rights reserved. Except as permitted under the U.S. Copyright Act of 1976 and the United Kingdom Copyright act of 1956 and 1988. No part of this publication may be reproduced, distributed or transmitted in any form or by any means, or stored in a database or retrieval system without the prior written permission of the author.

Cover by Robin Ludwig Design Inc.
http://www.gobookcoverdesign.com

ISBN-13: 978-1-938988-40-0

(Ragz Books)

ISBN: 193898840X

Library of Congress Control Number: 2014933410

Disclaimer: This is a work of fiction. Names, characters, businesses, places, events and incidents are either the products of the author's imagination or used in a fictitious manner. Any resemblance to actual persons, living or dead, or actual events is purely coincidental.

DEDICATION

To my father, Edward...

You showed me love, and you made me smile.
You protected me as best you could,
and I cherish every memory I have of you.
I miss you, Dad. I miss your silly laugh and your funny jokes.
I miss the scent of your cologne, and the warmth of your hugs.
I wouldn't be where I am right now if it hadn't been for you,
and I want you to know that I did this for you, Dad.
I did this to prove you right.

And to God...for giving me a reason.

ACKNOWLEDGMENTS

Give Me A Reason isn't *exactly* a short story, so a tremendously large "Thank You" goes out to those who spent their days, nights *and* weekends reading my words. Some may call them betas and some may call them editors, but to me, they are much more than that. They are my friends.

So, to Susan, Marian, Mike, Joyce, Bron and Candice...I simply could not have done this without you. You kept me true.
You kept me sane. You rock!

CHAPTER ONE

She had lost track of time as she sat in the dark listening to the noise of the night. Winter was coming to an end, but like she had done every night as the months had passed, the windows were open an inch, allowing the cool dampness to invade the room and saturate her soul. She didn't mind. She had forgotten what it felt like to be warm.

She turned on the floor lamp, the bulb flickering for a moment before the connection was made, but its brightness was lost behind a shade stained with the yellowness of age. It was used, bought second-hand like the few other necessities that took up space in the tiny flat she called home. A small couch, barely large enough to hold two people, its upholstery faded and frayed just like her, sat in the middle of the room while a mismatched chair stood desolate in a corner. Purchased for the comfort of guests, it had yet to be used except for the occasional piece of clothing dropped on its lonely cushion. Books were scattered and stacked around the room, some piles neat while others leaned to the left or right, waiting for the effect of gravity to announce itself. There was no need for a bookcase, just another piece of clutter, just another problem for someone else to clean up. There wasn't a reason for buying new. Why burden someone with your belongings when it would be so much easier to discard them when you're gone?

Going into the kitchen, she switched on the light, the fluorescent lamp sputtering and groaning as it was awakened from its sleep.

Squinting at the brightness, she turned it off and took a few short steps to open the tiny fridge tucked under the counter. It was a paltry room, large enough for one, but too small for two. She liked that.

Taking a bottle from the shelf, she returned to the lounge and placed it on the coffee table, staring at its milky contents and wondering if tonight would be the night. Lighting another cigarette, she slowly exhaled and watched as the smoke floated over her head until it disappeared into the shadows. She glanced at the bottle again. Picking it up, she examined some particles that had settled to the bottom, awaiting their turn to be dissolved by the clear liquor inside. Inhaling a lungful of smoke, she carefully set the bottle down, within reach if the mood struck, but far enough away to keep it safe from harm. Opening her briefcase, she pulled out a packet of papers and took a sip from the bottle of beer she had been nursing for over an hour. As she read over the first essay, she grimaced. Her student had yet to comprehend the lessons being taught. Picking up a red pencil, she began to make notes and corrections in the margins. Taking an occasional drag from her cigarette, she worked through the small stack until all were graded and tucked safely back into her attaché.

Getting up, she went to the window to close the sash and paused for a moment to peer through the glass. Three stories above the street, she could still hear the sounds of tires against wet pavement and the occasional shout of a fond farewell as nightlife left the pubs and stumbled to find their way home. Letting out a long breath, she carried the bottles to the kitchen, throwing one away and placing the other safely back in the fridge, shaking it a few times to assist the remaining granules in their disappearance. Unbuttoning her blouse, she walked silently to the bedroom, and after tossing the shirt in the wardrobe, she pulled down the brightly-colored duvet on the bed, its vibrant hues in sharp contrast to the rest of the flat. Having spent too many nights lying awake on sheets and mattresses used by others, their bodily habits leaving stains and scents behind, this mattress and linens were purchased new. Although the sheets were now two years old and their colors were faded by washing, they still felt good to her.

As she lay in the darkness, she wondered how she could feel so lost in a space so small, but then again, she felt lost everywhere. The flat was simply a place to exist until the next day dawned, and tomorrow *would* dawn. Tomorrow she had work to do...so it wouldn't be tonight.

***

"Are you going to work all night?" he asked, stomping into the kitchen for the third time in the last hour.

"Duane, you know I start tomorrow, and I need to get my thoughts in order," she answered, looking up from her laptop.

Frowning, Duane said, "It's just that your work always seems to come first. There's never anything left for me."

"I'm sorry, but you know how I am."

"You mean a workaholic?"

"Yeah. Sorry."

"Look, I love that you're focused on this, and I love you. It's just that I've spent the last two days watching the telly, and I'm bored."

"And I want to make a good impression on my first day. I promise, once I get settled at Calloway, I'll give you all the time you need."

"I need time now, babe. I feel like I've wasted my whole weekend over here."

"Well, if I'm not mistaken, you invited yourself over here this weekend, not me."

"I didn't think I *needed* an invitation!"

Realizing she could have been more eloquent in her response, Laura rubbed the bridge of her nose, trying to think of a way to avoid yet another endless argument about her wants versus his needs.

Laura MacLeod was thirty-two years old, and although born in Scotland, she had moved to England six years earlier to take a rather lucrative teaching position at a small private academy in Surrey. She had always wanted to teach, to instill values and knowledge in youthful minds, so it was a dream come true...and the paycheck didn't hurt either. She was smart. She was young, and she was rapidly building a hefty nest egg.

During one summer break, a fellow teacher suggested that Laura join her in volunteering at a local women's prison. Although doubtful that incarcerated women would be as willing to learn as the boys behind ivy-covered walls, Laura reluctantly agreed. It was a decision that changed her life.

Having always taken great delight in educating others, it wasn't until she saw the appreciation in the eyes of the inmates that Laura realized she had found her niche. There was a profound difference between instructing children raised with silver spoons in their mouths, to enlightening women whose lives seemed to hold only despair. Before autumn arrived that year, she had left the pristine palace of expensive education, and taking a position at HMP Sturrington, Laura MacLeod entered the world of Her Majesty's Prison Service.

Laura enjoyed her time at Sturrington, as much as anyone could enjoy being locked behind thick stone walls for eight hours a day. Most of the women were eager to learn, and although there was an occasional conflict, more often than not it was just frustration on the part of the inmate. Laura could walk out of the gates every afternoon while they stayed behind, locked in their cells, with only their thoughts to keep them company. She understood that feeling all too well…that was until she met Duane York.

With a healthy bank account to back her up, Laura purchased a small home in the borough of Barnet and spent her free time renovating and decorating it to make it her own. Visiting a local nursery one weekend, she accidentally bumped into a man carrying a shallow tray of flowers, sending him and the plants to the ground. Profusely apologizing, when she offered to buy him a cup of coffee while waiting in the queue to pay for their purchases, he agreed, and one week later, Duane York called to ask her out on a date.

Laura's attraction to Duane wasn't instantaneous, but like the flowers she planted around her house, it grew over time. He was an attractive man, a half foot taller than her five-foot-four-inch frame, and although slender, years of playing football with his mates had afforded him a workout that defined his muscles quite nicely.

It was a comfortable, slow-moving relationship, but when he had proposed to her a few months earlier, Laura was stunned. They were good together. In and out of bed, they were good together, but marriage meant love, and Laura wasn't sure she really loved Duane. She liked him. She liked him a lot, but a commitment of that magnitude needed more than just like, it needed love, so she told him no. Heartbroken and angry, he left her house that night saying he'd never return.

At first, it was odd not having Duane underfoot, rummaging through her pantry for nibbles or relaxing in the lounge while she fixed dinner. However, as each day passed, Laura realized that it was nice to do what she wanted *when* she wanted to do it. It was refreshing to open the refrigerator and still find it stocked with what she craved, and when she came home after a long, hard day, her house was exactly in the order she had left it that morning. There were no surprises anymore, and for the first week, it was a nice change, but by the start of the second, Laura began to miss having Duane around. She missed his laugh and his warmth, and the way they'd snuggle on the sofa together, watching the telly as they talked about their days. She missed making meals for two and evenings in the pub with friends, and she missed the love they made, even though she wasn't sure, at least for her, love had anything to do with it. So, when Duane called to apologize ten days after he walked out of her house, Laura accepted it and things returned to the way they were.

During those two weeks of solitude, Laura received a call from an old friend. John Canfield was the former governor of HMP Sturrington, but he had resigned his position at the prison two years before, deciding that he no longer wanted to live ten hours a day behind locked doors. Still passionate about helping those who could not yet help themselves, he had accepted a position as the director of one of the largest bail hostels in London whose primary focus was on education.

Two days after receiving John's phone call, Laura sat in a bustling coffee shop listening as the man across the table chattered on about Calloway House. Not just a hostel to spend the night, the week or the month, Calloway offered its occupants more than just a roof over their heads and a curfew. With the current curriculum, the residents could learn to read, to write, to balance a checkbook and even fix a car if they so desired. It gave them hope and with it, self-worth.

Over their second cup of coffee, John explained that he currently had a staff of four full-time and two part-time teachers, but he needed someone to oversee not only them, but also the course schedules. He needed a person with focus, steadfast in their belief about what learning could accomplish. He needed someone who could follow rules, adhere to the strict guidelines set by the Department of Education and Skills, and he needed someone who would be willing to take the steps necessary in order to insure that Calloway would continue to receive funding. In other words, he needed Laura MacLeod.

When they had first met at Sturrington, although impressed by the petite woman with the green eyes and infectious smile, John believed that her enthusiasm to teach convicts would be short-lived. He could not have been more wrong. While many a teacher had turned cynical behind the stone walls and barred windows of the prison, Laura had not. She thrived on teaching those who craved to be taught. She adored her students and they adored her, and it didn't take long before Laura MacLeod became one of John's most trusted and valued educators. When funds were allocated to increase his staff at Calloway by one, John picked up the phone and called Laura.

Before they finished their third cup of coffee, Laura accepted the position, and when Duane York once again became part of her life a few days later, their already fragile relationship began to show even more cracks.

"Laura!"

Startled from her thoughts by Duane's outburst, she looked up from her notes. "I'm sorry, what?"

"You haven't heard one bloody word I've said, have you?" he shouted, grabbing his jacket. "That's just great!"

Flinching as the front door slammed shut, she sighed. "Shit."

***

After parking in an area marked For Employees Only, Laura climbed out of the car, gathered her briefcase, laptop and lunch, and turned around to gaze at the six-story building in front of her. Located on the outskirts of London, Calloway had been converted from an old apartment building to a halfway house nearly twelve years earlier. Showing its age in its architecture, the brick facade was broken up by tall, narrow windows, all of which were capped with thick pediments of stone, and along the roof line was a bulky cornice supported by brackets jutting out every few feet. Slightly ominous in its appearance, Laura took a deep breath as she headed to the entrance. Pulling open the heavy door, she walked inside.

Well aware that if Laura MacLeod had a fault, it was one based on time, John Canfield had been patiently waiting in a doorway off the entry. Watching as his new hire walked into the lobby, before she could say anything to the elderly man sitting behind the front desk, John called out, "Glad to see you could make it."

Looking in his direction, Laura smiled. Pushing six-foot-six, John Canfield was in his late fifties with very little hair left to speak of, but his cheerful personality and boyish charm subtracted years from his age. Gangly and soft-spoken, while they had only worked together at Sturrington for a short time, it was long enough for Laura to see John as more than just a friend, and only slightly less than a father.

"Sorry. Am I that late?" she said with a weak grin, shrugging her laptop bag off her shoulder.

"Only a few minutes," he said, taking the satchel from her hands. "Come on. Let me show you around."

Before starting the tour, John quickly introduced Laura to the old man sitting behind the desk. As with most bail hostels, or Approved Premises as they were now being called, several of the residents had strict curfews. During the week, it was Martin's job to keep track of who came and went, while at night and on the weekends, other retired prison officers took his place.

Rail thin and with his scraggy face displaying a two-day-old stubble of stark white hair, Martin grumbled a curt hello before looking back at the daily tabloid he held in his withered hands.

Rolling his eyes at the watchman's gruffness, John led Laura through a large doorway to the right of the entry as he explained that the two lower levels of Calloway held the staff offices, classrooms and community areas while the upper four floors housed the residents. Believing that part of their rehabilitation involved giving the women their privacy, although he and a few other employees were allowed to visit those who lived above their heads, he made it clear that unless she was invited, there was no need for Laura to travel higher than the second floor.

Nodding in agreement, it wasn't until they came to a stop just inside the doorway when Laura took in her surroundings. Three large sofas filled the middle of the room while a pool table stood in one corner with a ping-pong table in another. Vending machines were lined up along the back wall, and to her left, from floor to ceiling was a battered bookcase, its shelves dotted with a sparse collection of paperbacks.

Going over to it, Laura tilted her head to scan some of the titles and was surprised to see that most were fiction, and by the appearance of their covers, they had been read hundreds of times. "These have seen better days," she said.

"Yes, they have," John said, motioning for her to follow as he walked from the recreation area. "Unfortunately, most of the funding we receive has to be used to cover the cost of school books, food and salaries, so when it comes to the non-essentials, it's up to us to find them. All the books in there were either donated or left behind by someone when they moved out. Part of our job is to drum up more donations, so I hope you're ready to spend a great deal of your time on the phone."

Smiling, Laura said, "I am."

"Good."

"John?"

"Yes?"

"Where is everyone?" she asked, glancing around the empty lobby. "I know you told me that the residents had to have jobs or be in class, but I expected to see at least a few stragglers."

"Not a chance," John said, leading Laura to a corridor on the other side of the room. "Most of the women here know that we offer a hell of a lot more than most bail hostels. We're giving them a free education and a chance at a better life if they apply themselves, so most take our rules fairly seriously."

Walking down the expansive hallway, John stopped in front of a desk tucked into a small alcove. Sitting behind it was a woman in her mid-fifties with strawberry blonde hair.

"Laura MacLeod, let me introduce you to our office manager, administrative assistant and saving grace, Irene Dixon," John said. "Without her, I'd be lost."

Dismissing his compliment with a shake of her head, Irene extended her hand. "Welcome to Calloway House, Miss MacLeod."

"Call me Laura, and it's very nice to meet you. John's told me a bit about you. He says that you run Calloway, but they gave him the title."

Laughing, Irene's cheeks turned a soft shade of pink. "Oh, well, I don't know about that. I just try to do my best."

The phone on her desk rang and Irene excused herself to answer it, allowing John to continue the tour. Continuing past a few doors, when he came to one opposite another stairway, he opened it and ushered Laura inside.

"This is your office," he said, adjusting the blinds to let the sunlight wash over the room.

"Wow!" Laura said, her eyes opening to their fullest at the sight of the spacious office. About to express her delight, she stopped when the room was filled with the sound of chirping.

Quickly pulling his mobile from his pocket, John silenced the alarm. "Sorry, but I've got an appointment in a few minutes," he said, placing her laptop case on the desk. "Why don't we meet in my office at noon, and I'll introduce you to the rest of the staff and finish the tour. Okay?"

"That works for me," Laura said. "See you later."

As soon as John left, Laura returned her attention to her new office. In addition to the massive desk opposite the door, fronted by two upholstered chairs, several file cabinets filled one wall, and a small leather sofa ran along another. With the slightest hint of fresh paint in the air, Laura assumed the light mauve coating on the walls was new, and the wood flooring appeared to have been scrubbed and polished until it shined.

"I'm sorry to interrupt, but these just came for you," Irene said as she walked in carrying a vase filled with roses.

"Oh my," Laura said, blushing slightly at the amount of long-stemmed reds. "They're lovely."

"Yes, they are." Placing the vase on the desk, Irene leaned closer to inhale the fragrance, but before she could take another sniff, the phone in the outer office began to ring. "Oh, I'd better get that. Call me if you need anything."

"I will. Thanks," Laura said, plucking the card from the roses. Reading the words inside, her face spread into a smile.

Good luck on your first day. I know you'll be brilliant! Love, Duane

***

Before she left Calloway that night, John had introduced Laura to four of the members of the teaching staff, explaining that the missing part-time teacher was at his regular job, while the other full-time teacher had been unavoidably detained.

The first to meet the new department head was Susan Grant. A tall woman with blonde hair, Susan taught mathematics and accounting skills to their residents, and upon being introduced to Laura, she warmly shook her hand and welcomed her on board.

Next was Jack Sturges. An imposing figure of a man, although not terribly tall, he was broad-shouldered and brooding. He sported a flattop crew cut of salt-and-pepper hair, and adding to his menacing appearance was a jagged scar running down the right side of his face. Responsible for teaching history and languages, Laura was impressed to hear him move from Spanish to Italian to French and then to German effortlessly.

When she was introduced to Charlie Cummings, it was all Laura could do to keep her smile to a minimum. A portly man in his mid-forties, without the bright-red suspenders holding up his trousers, she feared that they would hit the floor in an instant. Hired on as a handyman, when John noticed the women asking Charlie questions about home maintenance and the like, he convinced the contractor to add teaching to his repertoire. Now, two days a week, he instructed the ladies of the house in basic home and automotive repair…and he enjoyed every minute of it.

Last was Bryan O'Neill, the youngest member of the teaching staff. Dressed in jeans and a red polo shirt, he shook Laura's hand eagerly, his grin toothy and his blue eyes smiling back at her like a puppy awaiting a treat. In charge of the classes on computer technology and sciences, Bryan had been handpicked by John when they had met at a teaching conference one year earlier. Fresh out of university and unemployed, Bryan had attended almost every seminar given that week and John had taken notice. Even though the young man's experience was lacking, his dedication to his profession was not, and before the conference had ended, Bryan had a job.

In the early hours of the evening, Laura left work, but only after filling her attaché with various reports and schedules that would keep her awake until late that night. As she grabbed her teachers' personnel files and stuffed them in her case, she wondered why she could only find five.

CHAPTER TWO

By mid-week, Laura MacLeod was awash in paperwork. Trying to find some rhyme or reason in the filing system, old files and new ones were now scattered about her office as if a tornado had just visited.

Hearing a knock on her door, Laura shouted, "Come in," as she continued to sort through paperwork, only stopping when she heard the door open. Looking over her shoulder, she saw John grinning back at her.

Puffing out a bit of air to blow a strand of hair from her cheek, she said, "Hiya, John."

"So, you making sense of all this yet?"

"Give me another week and then ask me that question."

"I heard you met Christopher yesterday. How'd it go?"

"Oh, he's a sweetie," she said, standing straight. "And I'm told the women love him."

"Yes, they do. He's quite a charmer, that one."

Pausing for a moment as she remembered the soft-voiced man with curly blond hair, she said, "So, is he as gay as I think he is?"

"I believe they call it flaming," John said with a hearty guffaw. "Luckily, no one here seems to care, and the students absolutely adore his wit and his cooking skills."

Dusting off her hands, Laura said, "John, when am I going to meet...ah..." Pushing some files aside, Laura looked at the notes she had written the night before. "Antoinette Vaughn?"

Thinking for a moment, he asked, "You have any plans after work today?"

"Nothing comes to mind. Why?"

"Well, Connie is out of town visiting one of the kids. How about you and I go get something to eat and I'll fill you in?"

"Sounds like a date to me."

***

As their dinner plates were cleared from the table, Laura leaned back in her chair. The evening had been pleasant, filled with easy conversation and a delicious meal, but through it all the subject of her missing teacher had yet to be brought up. Eyeing her boss, Laura said, "Okay, John, you've stalled long enough. Tell me about Antoinette Vaughn."

Letting out a heavy sigh, he signaled the waiter for more coffee and then returned his gaze to Laura. "She's probably one of the most gifted teachers I've ever known," he said quietly. "She has the ability to light a spark in a student, and like a wildfire, it spreads through the room, and before too long, everyone is chiming in on whatever it is they're discussing. It's really quite amazing to watch. The women flock to her classes, and if there's one person in Calloway that has the respect of each and every resident, it's Toni Vaughn."

Something in the tone of John's voice piqued Laura's interest. "And why's that?"

"Because she was once one of them."

Raising an eyebrow, Laura processed the information. "What was she in prison for?"

Knowing that when he hired Laura, they would eventually have this conversation, there was no reason for John to hesitate any longer. His eyes met hers, and in a tone filled with sorrow, he said, "Murder."

Before Laura could say a word, John reached down into his briefcase and extracted a manila folder which he slid across the table. Getting to his feet, he said, "Why don't you give that a read while I visit the gents?"

As John walked away, Laura opened the file and lost herself in what it contained. Filled with information on Antoinette Vaughn's background, education and work history, before Laura reached the last page, she was impressed...and she was confused.

A short time later, John returned to the table. Noticing Laura's slack-jawed expression, he grinned. "Not what you were expecting was it?"

"No," she said, closing the folder. "Please don't take this the wrong way, but I find it hard to believe that with her credentials, she'd want to work at Calloway. I would think that at least one university in this country would give her another chance."

"There are dozens who tried to hire her, but she refused them all." Taking a quick gulp of coffee, he leaned toward Laura, keeping his voice low as he began to explain the history of one Antoinette Vaughn. "Do you remember...well, let's see...about six years ago, a story in the paper about a professor arrested for murder?"

Shaking her head, Laura said, "No, but I had just moved here and was busy trying to get settled. I honestly don't think I even looked at a newspaper for months."

"Well, as you've already read in that file, Toni came from an affluent family and was quite the prodigy, finishing two years ahead of her class before going to university. By the time she was twenty-five, she was a published author *and* a respected professor at one of the finest universities this country has to offer. It didn't seem like anything could stop her, but a few months after her second book hit the stands, her life took an unexpected turn."

"How so?"

"She received a call late one night from a close friend who owned a club in Stoke Newington. Apparently, the woman's car wouldn't start, and since she needed to go to the night depository to drop off that day's earnings, and didn't feel safe calling a taxi, she called a friend instead. Toni drove to the club, but when she went inside, she found the woman being assaulted by a man. Toni apparently tried to pull him away, but he was too strong, so she picked up a chair and struck him with it. It shattered, and a part of it lodged in his neck."

"Jesus," Laura said under her breath.

"Toni tried to stop the bleeding, and her friend called for help, but by the time anyone got there, the man had already bled out. They gave the local constabulary their story, but when the police found the surveillance video machine from the club empty, and it was discovered that the dead man was an off-duty copper who had visited the club several times for possible drug violations, things seemed to go from bad to worse. Toni was arrested the next morning, and before the year was out, she was sentenced to life for murdering Harlan Leavitt."

"Life? Then how did she get out of prison?"

After signaling the waiter to bring yet more coffee, John said, "A little over two years ago, a police officer by the name of Gordon Jacoby was killed in a car accident while driving home from work. When his supervisor went to clean out his locker, he found two video tapes, and not knowing their contents, he took it upon himself to watch them. They were the missing tapes from the night Leavitt was killed."

"But how—"

"Jacoby had been Leavitt's partner, and he was one of the first officers to arrive that night. He apparently stole the tapes in order to protect Leavitt's reputation and just never got rid of them. Needless to say, they proved Toni's innocence, but unfortunately, the damage had already been done."

"What do you mean?"

"She was in Thornbridge," he said quietly.

Cocking her head to the side, Laura said, "I'm sorry, John, but I've never heard of a prison called Thornbridge."

"Actually, I'm not surprised," he said, leaning back in his chair. "It was a medium-sized facility in the north of England that was opened in the late sixties, and then privatized about twenty years ago. It was meant to house only the criminally insane, the women deemed too unstable to be among the general prison population, but Fagan and Dent had other ideas."

"Fagan and Dent?"

"The company that ran it."

"Oh."

"Anyway, the more prisoners you have the more money you make, and since Thornbridge had a lot of empty cells and our prisons were overflowing, Fagan and Dent began taking in the worst of the worst. It was a maximum security facility, and what better place to send the dregs of society than to a prison so far away that they could easily be forgotten. Nobody cared about the women incarcerated in that place, so eventually Thornbridge slipped under the radar."

"In what way?" Laura asked cautiously.

"I'm afraid Thornbridge became the last bastion for those with the spare-the-rod, spoil-the-prisoner mentality. Since no one was watching them, the guards could do whatever they liked."

"I don't like the sound of this, John. How long did it go on?"

"Too long," he said, hanging his head. Thinking back to the reports he had read, he closed his eyes and tried to rid himself of the images, but they were there forever. Taking a deep breath, he looked up and offered Laura a sympathetic grin. "Where was I?"

"You said it had gone on too long."

"Right," he said with a nod. "Well, due to their sentences or mental instability, it was rare that an inmate ever left Thornbridge, but there were a few. One woman...oh what the hell was her name?" he grumbled, pausing to take a sip of coffee. "Oh, yes...Lucy. Lucy, that was it. This woman, Lucy, was visiting her probation officer and during their meeting, he noticed some scars on her arms. He mentioned them, and she told him that she had been punished by the guards for something or another. Now Lucy, poor thing, wasn't the sharpest tool in the shed, and she had no idea that the *punishment* she had received wasn't *normal* prison policy. Fortunately, her probation officer knew better. He informed the authorities immediately, and as they say, the snowball started rolling down the hill."

"What happened?"

"An undercover officer was sent inside, and in less than a month, the doors to Thornbridge were closed. Many of the officers were arrested and are now serving time in prison for their crimes, and those that aren't...well, they're probably stocking shelves in your local supermarket."

Although she was afraid to ask the next question, she did. "What kind of crimes?"

John's shoulders slumped. "Extended periods of time in solitary and—"

"What do you mean *extended*?"

"I heard weeks, possibly months."

"Oh, my God..."

"And there were beatings, many of which ended with the prisoner in the infirmary."

"Jesus Christ!" Laura blurted. "How could this happen, John? There are monitoring boards for Christ's sake, not to mention privatized prisons are supposed to be inspected!"

"Laura, like I said, Thornbridge was in the middle of nowhere. Since those boards are made up of locals, and most of the prison staff lived in the area, it wasn't long before *that* board consisted of nothing but friends and family of the officers who worked behind those walls. And as for the inspections, it was so remote, they didn't happen that often, and when they did, they were scheduled. It's easy to make it appear that everything's the way it should be when you have ample time to do so."

"Okay, fine, but that still doesn't explain why someone like Antoinette Vaughn would end up in a place like that. There's nothing in this file about her ever being violent."

"Originally, she was sentenced to Sutton Hall, but within a few months of her arrival, the Home Office began getting reports from a guard over there stating that she was disruptive, argumentative *and* violent. After the fourth report, she was deemed unsafe for the general population and was immediately transported to Thornbridge."

"How long was she there?"

"Almost four years. The information about her innocence came to light only a day or two before they closed Thornbridge, so she was there until the end. She was put into a holding facility for a few weeks while they sorted out the details, and then she was given a full pardon and set free."

"How do you know all of this?"

"When she arrived for her first day of work, she had a friend with her, and after we got Toni settled in her classroom, her friend and I had a chat. She filled me in on some of the details, and the rest I already knew from working at Sturrington."

"At Sturrington? I don't understand."

"In my position as governor there, I was privy to most of the reports that were funneled through the Home Office, and when I read the one about Thornbridge, it made me ill. It's the reason I left. I didn't want to work *behind* the walls any longer. I needed to do more. I wanted to open some doors instead of locking them all the time, and what better way to do that than to work in a place like Calloway."

"Okay, so you tracked down Miss Vaughn and hired her, but that still doesn't explain why I haven't met her yet."

"I didn't track her down," John said, shaking his head. "As fate would have it, my first priority when I came onboard was to hire replacements for two of the teachers who had left, so I placed an advertisement and Toni answered it a few weeks later. Things were quite hectic back then. New job, new responsibilities and we were understaffed, so I honestly didn't remember who she was until after the interview, and to tell you the truth, I almost *didn't* hire her."

"What!"

"Even though her credentials were impeccable, all during the interview, she never once made eye contact. She stared at the floor, the desk...anywhere but back at me, and even though I know that some people are nervous when it comes to applying for a job, she was downright terrified. You could see it in her posture, the way she set her jaw, the way her hands were clenched in fists, and she was so introverted that she could barely answer anything I asked in a sentence consisting of more than just a few words."

"Then why hire her?"

"To this day, I have no idea why, but after the interview, I took her on a tour of Calloway. I already knew that I wasn't going to offer her a job. It was ludicrous to imagine that someone so withdrawn could ever teach reading and writing, let alone literature, but nevertheless, I showed her around. When we got to one of the classrooms, we walked in on a discussion that some of the women were having about a book they were reading. Don't ask me what it was called, but as Toni and I stood there listening to their conversation, I noticed excitement in her eyes, and before I knew it, she had immersed herself in the discussion."

"Just like that?"

"It was quite remarkable, actually," John said, his eyes creasing at the corners. "This reclusive creature, who moments before could barely utter two words, had changed into this brilliant educator. Sitting on the edge of a desk, motioning with her hands, she was so passionate about the discussion they were having, and within a few minutes, I knew I had found my teacher."

"So, I'm guessing she's still reclusive?"

"Yes, I'm afraid so. She doesn't associate with any of us, and her classes start and finish earlier than all the others."

"I don't understand. Why?"

"In the classroom, Toni's comfortable and confident, at least with her students. However, among the teachers and especially strangers, she simply can't handle it. Therefore, I arranged for certain liberties when it comes to Toni. By allowing her classes to start earlier and end sooner, she can come and go when the halls are nearly empty. It seemed a small price to pay to have someone like her on our staff."

"Are there any other liberties that I should know about?"

"I'm the only one she allows to monitor her class."

"What?" Laura said, leaning forward in her chair. "John, as head of the department—"

"I know what you're going to say, Laura, and you're right, but Toni is a tremendous teacher, and I don't want to lose her."

"And you think she'll quit if I try to do my job?"

"Honestly, I don't know, but the woman is frightened of her own shadow, and I don't want to inflict any more harm on her. I have to ask you to take it very, *very* slowly where Toni is concerned. I promise that I'll arrange for you two to meet soon, but as for you doing your job, as you put it, that will take a bit of time, I'm afraid."

"What about the monthly reports?"

"For the time being, I'll continue to monitor her classes, just like I've been doing."

"If she's this scared, why does she trust you?"

"I have no idea."

***

On Friday, John Canfield came to work an hour earlier than scheduled and headed to the second floor. Lightly tapping on the doorframe before entering, he smiled at Toni when she looked up from her desk, and a tiny grin of acknowledgement crossed her face.

"Good morning, Toni."

"Hi, John," she said quietly, glancing down at the papers in front of her.

"I'm sure you've heard by now that we have a new department head."

Nodding in reply, Toni rearranged some papers and then picked up her coffee cup, her hand trembling slightly as she lifted it to her lips.

"She wants to meet you."

Once again, she nodded an acknowledgment, but said nothing.

"I thought I'd bring her up next week some time, so that could happen."

In a whisper that was barely audible, Toni said, "I suppose I don't have a choice."

His heart heavy with sadness for the broken woman, John walked over and knelt by her desk. "Toni, you know if I didn't need to do this, I wouldn't. She's a nice woman with lots of good ideas. Just give her a chance. Okay?"

Toni slowly raised her eyes and stared blankly at the man next to her. "Sure...like I said, I don't have a choice."

***

Krista Nielson parked her car and glanced out the window at the rundown apartment building in front of her. It was just another Friday in a long line of Fridays, and tonight would be no different than it had been for the past two years. She had visited the local supermarket and picked up the usual things, just enough to last a week, nothing more and nothing less. Going against the rules, she had also tossed in two new items, but they were small, and Kris hoped they would go unnoticed until she left the flat.

She knew the rest of her short time here would be the same as the groceries, repetitive and limited. With her best friend's identity all but erased by prison walls and corporal punishment, their conversation would be cordial yet stilted. It pained her to see Toni this way, but unlike all the others who had walked away from the cold, empty woman who lived three floors up, Krista could not. Until her dying day, she would never give up on the woman who had saved her life.

Filling her arms with bags, Kris walked into the building and climbed the three flights of stairs, wishing that once she arrived at 3-D, she could playfully joke about the tiresome ascent, but she didn't dare. She knew she couldn't cross that line because it would give Toni a chance to send her away. Along with everything else, Toni's sense of humor had disappeared.

Arriving at Toni's door, she tapped on it with her foot, and seconds later it was opened by her tall, dark-haired friend, dressed as she always was, in clothes that were worn, faded and two sizes too large. Stepping aside, Toni allowed Krista to enter.

"Hi, Toni," Kris said, leaning over to kiss the woman on the cheek, and even though Toni backed away, Kris followed until her lips softly grazed Toni's face. "How you doing?"

"I'm okay," she said, her voice still as dull and lifeless as it had been since the day Krista drove her away from the holding facility.

As Toni aimlessly headed back to the lounge, Kris went to the kitchen to put away the groceries. Emptying her meager purchases into the cupboard, she quickly stashed the new items behind the old and opened the refrigerator. Noticing that it only contained beer, water and one bottle of vodka, she called out, "Did you eat tonight?"

Not hearing a response, Kris checked to make sure there was more beer in the crate on the floor and then walked into the lounge to check on Toni. Finding her sitting on the sofa, looking through a stack of papers, Kris repeated, "Toni, did you eat tonight."

"I had a sandwich delivered," Toni said, without looking up.

Aware that the woman could easily go without food for more than just one day, Kris glanced at the door. There were three restaurants in the area that delivered and long ago, Kris had made arrangements with all of them. Explaining that her friend was a shut-in, she instructed them to knock four times and Toni would slide a brown envelope containing payment under the door. Once they received their money, the food was left in the hallway, and Toni would retrieve it, but only after she watched from her window to make sure they had left. Noticing the money envelope, along with a take-away menu sitting near the door, Kris breathed easier. At least she was eating.

"I checked the beer. You have about a dozen bottles left so I'll bring you over a new crate early next week. Okay?"

"I only drink one a night. You don't have to make a special trip."

"I don't mind," Kris said, sitting on the arm of the sofa. "Toni, I was thinking...maybe we could go out and see about getting you some new clothes."

"I don't need anything new. These are fine."

"Well, they are getting a bit worn, don't you think?"

Raising her eyes to glare at the woman, Toni said, "I don't *need* anything new, Krista. We've gone through this before."

The room went silent, and chewing on her lip for a moment, Kris said, "Hey, I have an idea. Antonio's is right down the street. How about I order a pizza, and we have dinner together. Like old times. I'll even buy a bottle of wine. How's that?"

"I told you, I already had a sandwich."

"Oh, right," Kris said. Noticing the pile of papers on the coffee table, she said, "It looks like you have a busy weekend planned."

"Yeah. I have essays from two classes to grade. I need to hand them back on Monday."

Breathing a silent sigh of relief, Kris tried to think of something else to say. Years before, they could spend hours talking about a recent bestseller, a new shop or people making headlines, but that was no longer the case. The books scattered around were old and used, and although popular in their day, Krista hadn't read any of them in years. Toni refused to have a television or radio in the apartment, and whenever Krista brought over a magazine or a newspaper, it left when she did. The world held no interest for Toni any longer, and she showed no curiosity over technology or the latest novel to hit the stands. The classics were safe, providing a warm cocoon where she could hide amongst the words she had read a hundred times before, allowing her to forget, if only for a moment, the ugliness that lay beyond the door to her flat.

Knowing that their limited conversation had come to an end, Kris reached out and touched Toni's sleeve, the simple action causing the woman to jerk away. Refusing to allow her sadness to show, Kris said softly, "I know I say this every week, but if you ever need anything, if you ever just want to talk...I'm here for you."

"I know you are," Toni whispered.

Looking into Toni's dark brown eyes, Krista felt her emotions begin to rise to the surface, remembering a time when those eyes, now dismal and empty, once sparkled with life, love and mischief.

"I love you, Toni," Kris said as she walked to the door, needing to leave before she broke down like she always did. "Please call me if you need anything...anything at all."

A few moments later, Toni murmured, "See ya, Krista."

She hadn't noticed that her friend had already left.

***

With Duane out of town visiting his parents, Laura spent most of the weekend going through paperwork and getting a grasp on the monthly reports, so by the time she returned to work on Monday, she was raring to go. Even though there seemed to be a mountain of forms and requirements to adhere to, she quickly came up with a schedule that would allow her ample time every month to monitor the teachers, submit her reports and bring a few of her own ideas to Calloway House.

On Wednesday morning, as Laura sat in her office drinking her third cup of coffee, John appeared in the doorway. "Good morning."

"Hiya, John."

"Do you have a few minutes?"

"Sure, what's up?" Laura said, putting aside her paperwork.

"I thought it was time that you meet Toni."

Instantly grinning, Laura popped out of her chair, and quickly followed John out of the room and up the stairs.

Pausing once they got to Toni's classroom, John said, "Laura, don't expect too much, all right? I mean, I doubt that she'll say more than a few words, if that."

Laura was nervous, and she didn't know why. The woman she was about to meet technically worked for her, so taking a deep breath, she straightened her suit jacket. "I understand, John. It'll be fine."

"Good."

Hearing the hushed voices in the hallway, Toni recognized one as John Canfield's and immediately knew that she was about to meet the new head of her department. Sighing, she took a few deep breaths to steady her nerves. She hated this...this requirement of life that she couldn't avoid. Meeting people, strangers until they weren't, but they were all strangers to her. She didn't trust them. She couldn't trust them. They would hurt her. Maybe not with a fist or a foot or a belt, but somehow, in some way, they would hurt her.

Entering the room, Laura saw her sitting at the desk, and while most people would have looked up to acknowledge their visitors, Toni Vaughn did not. Several moments passed and Laura began to feel awkward, unsure as to why John hadn't said anything and the woman behind the desk hadn't moved an inch. Biting her lip, Laura began to take another step forward when John reached out and touched her arm. Shaking his head, he whispered, "Wait."

Another minute passed before Laura heard the screech of the wooden chair across the tile floor, and she watched as the apprehensive woman stood and took a few hesitant steps toward them.

Since their discussion the week before, Laura had built an image of this woman in her mind. She believed that Toni Vaughn would appear hard and much older than her age, downtrodden by her time in prison and the brutalities inflicted upon her, but Laura couldn't have been more wrong.

Appearing to be nearly six feet in height, with short black hair that had a style all its own, Toni Vaughn was an attractive woman. Although gaunt, her features were striking and natural. Her jaw was strong and her nose narrow, and while dark circles appeared under her eyes, they couldn't offset the whole. Even though John had explained that the years behind bars had taken their toll on her psyche, as far as Laura could tell, they had done little to affect Antoinette Vaughn's beauty.

"Toni, I'd like to introduce you to our new Education Administrator, Laura MacLeod."

Laura watched as the woman dipped her head a millimeter, but continued to stare at the floor.

"Laura, this is Toni Vaughn, one of our most popular teachers."

Extending her hand, Laura smiled. "Nice to meet you, Toni."

Taking a quick step backward, Toni shoved her hands in her pockets. Refusing to look in Laura's direction, instead she raised her eyes to glare at John. Abruptly turning her back on both of them, she walked to the window and stared out the glass, desperately trying to hold it together. They needed to leave. They needed to leave *now*.

With a frown, John motioned toward the corridor, and they left the room without saying a word. As soon as John closed the door to Toni's classroom, Laura asked, "Did I do something wrong?"

"No," he groaned, pinching the bridge of his nose. "But I did."

"What do you mean?"

"I forgot to tell you. Toni doesn't like to be touched."

CHAPTER THREE

Four weeks later, Laura MacLeod couldn't have been happier about her decision to work at Calloway House. Except for those taught by Toni Vaughn, she had managed to monitor every class and found herself duly impressed by the patience, intelligence and fortitude of her staff.

Seeing Susan Grant heading outside for a smoke, Laura grabbed her coat and followed her out the rear exit of the building.

"Hard day?" Laura asked as she sat down next to Susan on the step.

Chuckling softly, Susan said, "I've got one woman who can't grasp addition sitting next to another who could do calculus in her sleep. You tell me."

Laura knew all too well that while all the residents at Calloway had spent time in prison, that's where their similarities ended. A melting pot of ethnic backgrounds, incomes, educations, religions and mental aptitudes, they presented the teaching staff with a smorgasbord of challenges.

"Sounds difficult," Laura said.

"You think?"

"What can I do?"

"Oh, Laura, there's nothing you can do. There aren't enough hours in the day to have classes for each level, at least not until John can scrounge up enough funding to hire a few more teachers. Until then, we just have to muddle through."

"And make sure *you* don't run out of cigarettes," Laura said, watching as Susan lit her second.

"Yeah, that too," Susan said with a laugh. "So, how about you? How are you doing?"

"Well, the paperwork was a little overwhelming at first, but I'm getting the hang of it."

"I heard that John introduced you to Toni," Susan said, taking another drag of her smoke.

"Yeah, last month."

"What do you think of her?"

Tilting her head, Laura asked, "Are you asking me about her teaching abilities or about *her*?"

"If you ask any one of those women inside as to whom their favorite teacher is, Toni would win hands down. We all know that. I'm talking about the woman, *not* the teacher."

Thinking for a moment, Laura shrugged. "Honestly, I don't know what to say. When we met, she didn't say a word, and then I tried to shake her hand—"

"Didn't John tell you that she doesn't—"

"He forgot."

"Ouch."

"Yeah," Laura said with a sigh.

"You know, every time I see her, she just seems so lost, so hurt. It's almost painful—"

"Wait," Laura said. "I've been here over five weeks and the only time I've seen her was when I was in her classroom."

Holding up her pack of smokes, Susan said, "I occasionally bump into her out here."

"Does she talk to you?"

"No," Susan said, shaking her head. "On second thought, there've been a few hellos over the past two years, but nothing more than that. Honestly, Laura, I think she's terrified of everything and everyone. Absolutely, positively terrified."

"Bastards," Laura said under her breath.

"You got that right."

"You know about...about what happened to her?"

"Given her background, John wasn't sure about her...um...her *stability*, so he pulled us all aside one day and told us about what she had gone through. Of course, he didn't go into details, and seeing the way she is, I honestly don't think I wanted to hear any."

"She just seems so fragile," Laura said.

"At first, I tried to help her," Susan said, taking a drag of her cigarette. "I mean, she must have been put through hell to end up like that, and I thought the least I could do was to try to become her friend. So, I'd stop by her classroom to chat, and I even invited her to the pub a few times, but she always refused, and eventually I stopped trying. There are a lot of wounded people in this world, including many of our students, so I decided to stop trying to help someone who obviously didn't want my help, and moved on to others who did."

Hearing the bell signaling the start of the last class of the day, they both walked back inside. Going their separate ways, Susan climbed the stairs and Laura headed to her office, but when she saw John at the end of the hall, she called out to get his attention. Jogging down the corridor to catch up to her long-legged boss, she said, "I just wanted to remind you that I'm going to need those reports for Toni Vaughn's classes. They're due next week."

"Which ones do I owe you?"

"Remedial reading and the university-level creative writing course."

Quickly stepping into his office, he returned with a file. "This is the one for the writing course, and I'll get you the other one early next week. Will that work?"

"Absolutely," she said, taking the file. "Have a good weekend."

"You, too."

Returning to her office, Laura glanced at her watch and then at her desk. Grinning, she gathered her belongings, filled her attaché with work she could do from home, shut off the light and left. For the first time in weeks, she would get home before the sun went down.

***

Irene looked up when she heard the sound of heels tapping down the hallway. As Laura came into view, dismissing the usual morning greetings, Irene said, "Silly man should have known better than to try to trim the tree himself."

"I think that falls under the heading of hindsight," Laura said, glancing at the mail piled on Irene's desk. "I hope you know I'm going to be depending on you a lot in the coming weeks."

"Of course. I'll do whatever I can. Have you come up with a plan of attack?"

"Well, I'll need to see his calendar, and then we can start rearranging some appointments."

"I know which ones are the most important, so let me get his diary, and I'll make some notes. That way, we'll know who to cancel and who to coddle," Irene said with a smirk, knowing all too well the politics that went along with funding.

"Good idea," Laura said, heading to her office. "I'll check my schedule and start making calls."

Two days earlier, while enjoying a quiet Saturday night with Duane, Laura received a phone call from Constance Canfield telling her that John, whilst trying to trim a tree, had fallen from the ladder and broken his leg. His prognosis was good, but until the hip-to-toe cast was removed, returning to work was impossible. After visiting John in the hospital and being told she was now in charge, Laura spent the rest of the weekend making notes, checking her schedule and calling her staff to inform them of John's accident, leaving Duane to fend for himself. He was *not* happy.

With Irene's help, before she left work Monday evening, Laura knew what the rest of the week would bring, and it wasn't good. Having already cancelled all the appointments she felt were inconsequential, when she looked at what was left, Laura sighed. It was going to be a very, very long week.

***

Four days later, Laura looked at the reports piled on her desk, and debated only for an instant before stuffing them into her briefcase and grabbing her jacket. Having spent the whole week coming in early and staying late, she was finally making a dent in the combined workload. Sorting out John's share of the monthly reports had taken her the entire day, and even though there was still more to be done, as far as Laura was concerned, it could be done at home. The idea of having her tired feet propped on a pillow with a glass of wine at the ready as she shuffled through the rest of her paperwork sounded heavenly.

Getting into her car, she turned the radio off as she pulled out of the car park, enjoying the silence and the sound of the tires on the road, and by the time her house came into view, she was relaxed and looking forward to a quiet night. Pulling into her drive, she noticed Duane's car parked on the street and her shoulders fell. Momentarily regretting that she had ever given him a key, she pushed away her annoyance and gathered her things. Climbing out of the car, Laura schlepped up the walk and into the house.

Duane was coming off a very bad week. As a matter of fact, it was the fourth in a row. As a car salesman at a high-end dealership in London, he normally could hold his own, selling more than his fair share of shiny imports without blinking an eye, but the tide had turned, and he was stuck in the undertow.

Like most commissioned salespeople, he took the first week in stride. Customers come, customers go, and customers change their minds—that's life, so he sat back as others sold vehicles and smiled politely. He knew things would change soon enough. He knew his time would come, or at least that's what he thought.

Another week passed and then another, and with no sales to his name, when his manager asked Duane to cover while another salesperson was on holiday, Duane leapt at the chance. Knowing Laura would be working extra hours in John's absence, he walked into the dealership on Monday morning with his head held high, confident that he would sell a car. Unfortunately, Mother Nature had other plans. With an entire week of rain washing away any possibility of selling an automobile, Duane spent the last four days in a desolate car showroom, doing only one thing...looking forward to Friday night.

Hearing the front door open, Duane bounded down the stairs. "How long will it take you to get ready?"

"What are you talking about?" Laura said, tossing her things on a chair.

"We're meeting Seth and Julie at the pub."

"Oh, sweetheart, I wish you would have called me first."

"I texted you hours ago."

Furrowing her brow, Laura pulled her mobile out of her handbag. "Shit. I turned it off. I had meetings all day."

"Well, no worries. Just get changed and we'll head on over. I've had a hell of a week, and I need to unwind."

"Duane, I'm sorry, but I can't. I have work to do. Go without me."

"This is *really* becoming annoying. Do you know that?"

"Sweetheart, please don't start," she said as her head began to pound. "You know John's out with a broken leg, and we have four new women coming in on Monday. I have to get the job notices sorted and their class schedules—"

"And *I* want to go out with *you* and meet some of *our* friends for a drink!"

When Laura was a child, her hair was the color of a dark chili pepper, and her temper was just as spicy; however, as she grew older, the deep red gradually faded to a medium auburn. Unfortunately for Duane, that was the only thing that had faded.

"What the hell is your problem?" she shouted. "From the minute I took this job, all you've done is bitch and whine about it, and frankly, Duane, I'm tired of hearing it."

"I hate your bloody job!"

"Well, I don't care, because I love it!" Laura said, placing her hands on her hips.

"I have no idea why you continue to waste your time trying to help criminals," he said, walking away.

"What did you say?"

Spinning around, he said, "You heard me. Seriously, Laura, those women aren't going to make a difference in this world, so why the *hell* are you wasting your time?"

"Good point," Laura said, quickly turning on her heel and stomping into the lounge. Picking up his jacket, she searched through the pockets until she found his keys. Removing one, she placed the rest back in the pocket and calmly walked over and held out the coat. "Take it and get out."

"Laura—"

"I said get out, Duane, because you're absolutely right. I am wasting my time, and I have no intention of wasting any more of it. Now please leave."

For a few seconds, he tried to stare her down, but when Laura didn't even blink an eye, he snatched the jacket from her hands and stormed out of the house.

A short time later, after a long bath and healthy dose of Pinot Noir, Laura padded down the stairs wearing her favorite flannel pajamas and a grin. Making herself a sandwich, she refilled her glass and sauntered to the lounge where she plopped on the sofa and opened her briefcase. Diving into her work, two hours later, she poured herself another glass of wine to celebrate her progress. Picking up the list she had made, Laura merrily began to check off item after item, but when she read the last notation, her heart sank.

"Shit," she moaned, reading the note again. "Shit. Shit. Shit. Shit. *Shit!*"

***

Under the misconception that the names given to coffee actually meant something, Laura was half-tempted to turn her car around and return what was left of her Fog Lifter to her local coffee shop. Since discovering which report had yet to be completed, sleep had eluded Laura the entire weekend. With her thoughts solely on Toni Vaughn and how the troubled teacher was going to react to the news, even with the help of alcohol, Laura had spent two nights tossing and turning, trying to think of a way out. The last thing she wanted to do was to intrude upon the fragile existence of the woman, but the monthly class reports were mandatory. Laura didn't have a choice.

Still in the shadows of Monday's dawn, Laura pulled into her parking space at Calloway. The lot was empty except for a rundown Jeep, dented and scratched. Parked where it always was, nearest the rear exit of the school, it could have been easily mistaken for an abandoned vehicle, if it weren't for the parking permit affixed to its windscreen.

Barely acknowledging the night watchman as she walked into the building, Laura dropped her things in her office and then slowly climbed the stairs. The classrooms were dark save for one, and the only sound she could hear was the hum of the fluorescent fixtures dangling from chains above her head. Silently, she walked to the classroom, and pausing in the open doorway to gather her thoughts,

Laura gazed at the teacher who was not yet aware that she wasn't alone.

She looked unaffected. Normal. Relaxed, and shuffling through papers while she sipped coffee from an insulated mug, Toni Vaughn could have been any teacher, in any school, anywhere. But Laura had read her file and knew she wasn't just *any* teacher. After her dinner with John, Laura had rushed home that night and turned her house upside down until she found the two books by one A. L. Vaughn.

Pulling the dog-eared paperbacks from the shelf, Laura flipped them over, wondering if there was a photograph of the author, but only a brief synopsis and some reviewer's quotes filled the back cover. Most likely found under the heading of *Education and Reference* in bookstores, one had been written with the student in mind and the other, the teacher.

Inside, the pages were filled with helpful hints, guiding the undergraduate and the novice educator through their first years at university. The author spoke of what to expect, what not to expect and what could be achieved, and through the words, wit and guidelines they contained, both books had eventually become bestsellers in the world of academia. As Laura flipped through the pages, she smiled at the notes she had written in the margins years before. Pausing to reread a few paragraphs she had highlighted and underlined, she remembered why she liked the books so much. They had helped her learn, and they had helped her study, but more importantly, they had helped her teach. As she stood in the hallway still watching the woman sitting behind the desk, Laura wondered if a book existed that could possibly help Toni Vaughn.

As minds do, Laura's continued to wander, and seeing Toni hunched over her desk, Laura realized that she had yet to see the woman's eyes. Were they blue or were they brown? Did she ever wear glasses? Did she ever smile? Did she have friends? Was there someone special in her life that helped her, took care of her...loved her? Silently admonishing herself, Laura cleared the thoughts from her mind. It wasn't her place to worry or even care about Toni Vaughn the person. Laura had a job to do, and right now it involved one of her teachers, simple as that. Taking a deep breath, she walked into the room, and in a fraction of a second, Toni Vaughn went rigid. Placing her hands palm down on the desk, she sat like a statue, stiff and mute.

"Hiya, Toni," Laura said quietly as she moved closer, but when she saw the woman pale, Laura came to an abrupt stop. Pausing for a moment, she turned around and took a seat at one of the desks nearest the door. Keeping her tone low and calm as if she were speaking to a frightened child, Laura said, "I don't know if you've heard, but John broke his leg last week." Seeing Toni's infinitesimal nod, Laura said, "So he won't be able to sit in on your classes for a while."

Laura didn't think it was possible, but Toni became even more rigid. The muscles in her neck grew taut as her spine stretched to its limits, and Laura felt horrible. This wasn't what she wanted, but there was no other way. "Toni, I'm sure John told you that eventually I'd be the one monitoring all the classes, and due to his accident, it's going to be sooner than expected. I came up to let you know that I'll be sitting in on your one o'clock reading class today."

As she sat staring at the top of her desk, Toni tried to think of a way out. The only things they couldn't destroy were her mind and her love of teaching. Even though the option to quit was hers, if she quit, it meant they had finally won, and she was not yet willing to let that happen.

Quickly, she glanced up to look at the stranger who would soon be interfering in her world and invading the sanctity of her classroom. By the sound her thick heels made on the tile floors, Toni had pictured a woman of John's age, and although she found the woman's Scottish accent compelling, it hadn't been enough to acknowledge her existence.

A brief glimpse was what she had intended, but when Toni raised her eyes, they widened at the sight of the woman who, for the moment, was looking in the other direction. Where she had expected to see gray hair twisted tightly into a chignon, Toni found hair the color of chestnut. Shimmering in the brightness of the classroom lights, the finely-textured style was modern and just long enough to brush the woman's shoulders. And even though a quick glance at her footwear confirmed that it was heavy-heeled, Laura MacLeod could not have been more than thirty years old. Doing her best to safeguard herself from the ugliness of the world and the pain of memories etched into her soul, Toni had forgotten the definition of beautiful…until now.

Laura waited in silence, not even looking in Toni's direction for fear her stare would only further add to the stress she knew she had just created. Convinced that she would continue to be ignored, Laura decided to leave the woman to her thoughts and her anxieties. Rising from her chair, she headed to the door.

As Laura stood up, Toni cast her eyes down again, startled that she had allowed herself so much time to be exposed, but when she heard Laura move toward the door, Toni found it impossible to remain silent any longer. Looking up, she snapped, "And if I don't want you here?"

Laura's forward progress stopped when she heard Toni speak for the first time. Her tone was low, almost sultry, and her accent crisp and educated, but the cultured timbre could not mask the sound of the woman's annoyance. Laura heard it loud and clear, and for a split-second, she almost responded in kind, but then she remembered who she was dealing with. "Unfortunately, we don't have a choice," she said, turning around. "I'm sorry."

"Don't you mean *I* don't have a choice?" Toni growled, her hands now clenched in white-knuckled fists.

"Look, I know this is making you uncomfortable, and like I said, I'm sorry. I truly am, but there's no way around it. I'll just sit at the back of the room and listen. You won't even know I'm here. I promise."

***

By Friday, Laura was ready to scream. Even though she was filled with compassion for the woman whose soul had been stolen by immoralities unknown, each afternoon when Laura left Toni's class, she wanted nothing more than to return and throttle the hardheaded teacher.

Spying Susan Grant sneaking out the back door to grab a smoke, Laura quickly followed her into the late afternoon sun. Motioning at the pack of cigarettes in Susan's hand, Laura asked, "Do you mind?"

Surprised to find a kink in the woman's perfection, Susan raised an eyebrow as she handed Laura the pack. "Rough day?"

"Rough bloody week!"

"What's going on? I thought you had a handle on everything."

"Yeah, everything except Toni Vaughn!" Laura said, quickly lighting the cigarette.

"Toni? What in the world did she do?"

"It's what she hasn't done. That's the problem!"

"Sorry?"

Laura took another drag of her cigarette, exhaling the smoke as quickly as it went in. "All week long, I've sat in her one o'clock reading class, and every bloody day all she's had her students do is read."

"Isn't that what they're supposed to do?"

"No, you don't get it. She's having them read to *themselves*. No discussions. No talking. No nothing!"

Unable to hide her amusement at Toni Vaughn's cleverness, Susan snickered. "Oh my."

"Susan, if she keeps this up, what am I supposed to do about the reports?"

"I suppose you could lie and fill them in without actually seeing her teach. I mean, everyone knows she's fantastic."

"I thought about doing just that, but it doesn't cure the problem. What happens next time or the time after that?"

"Yeah, I guess you're right. When are the reports due anyway?"

"Today by five," Laura said, angrily stubbing out her cigarette.

"Ouch. Talk about pressure."

"I know."

"So, what are you going to do?"

Yanking open the door, Laura said, "The only thing I can do. Spend the next hour watching as a classroom of women read to themselves, and after that, who the hell knows!"

Stomping up the stairs, Laura entered the empty classroom, and glancing at her watch, she was surprised to find out she was early. She was even more surprised not to find her stubborn English teacher already glued to her chair as had become her custom. Heading to the back of the room, Laura took the seat she had occupied the entire week and opened her shoulder bag. Pulling out the same form she had placed on the desk for the past four days, she sighed seeing the notes and comments columns still as empty as they were on Monday. Hearing a noise in the hallway, Laura looked up just as the defiant Toni Vaughn strode into the room, walked to the blackboard and picked up a piece of chalk.

The scenario being all too familiar, Laura found herself looking at the teacher instead of the day's reading assignment. Lanky and obviously underweight, Toni's clothes only added to her emaciated appearance. Bunched around her waist by a belt pulled tight, her trousers were the same ones she had worn earlier that week. The once dark brown fabric, faded by washings, had turned to an earthy tan and the cuffs were ragged with threads dangling. Her oversized Oxford shirt had also morphed into another color, age bleaching its pastel yellow to cream, and the collar of the black T-shirt she wore underneath was frayed and stretched. As far as Laura could tell, Toni wore no makeup and the only jewelry in view was a wristwatch, and to complete her ensemble, barely visible under her trousers, were trainers, original color unknown.

As the students began shuffling into the room, Laura couldn't help but hear their collective groan as they glanced at the board to read the order of the day. Wearily dragging themselves to their desks, they slid into their chairs, making comments back and forth, all of which were loud enough for both Toni and Laura to hear.

All week Toni had tortured herself and her students with reading assignments, with no instruction, no discussion and no hands-on approach. The night before, she had sat in her darkened flat and opened the bottle to smell the aroma of death. There were other classes, other students being shown the way through her knowledge, patience and skill, but *this* was the class that kept her alive. This was what allowed her to sleep at night and rise the next morning. The first time she had seen the face of one of these adults finally able to read a sentence on her own, Toni knew *this* was the reason she had survived.

Still facing the chalkboard, Toni closed her eyes and filled her lungs to capacity. Dormant for years, emotions were beginning to rise to the surface, and due to Laura MacLeod's tenacity, anger was the first to arrive. Determined, Toni turned to face her class, glaring fiercely in Laura's direction for only a second before she began to speak, *and* she began to teach.

For the next hour, Laura sat mesmerized by the talented teacher, watching as Toni lectured, listened, and guided her students through their lesson, patiently dealing with each and every question regardless of its intellect or ignorance. So in awe of what she was witnessing, when Toni signaled that the hour-long class had come to an end, Laura found herself saddened that the time had gone by so quickly.

The students left as they had arrived, a group chattering and teasing amongst themselves, and within a few minutes, the room was empty except for two. Toni stood to erase the blackboard, praying that Laura wouldn't feel it necessary to talk, and when she heard the door close, Toni bowed her head and sighed in relief. Placing the eraser on the shelf, she turned to gather her things and her jaw dropped open. In the middle of her desk, sitting atop a stack of papers, was a shiny red apple.

CHAPTER FOUR

"Well, it's about bloody time!"

Kris glanced at the number on the door and then back at the woman standing in front of her. It was the right apartment. It was the right person, but it was the wrong attitude. Loaded down with groceries, she stumbled into the flat. "I'm...I'm sorry," she said, tilting her head to the side as she stared at Toni. "The store...the store was busier than usual."

"Whatever," Toni said, disappearing into the lounge.

Confused, surprised and somewhat tickled by Toni's demeanor, Kris quickly headed to the kitchen to put away the groceries. Noticing two empty beer bottles on the counter, she called out, "Are you pissed?"

"Get bloody real!" Toni yelled back. "It takes a hell of a lot more than three sodding beers to get me drunk. You know that."

Standing in the kitchen, Kris smiled. It had been years since she had seen even a glimpse of the woman she used to know, but as she listened to Toni mumble to herself while she stomped about the lounge, all the wonderful memories came rushing back. Gathering the bottles, Kris picked up the empty crate and then stopped. She closed her eyes and whispered, "I don't know what's happening, God, but whatever it is, please let it keep happening."

A minute later, Kris returned to the lounge, and noticing the beer crate in her hands, Toni asked, "Do you have time to get some more?"

"Absolutely," Kris said, walking to the door. Pausing for a second, she said, "Um...have you eaten? I could always grab us a pizza while I'm out, if you'd like."

"No."

Krista's shoulders fell. "Oh, okay,"

"No, I mean I *haven't* eaten, and a pizza sounds good. That is, unless you need to get home to Robin?"

Krista's bright blue eyes became even brighter, her cheeks turning rosy as her face lit up with joy. "I'll call her and let her know I'll be late," she said, rushing to the door. "Be back in a tick."

An hour later, Toni had consumed over half the pizza and another two bottles of beer while Krista watched in stunned silence. After carrying the empty box into the kitchen, Krista's curiosity finally won out. Returning to sit next to Toni on the sofa, she blurted, "Toni, what's going on?"

"What do you mean?"

"Well...you seem different tonight. Not a bad different, mind you, just...just different."

Thinking for a moment, Toni said, "I'm having a bit of trouble at work."

"Trouble? With one of your students?"

"No!" Toni said, jumping off the sofa. Storming into the kitchen, she grabbed a beer from the fridge. *"With bloody Laura MacLeod!"*

Kris pursed her lips, tilting her head to one side as she tried to decipher what Toni had said. Quickly giving up, she waited until Toni returned and sat down next to her. "So, who's Laura MacLeod?"

"The new head of the department."

"And she doesn't like you?"

"I have no bloody clue if she likes me or not, and frankly, I couldn't give a toss either way," Toni said, slamming her beer down on the coffee table. "What I *do* mind is the fact that she spent the entire fucking week in my one o'clock reading class!"

"Why?"

"Because of the fucking monthly reports, and since John is out, *she* felt the need to fill in for him."

"And you weren't comfortable with her being there, were you?"

"You know I wasn't," Toni said, looking at Kris for a second. "But I managed, because until today, all I had the women do was read to themselves. I didn't have to teach; all I had to do was just sit there and wait for the class to end."

"So what happened today?"

"I taught."

"What?"

"I taught the bloody class, like I always do."

"She wasn't there?"

"No, she was there. I just chose to ignore her."

"Wait. I don't understand. If you taught today and everything went okay, what's got you so wound up?"

Narrowing her eyes, Toni glared at Krista. "You want to know? Do you *really* want to know?"

"Yes, I really want to know," Kris said, grinning.

Grabbing her briefcase from the floor, Toni pulled out the apple. Placing it firmly in Krista's hand, Toni shouted, "*This!*"

Staring at the fruit, it was all Kris could do not to laugh. "You're angry at an apple?" she said, knowing the question was possibly the stupidest she had ever asked.

"No!" Toni said, grabbing for her beer. After taking a quick swig, she said, "And I'm not angry, Krista. I'm...I'm...oh, Christ, I don't know what I am!"

Placing the fruit on the table, Kris asked, "So...what's with the apple?"

"She gave it to me."

"Who?"

Toni's frustrations were solely her own, but it didn't prevent her from lashing out at Kris. "Are you actually *trying* to act this stupid or are you just yanking my chain?"

The comment was harsh and uncalled for, but Kris didn't mind. This was the feisty and hardheaded Toni Vaughn whom she adored. This was the best friend who had always been there for her, and Kris knew Toni didn't mean what she said. She was confused, upset, and in her own way, she was crying out for help for the first time since her release from prison. Placing her hand over Toni's, Kris said, "Honey, just tell me what happened?"

Taking a deep breath, Toni leaned back against the couch and ran her fingers through her hair. "After class, I heard her leave, and when I turned around, that was on my desk," she said, pointing to the apple.

"So *she* gave you that."

"Yes, and I don't know why, and it's turning my bloody head around."

"Maybe she was just trying to be nice. An apple for the teacher and all that."

"I didn't ask her to be nice. I don't trust her. I don't trust any of them," Toni said, and with every syllable, her voice faded as she slowly retreated back into herself.

Krista let out a sigh. Watching as Toni moved her bottle of beer to its coaster, and then picked up the papers she needed to grade, her actions and her silence told Krista that the evening had ended.

Leaning over, Kris kissed her lightly on the cheek. "Good night, Toni. Call me if you need me, okay?"

Toni nodded and then lit a cigarette, paying no mind as Kris gathered her belongings and quietly left the flat.

By the time Kris reached the stairs, her smile was wide and bright. For almost two hours, she had enjoyed the company of someone she never thought she'd see again. Even though she had no idea how the door to Toni's emotions had been unlocked, Kris was positive that a woman called Laura MacLeod held the key.

***

Hearing a knock on the door, Laura looked up as Irene walked into her office. "Laura, there's a woman outside who would like to talk to you, but she doesn't have an appointment."

"How's my day look?"

"You've got that conference call at eleven. Other than that, you're clear."

"Did she say what it's about?"

"No, just that she needed to see you about something very important."

"Well, I have a bit of time," Laura said, glancing at her watch. "I'll talk to her."

Laura was accustomed to unscheduled visitors. At least once a week, a parent or sibling of one of the residents would stop by to check on their loved one's progress or complain about their curfew, so she waited patiently for the door to open again. When it did, for a moment Laura simply stared at the woman smiling back at her.

Statuesque and blonde, she was dressed in an ivory skirt and jacket, and a shimmering pale green silk blouse open at the collar. Her makeup was flawless. Her jewelry was gold, and she had the lightest blue eyes Laura had ever seen.

Kris was pleasantly surprised when she walked into Laura MacLeod's office, and it showed on her face. The woman sitting behind the desk was younger than she expected, and it didn't hurt that she was also easy on the eyes...very easy. With the sunlight streaming through the window, Kris wasn't sure if the woman's hair was red or brown, but even the glaring rays couldn't wash out Laura MacLeod's finer features. Her complexion was clear and her jaw strong, and her full lips, enhanced by just a touch of lipstick, screamed soft and kissable. Remembering she already had a partner whom she loved dearly, Kris toned down her smile as she held out her hand. "Hi. I'm Krista Nielson."

Standing, Laura returned the handshake. "Laura MacLeod," she said. Motioning for her visitor to take a seat, Laura returned to her own. "What can I do for you, Miss Nielson?"

"Oh, please call me Kris or Krista."

"Okay, Kris, what can I help you with?"

Kris quickly glanced toward the door. "Before I answer that, is there any chance that Toni will be down here this morning?"

"Toni? Toni Vaughn?"

"Yes. If she knew I was here, she'd probably get a bit upset, and I wouldn't want that to happen."

Cocking her head to the side, Laura sat back in her chair. "No, Toni doesn't come down here," she said, carefully watching for the woman's reaction. When she saw Krista's posture relax, Laura leaned forward and said, "Now, since I just answered your question, you can answer mine. Who are you and what's this all about?"

Taking a minute to get her thoughts organized, Kris sat back and crossed her legs. "I've been Toni's best friend since we were kids, and since she got out of...out of Thornbridge, I've been taking care of her."

"In what way?"

"I get her groceries, take her car to get repaired, pick up medications if she needs them, and make sure she's eating. Things like that."

"Is it that bad? I mean, I know she's quite the loner here, but I didn't think—"

"She goes from work to her flat and back again. Nowhere else...ever."

Laura's mouth fell open as she stared at Kris, and several seconds passed before she found her voice. "I...I had no idea."

"That's because you don't know her like I do, or rather...I did."

"Did?"

"That woman upstairs looks like Toni and sounds like Toni, but since Thornbridge, she's become a stranger to me. I forgot what it was like to hear her laugh or joke, or even get angry. Christ, did she have a temper," Kris said with a snort. "But on Friday night, for the first time in over two years, I saw a glimpse of my old friend. It made me miss her even more, and I want my friend back. I want her back more than words can say."

"I'm sure you do, but I'm not sure why you're telling me this."

"Because I think you can help. That is, if you want to."

Since the day she first met the withdrawn teacher, Laura had found it difficult, if not impossible, *not* to think about the enigma called Toni Vaughn. There was something about the scrawny woman with lifeless eyes that piqued her interest, and although Susan Grant had given up, Laura was a wee bit more stubborn. After watching Toni teach, and seeing the enthusiasm in both the students *and* the teacher, Laura had made up her mind. If there were any way she could help Toni Vaughn, she would.

Leaning back in her chair, she asked, "What do you think I can do?"

"I'm not exactly sure, but Friday night, when I got to her place, she was absolutely livid, and it was because of *you*."

"Oh, God, this is because I monitored her class, isn't it? Kris, I apologize if I upset her. That wasn't my intention, and I'll tell her that myself if you think—"

"No!" Kris shouted, sitting up in her chair. "Miss MacLeod—"

"Call me Laura, please."

"Fine...Laura," Kris said, getting to her feet. "Look, I don't want you to apologize. The only emotion that Toni has shown since she got out of that place is fear. She doesn't smile. She doesn't cry. She doesn't get happy when things go her way or sad when they don't, and she certainly doesn't get angry...at least she didn't until Friday night."

"I still don't understand what you want me to do."

"Keep going to her class."

"What?"

"You heard. Keep going to her class."

"Kris, I did that because a report had to be filed. If I show up for no reason, Toni is going to get..." The rest of the sentence died in Laura's throat. Staring back at Kris, she said, "You *want* me to get her angry?"

"It's an emotion, isn't it?"

***

Reluctant to go along with Krista's idea for fear that playing amateur psychologist would do more harm than good, Laura agreed to meet Kris later that night to discuss it further. Parking her car, Laura walked two blocks and then rounded the corner which would lead her to a club called Exes. Seeing the long queue waiting to get in, she took a deep breath and continued on. Reaching the door, she was promptly stopped by a sequoia masquerading as a man. "Sorry, love," he said, holding out his arm. "You've got to wait like the rest of them."

"I'm here to see Kris Nielson," Laura said, handing him one of Krista's business cards. "I believe she's expecting me."

Recognizing his employer's handwriting on the back of the card, he opened the door. "There you go, love. Enjoy your night."

It took a minute for Laura to get her bearings when she entered the crowded club, mostly due to the fact that it was much larger than she expected. On two levels, the upper tier was just broad enough for a walkway and tables meant for two, while the lower held the dance floor and more seating. A standing-room-only bar ran along almost the entire back wall of the club, and there were people jammed three deep in front of it, shouting orders for lager, cocktails and wine. A little surprised that she saw very few men in the club, the observation left her mind as quickly as it had entered, and maneuvering through the throng, Laura reached the bar and grinned when she saw Kris smiling back at her.

"Glad to see you found us!" Kris called out over the chatter and the music.

"Yeah. This is quite a place!" Laura shouted back.

"What are you drinking?"

"Red wine. Something dry."

Giving Laura a thumbs-up, Krista grabbed a bottle and two glasses, and walked to the end of the bar. Waiting for Laura to emerge from the crowd, she led her down a hallway and into a small office. Kris motioned toward a loveseat placed along one wall, and as they sat down, she said, "I thought it would be easier to talk in here. Less noise."

"That's fine," Laura said, glancing around the room.

"Here you go."

Taking the offered glass, Laura said, "Won't your boss mind you drinking while on duty?"

"No, *I* don't mind at all."

"Wait. This is your club?"

"Actually, it belongs to Toni and me."

"Excuse me?"

Amused by Laura's bug-eyed expression, Kris said, "It was always my dream to own a club and Toni knew it. When this place became available, I told her about it and she offered to loan me the money to buy it."

"Wait a minute. Are you saying that Toni's rich?"

"Well, not stinking rich, but she inherited quite a tidy sum when her grandfather died. Between that and the money she made from her books, along with a few wise investments early on, she's fairly well off." Prepared for Laura's look of confusion, Kris said, "Let me guess. You want to know why she dresses the way she does, don't you?"

"I was kind of wondering about that. I mean, I know she's withdrawn—"

"*Withdrawn* doesn't even begin to describe her," Krista said. Taking a sip of wine, she said, "Toni doesn't trust anyone but me and to a certain extent, Canfield. And she's got this phobia about crowds and strangers that makes it impossible for her to go out, which is why I do all of her shopping and errands."

"So why not get her some new clothes or a new car? It sounds like she can afford it."

"I've tried, but she doesn't *want* anything new because she doesn't want to leave behind anything...unnecessary."

"What do you mean?"

Kris lit a cigarette, drawing the smoke into her lungs as she leaned back into the cushions. "When Toni got out of that place, I brought her home with me. The next morning, I thought I'd treat her to her favorite breakfast, so I went to a bakery and picked up some pastries. When I got back, I found her in the bathroom...trying to cut her wrists."

"What!" Laura shouted, jumping to her feet. "Oh, Jesus Christ, Krista! Are you *completely* mad? You asked me to go back into her classroom, knowing that if she gets angry—"

"Relax, Laura."

"*Relax*? How the fuck am I supposed to relax? I can't bloody believe you!"

"Look, I know how it sounds, but you need to trust me. I've spent the last two years taking care of her, and even though I know she *thinks* she wants to die, she truly doesn't."

In an attempt to slow her heart rate, Laura took several deep breaths as she paced around the room. After a few minutes of mumbling to herself, she returned to the couch and drank what was left of her wine. Glowering at the woman sitting next to her, she placed the empty glass on the table. "You had better start explaining yourself, and I mean now!"

It had been a long time since she had really thought about that day, and even though she could feel her emotions beginning to stir, Kris struggled to get the words out. "Well, like I...like I said, she tried, but...but she didn't get very far. When I found her, there were only a few hesitation cuts, but nothing deep enough to do...to do...to do any real damage."

Seeing that the woman was on the verge of tears, Laura reached out and took her hand. "Kris, I'm sorry. I shouldn't have asked for an explanation. I know you're her friend, and I'm sure that you think you know her better than anyone, but I can't risk—"

"I found her huddled in the corner of the shower," Kris said, snatching her hand away. Determined to get Laura to help, Kris angrily wiped the tears from her face. "The water was absolutely freezing, and she was just sitting under the spray, shivering. She didn't even realize I was there until I reached over and took the razor blade away from her."

"Did she try to stop you?"

"Not at all," Kris said, shaking her head. "It was as if she was in a trance. It didn't seem like she even knew she was hurt. I managed to get her out of the shower and wrap her in a towel. I was worried about her wrists and getting her warm, so I wasn't paying attention to anything else. It wasn't until I was helping her get dressed when I saw the scars."

"Scars? On her wrists?"

"No, on her back...they're all over her back," Kris said in a whisper. "And when she realized that I had seen them, she started to cry."

Remembering what John had told her about Thornbridge, Laura paled. "Oh, God."

"I held her for hours that day. I honestly can't remember how long she cried, but as each tear fell, a part of her disappeared," Kris said, hanging her head. "She dissolved in my arms and there wasn't anything I could do to stop it. By the next morning, she became the person you know now. Lifeless and detached...lost."

"Then how in the world did she ever manage to find a job?"

"I saw an advertisement for a teaching position at Calloway in the newspaper. I hadn't left her alone for a single minute after she had tried to...tried to kill herself, so over coffee one morning, I mentioned it. It took me days to convince her to apply. Christ, she was so scared, changing her mind every other minute, but she somehow found the nerve to do it. I don't know which one of us was more surprised when she got the job, but after a few weeks, she seemed better, like she was more at ease with living now that she had something to do. Eventually, she asked me to find her a flat, something cheap and small, and I did...and since then, nothing's really changed."

"So she never tried it again?"

"Suicide? No, but I know she still thinks about it."

"Why do you say that?"

"When she was in holding, before she was set free, the doctors there noticed that she had problems sleeping, so they prescribed some pills. After what she tried in the shower, I took them away from her...just to make sure she wouldn't get any ideas."

"Good plan."

"Thanks," Kris said, managing a thin grin. "Anyway, when she got her own place, she asked for them, but I refused. I still didn't trust her not to do something stupid; so instead, I stopped by every day to give her one to use that night. It seemed like a good idea at the time."

"It wasn't?"

"No," Kris said as she picked up her wine. Taking a sip, she let out a slow breath as she returned the glass to the table. "One day I went over like I always did. It was one of those shit days, you know? Everything was going wrong. I had just sacked a bartender, the sound system at the club had broken, and the weather was crap, so when I got to her place, I decided to have a drink. I knew she had vodka, so I poured myself some, but then I...I noticed that it looked odd. It was cloudy...almost dirty, and as I was standing in the kitchen, deciding on whether to drink it, she walked in. As soon as I saw the panic in her eyes, I knew what she had done. Here I was slogging over there every day for almost a year, thinking I was doing the right thing, and all along she was lying to me. She wasn't taking the pills. She was putting them in the bottle so she could have an easy way out if she wanted one."

Closing her eyes for a moment, Laura said, "Please tell me you took the bottle."

"I thought about it, but then I remembered I was the only person Toni trusted. I was the only one allowed in her flat, the only one bringing her food...taking care of her. If I had taken the vodka...if I had destroyed it, it would have destroyed the trust she has in me, and I wasn't willing to take that risk. So I left it there, along with the bottle of pills I had in my handbag. I told her that I loved her, but since she already had enough to do the job, there wasn't any point in me rationing them any longer."

"You're playing a very dangerous game, Kris."

"Don't you think I know that?" Kris shouted. "But, Jesus Christ, what else could I have done? If I took the vodka, she would have cut me out of her life. Without me, she doesn't eat. If she doesn't eat, she dies. So instead, I showed her that she could trust me. I showed her that I wouldn't do anything...*anything* to destroy her faith in me, and I go home every night, every *fucking* night and pray to God that I haven't made a mistake."

Burying her head in her hands, Kris began to weep, and feeling her own emotions starting to get the better of her, Laura went to the desk and grabbed a box of tissues. Taking one for herself, she handed the rest to Krista and then stepped away to give the woman some space. Drying her eyes, Laura walked over to look at some pictures hanging on the wall, and a grin slowly formed when she recognized both Toni and Kris in various poses of playfulness. It was obvious that all the photos were taken years before, but as she stared at the captured memories, a thought popped into her head. Thinking back to the amount of women in the club, she turned around and cocked her head to one side.

"I'm sorry," Kris said, sniffling back a tear. "It's just that I love her so much."

"Kris, are you and Toni...I mean, were you...were you partners?"

"No, we shagged a bit in school, but we realized that we were much better at being friends than being lovers."

Startled by the woman's honesty, Laura paused for a second. "You're...I mean, Toni's...Toni's gay?"

"Sorry, I guess there's really no reason why you would have known that, huh?

"No, but that explains all the women I saw when I walked in here tonight. This is a gay club, isn't it?"

Straightening her backbone, Kris said, "Is that a problem? Should I have *warned* you?"

Returning to the sofa, Laura poured a splash of wine in both glasses and handed one to Kris. "No, it doesn't bother me, Kris. I just wasn't expecting it. But honestly, it sounds to me like you're in love with Toni, and if that's the case, you should be the one working on getting her out of her shell, not me. I certainly don't want to give her the wrong idea. I mean...I'm not into women."

Smiling, Kris got up, grabbed a photo from her desk and handed it to Laura. "Her name's Robin and she's my wife. I'm in love with her, not Toni, but Toni and I have been through a lot, and I owe her my life."

"*You* were the one she saved that night?"

"How did you know about that?"

"I'm sorry. John let me read her file and then filled in some blanks. Being the way she is, he thought it wise."

"Smart man."

"John also said drugs were involved. That's why the copper was here that night."

Rolling her eyes, Kris let out a laugh. "When we first opened we had some issues with people bringing that shit into the club, but we always handled it ourselves. We made them leave and that was the end of it, but I guess the word got out on the street so the police started coming around every now and then. We didn't care. We weren't doing anything wrong, so when the copper came in that night, I didn't pay him any mind, but when I tried to lock up, he wouldn't leave. A few minutes later, I was fighting for my life, and that's when Toni walked in..." Kris stopped for a moment and drew in a ragged breath. "She tried so hard to stop the bleeding. She was pressing her hands on the guy's neck, trying...trying to make it stop all the while screaming at me to call the medics. It was all just a mistake, an accident...a stupid, *fucking* accident, and she paid for it with four years of her life in that hole...and she's still paying for it."

Leaning back on the sofa, Laura sighed. "Oh, Kris, I don't know what to do. I certainly don't want to push her over the edge—"

"Laura, she's not suicidal! Yes, she still has the fucking bottle in her fridge, but it's just a crutch. It gives her an option, but you have to trust me, Laura. She doesn't want to die! She's just stuck in this...in this prison she's made for herself, and she doesn't know how to get out. And as for Toni getting the wrong idea, as you put it, I'm her best friend and she won't even touch me, so I think you're safe."

"I don't know..."

"I'm not asking you to shag her, for God's sake. All I'm asking is that you be a friend and visit her class a few times a week. Just make yourself known. Please, Laura, I'm running out of options."

"I still don't know what makes you think that I—"

"Because you got to her! When you wouldn't give up and kept going to her class...well, I think she's met her match in you, and she knows it."

"Krista, if anyone has shown that they can be stubborn, it's you. You've spent two years by her side, and you said it yourself, she hasn't opened up to you at all. What makes you think I have the magic key?"

"That's simple," Kris said with a knowing grin. "I'm her friend, and I proved over the years that she can trust me. You, on the other hand, are a total stranger, and in five days you were able to get her to show an emotion. You got her angry, and that's something that no one, including me, has been able to do."

Laura stood and returned to the wall where images of a woman once alive and vital filled the frames. Her eyes went from one picture to the next, studying the Toni Vaughn who existed before Thornbridge. There wasn't a photograph where she wasn't smiling, and in her eyes Laura could see youthful confidence with just a hint of mischief. Laura's eyes darted back and forth across the photos as she chewed on her lip, and drawing in a slow breath, she said, "I'll still have to think about it, Kris. I've heard what you said, and some of it makes sense, but I don't want to do anything to upset her."

"Well, then you'd best not give her any more apples."

Spinning around, Laura's eyes flew open wide. "What?"

"She told me about the apple you left on her desk. Can I ask why you did that?"

With a snort, Laura said, "Because I had just spent an hour watching a paradox. One minute, she was rigid, mute and distant, and the next she was...she was *so* alive. I wouldn't have believed it if I hadn't seen it myself and after the class was over, I wanted to say something, but she had already shot me a dozen nasty looks during the lesson, so I decided against it. I was packing up to leave when I noticed the apple from my lunch was still in my bag, so when I left, I put it on her desk. It was just my way of saying thanks."

"That's what I thought."

"Are you saying I shouldn't have done that?"

Smiling, Kris shook her head. "No, I'm saying that the next time you go shopping...buy more fruit."

CHAPTER FIVE

Apprehensive about disturbing the world of a woman whom she believed was teetering on the edge, much to Krista's dismay, Laura refused to visit Toni's classroom unless it was required. It wasn't until ten days after she had met Kris at Exes when Laura found herself once again invading the troubled teacher's space to monitor her class.

Pulling the essays out of her briefcase, Toni was glancing at the papers when she heard the click of heavy heels coming up the corridor. Setting her jaw, she slowly raised her eyes, and when Laura MacLeod walked into her classroom, Toni's stare was cold and hard, and her message was clear. *Get out.*

Aware that her presence would not be welcome, Laura simply gave Toni a weak smile and then walked to the back of the room to find a seat. The students filed in, some saying their hellos as they took their places and opened their books, and a few minutes later, Toni gathered her wits and began to teach. Sitting silently, Laura listened to the lesson as she jotted down some notes, and when the class was over, she gathered her belongings and left without saying a word, but not before placing an apple on Toni's desk.

The scene was repeated the following week and the week after that, and the only thing that changed was the lesson being taught. No words were exchanged between the teacher and the department head. No looks of acknowledgement were given when Laura entered the classroom, and no good-byes were offered when she left. And even though she continued to place a shiny apple on Toni's desk after every visit, not once did Toni voice a thank you. Laura wasn't surprised.

When Laura wasn't buried in paperwork, glad-handing possible benefactors or monitoring classes, as part of her weekly routine, she made it a point of visiting with each of her teachers to discuss course schedules, grades and the like. Preferring relaxed, one-on-one meetings over lunch, rather than structured ones held in her office, she'd go to their classrooms, and over bagged lunches, they'd chat about their work. Having just finished such a meeting with Susan Grant, as Laura walked down the hallway, she noticed Toni's door open and decided it was time to test the waters.

Toni saw her standing in the doorway immediately, but she continued to grade papers without so much as a glance in Laura's direction. Without a file folder in her hand signaling a course review, Toni was confused as to why the woman was there, and when Laura approached her desk, Toni went rigid.

Silently admonishing herself for her own stupidity, Laura stopped and took two steps backward. "Hiya, Toni. I was just making the rounds and thought I'd stop by to see how things were going. I know you have three new students, and I wanted to make sure there weren't any problems."

Toni hated questions that couldn't be answered with a nod or a shake of the head, and for a minute, she sat motionless, hoping that MacLeod would simply go on her way. When another minute passed and Laura still hadn't moved, Toni sighed. "Everything's fine," she muttered, without looking up. "Now, if you don't mind, I'm busy." Picking up an essay, she returned to her reading as if the woman standing a few feet away from her didn't exist.

"Of course. I'm sorry I intruded. I'll let you get back to work."

Although amused by Toni's obvious brush-off, Laura didn't allow it to show until she walked out of the room. Shutting the door behind her, she broke into a smile that lit up the corridor.

It was the tiniest of steps, but it was a step nonetheless. Only a millimeter in length, across a space wider than a canyon, but the reclusive teacher had spoken, and she had spoken to Laura. From that day on, Toni's classroom became part of Laura's weekly rounds…whether Toni liked it or not.

As the days turned into weeks, both women found it impossible not to think about the other.

Alone in her darkened flat, Toni would sit with her cigarette and beer, staring at the bottle of vodka filled with poison, but not contemplating its contents. A student had made a comical remark one day, and from the back of the room came a chuckle, low and sexy. Toni knew in an instant it belonged to Laura MacLeod, and she found herself wanting to look up, to see the smile, the gaiety...but fear blocked her path. It was unimaginable to think she could allow a virtual stranger to become anything more. To trust was impossible, but as each day passed, Toni began listening for the footsteps and inhaling deeply at the scent of a stranger's perfume.

For Laura, finding a comfortable balance between work and leisure had never been her strong point, so bringing work home was nothing unusual. Although Duane had called once or twice, leaving messages on the machine asking for another chance, Laura hadn't returned the calls. Nightly, she immersed herself in her work, sipping a glass of wine as she moved through the papers, unconsciously saving the reports on Toni's classes until last. She'd open a file and get lost in its contents, remembering the lesson as if she were a student and the teacher as if she were a friend. Toni was so animated in her teaching that Laura found herself watching every move she made. How she waved her arms to make a point or clapped her hands when a student grasped a concept, and once, on an afternoon filled with sun and warmth, Laura had heard her laugh. She couldn't remember ever hearing anything sound so wonderful.

***

It was one of those days when you wanted to be at home, snuggled under the covers with a good book and a cup of tea, but that was a luxury that didn't apply to the working masses. Rain or shine, they came to work and did their time. As she stood under the overhang, cupping her hands against the wind to light a cigarette, Susan Grant wished that she were a member of the upper class if only to enjoy rainy days wrapped in the comfort of her duvet.

Hearing the door open, Susan moved enough to let Toni out, and as soon as the door closed, both women hugged the wall to prevent themselves from getting drenched. Lighting her cigarette, Toni took a deep drag and then looked at the sky. "Shitty day."

Stunned to hear the woman speak, it took Susan several seconds before she could find her voice. "Yes...yes, they say it's supposed to do this all weekend."

Toni didn't dislike Susan Grant. Like Switzerland, her feelings were those of neutrality where it concerned the blonde woman with the easy smile. Although she had never joined in the camaraderie that Susan had offered in the early days, a part of Toni appreciated the fact that she had tried to include her. Craving a cigarette for more than an hour, Toni, nevertheless, had waited until she saw Susan walk past her classroom door with jacket in hand before excusing herself from her class to grab a much-needed smoke. Having become accustomed to Laura's weekly visits, as Toni looked out into the storm, curiosity got the best of her. "Is MacLeod on holiday?"

"What?" Susan asked, glancing at Toni. Surprised that she was actually making eye contact with the woman, Susan said, "No...um...she's been at a conference for the past few days. She'll be back on Monday."

Flicking her cigarette into a puddle, Toni yanked open the door and went back inside.

***

After three days of listening to lectures, Laura was ready for the weekend. Running through the parking lot, she skipped over puddles, only to fumble for her keys for another minute before managing to get into her car. While the defogger cleared the glass, she checked her briefcase and sighed. She would have loved to spend the entire weekend vegetating in front of the television, but catching up on work would be far more productive. Knowing she had a stack of reports on her desk that needed attention, Laura pulled out of the lot and turned in the direction of Calloway House.

Arriving less than an hour later, as Laura pulled into her parking spot a shiver ran down her spine when she noticed two police cars driving away from the building. Ignoring the fact that the skies had opened up, she jumped out of her car and ran into the building.

Seeing Bryan coming down the stairs, Laura asked, "Bryan, why were the police here?"

"A couple of our residents got into a fight on the third floor. It was quite a row."

"What in the world happened?"

"We're not quite sure, but the flat's totaled, and Laura...one of them had a knife."

"A knife!"

"Yeah. As far as we can tell, she had it hidden in her mattress. She was already going to lose her probation because of the fight, so I guess she decided what the hell."

"Jesus Christ."

"Anyway, Jack got it away from her, and then we called the police."

"Well, thank God no one was hurt."

"Laura, I'm not so sure about that. Toni was the first one up there. By the time Jack and I arrived, the place was a mess. When we took over, she disappeared, and I'm fairly certain I saw blood on her shirt."

"Blood? Are you sure it was hers?"

"Well, other than a few scrapes, I didn't see any injuries on the women. After all the commotion died down, I went to Toni's classroom to check on her, but it was empty, and I looked in the car park. Her Jeep's gone."

"All right. Thanks, Bryan," Laura said. "I'll just go up and look around. Make sure you file a report before you leave, and email me a copy. Will you please?"

"Sure thing."

Trotting up the stairs, Laura rushed to Toni's classroom. Flicking on the light, her eyes darted around the empty room. Noticing a dark blue jacket hanging on the back of a chair, she walked over and picked it up. Undoubtedly Toni's, the threadbare collar and faded fabric announcing its ownership, Laura fingered the worn cloth as she debated on what to do, but then she noticed something at her feet. Amidst the gray and blue speckles of the white linoleum was something that didn't belong, and stooping over she touched the dark splotch with her finger. When it came back covered in blood, Laura blanched. "Shit."

Forty-five minutes later, she sat in her car outside a dilapidated old building, checking the numbers painted on the front step with the ones in Toni's file. Closing the folder, Laura glanced at the first-aid kit sitting on the passenger seat, trying to decide if she dare carry it inside. The torrential rain having not eased a drop, she took a deep breath before jumping out of the car and running into the building. Pausing long enough to push her soaked hair out of her face, she headed up the stairs. Three flights later, Laura walked down a dim hallway and stopped in front of a door with a crooked D nailed to its surface.

***

Having finished her last class of the day, Toni had been gathering papers to grade at home when she heard screams coming from upstairs. Running from the room, she took the steps two at a time and jogged down the hall toward a crowd of women congregating in front of one of the flats. Fighting her way in, she found the flat in shambles, and what was left of the meager furniture was now being used as weapons, the two ex-convicts trying to pummel the other with whatever they could grab. Acting on instinct, Toni pushed them apart and tried her best to keep them separated until help arrived.

One was small, almost spindly, but by the words she spewed, Toni knew that the woman's mouth had caused the fight, and it was all Toni could do to keep her in her place as the expletives continued to fly. The other was large and dumpy, with frizzy brown hair and insanity in her eyes, and while Toni struggled to contain the spindly woman, the other one continued to shout and threaten. Concentrating on keeping the one woman pushed against the wall, when Toni saw her eyes bulge, she turned around, but there was no time to react. The force of the chair rung hitting her on the temple knocked her to her knees.

Stunned, it took several seconds before Toni could gather her wits enough to stand, and that's when she saw the glint of a blade in the dumpy one's hand. Trying to avoid the knife now slashing in her direction, she raised her arms to ward off the attack. Toni dodged one way and then the other, her eyes darting around the room, trying to find something to use to protect herself, and then suddenly her arm turned cold. Confused, she lowered her eyes and watched as the pale yellow fabric of her shirt began to turn crimson.

Her heart felt like it was about to explode, the combination of adrenaline and fear causing her body to rush, and when she raised her eyes and saw the crazed woman coming at her again, Toni held her breath. For a few seconds, time seemed to stand still as the prey realized it was caught and the hunter moved in for the kill, but then shouts, masculine and deep, filled the room. Jack and Bryan stormed in, the language teacher quickly disarming the woman with the knife as Bryan shoved the other hard into a corner.

Pushing her way through the sea of women crowded around the doorway, Toni stumbled down the stairs. With her heart hammering against her ribs as her anxieties reigned supreme, she rushed into her classroom. Grabbing her briefcase, she staggered down the stairs and out into the pouring rain, the flood of water going unnoticed as she walked unsteadily to her car.

She drove home on instinct, barely able to see through the sheets of water and the glare from oncoming headlights. She was propelled through the night by the need to get to her sanctuary where no one could intrude, no one could hurt her...and no one could see the terror in her eyes.

***

In the safety of her flat, Toni stood in the kitchen, her blood mixing with water as it puddled on the floor. Focusing on the hum of the refrigerator compressor, she prayed that its thrum would drown out the sound of her heart pounding in her ears. She needed to concentrate to keep the horrors of her memories at bay, but then the rapping started, and it brought her back to now.

Someone was at the door, and the relentless knocking seemed to mirror the throbs of pain in Toni's body, and with each loud rap, her head felt one step closer to exploding. She needed quiet. She needed peace and darkness, and for a moment, her fear was replaced by rage.

Determined, Laura stood in the hallway with no intention of leaving until Toni answered the door. She had been there for ten minutes and with each tick of the clock, Laura's concern grew. There was blood on the door jamb and more on the tattered mat under her feet, and she instantly regretted leaving the first-aid kit in the car. Raising her hand to knock again, Laura stopped when she heard the door being unlocked. The hinges creaked as it opened a few inches, and Laura found herself looking at a ghost.

The color had all but drained from Toni's face and the dark circles under her eyes appeared almost black against her bloodless complexion. Soaked to the skin, the water dripping from her hair mixed with the blood on her temple, painting a macabre abstract as it made its way down the right side of her face, but she didn't seem to notice. She didn't seem to care.

Their eyes met for a moment, and Laura could see Toni's rage, but in a split-second, the woman's expression changed to one of fright. Sensing the woman's distress, Laura kept her voice low and calm. "Toni, Bryan said you might be hurt—"

"No!" Toni shouted as she tried to slam the door.

Laura had known she wasn't going to be welcomed and she had prepared herself for it. Although she flinched when the door pushed against her instep, she refused to move. "Toni, I just want to see—"

"No!" Toni shrieked, stumbling backward into her flat. Panic-stricken, her fear shrouded reality, and she no longer knew what was real and what was not, and who was a friend and who was an enemy.

Following Toni inside, Laura shut the door. "Toni, it's Laura, Laura MacLeod...from Calloway."

Muted by terror, Toni waved her arms in the air as if trying to avoid an invisible demon, and with each passing second, her breathing was becoming more and more labored.

Alarmed by the sight of Toni struggling to breathe, the sheer anguish etched on the woman's face told Laura all she needed to know. "Toni, you need to calm down. You're having a panic attack, and you need to slow your breathing. Please, just try to relax."

Gulping for air, Toni fell to one knee, inhaling again and again as she tried to fill her lungs with more.

"Shit!" Laura said, quickly glancing around the room. Dashing into the kitchen, Laura yanked open every drawer and cabinet until she found a small paper bag. Rushing back into the lounge to find Toni clutching her throat in agony, Laura didn't think twice. Falling to her knees, she tried to place the bag over Toni's mouth, but Toni panicked. Desperately trying to get away, she scrambled backward across the floor like a spider trying to hide, all the while gasping for air.

"Toni, you're going to pass out!" Laura said, crawling closer. "Please trust me. This will help," Laura pleaded. "Toni...please...please just trust me."

Their eyes locked, green ones filled with compassion gazing into dark-brown filled with anguish. "Relax, I won't hurt you," Laura whispered as she slowly put the sack over Toni's mouth.

Toni tried to fight. She wanted to fight, but the room was spinning and her body was no longer hers. Her strength was gone, but as her vision cleared for a moment, she grabbed Laura's wrists in a death grip. She was scared. Oh God, she was scared.

Expanding and contracting, the paper crackled in time with Toni's breathing as Laura hovered over her, mindless of the powerful hold Toni had on her wrists, but as Toni's breathing eased and her eyes fluttered closed, Laura let out a sigh of relief. Sleep was taking hold. The panic attack had ended. The worst was over.

CHAPTER SIX

Looking up from her coffee cup, Krista grinned when she saw Toni standing in the doorway of the kitchen. "Hey there. Feeling better?"

Confused, Toni nodded as she looked around. "How long have you been here?"

"Not long, and if you're looking for your friend, Laura, she left about fifteen minutes ago."

"She's not my friend."

"Well, she seemed friendly enough to me. She said you work together."

"Yeah, she's my boss," Toni said, scratching her head. "I...I thought it was a dream."

"It wasn't, and in case you're wondering, she's the one who cleaned you up and bandaged your arm."

Looking down, Toni raised her sleeve and found her arm wrapped neatly with gauze. Hesitantly, she touched her forehead and discovered yet another bandage taped to her skin. "She did this?"

It seemed to be becoming a habit, actual conversations instead of ones stilted by fear and mistrust, and Krista couldn't be happier. Convinced more than ever that it had something to do with Laura MacLeod, while the woman was cautious about pushing Toni's envelope, Kris knew two Toni Vaughns, and the one standing before her was an old and dear friend.

"Yeah, and by the bruises I saw on her wrists, you weren't a very cooperative patient."

"What? I don't remember—"

"Well, whether you remember it or not, you owe her an apology and a huge thank you for taking care of you."

"I didn't ask her—"

"Oh, don't you even start with that *I didn't ask for help shit*! You were hurt, and she cared enough to come over here and help you. The *least* you can do is to thank her for it."

"Okay...okay. I'll do it Monday."

"You won't have to wait that long. She'll be here tomorrow."

"What? Why?"

"Because Robin and I are going away this weekend, and someone has to change that bandage, so she agreed to come over and play nurse."

"I can take care of myself! You need to call her right now and tell her not to come!"

Laughing, Krista grabbed her jacket and walked to the door. "First, you don't have any bandages here. Second, you *can't* take care of yourself. And third, she wrote her number by your phone, so if you don't want her here, *you* call her!" Seeing the stunned look on Toni's face, Krista's shoulders fell. She had meant her words to be playful, totally forgetting that Toni no longer knew how to play. Walking over, she kissed Toni on the cheek. "I'm sorry, and if you want me to change my plans, I will. Just say the word."

With *you can't take care of yourself* still ringing in her ears, Toni shook her head. "No, I'll be okay. You and Robin have a good time."

Placing another quick peck on Toni's cheek, Kris said, "Thanks, Toni. See you next week."

As soon as the door closed, Toni stomped to the phone, dialing the number and listening as the connection went through. While it continued to ring, she stared at the scrap of paper, the phone number obviously written by Laura MacLeod for the strokes were strong and fluid and not at all like Krista's scrawl. As the answering machine picked up, Toni turned the paper over and when she read the words "*I just want to be your friend*" written on the back, her train of thought was lost. Hearing the beep in her ear, she quickly said, "Miss...Miss MacLeod, this is Toni...um...Toni Vaughn. Kris told me, well she said that you'd be stopping by tomorrow, but I don't need...I don't *want* you here. I...I appreciate what you did tonight, but I can...I can take care of myself. So...so thanks again. Good-bye."

***

Like the night before, Laura stood in the hallway for several minutes until her continual knocking produced the desired response. The door opened just enough to reveal a very sleepy Toni Vaughn, her short black hair tousled and pointing in every direction imaginable.

It was probably the worst case of bedhead Laura had ever seen, and her amusement showed on her face. "Hiya, Toni. How you feeling?"

Her brain and eyes still trying to adjust to consciousness, it took a moment before Toni realized she wasn't dreaming. "What are you doing here? Didn't you get my message?"

"Yes, I did, but I chose to ignore it," Laura said as she shuffled past and headed to the kitchen.

Closing her eyes, Toni took a deep breath to squelch her anxieties and then followed Laura into the other room.

"I brought you some coffee," Laura said, pulling a cup out of a cardboard carrier. "I didn't know what you liked, so I just ordered black."

"Have you got a problem taking no for an answer?" Toni asked.

"Only when it's the wrong answer."

The room went silent as they stood staring at each other, neither sure of the next step. Toni wanted nothing more than to banish Laura from her flat, but the smell of the coffee and the fact that the woman had helped her the night before was making it hard for Toni to say the words. Defeated, she asked, "So you're here. What now?"

Noticing Toni's rumpled clothes, Laura said, "Why don't you go get cleaned up, and when you're done, I'll change the bandages, and then I'll be on my way. How's that sound?"

"And if I want you to leave now?"

"You'll be in for one hell of an argument."

Clenching her jaw, Toni growled, "*Why* are you doing this?"

"Give me one reason why I shouldn't?"

Unable to think of an answer, Toni stomped to her bedroom, slamming the door behind her and throwing the bolt, leaving Laura grinning like a fool as she pulled the other cup of coffee from the carrier.

***

Having finished her coffee, Laura was just about to toss out the cup when Toni walked back into the kitchen wearing the same frown she had left with. Noticing that her hair was wet, Laura pointed to where the bandage on Toni's forehead used to be. "Did that fall off in the shower?"

"Yeah, but it's fine."

"I'll be the judge of that," Laura said, pulling out a chair. "Have a seat."

Toni's palms grew sweaty. Staring at the chair as if electricity were running to it, she said, "I can do this myself. I...I don't want you here. Why can't you understand that?"

Hearing the panic in Toni's voice, Laura asked, "Is this because you don't like to be touched?"

Toni's head snapped back, shocked and embarrassed that the woman knew so much. "I think you need to go...right now!"

"Toni, I'm not going anywhere, and I'm not going to hurt you. You need to trust me. Please, just sit down and we'll take it slow. I promise."

"And if I say no?"

Hoping to lighten the tenseness of the situation, Laura smiled. "Well, then I guess I'll just have to park my arse in this chair until you change your mind."

A snort of disgust escaped as Toni glared at the woman, but Laura simply crossed her arms and continued to smile. Her body language said it all. She'd stay all day if that's what it would take. Letting out a heavy sigh, Toni kept her eyes on Laura as she cautiously sat down.

Thrown by the woman's arrival, Toni hadn't taken notice of the first-aid kit until Laura put it on the table. Seeing the hefty case, Toni's curiosity was piqued. "Are you accident prone?"

Opening the case, Laura chuckled. "I took it from work last night. Hopefully, no one will stub a toe before I get it back on Monday."

Seeing that Toni's hands were now palm down on the table, and she had squeezed her eyes shut, Laura's movements were slow and precise. Peering at the cut on Toni's head, while her first thought was to brush a few strands of hair out of the way, Laura decided the less she touched Toni the better off both of them would be. Opening a tube of antibiotic cream, she put a small bit on her finger and as lightly as she could, coated the cut. "This doesn't look bad at all, actually. Typical head wound, lots of blood and hardly any damage. I won't cover it again, but you need to keep it clean."

Breathing in the scent of Laura's perfume, Toni relaxed enough to open her eyes and immediately felt like a voyeur. Laura's blouse had gaped open, and it was now presenting Toni with more than an ample view of the woman's cleavage. Quickly, she diverted her eyes and stared at the floor.

Toni hadn't thought about women in years. Her needs and wants for the warmth of another had been destroyed by thick walls, steel doors and scars. She was once a player, enjoying one-night stands with women of all shapes and sizes, but now...now she didn't even play alone. The touch of another used to make her body pulse, but now it trembled at even the slightest contact, so while Laura's touch was gentle, the only feelings stirring in Toni were ones of angst.

It felt as if her heart would break through her ribs at any moment, but frozen by fear Toni didn't move an inch until Laura sat down and reached for her bandaged arm. Acting as if a branding iron had been pressed against her skin, Toni jerked away, her chair rocking back with the force. Grimacing at her own reaction, Toni hung her head. She hated who she had become. She knew in her heart that Laura only wanted to help, but that knowledge did not stop her fear. Taking a stuttered breath, she put her arm back on the table as she raised her eyes to meet Laura's. "I'm...I'm sorry. Go...go ahead."

The sound of Toni's ragged breathing slowed Laura's movements even more, and as gently as she could, she removed the gauze wrapped around the woman's forearm. The crimson gash was long and deep, and the butterfly bandages that Laura had used the night before had done their job, but just barely. "You know, this really does need stitches."

"I don't like doctors," Toni said, glancing at the wound. "I've had worse. It'll be fine."

"Look, there's a clinic just down the road—"

"I said, *I don't like doctors!*" Toni screamed. Pushing back her chair to stand, she tried to yank her arm away and immediately regretted it.

The pain was intense, and as the gash reopened, blood began to spill out.

"Shit," Laura muttered, grabbing some gauze to stop the flow.

For an instant, their eyes met, and each tried their hardest to stare down the other. Scottish temper confronted by English anger was a lethal combination, but when Laura saw the amount of blood pouring from the cut, she reined in her annoyance. Narrowing her eyes as if daring Toni to move, Laura returned to the work at hand, giving Toni no choice but to sit in silence and watch.

As Laura tended to the wound, Toni's uneasiness began to disappear like the blood being blotted from her arm. She stole one glance and then another while Laura worked, oblivious that she was being watched. Her auburn hair smelled of strawberries, and the perfume she wore today was a bit more flowery than the one Toni was used to, but it still was pleasant and light. Looking down, she watched as Laura tenderly administered first-aid, and all of a sudden Toni realized that the woman's touch no longer felt foreign or dangerous.

"You'll need to keep this dry and clean. Okay?" Laura said, applying the last bit of tape to hold the gauze in place.

"Yeah," Toni said as she stood up with coffee cup in hand. Quickly drinking what remained, she placed the cup on the table and left the room without saying a word.

Laura knew Toni was telling her that her visit had come to an end, so gathering the kit, she walked to the door. "I guess I'll see you on Monday," she said as Toni opened the door.

"Look...um...thanks for doing this," Toni said, holding up her arm. "I don't...I don't know what I can do to repay you."

Without thinking, Laura said the first thing that came to mind. "Buy me dinner."

"What?"

"Buy me dinner," Laura repeated, grinning up at the woman.

Shaking her head, Toni said, "I-I-I don't think I can...I can do that."

"Well, you didn't think you could let me change the bandages, but you did. Just think about it. There's no rush," Laura said as she walked out. Looking over her shoulder, she said, "You have my number, so call me if you need anything."

Toni closed the door and looked down at her bandaged arm. Running a finger over the gauze, she closed her eyes for a moment as she remembered the feel of Laura's touch.

***

When she arrived at work Monday morning, Laura had only one thing on her mind...Toni Vaughn. As she expected, Toni hadn't called, so Laura spent the better part of the weekend worrying about a woman she hardly knew, but couldn't seem to get out of her head.

Deciding that her first stop would be Toni's classroom to see how she was doing, Laura's plans changed as soon as she walked into Calloway. Forgetting that she had appointments scheduled the entire day, for the next eight hours, Laura's time was spent in meetings and on conference calls. By the time she finished the last, it was nearly five o'clock.

"Shit," Laura said, looking at her watch. Aware that Toni always left at four, Laura had two choices. Drive to the woman's flat to check up on her or wait until the next day. As she weighed her options, she heard a light tapping and looked up to see Toni standing in the doorway. In an instant, Laura's face brightened. "Hiya, Toni."

"You're working late," Toni said, walking into the room.

"Apparently, I'm not the only one."

"Actually, I've been done for a while. I was just waiting for the halls to clear before I came downstairs."

Toni didn't visit the first floor unless it was to exit the building at the end of the day or to grab a smoke, and Laura knew it. Toni Vaughn had a routine, and it never, *ever* changed. Eyeing the woman, Laura asked, "What's up?"

Shuffling her feet, Toni looked at the floor. "Kris...um...the woman you met the other night in my flat. She's still out of town, and I...well...I don't have any bandages at my place. So...so I was wondering if I could borrow that first-aid kit for the night. I'll...I'll bring it back tomorrow. I promise."

"You haven't changed the dressing since Saturday?" Laura said, getting to her feet.

"No, I mean yes, but not...not properly."

Confused, Laura strode across the room and glared at Toni, defying her to say a word. Unbuttoning the cuff of her sleeve, Laura pushed up the material and her nostrils flared. "Are you completely mad!" she barked, seeing the washcloth being held in place by duct tape.

"I didn't have any bandages—"

"You had my bloody number!"

"I didn't want to bother—"

"Jesus Christ!" Laura shouted, pointing to the sofa. "Sit down."

"Look, if you just let me borrow—"

"I said sit *down*!" Laura said, before turning on her heel and stomping out of the room.

"Christ," Toni said under her breath as she hesitantly sat on the couch. She had never seen Laura MacLeod that angry before, and as she waited in silence, Toni hoped she'd never have to see it again.

Returning with the kit, and her blood pressure now well within the range of normal, Laura sat down. Attempting to be an obedient patient, Toni had rolled up the sleeve of her faded blue shirt, and this time, when Laura saw the shabby brown washcloth taped to the woman's arm, she snickered. Carefully cutting away the tape, Laura quickly discovered that Toni was telling the truth. Even though the bandage was indeed crude, the wound was clean, dry and healing.

As Laura worked, Toni's eyes wandered, and seeing faint, greenish-yellow bruises on Laura's wrists, she asked, "Did I do that?"

Looking up, Laura followed Toni's gaze. "Oh, yeah, but it's okay. They're almost gone."

"I'm sorry."

"You were in the midst of a full-blown panic attack. You didn't know what you were doing. It's fine."

"I didn't mean to hurt you."

"I know you didn't," Laura said softly. Sitting back, she tossed the scissors in the case. "Well, there you go. All finished."

Surprised to see that her arm was already freshly bandaged, Toni carefully pulled down her sleeve as she stood up. Noticing files scattered all over Laura's desk, she said, "I guess I should let you get back to work now." Reaching the door, she turned around. "Miss MacLeod?"

"Oh, Toni, please call me Laura."

"Um...I just wanted to say thanks for...for helping me."

"You're quite welcome, Toni."

"And about your idea for dinner."

"Yes?"

"I'm sorry, but...but that's not something I can do," Toni said in a whisper. "I'm sure you understand."

CHAPTER SEVEN

"What's that?" Toni asked, seeing a package she didn't recognize as Kris put away the groceries.

Inwardly, Kris groaned. Without turning around, she said quietly, "Oh...um...just some new biscuits. They were on sale. I thought you might like to try them."

"Oh, sure...whatever."

A month before, Krista would have been shocked to hear Toni accept change of any kind, but hairline cracks had begun to appear in the woman's cloistered existence, and aspects of her old friend had begun to slip through. Now, when Kris came over, they talked. Not long, in-depth conversations, but conversations nonetheless. The changes were subtle, and no one except Krista and perhaps Laura had noticed, but something other than despair had begun to take hold of Toni Vaughn.

Noticing a candy bar on the counter, Kris cocked her head to the side. "Where'd that come from?"

Toni followed her eyes, and the corners of her mouth turned up a fraction. "Laura."

"Laura gave you chocolate? Any particular reason?"

"She ran out of fruit," Toni said as she headed to her bedroom.

That day had started out like any other day for Toni. She woke up at five and shuffled into the kitchen to turn on the coffeemaker. Returning to her bedroom, she pulled on her trainers, jumped on her treadmill and jogged for an hour, and after showering and pulling on some clothes, she poured herself a cup of coffee and nibbled some biscuits while she prepared her lunch. Filling her thermal mug, she grabbed her lunch and headed out the door, triple-checking all the locks before she headed to work.

Toward late afternoon, she heard the familiar click of heels on the tile, and though her facial expression didn't change, in the deep recesses of Toni's brain, a smile was born. Looking up as Laura walked into the room, their eyes met for the briefest of seconds and Toni voiced a very quiet hello before returning her eyes to the papers scattered on her desk.

Since the day she had visited Laura's office to get the first-aid kit, the anxiety Toni always felt around people other than her students had eased, at least where Laura MacLeod was concerned. Knowing that she owed the woman something, and buying her dinner was out of the question, common courtesy would have to do.

Laura took her seat as Toni handed out test papers, and for the better part of an hour, the only sound to be heard was that of pencils scratching on paper. Sitting like she always did, her legs crossed at the ankles and tucked slightly under her chair, Laura's head remained bowed as she filled out reports, while Toni sat at the front of the room, occasionally stealing glances of the department head.

While Toni cared nothing about the clothing she wore, as she studied the woman at the back of the class, her lip curled just a hair. Partial to wearing skirts with jackets to match, today Laura was wearing the most basic of black...and it was basic. It seemed to fit her small frame perfectly, as if it had been tailored to her curves, but in Toni's opinion, it lacked a feminine softness. It spoke of authority and business, and even though it couldn't be considered masculine, without the white silk blouse unbuttoned just enough to show a hint of cleavage, as far as Toni was concerned, Laura's ensemble was downright boring.

The tests were gathered and class was dismissed. As the students shuffled out, Laura gathered her belongings and walked out of the room, but when Toni turned and saw no apple on her desk, a fissure opened and the person she once was made an appearance. "Oi!" she hollered. "Where's my bloody apple?"

Almost to the stairs, Laura stopped and then turned to look down the hallway. Her entire face spread into a smile as she slowly walked back, and as she entered the classroom, Toni wore an actual grin. It wasn't ear-to-ear or toothy or over-the-top, but it was definitely a grin...and it looked wonderful.

Opening her bag, Laura rummaged around until she found a candy bar, and placing it on Toni's desk, she said, "I haven't had time to shop. Hope you like chocolate."

***

Amused that Laura was now giving candy to her reclusive friend, Krista examined the wrapper for a second before dropping the treat on the counter and going in search of Toni. Finding her rummaging through her tiny closet mumbling unintelligible words, Krista said, "I'm going to be heading out, unless there's something else you need."

"No, I'm fine," Toni said, tossing another shirt on the bed. Turning around to find that Kris had already left the room, Toni jogged up the hallway to catch her. "Krista."

"Yeah?"

Stuffing her hands into the pockets of her jeans, Toni said, "I was wondering...well, I thought...I thought maybe, that is if you have the time, we might be able to go clothes shopping early one morning, before the crowds get too bad."

"We?"

"Yeah."

"As in you and I?"

"If that's okay?"

Kris told herself to keep her excitement to a minimum, but she just couldn't. Squealing, she ran over and pulled Toni into a hug. She expected what she received from Toni, which was nothing in return, but Kris didn't care. She didn't care one goddamn bit. Holding Toni at arm's length, Kris said, "Of course, it's okay, and there's no time like the present, so I'll be here bright and early tomorrow morning."

Raising an eyebrow, Toni stared back at her friend. "You don't *do* early."

"Are you serious about this? I mean, about going shopping."

"Yeah, I think so."

"Good, then I'll be here tomorrow bright *and* early!"

***

Wrapped in a towel, Krista softly padded into the bedroom. Trying her best not to make a sound, she opened the wardrobe door, but the hinge squeaked and seconds later, her wife squawked.

"What time is it?" Robin groused from under the sheets.

"A bit past seven, now go back to sleep."

"Seven? In the morning? On a Saturday? Are you crazy?"

"No, I'm not, now go back to sleep."

Switching on the bedside lamp, Robin propped a pillow behind her back and yawned. Rubbing the sleep out of her eyes, she said, "Honey, what's going on? You're never up this early on a weekend."

"I'm taking Toni shopping," Kris said, opening a dresser drawer.

"Oh, okay," Robin said, sinking into the pillow, but then the penny dropped. "*You're what!*" she screamed, sitting up in bed.

Beaming, Kris rushed to the bed, plopping down practically on top of Robin in her excitement. "She asked me last night, out of the blue, and I wasn't about to say no. I would have told you when I got home, but you were already asleep."

"Oh, my God, this is great! Do you want me to go with you? I don't mind. I can sleep anytime."

"Oh, baby, I know you love her and want to help, but I think she's going to be nervous enough without adding another person to the mix. Besides, you know how you get around her."

"Yeah, you're probably right."

Giving Robin a quick kiss, Kris headed back to the dresser, dropping the towel as she rummaged in her lingerie drawer. Hearing Robin's whistle, she turned around. "See something you like?"

"Several things, actually," Robin said, her eyes drinking in the view. Hopping out of bed, she grabbed her robe and then went over and playfully pinched Krista's bum before shuffling into the bathroom. A few seconds later, she called out, "What time are you picking her up?"

"Just before nine, but I was so excited I couldn't sleep. I thought I'd make some breakfast. You hungry?"

When no response was given, Kris shrugged and then stepped into her knickers. Hearing the door open, she glanced over her shoulder, and her mouth dropped open. Robin was standing in the doorway totally nude.

"As a matter of fact," Robin purred, pulling Kris into her arms. "I'm practically starving."

***

Although briefly sidelined by her oversexed wife, Krista arrived at Toni's flat just as promised, bright and early, and found that Toni's confidence level had dropped dramatically since the night before. In silence, Kris watched as Toni stomped about having an animated argument with herself. With her arms flailing about as expletives were growled, grumbled and shouted, she nervously paced back and forth and back again. Kris remained silent, clamping her lips together so as not to laugh, but when Toni handed her the list of clothes she needed, Krista found her voice.

"Sorry, Toni, that's not an option," she said, handing her back the list.

"I can't do this, Krista. Just get me a pair of jeans and a few shirts. That's all I need."

"No."

"Please—"

"No."

"Krista—"

"It's not happening, Toni."

"I can't do it."

"Yes, you can."

"No, I can't!"

"Yes—you—*can*."

"Why are you doing this?"

"I'm doing *this* because last night, *you* said you wanted to go shopping, and I didn't get my arse out of bed *early* on a Saturday so I can go out and buy you knickers! Now, get it together, Vaughn, because *you* and I are going out!"

Kris held her breath and prayed she hadn't pushed too hard. Even though over the past several weeks she had seen brief glimpses of her old friend reappear, she was also well aware of how easily Toni could pull back into herself. She was obviously scared, but she was talking, and shouting, and whether she knew it or not, she was becoming Toni again.

***

Less than an hour later, after spending ten minutes convincing Toni to get out of the car, they entered a small shop that offered its clientele the most basic of clothing. Its shelves were filled with jeans of every size and color, and racks bulged with T-shirts, Oxfords and the like. With only one other customer in the store, even though Toni was visibly nervous, Krista remained at her side while they rummaged through the stacks of denim. Feeling more like a bodyguard than a friend, Kris, nevertheless, stayed by Toni's side, and when clothes had to be tried on, Kris stood guard outside the changing room door.

Having already found a pair of jeans and two Oxfords, as they roamed the aisles, Kris noticed that Toni seemed to have lost interest in what the store had to offer. Browsing through the racks aimlessly, Toni hadn't stopped to look at anything seriously in over five minutes.

"Toni, what's up? I always get your clothes here."

"I...I just thought, well I mean...I...I—"

"Spit it out, Vaughn."

Hanging her head, Toni raised her eyes. "The other day at work, I noticed that most of the staff...well, I mean, Laura wears rather professional-looking clothes, and I'm always in jeans and T-shirts. So, I thought maybe I could try to look a bit more...a bit more proper, considering I'm a teacher and all."

Failing at hiding her excitement, Kris snatched the clothes from Toni's hands. "Why don't I go pay for this lot, and we'll go somewhere else? There are a few shops down the street I think you might like."

With Toni's credit card in hand, Kris quickly paid for the purchases, and then hooked her arm through Toni's as they left the store. Less than two blocks later, they walked into another shop; however, this one was upscale and trendy, its racks filled with the finest blouses, cardigans and trousers.

A bit busier than the last, Krista watched intently for any sign that Toni was beginning to feel tense. When she saw her hands turn into fists or her face pale, Kris would move in close, silently offering Toni her assurances that all would be okay, and all was.

While Toni moved through a rack filled with trousers in the finest fabrics, Krista stood opposite, fingering through one filled with leather. Pulling out a pair, she held them up. "How about these?"

"I don't think they're proper school attire."

"You used to wear them all the time when you worked at the university."

As soon as the words came out, Krista wanted to die. Promising Toni years before never to talk about her past life, Kris was afraid to look up and view the damage she had just caused. Several seconds passed, and then she heard Toni say, "Back then I was always on the pull."

Relieved that her misspoken words hadn't spoiled the day, Kris breathed easy. "That's true, but you never know when you'll need something for a special occasion."

Remembering Laura's suggestion about dinner, Toni glanced at the leather trousers and sighed. It had once been her favorite material, and before going to prison, half her wardrobe consisted of leather trousers, waistcoats and jackets, but that was when she cared. That was when she was alive.

"No, these are fine. I'll just try them on," Toni said quietly, holding up some dress trousers. Her mind occupied with thoughts of a life she no longer had, she walked to the dressing room.

Krista knew instantly that there was something on Toni's mind other than clothes for work. The woman was terrified of strangers, and she had just meandered through a boutique now filled with people as if they didn't exist. Trotting over to the changing area, Kris stood outside the door. "Toni, what's going on?"

Opening the door a few inches, Toni peered out, "What do you mean?"

Rolling her eyes, Kris said, "I wasn't born yesterday, Toni. You just walked through a crowded shop without batting a bloody eye. That tells me that there's something on your mind. Now, what is it?"

"It's nothing," Toni said, closing the door in Krista's face.

"You're lying and we both know it," Krista said as she tried the knob. Finding it locked, she stomped her foot. "Damn it, Toni! Open the sodding door and tell me what the hell is going on."

A few seconds later, Toni peeked out again. "Look, it's really nothing. It's just something Laura said."

"Oh yeah? What?"

"Well, she thought, I mean, she *suggested* that I could pay her back for helping me…by taking her out to dinner."

"Dinner?"

"Yeah, and if I did, not that I would, mind you, but *if* I did, I'd need something nice to wear."

"Are you thinking about it?"

"What's to think about, Krista? You and I both know it's impossible."

"You're managing to get through today, aren't you?"

"Sure, but I'm with you, and I trust you. You know how I am."

"And she doesn't?"

"Well, no, I'm sure she does, but you and I have a history together. If I freak out around you—"

"It's not as embarrassing as doing it in front of a stranger."

"Exactly."

"I don't know about you, but if someone came to my flat in the middle of the night to patch me up, I don't think I'd consider them a stranger."

"Yeah, but—"

"Toni, Laura seems really nice. If she's the one who suggested dinner, and she already knows how uncomfortable you are around people, it sounds to me like she's willing to take a chance. From where I'm standing, I think that makes her a friend. Don't you?"

Kris was right, and Toni knew it. Somewhere over the past weeks, Laura MacLeod had crossed the line between stranger and friend. Even though Toni still tensed when Laura walked into her classroom, and even though her palms would sweat and her heart would race, in the inner depths of her soul, Toni knew that Laura was no longer a stranger. Thinking for a moment, Toni said, "Kris, I don't know what to do."

"I do. Stay right there," Kris said as she disappeared back into the store. A few minutes later, she returned with a pair of leather trousers, two silk blouses and a rather large grin.

"What's this?" Toni asked, looking at the shimmering red and blue shirts.

"There's no harm in being prepared, is there?" Kris said as she handed the clothes to Toni. "And you can't very well wear cotton Oxfords with leather, Toni. It's tacky. Now go try these on." The changing room door had barely latched when Kris added, "And I want to see them!"

CHAPTER EIGHT

By the middle of the next week, Toni was a bundle of nervous energy. Her daily routine hadn't changed, but her mind was occupied with thoughts of venturing outside of her safety zone, and it was turning her head around. And if that wasn't enough, she had worn some of her new clothes to work, and all day long she had been receiving whistles and high-fives from her students.

Glancing at the clock, she gathered her belongings, took a deep breath and hesitantly went downstairs to Laura's office. It was a short walk, taking less than a minute, but by the time she stood outside the door, all of her courage had disappeared. She was about to turn and run when the door opened, and Laura stepped out.

"Toni, what a pleasant surprise!" Laura said.

As nice as it was to see Toni standing just outside her door, Laura couldn't contain her smile when she noticed Toni's new clothes. The blouse was still the woman's standard Oxford style, but this one was bright white, crisp and fitted, the side darts pulling the shirt tight against her skin. The gray tweed trousers were low on her hips, held in place by a narrow black belt, and her black boots were polished and new, with heels that pushed Toni slightly over six feet in height.

Nervously, Toni stared at the floor. She had practiced the words. She had even written them down, but now with Laura standing right in front of her, Toni couldn't think of a syllable. Luckily, Laura could.

"I'm sorry that I haven't been up to see you this week," Laura said, motioning for Toni to come into her office. "With John out, it gets a bit hectic at times."

Seeing the stack of papers on Laura's desk, Toni turned to leave. "I'm sorry. You're busy. I don't want to keep you from your work."

"No, Toni," Laura called out. "I was just coming up to see you. How's the arm?"

"It's fine," Toni said, once again staring at the floor.

"Yeah?"

Her fists tightening with determination, Toni raised her eyes. "Look, I just wanted to ask you, I mean, well I thought it was time that I pay you back for taking care of me."

"Okay?"

"Would you like to...would you like to have dinner on Friday night...with me?"

Without hesitation, Laura said, "Yes, I would, very much."

"Really? I mean...that would be great."

"So, where are you taking me?"

"Oh, I hadn't thought about that," Toni said quietly. "I don't really know—"

"I have an idea," Laura said, sensing the woman's dilemma. "Since you don't get out much, why don't I pick you up at six, and then we'll decide together. How's that sound?"

"That sounds good," Toni said, turning quickly to leave. "Well, I'd better let you get back to work now. See you on Friday."

"Toni."

"Yeah?"

"You look nice. I like your new clothes."

Toni acknowledged the compliment with a nod and then bolted from the room, leaving Laura sitting on the edge of her desk positively glowing. She had never seen Toni Vaughn blush before.

***

Immediately after her last class of the week, Toni raced home, showered and was partially dressed by the time Kris arrived with her groceries. After putting away the food, Kris walked to the bedroom and stood in the doorway as Toni debated on what to wear. Fifteen minutes later, Kris watched as Toni tried on the dark blue blouse for the third time.

"I like the red one," Kris said, watching as Toni took off the shirt.

"What the hell am I doing?" Toni muttered. Sitting on the edge of the bed, she tossed the blouse on the floor.

"You're just nervous," Kris said, picking up the shirt. "You haven't had a date in a long time."

"*A date!*" Toni shouted. "Krista, this isn't a date! This is just to thank Laura for what she did. Christ, you don't think that she thinks this is a date? Oh, that's not what I want…what I meant! Shit! I need to call her—"

"Toni, calm down. It was a poor choice of words on my part."

"But—"

"Relax, I'm sure Laura isn't thinking of tonight as a date. Just two friends going out to dinner. That's all."

"I don't know, if she thinks—"

"Will you *please* relax," Kris said, raising her voice just a tad. "Stop looking for excuses to call the whole thing off and get dressed. She'll be here in ten minutes, and I'm fairly certain that she'd appreciate it if you weren't half-naked. Then she'd *definitely* get the wrong idea."

***

Laura stood in her bedroom wearing nothing but her underwear as she tossed yet another outfit aside. She had tried on and removed three different dresses, and as she stared at the clothes in her wardrobe, she laughed. "What the hell am I doing?"

Quickly, she grabbed the next in line and slipped it on, smoothing the fabric and pulling up the zip before stepping into her shoes and returning to the bathroom. Glancing in the mirror, she brushed her hair, checked her makeup and then stopped and stared at her reflection. She was nervous, and she had absolutely no idea why. She knew that tonight would be difficult for Toni, but why was she feeling this way? She liked dining out. She liked having dinner with friends. She liked the restaurant she had chosen. She liked Toni.

A thought popped into her head, and Laura immediately pushed it away. She liked Toni. No big deal. She liked Abby and Susan and

Irene. No big deal. They were her friends and so was Toni, but then the thought returned, and Laura gritted her teeth. "Stop being daft," she said, glaring at her reflection as if *it* were to blame for what she was thinking. "She's a woman, for Christ's sake!"

Having spent the better part of the thirty-minute drive to Toni's convincing herself that she thought of the woman as a friend and nothing more, by the time Laura reached Toni's flat, she was calm, cool, *and* collected.

Knowing that Toni would undoubtedly be nervous and in need of moral support, Laura wasn't surprised when Krista opened the door and invited her in. As she walked past, Kris took a second—a *long* second—to admire Laura's attire.

The dress was emerald green, with a modest neckline and three-quarter length sleeves, and as Laura strolled into the lounge, Krista watched as the lightweight fabric swished around the woman's slender legs. Upon finishing her perusal, Krista came to a decision. Laura MacLeod was a babe.

"I was just leaving, but she should be out in a minute," Krista said quietly as she glanced toward the bedroom.

"Anything I should know?"

An easy smile played at the corners of Krista's mouth as she opened the door to leave. "She's nervous. She's scared, and I hope you two have a marvelous night."

A few minutes later, Toni appeared and Laura was stunned. She knew that Toni was attractive, but when she came into the lounge wearing snug, black leather trousers and a shimmering red blouse, attractive didn't come close.

"Hiya," Laura said.

"Hi."

Laura had two choices. Compliment Toni on her appearance, or get her into the car before she changed her mind. Laura chose wisely.

***

After maneuvering into a parking space, Laura turned off the engine and glanced over at her passenger. Since leaving the apartment, Toni had hardly said a word, and the farther away from her flat they traveled, the more anxious she had become. Now, nervously wringing her hands in her lap, Toni's breathing was becoming deeper with each passing second. Reaching over, Laura lightly touched the back of Toni's hand and instantly regretted it when Toni jerked it away.

Mentally chastising herself for her mistake, Laura said softly, "Why don't we go inside and see about getting you that steak dinner?"

Nervously, Toni shook her head. "I don't think I can do this. I think...I think I need to go home."

"Toni—"

"Look, I'm not stupid!" Toni shouted. "I know that you've talked to Kris and probably to John, so you know I've got a problem with...with *this*. Please...please just take me back to my place. I can't do this."

Toni's voice, although raised for a moment, had become a ragged, pleading whisper, and Laura's heart broke. "Toni, you can do this," she said, quietly. "I called ahead and asked for a private table, and I promise that I won't leave your side for a minute. I know you're scared, but you can do this. Please...for me?"

One minute passed and then the next as Toni sat looking out the window. She could see the entrance to the restaurant. It was only a few steps away, barely six strides, but almost five minutes passed before she managed to give Laura a nod as she reached for the door handle. Waiting until Laura appeared at her window, Toni cautiously got out of the car and keeping her eyes glued on the sidewalk, she took the longest walk of her life.

Once inside, Laura gave her name to the maître d', and as she had promised, he led them through the dining room to a secluded, corner table and Toni quickly chose the seat that put her back to the room. A menu was placed in front of her, and she was welcomed to the restaurant, but she didn't say a word or begin to peruse the selections until the man walked away.

Glancing in Laura's direction, Toni offered a weak smile as she picked up the menu. As she read the descriptions of the various entrées, her mouth began to water and her nerves settled, but when the waiter appeared seconds later, she instantly stiffened, placed her hands palm down on the table and lowered her gaze.

Seeing Toni's reaction, Laura quickly took charge. Ordering them both a glass of wine, once the waiter disappeared from view, Laura reached over and tapped the table to get Toni's attention. "I hope you like Cabernet."

Toni raised her eyes and took a breath. "I haven't had it in a while, but yes, I do."

"Good," Laura said, glancing at the menu. "So do you see anything you like?"

Toni looked at the choices again and then back up at Laura, their eyes locking for an instant before she answered. "I think I'd like the filet, but..."

"I can order for you, if you'd like. I don't mind."

"Thanks," Toni whispered, a slight blush appearing on her cheeks.

For the rest of the night, Laura took the lead, ordering them dinner and drinks as needed. Their conversation began hesitantly, but once Laura brought up the subject of teaching, for the rest of the meal, they chatted easily.

With bellies filled and warmed by wine, they walked to the exit wearing smiles, but as soon as they stepped outside, everything changed. When they had arrived, the street hadn't been crowded, but now it was overflowing with people coming and going from the various pubs and restaurants that lined the block, and Toni went absolutely rigid. As if cemented in place, she could neither move nor breathe.

Without giving it a second thought, Laura grabbed Toni's hand and pulled her through the crowd. Reaching the car, Laura got her inside as quickly as possible and then ran to the driver's door. As soon as the door closed, shutting off the noise of the street, Laura could hear Toni gasping for air.

"You need to relax, Toni. It's okay," Laura said quietly. "Just breathe easy."

Toni nodded, but when she continued to take too many quick breaths, Laura reached over, totally forgetting once again the woman's fears. As soon as she touched Toni on the leg, Toni flinched away, pressing herself hard against the car door.

"Damn it," Laura said, wincing at her mistake. "I'm sorry, Toni, but you need to slow your breathing. Just relax. You're okay."

"Please...please just take me home," Toni said, closing her eyes to try to block out her fear. "I want to go home."

***

All Toni wanted to do was lock herself in her flat and hide from the world, but when they reached her door, Laura suggested they have a cup of tea, and feeling obligated, Toni agreed. After setting up the kettle, Toni excused herself, disappearing into her bedroom in hopes that a few minutes of solitude would give her enough time to calm her nerves and lessen the weight of embarrassment now pressing down on her.

Patiently waiting for Toni to return, Laura looked around the lounge. Tilting her head to read the titles of the books stacked about the room, when the kettle began to whistle, she went to the kitchen and filled the mugs. Opening the fridge in search of milk, Laura stopped when she saw a bottle of cloudy vodka on the bottom shelf. Under the stark brilliance of flickering fluorescents, reality slapped her in the face.

"I don't have any milk," Toni said from the doorway. "Sorry."

Swallowing hard, Laura pushed away her thoughts and shut the door. "No worries. I can do without."

A few minutes later, sitting at the little table crammed into the corner of the kitchen, they sat quietly sipping their tea. Laura knew Toni was on edge, and hoping to offer some comfort, she reached over and touched Toni's hand.

As if she had just been burned, Toni snatched her hand away, the legs of her chair screeching across the floor as she pushed away from the table and jumped to her feet. "I do *not* like to be touched! Why can't you understand that?"

"Toni—"

"Oh, Christ, tonight was a huge fucking mistake," Toni shouted, storming from the room.

Quickly following, Laura said, "Toni, tonight was wonderful. I had a great time—"

"Did you, Laura? Really?" Toni said, crossing her arms. "Tell me, what part did you like the best? When you had to pry me out of the car to go into the bloody restaurant, or when you had to order my meal because I was too fucking *scared* to do it for myself!"

"Toni, you're being too hard on yourself."

"No, that's where you're wrong!" Toni shouted. "You see, I *know* where I belong and where I don't!" Waving her arms in the air, she yelled, "*This* is my life, Laura. Don't you get that? *This* is all I've got. I don't belong out there anymore, and I was an idiot for even trying."

"No, you weren't. You did great tonight! So you hit a few stumbling blocks—"

"Stumbling blocks? Stumbling blocks! I'm thirty-four years old, Laura, and I couldn't even go to the loo tonight because I was so bloody afraid."

"You could have asked me—"

"What? I could have asked you to hold my hand? Just how much humiliation do you think I can take?"

"Toni—"

"Laura, I want you to leave. Just go home. Go *back* to your life and stay the *fuck* out of mine!"

Knowing that her presence was only adding fuel to the fire, Laura reluctantly gathered her things and walked to the door. Looking over her shoulder, she gazed at the woman staring out the window, and even in the dimly lit room, Laura could see the tears rolling down Toni's face. "I had a wonderful time tonight, Toni, and if you need anything, you have my number."

"I don't *need* anything. Not from you, not from anyone! All I want is to be left alone, so do me a favor and *leave me the fuck alone!*"

Hearing the door close, Toni watched from the window as Laura got into her car and drove away. As it disappeared down the street, she rested her forehead against the cool glass, her breath fogging the pane as she struggled with her demons. Staring at the streetlights of the city, her eyes filled with tears as distant memories of nightclubs, friends and dancing came back to her. She was once so much more, but that person had been destroyed by the vileness of inhumane beings wearing prison uniforms.

"Fuck this!" she blurted through her tears as she stormed into the kitchen and yanked open the refrigerator door. "Fuck all of this!"

***

For the second Saturday in a row, Krista was up with the sun, and after a quick shower, and a promise to Robin she'd be back soon, she headed out the door. After stopping at a local coffee house, when she reached Toni's building, she took the stairs two at a time until she reached 3-D.

Rapping on the door, she waited and then glanced at her watch, somewhat surprised that Toni had yet to answer. Since her release from prison, Toni had been an early riser, and after a few more minutes of waiting, Kris took matters into her own hands. Juggling the coffee carrier, she fumbled for her keys and then let herself in.

The first thing she noticed was the air. It was thick with the smell of cigarettes, and the normally cool apartment was almost stifling. Glancing at the windows, she saw they were all closed, and then she noticed a table lamp lying on the floor and several stacks of books were now strewn about the room.

"Toni?" she called out, looking toward the bedroom. "You awake?"

When she heard no response, Kris frowned, and as she tried to remember if she had seen Toni's car parked outside the building, she made her way to the kitchen. Turning on the light, she was about to put down the coffee when she saw the empty vodka bottle on the counter. In a silent whoosh, the carrier fell to the floor, the hot coffee splashing on Krista's jeans, but she didn't feel the burn. Bringing her hands to her head, she pressed her palms against her temples and began to wail.

CHAPTER NINE

"Good morning."

"Hey there," Abby Parker said, turning just in time to see Laura yawn as she came into the kitchen. "Did you sleep all right?"

"Yeah. Thanks for letting me stay here last night."

"We were talking until three, Laura. I wasn't about to send you home at that hour."

After leaving Toni's, Laura had made it barely a mile before she stopped the car and used her mobile to call Abby Parker. A psychologist by profession, she was, more importantly, Laura's best friend, and by the time Laura arrived at Abby's home, there were two glasses of Chardonnay sitting on the coffee table. For the rest of the night, Abby listened while Laura talked about Toni Vaughn.

"I've been thinking about what you told me about your friend, Toni," Abby said, sliding a cup of coffee in Laura's direction.

"And?"

"First, I know you meant well, but playing amateur psychologist is a dangerous game."

"I was trying to help. She seems so alone and so hurt. I just wanted to be a friend."

A knowing smile appeared on Abby's face. "I know you were. You're one of those rare people who would stop to help an injured animal along the side of the road even if the poor thing was frothing at the mouth," she said. "And Toni is definitely wounded."

"So what can I do?"

"There's not much you can do unless she comes to you. And you mustn't invade her space again, because you saw what happened the last time."

"What the hell are you talking about?"

"Laura, that night when you went over to help her, her panic attack wasn't brought on by what happened at Calloway. It was brought on by you."

"Me?"

Reaching across the table, Abby took her friend's hand. "Laura, listen to me. Toni is fractured. She's just bits and pieces where once there was a whole person. She's lost the ability to trust. She doesn't feel safe *anywhere* but in her flat, and from what you've told me, until very recently she has shown little or no emotion. She goes through each day, regimented to a routine that allows her to exist in a world that terrifies her. When you intruded on her life by entering her flat *without* an invitation, she panicked. You see that's the *only* thing left under her control. *She* says who comes and goes, what books are there, even down to the food she allows to be brought inside. *She* controls it all. When you went there that night and walked in without an invitation, it pushed her over the edge."

"Jesus, I didn't mean—"

"Of course you didn't."

"So, that could have happened when I was sitting in on her classes?"

"No, I don't think so, because that's not a safe place for her."

Laura scrunched up her face and stared back at the woman. "Okay, now I'm confused. I've seen her teach, Abby. Trust me, she feels safe there."

"No, I disagree. If she felt safe, you'd see her roaming the halls or visiting the recreation area, but she doesn't do that. To a certain extent, she probably feels comfortable in her classroom, but that has more to do with her belief in her teaching abilities rather than having control over the situation like she does in her flat."

"You've lost me."

"What she has when she's teaching is confidence *not* control. She can't choose her students *or* the questions they ask, but she knows she can teach. So, she manages to overcome some of her fears and by doing that, she becomes the person she used to be. You said it yourself, it was like she was transformed into another person, when, in fact, all she was doing was allowing herself to be who she is, or rather *was*."

"That doesn't make sense," Laura said, burying her face in her hands. "If she can pull it together in the classroom, why can't she do it somewhere else, like last night at the restaurant?"

"That's simple—fear. Without talking to her, and without knowing what those bastards did to her, I can't give you a definitive answer, but you said that she's afraid of strangers and crowds, and I'm sure that's all based on trust. She believes they'll hurt her. She put her trust in the system, in her colleagues, and to a certain extent, in the guards who were in that prison to care for her. The system put her in that place. Her colleagues abandoned her, and the guards mistreated her. And if it wasn't for her friend, Kris, Toni probably *would* have killed herself that day, but Kris did what friends do; she showed her love and compassion. Believe it or not, by *not* demanding she get rid of that narcotic-laced crap in her refrigerator, Kris showed that she could be trusted. And you, by being your patient and caring self, *especially* last night, well, I'd have to say that she's probably starting to trust you as well."

"Then why lash out at me?"

"Embarrassment, pride, call it what you want. Laura, she's confused and she channeled that confusion into anger. Yes, she pointed the finger in your direction, but she was angry at herself. For the first time in years, outside the walls of her classroom and her apartment, she was doing what normal people do...and she liked it. When you left the restaurant, all her insecurities returned and reality slapped her in the face, and it hurt, probably more than either of us can even begin to imagine."

***

Sobbing, Kris ran to the bedroom, throwing open the door and stumbling inside. The room, like the lounge, was warm and still, and the duvet was smooth as if the bed hadn't been slept in. Hearing the shower running, images of a razor blade and bloody wrists flashed through Krista's mind as she slowly made her way to the bathroom. Holding her breath, she cautiously opened the door and walked inside. It was only a few steps to the tub, but it felt like an eternity before she was within reach of the shower curtain. Grabbing hold of the green plastic, she whipped it aside.

If there had been a contest for who could scream first or who could scream the loudest, it would have been a tie.

"Krista! *What the fuck!*" Toni yelled, grabbing for the curtain to cover herself.

"Toni!"

"*Get the fuck out of here!*"

"Toni!"

"Krista, *now!*"

***

Sitting in her noiseless flat with lights extinguished and windows closed, Toni aimlessly tapped the end of her cigarette into an ashtray, the sides of which already overflowed with ash. She didn't notice. She didn't care. She was single-minded. There were no more excuses to be made, no more hesitation as she faced the inevitable. She no longer belonged among the living, having died so many years before. She knew that now.

A brief flashback of dinner crept into her mind, and she pushed it away, not allowing it to enter into the equation of the night. The answer was cold between her legs, the bottle of death propped there an hour before, and as she took the last swig of her warm beer, she dropped the amber bottle to the floor and unscrewed the cap of the clear. Bringing it to her lips, she hesitated as her doubt surfaced again. The continuous mental masturbation that had brought her to this point again and again, but simply existing was meaningless now. No amount of students or books could take away her loneliness, but the vodka could take away her pain...couldn't it?

She placed it on the table, returning to the kitchen to get two more bottles of beer. There was no need for limits now. No need to save for tomorrow when tomorrow wouldn't be. She wondered if the hoppy liquid would give her the strength to take the next step, and as she sat back down, she dropped another empty bottle to the floor. The sound of a woman's laughter echoed in her head, a deep throaty chuckle filled with possibilities, and she grinned. She couldn't help it. It was only a small shard of time spent amongst the living, satisfying a thirst she didn't know she had, but the bar of life was set too high. Toni brought the clear bottle to her lips again, minutes ticking by as she sat frozen in her thoughts, and then a different terror entered her mind...and she began to cry.

***

Toni tugged jeans over her wet legs, donned a T-shirt and stormed out of the bedroom. Coming to a stop when she saw Kris in the kitchen, she screamed, "Who the fuck do you think you are barging in on me like that? Jesus Christ, Krista! I almost had a fucking heart attack!" Momentarily blinded by her anger, when Toni realized what Kris was doing, she shouted, "And why the fuck are you washing the bloody floor?"

The intensity of the morning caught up with Kris. Sitting back on her haunches, she began to weep uncontrollably, her shoulders rising and falling as her emotions overflowed.

"What the fuck?" Toni mumbled, kneeling by the woman. "Krista, what the hell is going on? First, you scare the crap out of me, then you decide to give my floor a wash, and now...now you're crying!"

Managing to get herself somewhat under control, Krista glared back and then slapped Toni's arm once, and then twice, and then again. "You scared the shit out of me!"

"Me? What the fuck did I do?" Toni said, rubbing her bicep.

Kris raised herself to her knees and pointed at the counter. "That."

When Toni saw the empty bottle, her entire body slumped. "Oh, Christ."

"I...I thought you...I thought you did it," Kris said, trying to hold back the tears. "I thought you were..." Overwhelmed by emotion, Kris started to cry again, and for the first time in forever, Toni reached out to *her*.

Pulling Kris into her arms, Toni held on tight. "Sshhh," she whispered. "Sshhh, Krista. I'm sorry. I didn't know you'd be here, but you don't have to worry. I poured it out. It's gone."

"You...you did?"

Toni leaned back and looked into eyes she'd forgotten were so blue. "I know I should be in a room with rubber walls, and my life is shit, but ending it isn't the answer." Waiting while Kris sniffled back a few more tears, Toni noticed that several of the floor tiles were now much brighter than the rest. "Hey, you made a clean spot."

Looking at the floor, Krista frowned. "I brought us some coffee, but I dropped it when I saw the bottle."

"Well, why don't I make us some, and you can go get cleaned up?"

"I'm fine," Kris said, wiping away her tears. With her mascara and eyeliner already drooping, Kris not only dried her tears, she also decorated her face with two large sweeps of black, one on each cheek.

"How am I supposed to have a serious conversation when you look like a bloody terrorist? Go get washed up," Toni said, getting to her feet and helping Krista to hers.

"A serious conversation?"

"Yeah. I think it's time. Don't you?"

***

"Can I ask you a question?"

"Sure."

"Why Toni?" Abby asked.

"What do you mean?"

"Well, it seems to me that there are probably lots of women at Calloway who could use this kind of attention. What makes Toni so special?"

An excellent question, and one for which Laura didn't have an answer. How could she explain something she didn't understand herself? All she knew was that from the first minute she met Toni, she felt drawn to the brooding teacher with the sad brown eyes. Rubbing the back of her neck, Laura said, "I honestly don't know. Maybe because she wasn't what I expected."

"In what way?"

"I pictured her as someone older, someone plain and rough, but she's not like that. She's our age and definitely *not* unattractive," Laura said. "Christ, that makes me sound so shallow."

"You wouldn't work where you do if you were shallow," Abby said, getting up to refill her cup. "It's human nature to gravitate toward things we find appealing, thus the need for chocolate."

Smiling, Laura took a sip of her coffee. "I think part of it is because I know her history. No one in Calloway has her education or her background, and to see someone who had so much going for them end up like Toni...well, it's sad," Laura said with a sigh. "I guess I thought she could use a friend."

"Well, speaking from experience, she couldn't ask for a better one, but you really need to be careful with her, Laura. You and Kris need to understand you can't play doctor. If Toni wants you to be in her life, to be a friend, you're going to have to follow her lead and let her take the first step. You can't push her. You can't even nudge, because if you do, she might just break."

"So I guess calling her is out of the question?" Laura said, slumping back in her chair.

"Yes, it most certainly is."

***

"Feeling better?" Toni asked as Krista returned to the lounge.

"Yeah," Kris said. Sitting on the sofa, she took the cup of coffee Toni was offering her. "Thanks."

"Thank *you*."

"Thank me?" Kris said, eyeing Toni curiously. "What for? Shocking you in the shower or cleaning your kitchen floor with gourmet coffee?"

"How about for taking care of me for the past few years, even when I didn't want you to; even when I told you to sod off."

"You didn't mean it," Kris said. Seeing Toni's eyes crease at the corners, Kris said, "Okay, so maybe you did mean it, but since when did I ever listen to you?"

Running her finger over a faint scar on her wrist, Toni asked, "Why'd you let me keep the bottle?"

"You don't know how many times I asked myself the same question," Krista said, leaning back into the cushions. "I guess I was banking on the fact that I knew you better than you knew yourself, and I never knew you to give up on anything *or* take the easy way out."

"It's hardly easy," Toni whispered, staring at the floor. "I tried a half-dozen times last night to drink that shit, but I just couldn't do it. Every time I got close, I'd think about you, and I knew you'd be the one to find me. I couldn't do that, not after all we've been through. I wouldn't have just destroyed me. I would have destroyed you, too, and I love you too much for that to ever happen."

A moment of silence passed between them, and then Kris reached over and took Toni's hand. "Talk to me, Toni. What are you thinking?"

"I'm scared, Kris," Toni said in a breath. "I don't want to die, but I don't know…I don't know how to live anymore. I don't even know where to start."

"I think you just did."

"Huh?"

"Start," Krista said, squeezing her hand.

"By pouring that shit down the drain?"

"Yes, and by going out last night with Laura, but I'm thinking that something happened at dinner that brought all this on. Or am I wrong?"

Raking her fingers through her hair, Toni let out a sigh. Getting up, she walked to the window and peered through the pane. "It was such a strange feeling being…being out there. I was so scared, but Laura, she was great. She never tried to rush anything or force me to do something I wasn't ready to do. She even ordered my meal and arranged for us to have a table in the back away from all the other people, just so I'd be comfortable."

"And were you?"

Turning around, Toni said, "At first I was. I was so busy talking to her and noticing things…things that I had forgotten."

"Like what?"

"Lots of stuff. The taste of a good steak and Cabernet. The way linen tablecloths feel, and how the flame of a candle flickers at the slightest breeze. Even the bloody silverware felt heavy in my hand, and for a little while, I felt…normal."

"But?"

"But when we left the restaurant, there were people everywhere and I panicked…and everything went to shit."

"What happened?"

Walking over, Toni sank into the sofa. "I fucking froze. I couldn't walk. I couldn't talk. I couldn't even breathe. Christ, I must have looked like a bloody fool standing there like a statue. I don't even know how she managed to do it, but Laura got me into the car and brought me home, but by the time we got here, I guess my embarrassment turned into anger and I…I sort of directed it all at her."

"Sort of?"

"I lashed out at her. I told her I didn't want her around and for her to stay the fuck away from me," Toni said, hanging her head. "All I keep seeing is her face when she left. She looked so hurt. All she wanted to do was be my friend, but I don't know what that means anymore. It's so hard for me to trust anyone, to believe that they won't hurt me."

"Do you really think she would?"

"No, not intentionally, but it doesn't really matter, does it? I fucked it all up."

"You could apologize."

"What good would that do? It doesn't make what I did right, and I can't expect her to just accept it and still want to be...to *try* to be a friend. Friends don't treat friends that way."

"Sure they do," Krista said softly. "You've been a pain in my arse these past few years. Hardly talking to me, most of the time not even acknowledging I was here, but I'm still your friend, and I always will be. I know you're hurting, and I know you're confused. You don't know which way to go, but I think Laura understands that, and in a way, we both grade on a curve when it comes to you."

"Must be one hell of a curve!"

"Yes, it is, but you're worth it. So why don't you pick up the phone and call her. Apologize and see what she says. You've got nothing to lose."

"I can't do that."

"Why not?"

"I burned her number last night."

CHAPTER TEN

For the third time in as many minutes, Toni glanced at the clock, and she still wasn't sure what time it was. She had spent the entire day finding it difficult, if not impossible, to keep her mind on her work, her thoughts always drifting back to an auburn-haired woman whose office was one floor below. Having every intention of apologizing when Laura arrived that morning, as usual the woman was late, which left Toni with only one option. As she looked up and saw five minutes remaining for the class, she took a deep breath and began gathering papers.

Laura couldn't remember a worse Monday. After begrudgingly heeding Abby's advice, although Laura didn't try to contact Toni over the weekend, not thinking about her was another matter entirely. Unable to sleep more than a few hours on Saturday night and even less on Sunday, Laura arrived at work later than her usual lateness and then proceeded to spill not one, but two cups of coffee before the little hand pointed north. She had left her lunch sitting on the kitchen counter. John had called to say his sick leave would be extended three more weeks, and the over-the-counter painkillers she had been popping the entire day, while marvelous for a headache, seemed to have little effect on cramps. Long story short...Laura wanted to scream.

Noticing the time, Laura's first thought was to visit Toni before she left for the day, but remembering Abby's edict, she gritted her teeth and looked at the stack of files on her desk. Deciding that working from home sounded much more appealing than staying at Calloway, she began cramming papers into her attaché as she said under her breath, "Fuck it!"

"Bad day?"

Startled, Laura looked up to see Toni standing in the doorway. "Toni! Hi!"

"I'm...I'm not disturbing you, am I?"

"No!" Laura blurted. "I mean...um...no, of course not. Please...please come in."

As Toni walked inside, she kept her eyes on the floor and her hands stuffed deep in her pockets, but when she hesitantly looked up and saw Laura's smiling face, the weight of uncertainty was lifted. Where she had expected to see anger and resentment, there was only friendship and compassion, and all the words Toni had practiced for the past two days came rushing back. "I...I want to apologize for Friday night. I had no right to say what I did and take my...my frustrations out on you. I had a really great time at dinner, but when we left, it all turned to shit, and by the time we got back to my place I was...I was..."

"Angry?"

"Yeah, and embarrassed," Toni said quietly. "And I'm sure I embarrassed you as well."

"You did no such thing," Laura said, shaking her head. "You were right. John and Kris did talk to me about you, so I know that Friday night wasn't easy for you. But all things considered, I think you did great, and you didn't embarrass me. Not at all."

"That still didn't give me the right to say the things I did, and I'm truly sorry."

"Well, apology accepted," Laura said, reaching for the painkillers.

Seeing the bottle on the desk, Toni picked it up and looked at the label. "Headache?"

"Um...no," Laura said, her cheeks darkening slightly as she held out her hand.

"Oh, right," Toni said, handing Laura the bottle. "You know? Those aren't really good for that."

"Where were you yesterday afternoon when I was buying them?"

"In my flat, practicing my apology," Toni said with a twinkle in her eye. "I have something in my desk that works a lot better than these. I'll be right back."

Before Laura could say a word, Toni bolted from the room, returning less than two minutes later with a small plastic container in her hand. "Take two of these and you'll feel better. I promise."

Arching an eyebrow, Laura glanced at the bottle only momentarily before unscrewing the cap and downing two of the capsules. As she handed the bottle back to Toni, their eyes met and then Laura held out her hand. "Friends?"

Toni stared at Laura's outstretched hand. Her lips parted as the need for air became great, and then ever so slowly, she reached out and shook it. "Yeah, I think so."

A small, friendly grin appeared on Laura's face, but remembering what Abby had told her, deep down, Laura was positively beaming. Toni had just taken a step...*all* by herself.

***

"Hiya."

It was a habit that Toni was having a hard time breaking, because when she looked up from her desk and saw Laura, she smiled. "Hi."

"Done for the day?"

"Yeah, I was just getting ready to leave."

"How'd you like to join me for a cup of coffee?" When Toni's only response was a blank stare, Laura said, "I found a small shop the other day. It's really quite quaint. Since most people won't be out of work for another hour or so, I wouldn't think it would be too crowded, and it's only a few blocks away. I thought, perhaps, we could walk."

Toni stiffened. "I don't walk."

"Okay, so we drive over."

"I'm not sure—"

"I promise, if it's too crowded, or you don't like it, we can leave."

Toni lowered her eyes and scowled. It was the simplest of offers, but within seconds of hearing it, her palms began to sweat, and her heart began to race. There was nothing simple about going somewhere new. It would be unfamiliar and filled with strangers and noise...and Laura. Looking up, Toni saw Laura smiling back at her, and in an instant, saying no became impossible. "O-Okay, but you're buying."

A short time later, they walked into the coffee shop and within minutes, Toni began to relax. Just as Laura had said, the place was charming, and with small round tables scattered about, each having only two chairs surrounding it, the café reminded Toni of an old-fashioned soda shop.

Quickly leading Toni to a table in the far corner of the room, Laura gave her a reassuring wink as she went to the counter to order their drinks, returning a few minutes later with two coffees and the largest croissant imaginable.

"I'd thought we'd split it," Laura said as she placed it on the table.

"I'm not really hungry. I had a rather large apple for lunch today," Toni said, her eyes creasing at the corners. Watching as Laura tore off a piece of pastry, Toni said, "Can I ask you a question?"

"Sure."

"That first time, why did you leave me the apple?"

"It was all I could think of to do. I knew how difficult it was for you to trust me, to allow me to see you teach, and after the class was over, your body language screamed for me to stay away. Then I saw it in my bag and figured what the hell."

"And now?"

"Now? Now it just makes me smile."

***

Knowing that the process of extracting Toni from her shell would be long, arduous, and at times frustrating, both Laura and Kris agreed that they would do whatever it took, but they would do it slowly. After two weeks of playful badgering, Kris finally managed to take Toni to a local market to buy her own groceries, and like they had done when they had shopped for Toni's clothes, they entered the small store just as it had opened. A neighborhood market, with narrow, cramped aisles, it offered its customers a limited selection, but with only three other people in the store, Toni soon relaxed and began wandering the aisles with Kris by her side. Having not stepped foot in a grocery store for over six years, she marveled at all the new products, and Kris couldn't help but snicker, thankful she hadn't taken Toni to one of the larger chains. Though Toni still refused to purchase any more than what she could use in a week, by the time they left, the bags they carried contained more new products than old.

Between shopping with Krista and meeting Laura for coffee on the occasional afternoon, Toni's comfort zone slowly began to expand. She made a point of visiting Laura's office a few times a week just to say hello or drop off grades, and even began chatting with Susan Grant on her cigarette breaks. Although not yet comfortable to talk to Susan about anything other than the weather, Toni's conversations with Kris and Laura were no longer stilted or stuttered. She still remained in her flat every night, bolting the door against the terror that lurked outside, but in Toni's own small way she was learning to live again…and she liked it.

∗∗

They arrived at the coffee shop later than normal and found it already beginning to fill with people grabbing their fix of caffeine before driving home. After finding a secluded table, Laura left Toni for only a moment to get their coffee, but when she returned Toni appeared edgy and frightened. Like the tide, Toni's anxieties seemed to ebb and flow. Laura knew the warning signs, and right now they were flashing brighter than neon. Sitting down, she slid a cup in Toni's direction. "Are you okay?"

Staring at the tabletop, Toni shook her head and then repeated the motion again and then again.

Puzzled, Laura leaned back and looked around the shop. Noticing a rather obese man sitting at the counter, his tonnage stuffed into a prison officer's uniform, she paled. Leaning closer to Toni, she whispered, "Should we try to leave?"

A few seconds passed before Toni managed to look up, and when Laura saw the absolute terror in her eyes, she said, "The ladies' room is right behind us. Can you make it there?"

All Toni could do was respond with a jerk of her head, but it was enough for Laura to spring into action. Standing, she waited until Toni did the same, and tugging on the woman's sleeve, Laura said, "Come on. Let's go."

Once inside the small tiled restroom, Laura let go of Toni long enough to latch the door, and by the time she turned around, Toni was sitting on the floor. Her arms wrapped tightly around her knees, she was struggling to control her breathing, but she was rapidly losing the fight.

"Just relax, Toni. Slow, even breaths. Okay?" Laura said softly, kneeling by Toni's side. "You can do it. Nice and easy."

Toni tried to listen, but her fear was too strong. Her lungs emptied and filled as she struggled for air, and feeling as if she was suffocating, she tried to suck in more.

"Shit," Laura said, opening her handbag. Pulling out a neatly folded paper bag, she shook it open and placed it over Toni's nose and mouth. "Relax, Toni. Remember this? This will help. Just look at me. Look at me, Toni. It's going to be okay. Just breathe easy. Slow and easy."

Like the night in her flat, Toni grabbed Laura's wrists, but this time there wouldn't be any bruises. Concentrating on Laura's Scottish lilt, after a few minutes, Toni's heart slowed and her breathing returned to normal.

Setting aside the bag, Laura reached up and brushed a few soaked strands of hair from Toni's forehead, mentally berating herself when Toni shrunk away from her touch. "Feeling better?" Seeing Toni's eyes fill with tears, Laura said, "This one wasn't too bad. Please don't feel embarrassed. It's okay. We're friends. Remember?"

"And friends always carry paper sacks in their handbags?"

"Well, I can't speak for everyone, but since *I* have a friend who has a tendency to hyperventilate when she gets stressed, I figured it was the least I could do," Laura said with a small grin.

Leaning her head against the tile wall, Toni closed her eyes. "I'm a fucking nutcase."

"Oh, stop being so hard on yourself. If I had been through what you've been through, and I saw a...a screw, I'd probably lose it too."

"Did you actually just say *screw*?" Toni asked, opening one eye.

Sniggering, Laura sat on the floor. "Yeah, I guess I did."

"The thing is I felt really good today. I wasn't nervous or stressed, and if it hadn't been raining its arse off, I was going to ask to walk."

"Really?"

"Yeah, I used to like to go for walks."

"You did?"

"Yup, but now the only ones I take are on a treadmill."

"I take it that it's in your flat?"

"Yeah. Krista thought I needed something to do for exercise, so when I moved in, she bought it for me."

"Smart woman."

"I guess. I did try climbing the walls once or twice, but I kept falling off."

Laura beamed at Toni's attempt to lighten the mood. "So, you ready to get off the floor or do you need some more time?"

The day had been a small step backward, but after a few more had passed, the incident with the HMP officer was forgotten. Laura and Toni returned to their routine, altered by only one thing. If the weather permitted, they walked, rather than drove, to the coffee shop.

***

"I know it's not our regular day, but are you up for getting a cup of coffee today? I'll buy," Toni asked as she poked her head in Laura's door.

"Oh, sorry, Toni," Laura said, looking up from her computer. "I can't today. I have a date."

"Really?" Toni said, striding into the room. "Do tell."

With a laugh, Laura said, "His name is George, and I met him at a conference a while back. He's in town for a few days and called to ask me out. Since you and I don't usually have coffee on Thursday, I didn't have any reason to say no."

"Wait," Toni said, tilting her head. "You're not turning down dates because of me, are you?"

"What do you mean?"

"You *know* what I mean," Toni said, approaching the desk. "You can't *not* live your life because of me."

"Oh, Toni, don't be silly. It's not like I get asked out every day or anything."

"How many times?"

"What?"

"How many times have you said no because of me?"

"Toni—"

"Damn it, Laura, answer the bloody question!"

After hesitating for a moment, Laura whispered, "A few."

"Oh, that's just bloody great!" Toni shouted, throwing her arms up in the air.

Before Laura had a chance to speak, Toni marched from the room, slamming the door so hard that the glass rattled in its frame. Letting out a sigh, Laura got to her feet. "Shit."

Getting to her classroom, Toni angrily snagged papers from the desk, forcing them into her briefcase as she grabbed her jacket from the chair.

"I'm sorry if I've done something to make you angry," Laura said.

Toni's nostrils flared as she spun to face Laura. "What you've *done* is turned me into a needy child instead of a friend!"

"No, I haven't."

"Oh, yes, you have! You just told me that you turned down *dates* so you can babysit me!"

"I don't consider going out with you babysitting."

"Oh? What do *you* call sitting in a loo holding a paper sack over my face—a date?"

"I call it being out with a friend."

"Well, this *friend* is going home!" Toni said, slinging her jacket over her shoulder. "And don't worry. You don't have to hold my hand. I can make it to my car just fine without you!"

Storming past Laura, Toni ran down the stairs and out the rear door, never once looking back.

***

They stood in the small flat, watching as people no longer needed or wanted, disappeared from view. An hour before, nosy neighbors grumbling about being woken from their sleep were shooed back to their apartments, the wave of plaid and flowered flannel shuffling down the hallway and stairs, and disappearing behind dingy doors with crooked numbers. The paramedics had also gone, ordered to leave by the victim who still cowered in the corner of the bedroom, her visible injuries slight compared to the ones hidden from view. The only strangers who remained were the two constables, summoned to the building by the next-door neighbor, his frantic phone call to report a woman screaming, bringing them to apartment 3-D almost two hours before. They weren't the most seasoned of officers, both younger than thirty with freshly shaved faces and smelling of popular cologne, but it didn't take experience to deal with what they had faced that night; it took compassion. And as they stood by the doorway, glancing at the two women in the lounge, the uniformed officers looked sad and helpless. There were no witnesses to interview and no items to report as stolen. How could they have known that what was stolen that night was more valuable than any trinket money could buy? When the nameless, faceless man broke in, although he left with empty hands, driven from the apartment by the blood-curdling screams of a woman in blue pajamas, he took with him her safety net. The only place she had felt safe…was safe no more.

Krista's number had been by the phone, written and posted on the wall under the heading of *In Case of Emergency* the day Toni moved in. She was the one they had called in a panic, professionals supposedly trained in all situations, but still unable to quiet a victim who continued to rant and rave. How were they to know they shouldn't touch? How were they to know that it was their unfamiliar faces that caused her to lash out? Striking in fury and fear, she drove them away, and by the time Kris arrived, Toni's screams had turned to silence.

Krista escorted the last of the officers to the door, and the tall fellow with sandy blonde hair and blue eyes handed her his card and offered his apologies. He had never experienced a victim so frightened of him before that night, and her terrified screams would haunt his dreams for weeks to come. Closing the door, Kris pulled on the knob and forced the jimmied latch back into the keeper before turning around to face Laura.

CHAPTER ELEVEN

The lounge appeared as if it had been visited by a tornado. The small sofa sat at an odd angle, the coffee table lay on its side, and books covered the floor. One lamp was shattered, while the other still stood in the corner, its yellowed shade torn open to reveal the stark brightness of a single bulb. The intensity of its light cast long shadows across the discolored ceiling, and as Laura looked around the room, it seemed filled with despair. Hearing the door close, Laura looked over at Kris. "How bad is she?"

"She hasn't moved or said a word since I got here."

"Is she okay? I mean, physically?"

"Honestly, I don't know. The police didn't think she was hurt, but no one could get near her to really check. She calmed down when she saw me, so I just closed the bedroom door until I could get everyone out. You know how she is around strangers."

Bending down, Laura started to pick up some of the books and then realized how pointless it was. "This place is a wreck. She can't stay here."

"I know."

"Does she have a suitcase?"

"I think so. Why?"

"Because she's coming home with me."

"Don't take this the wrong way, Laura, but she'll be much more comfortable at my place. She's been there before and—"

"Are you planning to leave her alone?"

"Of course not! How could you even ask that?"

"I'm sorry, but the other day I thought Toni said you were going on holiday."

"Oh, crap," Kris said. "With all the commotion, I totally forgot about that. We fly out tomorrow afternoon."

"So that leaves us with only one option."

"No, it doesn't. I'll call Robin and have her cancel the tickets."

"You can't do that."

"Why the hell not?"

"Because earlier today, Toni found out that I had turned down some dates. I didn't want to disrupt our normal coffee outings by having to cut them short, so I said no a few times. She was more than just a little angry. She accused me of babysitting her, so if you cancel your holiday—"

"She's going to think I'm doing the same thing."

"Exactly."

"Okay, so any idea how we're going to do this?" Kris said, heading in the direction of the bedroom.

"Absolutely none," Laura said, following Kris to the door. "Let's just play it by ear."

After glancing at Laura for a moment, Kris held her breath as she opened the bedroom door. It was the first time Laura had seen Toni since she arrived, and it was all Laura could do not to cry. Toni had pressed herself into the corner of the room. Sitting on the floor with her knees pulled tight to her chest, she was staring off into space as she lightly tapped her head against the wall, over and over and over again.

"Find the suitcase," Laura whispered over her shoulder as she took a hesitant step toward Toni. It was as if she had stepped on an invisible switch, because as soon as she took that step, Toni began knocking her head harder against the plaster. Pained by the sound, Laura grabbed a pillow from the bed, and slowly placed it behind Toni's head. Unsure of what to do or what to say, Laura knelt down and gently touched Toni's arm. It was the wrong thing to do.

Toni came to life in a fury, and before Laura could react, she found herself being shoved away, the force so strong it sent her stumbling backward across the room. With a thud, she landed at Krista's feet.

"Christ, are you all right?" Kris asked, kneeling by her side.

"Yes, I'm fine," Laura said, getting to her feet.

"For a string bean, she sure is a strong bugger, isn't she?" Kris said with a snigger.

Laura glared at Krista. "You think this is funny?"

"Sorry. When I get nervous, I tend to make jokes."

"Right," Laura said, taking a deep breath. "Have you found the suitcase?"

"No, I was too busy picking you up off the floor."

"Krista!"

"Sorry."

Laura looked in Toni's direction and then back at Kris. "Let's try this again, shall we?"

Cautiously, Laura approached Toni again, and as carefully as possibly, she knelt by her side making sure she wasn't close enough for them to touch. Concentrating on her proximity rather than the woman's reaction, Laura didn't notice that Toni's hands had turned to fists until it was too late.

In an attempt to dodge the blow, Laura scrambled to get to her feet, but her movements were slow and Toni's, unfortunately, were not. Laura had never been hit before—not really. Playful slaps between friends were one thing, but a solid punch to the jaw was quite another. Again, Laura stumbled across the room, but this time Kris caught her before she hit the floor.

Her Scottish temper now at a rolling boil, Laura rubbed her jaw and gave Kris a cold, hard stare. "If you make one sodding joke—"

"Wouldn't think of it," Kris said, holding up her hands. "Are you okay?"

"Oh yeah, I'm just peachy!" Laura said through clenched teeth.

"If it means anything, I've never seen her like this. Back in the day, she did have quite a temper, but that was more just shouting and tossing books about. I don't think she's ever hit anyone before."

"Is that supposed to make me feel better?" Laura asked, moving her jaw left and right to work out the ache.

"No, I just thought you'd want to know." Seeing Laura take a step in Toni's direction, Kris pulled her back. "What are you going to do?"

"Give her a taste of her own medicine!"

Three quick steps and Laura was at Toni's side again, but this time, there was no hesitation. Anger set the pace, and it was quick and unexpected. Dropping to her knees, before Toni had a chance to react, Laura grabbed her wrists and held on tight. Eyes, now dark and smoldering with anger, stared back at her as Toni began to struggle to free herself from Laura's grasp.

"Knock it off, Toni," Laura shouted, tightening her grip. "I'm not going to hurt you, and you know it!"

Toni continued to fight until Laura's temper finally got the best of her. Shoving Toni hard against the wall, Laura said, "For Christ's sake, stop acting like a goddamned child! I know you're scared, and what happened tonight was shit, but *this* isn't helping! I didn't come here tonight to become a punching bag. I came here because I'm trying to be your friend. Now, will you please just calm the fuck down and listen to me!"

Toni tried to pull away again, but she had run out of steam and Laura had not. Giving Laura a menacing glare, Toni stopped fighting and rested her head against the wall.

"That's better," Laura said, letting out the breath she had been holding. "This place is a mess, so I've asked Kris to gather some of your things, and we're going to take you back to my house."

Instantly, Toni's eyes widened in fear, and she struggled to get away.

"Goddamn it, Toni, will you please listen! I'm not going to sit here and fight with you about this. Your flat is a wreck, and the front door is broken. You cannot stay here. It's *not* safe!"

Toni wondered how Laura could believe she was that stupid. Toni knew it wasn't safe. Although most had acted like she didn't exist, or she couldn't hear or comprehend, she had heard every word. The constables had offered apologies and asked for explanations. The medics had suggested drugs, doctors and observation, and her two friends, or the ones that professed to be her friends, stood by and listened intently. But none of them knew what had happened. None of them understood. They were guessing. They were clueless. They weren't the one awoken in the middle of the night by the sound of splintering wood. They didn't smell the foul body odor mixed with alcohol and cigarettes that permeated her flat when he crept inside. They had never experienced the sheer helplessness of having no escape...again. They had homes, secure and warm with thick doors to shut out the cold and the danger. She had nothing, at least not anymore.

Toni felt Laura relax her grip, and for a second their eyes met, and they both knew words were no longer needed. Sensing the argument had ended, Laura got up and walked to the door, and looking back at the woman cowering in the corner, she said softly, "I'm sorry, Toni, but you don't have a choice."

Laura was halfway across the lounge before Krista caught up with her. Grabbing her by the shoulders, Kris spun her around.

"Who the *fuck* do you think you are speaking to her like that? Do you have any idea what she's been through tonight? She's not just scared, Laura, she's fucking *terrified*! When I got here, she was hiding in the goddamn closet, for Christ's sake! I called you because I thought you could help. I *thought* you wanted to be her friend. But I don't think you know what that means. Rain or shine, rich or poor, for better or for *fucking* worse, that woman in there is my best friend, and I will never give up on her, but apparently *you* have! So why don't you get the fuck out of here before *I* take up where *she* left off!"

Although she was caught off guard by Krista's outburst, Laura couldn't blame her. Laura's day had gone from bad to worse and getting punched in the face had been the last straw.

Laura had spent the entire day up to her armpits in paperwork, followed by her argument with Toni and ending with her date with George Portman. Prior to that night, she had only known George as an accountant who worked for the Home Office, and after spending an enjoyable lunch together while attending a conference, going out on a date seemed like a good idea. Not an extraordinarily handsome man, he was of average height and weight, had average brown hair and brown eyes, and drove an average car. Look up average in the dictionary and you would see George Portman's face. But he had a nice smile and a hearty laugh, so when he called, Laura couldn't think of a reason not to accept his invitation.

Hindsight being twenty-twenty, when he showed up at her door promptly at seven and then huffed when he found out she wasn't ready, Laura should have called off the date then and there. But hindsight is called hindsight for a reason, so the date proceeded as planned...all the way down the hill.

Laura liked coupons. She liked them a lot. They saved her money on groceries, books and even greeting cards, but when it came to choosing a restaurant, they had never been her first priority. It was your typical sports bar, with a hundred flat-screen LCD televisions hanging on the walls, each flickering with images of sporting events from around the world. Sportscasters dressed in garish ties and loud jackets, had their words inching across the bottom of the screens, and patrons sat with heads at odd angles, trying to read each and every syllable.

Walking into the noisy pub, Laura looked down at the pale green dress she had chosen to wear and sighed. It was a dress meant for a quiet dinner and relaxing conversation amidst candlelight, and her shoes, although modest in style and height, were meant for dancing the night away. As she slipped into the booth, across vinyl cracked and repaired by strips of colored tape, she found herself missing her trainers and jeans.

She didn't plan to spend the evening watching sports in a noisy bar, having little if any conversation with her date. She had wanted to unwind, relax and have a few drinks, but George wasn't interested in unwinding, and he certainly wasn't interested in drinks. A frugal man, he preferred water with lemon, and as soon as they sat down, he ordered two, stating that alcohol in bars was overpriced and overrated. Laura's dinner selections were also limited due to the crinkled coupon he proudly held in his hand, and reaching over, he eagerly pointed to the six items from which she had to choose. It was past eleven before he brought her home, tired, cranky and totally sober, and as Laura walked up the steps to her house, there was only one thing on her mind...the location of her corkscrew.

Closing the door on one of the worst nights of her life, Laura opened a bottle of wine, poured herself a large glass and wearily trudged up the stairs. Changing into her most comfortable pajamas, she settled under her warm duvet for a much-needed rest. The horrible day had finally ended...at least that's what she thought. Two hours later, Kris called.

Laura felt like shit, and the pain in her jaw was the least of her worries. She had let the anger of the day creep into the night, and Toni had just paid the price. Her words and actions, no doubt, had done more harm than good and there was no taking them back. Life doesn't have a rewind button.

"Laura, did you hear what I said?" Krista shouted. "I told you to leave!"

"Is that what you want to do, Laura...leave?"

Both women turned and saw Toni standing in the bedroom doorway, her blue pajamas crumbled and askew, and her face pale and streaked with dried tears.

"Toni," they said in unison, both wondering if she had heard their argument.

"Answer the question, Laura. Do you want to leave?"

Pulling away from Kris, Laura walked toward Toni. "No, I don't. I want to be your friend and help you through this, but you've got to trust me. You've got to trust us. We care about you, Toni, and neither one of us is going to give up. What I said in there, what I *did* in there was wrong, but I did it for all the right reasons."

Toni's eyes were glassy, filled with tears she refused to let fall, but as she stood in the doorway looking back into faces filled with sorrow and worry, she knew if she was to live again, she needed their help.

"My suitcase is under the bed," she said in a whisper, and then she turned, returning to her corner where she sat in silence while they packed up her world.

***

They hadn't had much sleep, but that didn't factor into the night. They moved slowly, packing up Toni's life. The fabric suitcase, worn and tattered, was found under the bed and filled with the items from the dresser, and the clothes hanging in the wardrobe were carried down the stairs and placed in their cars. Laura gathered the papers, pencils and pens that had been scattered by the scuffle, placing them back into Toni's attaché, and toiletries were collected, along with shoes, a jacket, and a carton of cigarettes that had been sitting on the counter. They had worked quietly, one or the other checking on Toni every few minutes, but she remained in the corner of the bedroom, shivering under the blanket that Laura had wrapped around her an hour before.

Finally, Kris returned to the bedroom, and cautiously approaching Toni, she sat on the floor and held up a pair of trainers and socks. They had already asked her if she wanted to change, but Toni didn't have the strength. So, a few minutes later, dressed in wrinkled pajamas, trainers and an overcoat, Toni Vaughn left her flat...and her world.

Laura drove down her street, the pavement glistening from the rain which had fallen hours before, and as she pulled into her drive and climbed out of the car, the only sound she could hear was the low hum of the streetlamps. Like a patient just released from the hospital, they guided Toni up the path and into a house that was warm and smelling of vanilla. Laura turned on some lights and her shoulders instantly fell. Not one who could be labeled either neat or sloppy, but rather somewhere in between, the work Laura had brought home still covered the coffee table and the sofa. She weakly grinned in Krista's direction, and the woman replied with her own feeble smile.

They led Toni to a chair, and she sunk into its softness, and while Kris remained at her side, Laura went about gathering fresh sheets and towels. The guest room off the lounge had an en suite bathroom, so after changing the linens and turning down the duvet, the two women practically carried Toni into the room.

Sitting on the edge of the bed, Toni blurted, "I need a book!"

"I've brought one," Krista said, opening her bag and pulling out a small, hardcover book. Paying no mind to the confused look Laura was giving her, Kris placed the novel on the nightstand. "It's there if you need it."

More concerned with her houseguest than the reasoning behind the book Toni didn't have the strength to read, Laura stepped in and cupped the woman's head, gently lowering her to the cool linen, and as Toni's head hit the pillow, their eyes met. Seconds ticked by as they stared at each other, and offering Toni a soft smile, Laura stood straight and tucked the duvet around her.

Snuggling into the crisp scent of her surroundings, after one quick glance at the book on the nightstand, Toni allowed exhaustion to take her to darkness.

***

Early the next morning, Laura called Calloway and spoke to Irene, apologizing for her absence and that of Toni Vaughn's. After hearing what happened, Irene took control. Before Laura hung up the phone, Irene had figured out how to rearrange the teachers' schedules to cover Toni's absence, and she promised that within the hour, Laura's appointments for the day would either be cancelled or moved. Hanging up the phone, Laura returned to the sofa and fell asleep...again.

Two hours later, Laura's eyes popped open, and she quickly went to check on Toni for the umpteenth time. Finding herself an inch between awake and asleep throughout the night, she'd climb off the sofa to peer through the shadows, making sure Toni hadn't woken up, and then she'd return to the couch to toss and turn some more. Her bed was comfortable and warm, but it was one floor up, too far away if Toni cried out in the night or stumbled in the dark, but Toni had hardly moved. With her black hair peeking out from under the duvet, she had remained asleep, eerily quiet for a woman who had gone through hell only hours before.

Seeing that Toni was still in the same position she had been the entire night, Laura quietly closed the door and yawned. Looking at her less-than-tidy lounge, she straightened up a bit, made a pot of coffee and then checked on Toni again. Convinced that she was still asleep, Laura ran up the stairs for a much-needed shower. Normally one who took great pleasure in long, steamy showers, Laura was in and out in an instant, quickly pulling on jeans and a T-shirt before jogging down the stairs to make sure Toni was all right.

Going to the kitchen, Laura sat at the table, drinking endless cups of coffee as she thought about her houseguest. When she was about to make another pot of coffee, the doorbell rang, and sprinting toward the noise, she opened the front door before the bell rang again.

Introductions were made with weak smiles and whispered words as Laura led them to the kitchen. Krista's partner appeared to be in her early thirties and matched Laura's height and weight almost exactly. Her dark brown hair was wavy and cut short, and her steel blue eyes were framed by gold wire-rimmed glasses that made her appear bookish and smart.

Coffee was poured and they gathered around the kitchen table, talking in hushed tones as they discussed the possibilities. They knew Toni couldn't return to her apartment. Even if the door was repaired, the damage had been done. Toni would never feel safe there again. Robin and Kris volunteered to change their plans, but altering their holiday was out of the question. With the babysitting argument still fresh in her mind, Laura wouldn't allow them to make the same mistake. Toni needed a roof, a bed and a friend, and until Robin and

Kris returned, Laura would offer all three. Finishing their coffee, they spoke itineraries, giving Laura all their information, and then Krista crept into the bedroom and placed a soft kiss on Toni's forehead, and in a whisper, they were gone.

CHAPTER TWELVE

Laura looked up from her book when she heard the bedroom door open, smiling instantly at the woman in the rumpled sleepwear. "Hey there. How you feeling?"

"I'm...I'm okay," Toni said quietly. Seeing a bunch of her clothes stacked on a nearby chair and her small suitcase sitting next to it on the floor, she asked, "Why's my stuff here?"

"Kris and I didn't think you'd want to go back to your place, so we grabbed everything we could carry last night and brought it over here for safekeeping."

"Oh."

It was clear to Laura that Toni was totally out of her element. Her eyes darted around the room as she continued to clutch her pajama top tight against her bosom, and her face, already pale, grew more ashen. Believing that the last thing the woman needed was to be mothered, Laura stayed on the sofa, giving Toni a few moments to get used to her surroundings, but when Toni began to sway, Laura jumped up and ran to her side.

"I think you had better sit down before you fall down," she said, guiding Toni to the couch.

"I'm fine," Toni said, sinking into the sofa.

"So you're saying you always sway like that."

"Just a bit unsteady. Still waking up. What time is it?"

"Almost five."

"Oh. I...I should get ready for work," Toni said, trying to stand. "Can you take me to get my car?"

"Toni, it's Friday *night*."

"What?"

"You were exhausted and I didn't see a need to wake you. I called work this morning and had Irene rearrange our schedules."

"Oh...okay," Toni said, staring off into space. "That's fine."

Eyeing the woman for a moment, Laura tried her best to remain nonchalant. "Hey. You hungry?"

"What?"

"Toni, when was the last time you ate anything?"

"Huh?"

"Did you have dinner last night?"

"Oh...um...no, I don't think so."

"Well, how about I make us something to eat?"

Thinking for a moment, Toni said, "If it's okay, I mean...I'd like to get cleaned up a bit. That is, if you don't mind?"

"Of course I don't. Bath or shower?"

"What?"

"Do you want a bath or a shower?"

Toni was uncomfortable, and it was beginning to show. Coffee conversations were one thing, but sitting in Laura's lounge, dressed in pajamas, made her uneasy. She didn't like new. She didn't like change, and the more she looked around at the unfamiliar surroundings, the more nervous Toni was becoming. Running her fingers through her hair, she croaked, "I don't think I can do this."

"Yes, you can. Be right back," Laura said, picking up the suitcase. Giving Toni a quick smile, Laura ran up the stairs and left the woman alone with her thoughts.

Sitting tight-kneed and rigid on the overstuffed sofa, Toni nervously rubbed the back of her neck as she looked around the room. By the thick wood moldings and the high ceilings, it was clear that Laura's house had been built long before the age of "less is more." The front wall housed a bay window, the seat of which was covered in small, mosaic tiles of brown, tan and gold. A few houseplants sat near the panes of glass, and a row of votive candles, in glass cups of dark green, lined the front edge. In lieu of draperies, each window had Roman shades, and the fabric, a muted pattern of yellow, green and tan stripes, accented the soft yellow of the walls perfectly.

To her right was a small fireplace. Covered in flagstone, it was capped by a thick, white mantle and above it hung a simple watercolor of two lilies reaching for the sun. Like many of the older homes, built-in storage units flanked the hearth, but those in Laura's lounge were low to the ground and acted as window seats. The fabric on their cushions as well as the sofa was off-white, but while the ones under the windows were solid in color, the sofa's upholstery had a light olive leaf design running through it.

"Are these okay?"

Startled from her thoughts, Toni looked up to see Laura holding a pair of her pajamas in her hand.

"What?"

"Never mind," Laura said, handing Toni the clothes. Pointing to the stairs, she said, "First door on the left. I ran you a bath."

"I didn't ask you to do that."

"No, you didn't, but I think after the night you had, a long soak in a hot tub is just what the doctor ordered, don't you?"

"I shouldn't be here."

"What? All of a sudden you don't like my company?"

Shaking her head, Toni asked, "Why are you doing this?"

"Give me one reason why I shouldn't."

***

Toni couldn't remember the last time she had taken a bath. Her apartment had only a shower, crammed into the tiny bathroom as if an afterthought and Thornbridge had offered even less. There, her weekly wash took place in a large, tiled room filled with other women, all fighting for position under the shower heads suspended from the ceiling, hoping that the drizzly spray of tepidness could wash away a week's worth of dirt.

She couldn't help but grin at the mountains of bubbles that floated on the water and the smell of strawberries and cream that filled the air, but as she put her foot in the water, she hissed. It was hot, the type of hot that takes one's breath away, but nevertheless, you crave more. Toni wanted the heat to surround her, to soak into her pores and extract the tension of the last twenty-four hours, and as she lowered herself into the water, it did just that. She washed and scrubbed and then relaxed against the back of the claw foot tub, allowing seconds to turn into minutes, content in listening to the sound of the bubbles as they slowly faded away.

When the water cooled enough to cause goose bumps to appear on Toni's skin, she climbed out, pulled the chain and allowed the water to escape. Drying herself with a fluffy green towel that Laura had left folded on the sink, Toni stopped when she caught sight of her reflection in the mirror.

The bruises were long since gone, but she could still see them, and while many of the scars had also disappeared, they still existed in her mind. Under her left breast was one that would never go away, put there by a rotund guard whose belt was long and heavy-buckled. He had stood there in the shadows and chortled as he inflicted yet another punishment, and the sound of his laughter echoed through her brain. Running her fingers over the scar, she heard the crack of leather in the air and she winced, remembering the pain of that night.

Mentally, Toni shook her head and reached for the pair of pajamas Laura had picked out for her. They were Toni's favorite pair, and she wondered how Laura knew. Dark red and softened by dozens of washings, she pulled them over her long legs and smoothed the flannel, welcoming their comfort and their warmth. They made her feel safe...and she liked that.

As she gathered her things, making sure she hadn't forgotten anything, Toni noticed a pair of thick, wooly socks knotted in a ball on the sink. Soft and bulky, she knew they weren't hers, but she also knew they were meant for her. Pulling them on, she softly padded from the room.

Returning to the lounge, the first thing Toni noticed was her clothes were missing from the chair, and the second thing made her mouth water. Following her nose, she hesitantly walked into the kitchen and silently watched as Laura fiddled with something on the stove.

It felt odd to be there. To be in a place cozy and filled with home-cooked aroma was new. She knew that just under the surface her fears existed, but for now, for this split-second of her life, it felt good to be alive.

Laura turned and discovered Toni standing in the doorway. "Hey there. Feel better?"

"Yeah," Toni said, looking down. "Thanks for the socks."

Laura glanced down and smiled. "The floors get cold, and I couldn't remember packing any of your slippers."

"I don't own any," Toni said as she looked toward the lounge. "Speaking of packing, where are my clothes?"

"Oh, I put some in the wardrobe in your room and the rest are on your bed. The dresser is empty, so feel free to use it."

"You act as if I'm going to be here for more than just today."

"Well, Kris said they were going on a two-week holiday, and between my schedule and yours, that doesn't leave a lot of time for apartment hunting, so I thought we'd just wait until they got back."

"Two weeks? I can't stay here for two weeks!"

"Why not?"

Toni stopped and tried to come up with a valid argument. The only place she had ever felt safe was safe no longer. Her flat held memories of an intrusion now, a violation of her existence and no matter how many new locks could be put on the door, it would never be enough. "I...I just don't want to intrude. That's all."

Placing some plates on the table, Laura chuckled softly. "Toni, you're not going to intrude. This house isn't huge, but there's plenty of space for both of us. Now what do you want to drink with dinner?"

***

Laura had made a chicken and rice casserole, and while it was a simple recipe, her guests had always asked for seconds, all of them except for Toni.

"Let me get you some more," Laura said, reaching for the pan.

"No, I'm fine, Laura. I don't really eat very much."

Laura knew Toni was telling the truth. She had stopped by Toni's classroom enough in the past few months that seeing her eat half of a sandwich for lunch had become commonplace. Even when they had gone out to dinner that one time, to a restaurant known for its large portions, Toni had ordered the smallest filet on the menu.

About to clear the dishes, Laura stopped when she noticed Toni frowning. "What's wrong?"

"I...I want to apologize for what happened last night," Toni said, staring at the table. "I didn't mean to hit you or...or push you. I was just scared."

"I know you were."

Raising her eyes to meet Laura's, Toni whispered, "I still am."

"Of me?"

"Of everything," Toni said, drawing in a ragged breath. "Of being here. Of not being able to go back to my flat. Of people and strangers, and places I haven't been. Everything."

"Toni—"

"Look, I was thinking, maybe I can get a room at Calloway for a while."

"There aren't any rooms open, and even if there were, you can't stay there. You don't belong there."

"I don't *belong* anywhere."

"You used to."

Toni sat in silence, trying to remember what it was like to be whole...to be her. That person had all but disappeared now, but like dust particles floating in the air, tiny fragments of memories swirled in her mind. Remembrances of dinner parties with colleagues and drinking with friends and brief flickers of evenings requiring tuxedos, and mornings when she awoke in the arms of another went in and out of her mind at breakneck speed. The collage of images seemed familiar, but they also felt foreign and false, as if they'd been put there by somebody else.

"That person is dead, Laura," Toni said with no emotion in her voice. Getting to her feet, she went to her bedroom, closing the door on her memories, her pain, and on the woman who was trying to be her friend.

***

Saturday was a quiet day in the MacLeod household. Laura tapped away on her laptop, entering information, working on reports and compiling data while Toni remained sequestered in the guest room, making an appearance only once when she came out for coffee.

By early afternoon, Laura began to worry. Scanning over the travel plans that Kris had left her, she picked up her phone and called Toni's best friend.

"Hi, it's Laura."

"Hey. How's Toni? Everything all right?"

"It's kind of hard to tell. She's only come out of her room for dinner last night and coffee this morning."

"She's out of her element."

"Tell me about it," Laura said with a sigh. "Kris, what do you know about her not eating?"

"She's not eating?"

"Well, no, last night she had some dinner, but honestly, a three-year-old could have eaten more, and this morning, all she's had is coffee, and when I offered to make her something, she refused. Said she wasn't hungry."

"Honestly, I'm not sure. She's been like that since she got out of Thornbridge. She only eats so much, and that's it, except when she was pissed off at you over that apple thing. She devoured half a pizza that night."

"She likes pizza?"

"Doesn't everyone?"

"Kris, do you know what her favorite food is?"

"Oh, that's easy. Lasagna."

"Lasagna?"

"Yeah, back in the day, she could finish off a whole one all on her own."

"Wow."

"Tell me about it. It used to piss me off how much she could eat without gaining any weight. She's got the metabolism of a bloody horse, that one."

Although tickled by the jealousy she heard in Krista's voice, Laura stayed on track. "Anything else?"

"Sorry?"

"Foods, drinks…snacks?"

"Laura, what are you trying to do, fatten her up?"

"No, I'm trying to get her to talk to me."

"By feeding her lasagna?"

"Well, it's better than an apple, isn't it?"

***

Toni spent her day lying on the bed, staring at four walls and a window. It had been easy to construct walls around her mind and her heart. Prison had taught her that, and over the past few years, she had managed to keep Krista at bay, her questions silenced by a look or a threat, but Laura was different and Toni didn't know why. Hearing the knock, Toni sighed. It wasn't even easy to keep doors closed when Laura was around. "Come in."

The door opened just a smidge and Laura peeked in. "Dinner will be ready in fifteen minutes, and I'm not taking no for an answer."

"I'm not—"

Pushing the door open, Laura glared at the woman on the bed still dressed in red pajamas. "Don't start with me, Miss Vaughn. I didn't spend my afternoon making you your favorite dinner just to have you tell me you're not hungry. Now get out of that bed, put on some clothes, comb your hair and meet me in the kitchen."

Before Toni could utter a syllable, Laura closed the door on the conversation leaving Toni to contemplate the consequences if she didn't follow the orders she had just been given. Remembering Laura's temper when her arm was injured, Toni climbed out of bed and began to get dressed.

After putting on jeans and a T-shirt, along with what was rapidly becoming her favorite pair of socks, Toni opened the door and found herself surrounded by the smell of something delicious. Quietly walking to the kitchen, she saw the table set with plates and glasses, and a bottle of Chianti at the ready.

"You're late."

Laura meant it as a joke. Something to lighten the mood and calm Toni's worries, but her playful reprimand had done just the opposite. Toni immediately stuffed her hands in her pockets and stared at the floor.

"Toni, I'm sorry. I was just kidding. You're not late and even if you were, it's okay. That's what they make microwaves for."

Raising her eyes, Toni noticed a foil-covered casserole on the counter. "What's that?"

"Lasagna. I was told it's your favorite," Laura said, removing the foil.

"You talked to Krista?"

"Yeah, I called her this morning."

"Why?"

"Oh, I don't know," Laura said, carrying the food to the table. "Maybe because she's your friend, and she's worried about you. I wanted to let her know that you were doing okay."

"And she just happened to mention that I liked lasagna?"

"No, I asked her what your favorite food was."

"Why?"

It would have been easy to make up a story, but lying to Toni would never, ever be an option and Laura knew that. "Because I wanted to fix you something that you wouldn't be able to say no to. That's why."

"Why are you doing this?" Toni asked, but remembering Laura's patented response, she held up her hands. "I know. I know. Give me a reason why you shouldn't."

Positively beaming, Laura motioned for Toni to sit. "It's nice to see that you've been paying attention."

***

An hour later, Laura covered the barely eaten casserole, picked up her glass of wine and went to the lounge where she found Toni sitting in the corner of the sofa, staring off into space. "I guess you didn't like it."

Slowly, Toni looked in Laura's direction. "No, it was good."

"You hardly ate anything."

"I'm fine."

Abby had cautioned her not to push Toni too hard, but Laura's heart told her she needed to push. So, remembering that anger was definitely an emotion, she said, "You certainly like playing the martyr, don't you, Toni."

Toni's head snapped up, and jumping off the sofa, she glared at Laura. "What the fuck gives you the right to say that? You have no idea what I've been through! You've got no *fucking* clue!"

Storming to her room, Toni slammed the door and began gathering clothes, emptying drawers and hangers like a dervish out of control. Tossing everything on the bed, she didn't stop until the door opened and Laura came in. "Talk to me, Toni."

"*No!*"

"Toni, please—"

"No!"

Seeing the pile of clothes on the bed, Laura asked, "What are you doing?"

"I'm leaving!"

"You can't."

"Why the fuck not?"

With her face filled with sadness, Laura looked at Toni and waited until reality struck home.

It only took a second, but then Toni remembered she had no other place to go. "Fuck!" she said, collapsing on the edge of the bed. "*Fuck!*"

"Toni, please talk to me."

"I can't."

"Why not?"

"Because it hurts!" Toni shouted, glaring in Laura's direction.

Laura's heart broke when she saw the anguish in Toni's eyes. Quietly, she said, "It can't possibly hurt more than holding it in."

"Leave it be, Laura. Please, just leave it be."

There it was. Laura couldn't believe it when she heard it, but there was the slightest inflection of wavering in Toni's voice. A hint of maybe, a sliver of yes, an octave change telling Laura what she needed to know...Toni was no longer sure she *could* hold it in.

Hesitating for only a moment, Laura whispered, "Tell me why you ration your food?"

Toni's lungs emptied in a rush. Bowing her head, she said in a breath, "Please...please don't do this."

In that instant, something changed between them. Laura was a hair's breadth away from getting Toni to talk, and they both knew it...and they were both scared.

Unsure of what to do or what to say, Laura didn't move. Twice she opened her mouth to speak, but the words weren't there until Toni raised her eyes. Darkened with despair and glassy with tears, they told Laura what she needed to know. Going over, she sat on the bed and without hesitation, placed her hand over Toni's. "Talk to me, Toni. Make me understand."

"Oh, God...please. Please, I can't do this."

"Yes, you can, Toni. Yes, you can."

Toni swallowed hard. Her mind was a hurricane of thoughts, of reasons why and of reasons why not, and the barrage was dizzying. She took a deep breath and then another, trying to decide. Could she do this? Did she dare? Was it worth it? Would it help? Glancing at Laura for a moment, Toni lowered her eyes, and in a voice soft and calm, she did what Laura asked.

"It was one of their mind-fuck games. It was one of their *many* mind-fuck games. There were a few like me, put there because they had pissed off the wrong guard, but we weren't insane and the screws knew it. They had ways of getting to all of us, trying to break us, to make us like those poor women in the padded cells...the ones that screamed all night long. The guards would watch us, wait for us to make the tiniest mistake, and then they'd send us down the block." Looking up, Toni asked, "Can I smoke in here?"

Without giving it a second thought, Laura said, "Sure. Hold on." While Toni quickly lit a cigarette and hungrily pulled the smoke into her lungs, Laura got up and opened a window. Retrieving an ashtray from the kitchen, Laura rushed back into the bedroom, handing it to Toni as she sat down.

"Thanks."

"You're welcome."

Taking another drag, as the smoke slowly exited her nose, Toni said, "You're supposed to get three meals a day on the block, at least that's what it said in the rule book, but they made up their own rules in Thornbridge."

"What do you mean?"

"Sometimes I'd only get two, and sometimes only one. There was no pattern, so there was no way of knowing when I'd get my next meal, or *if* I'd get my next meal. There were days when I'd get breakfast and dinner, but they'd skip lunch, and other times I'd get lunch and dinner, but no breakfast...and then they started skipping entire days."

"Jesus Christ," Laura said under her breath.

"At first, it was only a day, but then one morning I woke up to find a pitcher of water in my cell, and I didn't see anyone for two days. It didn't take me long to realize I had to ration what they gave me, so I'd separate the food into small piles. Things that would spoil quicker, I'd eat first, but stuff like bread and vegetables, they'd last longer. Sometimes I was wrong and I'd get sick, but after a while, I got pretty good at it."

Toni stubbed out her cigarette and looked Laura straight in the eye. "You don't know how it feels to think you're going to die. To count the hours, knowing that as each one passed, you're getting closer and closer to death...and there's nothing you can do about it. I was in a place where no one could hear my screams. Surrounded by stone walls, damp with mold, and toilets that didn't work, and silence that was so fucking deafening, so deadly...and each day I'd make my peace with God, expecting it to be my last, but it never was."

She had spoken as if she had been reading from a book, refusing to allow emotions long since buried to appear, but when Toni saw the tears in Laura's eyes, her resolve was destroyed. Choking back her tears, Toni said, "I'm afraid that if my belly gets filled, someone will take away the food again."

"Oh, Jesus," Laura said, her eyes overflowing with tears. "Oh, my God, Toni. I'm so sorry. I'm so, so sorry."

"I know what happened was a mistake. I know that I'm free and cleared of everything, but I keep thinking that someone's going to change their mind, and I'm going to be sent back to that place...and I have to be ready."

"Toni, they closed Thornbridge. I thought you knew that."

"I know it's closed, but it still exists up here," Toni said, tapping her head. "Every day and every night and every meal...it's *still* there."

"So, are you saying that what you ate tonight is enough for you? I mean, that you're not still hungry?"

"I'm always hungry, Laura," Toni said, wiping the tears from her face. "But it's enough to keep me alive."

Taking a shuddering breath, Laura squeezed Toni's hand. "Come on. Let's go get you something more to eat."

"I know you mean well, but it's not that easy. It's like my stomach's full, and I can't...I can't take another bite. I just can't."

"Well, then how about you keep me company? I'm still a bit hungry, and I hate to eat alone."

"I won't be having any more."

"Okay, but you can have another glass of wine, can't you?"

"I know what you're doing," Toni said, getting to her feet. "Like I said, it's not that easy."

Smiling, Laura stood up and walked to the door. "But there's no reason why we can't try, is there? Besides, we have a bottle of Chianti to finish."

CHAPTER THIRTEEN

If it had been up to Toni, she would have remained locked in her room thinking about a life she didn't have, but that wasn't to be. Craving coffee, she quietly opened her door Sunday morning, intending to sneak to the kitchen without waking Laura, only to find the homeowner busy cleaning the lounge.

Looking up from the stack of magazines she was straightening, Laura's face lit up. "Good morning. Did you sleep okay?"

As normal as it was, Laura's greeting caught Toni by surprise. Staring blankly back at the woman, she scratched her head. "Sorry, I'm not used to waking up with someone."

Laura's smile widened at the look of befuddlement on Toni's face. "If the truth be known, neither am I. There's coffee in the kitchen, if you're interested."

Giving Laura a quick nod, Toni went to get some coffee, and after pouring a cup, she noticed the dishes still stacked in the strainer. There were two plates, two glasses and an empty glass casserole.

When they had returned to the kitchen the night before, Toni wasn't surprised when Laura put more food on both of their plates. Frowning at the gesture, Toni sat down and immediately pushed the plate away. She was only there to keep Laura company and have a bit more wine, but the Chianti flowed easy, and the aroma of her favorite food was too hard to resist. It took two hours and almost two bottles of wine, but when Toni stood on wobbly knees to return to her bedroom, the casserole was empty, and for the first time in years, her belly was full.

Laura grinned as she followed Toni to her bedroom, making sure the tipsy woman didn't trip or run into any furniture, and when they got to the door, Laura said, "Thank you. You did good."

"It's just one meal, Laura. It doesn't change anything."

"It's a start, isn't it?"

"Are you always this optimistic?"

"Give me a reason why I shouldn't be."

***

Putting the last dish in the cupboard, Toni refilled her mug and then walked quietly to the doorway, watching in silence as Laura rearranged knick-knacks and photos in the lounge.

Toni didn't know if it was because she hadn't woken up hungry or the fact that the sheets on her bed were soft and smelled of roses. She didn't know if it was because the house was warm and lived-in, or maybe she just enjoyed starting out her day seeing Laura, but standing there in socked feet and wearing her favorite red pajamas, Toni felt more normal than she had in forever...*and* she felt safe.

Getting to the mantle, Laura struggled to remove the items above her head, and when she turned to get a chair, she ran right into Toni.

"Shit. Sorry. I didn't know you were there."

Taking the dust cloth from Laura's hand, Toni said, "Why don't I get the high spots?"

Smiling up at the woman who was at least six inches taller than herself, Laura placed her hands on her hips. "Is that a short joke?"

Laura's mood was infectious and Toni's face brightened. "Me? Make a short joke? I know which side my bread's buttered on."

"Whatcha mean?"

"You've offered me a place to stay for two weeks, haven't you?" Toni said, handing Laura some photographs from the mantle.

"Yeah. So?"

"I'd hate to have my arse booted out on the second day just because I made a short joke."

"Oh, I don't know," Laura said, checking out the woman dressed in red flannel. "I think I'm going to like having your arse...um...*you* around."

Placing the photos on the coffee table, Laura disappeared into the kitchen to refill her coffee. Standing at the counter, she felt her cheeks flame. Why did she just flirt with Toni?

***

By the middle of the next week, a routine had been born. Fixing coffee and toast, Toni would wait in the kitchen for the arrival of a very sleepy woman. With puffy eyes and auburn hair uncombed and wild, Laura would shuffle into the kitchen yawning like there was no tomorrow, and after handing her a cup of coffee, Toni would bid her farewell. At Calloway, they'd see each other occasionally, and then at night they'd eat their dinner and go their separate ways. Toni's comfort level had expanded to include Laura's home, but at night when Laura put her work aside and flipped on the television, Toni would disappear into her room, content to spend her night reading alone. It was a comfortable co-existence for a woman who hadn't felt comfortable anywhere or with anyone in a very long time.

Late on Friday afternoon, Toni stood in her classroom until she was sure the hallways were clear. Making her way down the back stairs, she walked outside only to turn around and walk back in. Forgetting that she had carpooled with Laura that morning because her Jeep had a flat tire, Toni acknowledged Irene with a weak grin as she went over and knocked on Laura's door.

"Come in."

"Hey," Toni said, sticking her head in the door. "Is it all right if I stay in here until you're ready to go?"

"Yeah, just give me a minute," Laura said, gathering her things.

Tilting her head to the side, Toni watched as Laura began filling her briefcase. "Laura, what are you doing? It's only four."

"I'm leaving early."

"You okay?" Toni said, stepping into the room. "You look pale."

"I'm not feeling very good," Laura whispered, coming around the desk. Dropping her keys in Toni's hand, she asked, "Do you mind driving?"

"No, of course not," Toni said, taking the attaché from her hand. "Come on. Let's get you home."

A short time later, Toni pulled into the driveway. Laura mindlessly climbed out of the car, and appearing as if the weight of the world was on her shoulders, she trudged up the path and into the house.

After grabbing the briefcases and Laura's laptop, Toni followed, but stopped briefly at her Jeep to kick the tire the breakdown crew had fixed earlier that day. Happy to hear the solid thump when her foot hit the rubber, she continued on her way, almost bumping into Laura as she was coming back out the door.

"I've got your stuff," Toni said, holding up the cases.

"No, I need to go to the store. I forgot I was supposed to get groceries tonight."

"Don't be ridiculous," Toni said, blocking Laura's path. "You're not feeling well, and I'm sure we can find something to eat. If not, we can just order take-away."

"Are you sure?"

"Positive. Now, go get comfortable and I'll make you some tea."

Toni waited until Laura disappeared up the stairs before going to put the kettle on. While the water heated, she looked in the refrigerator for something to eat only to find barren glass shelves staring back at her. "Looks like it's take-away," she mumbled as she went over and opened the junk drawer.

Overflowing with gadgets, pens, paper bags and everything in between, she tugged at the wad of folded menus that had somehow found their way to the back. Managing to break them free, Toni scanned the pages and sighed. The faded pictures of entrées didn't look at all appetizing, and the fact that she'd have to open the door to a stranger made her heart race. Tossing the menus on the counter, she went about making the tea, and a few minutes later, she carefully carried a steaming cup of Darjeeling to Laura's room and rapped lightly on the door.

"Come on in, Toni."

The small bedside lamp provided only a minimal amount of light, so after slowly stepping over Laura's discarded clothing covering the floor, Toni placed the cup on the nightstand. Seeing no sign of the woman except for the lump under the covers and a splash of auburn hair on the pillow, Toni said, "Um...I brought you some tea if you're up for it."

"Thanks," Laura said, pushing down the duvet to reveal her flushed face. Seeing Toni's brooding expression, she asked, "You okay?"

For a moment, Toni didn't say a word, and then hesitantly she reached over and placed her hand on Laura's forehead. A few seconds later, she pulled it away. "I'm fine. You're the one with a fever. Did you take anything?"

"Yeah, a few minutes ago. Did you find the menus?"

"Yes, but I wasn't sure what you felt like eating."

"Soup would be nice."

"Soup?"

"Yeah."

"What kind?"

"Chicken, of course," Laura said through a weak grin.

"I don't know if there's a place that has that on the menu."

"No worries, Toni," Laura whispered, rolling to her side as she pulled the duvet over her. "I'll be fine."

***

"Can I help you, dear?"

Toni spun around and lowered her eyes. A woman barely five feet in height, her face wrinkled and her gray hair pulled tightly in a bun was standing only a few feet away wearing a large gap-toothed smile as she gazed back at Toni.

"Were...were you talking to me?" Toni asked.

"Yes, dear. You look a bit lost."

"Oh, um...I've never been here before."

"Well then, welcome to Lenders Corner Market. We're not as big as all the rest, but we do try our best," she chirped. "I'm Gertrude, and I'm the official greeter."

"Official greeter?"

Taking a step closer, Gertrude lowered her voice. "Actually, my grandson owns the store. I just come in every now and then to keep myself busy. He hates it, but I'm old, and he can't say no."

Her words went unheard as Toni looked around the store, her eyes darting from one aisle to the next, all of which were filled with customers. A few came closer than Toni would have liked, and she flinched when one brushed against her.

"Pardon me for saying this, dear, but you do seem a bit jumpy. Is there anything wrong?" Gertrude asked.

"It's just a bit crowded in here. That's all. I think maybe I should come back later," Toni said as she turned and headed toward the exit.

"Oh, please don't go," Gertrude said, shuffling to keep up. "I'll help you if you'd like. I know where everything is, and you'll be in and out in no time."

Turning, Toni asked, "Why would you want to do that?"

"Can you think of a reason why I shouldn't?"

Toni jerked back her head as she stared at the woman. "What did you say?"

"Oh my, it wasn't my intention to get you angry, dear. I'm sorry."

"No. No, I'm not angry. It's just that I have a friend who says that all the time."

"And do you ever give her an answer?"

"No, not normally," Toni said with a snort.

"Well then, it appears that we have some shopping to do," Gertrude said, clapping her hands together. "Now, do you have a list?"

Pulling a take-away menu from her pocket, Toni pointed to the margins where she had scratched some notes. Scanning the items, Gertrude said, "Looks to me like you're making chicken soup."

"I have a friend who's not feeling well."

"Have you ever made it before?"

"No, I copied that from a cookbook."

Crumpling up the menu, Gertrude stuffed it in her pocket. Standing as straight as her frail frame would allow, she said, "I have a much better recipe than this. Follow me. I'll explain as we shop, and don't dawdle. I believe you have a sick friend you need to take care of."

***

Padding into the kitchen Sunday afternoon, Laura opened the refrigerator. "Is there any soup left?"

"No, you finished it off last night," Toni said, looking up from the morning paper.

"Oh," Laura said, sitting down. "Thanks for making it and for going shopping. That couldn't have been too easy."

"It wasn't, but I managed."

Concerned with Toni's monotone delivery, Laura reached over and touched her arm. "I mean it. Thanks for taking care of me and making the soup. It was delicious."

"You're welcome," Toni said, yanking her arm away.

"Can I ask you a question?"

"You just did," Toni said, folding the paper and tossing it on the table.

"I'm serious."

Exhaling, Toni leaned back in her chair. "Let me guess. You want to know why I have a problem in stores. Don't you?"

"Yes, I do."

With a huff, Toni got to her feet. "Well, that's too fucking bad! Stop trying to get into my head. I told you about the food, and that's it!"

"But—"

"There aren't any buts! I don't want to talk about it...*ever*! Not with you, or a shrink, or the chaplain down the fucking street. It's none of their business, and it's certainly not yours!"

Shocked, Laura watched as Toni stormed from the room, jumping in her chair at the sound of the bedroom door closing with a bang. "Shit," Laura muttered to herself. "What the hell just happened?"

Thousands of people across the country did it every Sunday without even thinking, but Toni wasn't them...and she forgot that. Sipping her tea, she had picked up the Sunday newspaper without giving it a thought, and that was her mistake and her trigger. The pages were filled with violence. Horrible stories about horrible people and their horrible crimes, and in her head, steel cell doors banged shut, women screamed, and keys on long chains rattled as baritone voices shouted threats that eventually would turn into reality.

Toni threw herself on the floor in the corner of the room. Burying her head in her hands, she tried to quiet the sounds that haunted her, praying that Laura wouldn't find her this way. This was her worst. This was shaking and pale and terrified. This was tears that wouldn't stop, and pain so deep inside her psyche, she dared not move for fear her heart would give out. This was when she prayed to be back on the block where no one could hear her scream. God, how she wanted to scream.

***

"That doesn't make sense."

"You're telling me!"

"Laura, you had to say something or *do* something for her to fly off the handle like that."

"Abby, I'm telling you, I thanked her for taking care of me, and when I started to ask her about her fear of people, she tossed down the newspaper, screamed at me and then stormed out of the room."

"And you and she have been getting along okay?"

"Yes, I told you that! It's been great. We haven't had any problems until this afternoon."

Sipping her coffee, Abby leaned back on the sofa, replaying what Laura had told her in her mind. Sitting up straight, she said, "Christ, I'm being stupid!"

"What?"

"Stay here. I'll be right back," Abby said as she jumped up and ran in the direction of the kitchen. Moments later, she returned, carrying a newspaper and a black marker. Sitting back down, she began scanning the pages.

"What are you doing?" Laura asked.

"Just give me a minute," Abby said, drawing black circles around articles as she scanned a few pages.

"Abby, what the hell are you doing? Looking for a job?"

Capping the marker, Abby tossed it on the coffee table along with the newspaper. "She forgot."

"What? Who? Abby, you're talking in riddles."

"When you first told me about Toni, you said that she was very specific about what was allowed in her flat, right?"

"Yeah. So?"

"Besides choosing the food that could be brought in, you also said that her friend Kris told you that Toni didn't read newspapers or magazines, and she didn't own a TV or radio. Yes?"

"What's that got to do with anything?"

With a sigh, Abby said, "Oh, Laura, she made herself a world she could survive in. Without newspapers or television, Toni didn't have to read or hear about the atrocities that take place almost daily. You told me that she owns a lot of books. Let me guess. They're all classics, written long before writers felt the need to shock or awe."

"How'd you know?"

"Because they don't hold any surprises for her. She's probably read them dozens of times, virtually memorizing them, so when she turns the page, she knows what to expect."

"So?"

"This morning, Toni sat down like the rest of the bloody population, poured herself a cup of tea and began to read the Sunday paper, totally forgetting that she can't do that."

"Why not?"

Handing Laura the newspaper, Abby said, "I haven't even made it to page three and there are at least a half-dozen articles about murder, rape or other acts of violence. You and I have become numb to those types of stories. We grimace at the details and wonder how people can do that sort of thing, but Toni *lived* with those people. She spent four years amongst the most violent *and* vile women this country has to offer, housed in a prison run by bastards who made up their own rules and their own punishments. When Toni picked up the paper and began to read those headlines, all those memories, all those terrible, terrible memories came rushing back."

"So when I brought up the market—"

"It had nothing to do with you, Laura. Nothing at all. She was most likely unraveling before you ever stepped foot in the kitchen."

"Unraveling?"

"Yeah, she's probably having quite a hard time right now."

"Oh my God, I've got to get back home," Laura said, jumping to her feet.

"Not so fast," Abby said, grabbing her arm and forcing her to sit back down.

"Abby, you just said—"

"I know what I said, but I also know that as hard as it is to imagine, this is just what she needs."

"How can you say that? That's cruel!"

"Laura, if Toni wants to have some semblance of a normal life, she has to start facing some demons. I suspect that she's been able to keep most of them away by living the way she did, but that's no longer possible. Toni told Kris that she wanted to start living again, and if that's true, which, by what you've told me, I expect it is, what happened today was unavoidable. You can't live in the real world and not be exposed to some sort of human brutality. Toni has to learn to live with it *and* to deal with it."

"That doesn't mean that I can't be there for her," Laura said, snatching her arm from Abby's grasp.

"No, it doesn't, but I honestly think that she's probably better off alone right now. You managed to get her to open up to you about the food issue, but you can't think that because she trusted you with that, she'll trust you with this. Laura, she's wounded, and right now that wound is open and ghastly, and I don't think she's ready for you to look inside. As a matter of fact, she may never be ready for that."

"What are you saying?"

"I'm saying that there's a very good chance that she'll never open up to you or to anyone."

"But you just said she has to start facing demons if she wants a normal life."

"Laura, you're probably not going to like what I have to say, but Toni may never have a normal life, at least not what you and I would call normal."

"You're right. I don't like it!" Laura shouted. "I don't like it at all. How can you say that? You've never even met her!"

"That's true. I haven't. I'm basing my opinion solely on what you've told me about her and what I know about posttraumatic stress."

"Well, I refuse to believe she won't get better, and I can guarantee that Kris won't believe it either."

"Good, because Toni's going to need all the help she can get."

CHAPTER FOURTEEN

"What do you mean she's not here?"

"I needed to drop off something to one of my students who goes to Toni's seven o'clock. I walked in to find a room filled with students, but no teacher. I assumed you two were just running late, but I just checked her eight o'clock, and she's not in there. She's still staying with you, isn't she?" Susan asked.

"Yes, but when I got up this morning, she was already gone. I just assumed she came to work."

"Well, she's not one to roam the hallways, and I checked the car park. Her Jeep's not out there."

"Shit."

"Can you call her?"

"She doesn't have a mobile, and she refuses to pick up my home phone," Laura said, tossing her pen on her desk. "Susan, do me a favor. Go up and tell the women that Toni's classes are cancelled for today. Okay?"

"Sure, but what are you going to do?"

"First, I'm going to call home and leave a very loud message telling her to call me, and after that, I have no bloody idea!"

***

GIVE ME A REASON

Slamming the front door, Laura strode through her house. Moments before, when she drove down her street and saw Toni's Jeep, she was relieved, but by the time Laura pulled into the driveway, she was livid. She had spent the entire day on the phone, calling hospitals and hostels in search of Toni, and as each hour passed Laura's concern grew. Thoughts of accidents and suicide raced through her mind, and more than once tears rolled down her face when her imagination spiraled out of control. Having run out of numbers to call, and unable to keep her mind on work, at half past three, Laura filled her briefcase and stormed out of the building.

Finding the lounge and kitchen empty, Laura marched to Toni's bedroom and rapped hard against the wood. A few seconds later, Toni opened the door a crack and Laura erupted. "Where the hell have you been?"

"What?"

"Toni, where the fuck have you been all day!" Laura yelled. "Do you have any idea what I've been going through? I called every hospital in London looking for you!"

"I'm sorry—"

"Sorry doesn't cut it, Toni!" Laura said. "First and foremost, you are one of my teachers, and you have a responsibility to Calloway, which includes calling in if you're not going to be there." Glaring at the woman, Laura was about to utter her second argument when she realized Toni's face had turned ashen. Letting out a long, audible breath, Laura said, "Look, I'm sorry. I didn't mean to yell, but you really scared me today."

"I didn't mean to," Toni said quietly. "I'm...I'm just not used to having to answer to someone."

"You don't need to answer to me, Toni, but the next time you decide to disappear for the day, you need to at least call work. Okay?"

"I didn't disappear. I went back to my flat."

"Your flat? Oh, Toni, I had Charlie fix the lock, but it's only temporary. You can't stay there."

"I know. I just went to get my books. I needed my books."

Peering through the open door, Laura saw a stack of worn paperbacks on the nightstand with a few more lying on the floor.

"Did you get all of them?"

"No, I only grabbed a few. I didn't like it there. It didn't feel safe."

"Well, how about tomorrow, I drive over and get the rest?"

"I can't ask you to do that."

"You didn't ask. I volunteered," Laura said with a small smile. "So, now that we have that settled, how about dinner? Have you eaten yet?"

"Um...no."

"Have you eaten today?"

Thinking for a moment, Toni said, "Wasn't hungry."

For a split-second Laura's smile drooped before she forced it to return. "Well, I'm starving, so why don't I fix us some dinner. You like spaghetti?"

"I'm not really hungry, Laura. I just want to read."

"You can read while you eat. I won't mind."

"Laura—"

"I'm not taking no for an answer," Laura said, walking away. "Now go and read for a while, and I'll call you when it's ready."

***

Toni was sure it wasn't Laura's intention, but once she sat down for dinner, she found it impossible to read while trying to twirl spaghetti on her fork. Setting her book aside, she listened as Laura rambled on about work, eating what was put in front of her...twice.

A short time later, Laura carried two cups of tea into the lounge. Placing one on the coffee table in front of Toni, she went to the opposite end of the sofa and curled up in the corner. "What are you reading?"

"Pride and Prejudice."

"That's one of my favorites."

"Yeah, me too."

Leaning back into the cushions, Laura tilted her head to the side. "Are you doing okay?"

Toni let out a sigh as she leaned over and placed her book on the coffee table. "I owe you an apology."

"You already apologized, Toni."

"No, I meant about yesterday."

"Don't worry about it."

"I shouldn't have yelled at you."

"It's okay."

"No, it's not. I don't know why, but you have this way of...of—"

"Getting on your nerves?"

Toni snorted, smiling ever so slightly as she looked at the woman. "No, I mean, yeah, but not on my nerves. More like in my head."

"What do you mean?"

"It's been a long time since I've had anyone other than Kris to talk to, and I know her. I know what to expect with her, but with you...with you, it's different. You do things and ask questions that she wouldn't, and it does my head in."

"I don't mean to, but I haven't known you for as long as Kris. I don't know the boundaries until I've already crossed over them, and then it's too late. I'm sorry about Sunday—"

"That wasn't you. I just...I just did something stupid, and my head started filling with all this shit."

"I'm sorry," Laura said in a whisper.

"It's not your fault."

"It's not yours either."

"How do you figure that?"

"All you did was read the paper. Most of us do it every day."

Toni's head jerked up, her eyes turning to slits as she studied the woman sitting a few feet away. "You're surprisingly intuitive tonight."

"Oh...um...I have a friend. Her name's Abby, and when you did what you did on Sunday, I went and talked to her. She's a psychologist." Noticing that Toni seemed to stiffen, Laura said, "Please don't get angry. I just needed someone else's opinion—"

"And since she's a bloody shrink—"

"She's my friend, Toni. My *best* friend, and whenever there's something bothering me, just like you talk to Kris, I talk to Abby."

"Maybe I should find another place to stay."

"Why? Because my best friend's a psychologist?"

"No, because the next thing you're going to suggest is that I should go talk to her!"

"Don't put words in my mouth."

"Are you saying I'm wrong?"

"Yes, I am."

"Bollocks."

"I don't appreciate you calling me a liar," Laura said, sitting up and placing her cup on the table. "I've never once lied to you or done anything that wasn't in your best interest. I talked to Abby because I was worried about you. You're not exactly the easiest person to read sometimes, Toni, and up until Sunday morning, we were doing great. Then, all of a sudden...*bam*...you fly off the bloody handle, and I had no idea why or what to do about it."

"Who asked you to do anything about it? People have moods, you know?"

"Yes, they do, but Jesus Christ, Toni, you have bloody tidal waves!"

As Laura shouted, Toni found herself listening more to the woman's rapidly thickening accent than to the words actually being said, but when Laura's tidal wave analogy hit Toni's ears, her eyes creased at the corners. "And I suppose what you're doing right now doesn't fall under the heading of tsunami?"

Whatever Laura was planning to say got trapped when her jaw snapped shut. Staring back at Toni for a moment, the corners of Laura's mouth turned up ever so slightly. "If I didn't know better, Miss Vaughn, I'd think you just made a joke."

Toni returned the smile for a few seconds, but then it disappeared. "I shouldn't have called you a liar, but Kris has tried more than once to get me to talk to a doctor and I just assumed you wanted me to do the same thing, and I can't. I won't."

"Okay."

"That's it?"

"What else would you like me to say?"

"I don't know. I just...I guess I thought you'd argue a bit more. Kris always has."

"I'm not Krista," Laura said, picking up the empty cups. "I'm going to get another. Would you like one?"

Toni glanced at the book on the coffee table and then back at Laura. The idea of locking herself in her room to read all night long suddenly lost its appeal. "Yeah, that would be great."

***

"You can't be serious."

"Why not?"

"Because...because it just wouldn't work!"

"It's working now, isn't it?"

"Laura, there's no way I'm going to live with you."

"Give me one reason why you can't?"

"I can give you plenty!" Toni shouted. Instantly regretting that she had raised her voice when the noise level in the coffee shop plummeted drastically, Toni leaned in Laura's direction and said quietly, "First, I don't need a babysitter."

"When, over the past two weeks, have I babysat you?"

"You know what I mean."

"No, I don't. You have your own key, and you come and go as you please. I haven't once tried to coddle you or protect you or...or even shop for you."

"That's because you make me go with you," Toni said with a playful pout.

"Exactly! Toni, you're not a child, and I haven't treated you like one. I'm just suggesting that since this is working, why change it?"

"You won't have any privacy."

"That's a bunch of crap, and you know it."

"Do I? Laura, what happens when Mr. Right comes along? What happens when you bring him home and cook him a meal and...and he stays."

"What do you mean?"

"Don't be coy. You know exactly what I mean. What happens when you meet a man...when you meet a man who you want to sleep with?"

"I don't see that happening anytime soon, Toni, and when it does, I'll go to his place."

"Are you cancelling dates because of me?"

"What?"

"You heard me, Laura. Are you cancelling dates because of me?"

"No, I'm not. I did that once and have no intention of doing it again."

"I don't believe you."

"Why not?"

"Because you're gor—"

Toni stopped, retracting the last syllable before it escaped. Surprised that the word had even entered her mind, Toni regrouped, or at least she *tried* to regroup. "I...I mean you're an...an attractive woman, Laura, and I can't believe that men aren't...well, they aren't...they aren't knocking down your door to...uh...what I mean to say is, is that I...I find it hard to believe that—"

"Are you going to make a sentence anytime soon or should I order us some more coffee?" Laura said, her eyes twinkling with mirth.

Setting her jaw, Toni blurted, "Damn it, Laura, you're a beautiful woman, and I can't believe there isn't a man in this bloody city who wouldn't want to date you! What are they, blind?"

The fact that Toni found her attractive made Laura's heart skip a beat, but quickly shaking off the feeling, Laura said, "Thanks for the compliment, but since John's been out, I've been putting in some long hours, so I haven't really had a lot of time to socialize. Now have I?"

Thinking for a moment, Toni said, "No, I suppose not."

"If it makes you feel any better, I do have a date on Saturday."

"You do?"

"Yes. My ex called me the other day, and we're going to meet for drinks."

"Your ex?"

"His name's Duane. We were together for a couple of years, but when he asked me to marry him, and I said no, things started going downhill."

"Wait. He proposed?"

"Do you find that surprising?" Laura said, cocking her head to the side.

"No. No, of course not, it's just that you never mentioned it."

"That's because it wasn't worth mentioning."

"Oh."

"Anyway, we tried to make it work for a while, but then everything went to shit."

"Then why see him again?"

"Because I really like him, and we have two years of history together. The fight was as much my fault as it was his. I was working some really long hours, and I knew Duane was having problems at his job, but I wasn't giving him the time he needed. So, one night I came home a bit grumpy. He was there, also a bit grumpy, and we ended up having a grumpy explosion."

"Sounds messy."

"It was," Laura said with a laugh. "We both said things we didn't mean, and when he called on Monday, he apologized for everything and said he'd like to try again."

"And I'm assuming you do, too?"

Laura shrugged. "It depends on the day, but we were so good together once. I'd love to get that back."

"Well, I hope it works out then," Toni said, picking up her coffee. After drinking what remained, she placed the cup on the table. "So, you ready to go?"

"Not so fast, Miss Vaughn."

"Huh?"

"You never answered the question."

"What question?"

"Now who's being coy?"

"Laura—"

"Give me one reason, Toni. One reason and I'll shut up."

Toni took a deep breath and ran her fingers through her hair. Whether she cared to admit it or not, Laura was right...it *was* working.

***

Finishing off her dinner, Toni pushed the plate away and turned back to her book. It was the second she had read that day. After spending a few hours of the morning helping to tidy up the house, while Laura ran errands and prepared for her date, Toni had spent the day in her room until her stomach made itself known.

"There you are," Laura said, walking into the kitchen.

Toni looked up, and her eyes widened. Gone was the normal business suit she was used to seeing Laura wear, and in its place was a pale blue summer dress. The skirt was loose and flowing, but the halter bodice fit Laura like a second skin, accentuating her upper half as it plunged low between her breasts. It had been years since Toni found herself admiring a woman, allowing her eyes to wander and her imagination to soar, and when she realized what she was doing, she became annoyed. She didn't have the right to look. She didn't have the right to even imagine. That part of her had died, and she wanted it to remain that way. Burying her head in her book, she said, "I assumed your date included supper, so I didn't make you anything."

"Yes, it does," Laura said, looking at the empty plate on the table. "Did you get enough to eat?"

"Two servings," Toni muttered as she turned the page of her book.

Deciding that Toni was just having a rough day, Laura tried to lighten the mood. Twirling around, she said, "Well, you could at least tell me if I look okay?"

"You look fine."

"I was going for something more than *fine*."

With a sigh, Toni closed her book and looked up. "I don't see why it matters what I think. It's him you're trying to impress."

"Do you have a problem with that?"

"No. It's none of my business."

"You're right, it's not, but I thought since Duane made the effort to apologize, I could at least make the effort to look nice. Do you have a problem with me going out tonight or have I done something that deserves your attitude?"

Realizing she was now directing her own annoyance toward Laura, Toni leaned back in her chair. "I'm sorry. You look great, and you haven't done anything wrong. I'm just having a bit of a bad spot today. I hope you have a great time."

"Are you sure?"

"Positive. You and I are fine."

Grinning, Laura said, "Well, he's going to be here in a few minutes, but I don't know where we're going, so if you need anything, you have my mobile number. All right?"

Tilting her head to one side, Toni asked, "Is this the part where you *don't* treat me like a child?"

Chuckling, Laura's cheeks darkened. "Touché."

Toni smiled as she returned to her book, but when she heard a car horn beep, she jerked up her head. "What? He can't walk up to the door and knock?"

"It's a joke," Laura said, grabbing her handbag. "I always run late and he thinks if he keeps the car running, it'll make me move faster."

"Does it?"

"Do I look like I'm moving fast?" Laura said, casually sauntering to the door.

CHAPTER FIFTEEN

Hearing the front door open, for a split-second Toni went rigid until Laura quickly called out, "It's me." Waiting until she walked into the room, Toni asked, "What are you doing home?"

"Last time I checked, I lived here."

"I know that, but for the past couple of weeks, you've been spending the weekends at Duane's."

"Well, not this weekend."

"Problems?"

"No, not really," Laura said. "I'm going to put on something comfortable and have some wine. Would you like a glass?"

Tossing her book onto the coffee table, Toni said, "You go change. I'll get the wine."

A few minutes later, Laura returned wearing track pants and a T-shirt, and flopped down on the sofa next to Toni. Opening the painkillers she had in her hand, she tapped out two, popped them in her mouth and washed them down with a full-bodied Merlot.

"I'm fairly certain that those aren't supposed to be taken with that," Toni said, pointing at the pills and then the wine.

"Ask me if I care."

"What's wrong?"

"Nothing."

"Is this the part where you'll never lie to me?"

"Must you remember everything I say?"

"Must you always ask me to give you a reason?"

With a sigh, Laura leaned into the cushions and pinched the bridge of her nose. "Duane and I had a bit of an argument tonight."

"A bit?"

"A row."

"Can I ask why?"

With a snort, Laura leaned over, picked up the painkillers and shook the bottle.

Toni's brow wrinkled as she tried to decipher the clue. "He got mad because you have cramps?"

"Not exactly, but you're close."

"I'm lost."

"When he saw me take the pills he asked me what was wrong, and I told him, and then his whole attitude changed. He said if he had known, he would have skipped tonight and gone out with his mates."

"Why?"

"Because having sex during my cycle is a *major* turn-off for him, and he realized he wasn't going to be getting any tonight."

Toni's mouth dropped open, staring back at Laura as if she was in a daze. "You've *got* to be joking."

"Am I laughing?"

"That's bollocks!"

"I know!"

"Well, so much for him being a nice bloke."

"That's the problem, Toni, normally he is. These past few weeks have been great. I mean, *really* great and we've been having a blast, but then something stupid comes along and turns it all upside down."

"So what are you going to do?"

"What do you mean?"

"You going to see him again?"

"I don't know."

"You deserve better," Toni said under her breath as she took a sip of wine.

"What did you say?"

"Nothing."

"Yes, you did."

"Fine. I said you deserve better."

"You think?"

"You don't?"

"Sometimes I wonder."

"A bit down on yourself tonight, aren't you?"

"Must be the company I'm keeping." As soon as the words slipped from her lips, Laura frowned. "I'm sorry. I didn't mean that, Toni."

"It's okay. I'm not exactly what most would call an exuberant housemate."

Thinking for a moment, Laura asked, "Can I ask you a question?"

"It depends."

"Don't you miss it?"

"What?"

"Sex."

"Oh."

"Sorry, that's probably under the heading of crossing the line, huh?"

"Not yet, but you're close," Toni said, quickly following it with another taste of wine.

She was enjoying Laura's company, and she didn't want it to end, but Toni's heart rate was increasing by the second. She knew where the conversation was going, and Toni hoped Laura would pick up on her nervousness without having to point it out. Unfortunately, Laura didn't.

"So, do you? Miss it, I mean?"

"I don't really think about it anymore," Toni answered, her voice now barely a whisper.

"Why not?"

Unable to handle any more questions, Toni gritted her teeth and sprang to her feet, glaring down at Laura as she tried to control her anger. "It's none of your fucking business!" After downing what was left of her wine, Toni stomped to her room and slammed the door.

"Shit," Laura said. Shaking her head at her own stupidity, she picked up a nearby pillow and promptly threw it across the room. "Shit. Shit. *Shit!*"

***

The next morning, Laura awoke to two surprises. The first she discovered when she shuffled into the kitchen for coffee only to find Toni hard at work making them a scrumptious breakfast of bacon, eggs and toast. Apologies were quickly exchanged and accepted, and by the time the meal had ended, the argument had all but been forgotten.

The second surprise came an hour later, when a dozen red roses were delivered with a lengthy apology from Duane attached. After a dozen texts and two phone calls, Laura agreed to meet him for drinks Monday night, and by the time Tuesday rolled around, Duane and Laura were, once again, an item.

Laura swung the Jeep into the driveway, slipped it into park and shut off the engine. "Thanks for letting me drive," she said, handing Toni back her keys.

"That's fine, since *I* never went to the Le Mans School of Driving."

"I wasn't driving that fast."

"You weren't driving that slow either," Toni said, climbing out of the car.

"Duane told me I can't be late," Laura said, trotting up the stairs.

"I still can't believe you're giving him another chance."

"Well, he did apologize and I wasn't in the greatest of moods that night anyway, so it was as much my fault as it was his."

Unlocking the front door, Toni pushed it open. "How the hell do you figure that? Where is it written that a woman has to tell her date when she's on before accepting an invitation?"

"All I'm saying is that I could have handled it better."

"So could he."

Dropping her things on a chair, Laura ran up the stairs, stopping when she reached the top. "You okay with dinner?"

Looking at the bag of Chinese take-away in her hand, Toni said, "I'm fine. Go, you've only got three hours to primp."

"Are you making fun of me?"

"Wouldn't think of it," Toni said with a small grin. "Of course, it would be a hell of a surprise if you were actually on time for once."

"Oh, that reminds me. There's a surprise in your room."

"What?"

"Charlie had an early day today, so I gave him your keys, and he packed up the rest of your books. They're in your room."

"Really?"

"Yep, and I thought maybe this weekend we could go out and try to find a bookcase so you have some place to put them."

"I can't ask you to do that."

"You're not. Besides, you'll be paying. Consider it rent," Laura said, giving Toni a quick smile before she disappeared into her room.

***

"So, how do I look?"

Toni glanced up from her book, and her mouth dropped open. "Wow. You look amazing."

Laura felt herself blush, and surprised by it, it took a moment to find her voice. "Um...thanks."

It was your basic little black dress, but the color was the only basic thing about it. A mixture of jersey and silk, the chiffon overlay added an air of sophistication to the simple frock, and the knotted detail gathering the fabric at the base of the plunging neckline left little doubt that Laura was all woman. Sleeveless and stopping just short of her knee, the dress was beautiful, but it paled in comparison to the woman who wore it.

"Can I ask you a favor?" Laura asked.

It took a few seconds for Toni to realize that Laura had spoken, and raising her eyes to meet Laura's, she said, "A...A favor? Sure, if I can."

Holding out a thin gold chain, Laura said, "I can never work the clasp. Do you mind?"

"No, of course not," Toni said, taking the necklace from Laura. "Turn around."

Laura did as asked and a few seconds passed before Toni said, "This *is* a bugger."

"And here I thought it was just me."

"I've got it," Toni said. "You'll have to lift your hair."

Laura held up her hair without giving it a second thought and Toni reached around, draping the necklace so she could fasten it. It seemed so innocent and normal to Laura, one friend helping another, but when Toni rested her fingers on Laura's neck for leverage, the sensation Laura felt didn't *quite* fall under the heading of friendship.

"Are you cold?" Toni asked, noticing goose bumps on Laura's skin.

"Um...maybe a bit. Have you got it yet?"

"Just did."

About to step away, Laura drew in a quick breath when she felt Toni's fingers on the zipper of her dress.

"You missed the hook," Toni said, patting Laura on the shoulder. "All better now."

"Thanks."

"Anytime."

Watching as Toni returned to the table to finish her meal, Laura asked, "Have you started unpacking your books yet?"

"No, I thought I'd do that after dinner. Maybe try to organize them by author or title."

"Sounds like a plan."

A car horn beeped and Laura immediately grinned at the sight of Toni's scowl. "Toni, relax. I told you, it's just a joke."

"Right."

"Well, I'm out of here. You have fun alphabetizing, and I'll see you later. Okay?"

"Yeah, and I hope you have a great time tonight."

"Thanks," Laura said, heading to the door. "Don't wait up."

"Don't worry, I won't."

***

Laura was duly impressed with Duane's choice of restaurant, and as they were led to their table, she couldn't help but admire the award-winning Reading Room. Located in Shoreditch, the restaurant was known for both its ambiance and its international cuisine. Set in what used to be an old book depository, the owners had spared no expense in making the upscale eatery true to its name. The walls were covered in bookcases, overflowing with volumes old and new, and the martini bar set off from the entry was filled with overstuffed sofas and chairs where patrons could sip their gin or vodka while they nibbled appetizers served to them on silver platters.

The main dining area was spacious and filled to capacity, but the noise of the busy restaurant was absorbed by the stately bookcases lining the walls and the domed skylights two stories above their heads. Simple, yet elegant tables covered in white linen filled the room, and atop each were crystal goblets standing proud near polished silverware, all reflecting the flickering light coming from candles set in glass globes in the center of the tables.

After the waiter had taken their drink order, Laura asked, "How did you ever manage to get a reservation? I heard this place was booked for months."

"It's all about who you know, babe. Besides, nothing's too good for my girl."

"Is that right?" Laura said, sitting back in her chair.

A gurgle of laughter escaped Duane's lips as he held his hands up in mock surrender. "All right, the truth is the reservation belonged to one of my mates, but his girlfriend dumped him last week. Since he wasn't going to use it, I asked him if I could because I wanted to take you somewhere special. Somewhere we could have a nice quiet chat and talk about our future."

"Our future?"

"Laura, you've got to know that I love you, but this isn't working. You need to get rid of your lodger so we can get back to having a life together. I'm tired of just crumbs, Laura. I want it all. I want you to be my wife."

"What are you talking about?" Laura said, leaning closer to keep her voice low. "Duane, the only reason I started going out with you again was because you promised all you wanted was casual. And as far as Toni's concerned, I have no intention of asking her to leave. I like having her around."

"So where the hell does that leave me?"

***

Carefully carrying a cup of coffee into her bedroom, Toni placed it on the nightstand and glanced at the stack of boxes in the corner. Scratching her head, she knelt on the floor, opening the first and peering inside to see what secrets it held. Smiling at the familiar titles, she began stacking the volumes on the floor, deciding that sorting by author instead of title would be easier. The first box was emptied in no time, as was the second, but as she came upon the next in line, she stopped and stared.

It was different in shape and color, and the tape sealing the lid had been yellowed by age. Tilting her head, Toni tried to remember what it contained, and after taking a quick sip of coffee, she began picking at the brittle cellophane until it gave way. Opening the flaps, she looked inside and the silence of her room was shattered as she drew a quick, hissed breath. She didn't notice the minutes slipping by as she sat cross-legged on the floor. She didn't feel her legs begin to cramp from the position, or the dryness of her mouth as she sucked in air through parted lips. And if blinking hadn't been a reflex, Toni's eyes would have turned to dust, for in the box were her ruins from Thornbridge.

She had been on the block when it happened. Men dressed in long, heavy coats and wearing angry faces, arrested the guilty and gathered the convicted. Those too violent or crazed were put into strait jackets, while others were placed in shiny cuffs and escorted to vans lined at the ready, and personal effects were packed, sealed and labeled with the names and numbers of inmates, so they could be shipped to a holding area to await redistribution. Within weeks, prison records were corrected, and the packages were sent to the appropriate prisons or mental facilities, but in Toni's case, hers had been shipped to Krista's where it had been stuffed into a closet and forgotten.

Mixed in with other boxes of Toni's belongings, it had travelled from Krista's house to Toni's flat, where it had stayed on the top shelf of her closet until Charlie had found it while boxing up Toni's books. Taking it upon himself, he brought it to Laura's, and now it was at Toni's side, gaping and showing its contents like an open wound.

A clear plastic bag was on the top. Sealed with a zip, it contained the wallet taken from her when she entered Sutton Hall to begin serving her life sentence. Pulling it from the bag, Toni paused. The leather was smooth and rich, and she had forgotten she ever owned anything so fine. The license inside had long since expired, and hearing a clink of change, she opened the side pouch. A few coins fell out, and she watched as they rolled across the oak floor, weaving back and forth until they disappeared under the bed as if trying to hide. With a sigh, she dropped the wallet to the floor, and it opened to a photograph that had been taken when she and Kris had visited Spain on holiday. Snapped by a stranger, it showed them posing on a beach, arms wrapped around each other with smiles broad and bright, seeming to have not a care in the world. As Toni stared at the photo, tears began to form.

Tossing the bag aside, she fingered the T-shirt she found underneath. Discolored by foul soaps and dried blood, the collar was ragged and thin from too many times worn and too many times washed. Wincing at the ugliness, she moved it aside and then all the air her body contained came out in a whoosh when she saw a tattered book. The acrid odor emanating from its yellowed pages so vile that she choked on the smell, she gingerly lifted it from the box and tossed it aside, and one by one other scraps of Thornbridge were discovered. A sliver of soap meant to last for weeks, a crushed pack of fags, non-filtered and cheap, a bit of powder, and the remaining pieces of clothing that she had worn over and over and over again. There was no stopping the tears now. They came so violently that her shoulders heaved at the intensity, and as she wailed, the breaths she tried to take were becoming frightfully painful.

***

"Laura, answer the bloody question. Where does that leave me?"

In an instant, Laura knew she had made a mistake, because when she heard his question, the answer came to her far too quickly. She didn't want to make more time for Duane in her life. She didn't want to marry him. She didn't want to live with him. Their relationship was over, and her mistake was not ending it months ago...permanently.

Laura placed her napkin on the table as she pushed out her chair. She needed time to find the right words to let Duane down easily, and sitting across from him while he glared back at her wasn't helping. "I'm sorry. I need the ladies. I'll be right back."

Before Duane could say a word, Laura grabbed her clutch bag and was out of her chair. Halfway across the lobby, she changed her mind and slipped outside instead. Standing just off the entrance, she breathed in the warm August air, trying to think how to answer Duane's question honestly, but without starting a fight in the middle of the restaurant.

Five minutes later, Laura still didn't know what to say, and with a heavy sigh, she turned to go back inside, but as she did her mobile chimed from inside her bag. Pulling it out, when she saw the number on the display, she blanched and quickly answered the call.

"Toni?" she said in a rush, covering her other ear with her hand to block out the sounds of the busy street. "Toni?"

Laura waited for a second, but when she heard Toni gasping for air, a chill ran down her spine. "Toni, talk to me. What's wrong? Answer me, Toni. Please, answer me."

"Can't...can't..."

"Okay, you need to calm down. Just listen to my voice."

Suddenly, the street noise became louder. Whipping around, Laura glared at the group of people jabbering nearby. "Will you please shut up?" she shouted. "I can't hear a bloody word!"

Ignoring the dirty looks they sent her way, she turned her back on the crowd as she pressed the phone against her ear. "Toni, please just try to relax. I'll be there as fast as I can. I promise. I'll be there as fast as I can."

Hearing a click, Laura looked at her phone, frowning when she saw the call had ended. Dashing back into the restaurant, she paused long enough to ask the doorman to call her a taxi, and then slowed her walk only slightly as she headed to the table.

"I'm leaving," she said, as she picked up her wrap. "Toni needs me."

Duane's entire body stiffened. "Excuse me?"

"I said I'm leaving. Something's wrong with Toni."

"Oh, for Christ's sake, she's a grown woman, Laura. Sit down and let's talk about us."

Although Duane's voice had raised a notch in volume, Laura's did not. Leaning closer, she looked him in the eye. "Duane, I'm sorry, but there's nothing to talk about. I don't love you. I can't give you what you want, and we both have to stop thinking that things will change, because they won't. It's over, and it has been for a long time. I just refused to see it. I'm really, really sorry, Duane, but please don't call me again because I won't be calling you back."

CHAPTER SIXTEEN

Rushing into the house, Laura slammed the door behind her and screamed, "Toni!"

Getting no answer, she tossed her handbag and wrap on a chair and ran into the lounge, but finding it empty, she hurried to the guest bedroom, bursting through the door as panic began to set in. One quick glance told her that Toni wasn't inside, and after checking the bathroom, she darted from the room and headed to the kitchen. Seeing Toni sprawled on the floor near the table, Laura's heart practically stopped. "Oh, shit," she said, dropping to her knees by the woman's side. "Toni? Toni, can you hear me?"

When Toni didn't respond, Laura glanced at the phone on the wall, debating on whether to call emergency services. Taking a moment to gather her thoughts, she looked around the kitchen. Dried dishes were in the rack and a bottle of wine, the cork still in place, was on the counter, and then she noticed the junk drawer. Pulled open as far as it would go, its contents now littered the floor.

Hearing a soft moan, Laura returned her attention to Toni and carefully rolled her to her back. "Toni, can you hear me? Are you all right?"

"Laura?"

Letting out a sigh of relief, Laura said, "Yeah, Toni, it's me. Are you hurt?"

Struggling to sit up, Toni said, "I...I don't think so."

"Wait," Laura said, coaxing her back to the floor. "Give yourself a few minutes to get your bearings."

"I'm fine."

"Did you hit your head?"

"What?"

Wrinkling her brow, Laura said, "Open your eyes. I want to see them."

"I'm not pissed if that's what you think."

"I want to make sure you haven't got a concussion."

"You a doctor?"

"No. Can I call one?"

"No!"

"Then stop being a pain in the arse and let me look at your eyes!" Laura said, wincing instantly when she realized she had raised her voice.

It was pointless to argue, and Toni knew it. Opening her eyes, she stared defiantly back at Laura. "Satisfied?"

Tickled by Toni's tenacity, Laura leaned closer, easily seeing that Toni's eyes were reacting to the light in the room. Getting to her feet, Laura said, "Stay there. I'll be right back."

"Laura—"

Stopping in the doorway, Laura turned around. "Do we have a problem here?"

Any argument Toni had brewing was trumped by Laura's tone. Resting her head on the floor, Toni closed her eyes. "No. I won't move a bloody muscle."

"Good. Be right back."

When Toni heard Laura return a few minutes later, she opened her eyes. "Needed the loo, did you?"

"Actually, I did, but I went up to get this," Laura said, holding up a small wicker basket. "It's where I keep all my first-aid stuff."

"I told you, I'm fine," Toni said, sitting up. "See."

"And what about that cut on your cheek?" Laura asked, helping Toni to her feet.

Touching her face, Toni flinched. Staring at the blood on her fingers, she asked, "How'd that happen?"

"I don't know, but let's get you into the lounge so I can look at it."

After slowly guiding Toni to the couch, Laura returned to the kitchen and poured two glasses of Scotch. Returning to the sofa, she handed one to Toni. "Here, take a sip."

"What is it?"

"It's Scotch. It'll take the edge off."

Toni took a taste of the amber liquor, and immediately welcomed its warmth as it made its way to her stomach. After a few more sips, she rested her head on the back of the sofa and closed her eyes. When the cushions to her left dipped, she didn't acknowledge it, but when she felt Laura touch her face, Toni's eyes flew open. Pulling away, she said, "What the hell are you doing?"

"I was just trying to take a look at that cut."

"It's fine."

Drawing in a long breath, Laura let it out slowly as she grabbed a throw pillow and put it on her lap. "Toni, just lie down and put your head here. I'm not going to hurt you, and you know that. Now, how many times am I going to have to say it before you believe me? I have all night, if that's what it's going to take."

Too tired to argue, and well aware that Laura wasn't about to back down, Toni swung her legs over the arm of the sofa and rested her head on the pillow in Laura's lap.

"Good girl," Laura said in a whisper. Opening an antiseptic wipe, and moving slowly so as not to put any undue stress on her patient, Laura lightly dabbed at the scratch on Toni's cheek. More a graze than an actual cut, it only took a few minutes before Laura was satisfied it was clean and not in need of a bandage. Tossing the wipe on the table, she said, "This doesn't look bad at all. Do you remember what you hit it on?"

When Toni didn't answer, Laura was about to repeat the question when the sound of Toni's breathing stopped her. Glancing down, the smallest of grins appeared on Laura's face. The woman who hated to be touched had fallen asleep in her lap.

For almost two hours, Laura sat there in silence, sipping her drink and finding it impossible to look away from Toni. She was at peace. Her brow wasn't furrowed with worry or panic now, and her breathing was steady and strong. The comfort of sleep had erased her rigid edges, and in their place was softness and beauty. Unconsciously, Laura ran her fingers lightly over Toni's short black hair, pushing strands about and marveling at the silky texture, and then suddenly, as if burned by her thoughts Laura snatched her hand away, and the abruptness of her movement caused Toni to stir and open her eyes.

"Hiya," Laura said. "Feeling better?"

Shocked to see Laura gazing down at her, Toni scrambled to sit up. Moving to the far end of the sofa, she said, "Yeah. Yeah, I'm fine."

"Good," Laura said, placing her empty glass on the coffee table. "So, do you mind if I ask what happened?"

"I passed out."

With a chuckle, Laura said, "I figured that part out, what with finding you on the kitchen floor. I was actually going for what brought on the panic attack. I'm assuming that's why you passed out."

"I just...I got nervous."

"Nervous? Toni, when you called me at the restaurant, you couldn't even talk."

Staring back at Laura for a moment, Toni said, "Christ, your date. I must have ruined it. I'm sorry."

"You didn't ruin my date. Trust me."

"Oh, well that's...that's good, I guess," Toni said, staring off into space.

Sensing Toni's exhaustion, Laura decided any further questions could wait until morning. "I think we need to get some sleep. How about I make some tea and bring yours to your room?"

"No!" Toni shouted. "No. I can't...I can't...I can't go in there!"

Rattled by the absolute panic in the woman's voice, Laura asked, "Toni, what's wrong? What do you mean?"

"Don't...don't ask me to go in there. I-I-I can sleep here," Toni said, patting the sofa. "I can sleep here tonight and...and tomorrow you can find me a place. Any place will do. I-I don't even care if it's a hospital. I just can't go in there. Please don't make me go in there."

Staggered by Toni's pleas, Laura quickly said, "Okay. Okay, relax, Toni. Relax. You don't have to go anywhere you don't want to. I promise." Thinking for a moment, Laura said, "Why don't you take another sip of your drink, and I'll get you some pajamas. Is that okay?"

"They've got to be clean. They mustn't smell. They...they can't smell."

Laura's mouth fell open and for a few seconds, her confusion froze her in place. "Um...of course," she said quietly. "I'll...I'll make sure they're...they're fresh."

Hoping that the liquor would help steady Toni's nerves, Laura waited until she saw her take a few more sips before she went to Toni's bedroom and cautiously walked inside. Laura wasn't exactly sure what she expected to see. Other than the empty cartons in the corner and the stacks of books neatly lined up against the wall, nothing had changed. Opening the dresser, she retrieved a clean pair of Toni's pajamas, but as she was about to leave, she noticed a jumble of odds and ends scattered on the floor near the boxes. Going over, the first thing Laura noticed was the prison-issue plastic zipped bag, and the second thing was the stench rising from the pile. Wrinkling her nose at the smell, she pushed a piece of clothing aside with her toe. Uncovering a worn and tattered book, its pages stained and wrinkled as if it had been soaked in water, Laura cocked her head to the side.

"What in the world?" she whispered, bending down to pick it up, but when she recognized the odor, bile rose in her throat. "Jesus Christ!" she said, kicking it aside. "Jesus...*Jesus Christ*!" Pressing her lips together so the screams growing inside her couldn't escape, when a few tears slid down her face, Laura angrily wiped them away. "Fucking bastards!" she said, her hands turning into fists. "You no good, fucking *bastards*!"

Stumbling backward, Laura sat on the edge of the bed, sniffling back her tears as she tried to make sense of things unbelievably horrid. After a few minutes, she went into the bathroom and wiped away smudges of makeup and then calmly washed her hands, taking all the time she needed to pull herself together. Toni couldn't see her like this. Laura needed to be strong. She needed to be strong for Toni.

Returning to the bedroom, Laura glanced at the pajamas she had left on the bed. They were clean, but in her mind, they were no longer clean enough. Deciding she'd find something of her own for Toni to wear, Laura went back to the lounge, and seeing Toni resting across the sofa with her eyes closed, Laura crept up the stairs without saying a word.

As she pulled a T-shirt from her dresser drawer, Laura's thoughts returned to Toni's room, and she decided that tomorrow she would clean. She would scrub the walls and woodwork, and paint them if necessary. She would burn the bed linens and draperies, and replace them with new. And she would destroy everything associated with Thornbridge. Laura didn't believe in burning books, but tomorrow she would have a bonfire.

***

It was a restless night for Toni. Lying on the sofa, she tossed and turned, waking a half-dozen times in as many hours. But each time she awoke, Laura was at her side, soothing her with quiet words of comfort until sleep took hold again.

Wide awake, Laura had remained sitting a few feet away, first sipping Scotch and then tea as daybreak approached. Her mind alive with a prison called Thornbridge, in the middle of the night, she quietly opened her laptop and searched the Internet for details, but she found almost nothing. Fagan and Dent had done itself proud, erasing all information about the hellish prison, and the only thing that was left was an estate agent's listing for the abandoned property which had been on the market for years.

At seven in the morning, Laura called Irene. After apologizing for the early hour, Laura informed her that she and Toni would not be at work that day, and after hanging up the phone, she made a pot of coffee and grabbed a pad of paper. Returning to the lounge, Laura sipped from the mug as she began making a list. Lost in her thoughts, she didn't realize that Toni had woken up and was now watching her from across the room.

"What are you doing?" Toni croaked.

Looking up, Laura grinned. "I'm making a list of things we need to do and to buy."

"We?" Toni asked as she sat up and ran her fingers through her hair.

"Yes, as in you and me."

"I don't understand."

Putting down her list, Laura walked over and sat on the coffee table within inches of Toni, invading her space on purpose, and just as she suspected, Toni backed away. "I want to say some things, and I want you to listen without interrupting. Okay?"

"I told you last night, I'll leave," Toni said, hanging her head. "I'll call Kris and—"

"Toni, please stop second-guessing me. You're awful at it."

"I just thought—"

"Will you please just be quiet and listen to me for a minute?"

Letting out a breath, Toni said, "Yeah. Sure."

"First, I don't want you to move out."

"I can't—"

"I asked you not to interrupt me."

"Sorry. Won't happen again."

"Good. Now, as I was saying, I don't want you to move out, but you can't keep sleeping on the sofa either. I called Irene this morning and told her that you and I wouldn't be in today, but I'm going to call her back and change that."

"You can go to work if you want. I'll be..." Realizing she had just interrupted again, Toni offered Laura a weak grin and motioned for her to continue.

"I'm going to call her and tell her that we won't be in for the rest of the week."

"What?"

"That will give us time to do what we need to do."

"I'm confused."

"You're also interrupting."

"Well, I can't keep quiet—"

"Will you please shut up!" Amused and exasperated by the woman who once wouldn't talk, but now wouldn't remain quiet, Laura reached over, and without thinking twice, clamped her hand over Toni's mouth. "I'm starting to think I liked you better when you didn't speak."

For a moment, Laura's hand remained, and she could feel the warmth of Toni's breath on her palm. Their eyes met, and a silent agreement was formed. When Laura removed her hand, Toni didn't say a thing.

"As head of the department, I know that you've never taken a holiday, and with summer coming to an end, I'm sure your students wouldn't mind a few days off if Irene can't find anyone to substitute. You know that all your classes are up-to-date, if not ahead of schedule, and my calendar is clear for the next few days, so there is no reason why we can't do this. Agreed?"

"I suppose, but—"

"Toni, if I have to ask you one more time—"

"You asked me a bloody question!"

"And you answered it, so pipe down and let me continue."

"Fine!" Toni said, throwing her hands up in the air. "Keep chattering away. I won't say another bloody word."

Toni's tone was gruff, but Laura could see the laughter in the woman's eyes. She was pleased that the conversation had turned lighthearted, but Laura knew that was about to change. Biting on her lip for a moment, she said, "Okay, now here's one of the parts you may not like. I want to get rid of everything in your room except for the furniture."

"What?"

"I'm going in there and taking everything out. The linens, drapes, and all of your old clothes, and then I'm going to give away what I can and the rest I'm going to destroy." Seeing Toni's puzzled expression, Laura said, "I'm going to burn your books, Toni. All of them."

"You can't do that. They're mine!"

"Toni, we'll get you new books, and some of the titles I saw in there are ones I own myself, so until we can replace them, you can read mine. But you need to start getting rid of things that remind you of Thornbridge, and since all the books you have are second-hand, they're musty and stained, and they need to be replaced. What you need is new, not old."

A flicker of pain crossed Toni's face at the mention of Thornbridge, and even though Laura saw it, and her heart ached for the woman, there was no turning back. "I know you have a few new things, but most of your clothes are faded and tattered, and that's not who you are any longer. Is it?"

"I...I hope not."

"Then you need to rid yourself of things that remind you of that place. It doesn't matter that you didn't have those clothes in Thornbridge, or even read the books there—"

"I did read them."

"What?"

"I read them in here," Toni said, tapping her head. "I kept them where the screws couldn't get to them or...or piss on them."

"Then that's all the more reason why we should buy new ones. I know the words won't change, but the smell will. They'll be brand new and untouched by that place in any way."

"Can't we donate them? Give them to someone? I mean, not all of them are in bad shape. Please?"

Thinking for a moment, Laura said, "How about we donate what we can to Calloway? I'm sure some of the women would enjoy reading a few of the classics. Will that work for you?"

"Yeah, that's better. Thanks."

"Don't thank me yet."

"Why?"

"Because I'm not finished."

"Oh."

"After we empty the room, I'm going to ask you to help me clean it up. I want to wash everything down and then get some paint and change the colors."

"To what?"

"I don't know. You tell me."

"Huh?"

"It's your room. So it's your choice."

"But it's your house."

"Are we going to argue semantics?"

"Maybe," Toni said, easing into a grin.

Laura laughed, and both relaxed, returning to the comfort of a friendship that was growing by the minute.

"So, you and I will need to go shopping. We'll need to buy a new duvet and curtains, and we might as well spruce up the bathroom while we're at it. Don't you think?"

"Why do I feel like there's a *but* coming?"

"It's not really a but; however, I'm fairly certain...actually, I'm positive that you're not going to like it."

"Okay?"

"After it's all said and done and the room is clean, and we've replaced your books and your clothes, I'm going to break a promise, and I'm letting you know that right now so there won't be any surprises."

Toni eyed Laura for a moment. "What promise?"

"I want you to trust me enough to tell me what happened at Thornbridge."

"No!" Toni shouted, jumping off the sofa. "I will *not* do that!"

"Toni, you've got to talk about—"

"Fuck you, Laura! I can't, and I won't!" Toni screamed, glaring at the woman. "Don't you bloody get it? Every time...every *fucking* time I think of that place, I can't breathe and my head fills with the stench of that fucking hole. You were in my room. Didn't you smell it? Didn't you see what they did to the *only* fucking book I had? How can you ask me to relive that nightmare? How, *goddamn it*, how!"

"You need to get this out."

"*You* need to go to hell," Toni yelled, heading toward the kitchen.

"Toni, please, it will help. It will be like...I don't know...cleansing."

"What? Like washing it away, you mean? Talk about it and it goes away?"

"In time it will, yes."

Turning her back to Laura, Toni ripped the T-shirt from her body, exposing the brutality of a place called Thornbridge. "Will it make these go away, Laura? Will it? Or how about the ones on my legs or on my chest...or in my *fucking* mind? Will they all just disappear if I just *talk* about it!"

Toni crumpled to the ground and began to wail as she pulled herself into a ball. Pounding her fist on the floor as she continued to weep, she prayed to God that he'd take her...and take her now.

CHAPTER SEVENTEEN

Ignoring the scars, Laura managed to get Toni to her feet. Covering her with a throw from the sofa, she practically had to carry her up the stairs, the woman leaning so heavily on her that Laura's knees shook from the strain. Once inside her bedroom, Laura pulled down the duvet, and Toni fell into the softness that lay underneath, immediately returning to a fetal position as she continued to cry. Her own tears unstoppable, Laura stood over Toni, unsure of what to do to make the pain go away. Refusing to leave her alone, Laura climbed across the duvet and spooned against the woman who didn't like to be touched, but this time Toni didn't pull away. Spent and exposed, she felt as beaten as she had when the belts had left their marks, and when Laura reached around, lacing her fingers through Toni's, the broken woman returned the grasp more tightly than it was being given.

There were no words of comfort Laura could give, or soothing reassurances to be spoken, so she said not a word, and simply held Toni tightly as their tears fell together and their sobs became one. Finally, emotionally exhausted, they fell asleep, Toni slipping into darkness seconds before Laura, but their fingers remained intertwined and their bodies molded, back to front, until the sound of the phone woke Laura up a few hours later.

Hearing the click of the answering machine, Laura extracted herself from Toni's grasp and crept to the bathroom to empty her bladder, brush her teeth and wash the dried tears from her face.

Staring in the mirror, Laura reached out and ran her finger over the glass, outlining her face as she thought about her feelings for the woman lying in her bed. Between friends, especially best friends, emotions such as love and trust were commonplace, and even anger, sadness, and at times, disgust could be present. Over the years, her relationship with Abby had produced a rainbow of emotions, from the joy of seeing her friend at the holidays, to the disgust at her poor choice in men, but through it all, one emotion prevailed...love. She loved Abby as best friends do, but when Laura was lying next to Toni, she found herself thinking about more. She wondered about how it would feel to kiss Toni's tears away, instead of just holding her hand, and about slipping under the duvet to press herself against the woman's curves and feel Toni's warmth radiating against her own.

Shaking her head to clear her thoughts, Laura rationalized again. "Stop being daft," she said in a whisper. "She's hurt and you want to help. That's all."

Still wearing what was now a rather wrinkled little black dress Laura tiptoed back into the bedroom to find clothes suited for cleaning. After changing in the bathroom, she emerged to find Toni sitting up in bed, covered up to the neck with the duvet.

"I need a T-shirt or something," Toni said in a raspy voice.

"Of course. Hold on," Laura said, opening the dresser. Handing Toni a T-shirt, she said, "This should fit. I'll get your things and start a load of laundry, so you'll have something of your own to wear by tonight. Okay?"

"Sure," Toni said flatly, refusing to look in Laura's direction.

"I'll be downstairs if you need me, and I put some fresh towels by the sink in case you want to get cleaned up."

"Thanks."

At the door, Laura turned. "Toni?"

"Yeah?"

"There's nothing that I can say or do to take away those scars, but please believe me when I tell you that they don't matter to me. They don't define the woman I've come to know, and even though I know you're angry with me, that doesn't change how I feel about you, and it never will. You may have lost some friends because of this, but I'm here to stay. I can't promise that I still won't want answers to questions, but I'll wait until you're ready to talk. I'm not going anywhere, so if ever you need a shoulder to cry on or a hand to hold, I'll be there. I promise."

***

After fixing a pot of coffee, Laura filled a large mug and took a few sips before heading to Toni's room. Deciding the best place to start would be with the books, she grabbed an empty box and began filling it, glancing at each title as she packed them away, and a few minutes later all the books Toni had arranged by author the night before were once again in cartons stacked near the door. Looking at the pile from Thornbridge, Laura decided rubbish bags were in order, but when she went to the kitchen to fetch a few, she stopped when she saw Toni sitting on the stairs, looking forlorn and emotional.

"Are you okay?" Laura asked softly.

Slowly, Toni shook her head. "I'm scared."

"Of what?"

"Of never being the person you want me to be."

"Oh, Toni," Laura said, sitting down beside her. "All I want you to be is yourself, with all the faults and quirks that come from being human. If you want to cry, then cry, and if you want to laugh, I'll laugh with you, and if you want to be angry for what those bastards did to you, then be angry, Toni, because you have a right to be! What they did was wrong. Terribly, terribly wrong, but you'll never get past it if you don't let it out."

Toni stared at the floor as if she didn't hear a word that had been said, and with a sigh, Laura got up to walk away, but before she took a second step, Toni grabbed her hand. At first, Laura did nothing, but when she felt Toni tighten her grasp, Laura turned and saw tears rolling down Toni's face. Returning to the step, Laura put her arm around Toni to offer comfort, and the floodgates opened. Unabashedly, Toni buried her face in Laura's shoulder, gasping for air in between loud, ragged sobs.

***

After the tears had stopped, Laura jogged up the stairs, returning a minute later with a box of tissues in one hand, and a crumpled one in the other. Sitting down beside Toni, Laura handed her the box, and in unison they blew their noses, the impromptu concerto causing both to snicker under their breath.

"Feeling better?" Laura asked quietly, pulling another tissue from the box.

"I can't ever remember crying this much. Sorry."

"There's absolutely nothing to apologize for, Toni."

"Not even the fact that I told you to go to hell earlier?"

"No, I'll even let that slide...this time," Laura said lightly.

"I could use a drink," Toni said matter-of-factly.

"We have Scotch, wine or beer. What's your pleasure?"

"Beer would be good."

"Be right back."

Leaning against the stairs, Toni closed her eyes, hardly moving a muscle until she felt Laura return to her side.

"Here you go," Laura said, handing her a bottle.

In silence, they sat hip to hip and sipped their beer until the bottles were empty, and without asking, Laura returned to the kitchen and retrieved two more.

"How far did you get?" Toni asked as Laura sat back down.

"Whatcha mean?"

"With the packing in my room."

"Oh, I got the books boxed up, and I was coming out for some bin liners when I saw you on the step."

"Bin liners?"

"For the stuff from Thornbridge."

"Oh, right."

"Was there anything in there you wanted to keep?"

"There are a few pictures in my old wallet I'd like, but the rest can go."

"Okay. You'll have to help me with your clothes. I don't know what's old and what's not."

"Can you bring them out here?"

"Absolutely."

"Can I ask you a favor?"

"Of course."

"Can we light some candles, scented ones, and maybe let them burn in there for a while?"

Laura leaned against Toni's shoulder and said, "I'll burn dozens if that's what you want."

"Thanks."

"No problem."

Taking a swig of beer, Toni said quietly, "So what now?"

"Well, I'm going to go get the bin liners and finish what I started, and you can work on finishing that beer."

"I feel like I should help you, but I don't know how."

Seeing the exhaustion in Toni's eyes, Laura said, "Actually, you can help by going back upstairs and lying down for a while. There's nothing you can do right now, and I don't think you need to see any of that stuff again, even if it's just me taking it to the rubbish bins, right?"

"I'd rather not."

"Good, then go lie down. I'll call you when I get things sorted, and then we'll go through your clothes."

"I still have no idea why you're doing all of this."

Without giving it a second thought, Laura leaned over and placed a light kiss on Toni's cheek. "Give me a reason why I shouldn't."

***

Between filling rubbish sacks and carrying Toni's clothes to the lounge, it was nearly four o'clock before Laura opened another bottle of beer and headed up the stairs. The bedroom door was open and when she walked inside and saw Toni sprawled across the bed, a small grin appeared on her face. About to turn and leave, she heard her mumble, "I'm not asleep."

"Great imitation," Laura said, chuckling to herself.

"What time is it?"

"Just after four. I was thinking about ordering some pizza, and then afterward we can sort out your clothes."

Swinging her legs over the side of the bed, Toni yawned. "That works for me. Just let me get cleaned up and I'll be down."

"See you in a bit."

After using the facilities, Toni splashed water on her face and combed her damp fingers through her hair, trying to make at least a few strands go in the right direction. Looking at her reflection in the mirror, she frowned. Although she had changed into one of Laura's T-shirts the night before, the jeans she was wearing, she had worn for over a day. She had never noticed how faded and threadbare they had become, or how baggy in the seat and the leg, and she sighed. She used to care about how she looked, always shopping in the better stores and buying the newest styles. She'd have them tailored to fit her long legs and narrow hips, but she hadn't given it a second thought for years...until now.

Toni felt oddly calm for having such a tormenting night and morning. Her eyes were bloodshot and glassy from the tears she had shed for so many hours, but when she inhaled, her lungs filled easily. She could breathe. Her life was packed away in boxes and rubbish bags, and for the first time in years, breathing came easy. Was this the cleansing Laura had talked about? Was this the start of becoming *normal*? Would there be a day when she didn't cringe at people or places she didn't know, or recoil from the touch of another human being?

Toni's eyes widened, remembering that she hadn't pulled away from Laura, but rather fell into her arms willingly. And when Laura had hugged her and held her tight, it had felt good, and it had felt right. After her tears had stopped, she had kept her head buried in Laura's shoulder, breathing deep a blend of scents unfamiliar yet wonderful. Strawberry shampoo and vanilla bath oil, perhaps? Or was it simply fabric softener smelling of flowers? And then, there was the perfume. The faintest hint of a fragrance that was feminine and soft, and it had struck Toni at the time that the scent seemed to match the texture of Laura's skin.

With one more glance in the mirror, Toni took a deep breath, flicked off the light and went downstairs, walking into the kitchen just as Laura was hanging up the phone.

"I hope you like pepperoni and sausage."

"That's fine."

"You doing okay?"

"A bit wiped out."

"Understandable," Laura said. "I've got to go pick up dinner. Do you want to come with me? Get out of here for a few?"

Looking at her rumpled clothes, Toni said, "Thanks, but if it's all the same to you, I'll just stay here."

"You sure?"

"Yeah, I'll be fine, Laura."

"Okay, I'll be back in a tick."

After grabbing a beer, Toni went to the lounge, but stopped in the doorway when she saw the disarray caused by a woman on a mission. Laura had boxes stacked in one corner, with trash bags neatly tied shut next to them, and all the clothes that had been hanging in Toni's wardrobe were now draped over chairs around the room. Even the drawers from the dresser were stacked behind the sofa, waiting to be emptied. Walking over to a pile separated from the rest, Toni couldn't help but grin. While Laura had said that she'd need help discerning new clothes from old, all the ones Toni had purchased with Krista several weeks before had been segregated to just one chair.

Taking a sip of beer, she started rummaging through the folded Oxfords and T-shirts, fingering the old fabrics as she decided what to keep, and spying an open bin liner on the floor, she scooped up the lot, save two, and dumped them inside. Trousers and jeans were next and after setting aside a couple of pairs, she tossed the rest in the bag before proceeding to the drawers stacked on the floor. Kneeling, Toni began to root through the socks, bras and knickers, and she felt her cheeks heat. Most of the socks were worn at the heel and had holes in the toes, and her assortment of knickers had loose threads or exposed elastic, but the bras were the worst. The only color she owned was white, but the white had long ago faded to gray. Straps were frayed and hooks were missing, and remembering that most were ill-fitting and loose, with one scoop, all but two were thrown into the bag. Choosing the best of the worst, socks and knickers followed, and other than a few pairs of the softest flannel pajamas known to man and a pair of track pants, the rest of her clothes disappeared behind the black plastic of a rubbish sack.

"It's me," Laura called out, walking in the front door. "Where are you?"

"Lounge."

Coming around the corner, Laura stopped. "You've been busy. I thought we'd tackle it after dinner."

"There wasn't much to do, really. It's all garbage except for that lot," Toni said, pointing to the chair. Inhaling deeply the aroma of pepperoni and cheese rapidly filling the room, she said, "Pizza smells good."

"Yes, it does," Laura said, glancing around at what was left of Toni's belongings. "I was going to suggest we eat in here, but if you'd be more comfortable in the kitchen, that works for me."

Looking around, Toni shrugged. "In here's fine."

Surprised that Toni didn't want to distance herself from the boxes and bags that held Thornbridge memories, Laura said, "You're really okay with this, aren't you?"

"What do you mean?"

"Getting rid of your stuff."

"Yeah, I think I am, but it means I'll need to go shopping again, and I'm not very comfortable with that."

"We'll figure something out," Laura said, putting the pizza box on the coffee table. "I'll just grab some plates and napkins. Do you want some wine or are you still nursing that beer?"

Picking up the bottle, Toni quickly chugged it down. "What beer?"

***

"What are those?" Laura asked, pointing at a small pile of old clothes neatly folded on a chair.

"I figured since we'll be cleaning and painting, I'd keep a few things around so I don't ruin my newer clothes, not that I have a lot of those to ruin."

"Just to let you know, I had candles burning all day and everything's gone in there. All that's left is the bed, dresser and nightstand."

"You didn't have to get rid of the linens."

"Sure I did. That room is going to be yours for as long as you want it, so whatever memories you have while you stay here, I want to be good ones. Besides, I always hated that damned duvet."

"Oh, now I get it. You're using me as an excuse to redecorate!" Toni said, playing her mock outrage to the hilt.

"I'm thinking more along the lines of cheap labor."

"Oi!"

Giggling, Laura relaxed into the sofa, pulling her legs under her as she sipped her wine and gazed at the woman smiling back at her. "You have a nice smile."

Toni blushed slightly as she settled into the other corner of the sofa. "So do you."

"I'm sorry about pushing you so hard yesterday. I really didn't mean to upset you."

"What? Are you saying that you don't like women ripping their clothes off in front of you?"

"Well, I have to admit that was definitely a first."

"For me, too," Toni whispered. "And I'm sorry you had to see them."

"They're just scars, Toni, and you have nothing to be sorry for."

Feeling the slightest quiver of emotion beginning to start, Toni blurted, "So, what's the plan? For the room, I mean."

"I thought we'd get up early and clean, and then go out and pick up some paint."

"I haven't painted a room in forever. I'm not sure I remember how."

"Well, it's your room, so if you fuck it up, just remember you're the one who has to live with it," Laura said, her eyes squinting with amusement.

Letting out a laugh, Toni said, "And as far as decorating goes, I wouldn't even know where to start."

"That's simple. What's your favorite color?"

"Black."

"Do you want to live in a cave?"

"Not particularly."

"Then pick another."

Thinking for a second, Toni said, "Blue."

"There you go."

"Doesn't it matter to you that I could go pick out the most atrocious blue there is? I mean, after all, this is your house."

"Paint's cheap enough, and besides, I don't think you'll do that."

"Why do you say that?"

"Just a feeling."

Their eyes met, and for a second, Toni got lost in the ones looking back at her. "Thank you for not asking any more questions tonight."

"We've got all the time in the world to talk, and I know that when you're ready, you will."

"May be a long wait," Toni said quietly as she closed her eyes and rested her head on the sofa.

"You as tired as you look?"

"Must be the wine."

"How about I fix us some tea and then let you get some sleep. You can use my bed if you'd like. I can use the couch," Laura said as she got to her feet.

"No, I'll be fine here," Toni said, patting the sofa.

"Are you sure?"

"Yeah."

"That light in the corner has a low bulb so if you'd like to leave it on, feel free."

"Thanks, I might just do that."

"Oh, and if you need something to read, those books on the desk match a few of yours that I boxed up."

"You've thought of everything, haven't you?"

"I'm just trying to make you as comfortable as possible. I know you don't like change."

"You're right, I don't, and I can't promise you I won't wig out again," Toni said quietly.

"Well, if you do, I put the paper bags in the pantry."

"Now you tell me."

CHAPTER EIGHTEEN

The low wattage of a tiny bulb across the room provided just enough light to see the shapes and shadows in the lounge as Toni lay awake, telling herself that it was possible. Minutes ticked by as she thought about colors and patterns, new clothes and pristine books...and about spending the entire day with Laura.

They had spent afternoons over coffee and evenings over quiet dinners, enjoying light conversations about safe subjects like the weather, literature and work, and at first, that had been enough for Toni, but that was changing. Ever so slowly, that was changing. Nerves had given way to a soft smile and a Scottish lilt, anxieties squelched by a woman who needed no reason and offered words of encouragement with nothing expected in return. But Toni wanted to give back, and she had no idea why.

Her closest friend in the world hadn't been able to extract information about the hellish years at Thornbridge, but with Laura, Toni felt compelled as if somehow this woman, this *stranger* would make things better...and she had. Speaking of the horrors of starvation had eased Toni's nervous stomach and now more than one portion could be consumed before fear took hold. Not always, but it was a start.

Toni had been content in her life before Laura, complacent to a point of hermitage, and it had suited her. She hadn't wanted to know. She hadn't needed to discuss, and nothing and no one had held her interest. Krista was all she had needed, her lifeline to the world, but suddenly the world was getting bigger. Toni was becoming curious, intrigued by a woman with green eyes and auburn hair, and she found herself thinking about that woman...a lot.

Around Laura's home were framed photographs of friends and family, and Toni wondered if those people knew just how special Laura MacLeod was. Could they see past her beauty and brilliant emerald eyes? Had they discovered how her smile seemed to take away fear, or how a lighthearted comment could cause a grin to appear where tears had just traveled? Did they have a clue?

Lying in the darkness, Toni's thoughts moved to what tomorrow would bring, and a nervous excitement took hold. She wanted to do this. She wanted to spend the day with Laura, doing normal things and suddenly the idea of congested sidewalks and crowded shops didn't cause her heart to race. She wanted to purchase blues like they were going out of style. She wanted new silks against her skin, and new styles and smells. She *could* do this, and she went to sleep dreaming of things blue, of things new, and of things Laura.

***

"Feeling better?"

"I *feel* like a bloody fool," Toni growled as she opened her eyes.

"It wasn't that bad."

"No? You think customers always run out of paint stores in a panic?"

"I don't know. Some of those colors were beyond hideous."

Toni couldn't help but chuckle, and then shaking her head, she said, "How do you do that? How do you manage to make me laugh after I just acted like a total nutcase?"

"Toni, you asked to leave the store, and I brought you out here. I doubt anyone noticed, and if they did, so what?"

"Easy for you to say. You weren't the one with a sack over your face a minute ago."

Smiling, Laura folded the bag, returned it to her purse and pulled out the paint cards she had stuffed inside a few minutes earlier. Handing them to Toni, she said, "Why don't you take a look at these and pick out a color you like. I'll go back and get it, and then we can either go home or go find some bedding. Your choice."

Glancing at the strips, Toni said, "You really want to go through that again? Department stores are much larger than the one we were just in and my legs are longer than yours. You might not be able to catch me if I take off running. I might not stop until I reach the Thames."

"Stop being so hard on yourself."

"It's a habit."

"Break it."

"I'm trying."

"Good, now pick out a color."

Fanning out the cards, Toni perused the blues and finally pointed to one. "I like this. It kind of reminds me of blueberries."

"Blueberries?"

"Yeah, the color on the outside. The light hazy one."

Looking one more time at the small swatch, Laura said, "You know, you're right, and I like it. Are you still planning on painting the trim white?"

"Yeah, something bright to offset this."

"All right," Laura said as she took the card. "You going to be okay out here while I do this?"

"I'll be fine. I'll just lock the doors and take a kip."

Laughing as she climbed out of the car, Laura said, "I have no intention of being *that* long."

***

Intentions were just that. Goals that you set for yourself to complete a task in a timely manner or an orderly fashion, and while Toni's objective had been to go shopping that day, their first stop had almost become their last.

By the time they reached the paint store, Toni was nervous and not in a good way. Finally finding the courage to climb out of the car, she stayed by Laura's side and cautiously followed her into the store. It smelled of paint and thinners, and with only a few customers roaming the aisles, she strolled with Laura to a wall covered in paint chips, displaying hundreds, if not thousands of colors. Moving to the rows of blues, they began scanning the selections.

"See anything you like?" Laura said as she looked over her shoulder, feeling like Toni was more a parrot than a person at that particular moment.

"There're so many. I don't know where to begin."

"I always find it easiest if you just eliminate those you can't stand and then go from there."

"Okay," Toni said as she stepped around Laura to get closer to the display. Running her finger down the cards, she stopped every so often to remove one while leaving others behind. In a few minutes, she held a fan of blue in her hand.

"Are we doing the trim in the same color?"

"No, I was thinking white. Why?"

"Well, if you're going with white trim, you might want to stick to darker blues, so there's a contrast."

"Good point," Toni said, returning several strips to their holders.

"Can I help you two ladies with anything?"

When Laura heard the masculine tone, she quickly glanced at Toni and frowned. Toni's posture had turned rigid and worry lines were now creasing her forehead.

Turning to the store clerk, Laura grinned politely. "No, we're fine. Thank you. We'll call you if we need you."

"Okay, love, but if you need anything, anything at all, the name's Fred and I'll be right over there," he said, casually putting his hand on Toni's shoulder for a second before walking away.

Waiting until the clerk walked away, Laura whispered, "You still with me?"

Swallowing hard, Toni shook her head. "Barely," she said, handing Laura the paint cards. "But I think I'd best get out of here before I make a scene."

***

Sitting alone in the car, Toni had a decision to make. Crawling back into her shell and disappearing was tempting, but no longer easy. Her appetite for life was returning, and the zest was sweet. The flavor was erasing the foulness that had tainted her for so long, and the message it was sending was clear. Feed me life. Try again. You can do this.

Opening her eyes, she saw a familiar face smiling in her direction, and shoving her anxieties aside, Toni climbed out of the car.

"Least I can do is to carry those," she said, taking the cans from Laura's hand.

"So what did you decide?" Laura asked, opening the boot and dumping the supplies inside.

"I don't think sleeping on a bare mattress is an option, is it?"

"No, it's not."

Letting out a long breath, Toni shut the boot. "Well, I guess that means you'd better make sure you keep that paper sack handy."

"It's right in here," Laura said, patting her handbag.

***

It was one of the largest stores in the area, the bedding department alone covering almost an entire floor. Riding the escalator up, Laura kept her eye on Toni, and Toni kept hers on the customers milling about.

When they reached the second floor, even though Toni didn't say a word, Laura could sense her relief. The aisles were spacious, eliminating the possibility of a stranger's accidental touch, and the racks of shelving were low enough for even Laura to see over. Noticing that the customers nearest them seemed intent on their purchases, paying little if any attention to the two women standing just off the escalator, Laura tugged on Toni's sleeve, and slowly they began to shop. Less than an hour later, they rode back down, their hands filled with bags containing sheets, drapes, pillows, and one scrumptiously soft quilt.

Their plans had included shopping for clothes, but the stores were getting busy, and Laura knew Toni was on edge. After dropping their packages into the boot of the car, Laura gave Toni the option on whether to go home or continue.

Between the clothes she had purchased with Krista and those she had kept of the old, Toni knew she'd have enough to make it through a week without having to do laundry, so she almost asked to go home...almost. Remembering the dire straits of the few undergarments she had remaining and knowing that the socks inside her trainers were filled with holes, she sighed. "Could we get lunch first?" she asked quietly. "Build up my strength, so to speak."

"That's a great idea. I'm starving," Laura said, looking up at a signpost to get her bearings. "You know, there's a small bistro up the street. I've never been there before, but I've heard the food is good. We could walk if you'd like, unless you prefer we drive?"

"How far is it?"

"If we walk? Less than ten minutes."

As much as Toni would have preferred to drive, seeing Laura's smile made it impossible for Toni to suggest it. "Okay. Let's go."

"You sure?"

"No, but what doesn't kill you makes you stronger. Yes?"

"That's what they say."

"I hope they're right."

***

The tiny bell over the door chimed as they walked inside, and spotting a table in the corner, they went over and sat down. Scanning the menu, by the time the waitress appeared, Laura wasted no time in placing their order. A few minutes later, two rather large salads were placed on the table.

Leisurely crunching away, Laura asked, "Can I make an observation?"

"Is there any way of stopping you?"

"You could always...what did you call it, wig out?"

"No, I'm not in the mood," Toni said, popping an olive into her mouth.

"Good to know. Actually, it's not really an observation. It's more a question."

"Okay."

"I watched you today, and you seemed much more comfortable when we were buying the linens than when we were picking out paint. I noticed there were no men around in the bedding department, so I'm thinking it has something to do with the fact that you probably trust women more than men...because you're a lesbian, I mean."

Stopping mid-chew, Toni stared back at Laura. "How did you—"

"Kris told me ages ago."

Pursing her lips, Toni took a moment to ponder Laura's question. "So along the same lines, you're saying that you trust men more than women because you're heterosexual?"

As soon as the last word slipped from Toni's lips, Laura felt her cheeks redden. Hanging her head, she raised her eyes to meet Toni's. "Is that your way of politely telling me that I just asked a really stupid question?"

"What do you think?"

"I think I just asked a really stupid question."

"I'd have to agree."

"Should I change the subject?"

"That depends."

"On what?"

"On whether you want to continue down the road of stupid or not."

Smiling, Laura snatched the check from the table. "Why don't I take care of this, and we can get out of here?"

Watching as Laura scampered away from the table with cheeks still ablaze, Toni grinned. "Nice out."

***

The sun had been replaced by the moon when Laura finally awoke from her nap. Nestled in the corner of the sofa under a tartan throw, she tried to decide if getting up was really necessary. The light coming from the kitchen enabled her to see the bags still piled on the floor, put there a few hours earlier by two women, one of whom was exhausted from shopping, and the other, from stress.

By the time they returned to the store, the afternoon shopping rush had begun, and they barely had enough time for Toni to find some jeans, T-shirts and undergarments before her anxieties kicked in. Although they managed to get through the check-out line without issue, after trekking through the crowded store and down the busy sidewalk, Toni was gasping for air. In a cold sweat, she sat in the passenger seat of Laura's car, listening as Laura calmly soothed her fears with words of encouragement until finally, she could breathe again. Closing her eyes to the world, she reclined her seat and listened to the sounds of the traffic as Laura drove her home.

It took three trips to the car to bring their purchases inside, and after agreeing they could both use a short rest, Laura prepared some tea, and they collapsed on the sofa together. Sitting in opposite corners, they sipped their tea quietly, and before the liquid had a chance to cool, they had both fallen asleep.

As Laura lay in the dimly lit lounge, she noticed a scent hanging in the air, and sniffing again, she glanced over at Toni's door. Seeing light streaming out from underneath it, she tossed aside the throw and went to investigate the smell of fresh paint. Slowly opening the bedroom door, she squeezed her eyes shut to block out the brightness of the stark naked bulbs from the overhead light, and when she finally opened them again, she saw Toni rolling paint on the wall, her old red T-shirt now marred by streaks of blue.

"What are you doing?"

Turning toward the sleepy voice, Toni said, "I'm fairly certain it's called painting."

"What time is it?"

"A bit after nine, I think."

"Nine? What the hell are you doing painting at nine o'clock at night?"

"I woke up a few hours ago and thought...why not."

"Why didn't you wake me?"

"Um...because you were sleeping."

"You know what I mean. I could have helped."

"You were exhausted."

"So were you."

"True, but I woke up feeling fine, and since I can't put away any of my clothes until this room is done, I broke open the cans."

"Did you eat anything?"

"Not yet, but we have that pizza from last night. I thought I'd just heat it up."

"I'll do it," Laura said. "Beer or wine?"

"Beer would be good. Thanks."

Trotting up the stairs, Laura changed her clothes, splashed some water on her face and headed back down. Turning on the oven, she slid the leftover pizza inside, grabbed two beers from the fridge and went back to Toni's room. "What can I do to help?" she asked, stepping inside.

"How about handing me that beer?" Toni said with a grin as she put down the roller.

As she gave Toni the bottle, Laura looked around the room. "Wow! This looks great."

"Thanks. I figure I can finish the walls tonight and then do the trim and the bathroom tomorrow."

"We didn't buy any paint for the bathroom."

"I know, so we'll have to go back out. I mean, if that's okay?"

"It's fine, Toni," Laura said, a smile spreading across her face.

Noticing Laura's expression, Toni asked, "What?"

"Nothing."

"You're smiling like a bloody fool. Now come on, out with it."

"It just seems to me that you're enjoying redecorating my house."

The grin faded from Toni's face. "I'm sorry. I overstepped my bounds."

"What the hell are you talking about?"

"I shouldn't have started anything without first talking to you."

"Oh, Jesus Christ," Laura said, rolling her eyes. "Toni, we both agreed that this was *your* room. Remember?"

"Yeah, but—"

"And you're giving me something to help cover bills and food, aren't you?"

"Well, yes, but—"

"So, that means you can do what you want in here."

"It's still your house."

"Look, let's make a deal, shall we? This is your space, and in it you can do whatever you'd like. My bedroom is my space, and the same thing goes. The lounge and kitchen are community areas, shared by both, so if you want to read a book or cook a meal, feel free, and if I want to watch the telly or burn a meal, I can. And if either of us wants to bring a *guest* home, the other will make herself scarce. Agreed?"

"I don't see that happening."

"What? You don't think I can pull?" Laura said, placing her hands on her hips.

"I wasn't talking about you."

"Toni, trust me, there'll come a time when you'll want a woman's company again and when you do, I'll sequester myself in my room, and you won't even know I'm here."

"That part of my life is over, Laura," Toni said flatly. "And I know this arrangement won't last forever, so when I start getting underfoot, let me know, and I'll ask Krista to find me another place to live."

"That's a bit cynical, don't you think?"

Toni shrugged. "It's just the way it is, and speaking of the way it is, you do know that you're burning the pizza, don't you?"

Sniffing the air, Laura's eyes widened. "Shit!" she said, running out of the room.

Toni picked up the roller and turned back to the task at hand, covering old paint with new and trying not to think about a life she'd never have.

CHAPTER NINETEEN

"I've missed you."

"Really? I thought you'd like not having to babysit me anymore."

"I never *ever* considered it babysitting, and you know it."

"I know," Toni said. "Speaking of babysitting, why aren't you at home taking care of Robin?"

"You couldn't have possibly forgotten how whiny she gets when she has a cold," Krista said with a titter. "Besides, she told me to come over. She knows how much I love your lasagna."

"To be honest, I wasn't sure I'd remember how to make it, but it didn't turn out half bad," Toni said, pushing away her plate. "Remind me later and I'll pack up some for you to take to her."

"She'll love you forever."

As Toni began to clear the table, Krista pulled the cork from the Chianti and refilled their glasses. Putting the bottle aside, she asked, "So, where's *your* other half?"

"Sorry?"

"Laura. You know, the woman you live with."

"I rent a room from her, Krista. It's not quite the same thing."

"Okay, fine, but where is she?"

"She had a date."

"Oh yeah? Anyone I know?"

"You and Laura travel in the same circles, do you?"

Her face splitting into a grin, Krista said, "No, I guess we don't. But come on, who is he?"

"Well, if you must know, his name is Phillip Hoult, and he's a doctor."

"A doctor? Laura's okay, isn't she?"

"Yes, she's fine. A few weeks ago, one of the residents at Calloway twisted her ankle and Laura drove her to the walk-in clinic. Apparently, Hoult splits his time between there and the hospital, and they got to talking. One thing led to the other...blah, blah, blah."

"Is it serious?"

"I have absolutely no idea," Toni said, shutting the refrigerator. "She seems happy."

"And how about you? Are you happy?"

"I'm getting there," Toni said, starting the coffeemaker. "I've got my own room and my books. That's all I need."

Before Krista could speak, her mobile rang, and excusing herself, she disappeared into the lounge.

After tidying the kitchen, Toni placed a hefty portion of lasagna on a plate, and she was just finishing wrapping it in foil when Kris came back into the room.

"I'm afraid I'm going to have to cut our night short."

"Is Robin okay?"

"Yeah, but she feels absolutely awful and is requesting soup, so I'm going to hit the market and head home. I'm sorry."

"Don't be sorry," Toni said, handing her the plate. "Take this with you. There's enough for both of you if you decide you want to share it."

Krista leaned over and kissed Toni on the cheek. "I'll make it up to you. I promise."

"No worries, Krista. Go take care of Robin."

***

It had been two weeks since Toni's bedroom had been redecorated, but when she went in and flicked on the light, she smiled as if she'd never seen it before. Laura was right. The new had helped. Gone was the smell of musty books that had reminded her of an apartment she couldn't return to, and clothes long past their prime had been replaced by ones crisp, their colors still true and vivid. Eyeing the small pile of books neatly arranged on the dresser, Toni almost didn't want to disturb their newness. Although her recently purchased collection had yet to grow beyond a dozen, their covers were glossy and unscratched, and their pages had yet to curl from use.

Deciding that it didn't matter which she chose because she knew what each contained, Toni picked up the one on top of the stack and returned to the lounge where her coffee was waiting. Taking a sip, she sat down and propped her legs on the coffee table, but before she could open the book, she heard the front door open.

"It's me," Laura shouted.

"You're home early. Something wrong?" Toni asked when Laura appeared in the doorway.

"No, Phillip got called back to the hospital, so he put me in a taxi, and here I am," Laura said, slipping out of her high heels. "Where's Kris?"

"Robin called and requested soup to help fend off her cold, so she left a few minutes ago. You just missed her."

"Oh, that's too bad. There wouldn't be any lasagna left, would there?"

"Half a tray," Toni said, placing her book on the end table. "It's still on the stove cooling down. Why don't you go change, and I'll fix you a plate?"

"Thanks." Grabbing her shoes, Laura ran up the stairs. "Be right back."

A few minutes later, wearing track pants and an oversized jersey, Laura came into the kitchen. "Is there any wine open?"

Toni pointed at the glass on the counter filled with Chianti. "I already poured you some, but I wasn't sure whether you wanted to eat in here or in the other room."

"Lounge works for me," Laura said, taking her wine and food and disappearing through the doorway.

Tickled by Laura's apparent need for sustenance, Toni poured herself what remained of the Chianti and headed back to the lounge. Sitting down, she tried her best to hide her amusement as she watched Laura devour her dinner.

Noticing a glint of humor in Toni's eyes, Laura asked, "What?"

"Nothing."

"Do I have tomato sauce on my face?"

"I doubt that it was quick enough to escape your mouth."

Laughing, Laura put her plate to the side. "Sorry. I didn't have lunch."

"I thought I was the only one with an eating disorder."

"I've noticed you're doing a bit better with that."

"All depends on the day."

"Why?"

"It's a hard habit to break. I'm a trained dog, Laura. I was taught to ration my food in preparation for days when there wouldn't be any. So, some days I manage to eat my lunch, and others, I can barely finish half of it."

"But at dinner, you're fine."

"That's because I know you're watching me," Toni said with a grin. "Honestly, I'm doing better than I was. Habits just take time to break. And speaking of time, you seem to be spending a lot of time with your new boyfriend. How's that going?"

"It's still early on, but it seems to be going okay, I guess."

"You guess?"

"I've not had a lot of luck in the boyfriend department in recent years, so I'm a bit wary of moving too fast."

"And he wants to?" Seeing Laura instantly blush, Toni said, "Oh, I see."

"It's not that I'm a prude or anything, but I don't see the need to fall into bed with someone I barely know just because he's a handsome doctor."

"A bit full of himself, is he?"

"Not really, but I get this feeling that he likes the title a bit too much."

"How so?"

"Like tonight," Laura began, tucking her legs under her as she sipped her wine. "He forgot to make a reservation, so when we got to the restaurant we were going to have to wait in the queue, so he told the maître d' that his name was *Dr.* Phillip Hoult."

"Well, that is his name."

"I know, but it was just the way he said it, like he wanted preferential treatment because of it."

"It could also be because he knew he was on-call and was afraid he'd have to go back to work."

"Are you defending him?"

"No. I'm simply saying that in this day and age, I would think that a handsome doctor would be a good catch."

"Who said I'm fishing?" Laura said with a huff.

Smiling, Toni said, "You're in a mood tonight."

"No, I'm not! I just don't want to be pushed into a relationship simply because he fits into the mold of what some people think women want!"

"Whoa. Whoa. *Whoa*," Toni said, trying not to laugh. "Where the hell did that come from?"

Realizing that she'd been shouting, Laura sighed. "Sorry, but for a minute there you sounded like my mother."

"Well, by your reaction, I'm thinking that's not a good thing?"

"Toni, I love my mum, but sometimes it seems like she's pressuring me to get married and have kids. Like that's what a woman needs to be happy."

"I think they call that old school."

"Well, she needs to graduate!"

Laura had never seen Toni laugh—*really* laugh—until that moment, but watching her toss back her head and roar brought a smile to Laura's face. Waiting until Toni's merriment subsided, Laura said, "You have a nice laugh."

"Thanks," Toni said as she stood up and picked up the empty plate. "I'm going to get some wine. Would you like some more?"

"Yes, please."

Returning a few minutes later with a freshly opened bottle, Toni filled Laura's glass and settled back into her corner of the sofa.

"Can I ask you a question?" Laura said as she sipped her wine.

"I've yet to figure out a way to stop you, so go ahead," Toni said with a chuckle.

"What did you mean when you said that part of your life was over?"

"Huh?"

"That night, when you were painting your room. I was talking about you bringing a woman home, and you said that part of your life was over. Why'd you say that?"

"Because it's the truth."

"Just like that."

"Yep."

"Don't you ever think about it?"

"What?"

"Sex."

Stopping for a moment, Toni took a sip of wine. Quietly, she said, "No, I don't."

"Really?"

"Why do you find that so surprising?"

"Well, for one thing, you're young and attractive, intelligent and—"

"Don't forget my finer features. Let's see...afraid of crowds and strangers and of course, there's the little issue about being touched."

"But that can change."

"I don't ever see it happening."

"Why?"

Abruptly, Toni stood up and emptied her glass in one swallow. "Refill that, will you? I need to use the loo."

Going into her bathroom, Toni shut the door, and leaning against it, her hands turned into fists. Why couldn't Laura let it go? Why did she need to know answers to things better left unspoken? Yes, talking about the food had helped, but this wasn't about hunger. This was about pain. This was about depravity and scars and pain. Closing her eyes, Toni tried to keep her annoyance at bay, but with every breath she took, it grew. Laura wasn't going to let go, and Toni knew it. If it wasn't tonight, then it would be another night. If it wasn't *this* question, then it would be another...and then another. Shaking her head, Toni opened her eyes. It was time to get off the carousel and give Laura answers to a few questions. Maybe then she wouldn't ask any more.

Returning to the lounge a few minutes later, Toni sat down, picked up her wine and nearly drained the glass.

"Are you trying to get pissed?" Laura asked.

"No," Toni said, holding out her glass for a refill.

Scrutinizing the woman as she topped off her glass, Laura asked, "What's going on?"

"Liquid courage."

"What?"

"False bravado. Alcohol makes you feel invincible, or so I've read."

"Why do you need to feel like that?"

"Because I'm about to answer your goddamn questions."

If it weren't for the words she had just heard, Laura would have reprimanded Toni when she saw her pull a pack of cigarettes out of her pocket. They both had agreed that Toni wouldn't smoke anywhere but in her own room, but as Laura watched her light the cigarette and pull the smoke into her lungs, she decided not to argue the point. Grabbing an empty candy dish from the end table, she placed it in front of Toni.

Taking another drag, Toni followed it with a gulp of wine and then turned to look at Laura. "That's the way I used to be," she said, her voice low and steady. "Invincible. I wasn't afraid of anything...not anything. I could walk into a crowded auditorium, stand on the stage and face hundreds of people, and my blood pressure wouldn't raise a notch. Not one fucking notch. I'd go places I'd never been without giving it a second thought, and I'd shop in the finest stores, eat at the fanciest restaurants and dance in the loudest clubs this country has to offer without a care in the world. And I was educated. I was smart. I was too smart.

"They say that a good education is what you need to make it in this world, but mine almost killed me. Because with that intelligence, with that learned background of mine, when I walked into Thornbridge, I walked in with the confidence that I could handle anything...*anything* that came along. But I was wrong. Confidence to a Thornbridge screw was like catnip to a cat."

Stopping to pull more nicotine into her lungs, Toni tried to decide what Laura needed to know and what she didn't, but Toni's mind was a jumble, so as thoughts entered, she spoke them as if she were reading them from a book. "I was in Sutton Hall long enough to learn the rules, but Thornbridge had its own set, and it didn't take me long to realize that Sutton Hall was five-star compared to that hole in the north of this country. Sutton was relatively new, so the cells were modern and clean, but Thornbridge was over a century old. The cells were cramped and dank, and the mattresses were ghastly. They were barely an inch thick and stained with God knows what. They smelled like death...or something far worse. The plumbing was horrid, and the stench of human waste hung in the air like a shroud. And it was cold. It was *so* fucking cold.

"Each cell had a window no bigger than a shoe box. I remember thinking how stupid it was that they actually put bars in front of them. Like somehow we could slip through something that small and get away. Most of the glass was broken, and the cracks were covered over with tape. In the summer when the sun was high, it was like looking through a kaleidoscope. But in the winter...in the winter you'd have to stuff as much clothing as you dared into that space to try to keep the cold from coming in, but it always found a way. It was like it just snaked its way through the mortar."

Stopping to take a sip of wine, Toni stubbed out her cigarette and lit another. "I thought the meals at Sutton Hall were bad, but nothing could have prepared me for Thornbridge. Half the time what they gave us tasted like detergent, and when it didn't, it had been cooked for so long it was like a putrid pudding. The only good thing about being sent down the block was the fact that they made our trays first. When we *did* get food, it still looked like food.

"I couldn't believe anything like Thornbridge could exist in our country, but I knew that once I talked to Kris, she'd get in touch with the authorities and tell them what was going on. In Sutton Hall, we got our phone privileges in a week, but in Thornbridge, they made you wait for a month. So, I waited. Patiently counting down the days, but my counting stopped on day twenty-nine."

"Why?"

"Late in the afternoon, I was escorted to the governor's office and shown over a dozen photographs of cons, or should I say *dead* cons. Lying on steel tables, with their naked shoulders and faces whiter than white, I knew in an instant that they had been taken in a morgue. I still had no idea...no *fucking* clue why he wanted me to see them, but then he explained. He said most of the women in Thornbridge had no connections outside the walls. The nutters' families had long since forgotten them and the sane ones, well their crimes were so heinous that their families refused all contact, but he knew there were a few of us who didn't fall into those categories. He said he wanted to make sure I understood that he wasn't about to lose what he called his lucrative career because of a con who couldn't keep her mouth shut. He told me the women in the photographs all believed they were smarter than he was, but all of them...*all* of them died before they ever got a chance to make their first phone call."

"Oh my God," Laura said in a ragged whisper.

"The next morning, when I called Krista for the first time, I stood outside the officer's lounge on the only phone we were allowed to use, and I talked to her about the weather. She kept saying she wanted to visit, wanted to see how I was doing, but I couldn't risk it. I just couldn't, so no matter how many times she asked for a visiting order, I'd never send one. I wasn't about to die like those women. I was smart and *I* was going to survive, but it didn't take me long to realize that the screws weren't my only enemies.

"You can't erase the air of a proper upbringing in a day or a week, or even a year, and those women inside those walls hated me for it. I wasn't like them. I wasn't hard and angry. I wasn't vicious. I had a conscience, and they didn't. In Sutton Hall it wasn't like that. There, the women were all just trying to do their time until they got out, but in Thornbridge, all the cons had was time, so they used it the only way knew how. They'd spend their nights making shivs out of toothbrushes or plastic cutlery stolen from the servery, and whenever they got a chance, they'd try to stab you...just because they could," Toni said in a whisper. "They got me over a dozen times."

Hearing Laura's gasp, Toni looked over. "You said you wanted to know, but I'll stop if you want me to."

Laura wiped a tear from her face and shook her head. Hastily drinking the rest of her wine, she reached for the bottle with a trembling hand.

Hearing the neck of the bottle tap against the rim of the glass, Toni reached over and took it from Laura. Steadily refilling both of their glasses, Toni stubbed out her cigarette and then paused to take a drink before she began to speak, her voice still as calm and emotionless as it had been when she started.

"I had been there almost two months before a screw came into my cell after lights out. It had rained all day, and I was lying in the dark listening to the water drip off the roof when I heard my cell door open. That place was so old, there wasn't a door that didn't squeak or a hinge that didn't squeal, and even though the lights were off, there was enough coming from the courtyard that I could see it was one of the men. He was tall and heavyset, but his face was in the shadows, so I never knew which one it was...and then he said, 'I heard you think you're pretty smart. Well, we don't like smart around here.' I didn't move. I didn't know what was happening or why he felt the need to tell me that, but then I heard a noise, and I knew he was taking off his belt. My first thought was that he was going to try to rape me, so I jumped up preparing to defend myself...and that's when the belt hit me across the face. Christ, it hurt, but before I could even cry out because of the pain, I heard the belt cutting through the air. I ducked and it glanced off my back, and when I heard that sound again, I knew he had no intention of stopping. I fell to my bed and curled up in a ball trying to protect myself anyway I could as he just kept whipping me. Over and over and over again until my entire body was burning from the sting...and then he just stopped. Just like that. I heard the door open...and he was gone.

"After that, every few weeks I'd be visited in the night for a bit of fun as they called it. Sometimes it would only be a punch or a kick, but there were some nights when it seemed to go on forever. And when they were in a really foul mood, they'd use the buckled end, and I'd end up going to medical to get stitched up.

"So, I started learning the *unwritten* rules of Thornbridge. If you didn't want the screws to notice you, you didn't notice them. You kept your eyes on the floor when they were around, never making eye contact. To them, it was a challenge, and they were more than ready to answer it. In the servery, if they came near you, you placed your hands palms down on the table, showing you were unarmed, and at night, you wore as many shirts as you could so the beatings wouldn't hurt as much."

Stopping for a moment, Toni finished the wine in her glass and lit another cigarette. After the third drag, she said, "But above all else, the one rule you always followed, the one you never, *ever* broke, was interfering when a screw was punishing a prisoner. The rule was to walk away, and I had learned to follow their rules...or so I thought.

"I had been there close to six months and one afternoon I heard screaming from the second level. When I looked up, one of the screws was holding a con named Betty over the railing. She was a twig of a woman with rotten teeth and a foul mouth, sentenced to life for murdering her parents in their bed. From what I could gather, she apparently spilled some tea on the guard as he was making his rounds, and he decided to teach her a lesson. He had her by her ankles, dangling her over the railing and laughing as he pretended to let go and then not, all the while promising that the next time, he'd let her fall. All the cons started disappearing into their cells, knowing there was nothing they could do, but I couldn't move. Something told me that the bastard was going to drop her...and then he did. I didn't have time to think about consequences or rules. I just reacted and somehow managed to break her fall, but in all the commotion, for a split-second, I forgot where I was. I looked up at that son of a bitch and called him every name...every *fucking* name I could think of...and then some guards grabbed me from behind and took me down the block. They beat me and they starved me, and when they finally took me back to my cell four weeks later, I thought the worst was over...but I was wrong."

Laura was staring at the glass in her hand as she listened. Revolted yet enthralled by Toni's story, it wasn't until she heard Toni's voice crack that she looked up, her breath catching in her throat at the sight of Toni's transformation. Her forehead and upper lip were now dotted with sweat, and her face had paled considerably. She held one hand to her stomach as if trying to keep something inside, while the other held a cigarette made almost entirely out of ash.

"Toni, it's okay to stop," Laura said. "You don't have to go on."

Clenching her teeth, Toni said, "You wanted to know."

"We can do this later."

"We do it *now!*"

Toni's belly had been on slow simmer since she began speaking, but now it was rolling. Dinner and drinks were tumbling, and the bile created rose in her throat. She winced at its sting, but forced it back down. She wasn't through. She would not let them win. She would *never* let them win.

Dropping the remains of her cigarette into the candy dish, Toni took a long, stuttered breath. "Just before lights out that night, Betty came to my cell. She said that she owed me for saving her life, and she wanted me to know that the screw who tried to kill her was going to visit me that night. So, I put on all the clothes that I could...and I waited. A few hours later, he showed up. Christ, he smelled vile. A mixture of cigars and alcohol and body odor, it was enough to make you gag, and then I heard the sound of his buckle being loosened..." Toni stopped, staring off into space as she remembered that night. "...and then I heard him unzip his trousers."

"Oh, dear God, no," Laura gasped, bringing her hand to her mouth. "Oh, please God, no."

"In that instant, in less time than it takes a person to blink, something inside of me just snapped. There was no way I was going to let that bastard rape me, and my fear turned into fury. I launched myself off the cot and dove into the darkness until I found him. I smashed my head into his face, and I just kept swinging at him...I just kept swinging at him over and over and over again.

"No con ever fought back, so I took him by surprise, but it didn't take long before he got the upper hand and began pushing me across the cell. When we stepped into the light, I could see blood all over his face. It was pouring out of his nose, but he didn't seem to notice...or maybe he didn't care. I don't know. When he got me to the wall, he pushed me hard against the rock, but I just kept fighting. I could taste blood in my mouth, and the stone was cutting into my face, but there was no way that bastard was going to take me like that. No *fucking* way! It was at that moment when I realized I had become what I had been convicted of being...a murderer. Because if there had been a weapon, if there had been something I could have used to kill him, I would have. I would have gutted that bastard without one ounce of remorse. I wouldn't have asked for forgiveness or offered an apology. I would have cut out his heart...just like that."

Toni's voice drifted off as emotions welled in her throat. Taking another deep, ragged breath, she let it out slowly. "It felt like an eternity as we stood there and fought. His hands were everywhere, groping and squeezing and hurting me, and his words were so filthy, so utterly appalling, but as each minute passed, I grew weaker. He was so fucking strong, and I knew I wasn't going to be able to stop him. I knew it was going to happen...and I wanted to die. I so wanted to die. Somehow...somehow I found this last bit of energy, and I pushed as hard as I could, trying to twist away from him...and then something...something let loose. I started to scream. Christ, it hurt. I didn't know what had happened, but I was...I was afraid to look. The bastard...it felt like the bastard had ripped off my arm. Jesus Christ, I had never felt pain like that before.

"For a second or two, he just stared at me. I guess I scared him. I don't know, but as he came at me again, my cell door swung open, and I heard a woman shouting. There weren't many women screws in Thornbridge, and up until that night, I thought them no better than the men, but she proved me wrong. Odd, how a few days earlier she had kicked me awake and now...now she was saving my life. I guess beatings were one thing, but rape...rape was something else. I crumpled to the floor when she pulled him away, and then they left. They closed the door, turned the key...and just left me there. I stayed on the floor until the next morning when they took me to medical to put my arm back in its socket."

Slowly, Toni got to her feet, swaying slightly as she stood tall. She held one hand hard against her stomach, trying in vain to quiet the churning, while the other had turned into a fist, and her jaw, once strong and defiant, now trembled uncontrollably. "You wanted to know why I don't see myself being with anyone," she said, her voice so weak Laura leaned closer to hear. "Because every time...every *fucking* time someone touches me, every time someone gets *too* close, all I feel is rage. I think of that night. I think of his hands. I think of his smell and the pain and the terror, and how much I wanted to kill him. How much I *still* want to kill him!" Clamping her hand over her mouth, Toni ran to her bedroom, pushing the door open with such force that it slammed against the wall. Bouncing back, it almost hit Laura as she ran to catch up.

Toni barely made it to the toilet before her stomach emptied, and standing in the doorway, Laura looked on in shock. A minute passed, and taking a hesitant step in the woman's direction, Laura said, "Toni—"

"Get out!" Toni screamed between heaves. "Get the fuck out!" Again, her stomach lurched, but there was nothing left to expel, and with a sigh, she sat back on her haunches. Sensing Laura was still in the room, Toni looked over and glared. "For Christ's sake, I'm begging you. Please...please just leave me be."

It was a plea Laura could not ignore. She had trampled on Toni's privacy again, and with regret etched on her face, she backed out of the room and shut the door. With a heavy heart, she walked to the bed and sat down, quietly waiting as she sniffled back her tears and worried about the woman on the other side of the door. She had no idea why Toni had chosen tonight to speak truths and terrors. Why she seemed so intent on getting every word out, but she had and the result wasn't uplifting. Laura had been the one pushing to hear the story, prodding for information and believing the result would be cleansing. It wasn't, and Laura felt dreadful. There was no epiphany to be found amongst the ruins of what Thornbridge had done to Toni. There was only more pain.

Taking a stuttered breath, Laura looked around the bedroom and the tiniest of grins appeared on her face. The room was vibrant and comfortable, and by Laura's standards, incredibly neat. The newly purchased books were carefully stacked on the dresser because the floor was no longer good enough for literature, and the bed was skillfully made with corners crisp, and pillows fluffed until they were perfect. There were no clothes scattered about or shoes on the floor, and the nightstand held only a clock, a lamp and Toni's wallet. The room was lived in, but just barely. Sitting there, Laura wondered if Toni would ever allow her world to include more than just four walls, some books and a carton of smokes.

Suddenly, a thought popped into Laura's head. It was a crazy idea...or was it? Before she could make up her mind, she heard the bathroom door open, and Toni walked out, looking disheveled and incredibly tired.

"Hey," Laura said softly. "I know you probably don't want me in here, but I couldn't leave until I knew you were all right."

For a few seconds, Toni just stared at Laura, and then she said quietly, "Please don't ask any questions. I can't handle any more tonight."

"I won't. I just wanted to make sure you were feeling better."

"Other than the fact that I just wasted perfectly good lasagna and several glasses of Chianti, you mean?"

"Yeah, besides that."

"I'll be okay, Laura. I'm just...I'm just really wiped out."

"All right," Laura said as she got up and walked to the door. "I'm going to make some tea. Would you like some?"

"That would be great. Thanks."

No sooner had Laura left the bedroom when her idea returned. Stopping a few feet from the door, she chewed on her lip as she weighed the pros and cons. Turning back around, she returned to Toni's room.

"Toni?" she said, standing in the doorway.

Staring at the floor, Toni looked up. "Yeah."

"How'd you like to go on a holiday with me?"

CHAPTER TWENTY

It had been a spur-of-the-moment idea, but lying in bed that night, the more Laura thought about it, the more it made sense. Toni had locked herself in a box. A dark, gray box filled with the noise and pollution of the city and the chaos of crowds, with buildings blocking out the sun and people too busy to remember what life was about. They had forgotten about green pastures and rivers swirling with life, and being lulled to sleep by the sound of insects buzzing in the darkness. They had dismissed from their minds forests filled with the wonderment of God, containing trees so tall they seemed to reach the clouds, and instead, they shuffled from pubs to cinemas, filling their bellies with alcohol and their minds with make-believe. They didn't know that tranquility was within their grasp. A short flight or a long drive would take them to a place where advertising didn't line the roads. Where air still tasted like air and where you could sit for hours amidst the fields of green...and feel safe.

Every week, they talked on the phone, and rarely a day went by without an email being exchanged, but Laura hadn't seen her mother in months. Too busy with work and with Toni, Laura had been remiss in her daughter duties, and she knew it. With her father deciding he liked the life of a fisherman more than that of a husband and a father, it had only ever been Laura and her mother, and Laura had no regrets. While she had complained about her mother's concern over her marital state or lack thereof, in her heart, Laura knew that her mother only wanted the best for her. So, in the wee hours of the morning, Laura picked up the phone and told her mum she was coming home for a visit.

Four hundred miles away, Eleanor hung up the receiver, slid her feet into her slippers and shuffled to the kitchen to make a cup of tea. Turning on her laptop, she opened her email account and began re-reading the dozens of messages she had received from Laura over the past several months. They spoke of a job she seemed to love and of boyfriends old and new, but those subjects seemed to be secondary to the one called Toni Vaughn. Although she had never met the woman, through Laura's words, Eleanor had come to know the elusive teacher, a woman wrongfully convicted and sentenced to hell, and it made her proud to know she had raised a daughter so willing to help someone so wronged. But as the emails kept coming, she began to wonder how long it would take Laura to realize what Eleanor already knew.

There had never been secrets between them. They only had each other, and with that came a trust that most parents would give their right arm for. Eleanor knew when her daughter had lost her virginity and to whom, and she knew about Laura's many boyfriends and all the failed relationships. She had heard the complaints, dried the tears and giggled at her daughter's stubbornness when it came to the male of the species. She also knew that until tonight, Laura had never asked to bring anyone home other than Abby, but Abby was Laura's closest friend. Toni Vaughn was not. She was something more, of that Eleanor was certain.

Laura was her pride and joy. Eleanor had raised a girl to be a woman the only way she knew how, and there had never been a day in her life when she wasn't proud that Laura was hers, and Eleanor was not about to start now. Other parents could turn their backs on their children, give them ultimatums or threaten their inheritance, but as far as Eleanor was concerned, they were idiots. Children are much too precious to be tossed aside simply because they want to live *their* lives.

Pushing aside the teacup, Eleanor opened a cabinet, got a glass and poured herself a small brandy. Going out the back door, she stood on the slate, looked up at the stars and smiled. Raising her glass to the sky, she silently thanked God for giving her such a wonderful child, finished her drink and then walked back inside.

***

"Why aren't you packed?"

"I can't bloody do this."

"Yes, you can."

"No, I can't," Toni said, sitting on the edge of the bed. "Laura, you're asking too much of me. You're pushing too hard."

Laura frowned. Toni was right. It had taken months to get Toni to take the tiniest of steps, and it had only been a few weeks since Laura had suggested they go to Scotland on holiday during the last break at Calloway before fall classes began. Sitting down next to Toni, she said, "I'm sorry."

"I know you mean well, but things like this are hard for me. I get so bloody scared."

"I lose sight of that sometimes," Laura said quietly. "You do so well around here and at work. I forget that you're still afraid of so much."

"I'm sorry."

"You've got nothing to be sorry about."

"Go without me. Okay?"

"Is that what you want?"

Hanging her head, Toni said, "Yeah. I think it's best."

"Then that's what I'll do, but I'll miss your company," Laura said, touching the back of Toni's hand.

As Laura walked from the room, Toni stared at the floor, unable to tell the woman that she'd miss her, too. When had Laura become so important? When did conversations over breakfast and dinner seem to make each day start and end so perfectly? When did pleasing someone else begin to matter?

Filling a travel mug with coffee, Laura tightened the lid and walked from the kitchen, but stopped short when she found Toni standing at the foot of the stairs with suitcase in hand.

Holding her breath, Laura asked softly, "Going somewhere?"

"Are you still planning to drive?"

"That was the plan."

"You...you still keep a paper sack in your handbag?"

"Never leave home without it."

"Well, then...you want some company?"

***

Although Laura had grown up in Stirling, after she had moved to England, her mother purchased a home in an area called Carron Bridge. Just north of Falkirk and south of Stirling, it offered a slightly quieter life in a country setting. Near enough to the cities that Eleanor could continue her duties as an estate agent, but far enough away that she could forget about work when she got home.

Since climbing into the car, Toni hadn't said a word. Preferring to just stare out the window and watch the world whiz by, it wasn't until they were two hours into the trip, when she finally spoke. "Does your mother know you're bringing a guest?"

Startled, Laura glanced at her passenger. "Yes, she knows."

"Does she know about me? I mean…the way I am?"

"I've told her a bit. She and I have never had many secrets, but I didn't give her all the details. I told her you had spent some time in prison, but you were released when evidence proved you innocent. I didn't tell her what they did to you. I just said you were shy around strangers, and you had some trust issues."

"That's putting it mildly."

"You're getting better."

"Around you."

"Well, she's just like me, only taller."

"Everyone's taller than you."

"Hey!"

"Just joking."

"I know. I like it," Laura said, giving Toni another quick glance. "So, you feeling better? Not so nervous?"

"We've only been in the car for a couple of hours. Ask me that again in about six more."

***

The trip was long and thankfully uneventful. As Laura expected, Toni never offered to drive, and Laura knew it was for the best. Her friendly banter was met with blank stares or mumbled replies, and when gas or restrooms were needed, unless the stations were small and practically deserted, Toni could not bring herself to get out of the car.

Having spent most of the trip either staring out the window or at her lap, when Toni felt the road conditions change, she raised her eyes. Peering through the windscreen, she saw they were on an unpaved road, and sitting straight in her seat, she said, "Are we there?"

"Yeah, well we are if I can find the bloody driveway," Laura said, slowing the car to a crawl. "Oh, there it is."

Turning onto the gravel drive, Laura drove up to the house and parked the car. Turning off the engine, she looked in Toni's direction. The sun had long since set, but between the brilliance of the full moon and the light streaming from the windows of her mother's home, Laura could see Toni's jaw was set. Reaching over, she placed her hand over Toni's. "So, you ready for this?"

"I guess asking you to turn around isn't an option, is it?"

Giving Toni's hand a squeeze, Laura said, "Afraid not, but if you feel the same way tomorrow, I'll take you home. Okay?"

"Yeah," Toni said in a whisper. After running her hands down her jeans to dry her palms, she reached for the door handle. "Right, well let's do this."

Laura quickly climbed out of the car and opened the boot, but before any luggage could be removed, she heard her mother's voice.

"That can wait just a bit, don't you think?"

Spinning around, Laura's face lit up, and running over, she fell into her mother's outstretched arms.

"Oh, I missed you, Laura," Eleanor said, giving her daughter a hug. "I'm so happy you're home."

"Me, too." Giving her mother a kiss on the cheek, she said, "You look great."

"It's dark, sweetheart. Wait until we get inside. I'm a wreck."

Watching from the car, Toni pulled the luggage out of the boot and took a deep breath. Aware introductions would have to be made, and ritual greetings exchanged, her heart began to race as she approached the two women.

Seeing the woman slowly walk toward them, Eleanor pulled out of Laura's hug and smiled in Toni's direction. Holding out her hand, she said, "I'm Eleanor MacLeod. You must be the friend Laura's told me about."

Pausing for a moment, Toni set the suitcases on the ground and cautiously held out her hand. "Toni Vaughn," she whispered. "It's very nice to meet you, Mrs. MacLeod."

"Likewise, my dear, and please call me Eleanor," she said, eyeing the tall woman standing in the shadows. "How about we go inside?"

Hustling them into the house, Eleanor shut the door and motioned toward the stairs. "Laura, why don't you take Toni up and show her where she'll be staying, and I'll make us some tea."

"Would you like some help?" Laura asked.

"Don't be ridiculous. I'm sure you both need to freshen up after that drive. Go up and get comfortable and I'll fix something for us to nibble on."

Watching as they disappeared up the stairs, Eleanor went to the kitchen and mentally chastised herself for being so stereotypical. The portrait of Toni Vaughn she had painted in her mind couldn't have been more wrong, and Eleanor couldn't have felt more stupid. With the knowledge that the woman was gay and had spent time in prison, she had imagined Toni to be rough, masculine and plain, but she was anything but. While her stooped shoulders and obvious hesitation even to shake hands had proved that prison had taken its toll, the woman was nonetheless, beautiful, and Eleanor found that Toni's soft-spoken ways seemed to add to her charm. Although many people would have reserved judgment until more than ten words had been spoken, after working nearly thirty years as an estate agent, Eleanor's ability to judge a person's character within minutes of being introduced was uncanny. Meeting and greeting hundreds, if not thousands of prospective sellers and buyers through the years, she had learned how to pick the winners from the losers...and Toni Vaughn was no loser.

Reaching the second floor, Laura led Toni down the hallway and opened the first door on her left. "This will be you," she said, leading Toni into the room. Seeing the woman's delighted expression, Laura added, "I thought you'd like it."

The room was just large enough to comfortably hold a bed, dresser, armoire and nightstand, and matching the walls, all the furniture, except for the bed frame, was white. The woodwork throughout the room had been stained a light cherry, as were all the tops of the furniture, and the brass hardware displayed on the doors and drawers matched the large shiny spheres sitting atop the corners of the black iron bed frame. The bedside lamp had a base decorated with a swirled blue and white design, and the colors were repeated in the patchwork quilt that covered the bed.

"Be careful of that wall though," Laura said as she pointed to the one slanted to follow the pitch of the roof. "I can't tell you how many times that I've walked into the one in mine."

"I'll do that," Toni said quietly, looking over at the sloped ceiling. "Speaking of rooms, where's yours?"

"Right next door," Laura said, opening a door in the room which led to a small bathroom.

"You're staying in the loo?"

"No, silly," Laura said as she pointed to another doorway across the small toilet. "That door leads to mine. I hope you don't mind, but we'll be sharing a bathroom."

"No...um...that's okay," Toni said, running her fingers through her hair.

"Hey, what's wrong?"

"Nothing."

"If you don't like the room, we can switch."

"No, the room's fine. I'm just a bit on edge. You know me."

"Yes, I do," Laura said softly. "How about we unpack and then have some tea? It might help calm your nerves."

"If it's all the same to you, I think I'd just like to stay up here for tonight. Get my bearings."

One of the many things Laura had learned over the past several months was when it came to dealing with Toni and her phobias, slow was the only option. Even after going to the market a half dozen times, all it took was a few too many people or a new employee, and Toni would retract faster than a switchblade.

"If that's what you want."

"Yeah, I...I just need a bit of time. That's all."

"Okay, well then I'll leave you to unpack and if you need anything, just knock on my door. Okay?" Laura said, opening the door to her bedroom and switching on the light.

"I'll be fine, Laura. See you in the morning."

***

"Where's Toni?" Eleanor said as Laura came into the kitchen.

"She's a bit out of sorts, and decided to call it a night."

"Oh my, she's not ill, is she?"

"No, she just gets a bit...a bit—"

"On edge?"

"You noticed?"

"It's fairly hard not to, actually," Eleanor said, motioning for Laura to sit. "I don't know what those bastards did to her, but I hope they were punished."

"Yeah, me too," Laura said, her voice drifting off as her thoughts returned to Toni. Startled when her mother placed a cup of tea in front of her, Laura looked up. "She's really not like that around me. Nervous, I mean."

"Well, by what you said in your letters, it's taken a great deal of time for you to earn her trust. I didn't expect her to walk in here and feel comfortable. She doesn't know me. She doesn't know this place, and she's yet to realize that, like you, I have no intention of hurting her."

"I can't ever imagine hurting her, Mum," Laura said quietly as she ran her finger along the rim of the cup. "I'd sooner die."

Holding back a grin, Eleanor said, "It sounds like you and she have something very...very special."

Eleanor thought that they would spend the night chattering away like they always did when Laura visited, but that wasn't going to be the case. Laura was so engrossed in her thoughts about the woman one flight up, she didn't even know her mother was there...and Eleanor didn't mind.

Like most mothers, Eleanor had only ever wanted the best for her daughter, but jealous of friends with grandchildren and son-in-laws, she had suggested to the point of annoyance that Laura needed to find a husband and settle down. What Eleanor forgot was that God works in mysterious ways, and gazing at her daughter, Eleanor knew that a husband would never be in Laura's future. A woman named Toni had changed that.

"So what are your plans while you're here?"

Shaken from her thoughts, Laura looked up. "I hadn't really thought about it."

"No? Since when haven't you planned every last detail of your holiday?"

GIVE ME A REASON

"It was kind of off-the-cuff. Toni had a really hard time a few weeks back, and I thought a change would do her good. I didn't think about what we'd do when we got here, other than maybe taking a few walks. Let her get some fresh air and see that the world isn't all gray and ugly."

"Well, there's a local artisan fair on High Street in Falkirk this weekend, or we could go to Stirling and do some shopping if you'd like."

"I'm not sure Toni will be up for doing that."

"Maybe you should ask her," Toni said from the doorway.

The last sliver of doubt that remained in Eleanor's mind slipped away, watching as the mere sound of Toni's voice changed her daughter's entire persona. Laura's frown changed to a smile, wide and bright, as her eyes twinkled back at the woman standing a few feet away.

"Hey, you," Laura chirped. "I thought you were going to get some sleep."

"I thought it was a bit rude to sequester myself up there. Besides, I could do with a cup of tea," Toni said, walking over to the table.

"I'll get it," Eleanor said, quickly going to fetch another cup. As she returned to the table, she said, "We were just discussing what your plans were. I suggested that we go shopping tomorrow, but Laura wasn't sure you'd be up for it."

Thinking for a moment, Toni looked at Laura and then back at Eleanor. "Well, there's only one way to find out."

***

Feeling as if someone were shining a light in her face, Laura slowly opened her eyes and saw slivers of brightness coming from around the bathroom door. Glancing at the clock on the nightstand, the blue digital display announced it was 2:47 in the morning. Climbing out of bed, she crept to the door, and hearing no sounds from within, she lightly knocked on the frame. Receiving no response, Laura opened the door, instantly recoiling at the brightness coming from the light bar over the mirror. Blinking to clear the spots in front of her eyes, she was about to turn off the switch when she noticed the door leading to Toni's room was ajar. Going over to it, she whispered through the crack, "Toni?"

"Go back to sleep, Laura," Toni said in a ragged whisper.

"Are you okay?"

When she heard no answer, Laura paused for only a moment before pushing the door open. Seeing Toni huddled on the floor in the far corner, Laura rushed over and knelt by her side. "Toni, what's wrong?"

Unable to hear her whispered response, she cupped Toni's chin in her hand, lifting her head so she could see her face. "Sweetheart, what's the matter?"

"I-I forgot to bring a book."

"You forgot to..." Laura stopped and her shoulders fell. Over the years, Laura had fallen asleep reading a book more times than she could remember, but Toni didn't need the words to lull her to sleep. She needed the comfort of knowing a book was nearby.

In Thornbridge, Toni's only connection to civilization, to a world that contained fairness, love and honesty, had been a torn and tattered paperback smelling of urine. It acted as a security blanket, proof that something existed outside the stone walls, and the words on its pages contained the power to calm her fears and still her nightmares. Old habits die hard, and this one would be with her until the day she died. Without a book within reach, falling asleep was impossible.

"Why didn't you wake me?"

"I didn't want to bother you."

"When are you going to realize that you don't bother me, Toni? What were you going to do? Sit on the floor the entire night?"

"I've done it before."

"Not anymore you don't," Laura said, getting to her feet. Holding out her hand, she said, "Come on. I've got some books in my room."

Hesitating for a moment, Toni took Laura's hand and allowed herself to be led to the other bedroom.

As soon as they walked inside, Laura pointed to the bookshelf. "Take as many as you'd like. I'm going to use the bathroom."

Distracted by the volumes filling the shelf, Toni didn't even notice that Laura had walked away. Taking a few books from the row, she sat on the edge of the bed and glanced from one to the other, deciding which to place on her nightstand.

Returning a few minutes later, Laura grinned at the sight of Toni sitting on the bed sound asleep. Taking the book from her hand, when

Toni opened her eyes, Laura said softly, "Let's get you to bed. Shall we?"

Guiding her back to her room, Laura turned down the bed, and without argument, Toni climbed under the sheet. Placing the book on the bedside table, Laura said, "It's here if you need it."

"I'm sorry I woke you."

"As long as you're okay, that's all that matters," Laura said, going over to turn off the lamp in the corner. With the help from the light streaming from the bathroom, she made her way back to the bed and sat down.

"What are you doing?" Toni asked.

"I thought I'd stay with you awhile, just until you fall asleep."

Narrowing her eyes, Toni stared back at Laura. "Are you going to read me a bedtime story, too?"

Amused at how rapidly Toni could change from needy to annoyed, Laura said, "Only after I'm done making you some warm milk."

Toni's agitation dissolved in an instant, and relaxing into the pillow she gazed back at Laura. "I'll never understand why you do things for me. I've given you so many reasons to tell me to sod off. Are you this nice to all the nutters?"

"Only the tall, dark and...um...*brooding* ones."

Noticing that Toni's eyelids had begun to grow heavy, Laura reached over and drew her finger along the woman's brow, pushing a few strands of hair from her forehead. "Get some sleep, Toni," she whispered. "I'm here."

Laura listened as Toni's breathing slowed, and although she was sure that she'd sleep until morning, Laura was not yet ready to leave. It was rare that Toni left herself so exposed, so vulnerable to another, but between them, a bond had formed. Even though Laura knew that Toni believed it was based only on friendship and trust, Laura now knew better.

Earlier in the week, she had met Phillip for dinner, but it was all Laura could do to keep her mind on her date. He was tall, dark and handsome, but so was the woman who shared her home. It was at that moment, while sitting in a crowded Indian eatery, when Laura realized her feelings for Toni were no longer platonic. And now, sitting in the dark, with Toni sound asleep, platonic was the last thing on Laura's mind.

Continuing to stroke Toni's forehead, Laura breathed deep, marveling in the texture of her skin. It was soft and warm, and she longed to run her finger down her cheek, to touch her nose, her chin...her lips. Were they as soft as Laura imagined? Would Toni taste of cigarettes and coffee or would it be something new? Something sweet and marvelous? Something dreams were made of?

Breathing deeply again, Laura blushed in the blackness of the room, feeling between her legs a pulse of awareness and want. Licking her lips, she stood quietly, knowing she needed to distance herself from the intimacy of the moment. So, after placing a chaste kiss lightly on Toni's cheek Laura crept from the room and returned to her own bed, praying her dreams could take her where reality could not.

CHAPTER TWENTY-ONE

Silently, Toni moved through the house, knowing that Laura and Eleanor were still asleep. The remnants of prison life clung to her like cobwebs, and sleeping was impossible after the sun peeked over the horizon. Grabbing her jacket and smokes, she walked out the back door, and before it closed behind her, the chill of the morning air erased the last bit of sleep from her soul.

The patio was covered in slate of gray, blue and green, and clay pots of every shape and size surrounded its perimeter. Some contained the remains of summer plants killed by the first frost, while others showed off the glorious colors of autumn. Glistening with early-morning dew, chrysanthemums in yellow, orange and white erupted from planters, and vibrant purple sedum cascaded over the sides of pottery, slowly drooping its way toward the ground.

Sitting on a small bench, Toni lit a cigarette and slowly exhaled. Her eyes followed a path of stepping stones leading through the garden just off the patio, winding their way to a Japanese maple with leaves so brilliantly red, they looked as if they were on fire. In the distance were tall sycamores and rowan standing proud with their branches stretching toward the sun. Their foliage, once green and full of life, had changed to yellow, red and orange, and as the breeze made its way through the branches, Toni watched as a few dried leaves drifted gracefully to the ground.

"Laura said you were an early riser," Eleanor said, coming out the door with two cups of coffee in her hand.

If it hadn't been for the fact that she had spent several hours the night before in Eleanor's company, Toni would have been scared. Although surprised that anyone else was up so early, Toni wasn't nervous. "Sorry. Did I wake you?"

"Of course not, dear. Unlike my daughter, I rather enjoy early mornings," Eleanor said, handing Toni a steaming cup. "Last night she mentioned you take it black."

With a nod, Toni took the cup. "What else has she told you about me?"

Sitting next to her on the bench, Eleanor said, "Only that you'd been in prison and were treated horribly, and you have a few foibles when it comes to new things."

"Oh."

"She also said that you were tremendously nice, and she liked having you as a housemate."

"Really? She said that?"

"You sound surprised."

"I...I have a bit of temper at times."

Laughing out loud, Eleanor leaned over and ran her shoulder playfully into Toni's. "And I suppose you've never seen Laura's temper?"

Smiling, Toni took a sip of coffee. "Your daughter is amazing. I hope you know that."

"I do. After all, she is *my* daughter."

"She looks like you."

"I'll take that as a compliment."

"It was meant as one."

"Well, then I'll say thank you."

"You're welcome."

"Can I ask you a question?"

Snorting, Toni shook her head. "Go ahead. Laura does it all the time."

"Are you going to be okay today if we go to Stirling?"

"I don't know."

"I appreciate your honesty."

"It's just hard for me. I try to convince myself that I can do something, and sometimes I can, but other times...other times I get so bloody afraid I can't breathe."

"That sounds awful."

"It is," Toni said quietly. "But I keep trying."

"That's all you can do."

"I just don't want to disappoint Laura."

"Oh, Toni, I doubt there's anything you could do to disappoint my daughter. She cares for you very much."

"I care for her, too. I never thought I'd have another friend in my life, and now I can't imagine having a life without her in it," Toni said, lighting another cigarette. "I know there'll come a time when we part. When she meets the man she wants to marry, but that'll be okay because it'll make her happy."

"You don't think she's happy now?"

"That's not what I mean. Sure, she's happy, but Laura's a marvelous woman, and she has so much to offer the right person. She can't waste her entire life taking care of me. I won't let her."

"Perhaps she doesn't think it's a waste," Eleanor said as she got up. Taking the empty cup from Toni's hand, she said, "I'll get you a refill."

Entering the house, as soon as Eleanor shut the door she snickered. "Oh my, and here I thought Laura was the only one in denial."

"Who you talking to?" Laura asked as she appeared in the doorway.

"Oh...um...no one. I was just muttering."

"Have you seen Toni?"

"She's on the patio," Eleanor said, handing Laura two cups of coffee. "Why don't you go join her?"

Smiling, Laura headed to the door. "I'm on my way."

***

With all of Toni's eccentricities, Eleanor had no idea what the day would bring when they left the house that morning, but by early afternoon, Toni's quirks were simply that.

They spent the day in Stirling, wandering the streets and shops, and flanked by Eleanor on her right and Laura on her left, for the most part, Toni enjoyed herself. Her anxieties flowed like the tide, coming and going at will, and after a few hours, even Eleanor could recognize the signals. Toni would set her jaw, pushing her hands deep into her pockets as she stared at the ground, concentrating on taking slow, steady breaths until Laura or Eleanor could come to her rescue. More than a dozen times, they locked their arms in hers, pulling her away from a crowd that got too close, and chattering at her until she forgot her fears, they'd venture into another store, casually strolling down the aisles filled with antiques, clothing and knick-knacks.

When she wasn't stressed by her surroundings, the sight of mother and daughter playfully arguing over clothing or perfumes brought a smile to Toni's face. Eleanor seemed to prefer the provocative while her child leaned toward the sedate. Although she didn't voice her opinion aloud, Toni agreed with Eleanor.

For her dates with Duane or Phillip, Laura had left the house dressed in feminine frocks designed to attract and flatter, but her day-in and day-out business suits did neither. Months before, Toni wouldn't have cared less, but now she found herself biting her lip every time Laura went to work wearing the same drab black, gray and brown suits. Watching as Laura searched a rack of white blouses, Toni finally spoke up. "You have enough white."

Halting her quest for the perfect blouse, Laura looked over her shoulder at Toni. "I do, do I? Well, what do you suggest?"

"Red, blue, green, purple...anything but bloody white."

"You don't like white?"

"I don't see the need to wear it every day. Everyone already knows you're the boss, so dressing like you do is rather pointless."

"Pointless?"

"Boring."

"Boring!"

Standing off to the side, Eleanor grinned at the exchange. The sparkle in Laura's eyes told Eleanor that she was thoroughly enjoying Toni's observations, and though the small boutique was rather crowded, Toni now seemed oblivious to the strangers milling about.

Slowly allowing her eyes to look over Toni's attire, Laura said, "And I suppose black trousers, a blue sweater and a rather old cloth jacket is your idea of trendy?"

"I wasn't talking about me."

As much as she tried, Laura couldn't hide her smile. Toni's comment about her choice in clothing could have been construed as an insult, but Laura knew that wasn't the intention. And the fact that Toni was actually noticing her wardrobe, as boring as it might be, made Laura's heart do a flip. Looking around the store, Laura said, "Well, Miss Vaughn, I'll make you a deal. You find something that you think I'd look good in and I'll do the same for you."

"I don't need any clothes."

"You most certainly do and you know it," Laura said with a laugh. "Besides, I'm not suggesting we buy each other new wardrobes. Just a blouse or a cardigan."

"Oh."

"So, is it a deal?"

As she thought about the offer, Toni looked around and when her eyes met Eleanor's, her decision was made for her. As if on cue, Eleanor moseyed over and hooked her arm through Toni's.

"Come on, dear," she said. "Let's go find my daughter something snazzy."

***

Sliding into the booth to sit next to Toni, Laura blurted, "So, what did you get me?"

"I thought we agreed we'd wait until later?" Toni said, her eyes seeking out Eleanor across the table. Seeing the amusement sweeping over Eleanor's face, Toni pressed her lips together to hide her own.

"You're no fun," Laura said, slouching in her seat.

Toni was about to respond when the waiter appeared, and falling into old habits, she bowed her head and immediately placed her hands on the table.

Without missing a beat, Laura placed her hand over Toni's and asked in a whisper, "What would you like to drink?"

With the drink order soon out of the way, the waiter disappeared and Toni looked up and began scanning the menu as if nothing had happened, and as far as Laura and Eleanor were concerned, nothing had. Lunch came and went, and after finishing their pints, they gathered their coats and left the restaurant.

"You seriously need a new jacket," Laura said, watching as Toni tried to zip the faded blue cloth coat.

"No, I don't," Toni said as she continued to struggle with her zipper.

"You need something warmer. More stylish."

"This one is plenty warm enough," Toni said. Giving the stuck fastener a strong tug, it broke free in an instant, quickly followed by the sound of something ripping. "Shit!"

Biting her lip in order not to laugh, Laura looked down at the torn fabric. "I bet it's not warm now."

"You did that on purpose."

"I didn't rip it. You did!"

"You jinxed me!"

"I did not!" Laura said, trying her best to stop giggling. Turning to Eleanor, she said, "Mum, isn't Barley's just around the corner?"

"Yes, I believe it is, and I must say that's a marvelous idea."

"What's Barley's?" Toni asked, eyeballing the two women smiling back at her.

"You'll see," Laura said, hooking her arm through Toni's. "You'll see."

***

"Is Toni still asleep?" Eleanor asked as Laura walked into the kitchen.

"Yeah, I checked on her before I came down. She was exhausted, so I expect she'll sleep a bit longer."

"Quite a stressful day for her, wasn't it?"

"At times," Laura said as she poured herself a cup of coffee. "Thanks for being patient with her."

"My pleasure."

"Mum, can I ask you a question?"

"Of course."

"Do you like Toni?"

"Yes, I do. She's quite charming. Why?"

"Just wondering," Laura said softly as she sat down.

Noticing that Laura appeared to be daydreaming, Eleanor stood and touched her on the shoulder. "Why don't you and I go for a walk?"

"It's almost dark," Laura said, looking out the back door. "And if Toni wakes up—"

"Toni will be just fine," Eleanor said, handing Laura her jacket. "Come on. Just a short walk down the path. We'll be back before she wakes up, I promise."

With a sigh, Laura quickly finished her coffee and then followed her mother out the door. Arm in arm, they walked silently down the winding path, past the Japanese maple and the sycamores, until they came upon a small iron bench. Brushing away a few dead leaves, Eleanor motioned for Laura to sit, and as they leaned back, Eleanor reached into her pocket and pulled out a pack of cigarettes.

"I thought you quit," Laura said, narrowing her eyes.

"I have one occasionally," Eleanor said, lighting a cigarette. Placing the pack on the bench, she looked out over the rolling meadows, the tall grass gently swaying in the breeze as the fading sunlight turned the green blades to gold. "I think this is my favorite time of the day. The sun paints the sky those marvelous colors, and it's so peaceful. I always come down here when I want to think. It helps put things in perspective."

"Yes, it's beautiful," Laura said, looking up at the orange and crimson clouds. "Toni would love this."

Eleanor looked at her daughter and secretly smiled. Laura was positively glowing, and it was all because she had mentioned another woman's name. Taking a deep drag of her cigarette, Eleanor decided the time was right. "Do you know what I'm most proud of?" she asked quietly.

Turning her attention to her mother, Laura shrugged. "I don't know. What?"

"Our relationship."

"What do you mean?"

"Well, to start, we've always been honest with one another. Don't you agree?"

Thinking back over the years, Laura grinned. "My friends always thought I was crazy."

"Why's that?"

"They'd spend all their time trying to hide things from their parents, and I was coming home and telling you everything. It boggled their minds."

Chuckling, Eleanor patted Laura on the leg. "I have a confession. My friends thought the same thing."

"Really?"

"They couldn't get over the fact that you and I had no secrets. I remember one afternoon when I was talking to Nancy on the phone. It was just after you slept with that boy. Oh, what was his name?"

"You mean my first...Kyle?"

"Yes, that's right. Kyle," Eleanor said, with a nod. "I told Nancy that you had lost your virginity, and she dropped the bloody phone. She was so shocked that you'd confess such a thing to your mother, and she was even more flabbergasted when I told her I was okay with it. After all, you were nineteen, and I knew it was only a matter of time. Oh, you should have heard her going on and on about your three cousins and how they'd *never* do such a thing at that age."

"Little did she know," Laura said under her breath.

Stubbing out her cigarette, Eleanor said, "Yes, I always wondered what would have happened if she'd found out that her girls had lost their cherries at sixteen."

"Coronary comes to mind," Laura said with a laugh. "Oh, speaking of Nancy, I guess I should try to schedule a day trip. Stop over and say hello."

"Well, if you do, you go alone."

"I thought you liked her."

"I do!" Eleanor said, her voice raising an octave. "But Dorothy just had her second, and if I know Nancy, she'll be prancing around spouting accolades about her glorious grandchildren, and there's only so much of that I can take before wanting to gag."

"I'm sorry I haven't given you any grandchildren yet. I know you want them," Laura said, looking back toward the meadow.

"Yes, I do, but *I* must apologize for always giving you such a hard time about it. Nancy just has a way of rubbing it in my face at times," Eleanor said, shifting in her seat. "But you have lots of time to have children, and luckily in this day and age, there are lots of ways for that to happen. Aren't there?"

Watching the sunset and in awe of the colors stretching across the sky, Laura was barely listening to what was being said, so a few seconds passed before Eleanor's words sunk in. Slowly turning to face her mother, Laura whispered, "What...what did you say?"

Taking her daughter's hand, Eleanor gave it a squeeze. "Does she know that you're in love with her?"

Laura's jaw dropped open, and a dozen lame denials ran through her mind. Their love had always been unconditional, but she couldn't help but think that this truth could destroy her relationship with the only parent she knew.

Seeing her daughter's jaw begin to quiver, Eleanor shook her head. "There's no need to get upset, Laura. I'm fairly certain that lesbianism doesn't fall under the heading of a dreaded disease. All it means is that I'll never have to worry about the toilet seat being left up when you two come to visit."

Laura's eyes flew open, and whatever fears she had were quickly eradicated by her confusion. Staring at her mother like the woman had just grown another head Laura picked up the cigarettes and quickly lit one.

"I thought *you* quit ages ago?"

"Yeah, well that was before *I* dropped a bombshell, and *you* didn't even blink," Laura said, taking a deep drag of her smoke.

"Technically, I was the one who dropped the bombshell," Eleanor said, snagging the cigarette from Laura's hand and stomping it out.

"Who *are* you?" Laura said, backing away slightly as she looked at the woman. "I mean, you're taking this awfully well."

"How else should I take it?" Eleanor asked. "It's not like you haven't given me months to come to terms with it."

"Months?"

"Oh, sweetheart, go back and read the emails you've sent to me since Toni came into your life. It was almost as if you were asking for my approval without saying the words. You'd go on and on about how much you liked having her around and how much joy you felt when she'd take another step. You were positively bursting with pride...and with love. You were with that Duane character for over two years, and you never once spoke about him like that."

"I just wanted you to see her how I see her. I wanted you to like her."

"I do, Laura," Eleanor said softly. "She's intelligent, articulate and attractive, but I get a feeling that she's also clueless as to how you feel about her, or am I wrong?"

"No, she has no idea."

"Can I ask why you haven't told her?"

"I don't know that I can."

"Laura, if you care for this woman as much as I think you do, you need to tell her."

"How can I do that, Mum? She's so afraid of being hurt and...and of being touched."

Raising an eyebrow, Eleanor said, "Well, you'd definitely have to get past *that*, now wouldn't you?"

Laura didn't need a mirror to know her cheeks were now fire engine red. Burying her head in her hands, she mumbled, "I can't believe you just said that."

"Like I said, I've had lots of time to think about it," Eleanor said, grinning at Laura's reaction.

"You're really okay with this, aren't you?" Laura said, looking up.

Eleanor leaned back on the bench and let out a sigh. "To tell you the truth, at first I was very upset. I mean, it's rather shocking when you realize that the one person in the world you thought you knew better than anyone, you didn't know at all."

"Mum, I'm still me," Laura said, leaning closer. "I haven't changed. I just fell in love."

"I know, sweetheart, but you fell in love with a woman, and I wasn't prepared for that. I walked around in a daze for a while, and then on one of the many nights when I couldn't sleep, I came down here to have a talk with God. Oh, you should have heard me, challenging him to tell me what I did wrong. To give me a sign, so I'd understand what mistake I made in raising you, and then a wave of shame swept over me that took my breath away."

"What do you mean?"

"I've always thought of myself as someone without prejudice, but there I was practically yelling at God to give me a reason, as if your love for Toni was somehow wrong...and it's not. I'll be the first to admit that my dreams for you didn't include a woman as a partner, but if this is what you want and Toni is *who* you want, then that's good enough for me. All that matters to me is that you're happy. You're my daughter and I love you more than life itself, and if I never get grandchildren, so be it."

"I don't know if Toni even likes children."

"Perhaps you should ask her."

"Oh, Mum, what am I going to do?" Laura moaned, again burying her face in her hands. "If I tell her about how I feel, it may be too much for her to handle. If I don't, I'm lying by omission, and I promised her that I'd never lie to her."

"From what you've told me, you know Toni fairly well, so you'll know when the time's right, and until then, I guess you'll just have to continue to be her friend and let God take care of the rest."

"Do you really think God approves of this? I mean, a lot of people think it's wrong."

"Do you think it's wrong?"

"No, I don't," Laura said, straightening her backbone.

"Neither do I and I'd like to think, since God created all of us...neither does He."

CHAPTER TWENTY-TWO

"Where are you taking me?" Toni called out as she came to a stop and looked up the hill.

Laura stopped and turned around. "It's just a little farther."

"You said that hours ago," Toni said, unbuttoning her coat to pull her smokes from the inner pocket.

"It was twenty minutes ago, so stop exaggerating, put those cigarettes away and get your arse up here," Laura shouted as she turned and trotted to the crest.

Glancing at the pack in her hand and then at the steep slope in front of her, Toni dropped the cigarettes back in her pocket, took a deep breath and began her ascent.

After having spent the last two days shopping and sightseeing, earlier that morning when Eleanor headed back to the city to meet a client, Laura and Toni decided to stay behind. After finishing their breakfast, they grabbed their coats and headed out the back door. Neither feeling the need to rush, they casually walked through the garden and past the stand of trees, occasionally pausing to admire the view. The autumn air was crisp, and breath could be seen, and even though the forecast called for rain for the rest of the week, today the sun was shining brightly. Aware of the seasons of Scotland, Laura had on her brown suede bomber jacket, worn to a softness that money could not buy, and Toni walked the fields wearing the leather coat she had purchased two days earlier at a store named Barley's.

Housed in an old brick building off of a side street in Stirling, Barley's had been in business for over a hundred years, selling to the locals the warmest wools and leathers needed to survive when the winter winds began to blow. When they had entered the well-known tourist attraction, Laura wasn't surprised at the overcrowded conditions, and immediately grabbing Toni's hand, she guided her to the back of the store where racks stood filled with leather coats of every length and design. Although unnerved by the throng of people roaming about, flanked by Laura and Eleanor, Toni's anxieties eventually calmed, and within an hour, they had walked out of Barley's with her wearing a thigh-length black leather coat.

"It's about time," Laura said, placing her hands on her hips as Toni finished her climb.

Unbuttoning her coat to allow the breeze to cool her body, Toni was about to reply when she noticed her surroundings and her eyes opened wide. Before her, overflowing with greenery, heather and tall wisps of tan grass were the rolling hills and meadows of Carron Bridge. A short stone wall, as old as the castles that filled the country, separated one field from the next, and a narrow river flowed over rock beds as it lazily wound its way through the countryside. As Toni gazed out over the scenery, she smiled to herself. All that was missing was the sound of bagpipes.

"This is amazing," Toni said.

"I thought you'd like it," Laura said, looking up at her. "When Mum bought the house, I came up to help her move, and one day we went for a walk and found this place. We ended up spending half the day here just enjoying the view."

"It's marvelous."

Hearing Laura move away, Toni turned and said, "I'd like to stay here for a bit, if that's all right with you?"

"I was just going to pull up a rock and sit down. Care to join me?" Laura said, pointing to a large boulder protruding from the ground.

Pleased that they didn't have to leave, Toni went over and sat down next to Laura, smiling as she felt the warmth radiating from the smooth stone beneath her. In unison, their eyes returned to the picturesque landscape, and they watched as the grass swayed in the gentle breeze.

Listening to the sound of the water as it rippled over the stones in the riverbed, Toni filled her lungs to their fullest with the fresh air. Glancing at Laura for a second, she whispered, "Thank you."

"For what?"

Pausing for a moment, Toni picked up a blade of grass, rolling it in her fingers as she thought about the words she wanted to say. "Where do I start?" she said quietly. "For bandaging my arm and not taking no for an answer. For being patient when most would have probably walked away, for giving me a place to stay where I feel safe...and for bringing me here. I'd forgotten that places like this exist outside the pages of a book."

"You're quite welcome," Laura said, the sun paling in comparison to the glow on her face.

Looking in Laura's direction, Toni said, "You look a lot like your mum. You've got her eyes."

"Yeah, but I don't have her height. Damn it!"

Grinning, Toni asked, "Can I ask where your father is?"

"He preferred fishing over family. They got divorced before I was two."

"Oh. Sorry."

"No need to be. Mum and I did just fine."

"So you never see him?"

"Sometimes I do. When I go to visit his sister, Nancy, a lot of times he's over there for dinner, so we chat."

"Must be awkward."

"No, not really, just different," Laura said with a shrug. "I mean, I know he's my father, but it feels more like he's an uncle or just a friend of the family. When I was a kid, I thought I had done something wrong because he didn't want anything to do with me, but my mum explained that there are just some people not cut out to be parents, and he was one of them. I didn't really buy it, but I wasn't about to argue, and then a few years ago I ran into him at my cousin's house. It was the first time we'd actually really sat down and talked. He asked about my job and how I was doing. It was nice, but then the kids woke up from their naps, and he became this bumbling, nervous man. He was *so* out of his element, and that's when I realized that my mum was spot on. He just doesn't like kids."

"Do you? Like kids, I mean."

"Yes, I do. How about you?"

"They're okay, I guess," Toni said, turning her attention back to the meadow.

"What's wrong?"

"I suppose now you want to know all about my family"

"Only if you want to tell me."

Shaking her head, Toni laughed. "When has *that* ever stopped you?"

When Laura didn't answer, Toni turned and found green eyes smiling back at her, and as much as she tried, Toni couldn't help but return the look. "I'll never in my life understand how you can get me to talk about things that I really don't want to talk about," she said. "It truly is aggravating."

"I prefer to think of it as a gift," Laura said, her cheeks turning rosy as she tried to suppress a laugh.

Fumbling in her pocket for her cigarettes, Toni said, "There really isn't that much to talk about, actually. My parents were rather well-off, so I grew up with the proverbial silver spoon in my mouth. We lived in Surrey in a pretentious Tudor home surrounded by acres of gardens, tennis courts and stables, and my education was very formal and *very* expensive. It was the ideal life, until I came home from university to tell them I was gay."

"I take it that didn't go so well?"

"My father was shocked. My mother was mortified and my sister…my sister was appalled. It wasn't long after that when my dad pulled me aside to inform me that I was to keep my depravity to myself and never bring the subject up again. My mother turned to drink, trying to drown her shame in vodka and my sister decided she'd shag anything in trousers just to prove she wasn't like me. Three people whom I thought I knew, and I loved with all my heart, turned into strangers.

"I went back to college, naively thinking they'd change or adapt or at least try to understand, but that didn't happen. I'm not even sure if it was intentional or just a knee-jerk reaction, but the next time I went home, it felt like I wasn't welcome there any longer. The staff smiled and said good morning, showing me more common courtesy than my own family, all of whom seemed to have disappeared behind their bedroom doors. I sat alone in a dining room large enough for twenty, eating my breakfast and trying not to cry. They were my family and I loved them, but what they wanted from me, I couldn't give them. I couldn't take back the truth. So, the next morning I left without even saying goodbye, and they never called to ask why. I went through the rest of my years at school like an orphan. They never called or sent a letter...not even a birthday card, but as they say, life goes on, and I had a good one until it all went to shit...and they still didn't call. During my remand, the trial, the prisons...they never once tried to contact me. Toward the end of my second year in Thornbridge, my father died from an aneurysm, and if it hadn't been for Krista seeing it in the newspaper, I'd never have known."

"I'm so sorry," Laura said placing her hand on Toni's knee. "I don't know what else to say."

"Well, that's a first." Stubbing out her cigarette, Toni stood and offered her hand to Laura. "How about we continue our walk and talk about something else? This is a great day, and I don't want to ruin it. Okay?"

Taking Toni's hand, Laura got up and gestured toward the meadow. "Lead the way."

"I don't know where I'm going."

Squeezing Toni's hand, Laura said, "That's okay. Together we'll find our way."

***

Eleanor arrived home late in the afternoon and immediately informed Laura and Toni she was taking them out to dinner. After suggesting they wear the new clothes they had bought for each other in Stirling, as the two women disappeared up the stairs, Eleanor sauntered to her room. Repairing her makeup in front of the bathroom mirror, she began to snicker.

While Toni seemed to prefer casual clothes for herself, when her assignment had been to buy something for Laura, casual seemed to be the *last* thing on her mind. Surprising Eleanor, she had skipped over simple cardigans and strode past shelves filled with cashmeres until she ended up amongst racks filled with silk blouses. Pushing aside the whites and the beiges, Toni stopped at the reds, and carefully inspecting each, she finally held up one to get Eleanor's opinion. Delighted by the blouse Toni had chosen, Eleanor promptly led her to the register. There was no reason to look any longer.

After touching up her makeup, Eleanor returned to the kitchen to make some tea while she was waiting for Toni and Laura, but before the water had a chance to boil, she heard someone come down the stairs. Turning as Toni walked in, Eleanor said, "Oh my, don't you look lovely."

The compliment bringing more than a hint of red to her face, Toni ran her hands down the sleeves of the top Laura bought for her. Made of soft jersey, the gathered knit hugged her torso like a glove, flattering every curve along the way, and the diagonally crossed neckline plunged lower than anything Toni had worn in years. Smoky blue in color, it complemented Toni's straight-legged black trousers and knee-high polished boots perfectly.

"Thanks, but can I ask you a favor?"

"Of course, dear."

"There's a tag in the back that's bothering me, but I don't have any scissors."

"No worries," Eleanor said, pulling a pair from a drawer. "Turn around and let me take care of that."

Toni turned, and Eleanor busied herself cutting off the manufacturer's label, hesitating for a split-second when a few of Toni's scars came into view. Her eyes clouded over with tears, but blinking them away, Eleanor finished the task at hand and patted Toni on the shoulder. "There you go, dear. All gone."

"Thanks," Toni said, rubbing her neck.

"Can I make an observation?" Eleanor asked as she returned the scissors to the drawer.

"Sure."

"You're quite a lovely woman, and I was wondering why you never seem to wear any makeup. I mean, you don't need to. Lots of women don't, but with those cheekbones of yours and that black hair, a bit of highlighting would be simply marvelous."

"I...I used to wear some," Toni said, a quick frown crossing her face. "To tell you the truth, I almost bought some the other day, but things got a bit hectic, and I didn't want to bother you or Laura with it."

"It wouldn't have been a bother."

Hanging her head, Toni said softly, "I feel stupid having to ask for help all the time."

"From what I've observed these past few days, Toni, you are anything but stupid. It takes a special person—a *strong* person—to know their limitations, and from what Laura's told me, you've made great strides in the past several months. Rome wasn't built in a day, young lady, and you need to remember that!"

Warmed by her words, Toni looked up. "I'll try."

Thinking for a moment, Eleanor reached over and took Toni's hand. "Come with me. I've got an idea."

Following the woman through the house, a minute later Toni was standing in Eleanor's bedroom while the woman rummaged through a cabinet. Pulling out a small wicker basket, she handed it to Toni. "I've got a friend who sells cosmetics, and she's forever giving me free samples. Why don't you take a look in there, and I'll go make us some tea?"

Before Toni had a chance to answer, Eleanor kissed her on the cheek, and as she walked from the room, she said, "And take your time, dear. If there's one thing you're probably well aware of living with my daughter, it's that Laura always runs late."

***

Standing in front of the cheval glass in the corner of her room, Laura gazed at her reflection as she fastened the last button of her new top. The blouse wasn't what she had expected, and it was more than Laura could have hoped for. The red silk shimmered in the light, and strategically placed darts snugged the fabric just enough to make a difference, making a simple blouse anything but. Feminine, soft and definitely sexy, the front dipped low, held closed by three oversized brass buttons, and the long sleeves were loose and flowing. Thankful that she had brought along a skirt, she pulled up the zip, fastened the gold buckle of her belt and then smiled at the result. Zipping up her black boots, Laura glanced once more in the mirror before heading downstairs.

As if all three women in the house were on the same schedule, Toni walked into the lounge just as Laura was coming down the stairs and Eleanor was exiting the kitchen, and simultaneously, their forward momentum stopped. Seeing Toni's jaw drop open, Eleanor glanced at her daughter, and her chest swelled with pride. Laura looked absolutely stunning.

Her black skirt was simple and straight, but the slit up the side which allowed Laura a bit more freedom, also allowed a bit more skin to show. One quick glance in Toni's direction confirmed what Eleanor already knew. Between the crimson blouse and the occasional flash of thigh, her daughter had captured all of Toni's attention, and Toni had captured Eleanor's. She didn't mean to stare, but once she looked at Toni she couldn't look away, and while the pride she felt wasn't that of a mother...it was damn close.

In Eleanor's jumble of cosmetic and hair care samples, Toni had discovered all that was required to transform her natural beauty into something so much more. Her brown eyes were now defined with black eyeliner and her lashes, enhanced by mascara, appeared almost twice as long as before. She had accentuated her cheekbones with blush, and with the help of some gel, she had slicked back her hair until it was shining and sculpted.

Believing that Laura was more beautiful than any woman had the right to be, Toni could not take her eyes off her as she descended the stairs, but when something deep within Toni stirred, something she believed had died years before, reality came rushing back. Squeezing her eyes shut, she silently admonished herself for the pang of awareness between her legs.

A few moments passed before Toni opened her eyes and by that time Laura was standing directly in front of her. Trying her best to act nonchalant, Toni took a step backward and stuffed her hands in her pockets. After giving Laura a casual once-over, she said, "Nice blouse."

Reality is where things appear as they should, rather than how one might wish them to be, but Laura could not have prepared herself for the reality of *this* moment. Toni stood before her as she used to be, a confident professor with styled hair, stunning features and a body to die for...and Laura so wanted to die. Her knees felt weak and her stomach fluttered, and never in her life had she been so titillated by the mere appearance of another. The only problem was that while Toni had managed to keep her feelings hidden, Laura's were now more than apparent through the thin red fabric of her top.

Suddenly aware that her body was betraying her, Laura felt her cheeks begin to burn. Quickly turning to get her coat, she said, "Thanks. You don't look half-bad yourself."

CHAPTER TWENTY-THREE

"Bloody weather," Eleanor said, staring at the black clouds through the window.

"I'm sorry," Laura said, closing her suitcase. "But you've got to work, and this storm isn't supposed to let up until Saturday. I just think it's safer if we get on the road now, before it gets too bad."

"You should have flown."

"That wasn't possible. Not with Toni."

Staring at her daughter for a moment, Eleanor said, "You've changed."

"Have I?"

"I can't remember a holiday where you didn't have something scheduled to do every single minute, but you showed up here with no itinerary, and you drove. The old Laura would have considered that a waste of time."

"As long as I'm with Toni, it's hardly a waste, and if I have to drive to Scotland from now on, so be it."

"Speaking of driving to Scotland, should I assume that if you come up for Christmas, you'll be bringing Toni with you?"

"I hadn't really thought about it, but yeah, I guess. Why?"

"Well, I was thinking that she's probably not had very many happy Christmas holidays for quite a while, so I thought perhaps if you were coming up, I'd go all-out and make it one she'd remember."

"What do you mean? You always go all-out."

"I haven't had more than a few baubles displayed in years, but you've been too busy to notice," Eleanor said quietly.

"What?"

"It's true. Ever since you moved to London, you've been so wrapped up with your work that you rarely stayed for more than a day or two, and then we'd spend most of it visiting Nancy and her girls. What I'm proposing is that you and Toni spend a few weeks up here at Christmas. That way, I get to know her better, we get to decorate until we drop, and maybe by that time, I'll be able to call her your partner instead of just your friend."

"What makes you so sure she'll...that she feels the same way?"

"They're called eyes, Laura, and I have two very good ones. Now, I know the woman has issues, but I can't believe you still haven't told her how you feel."

"No. No, it's too soon for that," Laura said. "When it concerns Toni, I've learned that going slow is the only option."

"Slow is the only option for what?" Toni asked as she walked in and returned the borrowed books to the shelf.

"For driving in the rain, of course," Eleanor said quickly, picking up Laura's suitcase. "I'll just take this down and fill up your flask."

Watching as Eleanor left the room, Toni said, "I really like your mum."

"Well, she really likes you."

"What's not to like?" Toni said with a shrug.

Grabbing her coat from the bed, Laura strolled over, stopping in front of Toni for only a moment. Allowing her eyes to travel slowly up and down the woman, Laura said in a breath, "Absolutely nothing."

***

After spending over eight hours driving through a storm that seemed to follow their every move, by the time they reached home, Laura and Toni were rattled and tired. With no garage or overhang to protect them, they ran through the onslaught of Mother Nature, stumbling into the house as if they were connected at the hip.

"Stupid, sodding rain!" Laura said, dropping her bags on the floor. "I'm soaked!"

"That makes two of us," Toni said, vigorously scrubbing her fingers through her wet hair.

"Hey!" Laura shouted when she got hit by the spray. "That's enough of that."

"Oh, sorry," Toni said, trying not to laugh.

Seeing the puddles forming on the floor as they removed their coats, Laura said, "I think we should put these in the kitchen until they're done dripping."

"Um...yeah. Good idea," Toni said, watching as Laura disappeared through the doorway.

Draping her coat over a chair, Laura turned around to take Toni's, but stopped when she noticed that Toni seemed intent on looking anywhere but back at her. Confused, Laura glanced down and quickly discovered the reason. Deciding to make the long ride home as comfortable as possible, she hadn't put on a bra that morning, and the soaked pale pink long-sleeved jersey she was wearing made that crystal clear.

"Oh shit," Laura said, crossing her arms in front of her chest. "I'd best go find something else to put on."

"Yeah, you...you do that," Toni mumbled as Laura ran past her. "I think I'm going to take a shower and try to get warmed up. See you later."

Once safely in her room, Toni let out an exaggerated sigh and sat on the edge of the bed, allowing her thoughts to return to a wet jersey and the gorgeous woman wearing it. Twice in as many days, Toni had felt her body react to the sight of Laura's curves, and it was doing her head in. Why didn't she tell Laura about her soaked jersey the second the woman took off her coat instead of waiting until she reached the kitchen? Why did she buy a woman she called a friend a provocative blouse meant for a lover, and why couldn't she get the image of her wearing it out of her head?

Silently scolding herself as her body again betrayed her, Toni walked into the bathroom, turned on the valves and while the water ran from cold to hot, she stripped and dropped her clothes on the floor. Peering into the mirror for only a moment, she held her breath as she turned around and looked over her shoulder at her scarred skin. A few minutes later, Toni stood under the hot spray and allowed it to wash away her tears. She had nothing to offer Laura. She had nothing to offer anyone.

***

Unpacking the assorted nibbles her mother had given them, Laura looked up to see Toni standing in the doorway, her black hair wet and shiny from her shower. "Hey there."

"Hey yourself," Toni said. Looking at the packages Laura had strewn all over the counter, she asked, "What are you doing?"

"I thought we'd have this stuff for dinner, if that's all right."

"Yeah, it works for me. Anything I can do to help?"

"Well, if you'll open the wine, I'll go and see what I can do about warming up the house."

"I thought it was just me," Toni said, briskly rubbing her hands over her arms.

"No, this place is old and a bit drafty, which is why I keep the fireplace well stocked."

By the time Laura returned, the wine glasses were filled, the last package of cheese had been unwrapped and sliced, and Toni was placing crackers on the tray. Licking her fingers as she looked up, Toni said, "I'm assuming we're eating in the lounge?"

"Well, I don't want the fire to go to waste," Laura said, grabbing the wine and glasses. "You bring the food. I've got the tipple."

A short time later, snuggled into what was rapidly becoming *her* corner of the sofa, Toni popped the last piece of cheese into her mouth. "I wish I had known about this stuff when we were up there. I would have bought more."

"Well, you may have your chance."

Refilling their glasses, Toni handed one to Laura. "What do you mean?"

"Mum thought...well, she suggested that we spend our Christmas break in Scotland. I've been a bit lax about visiting, and I know she'd be thrilled if we accepted."

"Oh," Toni said quietly as she relaxed into the cushions.

Sensing Toni's hesitation, Laura leaned over and touched her on the leg. "What is it? What's wrong?"

"I haven't celebrated Christmas in quite a while. That's all."

"But you're not opposed to it, are you? I know that...I mean...at least I think I know...that is I'm fairly certain—"

"I thought I was the only one with a stuttering problem."

Playfully glaring at the woman, a hint of added color crept across Laura's face. "It's apparently something I just recently developed, and you didn't answer the question."

"Laura, I haven't celebrated anything in a very long time. There weren't any Christmases or birthdays where I was, and it's hard for me to imagine having them again."

"You won't have to imagine if you say yes."

Toni was torn between listening to her head or listening to her heart. In the shower, she had told herself that the feelings heating her blood were wrong, but with Laura's hand on her knee, those same urges returned in force, and when she looked into Laura's eyes, all her strength seemed to disappear. "Exactly what would Christmas entail at your mother's?"

"Well, she told me she'd like to go all-out. And if I know my mum, that means we'll spend our days putting up lights and garland, and our nights making biscuits for the family and her church group."

"Biscuits, eh?"

"Don't tell me you don't like Christmas biscuits."

"I've got a confession."

"Okay?"

"I've never actually baked a biscuit."

"You've got to be joking."

"Nope."

"Not even when you were a child?"

"Rich family, remember? The staff baked. The Vaughns did not," Toni said. Taking a sip of wine, she looked at Laura. "I'll go if you want me to."

"I want you to do what *you* want to do, Toni."

"And if I say that I want to stay here, but you can go. Will you?"

"That depends."

"On what?"

"On whether or not you can give me a reason."

Already annoyed that she couldn't keep her eyes from traveling to the plunging neckline of Laura's sweater, when Toni heard Laura's question, she erupted, "Here we go again," she shouted, jumping off the sofa. "You and your goddamned reasons!"

Sitting up straight, Laura placed her glass on the table. "Toni, it's just a question."

"Yes, it is, and it's one that you've asked a dozen times. Isn't it?"

"Yes, I have, but there's no need to get upset. Like I said, it's only a question."

"Well, let's turn the tables, shall we? Toni barked back. "Stop answering my question with a question and give *me* a reason!"

"For what?"

"Tell me why you want to spend all your time with me instead of the good doctor?"

"Because he's a bore."

"Oh, and I'm the life of the party?"

"No, but you're getting better," Laura said, displaying a devastating smile.

"Don't flash that bloody smile at me, Laura. It won't work."

"Sorry," Laura said, trying to hide her amusement.

"Tell me why you took me to Scotland."

"Because I wanted to show you that the world isn't as gray and dark as you think it is."

"And why did you want to do that? Why do you want to waste your time on someone as fucked up as I am?"

"You're *not* fucked up!"

"Oh, trust me, Laura...I am."

"Toni, we've gone over this before. You have every right to be afraid of strangers and the like. That doesn't make you fucked up. It makes you human!"

"That's not what I'm talking about."

"No? Then explain it to me."

Turning toward the hearth, Toni stared into the flames. "Laura, look...things are just starting to get a bit muddled for me. Okay?"

Going over to join Toni by the fireplace, Laura looked up at her. "In what way?"

"It's nothing. I...I just need to sort something out."

"Have I done something wrong?"

"You haven't done anything, Laura. It's me. Like I said, I'm fucked up."

Tugging on Toni's sleeve, Laura forced her to turn around, and cupping her chin, Laura looked her in the eye. "Please stop saying that. You're scaring me."

"That makes two of us."

"What are you scared of?"

"Do you want a list?"

"Stop being flippant and answer the question. Why are you so down on yourself tonight?"

"I'm just having a bad day. I'll be fine in the morning," Toni said as she walked away.

Grabbing Toni's hand, Laura spun her around. "What did you mean by things are getting muddled? What things?"

"Laura, I'm tired. Please, just drop it. Okay?"

"Tell me."

Shaking her head, Toni sighed. "I miss who I once was, and I just realized that I can never be that person again."

"Why not?"

"Because she's dead, and there's nothing I can do to make her come back from the grave. I just need to stop trying."

Moments before, Laura had been scared, but now she was terrified. Fearing that she was about to watch Toni plummet back down the rabbit hole of despair and darkness, Laura didn't think about consequences or consider the passage of time. She listened to her heart and acted on her feelings. Pulling Toni's face to hers, Laura kissed Toni squarely on the lips.

Stunned, for a split second Toni stood with her eyes open, staring back at the woman whose mouth was pressed against hers...and then instinct took over. Slowly closing her eyes, Toni savored the moment, allowing it to continue even though she could feel rage growing inside her.

Laura knew that there wouldn't be a difference between kissing a man and kissing a woman, so there was no hesitancy in the pressure she was applying to Toni's lips, but Laura had forgotten one thing...and it was important. She had never been in love with the men she had kissed, but she was totally and unequivocally in love with Toni Vaughn.

The flavors of their meal swirled between them as they separated for a second and then their lips met again. Laura could taste the Cabernet, oaken and spicy on Toni's lips, and the mellow nuttiness of the Scottish Cheddar blended with something new and wonderful...the taste of Toni. Unique and heady, her flavor blended with the others to form a combination that Laura could live on for weeks. She could smell the sandalwood soap she had placed in Toni's shower. Purchased on a whim months before in a shop promoting all things natural, its scent brought back the memories of a field in Scotland, and Laura breathed it in. It was glorious.

The only sound in the room was that of their breathing and the occasional crackle of the fire, and losing herself in her dreams, the tip of her tongue touched Toni's lips. In an instant, Laura's dreams were shattered when Toni jerked away. Seeing the anger in her eyes, Laura said, "Toni, I'm...I'm sorry."

Taking another step backward, Toni almost tripped over a chair as she tried to put space between them. Angrily wiping the back of her hand across her mouth, she glared at Laura. "What the *fuck* do you think you're doing?"

"Toni—"

"Why the fuck did you do that? What the fuck is wrong with you!"

"I'm sorry, Toni. I made a mistake."

"Yes, you did, Laura. Yes, you bloody well did!" Toni yelled, storming into her room and slamming the door before Laura had a chance to say another word.

***

Laura sat alone in the kitchen, nursing her second cup of coffee and feeling absolutely horrible. Unable to sleep, she had tossed, turned and paced for hours. Finally dozing off at four in the morning, she woke up two hours later feeling more tired than she had when she'd fallen asleep. Resting her head in her hands, Laura closed her eyes and waited for the painkillers to take away the ache between her temples.

Hearing Toni's bedroom door open, Laura looked up just as she came into the kitchen, but instead of their usual exchange of morning greetings, there was nothing but silence. With a sigh, Laura lowered her eyes and stared at the mug in her hands.

Toni poured herself a cup of coffee, and turning around, she leaned against the counter and stared angrily in Laura's direction as if daring her to look her in the eye. Seconds turned into minutes and as each passed, Toni found her annoyance returning.

Fueled by anger, frustration, and hormones that seemed to have a mind of their own, Toni had spent the better part of the night trying to convince herself that what had happened—hadn't. She had silently berated, audibly scolded, and stomped about her room for hours, but as hard as she tried, she could not get the memory of the kiss out of her head...or out of her heart. Never daring to dream that she'd ever know what it was like to kiss Laura MacLeod, the thought of it was now etched in Toni's soul. She would never forget the tenderness of lips so pink and smooth or the hint of a perfume, earthy and crisp, but what lingered and filled her body with warmth was the flavor of the woman before her, and knowing that she'd never taste it again filled her with rage.

Deciding that an apology might break the ice, Laura looked up. "Toni, about last night—"

"*I thought you were straight!*" Toni yelled, taking a step toward the table.

Flinching at the anger in her voice, Laura said softly, "I thought I was too."

Setting her jaw, Toni leaned over the table and growled, "If you ever fucking do that again, I'll move out. Do you hear me? I'll quit Calloway, and you will *never* see me again!"

Standing straight, Toni glared at Laura for only a moment before she strode from the room, and seconds later the front door closed with a bang, leaving Laura alone with her tears.

CHAPTER TWENTY-FOUR

"You did what!"

"You heard."

"You kissed Toni?"

"That's what I said."

"When did this happen?"

"Abby, I really need you to pay attention here. I told you, last night."

"I'm not talking about *when* you kissed her. I'm talking about..." Abby stopped for a moment, trying to find the words. "I'm talking about when you started playing for the other team, because the last time I checked, you were *hetero*sexual."

"Oh."

"Laura, I'm serious. What the hell were you thinking? The woman is damaged enough without you deciding it was time to experiment!"

"I *wasn't* experimenting!"

"No?"

"No," Laura said. Sinking to the sofa, she put her head in her hands. "Oh, Abby, what am I going to do?"

Abby had graduated first in her class, evidenced by the degrees and certificates hanging on her office wall. She had given lectures, treated the rich and famous, and had even written articles for various medical publications, but as she replayed the dozens of conversations she had had with Laura over the past several months, Abby Parker came to the conclusion that she was a daft cow. "Oh, my God, you're in love with her?"

Appearing as if she was bobbing for apples, Laura nodded several times before finally peeking through her fingers. "Yes, and I think I ruined it."

"Why? What happened?"

"Oh, Abby, I moved too fast. She wasn't ready. How could I have been so bloody stupid!" Laura shouted as she got to her feet and paced around the room. "Why the fuck didn't I just leave her be? I mean, she's had moods before, and they've always passed, but I pushed her. I went too fast and now she hates me. She fucking hates me!"

"Laura, calm down."

"I am calm!"

"No, you're not, and I can't help you if you don't slow down and start making some sense. Now sit back down and tell me what happened."

Throwing herself onto the sofa, Laura picked up her wine, tucked her legs under her and glared at Abby. "There—you satisfied?"

Fighting the urge to laugh, Abby picked up her own glass, taking a sip as she settled into the corner of the sofa and looked at her exasperated friend. Thinking for a moment, she said, "Okay, so last night something happened and you kissed Toni. Yes?"

"Oh, so you *were* paying attention," Laura snarled. "It's about bloody time."

"You *are* in a mood, aren't you?"

Realizing she was taking her frustrations out on Abby, Laura frowned. "I'm sorry. That was totally uncalled for."

"Apology accepted," Abby said with a smile. "Now, what exactly happened last night?"

"I told you. I kissed—"

"Not that part. I'm talking about *before* the kiss."

"Oh."

"You said that Toni was having a bad day, right?"

"Not at first," Laura said, unfolding her legs. "When we left Scotland, she was fine. She was quiet during the drive, but she's always like that. When we got home, we both unpacked, had some dinner, and then we just sat around and talked."

"About what?"

"I told her that my mother wanted us to come back at Christmas and spend a few weeks with her."

"Does your mother know?"

"I wasn't lying, Abby. My mother is the one who extended the invitation."

Abby tried not to laugh, but promptly failed. Quickly collecting herself, she said, "Laura, does your mother know about your *feelings* for Toni?"

"Oh...oh, yeah, she knows. We had a long talk one night, and she seems okay with it."

"All right, so you were chatting about returning to Scotland for Christmas, and then what?"

Thinking for a moment, Laura said, "She asked me if I would go without her, and I told her that it all depended on what her reason was for staying home alone. That's when she got angry."

"Why?"

"From the start, she's always asked me why I do the things I do for her, and I always say—"

"Give me a reason?"

About to take a sip of wine, Laura stopped before her lips touched the glass. "How in the world did you know that?"

"Because you've used that same line on me a hundred times."

"Oh."

"It's okay, Laura. It's part of who you are, and I love it, but by the sounds of Toni's reaction, she doesn't feel the same way."

"Oh, Abby, she got so angry and started rattling off all these questions. Why did I do this and why did I do that, and then she said things were getting muddled. When I asked her what she meant, she said she needed to work it out on her own."

"And you didn't let her."

"No, I guess I didn't," Laura said with a sigh. "I kept pushing her and she finally said that she realized that she'd never be the person she once was. When I asked her why, she said it was because...it was because that person was dead."

"I see."

"Oh, Abby, she looked so sad. So, so sad, and I thought...I thought she was going to slip away, disappear back into her books and close all the doors that had finally opened, and I didn't want to lose her. I wanted her to know that she wasn't dead, that she was loved...so I kissed her."

"Did she kiss you back?" Noticing that Laura instantly blushed, Abby grinned. "Laura, I'm not a sex therapist so you can skip the gory details. Just tell me what she did."

"She didn't *do* anything. She didn't pull away, and for a second or two, I thought things, well I thought things might go further, but then she backed off and got really, really angry. I tried to apologize, but she wouldn't listen, and then she ran to her room and slammed the door."

"And you haven't spoken since last night?"

"We had a brief exchange this morning, but it didn't go very well," Laura said, rubbing the bridge of her nose.

"What happened?"

"I thought maybe I should try to apologize again, but I barely got started before she began screaming. She told me if I ever tried it again, she'd quit her job and move away. Then she just stormed out of the house."

"Really," Abby said pensively. "That's interesting."

"What do you mean?"

Taking a sip of wine, Abby got her thoughts in order. "Our relationship, you and I, we're close friends, wouldn't you agree?"

"The best. You know that."

"Okay, and taking away the fact that you're in love with Toni, would you say she falls under the same heading?"

"Sure. Why?"

"Laura, in all the years you and I have known each other, we've had our share of disagreements, but neither of us has ever seen the need to give the other an ultimatum. Between friends, especially close friends, there's an honor, if you will. You tell me you don't like something, and I accept it and move on because I care about you, and I value our friendship. I don't need to threaten you. I just need to ask, because I trust you, and you trust me."

"So, what's your point?"

"I think Toni's in love with you."

"What?"

"You heard me."

"Abby, are you on drugs? Have you heard a single word I've said? She was furious!"

"Yes, but not at you," Abby said. Drinking what was left of her wine, Abby set the glass aside. "You said it yourself. At first, she didn't pull away when you kissed her. I don't know about you, but if someone tries to kiss me, and I don't want them to, I don't just stand there and let it happen. That tells me she has feelings for you."

"Then why did she get so bloody angry?"

"Probably the same reason she gave you those ultimatums. She doesn't want it to happen again."

"She doesn't want to be loved?"

"Probably more along the lines that she doesn't think she has anything to give to a relationship being the way she is, and if she could ever get past that, you're still left with the scars."

"Oh, that's bollocks! I don't care about the bloody scars!"

"Of course you don't, but *she* does. Laura, you keep forgetting that Toni has very little, if any, self-worth. Sure, she's a fantastic teacher, and she knows that, but as far as being in a relationship—no way. She looks in the mirror and sees nothing but those marks, and most likely remembers every bloody detail. And as hard as she might try, she simply can't imagine ever being with anyone who can look past them or accept all of her eccentricities."

"I can."

"Sweetheart, I'm sure you can, but I'm not Toni."

"Well then, what do I do?"

"First, I need to ask you something, and I want you to wait until I'm finished before answering. All right?"

"Okay?" Laura said cautiously.

"In my profession, or should I say, in the medical profession, there is a lot of care and nurturing that goes along with the job. Because of that, it's not unheard of that a doctor falls for their patient or vice versa, and whilst you're not a doctor and Toni is not your patient, your relationship has quite a few similarities to that of a doctor and patient."

Noticing Laura was about to interrupt, Abby held up her finger to stop her. "With that being said, I need you to assure me that you're not trying to develop an intimate relationship with her simply because you think by showing her that sort of affection it will make her, for the lack of another word...better."

"I'm not," Laura answered quickly.

"Are you sure?"

"Yes."

Studying her friend, Abby said, "Convince me."

Laura took a sip of wine and then placed her glass on the table. Turning to Abby, she said, "You see her as damaged...broken, but I see her as a survivor. She managed to get through something we can't even begin to fathom. I'm not blind, Abby, I know Toni has issues...and I don't care.

"It doesn't matter to me if Toni can't go shopping by herself, because all that means is that we'll get to spend more time together than most. I don't care that she prefers intimate restaurants over loud, crowded pubs, because that way I'll never miss a word she says. If she can never find the courage to order her own food in a restaurant, that just means when we're old and gray, I'll be able to make sure she's eating properly. And not opening doors to strangers? Well, in this day and age, I think that's pretty smart. Don't you?" Pausing for a moment, Laura said quietly, "You ask me if I'm trying to make her better, and I wonder what you mean, because to me...to me, she's perfect."

Staring back at Laura, goose bumps appeared on Abby's arms. "Wow."

"You believe me now?" Laura whispered.

"Yes, I do."

"So, what do I do?"

"Unfortunately, there's nothing you *can* do, Laura. It takes two people to make a relationship, and even though I'm convinced Toni has feelings for you, she may never be able to act on them."

"That's not what I wanted to hear."

"I know, and I'm sorry, but as your friend, I'm not going to lie to you. If you want Toni in your life, you're going to have to settle for friendship, because that's all she may ever be able to give you."

"So I just pretend it didn't happen?"

"Basically, yes. She's probably not going to be very talkative for a while, so when you get home, if I were you, I'd just go about doing the usual things and not say anything. When she's ready to talk, she will."

"Well, that won't be difficult, since she's not home."

"Oh, that's right, you said she stormed out. Do you have any idea where she went?"

"Yeah, Kris sent me a text. Toni showed up at her place."

"It sounds like you weren't the only one who needed to talk."

***

"She did what?"

"You heard me."

"Laura kissed you?"

"Yes."

"On the lips?"

Exasperated, Toni said, "Would you like me to draw you a picture?"

"Can you?" Krista asked with a gleam in her eye.

"Oh, bloody great! My world is falling apart, and *you're* making jokes!"

"From where I'm sitting, it looks to me like your world is improving by leaps and bounds."

"Are you daft?"

"No, I'm not, and I'm not blind either."

"What's that supposed to mean?"

"Hello? Toni, I may not be allowed to touch, but I can still look, and Laura's a fox."

"Oh, get real, Krista."

"You don't think she's attractive?"

"That's not what I meant."

"Well, perhaps you need to explain, because I seriously don't see what the problem is."

"You don't?"

"No," Kris said, shaking her head. "Laura's a fox. She likes you, and you like her—"

"I *like* her as a *friend*!"

"Is that so?"

"Yes."

"Bollocks."

"Krista—"

"Toni, you saying that you like Laura *only* as a friend is like me saying I like chocolate *only* on occasion."

Narrowing her eyes, Toni said, "You love chocolate. You'd eat it all the time if you could."

Tilting her head, Kris wiggled her eyebrows and waited for Toni to catch up.

"I am *not* in love with *Laura MacLeod*!" Toni shouted. Jumping off the sofa, she headed to the door. "I'm leaving. I don't even know why I wasted my time with you."

Running after her, Krista grabbed Toni's hand and pulled her back. "Because I'm your best friend, that's why, and you've never been able to lie to me, so stop trying. Now, get your arse back on that sofa and talk to me."

Taking a deep breath, Toni let it out slowly as she returned to the couch. Sinking into its cushions, she looked over at Krista and when she saw the woman's obnoxiously large smirk, she blurted, "What?"

"Start talking."

"I've got nothing to say."

"Don't do that."

"Do what?"

"Disappear like you did before," Krista said angrily. "I've waited too long to get my friend back, and I'll be damned if I'm going to let you vanish again."

"I'm not going to vanish. I'm right here for Christ's sake."

"Then talk to me, because I know you want to."

"How do you figure that?"

"Because the only place you drive is to Calloway and back. You haven't stepped foot in this house since the day we moved you into your flat, but this thing with Laura apparently has you so wound up that you somehow found the courage to get here. That tells me you want to talk...so start talking."

After a minute passed without Toni saying a word, Krista softened her tone. "Toni, are you in love with her?"

Closing her eyes, Toni rested her head on the back of the sofa. "Yes, and I don't want to be."

"Why not? Laura's a fox—"

"Will you *please* stop saying that!"

"Well, it's true! And it doesn't hurt that she's smart, has a great job and is apparently totally in love with you."

"How the hell do you figure that? It was just a kiss."

"Yes, but it came from a woman who, until she met you, was straight. You don't cross over that bridge easily, Toni, and I don't think Laura is the type of person who experiments."

Leaning forward, Toni buried her face in her hands. "Christ, I don't want this."

"Can you kindly explain to me why not?"

"Because I can't give her the life she deserves."

"Oh, that's bollocks! Toni, you have more than enough money—"

"I'm not talking about money, Krista," Toni said, raising her eyes to look at Kris. "Laura deserves intimate dinners in five-star restaurants, but without her help, I can't arrange them. I can't surprise her with a special dinner at home, because without her help, I can't buy the food. And what do I do at Christmas or on her birthday? Ask her to buy her own present? She deserves to be wined and dined, and taken on holiday to exotic places where she can walk on white sand and feel the sun on her skin. How can I do that, looking the way I do?"

"Oh, Jesus, Toni, is that what this is all about...the scars? They're just some marks, and I'm sure Laura doesn't care about them. None of us care about them."

"But I do!" Toni screamed, leaping off the sofa. "I do, Krista. I don't need to even look at them anymore because I feel them. Don't you get that? I feel them! I remember when I got each and every one. I remember every fucking word that was said as the belts hit my skin. I remember wanting to die and forcing myself to eat spoiled food just so the bastards wouldn't win, and I remember one night that I fought so hard not to be raped that the bastard pulled my fucking arm out of its fucking socket!"

Toni had never told Kris about the horrors of Thornbridge. Although she had seen the scars, Toni had refused to give her any details knowing Kris would blame herself, and as soon as Toni saw Krista's expression, she realized her mistake. "Oh, Christ."

Toni's words burrowed their way through Krista's body, and when they reached her heart, it broke. Slowly, Krista shook her head as her tears began to flow. "Oh, my God," she said in a ragged whisper. "It's all my fault. It's all my fault."

Quickly kneeling by her side, Toni took Krista's hand. "No, Kris, please...please...it wasn't your fault. It was no one's fault."

"It should have been me. It should have been me."

"Don't say that. Krista. Even if I could go back and change things, I wouldn't. You could never have survived in there. You're not that stubborn."

"But what they did to you—"

"It's over Krista. The bastards got what they deserved, and even if they didn't, they never got me."

"They never...they never..."

"I was never raped, Kris. I swear."

"But you said—"

"I said he *tried*. I didn't say he succeeded."

"Is that the reason...is that the reason you don't like to be touched?"

"Something inside of me snapped that night, besides my arm, that is," Toni said, offering Kris a weak grin. "Since then I haven't had any...any feelings of...of..."

"Of want?"

"Yeah."

Wiping the tears from her face, Krista said, "But you do for Laura, don't you?"

Returning to sit by Krista's side, Toni said, "When we were on holiday, I bought her a blouse."

"A blouse?"

A small smile appeared on Toni's face. "Long story, but yeah, I bought her a blouse. One night we were going out to dinner, and when she came down the stairs, it was like I couldn't breathe. She was standing there looking so beautiful and suddenly...suddenly I felt...I felt..."

"Turned on?"

Toni's cheeks flamed instantly, and Krista couldn't help but snigger at the sight.

Amused by Krista's tittering, Toni said, "You know this isn't easy for me to talk about, so you laughing isn't helping one little bit."

"I'm sorry," Krista said, trying to contain herself. "But over the years, you and I have spent dozens of nights chatting about sex and our various partners, so you blushing because your knickers got a bit damp is kind of funny, don't you think?"

Toni snorted and shook her head. "Yeah, I guess you're right. It's just that I haven't felt anything like that in a long time. It kind of took me by surprise."

"Sounds like a nice surprise to me."

"It would be if I were interested in that type of relationship with Laura, but I'm not. I don't have anything to give her other than friendship. I just don't."

"So what are you going to do?"

"I told her this morning that if she tried it again, I'd move out and find another job, so I don't think she'll say anything more about it."

"So you and she will just remain friends?"

"Exactly."

"And when she goes out on a date and doesn't come home until the next morning, or better yet, *he* stays the night. You'll be okay with that?"

"Yes," Toni said quietly. "I don't have a choice."

CHAPTER TWENTY-FIVE

They spent over a week in silence, going about their days only exchanging good mornings and good nights, but when Toni's feet hit the floor Friday morning, she knew the silence had to end. She missed Laura's puffy eyes and rumpled pajamas as she shuffled into the kitchen in the morning. She missed their afternoon chats in the tiny café, and visiting Laura's office on a whim, just because she could, but most of all Toni missed the comfort of knowing Laura was her friend.

Pulling on a pair of socks, Toni padded into the bathroom and a few minutes later, she went to the kitchen to make coffee, only to be surprised to find Laura awake and sitting at the kitchen table.

Without lifting her eyes, Laura said, "Coffee's made, if you're interested."

"When don't I have coffee in the morning?" Toni said, pouring herself a cup. Turning around, Toni leaned on the counter and stared in Laura's direction. Taking a few hesitant sips of the steaming French Roast, Toni cocked her head to one side. "I've got a favor to ask you. Actually, I have two."

Stunned Toni was talking to her, Laura looked up. "All right?"

Going over, Toni pulled out the chair opposite Laura and sat down. "The first is to ask that we forget about what happened last week and move on. Let's get back to being just friends and leave all the other rubbish behind. Can you do that?"

While it wasn't what Laura wanted to hear, at least Toni was talking, and after a week of deafening silence, Laura was ready to agree to anything just to have Toni back in her life. "I'm willing to try, if that's what you want."

"It's what I want."

"Okay."

"Good, then that's settled."

While Toni took a sip of coffee, Laura asked, "What was the other favor?"

"Oh, I thought it was about time I re-enter the twenty-first century."

"How so?"

"I'd like to get a mobile. That is, if you have time to take me."

Instantly, Laura smiled. "I think that's a great idea. We can go this weekend, if you'd like."

"That would be great," Toni said. For a second, her eyes met Laura's, and then quickly getting to her feet, she said, "Right, well, I'm going to shower and get ready for work. Do you want to ride in together today?"

"Absolutely."

***

"I'm impressed," Laura said, standing in the doorway.

"Why's that?" Toni said, opening another box.

"We went to get you a simple mobile and came home with half the store."

"Well, you said it works better if you use a computer with it."

"I also said you could use my laptop anytime you wanted."

"True, but I haven't used a computer for years, and I'm sure they've changed a bit," Toni said, pulling a sleek laptop from a carton. "So, this way I can take my time learning the new stuff without interfering with what you need to do, and it'll give me a chance to read up on some things without having to open a newspaper to see all the rubbish."

"And you needed a printer why?"

"In case I want to print something, of course," Toni said with an exaggerated eye roll. Glancing at the instruction sheet in her hand, she asked, "So, you going to give me hand with this?"

"Sorry, but you're on your own tonight. I've got a date."

Although the words on the paper no longer held her interest, Toni refused to look up. "Anyone I know?"

"Phillip. He called yesterday, and I suggested we meet for drinks." Looking at all the boxes scattered in the room, Laura asked, "You going to be okay with all of this?"

"Sure. Piece of cake."

"Okay, well I'd better get ready. Don't want to be late," Laura said, leaving the room.

Waiting until she heard Laura run up the stairs, Toni tossed the instruction sheet aside and sitting on the bed, she grumbled, "Well, she didn't waste any time, now did she?"

***

"So, things are back to normal between you and Toni then?" Abby asked, eyeing her friend at the other end of the sofa.

"If by normal you mean that we're friends again, yeah."

"You don't seem too happy about that."

"I guess it's better than nothing," Laura said with a sigh. "I was hoping that when I went out with Phillip last Saturday, she wouldn't like it, but it didn't seem to faze her."

"I thought you weren't interested in him."

"I'm not. That's why I agreed to meet him for drinks. He's been calling, and I didn't want to break it off over the phone. Afterward, I just went to the cinema and stayed out long enough to make it look like I was on an actual date."

"Why the hell did you do that?"

"Grasping at straws, I guess."

"Oh, right. Playing the jealousy angle, were you?"

"Yeah, but like I said, it didn't work. And now she's so wrapped up in her computer I hardly see her."

"I wish there was something I could say to make you feel better."

"Me, too," Laura said, leaning back on the sofa. "I know I just need to get over it and move on, but I don't know how to do that."

"Well, I do."

"Yeah?"

"Let's go out…like old times."

"What? Go to a pub, get pissed and dance the night away?"

"Sure, why not? It's been ages since we've done that. What have you got to lose?"

Thinking for a moment, Laura said, "I'll need to go home and change."

"I'll pick you up at nine, and don't forget to put on your dancing shoes."

***

Laura stood in front of the mirror and forced herself to look happy. Wearing her favorite little black dress, she had no doubt that she'd dance the night away in the arms of strangers, but the idea had somehow lost its appeal between Abby's house and her own. Laura didn't want to be embraced by thick masculine arms or engulfed in colognes smelling of clove and oak moss. She wanted the arms of a woman around her. A woman who was tall and slender with eyes the color of cinnamon, and who needed no other scent than her own.

Realizing that she was again allowing herself to get lost amidst hopes and dreams, Laura's temper flared. "Fuck it," she said, stepping into a pair of three-inch, pointy-toed dress pumps. "It's time to go out and forget your troubles, MacLeod. One way or another."

With a bowl of crisps and a bottle of beer, Toni was heading to her room when Laura came down the steps, and although Toni tried to act disinterested, she failed miserably. Starting at the top of Laura's head, Toni's eyes slowly traveled down to her toes, but on the return voyage, she saw Laura's smirk, and knew she'd been caught. "I...I thought you were in for the night."

"Well, you thought wrong," Laura said. Seeing the glare of headlights sweep across the front of the house, she said, "And that's my taxi, so you have a nice night and don't wait up."

Without waiting for an answer, Laura swept past Toni, grabbed her coat and was out the door.

***

Glancing at the clock for the umpteenth time, Toni closed her laptop and pushed it aside. Having spent the first few hours of the night playing mindless games on the Internet, she had spent the next two surfing websites she deemed safe, reading recipes and gardening tips while trying to keep her mind off of a woman in a little black dress. It didn't work. Even though Toni had never personally met Duane York or Phillip Hoult, tonight Laura wasn't out on a date with a name Toni knew. Tonight, Laura was out on the town alone. Tonight, she was on the pull, and Toni didn't like it. She didn't like it one goddamned bit.

Deciding it was time to get some sleep, she jumped off the bed and yanked open her dresser. Snatching out a pair of pajamas, she tossed them on the bed, but then she froze when she heard a loud crash coming from the front of the house. Slipping her feet into her trainers, Toni silently crept to the bedroom door, her heart thundering in her chest as she pressed her ear against the wood. Hearing the sound of feminine giggles, she let out the breath she'd been holding, cautiously opened the door and stepped into the lounge.

"Sshhh...sshhh, Abby. You're gonna wake up Toni."

"I didn't knock over the bloody vase. You did!"

"I know, but we gotta be quiet. Don't wanna wake me lodger."

"Too late," Toni said dryly as she came into the entryway.

It was obvious by their silly grins, and the fact that both were having issues getting themselves out of their own coats, the two women staring back at Toni were pissed...to their earlobes. At first, she considered returning to her room to let them fend for themselves, but when Toni saw the shards of ceramic covering the floor, she changed her mind. "I'll get a broom."

"Whatever," Laura said, waving her hand through the air as she wobbled past. "You do the wife thing. I'm gonna turn on some music."

Paying no mind to the broken pottery crunching under her feet, Laura stomped through the foyer, leaving Toni and Abby standing in the hall staring at each other. As Abby started to take a step, Toni held up her hand. "No. Stay there until I get this cleaned up. Can you do that?"

"Yep!" Abby said proudly, giving Toni a thumbs-up. "Won't move 'til you tell me. Promise."

A few minutes later, with a dustpan overflowing with the bits and pieces of a broken vase, Toni turned toward the kitchen, but before she could take a step, the house was suddenly filled with music. Very, very loud music.

Startled by the thunderous hard rock blaring from the lounge, the dustpan slipped from Toni's hand, and as Abby watched in drunken delight, the pieces of shattered ceramic returned to cover the floor again.

"Jesus Christ!" Toni bellowed, storming into the lounge. "You're going to wake the entire bloody neighborhood!"

Unable to hear anything over the deafening sound of electric guitars, Laura stood in front of the stereo, fumbling with buttons and dials as she tried unsuccessfully to turn the volume down.

Pushing her way around the inebriated woman, Toni reached over and hit the power switch, sending the house back into silence. "What the hell are you doing? People are trying to sleep for Christ's sake!"

"I just wanna dance some more. I like dancing," Laura said, and feeling the need to demonstrate, she twirled around and immediately corkscrewed herself to the floor.

"Shit," Toni said, kneeling by her side. "Are you okay?"

Lying behind the couch, Laura said, "Yep. I'm *gooooood*, but it's really dusty under the sofa. You should see."

"I believe you," Toni said as she helped Laura sit up. "Can you stay here a minute while I get the entry cleaned?"

"You're not done wiff that yet! Whaz taken you so long? It was just an itty-bitty vase."

"Right," Toni said, getting to her feet. Seeing that Laura was once again lying on the floor, absorbed in her study of sofa dust bunnies, Toni returned to the front hall to find Abby tiptoeing toward the lounge.

"What the hell are you doing? I told you to stay put."

"I really gotta pee," Abby said, snickering as she grabbed hold of a nearby chair to steady herself. "Didn't think you'd wanna clean that up too."

Rolling her eyes, Toni said, "You're right. Can you manage on your own?"

"Yep, but best use the one in yours if you don't mind. Stairs probably wouldn't be a good idea right now."

"I couldn't agree more," Toni said, stepping back to allow her to pass.

Watching the woman carefully stagger toward her room, Toni waited until she disappeared behind the bedroom door before she returned to the task at hand. Glancing into the lounge to see Laura still sitting on the floor, now shoeless and fumbling with the buttons of her coat, Toni cleaned up the foyer, put some water on for tea and returned to the lounge.

Squatting beside Laura, she asked, "How you doing?"

Raising her eyes to meet Toni's, Laura's smile sloped to the left. "Just peachy...but me buttons are stuck."

Biting her lip to stifle a laugh, Toni's eyes sparkled with amusement. "Yeah, I hate when that happens. Why don't we get you off the floor, and I'll see about getting them unstuck?"

Taking Toni's hand, Laura got to her feet, and then looking up, her eyes grew large. "Blimey! You're a tall one, aren't cha."

"So I've been told," Toni said as she began to unbutton the misaligned coat.

"Whatcha doing?" Laura asked, looking down.

"Taking off your coat."

"You wanna see what's underneath, don't cha?"

"No, I want to get you out of it so..."

The word died in Toni's throat the second the hickey came into view. Running from the base of Laura's neck to her shoulder, it was a mottled mess of colors having not yet reached their prime. Setting her jaw, Toni tossed Laura's coat on the sofa. "Let's get you upstairs," she said flatly, her eyes avoiding the juvenile love bite in all its glory.

"Okay," Laura said, tottering to the stairs. "I'll race ya."

Taking two quick steps, Toni was at Laura's side before her foot hit the first step, and standing close enough to prevent her from falling, Toni followed her slowly up the stairs and into the bedroom. As Laura wobbled around the room, seemingly intent on examining each item on her bureau, Toni flicked on the bedside lamp, pulled down the duvet and then returned to Laura's side.

"Come on, let's get you to bed."

"Yougonnajoinme?"

"No, I'm going to tuck you in and go back down to see how Abby's doing."

"Abby? Is Abby here? Oh, I should go down...say hello," Laura said, staggering toward the door.

"You can say hello in the morning," Toni said, redirecting Laura back to the bed. "Right now, sleep is in order."

"You tired?" Laura asked as Toni guided her to the bed. "Me, too."

"Good, so we'll both get some sleep. Okay?"

"Okay!" Laura said as she sat on the edge of the bed and patted the mattress. "You first."

"My bed's downstairs."

"It doesn't have to be," Laura purred.

"You need to lie down and get some sleep."

"But I'm lonely," Laura said, adding a pout for good measure. "Stay with me. Please?"

Running her fingers through her hair, Toni sighed. "Sure. I'll stay until you fall asleep. How's that?"

"Good!" Laura said, falling into her pillow. Looking up at Toni, a lopsided smile appeared on Laura's face. "Toni?"

"Yeah?"

"Take off my clothes."

Laura's words acted like a sucker punch and Toni's lungs emptied in a whoosh. The little black dress was tight, hugging every inch of Laura's torso. It was definitely not designed as sleepwear, but the thought of assisting Laura in its removal made Toni's heart pound in her chest.

"It's already wrinkled. Just go so sleep."

"Fine, I'll do it myself," Laura said as she sat up and struggled to find the zip.

With a shrug, Toni walked to the door, but when she heard a resounding thud, she turned around to see Laura sitting on the floor in a heap.

"Christ, are you all right?" she asked, rushing over.

"I hurt my bum," Laura said with a long face.

"You're a pain in the arse. Do you know that?" Toni said, helping Laura get to her feet.

"Yeah, but it doesn't matter 'cause I know you love me."

Pushing those words from her mind, Toni spun Laura around by the shoulders. Making short work of the zipper, Toni tried her best not to look at what lay beneath the black jersey. She failed.

Against the onyx fabric, Laura's skin looked like Chinese porcelain, smooth, flawless and priceless, and it was all Toni could do not to reach out and touch it. Holding her breath, Toni pushed the dress to the floor, revealing undergarments of silk and spandex. Matching the color of the dress, Laura's bra was strapless, and as if she had been reading Toni's mind, Laura turned around...and Toni's lungs emptied.

Contoured spandex covered in satin and edged in lace covered Laura's breasts, but just barely, and the underwire lifted the creamy mounds as if they were an offering. Unconsciously licking her lips, Toni looked past the ivory swells to the matching bikini briefs, and her heart skipped a beat at the sight of the lace garter holding up nylons the color of charcoal.

"Like what you see?"

Brought back to reality by Laura's voice, Toni's head snapped up and when she realized Laura had been watching her, her face turned scarlet. Taking a deep breath, as she slowly exhaled, she cleared her mind of things not allowed and concentrated on the reality of things that were. Motioning toward the bed, Toni said, "Climb in, and I'll cover you up."

"But I still have clothes on," Laura said coyly, watching intently to see Toni's reaction. Even in a drunken stupor, when Laura saw the look on Toni's face, her inebriated playfulness disappeared.

Inwardly, Toni groaned as her center came to life, but within seconds, her want was replaced by rage. Her eyes narrowed, and pointing at the bed she growled, "Stop fucking around, Laura. You're drunk and you need to sober up, and I need to get some sleep. Knock this shit off and get into that fucking bed *now*!"

Without another word, Laura climbed under the sheets, and as Toni covered her, Laura whispered, "I'm sorry."

Closing her eyes for a second to push back the tears, Toni said softly, "So am I."

Toni waited until Laura fell asleep before going back downstairs. Hearing the kettle whistle, she went to the kitchen and made herself a cup of tea before going in search of the other drunken woman in the house. Noticing that the lounge was empty, but her bedroom door was ajar, Toni peeked inside and saw Abby passed out on the bed.

"Well, I guess I know where I'm sleeping," Toni grumbled. After covering Abby with the quilt and grabbing her book from the nightstand, Toni returned to the lounge, plopping down on the sofa with a sigh. Taking a sip of tea, she opened the paperback in hopes that the words would erase memories of a gorgeous body, marred by the love bite of another, and when that didn't work…she turned off the lights, settled into the cushions and cried herself to sleep.

CHAPTER TWENTY-SIX

Standing on the back porch of Laura's house under a small overhang, Toni smoked her cigarette and looked out over the garden filled with weeds and dried leaves. Sometime during the night, the rain began, and with the temperature dropping, signaling that autumn was here to stay, Toni's plans to clean and rake would have to wait. Having always lived in flats, she had never had the need to garden, or even to learn, but books were starting to lose their effect, and if the printed page could no longer lull her to sleep, then exhaustion would. It had to. Last night was the first night in years when a nightmare filled with the fractured images of men, belts and pain had found its way to her, and she awoke covered in sweat and gasping for air.

In Thornbridge, and even in Sutton Hall, Toni had listened as others awoke from their sleep, screaming at the images their minds created, but literature had always protected Toni. Remembering the lines from a sonnet, the dialogue from a play or the passages in a novel, she would fill her mind and sleep peacefully, but that was before she met Laura. Last night, lying in the darkness, Toni tried to concentrate on words written by authors long since gone, but memories of a kiss had invaded her thoughts and her body. The most basic of needs refused to lie dormant any longer, and when sleep finally came, Toni's mind conjured up images of gentle caresses and soft words, but then they morphed into a nightmare filled with schisms of pain and splashes of red.

Emptying her lungs of the smoke that remained, Toni stubbed out her cigarette and went back inside just as Abby came into the kitchen. For a second, Toni allowed her eyes to meet Abby's, but then she lowered hers, walked to the counter and refilled her coffee. The night before, her fear hadn't taken hold. Two drunken women were hardly frightening, but a new day had dawned, and not only was there a stranger in the house, the stranger was a psychologist. Toni's palms were sweating and her heart thumped hard in her chest, but she wanted answers that only this woman could provide. Holding her head high, she drew a slow, steady breath. "There's coffee, if you want some," she said over her shoulder.

"I'd kill for some," Abby said, slumping into a chair.

Toni filled another mug. Seeing the coffee ripple in the cup, she steadied her hand before she turned around and held it out. "Personally, I wouldn't recommend that," she said, keeping her voice low for fear it would crack.

"Oh," Abby said, her eyes widening as she took the mug. "Sorry. I didn't mean that the way it came out."

"Of course, you didn't."

After taking a sip of coffee, Abby said, "I'm also sorry about last night. It seems I took your bed without asking."

"Not a problem. I've slept on the couch before."

Toni's expression remained blank, but Abby could feel her anxiety. It filled the room, drowning out the noise of appliances, and even the clock on the wall seemed to quiet its tick when Abby looked up at it. Realizing that it was later than she had thought, she asked, "Is Laura awake?"

Leaning against the counter, Toni stared back at the woman in the rumpled dress with the crooked sequined belt. "No. I doubt she'll be down before noon."

"Understandable," Abby said. "She did have quite a bit to drink last night."

Crossing her arms, Toni said, "You know, I think it's pretty irresponsible of you to let her get that pissed, what with you being her *best* friend and all. I would have thought you'd have tried to slow her down."

"You obviously don't know what Laura's like when she's trying to pretend that she's happy."

"What's that supposed to mean?"

Pausing for a moment, Abby Parker considered the woman leaning against the counter. Over the years, Laura had dated lots of handsome men, but none of them could hold a candle to the slim, raven-haired woman standing before her. Others may not have been able to see past the beauty of this woman, but Abby could. Behind the soulful eyes, and masked by high cheekbones and feminine curves, an intelligence lurked. While Toni's question was seemingly innocent, Abby knew better. "I don't really need to answer that. Do I?"

Sizing up her opponent, Toni shook her head. "No, you don't."

"You know, you're not what I imagined," Abby said, placing her mug on the table.

With a snort, Toni walked over, yanked out a chair and sat down. Keeping her hands under the table so Abby couldn't see them shaking, Toni tried to hide her fear with arrogance. Glaring back at the woman, she said, "Is that so? Let me guess. Laura filled you in on all the gory details, and you thought I'd be some sort of monster?"

"Actually, that couldn't be further from the truth."

"No?"

"No. What I meant was, with what Laura's told me about your fear of strangers, I'm surprised you're speaking to me right now. That's all."

Abby wasn't the only one surprised, and if it weren't for the fact Toni still wanted answers, she would have run from the room. Deep inside she could feel her panic growing, but her need to know the truth kept her glued to the chair. Toni wanted to know who had put the mark on Laura's neck. Was this *best* friend more than just that, or had it been a stranger, someone who held Laura close while they danced in a smoky pub, his mouth pressed hard against her skin, leaving behind a bruise as if to claim her as his own?

Remembering the gruesome love bite, Toni dug deep. Leaning back in her chair, she sneered at Abby. "What's your point, or do shrinks only *ask* questions and never *answer* any?"

Abby had always prided herself on her patience and compassion, two required elements for her line of work; however, the need for a bath, toothpaste and headache tablets had got in the way, not to mention the belt she was wearing. While the broad sequined-edged sash was fashionable, after spending a night with it wrapped around her waist, it had become an annoyance. Without thinking, she got to her feet, yanked it off and tossed it on the table. Narrowing her eyes,

Abby said, "Well, I can't speak for *all* the psychologists, but this one has no problem answering questions! What would you like to know?"

With her hands on her hips, Abby waited for an answer, but it only took a few seconds before she realized she wouldn't be getting one. Her mouth dropped open, and she watched in stunned silence as Toni's Thornbridge persona returned.

Assuming the position of a prisoner on the verge of being reprimanded, Toni straightened her spine, bowed her head, and as the color drained from her face, she placed both hands on the table, palms down.

"Shit," Abby said, reaching over to push the belt off the table. Quickly kneeling by Toni's side, Abby's tone turned soothing and soft. "Toni, it's okay. No one's going to hurt you. I promise."

They were words offered for comfort, an assurance that all would be okay, but between the belt and her words, Abby had unwittingly transported Toni back to hell, and the result was painful to see.

As if Toni had been wearing the twin masks of theater, she had hidden behind the first, confident and strong, but words meant to soothe had ripped it away, revealing the tragedy that lay underneath. Abby watched in horror as Toni's face changed to one filled with terror, her entire body starting to shake as she struggled to take her next breath.

"Shit," Abby said. Jumping up, she ran in the direction of the junk drawer.

***

"I can find something stronger, if you'd like," Abby said, placing a cup of tea in front of Toni.

Shaking her head, Toni wrapped her hands around the cup and brought it to her mouth. Slowly sipping the steaming Assam, it wasn't until she heard Abby pull out a chair that she looked up. Pausing for only a second, Toni said, "I suppose now's the time when you're going to slide me your business card and suggest that I ring you up for an appointment. Yes?"

"No, actually I was thinking about giving you the names of a few books you might want to read."

"Books?"

"Yes. Both of the authors survived rather traumatic events, and the books deal with how they learned to trust again, and to live in a world that terrifies them." Seeing the confused look on Toni's face, Abby said, "Don't get me wrong. I do think you could benefit from some counseling, at least to help you manage those panic attacks of yours, but soliciting patients whilst fighting a hangover and wearing a dress I've slept in just doesn't seem professional to me. If you know what I mean?"

A hint of mirth found its way to Toni's eyes. "We have painkillers, if you'd like some."

"I'd kill...um...that would be lovely. Yes."

Retrieving the over-the-counter medication from a cabinet, Toni handed the container to Abby, and by the time Toni returned to her chair, Abby had already popped two white tablets into her mouth.

Quickly washing them down with warm tea, Abby capped the bottle and placed it on the table. "Thanks."

"I should be the one thanking you...for helping me."

"My pleasure," Abby said softly. "Do you mind if I ask what brought on the attack?"

"Panic."

Smiling, Abby said, "What I meant was, if it was because I took off my belt, I can assure you I didn't mean to upset you. That blasted thing was just uncomfortable."

"It wasn't just that," Toni said, pausing for a moment. "The screws would always say 'no one's going to hurt you'...and then they'd beat the shit out of me. Between that and the belt...I didn't stand a chance."

"Oh, God, I'm sorry."

"You didn't know," Toni said quietly.

Toni was right. Abby didn't know Toni's triggers. All she knew were the bits and pieces Laura had told her over the past few months...but therapy starts with bits and pieces. "Can I ask you a question?"

"That depends."

"On what?"

"On whether you're going to charge me or not?"

Grinning, Abby said, "It's on the house. I promise."

"Then go ahead."

"Did you suffer from panic attacks before you went to prison?"

"Never," Toni said, staring at the cup in her hands. "The first time was just after I got out. Krista wasn't home, and all of a sudden it felt like everything was closing in on me, like this massive weight was pressing down on me. I thought I was having a heart attack, but a short time later I...I woke up on the floor."

"Are they always as bad as the one today?"

Toni breathed deep, letting the air out slowly as she tried to decide whether to answer. Until this moment, she had never had the desire to talk to a professional about her problems, but a few minutes earlier, Abby had knelt by her side, calmly talking her back from a panic attack. Looking across the table at the woman in the wrinkled dress and smeared makeup, Abby didn't look the part of a doctor. She looked like a friend, and if there was one thing Toni knew she needed, it was friends.

"Some are worse than others," Toni said quietly.

"And this one? How'd you rate this one on a scale from one to ten?"

"I don't know, maybe a seven or an eight."

Stunned, Abby said, "But you almost passed out."

"Yeah, well, when I pass out, those are tens."

"You say that as if it's nothing, but I would think something like that would be terrifying."

"It is, but I don't have as many as I used to, and they're not nearly as bad. Laura helps a lot."

"How so?"

"She has a way of being able to calm me down by just talking to me, like you did, but she still carries a paper sack in her handbag just in case that doesn't work."

"Well, I'll be honest with you. I'm trained to talk someone through one of those, but after what Laura told me about you, my first reaction was to get a paper bag, but I couldn't find any."

"Laura put them in the pantry."

"Now you tell me," Abby said with a laugh.

Toni managed a tight-lipped smile and then lowered her gaze, mindlessly running her finger along the edge of her teacup. "If I...if I told you what happened to me, could you...could you help me? Could you make the attacks go away?"

"You mean, if I saw you as a patient?"

"Yes."

"It wouldn't happen overnight, Toni, but yes, I think in time they'd go away, or at the very least, you'd learn how to handle them better."

"Oh."

"Is that what you'd like to do? Become a patient of mine?"

"I don't know," Toni said, staring at the cup in her hand. "I have trouble going places."

"I'm sure we could figure out a way."

Fidgeting in her chair, Toni said, "Um...if it's all...if it's all the same to you, I'll...I'll need to think about it."

Hearing anxiety creep into Toni's voice, Abby said, "Look, why don't we just play it by ear, shall we? If you decide you'd like to talk to me, Laura's got my number. Okay?"

"Thanks, but I...I wouldn't want Laura to know."

"Can I ask why?"

"I...I don't want her to get the wrong idea, and think that this would somehow change things between us."

"Don't you want things to change?"

"No, of course not. Laura's my friend and I'd never want that to change."

"That's not what I'm talking about. Laura told me she kissed you, and you kissed her back."

"I did not!" Toni said, glaring at Abby. "That's bollocks! She caught me by surprise, and it just took me a minute to get things sorted. I think of Laura as a friend and *only* a friend."

A knowing grin spread across Abby's face. "Nice try, but the lady doth protest too much, methinks." The indignant look Toni gave her in return only added to Abby's amusement, and fighting the urge to laugh, she said, "Oh please, don't even think about telling me I'm wrong."

"Right or wrong, it doesn't matter. Laura's moved on," Toni muttered.

"And how did you come to that conclusion, may I ask?"

"It doesn't matter how I know—"

"Oh, yes it does," Abby said, sitting forward in her chair. "You're describing my best friend as a fickle tart and that couldn't be further from the truth."

"Really?"

"Yes, *really*."

"Then would you care to explain why she went out with Phillip a week after she kissed me, and then last night...last night she came home with a love bite on her neck the size of a bloody football!"

"She went out with Phillip to tell him face-to-face that their relationship was over. And as far as what happened last night, I invited Laura to go out for some drinks and dancing, hoping it would take her mind off of you, but it didn't take me long to realize that she didn't want to get buzzed, she wanted to get pissed out of her mind. When she came back to the table with that idiotic bruise on her neck, I put us both in a taxi and brought her home."

"So you didn't give her that hickey?"

"What? No, of course I didn't. Laura and I are friends. She's never been interested in any woman like that. Well, that is, until she met you. All she was trying to do last night was to escape from the feelings she has for you, if only for a few hours. Toni, you've got to know that she's fallen for you."

"She has a funny way of showing it."

"Oh, like you have any room to talk," Abby said, rocking back in her chair. "What's the difference between hiding in a glass of tequila and hiding in your room?"

"That's different."

"No, it's not. It's the same thing."

"How the hell do you figure that?"

"Because you're both *afraid*," Abby said. "You're afraid Laura can't get past your scars, and she's afraid she'll never be able to convince you that they don't bloody matter, but what Laura hasn't figured out is that you're not that vain, are you? I have no doubt the marks left by those belts aren't beautiful, but the ugliness you really don't want her to see is what lies underneath. It's the rage you feel, the hatred...the need for revenge. It's alive and well and living just under the surface, and you're afraid one day it will escape and seek retribution against those who hurt you. That's what you really don't want Laura to see, isn't it? That's what you don't want her to know."

Stunned that the woman had so easily seen through to the truth, Toni stared back at her for a moment, her eyes getting glassy as tears began to form. "I don't want to hurt her," she whispered. "I'm...I'm so afraid that I'm going to hurt her."

"Do you mean physically?"

"Yes."

"Why would you think that? She's not the one who put you behind those bars."

"Did she...did she tell you about the screw who tried to rape me?"

"Yes," Abby said, but then the room was filled with the sound of her gasp. "Oh, dear God. Are you saying that he did?"

Shaking her head, Toni said, "No...no...he didn't...he didn't—"

"Toni, did he penetrate you?"

Abruptly, Toni stood up. "I need a smoke."

Before Abby could blink, the woman stormed past her, grabbed her jacket and practically ran out the back door. Without thinking twice, Abby headed to the front hall to retrieve her coat.

Standing under the small roof, Toni watched the rain fall and when she heard the door open, she didn't turn around.

"Can I have one of those?" Abby asked.

Knowing if she looked in Abby's direction, the tiny thread holding her emotions in check would break, Toni placed the pack and lighter on the railing.

"Thanks," Abby said, lighting a cigarette.

They stood almost shoulder-to-shoulder, looking out at the overgrown garden while they smoked their cigarettes. When Toni lit the next, Abby did the same, but when the chill of the air finally made it through Abby's thin coat, and she shivered, Toni said, "You should go back inside. You're cold."

"Yes, well I have this problem with walking away from a patient in crisis."

"I'm not your patient."

"Yes, you are," Abby said, turning to look at Toni. "So talk to me."

"I don't want to talk."

"You and I both know you do. You're just worried that once those tears start to fall, they won't stop, but they will. I promise."

"Are you sure?" Toni said in a ragged voice. "Are you really sure?"

Flicking her cigarette to the ground, Abby placed her hand lightly on Toni's back. "I'm positive."

CHAPTER TWENTY-SEVEN

The tears came, and with them, a torrent of words filled with hatred and anger directed at the men and women who had abused her spewed forth. Toni pounded her fists on the railing so hard Abby feared she would break every bone they contained, but she didn't stop her. She stood a few feet away as Toni unloaded, tears angrily brushed aside as she used every name in the book to describe the people who had damaged her, and as Abby knew it would, the truth came out.

He had come into Toni's cell that night to violate her, to abuse her in ways that caused stomachs to empty, and even though Toni had fought him, not allowing him to rape her in the truest definition of the word, he had raped her mind. With his hands, he had destroyed memories of perfumed, gentle lovers, replacing them with painful gropes that had left the most tender parts of her body bruised and swollen for weeks. And with his mouth, he had annihilated remembrances of tender kisses and playful nibbles, and in their place were the feel of thick saliva on her skin, and the vile breath of an animal disguised as a man.

Between the raw emotions and the damp, cold morning air, it didn't take long before both women were shivering, and guiding Toni back inside to the table, Abby went in search of Scotch. Pouring a bit in two glasses, she placed one in front of Toni as she pulled over a chair and sat next to the woman with the tear-streaked face.

"Take a sip of that. It'll warm you up."

"A bit early for Scotch don't you think or do you always ply your patients with alcohol?"

Abby picked up a tumbler, her hand trembling so much that the amber liquid splashed about in the glass. "It's as much for me as it is for you."

For a few minutes, Abby sipped her drink in silence, allowing the heat of the alcohol to warm her belly and calm her nerves. A practicing psychologist for over ten years, Abby had heard her share of stories, and had dealt with patients trying to fight addictions, survive divorces or recover from abuse. Her experience with dealing with posttraumatic stress syndrome was notable, but sitting in Laura's kitchen, sipping malt whisky at ten in the morning, she knew she had her work cut out for her. Abby had never been so rattled by a patient's tale of woe before today. She had never been so disturbed by a person's anguish that her emotions got the better of her, but this morning they had. She hadn't been able to prevent tears from falling at the utter pain that seemed to envelop Toni as she spoke of Thornbridge, and it was at that moment when Abby made herself a promise. She was going to help this woman...no matter what.

"Feeling better?" Toni said softly.

Shaken from her thoughts, Abby looked up. "I should be the one asking you that."

"Perhaps, but I think in the coming weeks you'll be the one asking the questions, so I had better get mine in while I can."

Wary about reading between any lines no matter how much she wanted to, Abby asked, "So, are you saying I have a new patient?"

"Yeah, I think you do."

Struggling to keep her enthusiasm in check, Abby allowed only a ghost of a smile to appear before slowly letting out the breath she'd been holding. "Then I'd like to discuss a few things. That is, if you feel up to it?"

Taking a deep breath, Toni leaned back in her chair. "I'm okay. Go ahead."

"Well, first I want to say that I'll do everything I can to help you, but you've got to promise me you won't lie to me or hide things from me," Abby said, putting down her drink. "If I ask you a question, I want the truth. I don't want you to try to sugarcoat it in any way. Okay?"

Thinking for a moment, Toni said, "Okay."

"Next, what you tell me—stays with me. If you want Laura to know, you'll have to tell her. I may contact some of my colleagues if I have questions or feel I need their help, but they won't know your name or your situation. All right?"

"That's fine."

"The other day, Laura mentioned you bought a computer. Do you have an email address?"

"Yes. Why?"

"I have a questionnaire I give all my patients." Getting up, Abby went in search of a pen and paper, and returning to the table, she handed them to Toni. "Write down your email and when I get home, I'll send it along." Noticing that Toni had begun to fidget in her chair, Abby asked, "Are you all right?"

"Just nervous...never been shrunk before."

"Well, this isn't really the shrinking part," Abby said, flashing a quick grin. "It's more like the pre-wash."

Amused, Toni relaxed in her chair as she began to understand why the woman was Laura's best friend. "So, what's this questionnaire about anyway?"

"It's just for background information. Nothing too taxing, I assure you."

"Okay, and then what?"

"Normally I meet my patients at my office, but for the time being, I think we should meet here. You're obviously more comfortable in these surroundings and I don't think we need to put any undue pressure on you, or am I wrong?"

"No, here would definitely be better."

"Good," Abby said as she jotted down a note. "I'll check my planner and see what I can do. I'd like to see you at least twice a week to start, and if you think you can handle more, I'll make sure I have the time available. Will that work for you?"

"Yes. I usually get home just after four, but my classes on Monday and Wednesday end at two, so I could be here early on those days."

"Does Laura come home at the same time?"

"No, she works until at least five, and on Wednesdays, she has a staff meeting, so she's usually not home until after six."

"Aren't you staff?"

"I'm exempt."

Pausing for a moment, Abby said, "That's right. You don't do well in groups of people."

"Yeah."

"Okay, so let's plan on meeting here Monday at half past two, and we'll go from there," Abby said as she jotted down another note.

Running her hands on her jeans to dry her palms, Toni nodded. "All right."

"Can you handle a few more questions? I promise, just a couple more and then that'll be it until Monday."

"Um...sure. Go ahead."

"Do you take drugs?"

"Excuse me?"

Laughing, Abby said, "Relax, it's just a standard question. Nothing personal."

"Oh, um...no, I don't do drugs."

"Ever?"

"I smoked some grass in university, but I didn't like the way it made me feel."

"Okay," Abby said, adding to her notes on the paper. "How about prescription medication? Any of that?"

"No. Why, do you think I need some?"

"I don't believe in medicating patients unless it's absolutely necessary, Toni. The reason I'm asking about drug use is because I need you to be clearheaded when we talk. If you're taking something to alter your mood or using some narcotic to ease your pain, then the sessions would be pointless."

"This coming from a woman who just served me Scotch at ten in the morning," Toni said, a grin slowly forming on her face.

Chuckling, Abby said, "*Technically*, this isn't a session."

"Nice out."

"I thought so," Abby said, her eyes creasing at the corners as she picked up her drink.

***

With her head in her hands, she sat on the edge of the bed, trying to decide if opening her eyes or even moving was even possible. Awake for almost an hour, it took all Laura had to get herself into a sitting position, and after crawling out from under the heavy duvet, the pain in her temples forced her to stop. Cautiously opening one eye and then the other, she drew away from the thin streaks of light that had somehow found their way through the drapes. Slowly getting to her feet, Laura steadied herself on the nightstand and then on the dresser before she finally made it to the bathroom to empty her bladder.

Deciding that if she looked as bad as she felt, glancing in the mirror would *not* be a good idea, she walked past the vanity and turned on the shower. A few minutes later, she stepped under the hot spray and allowed the water to wash away the smell of alcohol and cigarettes.

Memories, fragmented by tequila, filled her mind. Snippets of pubs alive with laughter and loud music rushed in and out of her head, but as hard as Laura tried, she couldn't remember how many they had visited. The night was a blur of taxi rides, walks down crowded sidewalks and gargantuan men standing at doorways to usher them into rooms filled with the stifling heat of people on the pull. She had danced in the arms of strangers, arms that felt foreign, almost dangerous, but she found herself refusing none. Placating her nerves with clear liquor, she wanted to lose herself amongst the gyrating bodies on parquet floors, but the baritone voices that whispered promises did not hold her interest for long…so she drank some more.

Sometime during the evening, the music slowed and a man with black hair and eyes the color of milk chocolate took her hand and led her to the dance floor. He held her close, much too close, but fogged by alcohol, she allowed him to whisper, she allowed him to touch, and when he said he wanted to mark her…she let him.

The bar of soap slipped from Laura's fingers as her eyes flew open, and rushing to rinse the rest of the soap from her body, she shut off the taps, grabbed a towel and rushed to the vanity. Wiping the moisture on the mirror away with her hand, her entire body deflated. "Shit!" Slowly turning her head, when the magnitude of the vivid love bite came fully into view, all the color drained from Laura's face. "That's just great, MacLeod. That's just bloody great!"

***

A short time later, Laura came downstairs wearing her most comfortable track pants and her most uncomfortable high-neck cardigan.

Sitting on the sofa, Toni looked up from her book. "So, you *are* still alive."

"Barely," Laura said, collapsing into a chair.

"How's your head?" Toni asked, placing her book on the coffee table.

"It feels like I slept with it in a vise."

"Better than in a toilet, I suppose."

"Debatable," Laura said. Closing her eyes, she rested her head on the back of the chair.

"How about I make you some coffee?" Toni asked, and then holding up her bottle of beer, she said, "Unless you prefer the hair of the dog?"

Opening one eye, when Laura saw what Toni was offering, she blanched. "Not on your life."

Grinning, Toni got to her feet. "I'll put on a pot. Shan't be long."

She was trying her best to be a friend, but when Toni reached the kitchen, her grin disappeared. Laura's attempt at covering the bruise was admirable, but it didn't matter that Toni couldn't see the hickey. She knew it was there, and she was *not* happy. Silently berating herself for the jealousy flowing through her veins, Toni stayed in the kitchen until the coffee was done, and grabbing another beer for herself, she went back to the lounge with her annoyance in tow.

Handing Laura the cup, Toni returned to her spot on the sofa, and after taking a healthy swallow of the pale ale, she opened her book and leaned back into the cushions.

"Thanks for the coffee," Laura said.

"No problem."

"You okay?"

"Sure, why wouldn't I be?"

"I don't know," Laura said, eyeing the woman. "You seem a bit off."

"No more *off* than I usually am."

"Did I do something wrong last night?"

With a snort Toni looked up from the book she wasn't reading. "No, I always enjoy having to deal with two drunken women stumbling about the house at one in the morning. It's what I live for."

"Two? Abby was here?"

With a huff, Toni said, "You really don't remember anything, do you?"

"It's all a bit of a blur."

"Is the name of the bloke who put that mark on your neck a blur, too, or did you remember to get his number?" Seeing Laura touch the collar of her sweater, Toni blurted, "The frock you wore last night barely had enough fabric to cover your tits, let alone your neck."

Anger flashed in Laura's eyes as she sat forward in her chair. "There was absolutely *nothing* wrong with the dress I wore last night!"

"No, it just had *pull* written all over it," Toni said, tossing her book on the table. "I guess I should consider myself lucky you came home with Abby instead of your neck-sucking pub partner. I sure as hell wouldn't have wanted to come out here to find you fucking on the sofa."

"You are *way* out of line!"

"Am I?"

"Yes, you are," Laura said, getting to her feet. "I went out last night to have a good time. I wanted to dance and to laugh and to forget my troubles, and I ended up drinking too much. So what? I'm a big girl, Toni, and if I want to go out and dance the night away, I will! If I want to get drunk, I will, and if I decide to bring someone home, and we decide to fuck on the sofa, as you so eloquently put it, I suggest you either stay in your bloody room or look the other way when you come out!"

As Laura stomped to the stairs, Toni called out, "Since when did you become such a bloody tart?"

Stopping at the bottom step, Laura turned around. "Since you refused to give me a reason *not* to be!"

***

"So how's this work?" Toni asked, placing the tray of tea and biscuits on the coffee table.

"What do you mean?" Abby said as she picked up a cup.

"Do I lie on the sofa and tell you about my dreams or what?"

The corners of Abby's mouth turned upward as she leaned back on the sofa and crossed her legs. "How about we start with what's bothering you today?"

"What makes you think anything's bothering me?"

"Your body language screams it."

With a sigh, Toni sat down. "I had a fight with Laura."

"About what?"

"Her coming home drunk."

"Oh, I see. You don't like to see her get pissed."

"No, it's not that. We all need to unwind sometimes, and Laura's an adult, but...but—"

"Spit it out, Toni. Remember what I told you. Don't sugarcoat and don't lie, just tell me what's on your mind. I'm not here to judge you. I'm here to listen and to help."

Leaning forward, Toni rested her elbows on her knees, combing her fingers through her hair before she glanced back at Abby. "I'm jealous."

Abby couldn't help but smile. In the coming months, she knew many of their sessions would be filled with raw emotions and painful memories, but the biggest obstacle had just passed. Toni had told her the truth, and with truth comes trust.

"So, why don't you tell her how you feel?" Abby asked.

"You know why."

"Because you think you might hurt her?"

"Yes."

"Do you honestly believe with the feelings you have for Laura, you could ever possibly hurt her?"

"I can't take that chance."

"You can't take it or you *won't* take it?"

Hanging her head, Toni whispered, "I don't have anything to offer her."

"What do you mean?"

"She deserves better than me."

Thinking for a moment, Abby asked, "If you had met Laura six or seven years ago, would you have felt the same way? Would she have deserved you then?"

"Yes."

"Why?"

"Because I was a whole person back then, that's why!" Toni barked. "I had a career that was going nowhere but up. I had two books under my belt with plans for more, and I enjoyed going out to pubs for drinks and dancing. I liked myself back then. I liked the fact that I was attractive to women, and I liked the fact that I hardly ever came home alone."

"So you were a player?"

"If you want to call it that."

"What would you call it?"

"I don't know. Someone who embraced all life had to give, I suppose."

"And you don't want to embrace life again? You don't want to laugh or to drink or to dance? You don't want to write another book or bed another woman?"

"No, I don't."

"I asked you not to lie to me."

"I'm not lying."

"Yes, you are," Abby said, sitting up straight. "If you remember, on those forms you emailed to me, there was a question about suicide, and you told me about that night with the vodka. If you didn't want to live again, you would have guzzled it without giving it a second thought, but you didn't. You made a choice and that choice was to live, and as far as not having anything to offer Laura, that's just rubbish."

"How do you figure that?"

"Because you still have a career, those two books you wrote are still in print, and there's nothing to stop you from writing another. Laura is totally in love with you, Toni, and from where I'm sitting, you're head-over-heels for her. What you can offer Laura is love, and in case you haven't heard, love is *priceless*."

CHAPTER TWENTY-EIGHT

"Here, drink this," Abby said, handing Toni a glass.

"What is it?"

"Just some water," Abby answered, sitting next to her trembling patient.

More than a month had passed since their first session, and over those weeks, a strong doctor-patient bond had been formed. Meeting twice a week, and sometimes more, Abby had managed to get Toni to talk about her family, her feelings and, of course, Thornbridge. Today they had focused on the most vicious beating Toni had received when she was in solitary, the result of which put her in the infirmary for over two weeks.

"Sorry that today was a bit rough on you," Abby said softly as she picked up her cup of tea.

"I just can't understand it," Toni said, looking over at Abby. "I think about that night a lot. When he came into my cell, my first thought was that he didn't look evil. He looked...he looked normal. He wasn't unkempt or brutish like so many of the screws, and even though he only said a few words to me, I could tell he had received a formal education, but then he just...he just started hitting me, ripping me apart with that fucking belt. How can any man do that to a woman? How can any man do that to anyone? How do you beat someone like that and then just leave them on the floor, naked and bleeding, without giving it a second thought? How?"

"Was that when you stopped trusting people?"

"Yeah. My perception of him was skewed because of his looks and his accent, but he proved me wrong and I've always made it a point to learn from my mistakes. After that, I didn't trust any of the men."

"The men? What about the female guards?"

"They came later."

"Should I save that topic for another day?"

"If you don't mind."

"Of course, I don't," Abby said, leaning back on the sofa. "So, how are you and Laura getting on these days?"

"Do you know you ask me that every time we meet?"

"Yes, I do, but after the row you and she had the night we came home from clubbing—"

"We made up a few days later, just like we always do. I told you that."

"Yes, but I also know she had a date last Saturday, and I wasn't sure how that went."

"Well, she didn't come home drunk, if that's what you're asking."

"That *wasn't* what I was asking, and you know it."

"What do you want me to do? Ask her to put her life on hold while I try to figure out mine?"

"No, but I think you should at least tell her how you feel."

"And exactly what would that accomplish? I tell her that I like her—"

"Don't you mean love her?"

Folding her arms across her chest, Toni let out an exaggerated sigh. "I thought shrinks weren't supposed to put words in their patient's mouths. Isn't there a code against it or something?"

"I didn't put words in your mouth. I just corrected your use of one *particular* word."

Toni cast an evil glare in Abby's direction, but when she saw the psychologist's brilliant smile, her anger dissolved instantly. "Christ, you are as much of a pain in the arse as Laura. No wonder you're friends."

"You're trying to get off the subject."

"Perhaps I don't like the subject."

"Perhaps that's because you *love* the subject."

"Why is it so bloody important that I use that word? Can you explain that? Why isn't the fact that I *like* Laura good enough for you?"

"It would be good enough for me if it were the truth, but part of why you're doing all of this is because of your feelings for Laura, isn't it?

"I never said that."

"You didn't have to," Abby said, returning her tea cup to the table. "Toni, these past few weeks, you've poured your heart out to me. You've held nothing back, no matter how painful it was. I know you're doing this for yourself, but you're also doing it because you've fallen in love with Laura. So, please stop trying to deny it. You've come too far to start lying now."

Abby was surprised when Toni didn't respond. There had been plenty of times during their sessions when tough topics had caused Toni to go quiet, but this was only friendly banter. Studying the woman whose head was bowed, Abby noticed that she appeared pale. Reaching over, she placed her hand on Toni's forehead. "You're warm. You feeling okay?"

"Actually, I've felt a bit out of it all day."

"Why didn't you tell me? We could have cancelled the session."

"I didn't want to. I like talking to you. It helps."

"That's good to know, but these talks are tough enough on you without having to throw a fever into the mix, don't you think?"

"I'll be fine."

Deciding not to argue, Abby glanced at her watch, not at all surprised to see that their hour session had again lasted almost two. "I think I've put you through enough for today," she said, getting to her feet. "Why don't you go lie down? I'll tidy up and then show myself out."

"No, I'll do it."

"This isn't up for discussion," Abby said, sliding her notepad into her briefcase. "I'm quite able to clean up in here and get the house in order. Now, go lie down. I'll lock up when I leave."

Too tired to argue, Toni said, "Thanks. I owe you one."

"No, you don't. Now go."

As Toni disappeared into her bedroom, Abby gathered the cups and headed to the kitchen, but she stopped when she heard the front door open.

"I thought that was your car," Laura said, stepping into the house. "What's up?"

"You're early."

"What?" Laura said, tossing her coat on a chair.

"Oh...um...I mean, don't you have a staff meeting on Wednesdays?"

"Yes, but two of our teachers were sick, so we cancelled..." Stopping, Laura tilted her head. "How did you know I had staff meetings on Wednesday?"

Quickly, Abby disappeared into the kitchen. "Shit," she said under her breath, putting the cups in the sink.

"Abby, what's going on?" Laura asked, standing in the doorway. As she waited for Abby's response, Laura noticed a package of biscuits on the counter, biscuits that were Toni's favorite. Spinning on her heel, she quickly looked toward the lounge and then back at Abby. "Where's Toni? Abby, is something wrong with Toni?"

Hearing Laura's panic, Abby said, "No. No, Toni's fine, Laura. She's fine."

"Then why are you here?"

Abby's lungs slowly emptied as she leaned against the counter. "I was talking to Toni."

"About what?"

"I'm sorry, I can't tell you that."

"Why not?"

"Laura—"

"Damn it, Abigail, you're my best friend, and we've never had any secrets."

"This isn't really a secret."

"No? Well, then what the hell do you call it?"

Knowing that she had no way out, Abby sighed. "Doctor-patient privilege."

***

Too tired and achy to remove her clothes, Toni kicked off her shoes, climbed under the quilt and closed her eyes, hoping sleep would come so the pounding in her head would go away. Hearing a light rap on the door, she called out, "Come in, Abby." The door opened, and when Toni saw Laura looking back at her, her face dropped.

"Mind if I come in?" Laura asked.

"No, it's okay."

"Abby said you had a rough day, so I brought you some tea," Laura said as she walked over and placed a cup on the nightstand. Noticing the worry lines etched across Toni's forehead, she added, "And in case you're wondering, that's all she told me. Some silly nonsense about doctor-patient privilege."

"Oh."

"But she did say she thought you had a fever," Laura said, placing her hand on Toni's forehead. "Which, apparently you do. Have you taken anything for it?"

"No, not yet."

"Be right back."

Laura left the room, and a few minutes later, returned with a glass of water and a bottle of paracetamol. Putting two in her hand, she gave them to Toni and waited until she washed them down before taking the glass and putting it near the cup of tea.

"Why are you home so early?" Toni asked quietly.

Sitting on the edge of the bed, Laura grinned. "Abby asked the same thing. It appears that we may have a small outbreak of the flu at work, and since both Susan and Jack weren't feeling well, we rescheduled our meeting."

"Oh," Toni said, lowering her gaze. "I suppose you want to ask me some questions now, huh?"

"You know, you are absolutely terrible at second-guessing me, I think I've told you that, and whatever questions I may have will wait until you feel better." Reaching over, Laura pushed a few strands of hair from Toni's forehead. "You should try to get some sleep."

"I'm sorry. I'm sorry if I hurt you by not telling you."

"There you go again. Wrong as usual," Laura said with a little laugh. "I'm not hurt, Toni. Surprised...yes, but I doubt you could do anything to hurt me. You just don't have it in you."

"Laura—"

"Sshhh," Laura whispered. "Get some sleep. We'll talk later."

"Okay," Toni murmured as her eyes began to close, but when she felt Laura get up, she reached out and took her hand. "Please don't go. Abby was right. Today was rough and I could use the company, at least until I fall asleep."

"All right," Laura said, returning to her spot on the bed. Again, placing her hand on Toni's forehead, she said, "It looks like Jack and Susan aren't the only ones who have the flu."

"I thought I was just having an off day."

"Your off days usually include fevers, do they?"

"No, but I was trying to be optimistic."

Laura smiled, and as awful as Toni felt, she couldn't help but do the same. A few minutes of silence passed between them, until Toni's eyes grew heavy and sleep took hold. Tucking the quilt around her, Laura placed the lightest of kisses on Toni's brow before quietly walking from the room.

***

Absorbed in her thoughts, Laura sat cross-legged on the sofa as the mantle clock ticked away the hours. After leaving Toni's room, she had changed her clothes, made herself some dinner and then returned to the lounge with a glass of wine and a good book, but she couldn't focus on the words. Aware of Toni's vehement refusal to seek any kind of professional counseling, to discover that she'd been seeing Abby both delighted and confused Laura. She couldn't be happier that Toni had found the courage to do so, but she was also puzzled as to why Toni thought she needed to keep her sessions with Abby a secret.

Taking another sip of wine, Laura glanced over at the partially opened bedroom door and was surprised to see light streaming through the crack. Jumping off the sofa, she went to the kitchen to fix some tea. Filling a glass with water, Laura put both on a tray and headed to the bedroom. Knocking lightly, when she heard no reply, she cautiously walked inside, and noticing the bathroom door was closed, she gathered up the water and tea she had placed on the nightstand hours before and replaced them with the new. Hearing a door open behind her, she turned around and was shocked to see Toni dressed in jeans and a T-shirt.

"What are you doing in those clothes? You're sick, and you need to be in bed."

"I...I never got...I never got changed."

"What?"

Swaying in the doorway, Toni whispered, "I...I don't feel good, Laura."

In an instant, Laura was at Toni's side, and wrapping her arm around her waist, Laura guided her to the bed. "Let me find you something more comfortable to sleep in."

Quickly gathering Toni's pajamas, Laura returned and handed her the blue flannel. "I'm assuming you don't want any help?"

As if in a daze, Toni slowly raised her eyes and shook her head. "No. No, I can do it."

"Okay. Call me when you're finished," Laura said as she left the room, and closing the door behind her, she waited just outside. After a few minutes had passed, Laura's concern got the better of her, and rapping on the door, she called out, "Toni, are you all right?"

Hearing only a muffled response, Laura walked in and found Toni lying across the bed wearing a pajama top and blue jeans. Walking over, she placed her hand on Toni's forehead.

"Your hand's cold," Toni said quietly. "It feels good."

"Yeah, well your head is hot. Really, really hot," Laura said, quickly tugging back the quilt. "Come on, let me help you get out of these jeans, and we'll get you under the covers."

"I can do it."

"No, you can't, so stop arguing," Laura said. Unbuttoning Toni's jeans, she pulled down the zip. "Lift your hips." Waiting for a moment, Laura said, "Come on, Toni. I need a little help here."

Toni moved barely a few inches, but it was enough so that Laura could tug the denim down her legs. Seeing no need to redress her, Laura tossed the pajama bottoms to the end of the bed and pulled the quilt over Toni. "There you go. How's that?"

"It's good. Thanks."

"Can you manage some tea or water? You need to take a few more paracetamol."

"Water...just water."

Toni rolled to her side as Laura handed her the glass. Quickly taking the pills, the glass barely exchanged hands before she fell back to the pillow. Looking up at Laura, she said, "I have no idea what I've done to deserve you in my life."

"I don't know either, but I'm glad you did it," Laura said softly as she ran her finger down Toni's cheek.

***

Glancing at her watch, Laura decided she had waited long enough. For the better part of two days, she had tended to Toni, waking her every four to six hours to take more medicine and forcing her to drink water or juice whenever she could. She applied cold washcloths to Toni's forehead when the fever raged, and added an extra blanket or two when chills racked her body, but the night before had been bad and Laura knew it was time to call a doctor. Taking a deep breath, she climbed off the sofa and walked to Toni's room, but when she went inside and saw Toni looking back at her, alert and aware, Laura let out a huge breath. "Well, you're a sight for worried eyes."

"What do you mean?" Toni croaked.

Sitting on the edge of the bed, Laura placed her hand on Toni's forehead. "You've had a fever for two days, Toni. I was coming in here to tell you I was going to call a doctor, but apparently I don't need to. Your fever's gone."

"I don't like doctors."

"I know you don't, sweetheart, but you weren't giving me much of a choice. You were really sick."

"I'm sorry if I worried you."

"It's okay. How you feeling?"

"Tired," Toni answered sheepishly.

"More like exhausted, I would think," Laura said, getting to her feet. "Are you hungry? I can get you something."

Struggling to sit up, Toni said, "Yeah, I think I am actually."

"Good, then I'll go fix you some dinner."

"Dinner?"

"It's Friday night, Toni."

"Jesus, I don't even remember Thursday."

"I'm not surprised. Are you going to be okay if I leave you alone?" Laura asked as she headed to the door.

"Yeah, I can manage."

Waiting until Laura left the room, Toni extracted herself from the cocoon of blankets and sheets, and dangling her legs over the edge of the bed, she paused to catch her breath. While the fever had broken, the effects of the flu lingered, and feeling as if she had just run a marathon, Toni slowly walked to the bathroom.

***

Seeing Toni come into the kitchen, Laura said, "Go back to bed. I'll bring you a tray."

"I'd rather...I'd rather sit at the table, if that's okay."

"That's fine," Laura said suspiciously. "Are you all right?"

"I just feel, I don't know...out of it."

"Probably has something to do with the flu and the fact you haven't eaten in two days. Sit down, and I'll get you some tea."

"Thanks," Toni said as she sank into a chair. "So, what's for dinner?"

"Chicken soup," Laura said, placing a cup of tea in front of Toni. "I made it this morning."

"This morning?"

"Yeah. Why?"

Toni's jaw hardened as she stared back at Laura. "Why didn't you go to work?"

Pressing her lips together, Laura pulled out a chair, sat down and mentally counted to ten. "Let me guess. This is the part where you're going to accuse me of babysitting you again, right?"

"Well, if the shoe fits—"

"Well, it doesn't, and the only shoe around here is going to be the one I'm going to put up your arse if you don't stop accusing me of treating you like a child!" Laura said, the corners of her mouth easing upward. "After making sure you had something to drink with paracetamol at the ready, I went to work Thursday morning just like always, but when I got there, John told me that he had cancelled all the classes until Monday because *three* of our teachers were sick. At *his* insistence, I gathered up some reports I could do from here and came back home."

"You could have stayed at work."

"You're right. I could have, and I'm not going to lie to you and tell you that I wasn't worried about you, because I was. Toni, you were ill, and the only place I wanted to be was by your side, and I'm not going to apologize for that. I know you don't want to hear this, but I care about you, Toni, and there's nothing I can do about it. I can't just turn off my feelings simply because you've asked me to. It doesn't work like that."

"I know," Toni said, staring at her teacup. "I've tried."

"What?"

Looking up, Toni said, "It's why I started seeing Abby."

"I don't understand."

"I like you, Laura."

"Well, come on. What's not to like?" Laura said with a chuckle.

"That's not what I mean," Toni said quietly. "What I feel for you...well, it's...it's more than what a friend should feel toward another."

The humor faded from Laura's face as hope wrapped itself around her heart. "Really?"

"Yes, and it's one of the reasons I became Abby's patient. I've got a lot of things to work through before...before I'm ready for any kind of relationship. I thought if you found out...if you knew what I was doing...*why* I was trying to get better, then you'd...you'd get the wrong idea."

"What do you mean the wrong idea?"

"I didn't want you to think that I was...that because I was talking to Abby, it meant I was ready for...for..."

Laura had spent the last few days trying to come up with some reason why Toni had felt the need to keep her sessions with Abby a secret. As hard as she tried, she simply couldn't come up with a plausible reason...until now.

The sound of the chair legs screeching across the tile floor caused Toni to jump, and looking up, she tensed when she saw the fury in Laura's eyes.

"What?" Laura shouted, waving her arms in the air. "You thought if I found out I'd pounce on you or something! How dare you think that! Do you really think me that callous and single-minded?"

"Laura, I just wasn't sure—"

"You weren't sure? *You* weren't sure? How about me, Toni? Have you forgotten that I'm *straight*, or at least I was until I met you? I know you have issues, Toni, and I know that mine pale in comparison, but do me a favor and put yourself in *my* shoes. I've never felt this way about anyone, not *anyone*, and now that I do, I can't do a bloody thing about it!"

Storming out of the room with tears in her eyes, Laura reached the lounge and stopped. Her heart was telling her to turn around and apologize for her rant, but her temper still held the advantage. Spinning on her heel, when she saw Toni walk into the room, she yelled, "I think about you all the time, do you know that? I have thoughts running through my head that make me blush for Christ's sake, and I don't know the first thing about being with a woman in that way! But even though I have these feelings for you, I honored your wishes, didn't I? You told me to back off, and I did. I never once tried to do or say *anything* to change your goddamned mind!"

"Yes, you have," Toni said quietly.

"Oh, that's a bunch of crap!"

"You've been you."

Wiping a tear from her cheek, Laura said, "What are you talking about?"

"You've been you," Toni said, taking a step in Laura's direction. "You come into the kitchen every morning looking tired and rumpled, and then flash that smile of yours and my day's made, and I find myself looking forward to the next morning, just so we can do it all again. You force me to get out of the house and go shopping, but you do it in such a way, that by the time we get wherever it is we're going, I'm no longer afraid because I know you're right there, and you'll keep me safe. And even when I'm at my worst, even when I can't think of one bloody reason why you don't just walk away, you stay by me. You pick me up. You dust me off, and you make me want to live all over again. You haven't had to say or *do* a single thing to make me fall in love with you, Laura. You did it just by being you."

Taking another step toward Laura, Toni said, "It was wrong of me to think that you'd...that you'd try to move too quickly, and I'm sorry. It's just that if I were in your shoes, and you told me that you loved me, I'm not sure I'd have the strength not to act on those feelings."

Cocking her head to the side, Laura asked, "What do you mean *my* shoes?"

"You're normal."

"Oh, fuck you!" Laura said. Taking two quick steps, she intentionally invaded Toni's space. "When are you going to understand that you *are* normal? Toni, we all have problems and issues that we need to deal with. I'm afraid of heights and spiders scare the shit out of me, but that doesn't mean I'm not normal. It's just who I am."

"You're not afraid of being touched."

"Yes, I am," Laura said softly. "Yes, I am." Seeing the confusion in Toni's eyes, Laura said, "Trust me?"

A few seconds passed before Toni gave her answer with a nod, but when Laura took her hand and moved it toward her chest, Toni pulled away.

"Trust me, Toni. Please...just trust me." Their eyes met and when Laura saw Toni nod again, she took her hand and very slowly placed it above her left breast. "I'm afraid that when I'm finally in your arms, my heart is going to fail, because it beats like this every time I'm near you."

Toni could feel the strong, fast rhythm of Laura's heart, but what took her breath away...what froze her mind and heated her blood was feeling the slightest hint of the swell of Laura's breast beneath her hand. Hypnotized by the sensation, Toni stood in silence as seconds turned into minutes.

Laura's breathing grew short, and knowing her need could not yet be answered, she gently removed Toni's hand from her chest. "I know that whatever happens will happen when you're ready, but a minute ago, you told me that you loved me—"

"I do," Toni said in a breath, raising her eyes.

"Then I'll wait," Laura said softly. "I can't promise you I won't dream about you, and I can't promise you my heart won't race when you're near, but I can promise you that I'll wait for you, because you've just given me a reason to."

Pausing for a moment, Toni said, "Can I ask...can I ask that you don't date anyone else?"

A brilliant smile graced Laura's face. "Yes, you can, and no, I won't. Toni, I don't want to go out with anyone else. I only did it because you kept accusing me of putting my life on hold for you."

"But that's what I'm asking you to do now."

"No, you're not. You've given me hope that one day, whether it's next week or next month or next year...one day, I'll be able to show you how much I love you. I don't consider that putting my life on hold, Toni. I consider it...falling in love."

Allowing her concerns to rise to the surface again, Toni scowled. "And what if *it* never happens? What if I can never get past this?"

Knowing they would have lots of time to talk about their feelings, and hopefully lots of years to show them, when Laura heard the troubled tone in Toni's voice, she decided to lighten the mood. With a twinkle in her eye, she said, "Then I guess I'll be buying lots of batteries."

CHAPTER TWENTY-NINE

"Are you going to be all right?" Laura asked, putting on her coat.

"Is this the part where you don't treat me like a child?"

"No, this is the part where I treat you like a woman who just got over being sick."

"You sure you don't want me to come with you?"

"Since when do you volunteer to go shopping?"

"I just thought—"

"You thought that since you're offering to go, I'd jump at the chance to get you out of the house, totally forgetting you've been sick. Well, nice try, sweetheart, but you're staying home so you can rest."

"But I'm not tired," Toni said, slumping back on the sofa.

Amused by Toni's pout, Laura went over and placed a quick, light kiss on her cheek. "No, you're bored, but you're still not going. You're going to stay home and take a kip. That's an order."

Hearing the doorbell ring, Laura didn't wait for Toni's response as she trotted out of the room, and opening the door, she smiled at her guest. "Hey there. Come on in. You're just in time."

"Just in time for what?" Kris asked, unbuttoning her coat.

"To keep Toni company while I go shopping," Laura said, picking up her handbag. "She just got over the flu, and she needs to rest. I shouldn't be too long, but could you make sure she gets back to bed?"

Peeking into the lounge, Kris grinned at Toni and then looked back at Laura. "Consider it done."

"Oi! Don't I have a say in this?" Toni hollered.

"No, you don't," Laura said, giving Kris a quick wink before she walked out the door.

Tossing her coat on a chair, Kris went into the lounge. "You look awful."

"Thanks. Nice to see you, too."

"Flu, eh? You feeling better now?" Kris asked as she sat down.

"Yeah. Laura took care of me."

"Yes, it appears that she did," Kris said, reaching over and wiping away the smudge of pale pink lipstick from Toni's cheek. Seeing Toni blush at the discovery, Kris giggled. "It appears you've taken the old adage of bed rest and lots of fluids to a *whole* new level."

"Behave," Toni said with a scowl.

"What? I'm not the one with a smudge of Precious Pink on my cheek."

"Laura just kissed me good-bye."

"Really? Since when does Laura kiss you at all?"

"What are you, jealous?"

"No—intrigued."

"Oh."

"What's going on?"

"Nothing."

"Come on, Toni. You trusted me with the shrink thing, why not this?"

Pausing for a moment, Toni said, "Laura and I had a talk last night."

"About?"

"I told her how I feel. I told her I love her."

"What? Oh, Toni, that's great! " Kris said, giving her a hug. Glancing at the bedroom door, she said, "So, should I assume that last night you two...um..."

Following Krista's line of sight, Toni's eyes went wide. "No, of course not!"

"Why not?"

"Laura wasn't lying, you know. I *was* sick," Toni said, slouching into the cushions. "Besides, I'm not ready for anything else. I'm not sure I'll ever be ready."

"I thought you said your sessions with Abby were helping."

"They are, but Laura knows it's not something that's going to change overnight."

"Wait? Does Laura know about you seeing Abby?"

"Yes. She actually found out by accident, but she's okay with it."

"I told you she would be."

"I know. I just have a hard time believing she's willing to wait."

"It's called love, Toni," Kris said. "And it's wonderful."

"Yeah, I'm starting to figure that part out," Toni said quietly.

"So what now?"

"What do you mean?"

"Well, you told her that you love her, and I'm assuming she feels the same. So where do you go from here?"

"That's a question I've been asking myself since last night."

"Maybe you should ask Laura what she wants."

"I did. We talked about it, and we agreed we'll just take it day-by-day, like we've been doing. Nothing's really going to change."

"You don't think so?"

"No. Why should it?"

Kris sucked in her cheeks, successfully swallowing the laugh that tried to escape. "They're called hormones, Toni...in case you forgot."

***

"You sure I can't convince you to eat anything else?" Laura asked, walking into the lounge with a cup of coffee.

"No, I'm fine."

"You only had soup."

"I'm just not that hungry."

Snuggling into her corner of the sofa, Laura kept one eye on Toni. "This doesn't have anything to do with your eating issue, does it?"

With a snort, Toni said, "No, it doesn't. I just don't think my appetite's back yet. I'm fine."

"Okay," Laura said, gazing back at Toni. "You know, I was thinking. How would you feel if we invited Kris and Robin over one night for dinner?"

"That's a great idea, but I know they're both really busy right now."

"It's doesn't have to be tomorrow. I just thought it'd be nice if I could get to know them a little better."

"Well, I can guarantee that Krista will jump at the chance to spend an evening with us."

Cocking her head to the side, Laura asked, "Why's that?"

"Hormones."

"Excuse me?"

"I hope you don't mind, but I told her about our chat the other night."

"Of course, I don't mind, but what's that got to do with hormones?"

"Kris is having a hard time believing that we can...I mean, that we agreed to just take things day-by-day. Something about hormones getting in the way."

"I see," Laura said, trying to keep a straight face. "Well, they can be quite annoying at times."

"My friends or hormones?"

Letting out a laugh, Laura said, "Hormones, sweetheart. I like Kris and Robin."

"Just checking."

The room grew quiet and as Laura sipped her coffee, Toni reached for a book on the coffee table. Stopping mid-stretch, she said, "It's been almost seven years since I've been with a woman."

Raising her eyes, Laura said, "I've got you beat."

It took a split-second for Toni to get Laura's meaning, and forgetting about her book, she sat back and asked, "Does it frighten you?"

"What?"

"The possibility of you and I—"

"No, of course not," Laura said, placing her cup on the table. "I'll admit to being a bit nervous, but not frightened." Thinking for a moment, she said, "Actually, that's not entirely true."

"No?"

"When I first realized I was having feelings for you, I was terrified. No, I'll take that back. I was angry."

"Angry?"

"Oh, yeah," Laura said, nodding. "Until I met you, I had never even glanced at another woman in that way, and all of a sudden I wasn't just glancing. I was looking. Talk about confused!"

"So what happened?"

"Are you asking me when I fell in love with you?"

"No. Um...well, maybe."

Smiling, Laura thought about the question. "I don't know. One day I was telling myself I was daft and the next day...the next day it just felt right, and it still does."

"Good to know."

"How about you?"

"How about me what?"

"When did you know you were gay?"

"Oh, um...I was about thirteen, I think."

"And you didn't tell your parents until you were—"

"Nineteen, and you know what happened next."

"But a lot of time has passed and—"

"Don't go there, Laura. There's no point."

"People change."

"I'm living proof of that."

"That's not what I'm talking about. Somewhere out there you have a mother and a sister. I'm just saying maybe you should give them another chance."

Taking a deep breath, Toni let it out slowly. "You know, I actually think I would if it weren't for the fact that they never gave *me* another chance. They never tried to understand what I was going through. They never understood that I didn't have a choice. It's just who I was...who I am."

"Well, it's their loss if you ask me."

"You're biased."

"Sue me."

With a laugh, Toni tucked her legs under her as she gazed back at Laura. "Speaking of family, is that offer still good?"

"What offer?"

"The one involving you teaching me how to bake a biscuit."

Tilting her head, it took a few moments before Laura realized what Toni was talking about, and when she did, her face lit up. "Well, technically, you can't bake just one."

"I wouldn't know."

"Are you saying...are you saying that you want to go to my mum's for Christmas?"

"Yes, I think I do."

"You think?"

"What I mean is, I want to go, but I'm assuming the visit is going to involve more than just you, me and your mum, or am I wrong?"

Laura wished there were some way for her to temper the truth, but the trust Toni had in her was far more important than a visit to Scotland at Christmas. "No, you're right," she said softly. "We usually gather at my aunt's house. She has three daughters, all of whom are married with children, plus my father will be there, and I'm sure some friends and neighbors will be stopping by."

"Sounds like quite a crowd."

"Yeah," Laura said, unable to hide her frown.

Playing with an invisible speck on the sofa, Toni raised her eyes. "Well, I guess I'd best schedule more sessions with Abby then, huh?"

***

"When you see a man, what's the first thing you think?"

"I wonder what kind of belt he's wearing."

Wincing at Toni's honesty, Abby asked, "How about your co-workers? Some of them are men."

"True, and at first, I didn't trust any of them...except for John."

"Why John? He's your boss, yes?"

"Technically, Laura's my boss, but yeah, John runs Calloway."

"Why did you trust him?"

"I didn't at first, and it almost lost me the job, but John has this way about him. He's very calm and patient, almost humble, and even though I was a complete nutter during the interview, he still took me on a tour. That impressed me. I mean, he looked past what I am and saw...and saw who I was. It meant a lot to me. It still does."

"And what about the other men you work with? Tell me about them."

"Why?"

"Humor me," Abby said with a chuckle.

"Right, well...let's see, there's Jack. He teaches history, and Bryan, he teaches science and computers..." Stopping for a moment, Toni smiled. "And the two part-timers are Charlie and Christopher."

"Why do you like those two so much?"

"What do you mean?"

"You smiled when you said their names."

"Oh, um...well, I guess it's because they don't look or act the part."

"Explain."

Toni's eyes twinkled as she thought about the men in question. "Charlie has this big belly, kind of like Santa Claus. His cheeks are cherry red most of the time, and he's always laughing and joking with the women. You can just tell that he really enjoys what he does. It's just hard not to smile when you see Charlie."

Glancing at her notes, Abby said, "And what about Christopher?"

"He and I are cut from the same cloth."

"Excuse me?"

"He's gay."

"And that makes him trustworthy?"

"No, that's not what I mean," Toni said, scratching her head. "Maybe it is, I don't know, but he just has this...this aura about him. I honestly can't explain it other than that. He's just too queen to be mean."

Abby's face split into a grin. "Okay, I'll buy that," she said, laughing to herself as she jotted down some notes. "So...you and Laura still okay?"

"Um...yeah. We're fine," Toni said, waiting for Abby to finish, but when she saw her glance at her watch, Toni blurted, "So, I guess that's it for today then."

Abby slowly raised her eyes. "You trying to get rid of me?"

"No, but we always go over."

"I've been here less than a half-hour. Why are you rushing to end today's session?"

"I'm not."

"No?"

"No. Why would I want to do that?"

Laughing, Abby leaned back on the sofa. "You're answering a question with a question, and that's my job, so I'm thinking that something's going on. Now...what is it?"

"It's nothing."

"I'll be the judge of that," Abby said, folding her arms. "Come on. Out with it."

Pursing her lips, Toni raised her eyes to meet Abby's. "I told Laura."

"You told Laura what?"

"That...that I'm in love with her."

"Oh, my God, and you waited this long to tell me!"

"The subject just didn't come up until now. Sorry."

"'Sorry,' she says," Abby said, rolling her eyes. "So...how'd it go? Are you okay?"

"It went well. Laura's happy."

"Yes, well I figured she would be, but I'm more worried about how you're doing. That's a huge step you took."

"I'm okay."

"Just okay?"

"It's like...it's like looking through a shop window. You can see what you want. You know what you want, but you just can't bring yourself...you just can't find the courage to reach for it."

"You'll find it eventually."

Leaning back on the sofa, Toni raked her fingers through her hair. "I'm such a fucking coward."

Sitting up straight, Abby tossed her note pad to the side. "You are, without a doubt, the most courageous person I know. You've gone through more pain and more misery than any person should ever have to, and it was inevitable that it would leave some marks, but over time, those marks will fade."

"But how long does it take? How long before I can touch her without feeling fear or rage?"

"Oh, Toni, that's not a question I can answer, but you've made amazing strides. You've got to know that. Months ago, the idea of talking with a psychologist would have caused you to run from the room, but now we sit here, twice a week, and you tell me everything, holding nothing back. That takes a tremendous amount of trust and faith, but you need to realize that it's not just about the trust you have in Laura or the faith you've put in me. It's the belief you have in yourself, and one of these days...one of these days you'll find the confidence you need to take the next step. Of that, I'm sure."

"You're an optimist, aren't you?"

"No, I'm a psychologist whose best friend is in love with a remarkable, brave and beautiful woman, who just needs to be reminded of those facts every once in a while. Now, how about we make a pot of coffee? I have a few more things I'd like to talk about."

***

Eyeing the woman sitting on the opposite end of the sofa, Abby took a sip of coffee. "I'd like to discuss the women guards now. That is, if you feel up to it."

"I'm fine. What do you want to know?"

"Did they beat you like the male officers did?"

"They'd give me an occasional kick or punch, but it was never as bad as when the men did it. The women were slyer than that. They'd have others do their dirty work."

"Others? You mean the men?"

"No, I mean the cons."

"What?"

"Just like in school, prisons have their share of cliques. You have the smart cons versus the stupid ones and the strong ones versus the weak, and the women screws knew that. They didn't need to get their hands dirty. All they had to do was sit back and watch the show," Toni said, shaking her head. "How anyone can get off by allowing someone else to get hurt is beyond me."

"What did they do?"

"They knew who didn't get along, so they'd arrange that we'd all end up in the shower together. It's not easy to protect yourself when there's no place to run, standing there naked in front of four or five other women, most of whom hated your guts. It was hard to wash off the smells of that place, whilst trying to watch your back."

"Were you able to?"

"Rarely," Toni said, lighting another cigarette. "But the stench was so foul I needed to get it off my skin if only for a day. Getting beaten seemed a small price to pay for that."

Abby walked over and cracked open a window to allow the smoke to clear. If the need arose, Toni had always gone outside for a quick smoke, so her actions were both surprising and worrisome. Taking a moment, Abby looked over at Toni, trying to decide whether to continue. She was staring off into space, slouched on the sofa with her head bowed, and she seemed oblivious that Abby was even in the room. Returning to the sofa, Abby asked, "Would you like to stop for the day? We can continue this next time."

Looking up, Toni said, "No. I'm all right. I'd rather get it out now, if it's all the same to you."

"Okay," Abby said, glancing at her notes. "Did they do anything else? The women guards, I mean."

"They'd lie or try to humiliate me, and sometimes they'd just come into my cell and trash it, saying they were looking for drugs or weapons. They'd end up destroying the place, smashing my weekly pack of fags and making sure whatever clothes they did toss about ended up in the toilet. The bloody thing never flushed right, so after I scraped enough tobacco off the floor so I could have at least a few smokes, I'd spend the night trying to wash my clothes in a sink of rusty water."

"You said they lied to you? About what?"

"Anything...everything...it didn't matter. They'd say I had a phone call when I didn't, or that new evidence was found in my case, when there wasn't any. They'd tell me I had a letter or that a package had come in with my name on it, but it was all lies. I know it sounds like stupid shit, but shit like that matters when you're in a place like Thornbridge. Shit like that matters when every fucking day is a carbon copy of the one before."

"I expect it would," Abby said as she scribbled another note on her pad. Raising her eyes, she asked, "Was that what you meant about humiliation? The fact they had you believing things that weren't true."

"No," Toni said, closing her eyes. Taking a deep drag of her cigarette, the smoke slowly exited her nose as she opened her eyes. "They'd do...they'd do strip searches at all hours of the day and night. The rules say that the men can't be present when that happens, but they were. They'd leer at you as you stripped, all the while making vulgar comments about your tits or your arse, and even though they weren't supposed to touch...the rules said they couldn't touch, if you didn't bend over the table so they could have a...could have a closer look, the women screws would force you down, and then they'd...then they'd touch. Eventually, like everything else in that place, I grew numb to it. My humiliation turned into apathy. I didn't care that the men were there. I didn't care about their words, or about what the women screws were doing to me, so when their strip searches no longer got a rise out of me, they started shaving my head."

"They shaved your head?"

"Quite a few times, actually. I got used to that, too...took less time in the shower," Toni said as her voice trailed into a whisper.

Like folders in a drawer, Toni's memories of Thornbridge had been categorized, but she hadn't used the alphabet. She had used the pain. Overshadowed by boots and belts, the strip searches and beatings in the shower had been lost in the back of her mind...until now. Toni's head filled with the sound of cackling women and men shouting obscenities, and the hum of electric clippers as her hair floated to the floor. She could taste soap in her mouth, shoved there to quiet her screams, and the sting of lye cleanser as it leached into cuts and scrapes...and her stomach started to churn.

Noticing that the temperature in the room had started to drop, Abby went to the window to close the sash. Turning around, she was about to ask another question when she saw that Toni had gone ghostly white.

***

Walking into the house, Laura was surprised to see Abby heading to the kitchen with a mop and bucket in her hand. Tossing her coat on a chair, she said, "What, you cleaning houses now?"

"Not exactly," Abby answered quietly.

Following her into the kitchen, Laura cocked her head to the side. "Abby, what's going on? What are you doing with that stuff?"

"I was just...um...I was cleaning up the bathroom. Toni got sick."

"What?" Laura shouted. "Is she okay? What the hell happened?"

"She got a bit upset during our session, but she's fine now."

"Upset? *Upset*! Jesus Christ, Abby, the woman just got over the flu! Couldn't you have cut her some slack? I had her cancel Monday's appointment because of it, and I thought you'd have enough common sense to take it easy on her today."

"Laura—"

"Oh, I can't *believe* you!" Laura said, clenching her fists. "When did you become this heartless?"

"Christ, you have a temper!"

Laura spun around to see Toni leaning in the doorway with her arms crossed, and even though her face was pale, there was a glint of humor in her eyes.

"You should be lying down," Laura said, taking a step closer.

"Well, I would be except you were out here bellowing. Now I know what they mean about waking the dead."

"Toni—"

"Laura, I'm fine," Toni said, quickly glancing at Abby to offer her a weak smile. "I was a bit messy earlier, but Abby took care of me."

"But it's because of her—"

"No, that's where you're wrong. It's because of me. It's because I know I need to talk about this shit and it's not always easy. Christ, it's never easy, but it's something I have to do. We all know that."

"I just worry about you."

"I know," Toni said softly. "And I need your help to get through this, but squawking at my shrink isn't the way to go about it."

"I do *not* squawk," Laura said, narrowing her eyes.

"Okay, how about screech?"

Across the room, Abby stood quietly watching the exchange. Her smile was minimal, at least on the outside. She was well aware of Laura's temper having been on the receiving end of it before, but she had never seen the woman go from sixty to zero so fast. It was a pleasant change to see someone reel in Laura so quickly, and Abby had a feeling it was one that would be permanent.

"Well, I think this is my cue to leave," Abby said as she walked over.

"Will you have time to see me again this week?" Toni asked. "What with today's chat ending so abruptly, I mean."

"I'll check my planner and call you tomorrow," Abby said, glancing at her watch. "Oh my, look at the time. I'd better go."

"Not before I apologize," Laura said, touching Abby's sleeve. "I acted like a prat, and I'm sorry."

"Yes, you did, but you did it for all the right reasons," Abby said, patting Laura's hand. "Now, how about walking me out?"

"All right," Laura said, following her out of the room. When they reached the door, Laura pulled Abby to a stop. "Abby, I was wondering—"

"Laura, you know I can't tell you anything."

"I know," Laura said with a sigh. "I'm just worried about her."

"She's fine. We were just going down a road that we hadn't yet visited, and it got to her, but she's doing well, Laura. That much I can say."

"Yeah?"

Leaning over, Abby kissed Laura on the cheek. "Yes, now go back in there and take care of your woman."

CHAPTER THIRTY

Labeled by the estate agent as a home office, the small room situated under the stairs in Laura's house, just like the drawer in the kitchen, had held nothing but junk until Toni had moved in. Boxes of decorations meant to be stored in the attic had been stacked in one corner, and cartons filled with items not yet deemed to be junk, even though they were, had been piled in another, but once Toni's high-end treadmill was delivered, Laura decided to turn the space into a home gym. It became a place where both could visit to burn off excess energy or work out their frustrations, and since admitting their feelings to one another, the treadmill was getting a workout.

Shutting off the machine, Laura picked up her bottle of water and chugged it down. Wiping the sweat from her face with a nearby towel, she listened by the door for a moment before shutting off the light and heading to the kitchen.

"Have a good run?" Toni asked as Laura entered the room.

"Yep," Laura said, sitting at the table. "Did Abby leave?"

"Yeah, a few minutes ago. Thanks for giving up your Friday night for me."

"I didn't give it up," Laura said, glancing at the clock. "It's still early. I'm just glad Abby could see you tonight. You've been a bit out of sorts since your session on Wednesday."

"Yeah, I know. I'm sorry. That's the reason I asked to talk to her tonight. Try to clear the cobwebs."

"And did you?"

"I think so," Toni said quietly.

Thinking for a moment, Laura said, "Toni, if you don't want me asking about your sessions—"

"No, it's fine," Toni said. "I really feel bad that I kept my relationship with Abby a secret for so long, so if you want to know something, just ask. I don't want any more secrets. Okay?"

"Are you sure?"

"Yes, and speaking of not having any secrets, I also told Abby about us." Hearing no response, Toni looked up and saw Laura staring back at her. "What? Did I do something wrong?"

"No, it's just nice to hear you say *us*."

"Yeah, I kind of liked it, too."

Laura's heart fluttered, and for a moment she became lost as she gazed back at Toni, clueless that seconds were ticking by. Her mind wandered to things not yet known, but when her thoughts caused her body to pulse, Laura jerked upright in her chair. "I-I-I should go...go take a shower," she said, quickly getting to her feet. "You have any...um...any ideas about what you want to eat tonight?"

It was rare to see Laura rattled. Seemingly always in control and focused, for her to blush and stammer like a teenager caused a smile to form in Toni's heart, and slowly, it found its way to her face. Giving her reply in the form of an arched eyebrow, Toni watched Laura's cheeks darken a few more shades before she finally managed to stumble from the room.

For a few minutes, Toni sat at the table and just smiled. How could she not? Never believing that she'd ever be attracted to another, the reality of love was sinking in, and where once only fear lived, something else had begun to lurk...and she liked it. She enjoyed the banter that now seemed appropriate, the playful looks, the quiet talks, and she found herself wanting to know, wanting to touch, and wanting to love. Wiping her palms on her jeans, Toni let out a sigh and decided she'd best start dinner.

By the time Laura got upstairs, she was grinning like a fool. She had known Toni for months, and during that time, Laura had seen her happy and sad. She had seen her laugh and had seen her cry, but until now, she had never seen the flirtatious, suggestive side of Toni Vaughn.

For the most part, after admitting their feelings, their relationship had returned to that of friends, except for one thing. They both knew they were more, and things were starting to change. Mornings were no longer spent quietly sipping coffee, but instead they'd chat about their plans for the day, the meal they would cook when they got home and who was going to drive. Their evenings were spent on the sofa, each snuggling into their favorite corner with a glass of wine, and while both attempted to read the books they had chosen, more times than not, the pages didn't hold their interest. And when it was time to say good night, to bid farewell until the morning, their eyes would meet and their voices would become whispers.

Quickly stripping out of her clothes, Laura sauntered into the bathroom, her mind awash with all things Toni...totally unaware that she wasn't alone.

***

Gathering the ingredients for a salad, Toni grabbed a bowl and got to work. Laughing to herself as she remembered Laura's crimson face, Toni reached for a knife, but the blade slipped from her fingers when she heard Laura's ear-piercing shriek.

Running from the kitchen, Toni took the stairs two at a time and burst into Laura's bedroom without giving it a second thought. Finding it empty, she rushed into the bathroom...and then stopped as if she had run into a wall.

For a split-second, Toni's eyes opened wide and then, shutting them tightly, she spun on her heel and yelled, *"Laura! What the fuck!"*

Mistakenly believing that closed eyelids could somehow erase the sight from her mind, Toni tried her best to forget what she had just seen with less than favorable results. It had been years since she had seen the beautiful feminine form of another in all its glory, and while many a night Toni had been tempted to search the Internet for what she knew existed, she hadn't. Now, she wished she had. Swells of ivory with darkened centers and a dark triangle pointing to ecstasy would have been better viewed if they had belonged to strangers, but the images filling Toni's mind and heating her core belonged to Laura...lock, stock and glorious barrel.

Standing by the shower wearing nothing but skin, Laura quickly reached for a towel. "I saw a spider."

Brought back to reality by Laura's words, with her eyes still clamped shut, Toni shouted, "You saw a spider? *You saw a spider!* Jesus Christ, Laura, you scared the shit out of me!"

"I'm sorry, but I don't like—"

"Yeah, yeah, yeah, I know. You don't like spiders or heights. I remember."

"Could you get rid of it for me?"

Still cemented in place by the doorway, Toni asked, "Are you...are you decent?"

"Yes, I have a towel."

Toni opened her eyes and slowly turned around. Laura was indeed wrapped in a towel, but the fact that Toni had just seen what was underneath caused her body to throb...again. Trying to keep her eyes from devouring Laura, Toni asked, "Where is the bloody thing?"

"I don't know. I think it went over there," Laura said, pointing behind the toilet.

"Right," Toni said, snatching a tissue from a box on the vanity. "Let's see if I can find the bastard."

Looking this way and that, and believing the spider to be the size of a double-decker bus by the decibel level of Laura's shriek, when Toni noticed the microscopic, eight-legged creature in the corner, she said, "Laura, you can't be serious. This little thing scared you?"

"I don't like spiders."

"Okay," Toni said as she reached in and squished the bug with the tissue. "There you go. All gone."

"You killed it!"

Stunned, Toni looked at the crumpled tissue in her hand. "Well, what the hell did you want me to do? Invite it to dinner?"

"No, I just wanted you to get rid of it. Put it outside. I didn't want you to kill it!"

Tilting her head to the side, Toni tried to think of something to say. Unfortunately, pausing caused her eyes to wander...right up the gap in the towel that showed more than an ample amount of Laura's thigh and bottom.

Laura wasn't blind, but she was in love. When she realized where Toni was looking, Laura held back her grin and didn't move an inch. She was amazed at how Toni's perusal was affecting her, and under the pale green terrycloth, she felt her nipples harden at the sheer eroticism of the moment. She was being consumed by a look, and she liked it. She liked it a lot.

With a jerk, Toni came to her senses, and when she looked up and saw Laura staring back at her, the room suddenly felt a lot hotter. "Well...um...next time I'll try to save the little bugger, but this one's a goner," she said, tossing the tissue into wastebasket.

"Okay. Thanks," Laura purred, shifting slightly to further widen the gap in the towel.

Toni told herself not to look, but her eyes vehemently refused to listen. Finding the opening in the towel again, they ogled the flesh underneath. After a few moments, she returned to now with a jolt and immediately lowered her gaze. "All right then. The spider's gone, and I was...what I mean to say is that I'll go down and work on...work on making dinner. How's that?"

"That's fine, sweetheart," Laura said, trying to hide her amusement. "So I guess you decided on what you wanted to eat tonight?"

With a groan, Toni threw an annoyed glance in Laura's direction before taking two long strides and exiting the room.

Turning on the taps, Laura allowed the water to come up to temperature, and dropping the towel to the floor, she stepped under the hot spray. As the water heated her skin, Laura remembered the look in Toni's eyes, and the result heated her blood.

***

"What's wrong?"

"Who says there's anything wrong?" Toni asked, flopping down onto the sofa. "I'm fine."

"You're anything but, and I don't think I need to repeat—"

"I know. I know. No lies, no covering things up...blah, blah, blah."

"You are definitely wound up about something."

"*No*, I'm not!"

"Oh, Toni, who do you think you're talking to? You've been my patient for over six weeks, and that has given me more than enough time to study your habits."

"Oh, so now I'm something to be studied, am I?" Toni said, glaring back at Abby.

"Toni, our sessions always start with coffee and biscuits, but today you didn't offer me either."

"Maybe we've run out, or maybe I just wanted to be rude. Did you ever think of that?"

When Abby didn't answer, Toni looked in her direction and watched as the woman settled into the sofa and casually crossed her legs. Picking up her pen and paper, Abby knowingly smiled back.

"Christ, you're a pain in the arse!" Toni barked. Jumping to her feet, she began to pace around the room. "You know what? I don't want to talk today. How's that? Why don't you just get the hell out of—"

"Toni, knock it off."

"Abby—"

"You've come too bloody far to start this shit now! Now stop trying to avoid the subject and tell me what the fuck is wrong!"

As Abby knew it would, her outburst got Toni's full attention. She had never raised her voice in any of their sessions nor had she ever dropped the F-bomb, but she had just done both with the desired effect. Dumbfounded, Toni returned to the sofa.

"Now what's going on? Are you and Laura doing okay?"

"Yeah, we're fine. We're more than fine."

"Then what is it?"

Toni reached for her cigarettes, but then tossed them back onto the table. "Saturday is the anniversary of...of the day I went into Thornbridge."

"I see, and that bothers you?"

"Of course it does! It's the day I stopped being me."

"You mean it's the day when the person you used to be started becoming the one you are now?"

"Yes."

"Why is that so awful?"

"You're kidding, right?" Toni asked, angrily glaring in Abby's direction.

"No, I'm not," Abby said, straightening her posture. "Toni, I know that you think that the woman you once were is gone—"

"She's dead."

"You couldn't be more wrong," Abby said, putting down her pen and paper. "She's not dead, Toni. She's sitting right in front of me. Yes, she has a few more issues than she had years ago, and maybe a few more blemishes inside *and* out, but she's not dead. She's just evolved."

"Evolved? You call this evolved?" Toni growled back. "Correct me if I'm wrong, *Abigail*, oh wise doctor, but evolved normally means to improve, to change into something better than you once were, and that sure as hell isn't me!"

"It also means to develop or morph into something new. Sort of like a caterpillar into a butterfly."

"Great, now I'm a bug."

Snickering, Abby said, "Toni, I'll agree that parts of you were lost when you went into Thornbridge and other parts were damaged, but we're working on getting those back. Aren't we?"

"Yeah, I suppose."

"Have you always had problems with this? I mean, the anniversary of entering Thornbridge?"

"Yes. I tried not having a diary, but I had to keep track of my classes somehow."

"Tell me about it. Tell me about that day."

"Do I have to?"

"No, you don't have to, but I'd like you to."

Toni leaned back, exhaling slowly as she allowed her thoughts to return to Thornbridge again. "It was cold. Christ, it was so *fucking* cold, and the air tasted like...like wet leaves. The ground was frozen, crunching under my feet as if I was walking on gravel, but it was just dirt...hard, ugly dirt. The cons were shouting from the windows as I was led across the courtyard, cackling and swearing, and trying to intimidate me, but I hadn't yet lost my defiance...my confidence, so I looked up at those enormous stone walls dotted with windows and smirked at the faces I couldn't see. I was trying to be strong, but I was scared. I thought...no, I *knew* I was going to die behind those walls."

"But you didn't."

Toni glared at Abby. "So what's your point? I should be able to just put that day behind me because I was wrong?"

"No, but you didn't die, Toni. You survived. You bested the bastards, and you proved them wrong."

"It still hurts."

"Oh, I know it does, Toni. I know it does, but in time, it will become just another day."

"How do I do that? How do I *not* remember?"

"I wish I knew, but my job is to try to help you deal with those memories, and hopefully over time they'll fade, dulling into something you won't even recognize."

"Well, you've got your work cut out for you."

"I know, but I'm not going anywhere," Abby said softly. "No matter how many times you tell me to."

***

Toni stood in the doorway, looking at a man wearing a neon pink apron. Calloway had an enormous kitchen, and while staff members normally only used it to heat up their lunches, twice a week the room was filled with residents learning the basics of cooking. This was one of those days, but the class had already ended, so the only person left in the room was the teacher.

He whistled as he gathered dirty pots and pans from the counter, dropping each into a sink overflowing with bubbles. He had worked at Calloway for as long as Toni had, and even though she had never spoken to him, she now needed his help. Aware of his jovial nature and his vibrant wardrobe, Toni knew in her heart that Christopher Foster was just too flaming to fear.

Turning around to grab more soiled dishes, Christopher stopped mid-reach when he saw the woman standing in the doorway.

"Well, hello there," he said, displaying a big toothy grin. "If you're looking for Laura, she's not here." Seeing Toni cock her head to one side, he let out a laugh. "People talk, and besides, it takes one to know one. She may not be my flavor, but I'm thinking she's yours."

Feeling her cheeks begin to heat, Toni said, "I-I don't know if we were...if we were ever properly introduced. My name's Toni Vaughn. I'm the English teacher."

"John made the introduction a few years ago, but you were too busy staring at the floor at the time." Quickly drying his hands on the apron tied around his narrow waist, he stuck out his hand. "The name's Christopher."

John had spoken to the staff about Toni Vaughn, so Christopher was aware of her past and of her difficulties, but in his excitement to actually be talking to the woman, he had forgotten everything John had said. When he saw Toni flinch at his friendly gesture, his shoulders fell. Dropping his hand to his side, he frowned for a second, and then another smile graced his face. Daintily holding out the sides of his apron, he curtsied politely. "Pleased to meet you, miss."

Toni's face brightened, and even though her head dipped just a bit, she kept her eyes on Christopher. "Sorry. I have a problem with handshakes."

"No worries, love. Everyone has foibles," Christopher said softly. "So, what can I do for you? Looking to learn how to cook?"

"No. I...um...I know how to do that," Toni said, her eyes darting around the room.

Picking up on Toni's nervousness, Christopher grabbed a pair of yellow rubber gloves from the counter and tossed them to her. "Then you must be here to help me clean up, so roll up your sleeves, put on those Marigolds and give me a hand."

Looking over at the stack of dirty pans and dishes on the worktable, Toni said, "I thought the students would be assigned the cleanup duties."

"Normally they are, but it was Sally's birthday and the girls wanted to take her out to dinner. Since some of them have a curfew, I told them to scurry along, and I'd take care of it," Christopher said. Offering Toni his most dazzling smile, he placed his hands on his hips. "Now, am I going to ruin my manicure or are you going to give me a hand?"

Laughing at the man's effeminate air, Toni pulled on the gloves and headed to the sink. A few minutes later, they stood shoulder-to-shoulder amidst pots and pans needing a wash.

"You use a hell of a lot of pans," Toni said, grabbing another from the stack.

"I'll have you know it takes a lot to create greatness, and if you think this is bad you should see me at work. Thank God they've got a crew of washers at the ready."

"I heard you were a chef, and this is just a part-time gig for you. Is that right?"

"Yep."

"Can I ask why? I mean, why work here when you've got a real job?"

"You don't consider this a real job?"

"Yes, of course, I do, but...but most people don't give ex-cons a second glance, and here you are giving up your free time to teach them how to cook. I'm just wondering why."

"That's a long story."

Glancing at the pile of dirty dishes to her left, Toni said, "Looks like we have time."

Smiling back, Christopher grabbed another dish to dry. "I work in a fancy restaurant, very upscale, and part of my duties as the executive chef is to create new dishes for our clientele to enjoy. So, sometimes I go to work in the wee hours of the morning to mess around in the kitchen, and one day I found one of the women we recently hired as a dishwasher sleeping in the alleyway around the back of the restaurant. At first I thought she was a homeless person, but then I recognized her. It was funny, too, because I normally didn't pay much attention to our washers, but the night before, something about her caught my eye.

"I'm sure you probably think that washing pots and pans doesn't take a lot of brains, but where I work we use some high-end cookware, all of which requires special care. She was the only one—the *only* one who seemed to remember the instructions that were given to her. And while the other washers were scrambling to keep up, and re-washing what they didn't get clean in the first place, she never once faltered. Not once.

"Anyway, she woke up and I asked her why she was there, and she told me that she had missed the curfew at her hostel the night before and she couldn't afford to go anywhere else. I can't begin to tell you how *that* made me feel, so I suggested that if she wanted to earn a few extra quid, she could come inside and clean up after me."

"That was nice of you."

"I felt it was the least I could do, and she readily agreed. So, we went inside and while I was trying to decide what I wanted to create I told her to make herself breakfast if she wanted, and then she said the most astounding thing."

"What?"

"She said she didn't know how," Christopher said, shaking his head. "Can you imagine being in your twenties and not knowing how to make a meal? So, I sat her down and while she watched, I made her breakfast, and after she was done, I requested she make mine."

"Did she?"

"It was the best bangers and eggs I ever had," Christopher said as his eyes turned glassy. "God, you should have seen how happy she was. Right then and there I decided I was somehow going to try to help people like her, and eventually I ended up on John's doorstep, volunteering my services."

"Wait. Volunteering? You don't get paid for this?"

"No. I don't need the money, so I told John to spend it on the food we need for my class or something else for Calloway."

"That's quite impressive."

"That's what my boyfriend says," Christopher said with a wink.

Laughing, Toni returned to the task at hand only to discover she had managed to wash all the pots and pans while Christopher was talking. Pulling off her gloves, she said, "Looks like we're done."

"Not yet," he said as he pulled the pink latex gloves from his hands.

"What do you mean?"

"Somehow, I don't think you came all the way down here to wash dishes. Did you?"

"Oh...um...no, but it's not important."

Pulling two mugs from a rack, Christopher quickly filled both with coffee. "I'll be the judge of that," he said, handing one to Toni. "So, why are you so friendly all of a sudden? What's on your mind?"

Taking a deep breath, Toni said, "I need help."

"Well, you said you know how to cook, so that can't be it."

"No, but I thought, knowing what you do for a living, you could suggest a nice restaurant."

"I know several. What did you have in mind?"

"Huh?"

Pulling two stools from under the worktable, Christopher sat on one as he motioned for Toni to use the other. "I can give you the names of a dozen good restaurants, but it all depends on what you're looking for."

"You mean the type of food?"

"No, the surroundings. Do you want something with a pub-like atmosphere with dancing and music, or somewhere quieter, more intimate?"

"Oh, quiet is better."

"Can I ask the occasion?"

Pausing for a moment, Toni said, "I'm trying to change a memory."

"Excuse me?"

"Sorry, it's...um...personal."

"Okay," he said, cupping his chin in his hand. "Do you have a budget in mind?"

"Money isn't an issue."

Smiling, Christopher said, "Lucky girl, that Laura."

Feeling her face grow warm, Toni fiddled with her coffee cup, only looking up when she heard Christopher begin to speak.

"Well, if money isn't an issue, and you're looking for a romantic night out—"

"I didn't say anything about romance."

"You didn't have to," he said, rolling his eyes. "We've worked in the same building for over two years, and all of a sudden you show up down here, help me clean an enormous pile of pots and pans, all the while chatting away. Come on, do I really look like I was born yesterday?"

Sizing up the slender man whose head was overflowing with curly blond locks, Toni chuckled. "Actually, you do."

Holding his hand to his heart, Christopher said, "Oh my, if I ever feel the need to cross over the line, I'm going to look you up. What's your number?"

"Sorry, you're not my...my flavor either."

"Damn, I forgot," Christopher said, snapping his fingers. "So, where were we?"

"Money isn't an issue."

"Right. So, the sky's the limit, and you prefer romantic, or rather *quiet* places. Correct?"

"Yes."

"And when would this night on the town take place?"

"Saturday."

Jerking back his head, Christopher said, "Saturday?"

"Yeah."

"*This* Saturday?"

Toni paused, the tone of Christopher's voice telling her something she had forgotten. She had been out of circulation for too long, and while she had wined and dined several ladies in her former life, there had never been a need to go to the extreme. Casual dining had been fine...until now.

Disappointed, she hung her head. "I've waited too long. Anyplace worth going is already booked, isn't it?"

"Unfortunately, yes, but if you'd like, I can call where I work and see if I can arrange something. Will that do? I mean, if you're looking for opulent and trendy, you won't find anyplace better."

"I can't ask you to do that."

"You're not, and besides, give me one reason why I shouldn't?" he said. Setting down his coffee cup, Christopher hopped from the stool. "Be right back."

A few minutes later he returned and slid a note in Toni's direction. "That's the name of the club and the time of the reservation. I put it under Vaughn."

"I can't thank you enough for this."

"Can I be blunt?"

Pausing for a second, Toni said, "Sure."

"John told us about some of your history, so for you to be here right now, talking to me like you are, well, it makes me feel a bit like I did when I taught Kelly how to cook an egg, if that makes sense."

"Can I ask you a question?"

"Of course."

"What happened to Kelly?"

Smiling as wide as a human being could, Christopher stood proud. "She became my sous chef last year."

CHAPTER THIRTY-ONE

After waking from a lazy Saturday afternoon kip, Laura walked down the stairs just as Toni was hanging up the phone. Since Toni never answered the door or used the phone, Laura's brow creased. "Who called?"

"No one. I was calling for a taxi."

"A taxi? What's wrong?"

"Nothing. It's for tonight."

"Tonight?"

"Yes. I'm taking you out to dinner," Toni said matter-of-factly.

"You're taking me out to dinner?"

"Are you going to repeat everything I say?"

"Until things start making sense, yes, I am," Laura said, tilting her head. "Toni, what's going on?"

"I just told you. I'm taking you out to dinner, so I called to arrange a taxi so neither of us had to drive. That's all."

"That's all? *That's all?*" Laura muttered. "Who are you and what have you done with Toni?"

Mimicking the smile that now appeared on Laura's face, Toni said, "I'm still here, Laura, and I'm still nervous and scared and all those other things, but I want to do this. Okay?"

"Of course, it's okay. It's great!"

"Good."

"So, where are we going?"

"It's a surprise, but I can tell you that it's rather posh, so you'll need to dress accordingly."

Glancing at her watch, Laura said, "Wait. When will the taxi be here?"

"Well, the reservation is for seven—"

"Seven!"

"Is that a problem?"

"But it's already four o'clock."

"Nice to know you can tell time, Laura, but I don't see—"

"That only gives me a few hours to get ready. I have no idea what to wear, and of course, I need a shower—" Laura's mouth snapped shut when she realized Toni was laughing at her, but instead of getting angry, Laura's heart melted. Narrowing her eyes, she asked, "You did this on purpose, didn't you?"

"I just knew that if I told you about it earlier, you would have pestered me for details—"

"I do *not* pester."

"You most certainly do, and in case you haven't noticed, you're wasting valuable primping time," Toni said, pointing to the clock on the mantle.

Laugh lines appeared at the corners of Laura's eyes as she gazed back at Toni. "Give me one reason why I should run around like an idiot for you?"

Toni invaded Laura's personal space, and after placing a light kiss on her cheek, she said in a breathy whisper, "I hope to give you many."

***

With more than enough time to get ready, Toni took a leisurely shower and then puttered about the house in her robe for another hour before returning to her room to get dressed. With winter rapidly approaching, she pushed aside several blouses in her wardrobe and removed a gray cashmere, cowl-neck sweater. Pulling it over her head, Toni smiled at its softness as she adjusted the drape of the neck. Retrieving her leather trousers from the closet, she pulled them on and finished her ensemble with ankle-high black boots.

Looking at her reflection in the mirror over the dresser, Toni's shoulders drooped. She was in desperate need of a haircut, but

Krista's schedule hadn't allowed her to visit to do the deed. Thinking for a moment, Toni went into the bathroom and opened the cabinet. Pulling out a small bag, she emptied the contents on the counter and shrugged. Why not?

A short time later, Toni shut off her bedroom light, and glancing at the clock on the mantle as she came into the lounge, she went to the kitchen, opened a bottle of wine and filled two glasses. Taking a sip, Toni decided to grab a quick cigarette, and slipping on her coat, she stepped outside.

After a long shower, followed by an hour's worth of wardrobe selection, a petite Scottish woman stood in her bedroom wearing nothing but her underwear, her nylons and a worried look on her face. It was one thing to visit the café for coffee, or shop early in the morning before the crowds became too much, but tonight Toni was stepping outside her safety zone, *way* outside, and Laura was worried. Putting on her robe, she went downstairs, walking into the kitchen just as Toni was coming in from her smoke.

"You're not ready?" Toni said.

Laura knew her mouth was open, and she was fairly certain her eyes were a *wee* bit larger than normal, but Toni looked amazing. Her hair was shining with gel, the locks finger-combed and tousled until they were perfect, and like she had done in Scotland, her eyes were now emphasized by black eyeliner and her cheeks, with blush. She had finished the look with a blend of charcoal and gray eye shadow, and the result was both smoky and sensual.

Raising an eyebrow at Laura's bold and somewhat lascivious leer, Toni said, "Something wrong?"

"You look incredible," Laura said in a breath.

"Thanks. *You* look underdressed."

"Oh, I was thinking that maybe...maybe this might be too much for you."

"What do you mean?"

"Going out tonight. I know this is really hard for you, and if you're doing this for me—"

"I'm not. I'm doing it for me, and for us."

"Yeah?"

"Laura, this day, this *date*...it's the anniversary of when I entered Thornbridge, and I've always had a rough time with it, so I thought what better way to get rid of a bad memory than to replace it with a good one," Toni said, taking a step in Laura's direction. "Now, I'm not going to lie to you and tell you I'm not nervous, because I am. Christ, it took me half-dozen tries before I finally found the nerve to call the taxi company, but I did. I managed, and as long as you're there tonight, I think I'll be okay, and if I'm not, I know you'll take care of me."

"You know I will."

"Then please do me the honor of being my date tonight. It would really mean a lot to me."

Running over, Laura placed a kiss on Toni's cheek, and as she skipped out of the room and up the stairs, she called out, "I'll be down in five minutes. Promise!"

***

Four minutes and fifty-eight seconds later, Laura walked down the stairs wearing the red blouse Toni had bought her in Scotland, and the black skirt with the well-placed slit. Noticing that her legs had become Toni's focal point, Laura grinned. "I'm up here."

Raising her eyes, Toni shrugged and let out a laugh. "Sorry, but I really do love that skirt."

"Good to know," Laura said, all the while struggling to keep her eyes on Toni's face. Hidden by her jacket earlier, Toni's cashmere sweater was now in full view. It hugged her torso like a second skin, and the low drape of the cowl-neck piqued more than just Laura's interest. Prying her eyes away, Laura cleared her throat. "Um...new top?"

"Yeah. I got it when I went out with Krista," Toni said. "I poured some wine. I thought we'd have a drink before we leave."

"Do we have time?"

Without answering, Toni motioned for Laura to follow her and when they got into the kitchen, she handed Laura a glass. "I have a small confession to make."

"Yeah?" Laura said, raising the glass to her lips. "What kind of confession?"

"Well, knowing that you always seem to run a bit late, I told you that our reservation was for seven instead of half seven."

Eyeing Toni as she took a slow sip of wine, Laura smiled. "I'll get you for that."

Pleased with Laura's reaction to her ruse, Toni leaned against the counter and drank her wine, all the while staring at the most beautiful woman in the world.

Knocked slightly off-kilter by Toni's overt gawk, Laura asked, "Can...can I ask where we're going?"

***

Toni's anxieties began to appear almost at the same time as their taxi, but putting on a brave face, she donned her leather coat. Assisting Laura with hers, they walked silently to the waiting car. The sounds of the street and the traffic filled the cab's silence, and as Laura looked out the window at the lights whizzing by Toni took her hand and held on tight. No words were spoken or glances given, just a silent understanding that if Toni needed Laura's help, it would be there.

Having never actually eaten at The Reading Room, unless you could call a half-eaten salad a meal, Laura was thrilled when she realized she was returning to the restaurant for a second time. Getting out of the taxi, they looked up at the remodeled three-story warehouse and then slowly climbed the stairs that would take them inside.

Their coats were taken by the awaiting staff, but when Laura was about to approach the maître d' Toni touched her on the sleeve and shook her head. Drawing in as much air as her lungs could hold, Toni walked over, and in a quiet and shaky voice, spoke to the tall Indian man. Seconds later, they were led to a corner table on the mezzanine.

One floor above the largest dining area, the mezzanine was small and intimate, and far enough away from the bustle below that conversation could be whispered and still be heard. Keeping with the flavor of a book repository, the wall running the length of the upper floor was lined with bookcases that went from floor to ceiling, and each held on its shelves, volumes of literature in all shapes and sizes, covered in leather in a variety of colors.

Inhaling deeply the aroma of ink-filled pages, Toni could feel herself relax as they were seated at a linen-covered table awash in elegance. Smiling at Laura as the waiter placed menus in front of them, when he handed Toni the wine list, she didn't need to look at Laura to know that the woman was holding her breath.

After searching the Internet for two nights for all that she could find about the exclusive restaurant, like a child readying themselves for a speech in school, Toni had practiced what for most would have come easily. Quickly perusing the list of wines and champagne, she pointed to one. "I think this will do nicely."

Impressed by her choice, the waiter tucked the wine list under his arm, filled their water goblets and then went in search of the sommelier.

"You're doing great."

"Thanks, but that's just a bottle of wine. I'm not too sure about the rest of the meal."

"No worries, sweetheart. I'm here."

Opening the leather-bound menu, Toni asked, "So, what looks good to you?"

Raising her eyes, when she saw Laura's playful expression, the last ounce of Toni's fears disappeared. Sitting in an upscale restaurant surrounded by strangers no longer seemed threatening, and while her palms were indeed sweaty and her heart beat a bit too fast...neither could be blamed on The Reading Room.

**

Although Toni had found the courage to call for a taxi, order their drinks and then chat with the sommelier over the very expensive Pinot Noir she had chosen, Laura wasn't the only one surprised when the waiter returned to the table, and Toni found her voice again. Glancing in Laura's direction for only an instant, Toni took it upon herself to order their meal, perfectly pronouncing every dish, and when the young man finally walked away from the table, Toni picked up her wine and took a much-needed sip.

"I hope you don't mind," she said quietly as she steadied the shaking glass with her other hand.

"Give me a reason why I should?"

"Some might."

"They would be fools," Laura said. Noticing the wine rippling in Toni's glass, she asked, "You doing okay?"

"Yeah, just being me," Toni said with a snort as she carefully placed the glass on the table.

"You're doing great."

"Tell me that again in a few hours. Okay?"

"You got it."

***

They spent their time marveling at the architecture and atmosphere of the restaurant until the waiter returned to the table with two bowls of lobster bisque. Pouring a spot of brandy in each, he set them aflame, and a few minutes later, Laura and Toni were dipping their spoons into the creamy soup. For the main course, Toni had ordered tasting plates, one containing portions of pigeon, lamb and red deer, and the other, halibut, stir-fried crab claws and wild African prawns, and for the next hour or so, they delighted in the feast.

After dinner, they cleansed their palettes with a bit of lime-mint sorbet, and even though Laura let out a groan, emphasizing it by placing her hand on her filled belly, Toni insisted on ordering a tasting plate of desserts to complete their meal.

"So, did it work?" Laura asked, taking a sip of coffee.

"Did what work?"

"Are the cobwebs gone?"

It took a moment to understand the question, and then realizing that the memories of Thornbridge hadn't intruded upon their evening, Toni smiled. "Yeah, I guess they are."

"Good," Laura said, taking a small bite of one of the desserts. "Can I ask you something?"

"I still haven't figured out a way to stop you, so go ahead," Toni said, dipping her spoon into the chocolate mousse.

"I was just wondering...when you ordered dinner you did it so fluently."

"Silver spoon, remember?"

"How silver is silver?"

"Sterling."

After taking a sip of coffee, Laura's spoon found its way to the mousse. "What was it like?"

"What?"

"Growing up like that. I mean, Mum and I did all right, and I don't know that I wanted for anything as a child, but it sounds like you were a bit better off than most."

"I guess you could say that, and when I was young, I had no idea that other kids didn't have their own horse or tennis courts. I just thought everyone did."

"You had your own horse?"

"Actually, I had a few."

"Do you miss it?"

"My horse?"

With a laugh, Laura said, "No, silly. That kind of lifestyle."

"Oh...um...no, not at all. It was nice to have all that stuff, but once I was disowned it didn't take me long to realize I didn't miss it. I mean, family, yes, but not all the other crap."

"So, you do miss them?"

"At times, yeah, but it passes," Toni said. Pausing to take a sip of coffee, she looked back at Laura. "I envy you, your relationship with your mum. There doesn't seem to be a day that goes by when you're not talking to her or emailing."

"Speaking of my mother, I told her we'd be coming up for Christmas."

"Yeah? How'd she take the news that you were bringing your weird friend with you again?"

"You're not weird, and she was ecstatic. And she knows that we're more than friends."

"She does? You told her?"

"Yes, but she actually figured it out for herself when we were in Scotland."

"How?"

Smiling, Laura said, "She knows her daughter."

"And she's okay with it?"

Thinking back to their chat in the garden, Laura said, "Yeah. She just wants me to be happy, and she knows you make me happy."

"Good to know."

"Like you didn't already."

***

Toni's nervousness didn't reappear until they left the restaurant, and the cab ride home was quiet and introspective. Knowing that Toni had stepped way outside the boundaries of what she deemed familiar and safe, anxieties were bound to show, so Laura left her to her thoughts until they arrived home.

Walking in the door, Laura flicked on a few lights. "I'm going to make some tea. Would you like some?"

Placing her coat on a chair, Toni said quietly, "No, none for me. Thanks."

"You okay?"

"Yeah, I'm fine. Just...just tired, I guess."

"I'll bring it to your room, if you'd like," Laura said as she walked closer. "It's the least I can do after tonight."

"You don't owe me anything."

"I didn't say I owed you, Toni. I had a marvelous time tonight, and I just want to make sure you know it."

Lowering her eyes, Toni said, "I do and...and so did I."

"Good, because I'd hate to think our first date was our last."

Toni took a deep breath and then slowly raised her eyes. "Normally...normally dates end in a kiss."

All of a sudden, Laura understood Toni's nervousness. "Is that why you got so quiet when we left the restaurant?"

"I...I just didn't know what you expected and—"

"Toni, I *expected* to spend tonight at home, eating take-away and reading a book with you in one corner of the sofa and me in the other. I didn't expect to be taken to The Reading Room, or for you to arrange everything, and with that being said, how could I possibly expect anything else?"

"I guess you're right about me being a lousy second-guesser, huh?"

"Finally, she sees the light," Laura said, raising her hands up in the air.

Grinning, Toni ran her fingers through her hair. "Well, then, I guess I'll say good night."

"Good night, Toni. Sweet dreams."

Toni walked from the room, but before she made it halfway across the lounge, she stopped and closed her eyes. Taking one long breath and then another, she clenched her fists, opened her eyes and headed back to the kitchen.

Looking up as Toni walked in, Laura held up the tea kettle. "Change your mind?"

"Yes, but not about tea."

In the time it took for Toni to stride across the room, Laura's heartbeat went from normal to thundering, and when Toni came to a stop only a few inches away, Laura's eyes were drawn to the lips lowering to meet hers. Closing her eyes, she waited. Toni's cologne filled her senses and when their mouths touched, every nerve ending Laura owned sparked.

The kiss was soft and chaste, with just a hint of doubt, but as far as Laura was concerned, it was the best kiss she had ever received. Toni's lips were soft and full, tasting of coffee and mint sorbet, and even though she wanted the kiss to go on forever, when Toni pulled back, Laura didn't try to lean in for more.

Torn, her body craving the taste of the woman in front of her while her fear ordered her to run, Toni stood still for a moment, her eyes closed as she savored the flavor of Laura on her lips. Inhaling deeply the scent of Laura's perfume, Toni basked in the fragrance for as long as she could before giving in to her anxieties.

Opening her eyes to find Laura smiling back at her, Toni's face reddened ever so slightly. "Good night, Laura," she said in a breath.

"Good night, sweetheart," Laura said, lightly touching Toni's sleeve to acknowledge what Toni couldn't put into words.

CHAPTER THIRTY-TWO

While Laura hadn't had any expectations about the evening, Toni had, and as she shut her bedroom door, she growled under her breath, "Fucking coward!"

Since seeing Laura standing nude in the bathroom, desires that had remained dormant for years awakened with a vengeance, and Toni's libido refused to remain silent any longer. It had become impossible to look at Laura and not remember the feminine curves of ivory or the swells with dark pink centers, and digging deep Toni had finally managed to find the courage to kiss the woman she loved, but it was all she could do. Fear had won out again, so Toni did the only thing she could. She escaped to the safety of her bedroom.

Angrily getting undressed, Toni yanked on a pair of blue pajama bottoms and a white T-shirt, then stomped to the bathroom where she glared at herself in the mirror as she scrubbed her face clean of makeup. After making sure every speck of cosmetics had been washed away, she walked back to her bed and slumped on its edge. Looking around the room, she shook her head in disgust. This wasn't what she wanted.

Just like she had with her flat, Toni had turned the small bedroom into a sanctuary. She could close the door against the terrors of the world, but Laura was no longer a terror and Toni no longer wanted to shut her out. She wanted nothing more than to make love to Laura, to touch her, to taste...to feel, but she needed nerve for that. She needed a backbone not warped by memories of a filthy prison and despicable guards, and while over the past week, she had convinced herself that she could take the next step, she just couldn't.

With a sigh, Toni got up and opened her bedroom door a crack, hoping that the soft sounds of classical music could somehow ease her pain.

***

Lying on the sofa, her ankles crossed and her hands behind her head, Laura came to the conclusion that it was pointless. She had tried for the better part of an hour to rid herself of the smile she was wearing, but nothing had worked, and she was tired of trying.

After changing into her pajamas, she had poured herself a cup of tea, turned on the CD player and settled on the sofa. Believing that between a not-so-good book and the melodic tones of Bach, the nervous energy that filled her being would diminish, after an hour Laura gave up, tossed the book aside, stared up at the ceiling and let out a quiet laugh. She had never felt like this. Like a child high on sugar, Laura felt as if she could run a marathon or climb a mountain, and it was all due to one simple, delicate kiss.

Breathing deeply, Laura thought back over the evening and mentally patted herself on the back. She hadn't had any expectations, at least not any about a good night kiss. She *had* assumed that sometime during the night she would have to come to Toni's aid, helping her order food or drink, or possibly with a visit to the ladies' room, but that hadn't happened. And while her thoughts had drifted at times, and her body had quivered, Laura had pushed those feelings away, never once allowing them to intrude upon the evening. Memories of their first date were much too precious to ruin by pushing too hard or asking too much.

When Laura felt another flicker of awareness between her legs, she chuckled to herself and climbed off the sofa. Deciding she needed to burn off some energy if she planned to get to sleep before dawn, she headed to the kitchen. Putting some water on to boil, she went about rearranging the pantry, but when she saw a jar of heather honey on the shelf, her plans for tea changed. Spooning a bit of honey into her mug, she added a healthy measure of Scotch, and then filled it to the rim with boiling water. The scent of heather filled the room, and breathing in deep, Laura hesitantly tasted the drink and sighed at the familiar toffee flavor.

Carefully carrying her nightcap back to the lounge, when Laura noticed Toni's door was now open a crack, she debated for only a moment before going over and tapping lightly on the door frame.

**

Hearing the knock, Toni looked up to see Laura standing in the doorway dressed in gray and pink pajamas and once again, a ripple of desire ran through Toni's body.

"I thought you were asleep," Laura said, stepping into the room.

"No, I'm not tired."

"Me, either. A bit wound up from dinner, I guess. I made myself a hot toddy," Laura said, holding up the mug. "I can make you one, if you'd like."

Shaking her head, Toni returned her gaze to the floor. "No, that's okay."

Walking closer, Laura asked, "What's wrong?"

"Nothing."

"Liar."

"It's nothing, Laura...really."

Believing that Toni needed reassurance, Laura said, "Toni, I was telling the truth. I wasn't expecting anything else tonight. I really wasn't."

"Maybe I was," Toni said in a whisper.

"What do you mean?"

"Nothing."

"Please stop saying that it's nothing, and tell me what you're talking about."

Looking up for a split-second, Toni's heart skipped a beat when she found herself staring into Laura's eyes, and quickly returning her gaze to the floor, she blurted, "I love you, Laura. You're gorgeous, and I love you...and...and I want you, but I can't...I just can't find the courage. Do yourself a favor. Go find someone else to love, because I can't take the next step. I honestly can't."

With Toni's words ringing in her ears, Laura placed the steaming mug on the nightstand. Time seemed to stop as she stood there, watching the woman sitting quietly on the edge of the bed, and while

Laura had told herself a hundred times that she'd never make the first move again, she was about to do just that.

All Toni wanted was for Laura to leave so she could sulk in privacy. Refusing to look up, Toni waited and waited...and waited, and just when she was about to demand Laura's exit, a gray and pink pajama top floated to the floor in front of her.

A shockwave of want shot through Toni's body at the sight of the fabric on the floor, and the sound of her gasp filled the room. An eternity passed as she stared at the rumpled top, and even though she had told herself, *convinced* herself that her fears would always win out, they were about to be bested by an intangible thing called desire. With her heartbeat pounding in her ears, Toni slowly raised her eyes.

Laura was watching for any sign from Toni that she had made a mistake. Her palms were sweaty and her heart raced, but Laura didn't move an inch. Although a wee bit unnerved by her own nudity, when Toni looked up and their eyes met, Laura let out the breath she'd been holding. There was a need in Toni's eyes...and it was carnal.

They were perfect. In Toni's head, over and over the words kept repeating as she gazed upon Laura's breasts. Round and firm, with peaks taut and dark, they were absolutely the most beautiful breasts Toni had ever seen, and swallowing the moisture building in her mouth, she cautiously reached out and cupped one in her hand.

Laura had never added up the times she had made love, but over the years, she had experienced the pleasures of sex with several different partners. They had kissed her, plunged into her and made her moan. They had groped. They had licked. They had tasted, and a few had even made her come, but none of them with one touch had ever made her body rush with want. Feeling Toni's hand on her breast, Laura liquefied instantly.

Her hand surrounding the swell, with fingers split so as not to touch the hard and erect tip, Toni marveled at the plump softness beneath her palm. Caressing the fullness ever so slowly, she raised her eyes, and when she saw the desire in Laura's, something deep inside of Toni let loose.

She had never believed that she would ever find the strength to escape the tomb that had become her life. She had never imagined that she'd ever be desirable to another again, and she had never allowed herself to dream. She had never had a reason until now, and the reality of it, the deep-down truth that was unfolding in front of her caused Toni's emotions to erupt.

Her jaw trembled as her eyes filled with tears, and leaning forward, Toni rested her forehead between Laura's breasts and began to weep. She cried for the pain and the shame, and for the scars inside and out. She wailed for the loneliness and abandonment by family and for a bottle of vodka that she once believed would be her end. Tears flowed freely, falling from her eyes onto Laura's belly, and as she wept, Laura held her close.

Her body wracked with sobs and sniffles, it took Toni a while before she could pull herself together. Sitting back, she looked up at Laura and let out a ragged breath.

"You okay?" Laura whispered, wiping a tear from Toni's cheek.

Nodding, Toni looked at the near-naked woman standing in front of her. "You're gorgeous."

"So are you," Laura said, running her finger down Toni's jaw line.

Laura was in an odd place. While she had never been with a woman, she was smart enough to know she didn't need any instructions, but Toni had the experience and that fact caused butterflies to form in Laura's stomach. Part of her wanted to take the lead. To love this woman like she had never been loved before, but another part, the novice part, wished Toni would make the next move and teach Laura what she longed to learn.

Laura breathed deeply once and then again, hoping it would help settle her nerves, but when she looked into Toni's eyes for guidance and saw desire staring back at her, it was all the guidance Laura needed. Her eyes never left Toni's until their mouths were millimeters apart, and as their lips met, Laura slowly closed her eyes. The kiss was cautious and light, Laura allowing her lips to touch Toni's for only a few seconds before pulling away and starting again. Over and over she kissed her, and with each touch, their passion grew. In the back of her mind, Laura was preparing herself for when Toni would pull away, but when she felt the tip of the woman's tongue against her lips, Laura's center pulsed again.

When Laura had bent down to kiss her, fear caused Toni's heart to skip a beat, but then instinct and desire took hold. Her passion for Laura so strong that it squelched fears and annihilated doubts, Toni found herself wanting more. Sliding the tip of her tongue across Laura's lips, she asked for it, and when Laura opened them and invited Toni in, the silence of the room was broken by a sensual rumble snaking its way up Toni's throat.

Toni had never imagined Laura could taste so sweet. Her own flavor mixed with that of heather honey and Scotch whisky, it swirled like blended liquor and permeated Toni's entire being. Tongues danced, darted and teased as the kiss deepened, both women absorbed in the other's essence as they took from each other what both wanted to give. Finally, with lips swollen by passion they parted, and as they pulled air into their lungs, Toni's eyes lowered once more.

Laura couldn't move. She almost couldn't breathe. She was being devoured by Toni's eyes, and it was the most erotic thing Laura had ever experienced. She could feel her nipples harden, tightening at the want growing inside, and when she saw Toni reach out to her, desire flowed thick from Laura's core.

Toni sighed, her tongue darting out to wet her lips as she cupped Laura's breasts in her hands. They were to die for. She couldn't help but squeeze and fondle, for breasts this perfect were made for adoration, and unable to wait any longer, Toni ran her thumbs over the dark coral centers. Hearing Laura's throaty purr, deep inside Toni's psyche a leer was born.

Pebbled and erect, the hard tips rolled between her fingers, and spurred on by the sound of Laura's ever-increasing gasps for air, Toni licked her lips and placed her mouth over one swollen bud.

Passion soaked through Laura's knickers in an instant. "Oh, my God," she said in a rush of breath, instinctively arching in response. Enthralled by the sensations raging through her body, Laura looked down at the sight of Toni at her breast, and her knees began to shake as her imagination soared.

Tenderly, Toni suckled the tip, slowly flicking her tongue over the hardness before gently placing it between her lips and applying just enough pressure to make a difference. Between Toni's legs, the ache of her passion increased with each taste of Laura, and Toni knew one thing...she wanted more.

Lowering her hands to the waistband of Laura's pajamas, she waited only for a breath before pushing them to the floor. The aroma of Laura's desire rose in the air, and breathing it in, Toni looked up as if to ask permission. When she saw Laura gazing back at her, her face flushed and her lips parted, Toni hooked her fingers in the elastic of the black silk knickers and drew them down.

A feral groan escaped Toni's lips as all of Laura's womanly curves came into view. Her eyes traveled past the beautifully formed breasts to a belly with just a hint of roundness. They followed hips that curved perfectly, down to legs, smooth and sculpted, but then they returned to a patch of dark, curly hair and unconsciously Toni licked her lips again.

Laura had no idea how she was still managing to stand. Between her thighs lay an urgency that took her breath away. She felt as if she was being pulled into a vortex, a swirling paradise of sensuality that she didn't know existed, so when Toni guided her to the bed, Laura went more than willingly.

Together on the edge of the bed, they kissed again. With mouths opened, tongues glided in and out as they feasted on each other, but when Laura moved her hand under Toni's T-shirt, it was quickly pushed away.

Believing that their night was about to end, sadness swept across Laura's face, but when she saw Toni reach for the light on the nightstand, the problem became all too clear. "No, Toni," Laura said, grabbing her arm. "The light stays on."

"Laura…please, you don't understand."

Cupping Toni's chin in her hand, Laura said softly, "I'm in love with you, Toni, and I've never…I've never done this before. I'm not going to lie and say I'm not a bit nervous, but this is forever for me. What you and I have tonight…what we do tonight…what we *become* tonight is something I don't ever want to forget. I don't want the memory of our first night together to be filled with shadows and darkness. I want to remember this until the day I die. Please don't take that away from me. Please don't take that away from *us*."

Toni lowered her eyes, her body going limp as she let out a long, audible breath. Laura had never tried to push her too hard. She had never presumed. She had never lied, and she had never asked too much, and because of it, Toni knew she couldn't refuse Laura's request. Taking a deep breath, Toni looked up and nodded, and a few seconds later, Laura lifted the white T-shirt from her body.

In her dreams, Laura had imagined hesitation on her part, an awkward shyness of the unknown, an almost virginal moment of stumbling, but she was wrong. *Way* wrong. The sight of Toni's body added more fuel to the fire raging between her legs, and almost brazenly, she ogled the woman's near-nudity in amazement. Toni's skin was slightly darker than her own and her breasts slightly fuller, and although Laura could easily see a few of the scars, her eyes were drawn to the rose-red centers now rock hard with desire. Leaning in, Laura kissed Toni lightly on the lips before traveling down her neck and across her shoulders. Her fingertips danced softly down long arms and when she reached Toni's hands, their fingers intertwined. Lowering her head, she captured a hardened peak between her lips.

"Oh, Christ," Toni said in a breath. "Oh...dear God."

Totally aroused, Laura circled the dimpled center with her tongue before sucking hard against the tip. Again and again, she flicked and tasted, moving from one breast to the other, anointing each with equal attention until Toni pushed her to the mattress.

Everything Toni thought she had lost returned in force, and she wanted to make love to Laura until the dawn. She wanted to savor every inch and explore every crevice. She wanted it all, and when she saw the look of sheer want on Laura's face, Toni knew she would have it.

Forgotten was the fear of awakening the rage she knew lived deep within her, and mindless of her scars, Toni quickly stood and pushed her pajama bottoms to the floor. Returning to the bed, she carefully placed her knee between Laura's opened thighs, and in an instant...Toni Vaughn became who she once was.

Arching her back, Toni rubbed her body against Laura's. Breast-to-breast and pelvis-to-pelvis, she moved in a calculated slowness, and with each arch of her spine, she pressed her thigh against Laura's damp entrance. The tempo she set caused whimpers of satisfaction to fall from Laura's lips, and while Toni's pace had been one of gentleness, each time her thigh met Laura's center, Laura couldn't help but push harder in return.

Never so slick with want that she could feel it drip down her legs, Laura's thighs were coated, and desperate for release, her instincts turned animal. Opening her eyes, when Toni's breasts came within reach, Laura pulled a swollen tip into her mouth and sucked hard against the rigid point.

"Oh, Jesus," Toni hissed as lust hammered between her legs, and pulling Laura from her breast, Toni captured her mouth with hungry urgency.

Laura returned in kind, feeding on Toni's flavor and sucking against her tongue, with their legs intertwined and bodies becoming one, amidst breaths and thrums of pleasure, love-filled oaths were whispered.

Finally, the need for oxygen forced them to separate, and on outstretched arms, Toni gasped for air as she looked down at Laura...and then their eyes met. Answers were given to questions not needed to be asked, and while an infinitesimal glimmer of fear still nagged at the base of her brain, Toni slid her hand between Laura's legs, and slowly ran her finger through folds thickened and wet. Never remembering feeling anything so smooth, so soft and so slick, Toni gently rubbed Laura's sex, casually drawing her finger over every crevice, and when she finally entered Laura's body for the first time...their moans became one.

Laura was warm and tight, and deliberate in her strokes, Toni relished the feel of every millimeter of Laura's center. In and out her finger moved, pushing deep for a long, delirious moment before returning to the tender flesh soaked with want. Never wavering for a second, she continued to explore as Laura helplessly writhed under her.

Feeling as if the world were spinning out of control, Laura could do nothing but gulp for air while Toni took her to ecstasy. Each plunge seemed a bit quicker, each thrust a bit harder, and when Toni curled her finger, Laura grabbed fistfuls of sheet, arched her back and held her breath. It was building inside of her. Like a wave, it was rushing through her body to her core, and she wanted all of it.

"God, help me," she said as she pushed hard against Toni's hand. "Oh...God...help me."

An uncontrollable cry of satisfaction escaped as the orgasm swept over Laura, and trapping Toni's hand between her thighs, Laura rode every last wave of rapture with Toni's finger still inside her body.

***

Although not her intention, after a scrumptious dinner, several glasses of wine, and a climax that had rocked her senses, sleep took hold of Laura only seconds after the last wave of rapture ended. She had no idea how long she slept, but when she awoke, Toni wasn't in bed. Pushing aside the quilt, Laura quickly pulled on her pajamas and went in search of the woman she loved. Walking into the lounge, she was surprised to see a small fire blazing in the hearth and Toni sitting cross-legged on the floor, staring into the flames.

"I was wondering where you were," she said softly as she went over and knelt by Toni's side. "Sorry. I didn't mean to fall asleep." When Toni didn't respond, Laura touched her on the arm. "Hey, are you okay?"

Toni turned just enough to acknowledge Laura's presence, and seeing the dried track of tears on her face, Laura asked, "What's this?"

"It's nothing," Toni whispered.

Threading her fingers through Toni's, Laura said, "Talk to me, sweetheart. Tell me what you're thinking. Why were you crying?"

"It's...it's hard to put into words."

"Just say what's on your mind."

"Love."

"Love?"

"Yeah...love," Toni said again, staring into the flames. "Until tonight, I never understood the enormity of that word. I mean, it's just a word, right? A simple word describing how someone feels. People say it every day. They love their car or their cat, their new haircut or clothes. It's so multipurpose and common, isn't it?"

"I suppose, but there are a lot of levels of love."

"Then tell me what word I should use to describe how I feel about you?"

"I know how you feel," Laura said, giving Toni's hand a squeeze.

"No, you don't, because I'm not just talking about love."

"No?"

"I'm talking about reasons."

"What do you mean?"

Taking a breath, Toni let it out slowly. "I was watching you sleep, and all of a sudden I felt my emotions getting the better of me, so I figured I'd come out here and get my head together. Let you get some rest. So, I started a fire, and as I sat here watching it grow, I realized it reminded me of you."

"Me?"

"Yeah," Toni said softly. "At first you were just this flicker, this unexpected spark in my life, but just like the flames, you grew. And then I started thinking about all the times you asked me to give you a reason for something...so I asked myself the same question."

"I don't understand."

"Why do I feel so emotional tonight? Why do I feel like the world has stopped spinning so that I can finally catch up? Why do I know that I'd die for you without giving it a second thought?"

"Love?"

"No...hope," Toni said in a shaky voice. "You've given me hope, Laura. You've given me a reason to believe. You've given me a reason to want again, and to *need* again, and to love...for the first and *last* time in my life."

Covering her face with her hands, Toni began to cry, but this time the tears were those of joy, filled with the knowledge that humanity, her *own* humanity still existed. She was capable of love, but more importantly...she was capable of hope.

A short time later, Laura guided Toni back to the bedroom. Emotionally exhausted, before Laura had covered her with the quilt, Toni was asleep and Laura didn't mind. There would be plenty of time for love and discovery, but for tonight, Laura was content simply to hold the woman she loved. Tonight she would set aside her wants, her desires and her dreams, and take comfort in the love *and* the hope she had for the woman in her arms.

CHAPTER THIRTY-THREE

Her eyes opened, and staring into the darkness, she listened to the sound of steady breathing. Inhaling, she smiled at the fragrance of her lover's cologne, and then stealthily slid out from under the sheets. Creeping from the room, she padded up the stairs.

Laura had spent the night spooned against Toni, holding her tight and relishing the feel of feminine curves hidden beneath cotton and flannel. More than once she had been jarred from her sleep by dreams filled with erotic images, and although tempted to awaken Toni with soft caresses, Laura had simply snuggled closer and waited until sleep came again.

Stripping out of her pajamas, Laura took a quick shower, and wrapped in a towel, she headed back into her bedroom to get dressed. Opening the wardrobe, she was reaching for something to wear when she stopped and muttered, "What the hell am I doing?" Letting the towel drop to the floor, a minute later Laura left the room wearing nothing but a robe...and a smile.

Tiptoeing into Toni's bedroom, Laura was surprised to find the bed empty, and just as she began to turn toward the bathroom door, it opened and light filled the bedroom.

Still dressed in her pajamas and white T-shirt, Toni padded out, and seeing Laura standing before her dressed in a very short green silk robe, her jaw hit the floor.

Amused by Toni's expression, Laura quickly looked down and then looked back up. "What?"

"I woke up alone, and I thought...I thought it was a dream," Toni said, scratching her head.

"It wasn't a dream, sweetheart," Laura said as she walked over and pulled Toni's face to hers. "And here's the proof."

Fueled by a night filled with sensual dreams, the kiss was passionate and hungry, and as Laura wrapped her arms around Toni and pulled her close, their lips parted and tongues touched. Breathing turned ragged as hands began to fondle, but when Laura felt Toni loosen the tie of her robe, she pulled away. "And what do you think you're doing?" she asked as she moved backward toward the bed.

"Come here and I'll show you," Toni said, taking a step in Laura's direction.

"I have a better idea."

"Yeah? What's that?"

"How about you come here, and *I'll* show you."

A jolt of desire shot through Toni's body and for a moment she couldn't move...but only for a moment. Wetting her lips, she slowly walked over, and stopping in front of Laura, she croaked, "Here I am."

Laura slipped her fingers through Toni's and led her to the bed, and within seconds, she stripped the clothes from Toni and pushed her to the sheets. Gazing into eyes darkened with passion, Laura opened her robe and revealed herself, and the room was filled with the sound of Toni's gasp as Laura straddled her hips.

"I want you," Laura whispered as her lips moved close to Toni's, and as their breath mingled, their lips touched. For only a second, the kiss was light and then the passion which had begun the night before returned in force. Mouths opened and kisses grew deep as the sensual gluttony of lovers blossomed once again.

Minutes passed by until, hungry for more than just kisses, Laura sat back on Toni's thighs and looked at the woman beneath her. The green in her eyes morphed into the darkest of emeralds as she drank in the sight of Toni's breasts heaving below her, and with no hesitation, Laura cupped them in her hands. They were so full and supple, and Laura's mouth watered at the feel. Her eyes found Toni's as she tweaked, groped and squeezed, and urged on by the sound of

Toni's breathing as it grew quick and shallow, Laura massaged until the tips of Toni's nipples had become rock-hard points.

Unlike the night before when Laura had ignored the flaws left by belts, in the faint orange-red hues of early morning sun, she allowed herself to look...and to touch. Lightly, she traced a thick scar under one breast with her finger, and leaning down she ran her tongue over the welt. Another, thin and faint, was tasted with tenderness, and then she slowly bestowed butterfly kisses over Toni's shoulders, arms and chest before continuing her journey downward. Hearing Toni's breath catch in her throat, Laura secretly smiled.

Laura had awoken with a need to love. To give and to feel, to explore and to taste, and fueled by the sounds of Toni's sighs and her own desire building within her, Laura wanted to take the woman she loved to ecstasy. Things primitive meshed with things new and nerves disappeared as she moved lower, for the smell of Toni's desire was sweet, and the need to taste had become overpowering.

Already grasping the sheets in anticipation, when Toni felt Laura's hands on her thighs, she filled her lungs with air and opened her legs.

For a moment, Laura gazed at what lay before her. Glistening in the shadows of the room, passion-soaked folds beckoned her, and breathing deep the fragrance of Toni's desire, Laura tasted her lover for the very first time.

"Oh...sweet...Jesus," Toni cried out as her body arched off the bed. "Oh, my God."

Toni's flavor was dizzying. An enticing nectar of salty and sweet, Laura couldn't help but taste again and again, and placing her hand on Toni's belly to still her movement...Laura did just that. Drawing her tongue through the furrows, she lapped at the ambrosia that flowed from Toni's core. Drunk on the delicacy of the woman's flavor, Laura became bold, and spreading Toni's lower lips, she touched her entrance with her tongue.

"Oh...Christ. Laura...I'm...I'm...I need you. I need you now," Toni begged as her inner walls began to tremble. "Oh, please...oh, please now!"

Smiling at what she created, Laura wasted no time as she pushed a finger deep inside, but then suddenly she froze. She was inside the woman she loved, feeling for the first time Toni's slick, heated center and it took her breath away. For a few seconds, Laura relished the moment...and then she began to stroke.

Toni moved against Laura's finger with an urgency that even a novice could understand, and as she continued to plunder Toni with quick, even thrusts, Laura leaned down and flicked her tongue across Toni's aroused clit. In an instant, Toni's moans turned guttural and untamed, and as her bucks grew frantic, Laura sat back, and burying her finger again and again into Toni, she watched in amazement as she brought her to orgasm.

Laura felt every contraction as Toni was claimed by her climax, and as Toni rocked and groaned, Laura stared in awe. It was a pure and wondrous thing to watch another experience the sweetness of release, and squeezing her own legs together to squelch her need, Laura stayed still until Toni's movements quieted.

After Toni's breathing had slowed and her legs relaxed, Laura removed her hand and crept back up the bed. Unsure of how to ask or what to do, she lay there quietly until Toni opened her eyes.

When Toni saw the look on Laura's face, she slid her way down Laura's body and took her to orgasm...with her tongue.

***

The morning came and went with neither feeling the need to venture farther than the kitchen or the loo. Awakening each other's passion with a look or a touch, they snuggled, and they loved...and then they loved again, until, in a room filled with the brightness of afternoon, they fell asleep. A few hours later, Laura woke up to find Toni propped up on her elbow, staring back at her.

"Hiya," Laura said sleepily.

"Hi, yourself."

"What time is it?"

"Almost three."

"You okay?"

"Why do you ask?"

"Because you're staring at me."

"Is that a problem?"

"Depends on why you're staring," Laura said through a grin.

Toni brushed a strand of hair from Laura's forehead. "You're amazing."

"So are you," Laura said, her cheeks darkening slightly as she remembered the exquisite things Toni could do with just her tongue.

For a moment, they simply smiled at each other, each studying the other's features as if to memorize, but when Laura noticed a small scar on Toni's shoulder, she said quietly, "Turn over."

Taken aback, Toni cocked her head to the side. "Why?"

Laura's smile wavered just a bit, and then reaching over, she gently ran the tip of her finger over the scar. "I want to see the others."

Toni stared blankly back at Laura, unable to speak. She knew Laura had already seen some of the marks, but they were only halftones of the whole. Her back was the canvas. A masterpiece of horrors and pain, it displayed her agony in wide, deep brushstrokes of disfigured skin and corded flesh. Toni's heart began to race, but then she remembered the evening when she had ripped the T-shirt from her body. "You've already seen them," she said quietly. "That night in the lounge."

"I didn't look."

"Why not?"

"I didn't have a reason to."

"You do now?"

"Yes," Laura said in a breath, gazing into Toni's eyes. "Most definitely."

Toni wished it were dusk. Glimpses obscured by the shadows of evening would be easier, but the room was bright and there were no shadows in which to hide. Holding her breath, Toni rolled to her stomach and revealed her burden of truth.

Laura raised herself to her knees, her eyes filling with tears at the sight of the slashes. Some were thin and some were not, and some were faint while others were raised and brutal. There was no rhyme...there was no reason. They ran from side to side and from shoulder to hip. Several had cross-hatches, signs of sutures used to close gashes too deep and as Laura's tears fell to the sheets, she reached out and traced her fingers along a group of three that appeared almost identical. Running from Toni's right shoulder to her left hip, they were spaced apart like lines on a road. The outer two scars were thin and faded, but the center one was anything but. For a moment Laura assumed they had been made at different times, but then she saw another group a few inches long on Toni's left shoulder blade with the same pattern, and then another even shorter in length high on Toni's hip.

"It was the worst beating I ever got," Toni said in a ragged breath, feeling Laura's fingers on the scars. "It put me in the infirmary for over two weeks. He used a belt, but...but the buckle...he had done something to the buckle."

Tears flowed freely as Laura thought about the atrocities inflicted on the woman she loved. Violence wasn't in her nature, but in Laura's heart, anger raged. An outrage, a disgust, a contempt for those so cowardly and so, so cruel, and for a moment, for a sliver of time that came and went in the beat of her heart, Laura understood why those battered sometimes...*sometimes* took the lives of those who brought about their pain.

Leaning forward, Laura began kissing each and every scar, and as she wept and kissed, sobbed and caressed, Toni lay beneath her, her own cries quieted by a pillow.

***

"What's going on?"

"I have no idea what you're talking about."

"Are you high?"

Wide-eyed, Toni stared back at Abby. "Excuse me?"

"I asked if you were high."

"I don't do drugs. Remember?"

Leaning back into the sofa, Abby looked at the coffee and biscuits set out on the coffee table. "Then explain all of this."

Toni hadn't meant to be so transparent, and now she was worried. She had spent the weekend within a hairsbreadth of Laura, but not once had they discussed Toni's sessions with Abby. It was one thing to divulge her truths, but Toni wasn't sure she had the right to divulge Laura's as well.

Thinking quickly, Toni attempted to hide her good spirits behind an exaggerated scowl. "You know, I really don't get you. A few weeks ago, you were on my tits about not having any coffee or snacks, and now that I do, you're accusing me of taking drugs. There's simply no pleasing you, is there?"

"Nice try, Miss Vaughn, but I can see through your diversionary tactics, and they aren't going to work. You've been practically dancing around this house since I got here, and in all our sessions, I've never seen you smiling like you are right now. Now come on, out with it."

"Can't I just be in a good mood? I mean, don't I have the right to be happy, too?"

"Of course you do, and it does my heart good to see you like this, but as your doctor, I need to know what brought about this change."

"You're not going to let this go, are you?"

Amused, Abby shook her head. "Not on your life."

With a huff, Toni leaned back into the cushions and scratched her head, somehow hoping that the delay in answering would convince Abby to change the subject. Unfortunately, when she glanced at Abby and saw the psychologist still smiling in her direction, Toni gave in. "I slept with Laura."

Carefully, Abby processed the information. As Laura's friend, she couldn't be more thrilled to hear the news that the woman's relationship with Toni had moved to the next level, but as Toni's doctor, and knowing all the issues the woman had with physical contact and rage, she was more than a bit concerned. Gathering her thoughts, she took a sip of coffee and picked up her pen. "Should I assume by your mood that...that *things* went well?"

Blushing, Toni's smile slowly made an appearance. "Yeah...yeah, they did."

"What about your fear of becoming enraged when you're touched? Did that happen?"

"No, not really."

"Not really?"

"Well, I mean, I was scared at first, or maybe nervous is a better word, but then things started to change."

"Things?"

"It was...it was like Thornbridge never happened. One minute, all I could think about were my fears, and the next...it was like I became someone else."

"Who?"

"Me."

It took all Abby had to keep her grin to a minimum, and jotting down a note, she said, "You mean you became the person you used to be before Thornbridge. The one you said was dead."

"Yeah," Toni answered, glancing in Abby's direction. "Is this the part where you tell me I told you so?"

"No, not my style," Abby said, her eyes crinkling at the corners. "Besides, this isn't about who's right or who's wrong. It's about you learning how to put the past behind you and move toward the future."

"Speaking of the future, I told Laura that I'd go with her to Scotland over Christmas break."

"And now you're second-guessing yourself, aren't you?"

Constantly impressed with the woman's perceptiveness, Toni let out a long breath. "Yes, I am. I really want to go, but there'll be a lot of people around, and I don't want to ruin Laura's holiday by freaking out or something."

"You haven't had a panic attack in weeks, have you?"

"No. I've tried to stay focused when I get rattled, like you told me to, but there's no guarantee that will work away from here."

"Away from your comfort zone, you mean?"

"Yeah."

"Well, then expand it."

"Huh?"

"Expand your comfort zone."

"And how the hell am I supposed to do that? I don't know her family. How can I feel comfortable around people I don't know, or places I've never been?"

"*Make* them familiar. Talk to Laura and ask her to tell you about her family."

"What do you mean?"

"Ask her to tell you about who they are. Their names, their occupations, have her describe the way they look, the way they dress…their homes, their children. Anything you can think of."

"And what's that going to do?"

"It will make them familiar, or at the very least, it will help calm your nerves. We both know you're at your worst when you're around strangers or places you've never been, but in this house and at work, and even in the cafe where you always have your coffee, you do all right. Correct?"

"Most of the time."

"Then talk to Laura and have her tell you everything she can about her family. I'm not saying you'll be one hundred percent comfortable around them, but it should take enough of the edge off that you can enjoy your holiday."

"You think so?"

"There's only one way to find out, but with Laura by your side, what could possibly go wrong?"

***

Hearing the front door open, Toni waited until Laura shouted her "It's me" announcement before exiting the kitchen, and as Laura hung up her winter coat, Toni quietly admired the view. Her first thought was to walk over and pull Laura into her arms, but an unexplained awkwardness swept over her. So instead, she just stood in the doorway and waited for Laura to speak.

"Hiya," Laura said.

"Hi, yourself."

"Is Abby gone?"

"Yes, she left a while ago."

Slightly puzzled by Toni's cool demeanor, Laura asked, "Good session?"

"Yeah."

"Something smells good."

"Casserole...chicken and rice."

Making no attempt to hide the fact she was leering at Toni's body, currently wrapped in tight jeans and an even tighter long-sleeved jersey, Laura asked, "Do I have time to change?"

"Yes."

"Toni?"

"Yeah?"

"Kiss me."

Toni's face lit up, and by the time she took three quick strides to get to Laura, her awkwardness had disappeared. Pulling the curvaceous woman into her arms, Toni placed a gentle kiss on Laura's lips. Within seconds, *gentle*, just like Toni's awkwardness...also disappeared.

They hadn't touched since that morning, and their passion flamed instantly. Feathery kisses slowly turned into explorations, and as tongues met, hands found their way under clothing. Several minutes passed as they stood in the entry, and by the time they finally came up for air, neither had dinner on their mind.

"How long before dinner is ready?" Laura asked, glancing toward the kitchen.

With her eyes darkened by lust, Toni grabbed hold of Laura's hand and pulled her toward the stairs. "Long enough."

CHAPTER THIRTY-FOUR

"Thanks for seeing me."

"No problem. I always have time for you," Abby said, motioning for Laura to sit down. "But aren't you supposed to be at work?"

"I need to talk to you about Toni, so I left early."

Frowning, Abby sat back down at her desk. "Laura, you know I can't talk to you about—"

"No. No, it's not about your sessions. Toni tells me about them. It's...it's..." Stopping, Laura frowned. "I think I'm doing something wrong."

"In what way?"

"Sex," Laura said quietly, staring back at her friend.

Raising her eyebrows, Abby paused and leaned back in her chair. "Laura, I'm not *that* type of therapist."

"I know you aren't, but you're my best friend, and I don't know who else to talk to about this."

It only took a moment for the psychologist to disappear and Abby Parker, the best friend, to take her place. "Aren't you enjoying it?"

"Yes!" Laura said a little too quickly and a little too loud, her declaration causing Abby to rock back in her chair. Embarrassed by her own exuberance, Laura refused to acknowledge the heat now crossing her cheeks. "I'm enjoying it a lot. I just don't think Toni is."

"Why?"

"Because she hasn't touched me since Monday."

"What happened Monday?"

"Nothing out of the ordinary. We both went to work, and you met her for your session. I got home just after you left, and she seemed a bit distant, but then she relaxed, and we ended up..." Laura stopped, her face darkening yet another shade. "...we ended up burning dinner."

Tickled by Laura's obvious embarrassment, Abby asked, "And then what?"

"We eventually made it up to my room, but when I woke up in the middle of the night, she was gone."

"Gone!"

"No, I mean, she went back to her room to sleep. At first, I thought she just wasn't comfortable, new surroundings and all, but I don't think that's it. And since then, she hasn't even tried to kiss me or hold my hand or...or anything."

Mulling over what she had just heard, Abby asked, "You've been lovers since when? Last Saturday?"

"Yes."

"And you've..."

When Abby stopped, Laura looked up, and seeing her friend's obvious hesitation, Laura said, "Just ask me what you want. I'm not embarrassed."

"No, but I am," Abby said with a giggle. Pulling herself together, she said, "Okay, so...how many times have you made love since Saturday?"

Taking a moment to tally up the times, Laura said, "Seven or eight, I think."

"Between Saturday night and Monday?"

"Yeah."

Fighting to hide her smile, Abby said, "Oh my."

"Like I said, it's good between us. Well, at least it is for me."

"And you don't have any...oh, Christ, Laura, this is definitely not my forte," Abby said, running her fingers though her hair. Taking a deep breath, she said, "Okay. I'm just going to ask this and get it over with. You don't have any issues with things she may want to do...well, in the lovemaking department, do you?"

"No, none at all."

"And you return in kind?"

"Very much so."

The room grew quiet as Abby became lost in her thoughts. Allowing her friend to ponder, Laura got up and walked to the window. Staring down at the busy street, after a few minutes, she returned to her chair, drumming her fingers on the arm as she waited.

Finally, Abby looked up. "You're food."

"Excuse me?"

"You're food."

"What the hell are you talking about?"

"She's rationing you."

"What?"

"Laura, think about it. She's doing the same thing with your relationship that she did with food. She's preparing herself for when you're no longer there."

"I'm not going anywhere."

"She doesn't know that, or at least she hasn't come to terms with the fact that you *will* be there. She's afraid that if she loves you too much, wants you too much...*has* you too much, someone will take you away from her. She doesn't want to get used to having you for fear of losing you. And I'm fairly certain that she doesn't have any idea that she's even doing it."

"Why do you say that?"

"When she and I met on Monday, it was obvious she was happy. She finally admitted that you had become lovers, and I saw absolutely no sliver of doubt in her eyes, Laura. She loves you. She loves you a lot, so I'm thinking this is just a habit that's returned. A sneaky little bastard of a habit, but one that needs to be dealt with."

"Well, how am I supposed to do that? Have *Property of Toni Vaughn* tattooed on my bum?"

With a snicker, Abby said, "That *could* work, but I think maybe you should just talk to her. I told you a long time ago that there is no quick fix for what ails Toni, and unfortunately, this is a prime example. Where Toni is concerned, I'm afraid you'll be facing quite a lot of one step forward, two steps back throughout your life together. However, knowing your tenacity when it comes to her, somehow I don't think that's going to be a problem."

***

As was their norm, Friday night dinner for Toni and Laura consisted of curry take-away, and after finishing off most of what had been purchased, they sat quietly in the kitchen, sipping their wine and digesting their dinner.

"Do you consider me tenacious?" Laura asked.

"Is the sky blue?"

Laughing, Laura said, "I went to see Abby today."

"Oh yeah? Just catching up?"

"No, I went there to talk to her about you."

"Have I done something wrong?"

Laura's shoulders sagged. She could hear the worry in Toni's voice, and she wanted to cry. Reaching across the table, she took Toni's hand. "No, sweetheart, you didn't do anything wrong, but I was concerned because you've seemed a bit distant, so I wanted to talk to Abby about it."

"And what did she say?"

"She said I'm food."

"Excuse me?"

"That's exactly what I said, but then she explained that she believes you may be rationing your...your affection for me because you're afraid that you're going to wake up and discover this is all a dream."

"Oh."

"Is that true? Is that how you feel?"

Without saying a word, Toni pulled out of Laura's grasp and walked to the lounge, leaving Laura alone with her thoughts...and her wine.

Laura took a minute to reflect, and then finishing what was left in her goblet, she calmly refilled Toni's glass as well as her own. Carrying both into the lounge, she found Toni sitting in her usual corner of the sofa staring off into space. Considering her options, Laura placed the wine on the coffee table, and before Toni could react, she quickly straddled her lap and smiled at the surprised woman staring back at her. "This is where my tenacity comes into play."

As hard as she tried, Toni could simply not get angry, and slowly, her scowl turned upside down. "You truly are a pain in the arse sometimes. Have I told you that?"

"Lots of times, but who's counting?"

Gazing at Laura, Toni sighed. "I love you so much."

"I love you, too, sweetheart, and that's why I went to talk to Abby."

"I'm trying not to feel this way, but this is so surreal, you know? It's more than I ever thought I'd have after...after Thornbridge, and it's so bloody perfect that it scares me. I'm afraid that I'm going to wake up one day and it's all going to be gone. *You're* going to be gone."

"And what if I am?"

"What?"

"What if tomorrow never comes, Toni? What if tonight is all we have? What if something happens tomorrow and I'm gone?"

"Don't say that!"

"Toni, if this is the last night we have together, how would you want to spend it?"

"Laura, please—"

"Just answer the question."

Toni didn't have to think. "I'd want to spend it in your arms."

"Then stop wasting time. Stop thinking about tomorrow and concentrate on today, because if today is all we have, is this really the way you want to spend it?"

"No," Toni said quietly, and raising her eyes to meet Laura's, she became lost in the pools of green.

After a few moments of Toni staring back at her, Laura grinned. "This is the part where you're supposed to kiss me." Seeing the look in Toni's eyes, Laura knew she wouldn't have to say it again.

With a groan, Toni threaded her fingers through Laura's hair and pulled her down. Over and over they kissed, their heads tilting this way and that as they drank in each other's flavor. Invading with their tongues, they each eagerly took all that they could.

Finally, with their faces flushed and their lips swollen, they came up for air, and when Laura saw the fire in Toni's eyes, desire seeped from her core. In a voice filled with want, Laura said, "Take me, Toni. Take me here. Take me now."

Toni's response came in the form of a low, throaty growl. Quickly unbuttoning Laura's blouse, she tossed it aside and licked her lips at the sight of breasts hidden behind shimmering gray spandex. Cupping each in a hand, she squeezed and Laura squirmed, and then drawing the straps down, Toni exposed the plump rounds, their tips distended and ready for tasting. Covering one peak with her mouth while she tweaked the other with her fingers, Toni feasted on the nipple in all its erect glory. Flicking her tongue over the hard and beaded center, she pulled it gently between her teeth as she took Laura's words to heart. If this was to be their last day, it would be magnificent.

Laura was lost. She was being totally consumed by the woman at her breast, and between her legs an ache was growing at breakneck speed. Threading her fingers through Toni's hair, Laura held her in place as the woman sucked hard against her nipple, and when Toni began to pinch the other tip, torturing it with attention, Laura quickly found herself out of control.

Ravenous for the woman, Toni's hands found the waistband of Laura's trousers, and before she could ask, Laura raised herself to her knees to give Toni full access. Within seconds, the button was opened and the zip pulled down, and with Laura still on her knees, Toni pushed her hand inside.

"Oh...yes," Laura breathed as Toni cupped her sex. "Oh, Toni...yes."

Through the silk of Laura's knickers, Toni could feel the slick, wet heat of her lover, and cupping her hard, she smiled as Laura moaned above her. Again and again, she pressed and rubbed, never once venturing under the soaked fabric as Laura wriggled above her. With her breasts well within reach, Toni continued to suckle against one dark center while she relentlessly tortured Laura's center with divine friction until Laura could take no more.

"Please, Toni. Oh, God...I need you. Please...please..."

In an instant, Toni rolled Laura to the couch. Yanking down her trousers, Toni pushed aside the fabric of Laura's knickers and quickly pushed two fingers inside her lover's deliciously moist center.

Crying out in pleasure, Laura grabbed hold of the sofa cushions. Lifting and lowering her hips, she moved in unison with Toni's strokes, her needs turning wild as Toni drove into her again and again. Fingers were buried to the hilt, and each time Laura pushed hard to take them even deeper until finally she squeezed her legs around Toni's hand as spasms of pleasure erupted from within.

Toni gasped for air as she watched Laura shudder beneath her, and when she finally stilled, Toni slowly removed her fingers and climbed off the sofa.

Opening her eyes, Laura watched as Toni stripped in front of her, dropping each garment to the floor and exposing her body to the light of the room. Slack-jawed, Laura took in the view, and when Toni came within reach, Laura sat up and brazenly grabbed her arse to pull her closer.

Pressing her face into Toni's belly, she covered it with kisses as she kneaded Toni's firm bottom, and smelling the aroma of want, Laura burrowed through short dark curls and flicked her tongue across Toni's swollen petals.

"Oh, Christ," Toni breathed. "Oh, Laura. Oh...sweet Laura..."

Lustfully, Laura lapped against the tender flesh. She tasted and teased with lascivious abandon, but when Toni tugged at her hair, Laura sat back and looked up into the eyes of the woman she loved. The message they were sending was clear...foreplay was over.

With the taste of Toni swirling in her mouth, Laura knew what she wanted to do. A week before, Toni had taken her to climax with only her mouth, and remembering the feeling...remembering the absolute euphoria of that moment, Laura slowly lay back across the sofa and beckoned Toni with a curled finger.

In an instant, Toni knew Laura's intention. "Are you sure?" she said in a raspy voice.

Drinking in the sight of the nude woman standing before her, Laura licked her lips. "Oh, yeah."

Toni's jaw dropped open as she fought for more oxygen, and slowly straddling Laura's shoulders, she waited. Seconds later, her body arched as Laura covered her sex with her mouth.

Just as Toni had done to her, Laura probed with her tongue, gently pushing here and there before drawing it down one side and up the other. With Toni slowly gyrating above her, Laura uncovered what she sought and flicked her tongue over Toni's swollen clit.

The only sounds Toni could manage were unintelligible murmurs and gasps as Laura devoured her. Doing her best to take Toni over the edge with only her tongue, Laura was close to getting her wish. Between nuzzles, licks, and sucks against the engorged sex of her partner, Laura was pushing Toni to the point of no return, and frantically, Toni began to move against Laura's mouth. Each time Toni rocked, Laura teased with her tongue, flicking it here and there with abandon, and as the rhythm increased, she could feel her own center begin to tremble again.

A sound, guttural and deep, began to rise from within Toni, and unable to wait any longer, Laura parted Toni's swollen lower lips and pushed her tongue inside.

It was instant. Blood-rushing and not to be denied, it forced the air from Toni's lungs and the want from her body. Her moans grew loud as waves of splendor washed over her, and as she rode each one to its shuddering conclusion, Laura remained beneath her, tenderly lapping at the release.

A few minutes passed before, on shaky knees, Toni lowered herself to Laura's chest. Slowly opening her eyes, she gazed at the woman beneath her. "You're amazing," Toni whispered as she pushed strands of hair from Laura's forehead. "You are utterly...utterly amazing."

At the very least, Toni thought her compliment warranted a smile, but when she saw the look on Laura's face, Toni was the one who smiled. Slowly sliding off Laura's chest, Toni placed her leg between Laura's. "What do you want me to do?"

"I don't know," Laura said in an embarrassed squeak. "I can't believe...I can't believe this is going to happen again."

Stroking Laura's cheek, Toni whispered, "Fast or slow, darling? Tell me what you need, because I don't want to hurt you."

Laura's jaw dropped open, and taking a few quick breaths, she said, "Taste me, Toni. Taste me and take me to heaven."

***

Walking back into the lounge, Toni couldn't help but snigger at the naked woman sprawled on the couch. Coming to a stop in front of the sofa, she refilled their wine glasses. "Aren't you cold?"

"After what you just did to me? I don't think I'll cool off until spring," Laura mumbled as she slowly opened her eyes. Enjoying the sight of Toni dressed in only a T-shirt and knickers, Laura moved toward the back of the sofa. Patting the cushions, she said, "Sit. There's room."

Taking a sip of her wine, Toni handed Laura the other glass as she sat down. Amused by Laura's obvious exhaustion, Toni said, "I believe this comes under the heading of 'be careful what you ask for.'"

"You're telling me," Laura said, chuckling under her breath.

"You doing okay?"

"Yeah, I'm fine. I'm better than fine."

"Better?"

"I love you."

"I love you, too."

"So, are we going to have any more issues about this being a dream or worrying about what tomorrow will bring?"

"I can't promise *we* won't, but I'll do my best to try not to go down that road again."

"That's all I want."

"Really?" Toni said, her gaze slowly traveling over Laura's nakedness.

A tiny ripple of need announced itself between Laura's legs and shaking her head at the woman's overt perusal, she sat up. "Come on. Let's go to bed."

"Your place or mine?"

Toni's voice had turned husky, and the tone caused Laura's ripple to change into a throb. Wearing nothing but her smile, Laura got to her feet. "Yours. It's closer."

CHAPTER THIRTY-FIVE

"I can't believe you brought me breakfast in bed," Laura said, looking at the tray in front of her.

"I just thought it was appropriate, sort of like a celebration."

"A celebration?"

"Well, it is tomorrow and we're still here."

Smiling, Laura shifted over and Toni climbed under the sheets, pulling the tray close, so they could both nibble at the sausage and toast.

"So, any plans for today?" Laura asked, slathering a piece of bread with jam.

"Not really. Have you?"

"I thought I'd help you move."

"What?"

"From your room to mine," Laura said before taking a bite of toast.

"Oh."

"Is that okay? I mean, I just thought that since we're...we're—"

"Shagging like rabbits?"

Little bits of toast spewed from Laura's mouth. Washing what was left down with some tea, she wiped the remaining crumbs off the sheets as she playfully glared at Toni. "I was trying to be a bit more delicate."

"This coming from a woman who only a few hours ago asked for me to '*fuck her hard*.'"

Laura's face blossomed like the reddest of roses as she stared back at the woman casually munching on her breakfast. "So, does that mean you'll move into my room?"

Thinking for a moment, Toni said, "Yes, but new places are hard for me, so if I creep back down here in the middle of the night, please don't take offense. Okay?"

"That's a deal."

***

"Is that it?" Laura asked as she passed Toni on the stairs as she carried up another armful of clothes.

"This is the last bit from my wardrobe, and I think I have one more drawer to empty in the dresser."

"Do you mind if I get it?"

"Rummage through my knickers freely, Miss MacLeod," Toni chirped as she strode up the stairs.

Laughing, Laura went back to Toni's room, and after opening four other drawers in the dresser, she found the one still filled with bras and knickers. Somewhat surprised to see only a few, and that all were either white or beige, Laura gathered them up and closed the drawer.

"I see you found them," Toni said, walking into the room.

"Yeah, quite a limited selection," Laura said, looking at the cotton and spandex in her hands.

"I never thought anyone else would see them," Toni said with a shrug.

Laura would have replied, but her thought process was interrupted by a loud grumble coming from Toni's stomach. Studying the woman for a moment, she asked, "Are you hungry?"

"Maybe a bit, but I know you wanted to get this done."

Giving Toni the evil eye, Laura pushed the lingerie into her hands. "You put these away and I'll make us some lunch, and don't even *think* of saying no."

For a split-second, Toni's smile disappeared, only to return just as quickly when Laura leaned in to give her a peck on the cheek before sauntering out the door. Looking around at the empty room, Toni picked up the two books on the nightstand, shut off the light and headed back upstairs.

Walking into the bedroom, she stopped at the tall chest of drawers just inside the door, opened the top drawer and deposited her meager selection of undergarments inside. Slowly sliding the drawer closed, she turned and faced the room which had now become hers.

Like most of the other rooms in Laura's house, the master bedroom wasn't overly large, but it wasn't tiny either. With enough space to hold a complete bedroom suite, along with a small makeup table tucked into one corner of the room, it was comfortable, but not crowded.

Bright white woodwork accented walls the color of soft sage, and while the wood flooring was dark, most was hidden under a large ivory shag rug that ran just short of wall-to-wall. Two windows flanked the bed, and both were framed with drapes one shade darker than the walls. Ivory-tasseled tiebacks held open the curtains, revealing white venetian blinds that were cracked open just enough to allow the early afternoon sun to wash over the room.

The furniture all appeared to be oak, but the heavy grains had been softened by a stain in the color of buttermilk, and the duvet covering the bed pulled all the colors in the room together. On an ivory background, flowers of sage, gold and yellow weaved their way across the quilted spread, and while the pattern may have been considered busy by some, it had been calmed by a wide swath of tan fabric outlined in olive framing its edge. The bedside lamps were small and unobtrusive, and the minimal artwork on the walls consisted of only a few framed watercolors of flowers and trees. The room was feminine, but definitely not frilly.

Going to the bureau, Toni placed a few of her T-shirts inside and then perused the things covering its surface. A mirrored tray held a few bottles of perfume, a brush and the remains of a few price tags hastily removed from newly purchased clothing. Still zipped into tiny plastic bags, a collection of buttons was piled high in a shallow glass dish on one side, while on the other sat a small jewelry box, its lid opened to display a disarray of earrings, necklaces and bracelets. Smiling at the disorder, Toni walked to the makeup table and laughed out loud at the assortment of beauty products scattered about. Tempted to rearrange, or at least try to make some sort of order out of the pencils, bottles, tubes and eye shadow palettes that littered the small table, her thoughts were interrupted when Laura returned to the room.

"Sorry, it's a bit messy," Laura said from the doorway.

Turning around, Toni said, "That's okay, but I can't promise I won't try to tidy it up."

"I'll be forever in your debt if you do." Looking around the room, Laura asked, "You find places for everything?"

"Yeah, I don't really have that much."

"What about that?" Laura asked, pointing to a small box on the bed.

"Oh, that stuff goes in the loo," Toni said, picking it up. "Um...okay to put it in the cabinet?"

"Of course, and there's lots of room on the shelf in the shower if you need it."

Walking into the bathroom, Toni's thoughts returned to a day when a spider caused Laura to shriek. Amused by the memory, Toni gathered her paltry collection of toiletries in her hand and opened the cabinet above the sink just as Laura walked through the door. Tilting her head to the side, Toni smirked at the woman standing to her left.

Curious as to why she deserved such a look, Laura took another step, and when she saw the baby blue vibrator on the bottom shelf of the cabinet, she began to blush.

Tickled that Laura's face was rapidly turning into a beet, Toni picked up the toy and dialed the base, and when it didn't respond, she said, "It appears you need new batteries."

Her cheeks now flaming like a forest fire and her center quickly following suit, Laura reached up, and as she pulled Toni's mouth to hers, she whispered, "Not anymore."

***

It was a day when two became one. A day when the sun shined brightly, but neither craved its warmth. Lunch came and went, and the afternoon was spent between sheets of Egyptian cotton until bodies grew tired, and eyes grew heavy. Awakening to find that the sun was slipping from the sky, they joked about the late hour as they pulled on clothes and padded down the stairs. Weekend chores of shopping and cleaning had been forgotten, and with the pantry nearly empty and a refrigerator echoing the same, Chinese take-away would become their dinner. Over containers filled with chicken, duck and prawns, they sat at the kitchen table feeding each other morsels of food, and with bellies full, they retired to the lounge to sip their Chardonnay in front of a small fire blazing in the hearth. Taking up their usual corners on the sofa, they picked up their books, stretched out across the cushions and pretended to read.

With only the occasional crackle coming from the fireplace as wood turned to ash, it was quiet in the house. Pages were turned slowly, but no words were being read, and lost in their thoughts it wasn't until moisture opened a fissure in a log producing a loud pop that Toni was brought back to reality. Seeing that Laura seemed to be staring off into space, Toni nudged her with her foot, and when Laura looked up, Toni asked, "Where were you just now?"

Placing her book in her lap, Laura said, "I was thinking about the night when you broke up that fight at Calloway."

"Really? Why?"

"Because it goes against everything I know about you. I mean, you don't like strangers or crowds, and I'm fairly certain violence is pretty low on your list, too, so to do what you did goes against the grain, doesn't it?"

"Yeah, except you forgot one thing—instinct."

"What do you mean?"

With a sigh, Toni tossed her book aside. "There was nothing I could do when a screw went into a cell to inflict their punishment, but when it came to cons beating up cons, especially when it was just for kicks, I could never just stand by and watch it happen. When I heard those women fighting, I did what I did at Thornbridge..." Toni stopped, remembering all the bruises she had received trying to save another, and with a snort, she added, "...with basically the same results."

"Oh."

"And you've got to remember those women are my students, and I feel at ease around them."

"Why?"

"Because I'm one of them, or at least I was. I've been where they were, where they are. Lost and confused, and just trying to make it to the next day. I wouldn't consider most of them my friends, but in a way, they're my peers. They don't scare me like Bryan or Jack...or Martin."

"Martin! The doorman?"

"Does that surprise you?"

"Yes!"

"Why?"

"Toni, for God's sake, Martin is like a hundred-years-old! He's bent and frail, and dozes in that chair of his more than he's awake. How can you be afraid of him?"

Thinking for a moment, Toni asked, "Have you ever bought a book simply because you liked its cover, and then when you started reading it, you discovered it wasn't what you were expecting?"

Thrown off by the question, Laura thought for a minute before answering. "I guess. And now I suppose you're going to tell me that I shouldn't judge a book by its cover. Yes?"

"Exactly, and just like books, you shouldn't judge people by the way they look."

"I don't!"

"You believe Martin to be harmless because he's old."

"Oh, that's different."

"No, it's not. Granted, you're not judging because of color or disability, but you *are* judging."

"Fine," Laura said, holding her hands up in defeat. "But what's your point?"

"Laura, a lot of the screws in Thornbridge *looked* normal, and some were older, thin and frail as you call it. You wouldn't think that they'd harm a fly, but their belts were just as fierce and their blows were just as accurate. I'm not saying Martin is a bad man. I'm just saying he hasn't given me a reason to believe he isn't."

Accepting Toni's point with a nod, Laura leaned back into the pillows. "So, how about you?"

"Huh?"

"I wasn't the only one with my head in the clouds a moment ago. What were you thinking about?"

Smiling, Toni said, "Actually, I was thinking about you."

"Good thoughts, I hope."

"More like curious ones."

"Curious? About what?"

"I'm not sure I can put it into words without sounding…without sounding rude."

Intrigued, Laura said, "Try."

Toni reached for her Chardonnay, and after drinking the last mouthful, she placed the glass on the table and then ran her fingers through her hair. Turning to Laura, she said, "I was just wondering how someone...what I mean is...Laura, until you met me, you were straight. Right? I mean...I mean you were never with a woman before—"

"You know I wasn't," Laura said. "Does that bother you? Am I doing something wrong?"

"No! No, that's my point. You aren't doing *anything* wrong. Christ, you're doing everything right, more than right...but...but I was...I was just...oh, bloody hell!" Toni yelled, frustrated at her own stumbling.

Laura smiled. Months before, if Toni had shown the least bit of aggravation because of something Laura had done, she would have tried to calm Toni's nerves and apologize, but tonight, Laura didn't have anything to apologize for...and they both knew it. Amused by Toni's sputtering, Laura decided to save the woman from herself. "Is this because I give good head?"

It's one of the most natural reflexes, and a thousand times a day a person does it without even thinking, but occasionally a body can forget the most natural. Choking on saliva that had slipped down the wrong tube, Toni coughed and sputtered for almost a minute before her breathing cleared. Giving Laura an evil eye as the woman continued to titter at the other end of the sofa, Toni couldn't help but laugh. "Yes."

"I'm thinking that was meant to be a compliment?"

"You know it was," Toni said, settling back on the sofa. "But honestly, Laura, you just never seemed to have any issues with...with being with me."

"You mean about making love?"

"Yes."

"And the fact that I...that *we're* good together bothers you?"

"No, of course not. It's not that it bothers me. It's just...it's just that—"

"Spit it out, Vaughn. You're wasting moonlight here."

Narrowing her eyes, Toni said, "Would it be rude to ask what book you read on the subject?"

"I didn't read any book," Laura said as she sat up and swung her legs off the sofa.

"Then a video perhaps?"

"No, I didn't watch a video, either. Toni, you forget that I had a long time to come to terms with what I feel for you, and once I realized I had fallen in love with you, the other stuff...well, I guess you can say it just came naturally."

"Yeah?"

Laura paused, trying to find the words. "Sweetheart, being with you is different than it was when I was with a man."

"Let's not go there, shall we?"

"No, that's not what I mean. Look, taking the fact that I'm in love with you out of this equation, you and I are both women. Even though everyone has different erogenous zones, different turn-ons, wouldn't you say that most of ours are the same?"

"I suppose."

"And you've got to know how much I enjoy what you do to me, don't you?"

"Yes, I do," Toni said through a knowing smile.

"So why wouldn't I want to do the same for you? I love you, Toni, and I want to make you happy. It didn't take a book or a video or anything else to *show* me how to make love to you because I'm *in* love with you...and that's all the instruction I need."

***

"Tell me about crowds."

Toni looked up from her coffee. "They're large groups of people, normally found on busy streets or in shops running sales."

"Tell me about why they bother you."

"Besides the fact that they're normally made up of strangers, you mean?"

"Yes," Abby said, putting down her coffee. "Is this a tough subject?"

"No tougher than the others."

"Then tell me why you're so afraid of crowds."

Taking a deep breath, Toni leaned back into the sofa. "There were only about forty of us on the wing, and with three levels to wander around, there should have been enough room for everyone, but the only thing I had in common with the other cons was my gender. They were in for a multitude of crimes, some of passion and some of...some of pure hatred, and even though they weren't deemed insane by the court, trust me, they were. I mean, how can you kill your own children or mutilate or abuse someone and still be considered sane? And those women...they just seemed to feed on pain."

"What do you mean?"

"It was like a narcotic to them," Toni said, scowling as she shook her head. "I'd watch from across the way as they talked about what they had done and their eyes...I swear their eyes glazed over like they had just snorted crack. They got off on it. They got off on talking about the agony they had caused, and when talking wasn't enough, when their past no longer amused them, they'd look for new victims, so they'd have something else to brag about."

"And you were one of their victims?"

"They'd only strike when the wing was crowded, like during unlock in the morning or when the screws were herding us out to the exercise yard or to the servery, and sometimes I would just be in the wrong place. They were great at backing you into a corner and giving you a punch or two, but they really got off on it if they could stab you."

"What?"

"Maybe stab is too strong of a word," Toni said quietly. "They didn't have knives, just shivs made out of anything they could find, and when they got the chance, they'd use them. The first time it happened, I almost called a screw, but then I remembered where I was. Grass on another con and my days were numbered, that much I knew, so I just covered it with my hand until I could get back to my cell to repair the damage."

"How long did this go on?"

"How long was I in Thornbridge?" Toni asked, looking up.

"Wait, I don't understand. If you were stabbed, surely you went to the infirmary. Why didn't the doctors tell the guards?"

"I tried not to go to medical."

"Why not?"

"Because it was staffed by a bunch of incompetents, and the only doctor was an arrogant son of a bitch who caused me more pain than what I walked in with. I was never given a painkiller or anesthetic. He'd just pour on some alcohol, put in a few sutures and send me back to my cell. So, eventually I learned to take care of myself. The only time I went back was when I was almost beaten to death, and all

I got then was an IV with some fluids, clean sheets and a mattress slightly thicker than the one in my cell."

"Okay, but you still went a few times. Why didn't they at least tell someone what was going on?"

"You don't get it, do you?" Toni snapped. "It wasn't just the screws or the cons. It was everyone. They all wanted a piece of the pie, and as long as they kept their mouths shut, they got it."

"What do you mean by a piece of the pie?"

"Lucrative career."

"Sorry?"

"That's what the governor said he had, remember? In one of our first sessions, I told you about—"

"Oh...when he showed you those photographs?"

"Yeah, and whenever I thought about that day, all I could remember were the pictures of those poor women, but then one afternoon out of nowhere, his words popped into my head. What the hell did he mean by his *lucrative* career? I was fairly certain someone in his position couldn't take home that much money, but for the life of me, I couldn't figure out what he meant until late one night, it became crystal clear."

"What happened?"

"Earlier in the day, one of the cons had cut me, so I was standing near the window, trying to use the light from the courtyard to view the damage, when I heard a truck pull into the yard. My cell was one of the closest to the main gate, and I was forever hearing delivery trucks coming and going during the day, but never at night. So, I looked out my window and then watched as the screws filled it with the prison supplies."

"They were stealing food?"

"Not just food."

Pausing for a moment, Abby said in a breath, "They were stealing drugs."

"Yes. Judging by what they gave us to eat, I'm sure they took food as well, but it was mainly about the drugs. Thornbridge was first and foremost a prison for the criminally insane and violent psychopaths sometimes require—"

"Heavy-duty medication."

"Exactly, and that's the reason no one in medical said a word to the screws. They knew what was going on, and they didn't care."

"And that's the reason you don't like doctors?"

"You asked me once what was the first thing I thought of when I saw a man. Do you remember?"

"Yes. You said that you wondered what kind of belt he wore."

"So tell me, Abby, what do you think I see when I see a crowd or a doctor?"

Letting out a long breath, Abby said quietly, "Pain. You see nothing but pain."

CHAPTER THIRTY-SIX

"Hi there," Kris said as Toni opened the door. "Sorry I'm late, but traffic was a bugger."

"No problem," Toni said as she leaned over to kiss her on the cheek. "I just put dinner on the table."

"Speaking of dinner, what the hell is all over your shirt?"

Looking down, Toni laughed. "I had a battle with the tomato sauce, and it won. Why don't you pour the wine, and I'll be down in a minute."

"Um...okay...sure," Kris said, watching as Toni ran up the stairs.

A few minutes later, Toni returned to find her glass filled with wine and her plate practically overflowing with lasagna. "Thanks," she said, sliding into her chair.

"No problem," Kris said, regarding Toni quizzically for a second. "Sorry Robin couldn't come over."

"You know, this is the second lasagna dinner she's turned down. She's going to give me a complex if she doesn't show up soon, and Lord knows I don't need any more of those," Toni said, smiling.

"Trust me, she wanted to be here, but it was her mum's birthday, and her brothers insisted she make an appearance."

"Without you?" When all she received was an eye roll in response, Toni laughed. "Don't tell me that Chloe still hasn't accepted you yet?"

"Nope," Krista said, shaking her head. "Robin and I have been together for over seven years, married for five, and the woman still can't come to terms with the fact that her daughter is a lesbian."

"Technically, it's a civil partnership."

"True, but as far as Robin and I are concerned, we're married. Of course, as far as Chloe is concerned, we're housemates."

"Who shower together," Toni said through a grin.

"Exactly."

"I'm taking Chloe doesn't visit often then?"

"Oh, she pops in now and again, but never ventures past the first floor. I think she's afraid she'll see some lesbian paraphernalia lying about," Kris said, diving her fork into the lasagna.

The room got quiet as both continued to devour their dinner, and pausing to take a sip of wine, Krista asked, "And what about Laura? Where's she tonight?"

"On her way back from Runcorn."

"Runcorn?"

"Yeah, she and John had an appointment with the Department for Education to go over Calloway's numbers for the year, and they've got more meetings scheduled this week with some of our supporters."

"Problems?"

"No, nothing like that. It's basically a wine-and-dine thing. They thank them for all the money they gave us last year...and then they ask for more for this year."

"Oh, I see."

They returned to their meal, and after a few more minutes had passed, Toni pushed away her empty plate. Looking up to see Krista smiling back at her, Toni asked, "What's that for?" Quickly wiping the corners of her mouth with a napkin, she said, "Did I miss something?"

"No, but apparently I did."

"Huh?"

"Well, correct me if I'm wrong, but the last time I was here, you lived *downstairs*. So, I'm trying to figure out why you went *upstairs* to get a new shirt."

Toni's mouth fell open, and after fidgeting in her chair for a moment, she said, "Oh...right...well, there've been a few changes since last you visited."

Krista's first reaction was to jump out of her chair and shout out with glee, but first reactions aren't always the wisest, and as quickly as the thought entered her mind, it exited. This wasn't a conquest to giggle over or one where ratings would be applied. This was her closest friend in the world taking an unbelievably large step. Not wanting to jump to any conclusions, she cautiously asked, "Are you okay?"

Hearing the concern in Krista's voice, Toni said, "Yes, Kris. I'm very much okay."

"I'm so happy for you," Krista blurted, finally allowing her exuberance to show.

"Thanks."

"And I'm assuming Laura's okay, too? I mean, you were her first, weren't you?"

"Yes, I was, and she's fine. Actually, she's amazing."

Unable to resist, Krista leaned over and leered. "Exactly *how* amazing?"

"It took you all of what, two minutes to go there?" Toni said, laughing.

"I was pacing myself," Krista quipped.

Smiling at her friend for a moment, Toni reached across the table and took Krista's hand. Running her thumb over her knuckles, she brought her eyes up to meet Krista's. "Thank you."

"I didn't do anything."

"If it weren't for you insisting that Laura buy more apples, this may never have happened."

"She told you about that?"

"Yeah, the other night."

"You're not mad, are you?"

"Of course not, but I can't figure out why you thought she could help me?"

"I didn't know if she could or she couldn't, Toni, but after two years of seeing you show almost no emotion, when you got so bloody angry over that stupid apple, I figured what the hell. You were already so far gone I didn't think I had anything to lose, so I took a chance."

"I'm really glad you did."

"So am I."

***

Behind the walls and windows and doors of Laura's house, Toni had become who she once was. Swaggering and mischievous, her confidence level soared in the privacy of their home, but when morning rolled around, and it was time to go to work, reality always returned. After kissing Laura good-bye on Tuesday morning, Toni climbed into her old Jeep and drove to Calloway, easily returning to the routine that had enabled her to survive for so long.

Knowing Laura had meetings scheduled throughout the week, Toni didn't visit her office that afternoon. Instead, she sat alone in her classroom eating a sandwich and reading a book until she heard the sound of heels tapping their way down the corridor. Without looking up, Toni said, "You'd best have brought me an apple."

The sound of a low, sexy chuckle brought a smile to Toni's face, and it grew even larger when Laura placed an apple on the corner of the desk.

"I thought you had a lunch appointment?" Toni asked as she reached out and touched Laura's hand.

"I did. That's why I'm here."

Something in the tone of Laura's voice made Toni's smile disappear. "What's wrong?"

"Actually, nothing. Well, not really," Laura said, sitting on the corner of the desk.

"What do you mean, not really?"

"It seems our benefactors are quite impressed with our success rate."

"Yeah?"

"Apparently, out of all the rehabilitation programs out there, our repeat offender numbers are the lowest, and they're attributing our success to our teaching program...and to our staff."

"Why do I think I'm not going to like what you're about to say?"

Laura didn't have to say a word because the look on her face told Toni all she needed to know. As if the past several months had never happened, Toni straightened in her chair. Placing her hands palm down on the desk, she whispered, "Please don't do this to me, Laura."

"I tried everything I could, sweetheart," Laura said softly, kneeling by Toni's side. "But they want to meet our teachers and monitor some classes."

"You can't let them do that. You can't let them in here."

"Toni, it's because of them that Calloway exists. The government funds aren't enough, and if they like what they see, they're talking about opening another school."

"So I'm going to be on display like an animal in a fucking zoo?"

"It's not just you. They want to meet all the teachers and sit in on some classes. They'll only be here a few days—"

"Then I'll take a holiday. I have the leave time."

Laura placed her hand on Toni's knee. "Unfortunately, that's not going to work."

"Why not? I have plenty of leave. You know I have plenty of leave!"

"I know you do, sweetheart, and trust me, when they told me what they wanted to do, that was the first thing I thought of, but it simply won't work. You know how we ask all the students to rate the classes after the term is over?"

"Yeah…so?"

"Well, those forms are forwarded to the Department of Education and Skills, and copies are also sent to our sponsors, and it seems that your name kept coming up. Apparently, your students think you're a great teacher," Laura said with a weak smile. "So you see, even though they want to meet the entire staff, they especially want to meet you."

Allowing the words to sink in, Toni slouched in her chair. "Fuck!"

***

"Toni, you need to calm down."

"How can I be calm? Why couldn't she just tell them to sod off?"

"She can't do that. Those are the people that keep Calloway going, and Laura is smart enough to know that, as you should be."

"So in other words, what I want doesn't matter."

"Oh, now you're sounding like a spoiled brat," Abby said, tossing her notepad to the side. "Just because John gave you certain liberties when you went to work at Calloway doesn't mean you get to run the show, and don't forget that Laura convinced them that a full day of monitoring would be too disruptive. All you have to do is put up with them for an hour."

"That's one hour too many," Toni said as she threw herself on the sofa.

"Are you planning to allow Laura to protect you for your entire life?"

"What the hell's that supposed to mean?"

"Exactly what I said. Are your intentions to have Laura keep you safe from harm? To do all the shopping, order your food when you go out and buy you clothes when you need them?"

"No, of course not."

"Then why should you expect her to coddle you now?"

Abby's words sunk in, and with a sigh, Toni rested her head on the sofa and stared at the ceiling. "I'm scared."

"Of what?"

"Of fucking things up and making Laura look like an idiot."

"And how would you do that?"

"By freaking out in front of the suits."

"You didn't freak out when Laura monitored your class several months ago."

"True, but I doubt that I'll get away with having the class read to themselves for an hour."

"Point taken," Abby said. "So what are you planning to do?"

"I have no idea, but honestly, Abby, I just can't see myself glad-handing those people. I just can't."

***

Pulling apart the last bits of lettuce for their salad, when Toni heard Laura's "It's me" shouted from the entry, she called out, "You're late. Where've you been?"

Hearing rustling in the hallway, Toni looked up just as Laura walked into the kitchen carrying several bags filled with groceries.

"Sorry. I decided to stop on my way home," she said, placing a few of the bags on the table.

"But I thought we were going to go tonight?"

"Well, since I pass it on the way home, I thought I'd save us the bother of going back out."

"Oh."

Tossing her coat on a chair, Laura walked over and gave Toni a quick kiss. "Hiya. Whatcha making?"

"Salad…to go with spaghetti, if that's all right."

"Sounds good to me," Laura said as she started emptying the bags. "How'd your session go today? Did you tell Abby about the sponsors coming in on Friday?"

"Actually, we talked about it quite a bit."

"And?"

"She told me to stop acting like a spoiled brat."

Whipping around, Laura growled, "She *what*?"

Amused by Laura's quick temper, Toni walked over and rested her hands on Laura's shoulders. "Darling, as much as I hate to admit it, she's right. I can't keep expecting the world to stay out of my way, or for you to try to protect me from it. It isn't fair."

"I don't try to protect you from it."

"No?" Toni asked, glancing at the pile of groceries on the table. "Then why did you decide to go to the supermarket without me?"

With a sigh, Laura said quietly, "But I don't mind. I really don't."

"I know you don't, and we both know there'll be times when I'll need your help, but this shouldn't be one of them. I won't have you buying all our groceries simply because it's easier on me, and I can't let a few blokes in three-piece suits get in the way of something I love. Laura, I love to teach. I love to see those women learning to read and to write. I have no idea how I'm going to manage it right now, but come Friday, I'm going to teach my fucking class…just like I always do."

"Yeah?"

"Yep," Toni said as she placed a kiss on Laura's cheek. "Now, if I can only figure out how."

***

Relaxing in the lounge a few hours later, as Toni handed Laura a glass of wine, she said, "Tell me about your family."

"My family?"

"Yeah."

Taking a sip of the Chianti, Laura asked, "Where'd that come from?"

"Two places, actually. First, it'll get my mind off of meeting the suits on Friday and second, Abby suggested it."

"Why?"

"She thought that the more I knew about them, the more familiar they would be, and I might be a tad more relaxed...not so nervous when I meet them."

"That sounds like an excellent idea," Laura said as she sat up and crossed her legs under her. "What do you want to know?"

"Anything. Everything," Toni said with a shrug. "What they look like? What they do for a living? Stuff like that."

"All right. Where do you want me to start?"

"Well, I've met your mum. What about your dad?"

Pausing for a moment, Laura said, "Well, I'm not sure that I can tell you that much about him."

"Laura, he *is* your father."

"I told you before that I don't think of him as my father. I don't even call him Dad."

"Really?"

"No, I always call him Bill."

"And he's okay with that?"

"I don't know. I never asked, and I don't really care."

Surprised by Laura's response, Toni took a second to study her partner's face. Seeing that Laura's jaw was now clenched, Toni decided to tread lightly. "Okay...um...how about what he looks like then?"

"Oh...right. Well, he's a bit taller than my mum and slim. He's got sandy brown hair, like what you'd expect from someone who spent most of their life on the water, and, of course, he's permanently tanned. He's got..."

After waiting for a few seconds for Laura to finish her sentence, when she didn't Toni asked, "What's wrong?"

"I just realized I have no idea what color his eyes are."

"Well, it doesn't sound like you've spent a lot of time with him."

"No, hardly any. Just at family gatherings...birthdays and the like."

"Does he still work on the boats?"

"Um...no. Mum told me that he took a desk job a few years ago at one of the fisheries. He was apparently having some back problems and he couldn't handle working on the water any longer."

"Okay," Toni said, following it with a sip of wine. "And this aunt of yours, Nancy, she's your dad's sister, isn't she?"

"Yep, but you wouldn't know it by looking at her."

"Why?"

"Like I said, Bill is slender and about your height, whereas Nancy is taller and...and quite a bit heavier."

"A bit?"

Rolling her eyes, Laura said, "Okay, more than a bit."

Toni sat up, her eyes sparkling with curiosity. "Come on, out with it."

"She's just, well, a little over-the-top when it comes to clothes and things."

"Things?"

Trying to suppress a laugh, Laura said, "Right, so she's a bit large, and she has these really, *really* big breasts, and she tends to wear clothes that are quite flowery and bright."

"How flowery?"

"She could give Laura Ashley a run for her money."

"Oh my."

"And she's got red hair. Dyed, I'm sure, and she's quite, I don't know...bouncy."

"Well, with large breasts..."

Playfully slapping Toni's leg, Laura said, "That's not what I mean. She's like a bee that can't decide which flower to settle on. Whenever we visit, she's always flouncing around the house, doing this and that, all the while spouting praises about her daughters. Don't get me wrong, I love my cousins, but the woman *never* stops going on about them."

"Didn't you say she has three?"

"Yes. Alice, Dorothy and Peggy."

"Tell me about them."

"Well, let's see...Alice is thirty-six, and married to a man named Ron, who's her second husband. She has an eight-year-old daughter, Emma, from her first marriage and a one-year-old girl named Cara with Ron. She works in a restaurant, and Ron works in construction."

"She look like her mum?" Toni asked with a leer.

"No, actually she looks more like her dad. He was rather thin and tall, sort of like John."

"Was?"

"Larry died about ten years ago. Heart attack on a golf course."

"Oh, that's too bad."

"Yeah." Laura took a sip of wine and said, "Where was I?"

"You were saying that Alice looks more like her father."

"Yes, and her daughter, Emma, is the spitting image of her, right down to the freckles."

"Okay," Toni said, pausing to take a sip of wine. "Who's next?"

With her second eye-roll of the evening, Laura said, "That would be Dorothy."

"Let me guess, she's a bit like her mum?"

"The same, yet different."

"Do tell," Toni said, leaning forward in interest.

Smiling, Laura said, "Dorothy is built just like her mum, just not as heavy."

"Huge knockers, eh?"

"Will you behave!"

"*I'm* not the one who keeps bringing up breasts. You know, for a once upon a time straight woman, you sure pay attention to—"

"It's not that I pay attention. It's that...it's that they're pretty bloody hard to miss!"

Dissolving into a fit of laughter at the expression on Laura's face, it took Toni a couple of minutes before she was able to pull herself together. Wiping the tears from her face, she said, "I love it when you get flustered."

"And I love it when you laugh like that," Laura said, gazing back at the woman. "So, should I carry on?"

After allowing one last giggle to escape, Toni said, "Please do."

"Okay, so like I was saying, Dorothy is built like her mum and has the same taste in clothes, but she buys them in a much smaller size," Laura said, playfully glaring at Toni when she began to titter again. "She has red hair, too, but hers *doesn't* come out of a bottle, and she likes to wear lots of makeup, lots of jewelry, and lots of perfume."

"It sounds like she has *lots* of money."

"No, that's where her husband comes in. He's a..." The word died in her throat, and closing her eyes, Laura said, "Shit!"

"He's a shit?"

Laura shook her head. "No, he's a doctor."

"Oh, I see," Toni said softly. "Well, let's not worry about that, shall we? I mean, it's not like he's going to show up wearing a white coat with a stethoscope draped around his neck. Now is he?"

"I doubt it."

"Good, then let's move on."

"Okay, well, Dorothy seems to enjoy the fact that Bernard's a doctor—"

"His name's Bernard?"

"Yeah. Why?"

"The doctor at Thornbridge...his last name was Bernard."

"Well, this one's *last* name is Montgomery-Smythe."

Realizing her mistake, a flush crept across Toni's face. "Oh, right. Well, um...that's quite a mouthful, isn't it? Sorry...please go on."

After taking a sip of wine, Laura said, "They're actually very nice, but money has a way of changing some people, and ever since Bernard became the head of a private hospital in Stirling a couple of years ago, they've both become a bit...well, a bit showy."

"How so?"

"Fancy cars, fancy clothes and lots of holidays to places far, far away."

"Sounds like they're living the life."

"Oh, yeah, but like I said, they're good people, just a little overblown at times."

"They have kids, too?"

"As a matter of fact, Dorothy just had her second, Neville, this past July, which is actually kind of surprising because after Myles, I doubt I would have ever tried again."

"Why's that? Is something wrong with him?"

Laura's eyes creased at the corners. "Nothing that a good swift swat on the arse couldn't cure."

"A bit of a brat, I'm guessing?"

"Yes, but it's not really his fault. Everything seemed to happen for Dorothy and Bernard at the same time. Bernard was offered a job in Stirling, so they moved back to Scotland shortly before Myles was born, and not long after that, Bernard's career took off like a house on fire. So, while they were attending hospital functions, rubbing elbows with those who could help further Bernard's career, Myles stayed at home with his nannies. The problem was, whenever his parents did come home, they'd lavish him with gifts, and he apparently got used to it. Mum told me that Myles wasn't too happy to learn he'd soon have to share, so I can just imagine what he's like now."

"Well, we won't have long before we find out," Toni said, taking a sip of wine. "Okay, so far we've got a father you don't know, a cousin with freckles, a construction worker, a doctor, an aunt and a cousin who are both well-endowed, and a brat. Who's next?"

"That would be Peggy," Laura said with a smile. "She's my age and married to Stephen, who's a firefighter in Falkirk. They have two boys. Paul, who's five, and Gavin, who's three, and their third is due in February."

"Wow."

"Yes, well, Peggy always said she wanted a big family and so did Stephen, so I guess they're going to get their wish."

"And how about you? Do you want a big family?"

"I hadn't really thought about it."

"Liar."

"A bit too soon to talk about that, don't ya think?"

"It's just talk, and I think I'd best know what I'm getting myself into. Don't you?"

"Well, since you put it that way, yes, I'd like to have a few kids."

"How many, *exactly*, is a few?"

"I don't know, three or...or maybe four."

"Four!" Toni blurted. Quickly regrouping, she said, "Well, I guess I should consider myself lucky that you weren't going for an even half-dozen."

Biting her lip, Laura stared back at Toni.

"You've *got* to be kidding," Toni said, her eyes opening wide. "Six!"

"What can I say, I've always wanted a big family," Laura said quietly.

The room fell silent, and for a few moments, they simply stared at one another until Laura whispered, "Are we going to have kids, Toni?"

Toni tilted her head to the side as if to ponder the question, even though she already knew the answer. "Yeah, I think we are, but I can't promise—"

"I'm not asking for promises, Toni. Like you said, this is just talk. No worries."

Toni didn't think it was possible to love Laura any more, but it seemed as each day passed her love for Laura grew. She had become Toni's anchor. Weighted with honesty and caring, her words soothed and Toni knew there wouldn't be worries, not as long as Laura was by her side. Curling her finger at the woman, Toni said, "Come here."

Smiling, Laura slowly crawled across the sofa, and snuggling against the woman she loved, she pressed her mouth to Toni's. The kiss was slow and sensual, and with no need to rush, seconds turned into minutes as their lips touched again and again...and again. A short time later, their blood heated and their breathing ragged, hand in hand they climbed the stairs together.

CHAPTER THIRTY-SEVEN

Seventeen minutes. She had spent four days trying to ready herself for what was about to happen in seventeen minutes, and while she was sure that she had managed to clear one hurdle, the second was impossible. Toni was prepared to teach as she always had. To instruct, to listen and to guide would not be the problem, but the ritualistic greeting that so many took for granted would be her undoing...and she knew it.

Although it was their custom to carpool on Fridays, unsure if the contributors would want any additional time at the end of the day, Laura had suggested that they take two cars, and Toni jumped at the chance. Throughout the night, she had tossed and turned, and when she awoke, the thought of food had caused her stomach to flip, so after drinking a quick cup of coffee, she was out the door. And now, sixteen minutes before she would unravel in front of strangers, her belly began to boil over.

Feeling the bile rise in her throat, Toni jumped to her feet. Running out of the classroom as fast as she could, she sprinted down the corridor to the staff restroom. Fumbling in her pocket for the keys, when the door suddenly opened from within, she pushed past a startled Susan Grant and darted across the room. Sliding to her knees in front of the toilet, Toni emptied her stomach into the white porcelain fixture.

Susan didn't think twice. Locking the door, she grabbed some towels from the dispenser, ran them under some cold water and then went over to where Toni was kneeling. Blanching at the sound of the woman's heaving, Susan waited quietly by her side, and as she did, her eyes shifted to the gap between Toni's trousers and her cardigan. Quickly covering her mouth to prevent her gasp from escaping, Susan turned away as her eyes grew moist. She knew of Toni's past, but knowing and seeing were two different things and nothing could have prepared her for the horrific scars she had just seen. Realizing that Toni had quieted, Susan pulled herself together, knelt by Toni's side and held out the towels. "Here, take these."

Unaware that she wasn't alone, Toni's first instinct was to shrink away, but when she looked up and saw Susan, Toni relaxed against the wall and took the towels from her hand.

"Thanks," Toni croaked, wiping the sweat from her brow.

"Are you okay? Do you want me to call Laura?"

"No, I'm fine."

"But you're ill."

With a huff, Toni leaned her head against the wall. "I'm not sick. I'm nervous. There's a difference." Raking her fingers through her hair, she said, "Just leave me alone. I'll be fine."

A few months earlier, under an overhang in the rain, Susan had had her first conversation with Toni Vaughn. While it was hardly profound, centering mostly on the weather and the whereabouts of Laura MacLeod, it was still a conversation. Since that day, Susan had made it a point to take her cigarette breaks whenever Toni did, excited that the reclusive teacher had finally begun to come out of her shell. Now, kneeling on the floor next to her, leaving Toni alone was the last thing on Susan's mind. "Tell me what I can do."

"How about becoming me for the next hour," Toni said with a huff, tossing the damp towels in the rubbish bin.

Pausing for a moment, Susan asked, "Is this about Jacoby, Wilkinson and Bennett?"

"Who?"

"The men doing the tour today," Susan said. "You know, they really aren't that bad."

"They've already monitored your class?"

"Yes, first thing this morning. Laura brought them up and introduced them, and after a few handshakes, they went to the back of the room, took their seats and were quiet as mice for the entire hour. I didn't even know they were there, so I really don't think you have anything to worry about. Just teach your class like you always do, and you'll be fine."

"It's not the teaching part that has me worried."

"No?"

"I've spent all week gearing up for it, so I'm certain...well, I'm *fairly* certain I can handle that part."

"Then what made you just lose your lunch...or was that your breakfast?" Susan asked, dimples forming as she glanced toward the toilet.

Snorting, Toni said, "It was my breakfast. What there was of it."

"You know, if you tell me what's wrong, I might be able to help."

"No offense, but I doubt it."

"Then there's no reason why you can't tell me what's got you so wound up, now is there?"

Pausing for a moment, Toni let out a sigh. "I don't like to be touched. Okay? And I've got a huge problem with trusting strangers, especially men, and in..." Pausing to look at her watch, Toni's heart skipped a beat. "...and in nine minutes, three of the bastards are going to walk into my classroom and expect me to shake their hands, and I can't do it. I bloody can't do it!"

The fear in Toni's voice broke Susan's heart, and with the vision of Toni's scars still in her head, Susan was close to tears. In silence, she racked her brain, trying to think of some way to help, and then all of a sudden she jumped to her feet. "Stay here."

"What?"

"Lock the door when I leave and don't let anyone in. I'll be back in a minute."

"What are you going to do?"

Opening the door, Susan looked in Toni's direction. "I'm going to ask you to trust me, Toni. Just let me in when I get back, and I promise you, the...the *bastards* won't touch you."

***

"Got a minute?"

Looking up from her desk, Laura smiled as John walked into her office. Glancing at her watch as he sat in one of the chairs facing her desk, she said, "I've got about fifteen, or do our visitors need me?"

"No, they're fine. They wanted some one-on-one time with our students, so I dropped them off in the lounge."

"Oh, okay. So, what's up?"

"I'm not sure how I should say this," John said, rubbing his jaw.

"What's wrong? I thought they were enjoying their visit."

"What? Oh, no, Laura, this isn't about them."

"No?"

"No...it's about you, or rather it's about some rumors that are going around Calloway about you and Toni Vaughn."

"What kind of rumors?"

"Well, we all know that you two are housemates, but some of the women are starting to...well, they're starting to insinuate that you're more than just friends, if you get my drift."

Laura put down her pen, leaned back in her chair and folded her arms. "And what if what they're saying is true?"

John's eyes nearly came out of their sockets as he stared back at Laura. "Really?"

Without uttering a word, Laura simply nodded in reply.

"Well, I'll be damned," John said in a whisper.

"Is this going to be a problem, John?"

Noticing Laura's stern expression, John grinned. "There's a whole chapter in our rule book about consorting with students, Laura, but as far as I know, teachers are fair game."

Tickled by John's response, Laura asked, "And how about you? Is this going to bother you?"

"Laura, I'm a live-and-let-live kind of man. You should know that by now, and besides, if you remember, Christopher's gay and that's never bothered me. Why should this be any different?"

Smiling, Laura let out the breath she had been holding. "Thanks."

"You're welcome," he said as he stood up. "And speaking of Toni, how did she do today with the tour? Over the past few months, I've noticed a change in her, but I wasn't sure if she'd be able to handle strangers in her classroom yet."

"Actually, that's the next class they're monitoring."

"Oh, I would have thought you'd have arranged to get that out of the way first thing, for Toni's sake, that is."

"I would have, but they practically demanded to see her teach the remedial reading class, and unfortunately, that's her last class of the day. I couldn't very well say no, now could I?"

"Not with all the money they're talking about giving us."

"Exactly, and Toni seemed okay this morning. A bit nervous, but she's had the whole week to get ready for this, so I think she'll be just fine."

"And if she isn't?"

Seeing the worried look on John's face, she gave him a wink. "Don't worry, John. She'll be fine. Trust me."

***

Running into the house, Laura tossed her handbag on a chair and whipped out of her coat. "I'm home! Where are you?"

"I'm in here," Toni called back.

Rushing to the kitchen, Laura rounded the corner just in time to see Toni remove what was left of the bandage wrapped around her right hand.

"What the hell did you do to your hand?" Laura asked, quickly pushing aside the gauze to examine the injury. Seeing the skin clear of cuts or scrapes, she said, "I don't understand."

"It was Susan's idea," Toni said, throwing away the bandage.

"Susan? Susan Grant?"

"Yeah. I had a bit of a...well, a nervous stomach, and I ran into her in the loo."

"You were sick?"

"I was wound up, Laura, and when Susan asked me what was wrong, I told her. I knew I could teach the bloody class, but the handshaking. I just...I just couldn't do it, and she came up with the idea of the bandage. Apparently, a few years back, she had cut her hand just before a conference and spent the entire weekend unable to offer a proper greeting because of it."

"But you're okay?"

"I'm fine," Toni said, flexing her hand. "And I think I pulled it off. Don't you?"

Relieved, Laura let out a long, loud sigh. "You were amazing, and they loved your class. They couldn't stop talking about it."

"Then we should celebrate, and since I think I still have at least an ounce or two of courage left in me today, how about you take me out to dinner?"

"Really? Are you sure?"

"I'm sure. As long as it's quiet and not too busy. Okay?"

"Doable. Very doable. Just let me go up and change, and we can go," Laura said, quickly placing a kiss on Toni's cheek before she darted from the room.

Pouring herself a cup of coffee, Toni leaned against the counter and smiled.

Earlier that afternoon, Laura had led three rather distinguished gentlemen into Toni's classroom. Although she noticed Laura's eyes bulge at the sight of the bandage wrapped around her hand, Laura never said a word, but instead went about the introductions. The first man immediately offered his hand, and sheepishly Toni held up hers. Nodding his understanding, he expressed concern for her injury, which Toni quickly shrugged off, and after being escorted to their seats in the back of the room, for the next hour they watched and listened as Toni taught.

Toni's day had started with a belly churning with anxiety and absolutely no confidence, but as she sipped her coffee, she realized that not only had her confidence returned, it had done so with a vengeance. Placing her cup on the counter, she sauntered from the room, and as she trotted up the stairs, she had only one thing on her mind...and it wasn't dinner.

Getting to the bedroom, Toni leaned against the door frame and quietly sniggered at the mess Laura had created in only a matter of minutes. Her suit jacket and skirt had been tossed onto the bed, and her low-heeled black pumps had been kicked off near the wardrobe. A few clothing choices that had been pulled from their hangers now lay in a heap at the foot of the bed, and the assortment of makeup Toni had straightened just that morning was now, again, covering the surface of the low, boxy table.

Shaken from her thoughts as Laura walked from the bathroom wearing jeans and a brushed cotton shirt, Toni gestured toward the mess. "Couldn't decide what to wear?"

Well aware of her ability to destroy a room whilst picking out clothes, Laura giggled at the disarray. Sitting at the makeup table to make a few adjustments, she looked in the mirror at Toni's reflection. "I wasn't sure if you wanted formal or casual, and then I remembered that little bistro we pass on the way to work. I thought we'd try there tonight. Okay?"

"Sounds good to me," Toni said as she strolled across the room. Placing her hands on Laura's shoulders, Toni leaned down and placed a soft kiss on her neck.

Unconsciously, Laura moved to allow Toni more room. Enjoying the sensation of her lips against her skin, when Toni began to nibble her earlobe, Laura grinned. "What are you doing?"

"Saying hello," Toni whispered.

Laura's body reacted instantly to Toni's ministrations, and her words spilled out in a breath. "But you already did that."

"True," Toni said as she reached around and slowly began to unbutton Laura's shirt. "But I didn't use my hands."

Inhaling sharply as Toni's hands covered her breasts, Laura closed her eyes and leaned her head against Toni's chest, and as the woman continued to grope and squeeze, Laura felt her passion begin to stir.

Pushing the fabric from Laura's shoulders, Toni moved the straps aside, and as the brassiere loosened, she slid her hands under the beige material and began to gently tweak the erect buds that were now hardened to the point of ache.

"Oh...my," Laura said in a breath.

"You like?"

"You know I do...but...but we need to get there before it gets crowded. Don't we?"

"It's early, darling, and this won't take long," Toni said, removing her hands. "Now stand up."

It was an order, and Laura's jaw dropped open when she heard it, but unable to refuse Toni's demand or the urgent throb in her center, Laura did as asked. Getting to her feet, before she had a chance to take another breath, Toni unfastened her bra and threw it aside.

Wrapping Laura in her arms, one of Toni's hands found a plump breast while the other meandered downward. Tweaking and rolling the nipple between her fingertips, Toni smiled into Laura's neck as the woman squirmed in her arms, and as instincts began to take over, a primitive dance began.

Laura molded herself to Toni, grinding her bottom into Toni's pelvis as she felt Toni begin to work the button and zip on her jeans, and when Toni backed away to push the denim down her legs, Laura waited in gasping anticipation.

She thought she knew how accomplished Toni was as a lover, but standing there as she was being stripped of her clothing Laura felt as if her knees were about to buckle. This was new. This was different. This was about control...and Toni wanted all of it.

"I want to take you here," Toni said in a voice, hungry and deep. "Tell me I can take you here."

Hearing Toni's tone, Laura's desire surged. Standing nude in front the makeup table, as she felt the slickness of her excitement begin to coat her thighs, Laura answered in a ragged whisper. "Do it, Toni. Do it."

Behind her, Laura heard the rustle of clothing, and looking over her shoulder, she watched as Toni stripped herself of her shirt and bra. Her eyes locked on Toni's, and Laura's breath caught in her throat as she watched Toni kick the chair out of the way as she returned to her side. With one sweep of her arm, Toni cleared the surface of the makeup table, and the mascara, eye shadows and small mirror fell to the carpet in a muted clatter. Gently pushing Laura to the table, Toni placed her leg between Laura's and spread them wide.

For Laura, the position was new. If it had been anyone else standing behind her, she would have been frightened to be so exposed and submissive, but this wasn't anyone, this was Toni...this was the woman she loved. Their lovemaking had been voracious at times, but never like this, and Laura found herself excited to the point of nearly climaxing right then and there.

"Are you sure?" Toni asked in a breath.

"Yes...oh, God, yes."

It was all Toni needed to hear, and wasting no time she slid her middle finger inside Laura.

Grabbing the edges of the table, Laura held on as Toni pumped in and out of her, greedily accepting every thrust with fervor, and when she begged for more, Toni gave it readily. Probing deep and wiggling her finger, she'd then pull it out and slide it through grooves of pink, slippery softness, following every demand Laura voiced as their love turned feral.

The little table squeaked and groaned under their weight, but neither paid attention as again and again, Toni drove into Laura, and again and again, Laura pushed back in return. Mindless of the want soaking through her khaki trousers, Toni continued to give Laura everything she asked for, and as drops of sweat fell from her brow to Laura's glistening back Toni leaned forward and rubbed her breasts into the wetness.

Laura couldn't believe the feelings raging within her. She had never felt so uninhibited, so bawdy, so wanton. Naked and splayed, she was Toni's to do with what she wanted, and Laura found herself craving the unknown, the unbridled, and the years of practice ahead of them...to make perfect.

Suddenly, Laura felt Toni remove her finger and in a plea, quick and raspy, she said, "No, Toni. More...give me more."

Toni had every intention of giving Laura more. Pulling her off the table, she lowered her to the floor, and as their eyes locked, Toni spread Laura's legs wide.

"Oh...yes..." were the only words Laura could manage before Toni pushed two fingers inside, and relentlessly, she began again.

Raising her knees, Laura surrendered herself to Toni, lifting her hips to take everything Toni was giving. Feeling Toni's thumb against her clit, moving quickly back and forth against the hardened nub, Laura drew in a sharp breath, preparing herself for what was to come.

It happened within seconds, a powerful surge of pleasure that caused Laura's body to tingle and then go rigid. Her muscles tensing at the unstoppable, Laura cried out as her body released, and clamping her legs around Toni's hand, wave after glorious wave forced moans from her lips and want from her body.

CHAPTER THIRTY-EIGHT

"Did I scare you?"

"When?"

"Earlier tonight."

"No, of course not."

"Are you sure?"

"Toni, when I'm..." Laura stopped as the waiter approached the table with a small basket of bread. Waiting until he walked away, she pulled two rolls from under the cloth and placed one on each of their plates. "Toni, when I'm with you, the only thing that scares me, and I'm not even sure that's the right word, is the fact that *if* I had any inhibitions, they disappear when we're together."

"Is that a good thing or a bad thing?"

"You tell me."

Returning Laura's smile, Toni said softly, "I love you."

"I love you, too, sweetheart," Laura said, reaching across the table to take her hand. "And if I could, I'd give you the world."

"I don't think I'd want the world."

"No?"

"No, too many sloppy people to pick up after."

Narrowing her eyes in mock annoyance, Laura took a sip of wine, and then looked down at the menu. "See anything you like?"

"Yes, I do."

Laura didn't need to look up to know that Toni didn't have entrées on her mind, and pausing for a second, she lifted her eyes. "I'm talking about what's on the menu."

"Trust me, so am I."

Swallowing hard at Toni's inference, Laura quickly glanced again at the selections. "So, how hungry are you? Did you want to split something?"

"No, I think I'll be able to finish a plate on my own."

Five months of living together had afforded Laura time to get to know her housemate, and even though Toni's idiosyncrasies were many, when it came to her ability to go without food, Laura was now an expert. Slowly looking up, when she saw Toni's head buried in the menu, Laura knew the answer before she asked the question. "You didn't eat anything today, did you?"

With a sigh, Toni put down the menu. "No, not yet, but before you go jumping to any conclusions, I'm not falling back into old habits. When I woke up this morning, my stomach was in knots, and when we got home...well, I was *hungry* for something else."

Laura smiled, deciding the point could not very easily be argued. "Okay, but promise me something?"

"Anything."

"Don't order the smallest filet on the menu tonight."

"I actually have my eye on the Aberdeen Angus rib eye, if you must know."

Before Laura had a chance to respond, the waiter appeared, and while some of Toni's habits were disappearing, others were still alive and well. Having used up her remaining courage to walk into the crowded restaurant, Toni assumed the posture of an obedient prisoner, and without missing a beat, Laura quickly ordered their meals.

As soon as the waiter disappeared, Toni looked up. "Sorry. I know I should be better at this by now."

"Is that what Abby says?"

"No, she's never put a time limit on anything."

"Then why are you?"

"I just want to be norm—"

The word died in Toni's throat when she saw Laura go rigid, and quickly backpedaling, Toni said, "I just wish I could find the courage to make it through an entire day. I mean, it took me all week to get up enough nerve to face those blokes today, but I managed it. I felt really good about it, but then we get here, and I can't even order my own bloody meal. It's like I take one step in the right direction, and then two in the wrong. It gets downright dizzying sometimes."

"You're being too hard on yourself."

"Ya think?"

"I know," Laura said, reaching across the table to touch Toni's hand. "Sweetheart, six months ago you couldn't leave your flat, but tonight we're sitting in a crowded restaurant, and the only issue you've had was ordering your food. Now stop being so hard on yourself and remember that Rome wasn't built in a day. All right?"

"Your mum told me the same thing when we went up to visit."

"What do you mean?"

"I was wound up about something, and she told me that Rome wasn't built in a day."

"Smart woman, my mum."

"Yeah. I think she takes after her daughter."

Smiling, Laura said, "Speaking of my mum, I was wondering how you'd feel about going Christmas shopping tomorrow. She sent me a list of ideas for the kids, and I'd like to get as much of it out of the way as possible before we leave."

"I thought you were meeting Abby for lunch."

"I am, but that's not until one, so I thought maybe we could hit the stores early, but I'm afraid it's going to be busier than usual, so if you don't want to go, I'll understand."

"No, I'd like to, but as early as we can, if that's okay."

"It's fine, Toni. It's absolutely fine."

***

Abby walked into the restaurant, and allowing her eyes to get accustomed to the dim lighting, when she saw Laura waving at her from a booth, she took off her coat and went over. After kissing Laura on the cheek, Abby sat down. "I'm a little surprised not to see Toni here."

"I invited her, but she had a rough morning."

"Oh? What's happened?"

"Christmas shopping."

"Oh my," Abby said, slouching in her seat. "The crowds got to her?"

"She was doing okay for a while, but we ended up in a toy store. People were pushing and shoving to get the latest and the greatest, and she couldn't handle it."

"Did she have a panic attack?"

"No, I got her to the car and then home. She was feeling a bit down on herself and decided to take a kip."

"And how are you?"

"What do you mean?"

"Laura, you do know that she may never be able to handle certain things, don't you?"

"Yes, Abby, I'm fully aware of my partner's problems. We've had this conversation before, remember? Please stop doubting my love for her. Okay?"

"I'm not. I know you love her, but it has to be a bit disheartening for you when things like this happen."

"I'm not discouraged, Abby, quite the opposite. This just makes me love her more because even though it's difficult for her, she keeps trying. I don't care if it takes a hundred shopping trips, or a thousand dinners, we have lots of years ahead of us, and I plan to be there for her every step of the way, even if some of those steps are backward."

A waitress appeared, and quickly scanning the menu, they ordered their drinks and lunch. Waiting until the woman walked away from the table, Laura said, "Speaking of steps, I'm thinking about taking one, and I'd like your opinion."

"All right, but are we talking about my professional opinion or my personal one?"

"A little of both, I think."

"Okay, I'm listening."

Pausing for a moment, Laura said quietly, "I'm thinking about...about buying Toni a ring."

"A ring?"

Laura nodded and waited for the penny to drop.

"Are you talking about an *engagement* ring?" Abby blurted.

"Yes."

Smiling, Abby leaned back. "That's a hell of a Christmas present."

"It's got nothing to do with Christmas. I just love her so much, and I want her to know that I'm in this for the long haul."

"And you don't think she believes you are?"
"Sometimes, I'm not so sure."
"Why?"
"It's like today...we were out buying some gifts and I noticed a couple of things I thought would look good in the house. When I asked her what she thought, she said that whatever I wanted was fine, like she didn't care, but I got the feeling she didn't think she had the right to give her opinion."

"You mean, since it's your house and not hers."
"Yeah."
"And you think proposing will change that?"
"Well, it would definitely show her that I mean business," Laura said with a laugh. "I just don't know how else to convince her. One day, she seems secure and talks about children and forever, and the next, she won't even help me pick out a new set of towels."

"Quite multi-faceted, our Toni."
"Tell me about it," Laura said with a snort.

Abby's professional thoughts about Toni blended with her personal ones, and the result brightened her face. "Do you want to know what I think?"

"Yes."

"I think if you love her, then go for it. Go with your gut instinct, Laura. If there is anyone who knows Toni, it's you."

"But will she think I'm moving too fast? I know we've only been lovers for just over a month, but we've known each other for almost a year, and I honestly can't imagine ever being with anyone else. I just can't."

"Laura, have you forgotten about my parents? They got married less than five months after they met, and a few weeks ago, they celebrated their thirty-fifth anniversary. There's no time limit on falling in love. It just happens, and as to what Toni may think, yes, it's possible she could feel you're moving a bit fast, but from where I'm sitting, you're doing this for all the right reasons. You're not suggesting that this is a quick fix for what ails her. You're showing her that you're committed to your relationship."

Laura perked up in her seat. "Thanks, that's what I needed to hear."

"Now I have a question."
"Okay?"

"I've never shopped for an engagement ring before, so do you want some company?"

***

"I need your finger."

"I love it when you talk dirty."

"Behave. I'm being serious."

"So am I."

Grinning, Laura motioned toward the gift she was wrapping. "I need you to put your finger in the middle, so I can finish tying this ribbon."

Reaching over, Toni placed her index finger on the intersecting strands of red. "And here I was getting my hopes up."

"Your hopes will be answered later *if* we get all these presents wrapped tonight."

Looking at the piles of bags and boxes of toys stacked in the lounge, Toni said, "I don't know if I have that much energy."

"That'll be the day."

Smiling, Toni glanced back to the instructions in her hand. Squinting as she read the tiny printing for the third time, she let out a sigh and put them aside. "Girls or boys?"

"What?" Laura asked, looking up from her wrapping.

"Do you want girls or boys?"

"I just want them to be healthy. As for their sex, I'll leave that up to God."

"And the sperm bank."

"Yeah, I suppose."

"Will that be okay for you? I mean, not knowing the father."

"I didn't know mine, and I turned out all right."

"That's different."

"Not really. He never had anything to do with how I was raised. He wasn't there to teach me right from wrong, or to look both ways before I crossed a street. Everything I am, I owe to my mother."

"Except your DNA."

"I'll give you that, but from what I've read, we'll know almost as much about the father of our children as my mother did about my father, except for his name, of course."

"So, you've been reading, have you?"

"Just a little," Laura said quietly. "Do you mind?"

"Of course not. You need to know all the facts before committing yourself to this relationship. Weighing your options is smart."

Frowning, Laura pushed aside the package, got to her feet and headed to the stairs. "I'll be right back," she called out, running up the steps. "Pour us some wine. Will you?"

Although confused by Laura's quick exit, Toni did as asked and when she returned to the lounge a few minutes later, she found Laura sitting cross-legged in the middle of the sofa. Handing her a glass, Toni settled into her corner, but as she went to retrieve the toy instructions, Laura pulled them from her hand and tossed them aside.

"What's wrong? I thought my job was to assemble and yours was to wrap."

"Wrapping can wait."

"Oh, no it can't," Toni said, grabbing for the directions. "I have hopes, Laura, and you've made it perfectly clear that they won't be answered until all these gifts are tied up in pretty ribbons."

"I have hopes, too."

"I know. That's why I want to finish."

"I'm not talking about that."

"No?"

"No," Laura said as she handed Toni a box wrapped in gold foil.

"What's this?"

"Open it and find out."

"I thought tonight's goal was to wrap not *unwrap*."

"It was, but now it's not."

"Can I ask why?"

"Did you like those towels the other day?"

"Excuse me?"

"When we were shopping...those orange towels I said I liked. Did you like them?"

"What's that got to do with wrapping presents?"

"Toni, stop talking about the bloody presents and answer the question."

"But I don't understand—"

"Jesus Christ! Will you please just—"

"Okay. Okay. No, actually I didn't like them. Satisfied?"

"Why didn't you tell me?"

"I just did."

"No, I mean when we were in the store. I asked your opinion, and you said whatever I liked was fine. If you didn't like them, why didn't you just tell me?"

"I know that you want to include me on decisions, Laura, but this *is* your house."

Pursing her lips, Laura let out a slow breath as she stared back at Toni. "Open the present."

"Isn't it a Christmas present?" Toni asked, once again returning her gaze to the gift in her hands.

"No, it's not."

"But it's wrapped in foil."

"Do you see a candy cane or a reindeer on it?"

Glancing at the gold wrapping, Toni said, "Well, no, but since Christmas is just around the corner, I thought—"

"Do us both a favor. Stop thinking and open the box."

"It looks like clothes," Toni said, shaking the package.

"You're seriously trying my patience."

"I don't mean to."

"Then open the bloody box!"

Letting out an exaggerated sigh, Toni accepted defeat and began pulling away the ribbon and bow. Slowly removing the gold paper, she lifted the cover and pushed aside the tissue paper. Toni's eyes flashed to Laura and then back to the contents of the box, her eyebrows drawing together as she shook her head. "I...I don't understand."

"Look underneath."

For a second, Toni just stared at the stack of estate agent brochures before finally lifting them out. Moving aside a layer of tissue paper underneath, when she saw a rolled-up piece of paper held closed by a diamond ring, her mouth dropped open.

Reaching over, Laura pulled out the scroll, and removing the ring, she handed Toni the paper. "Read this."

"But—"

"Read it, Toni. Please."

Waiting while Toni opened the scroll, when Laura saw her begin to scan the words, she filled in the blanks. "It's an agreement I signed earlier this week with an estate agent."

"But...but why? You love this house."

"It's just a house, Toni, but I don't want a house. I want a home...and I want you." Opening her hand to display the emerald-cut diamond in a band of gold, Laura said, "And I want you 'til death do us part." When Laura saw Toni's eyes fill with tears, she cupped the woman's chin and looked her in the eye. "I love you, Toni, and I don't ever want you to doubt that. With everything you've been through, I know that words may not be enough for you, so I hope this is. Marry me, Toni. Marry me and give me a reason to smile...for the rest of my life."

Blinking back her tears, Toni said, "Are you sure this is what you want? It could take years of therapy, Laura, and even then, there aren't any guarantees—"

"I don't need guarantees, Toni. I need *you*...for better or for worse."

"It could be more worse than better."

"Sweetheart, there's nothing you can say that's going to change my mind. Now stop trying to give me an out...and give me an answer."

Looking into Laura's eyes, Toni grinned. "You're quite the pushy one, aren't you?"

"You have no idea."

"So, if I know what's good for me, I'd best say yes."

"Is that your answer?"

Pausing for a moment, Toni smiled wide. "Yes, I think it is."

If Toni thought about changing her mind, she had about a nanosecond to do it, because as soon as she said yes, Laura slipped the ring on her finger. Gazing at the diamond, Toni said with a leer, "Does this mean I get to unwrap something else now?"

"You're incorrigible."

"No...I'm just in love."

CHAPTER THIRTY-NINE

Normally a woman who enjoyed sleeping until noon if she got the chance, when the sun streamed through the blinds the next morning, Laura awoke with a smile on her face and more energy than she knew what to do with. Although tempted to take up where they had left off the night before, when she saw Toni sleeping peacefully, Laura silently chastised herself for her thoughts and crept from the room. Trying her best to keep her mind off the woman in her bed, she padded downstairs and proceeded to straighten the lounge, tidy up the kitchen and make a pot of coffee before the urge to return to Toni became too strong. Carefully carrying two mugs up the stairs, Laura quietly snuck back into the bedroom, placed the coffee on the nightstand, and dropping her robe on the floor, slipped back under the sheets.

Rolling to her side, she propped herself up on one elbow and admired the view. Her first thought was to run her fingers through Toni's tousled hair, but deciding to let the woman sleep for a little while longer, Laura instead allowed her eyes to wander. When they came to rest upon two hardened buds under the ivory cotton percale, she held back a grin as she gently moved the sheet aside.

Again, Laura was amazed how the sight of Toni's body ignited her desire in an instant, for when her eyes settled on the erect, pale pink crests, Laura's center awakened with a flutter. Swallowing the moisture building in her mouth, she leaned over and gently ran her tongue over the tightly beaded tip, and then watched as the already alert point seemed to grow harder before her eyes. After a quick glance to make sure Toni was still asleep, Laura grew bolder. Tasting again, she casually ran her tongue around the darkened center until she heard Toni's breathing change.

Without opening her eyes, Toni murmured, "What do you think you're doing?"

"Just saying hello."

"If I'm not mistaken, you said *hello* last night."

"Yes, I did, but this is a new day," Laura said, flicking her tongue across the pointed tip.

Sighing at the sensation, Toni stretched her legs and opened her eyes. Gazing at the woman smiling back at her, she said, "Good morning."

"Good morning," Laura said, running her hand across Toni's belly. "Should I let you go back to sleep?"

"What time is it?"

"Almost eight."

"Oh, I should get up."

"What's the rush?" Laura asked, covering Toni's right breast with her hand.

Enjoying Laura's tender tweaking of her nipple, Toni closed her eyes. "I'd...I'd like to go out today and buy my fiancée a ring."

Laura beamed. "Really?"

"Yes, really."

"I guess we should go early then, huh? Try to beat the rush," Laura said as her hand began to travel under the sheets.

"It makes the most sense given my...my...*oh*...fear of crowds," Toni said, shifting slightly as Laura brushed her fingers through the mound of curly hair between her legs.

"So you're saying we don't have time for this," Laura said, flicking her tongue across Toni's nipple again.

Arching her chest toward Laura's awaiting mouth, Toni said, "No, I'm just saying...we'll have to...we'll have to make it fast."

Fast was definitely an option Laura was willing to take. Quickly capturing Toni's nipple in her mouth, she sucked hard against the erect bud as she slipped her hand between Toni's legs. Amazed at the wetness she found, Laura snaked her fingers through the delicate softness until she reached her target. Easily dipping a finger inside, as Laura began to rub, Toni began to squirm.

The night before they had celebrated their engagement with tender foreplay that lasted long into the night before climax had been reached, but Laura wasn't the only one who had awoken with a need, so when she increased the tempo, Toni was more than receptive to the pace.

Within only a few minutes, Toni began to feel the distant thrum of her orgasm building within her, and hungry for release, she urged Laura to the mattress. Straddling her thigh, Toni forced Laura's hand between her legs, and as soon as Laura's fingers returned to her warm, wet center, Toni began to rock.

Thrusting her hips, Toni took Laura inside of her again and again, impaling herself in abandon until a rumbling, groan rose in her throat. She stilled for a second, waiting for completion and when it happened, it took her breath away. Collapsing on top of Laura, Toni rode out the spasms of her orgasm until, gasping for air and shining with sweat, she rolled to her side. Relishing the feel of the cool sheets against her heated skin, ever so slowly, her breathing returned to normal.

Laura waited as Toni returned to earth, and when her eyes opened, Laura asked, "Are you okay?"

"I will be in a minute," Toni said in a low, sexy voice as she slid off the bed.

"Where are you going?"

"I'm not the one who's going anywhere," Toni said as she pushed away the sheets. Curling her finger at Laura, she beckoned her closer. "Come here."

Toni's command packed a sensual wallop that settled soundly between Laura's legs. In an instant, Laura was on her knees, her breathing turning shallow as she crawled to the edge of the bed. With her eyes locked on Toni's, Laura took her hand, standing only for a moment before finding herself being lowered to the sheets again.

Placing a pillow under Laura's bottom, Toni leered at her. "It's time for breakfast, darling and I'm very...*very* hungry."

Kneeling on the floor, Toni gazed at what was in front of her. Feminine petals drenched with excitement awaited her, and wasting no time in sampling the banquet, Toni spread them with her thumbs and ran her tongue along a furrow. Delighting in the essence of

Laura's desire, Toni had no intention of taking the option of fast, and minutes passed by as she tasted, licked and probed until Laura raised her hips and pleaded, "Oh, Toni...please. Oh please...please do it now."

Toni purred at the plea. Easing a finger into Laura's slick center, she began to drive Laura insane. Toni was a quick study when it came to what would make Laura explode, and after only a few more minutes of tormenting her with long, steady strokes, Toni parted Laura's folds and began tickling her entrance with her tongue.

Air rushed from Laura's lungs. "Oh...oh...oh..." she gasped, placing her feet on Toni's shoulders. "Oh...oh...*yessss*."

Encouraged by the passionate response, Toni continued to tease with her tongue, all the while using her thumb to draw lazy figure eights over Laura's clit. Increasing the pressure with each circle of the swollen bud, Toni was unforgiving. She licked and teased while Laura moaned and bucked, raising her sex toward Toni's mouth with urgency until finally, Laura couldn't hold out any longer.

Grabbing hold of the sheets, Laura raised her hips again. "Now, Toni! Oh...God...now!"

Hearing the desperation in Laura's voice, Toni gave her what she knew she wanted. Exposing Laura's quivering center, Toni pushed her tongue inside.

Unmercifully claiming its victim, the orgasm took Laura's breath away, and as her body pulsed, pushing desire from her center, Toni tasted every drop. Gently licking away the ambrosial nectar, Toni waited until she felt Laura relax before she slowly climbed onto the bed, and brushing soaked strands of auburn from Laura's forehead, she placed her lips on Laura's.

Their feminine flavors mixed, and savoring the blend, it took everything Toni had to pull away. If it had been just another Saturday, spending the rest of the morning in bed with the woman lying naked across the sheets wouldn't have been a problem, but ever since Laura had slipped the ring on her finger, all Toni wanted to do was to return the sentiment. Jumping out of bed, she announced, "It's time to get your lovely arse in gear, Miss MacLeod. We have things to do."

"Give me one good reason why I should," Laura mumbled, opening one eye.

"Because I want to buy the woman I love an engagement ring, but without her help, I can't. That is unless you want me to ask Krista to run out and pick one up?"

Scrambling to her feet, Laura kissed Toni on the cheek. "Not on your life."

"Then you'd best get a move on. You know how I get in crowded stores."

"Give me five minutes."

Watching Laura sashay to the bathroom in all her nakedness, Toni smiled. "I'll give you ten."

***

Although they had several more gifts to purchase before their Christmas lists were completed, when Toni requested that the first stop be the jewelry store where Laura had purchased her ring, Laura happily agreed. Believing that she would accompany Toni into the store to choose the ring, Laura was shocked when Toni ordered her to stay in the car. With a confidence Laura had only ever seen behind the walls of her home, Toni exited the car and marched into the shop.

It was your typical jewelry store, filled with cases displaying gems from around the world. Behind the counters stood the sale staff wearing painted on smiles, assisting hunched-over customers who were pressing their fingers against the glass as they swooned over the selections.

Avoiding eye contact with customers and salespeople alike, Toni slowly walked around the shop until she found the cases displaying what she sought. Glancing at the ring she now proudly wore on her left hand, she took a deep breath and stepped closer to view the collection of diamond solitaires on velvet fingers.

"I'm glad to see you said yes."

Toni tensed. Slowly raising her eyes, she found herself looking at a woman in her early sixties who was standing on the other side of the counter. "I'm...I'm sorry?"

Pointing to Toni's engagement ring, the gray-haired woman said, "A few days ago I sold that to a young woman who said she wanted to propose to her girlfriend, and I'm assuming that's you."

Toni blushed, and with a nod, she whispered, "Yes. Yes, it is."

GIVE ME A REASON

Perplexed by Toni's nervousness, the woman asked, "I'm sorry, but is everything all right? Is there something wrong with the ring?"

"What? Oh, no. No, it's fine," Toni said, shaking her head. "I'm...I'm not...I'm just not very comfortable around crowds. That's all."

Glancing past Toni to the people rapidly filling the shop, the woman leaned closer. "Well, I'm afraid it's only going to get worse as the day goes on. It is the season for gifts of gold and silver."

"Yeah...yeah, I suppose," Toni said, going rigid when another customer leaned over to look into the case.

Smelling of gardenias and covered in glitz and finery, the woman didn't seem to care that she was invading Toni's space.

Taking a step back, it was all Toni could do to find her voice. "I-I-I think I need to leave."

Annoyed by the pompous matriarch's intrusion, the saleswoman said loudly, "Without getting your lovely girlfriend a ring?"

The dowager's head snapped up. Glaring down her narrow nose at Toni, she then turned her condescending look to the saleswoman. Curling her lip, she grunted in disgust and stomped away.

"Well, it seems we have the case to ourselves again," the saleswoman said, smiling brightly. "Isn't that convenient?"

With just a hint of a grin, Toni lifted her eyes. "You...you didn't have to do that."

"Give me one reason why that old biddy needs to peruse engagement rings," she said, using a cloth to wipe the woman's fingerprints from the glass. "Besides, it's about time we're allowed to marry those we love. Wouldn't you agree?"

***

An hour later, Toni emerged from the shop, shaky and pale, but with her purchase in hand. Sliding into the passenger seat, she closed her eyes and concentrated on slowing down her breathing.

"You okay?" Laura asked.

"Yeah. I just need a minute."

After a few moments of staring at the small white bag clutched in Toni's hand, Laura said, "So, I'm assuming you found something."

"Yes, I did," Toni said, opening her eyes.

"Can I see it?"

Amused by Laura's eagerness, Toni said, "No, you may not."

Inquisitive to the point of being comical, Laura tried her best to convince Toni to hand over the ring, but stating that the setting was neither romantic nor appropriate, Toni stuffed the package in her pocket and informed Laura she would have to wait. Slightly annoyed by Toni's decision, at first Laura tried to rush through the rest of the day's shopping spree, but as the afternoon progressed, stores got busier and Toni's anxieties flared. More than once, Toni had to return to the car to gather her wits, and in the ladies' room of an overcrowded toy store, Laura spent the better part of a half hour patiently talking Toni back from a panic attack. Although Laura's curiosity was still very much alive and well, she slowed their pace to a crawl, and Toni's nerves calmed.

After stopping by their favorite Chinese restaurant for take-away, they arrived home with the boot of Laura's car filled with packages and a paper bag overflowing with cartons of Eastern cuisine. Suggesting Laura start a fire so they could enjoy their meal in front of the hearth, Toni disappeared into the kitchen, returning a few minutes later carrying two glasses of wine.

Noticing Laura staring into the flames, Toni flicked off the table lamp, and when Laura turned in her direction, she walked over, placed the glasses on the table and knelt on one knee. Gazing at the woman she loved, Toni opened her hand to reveal the ring she had bought that morning, and in a whisper she asked, "I know this is just a formality, but will you do me the honor of becoming my wife?"

"In a heartbeat," Laura said in a breath. Holding out her hand, Laura's eyes overflowed as Toni slipped the diamond ring on her finger.

***

Abby noticed the ring on Toni's finger as soon as she walked into the house, but it wasn't until she was settled on the sofa that she made her observation known. "Nice ring," she said nonchalantly as she sipped her coffee. "Laura has good taste."

"In rings or fiancées?"

"Both, I think."

"Do you think we're ready for this?" Toni asked, holding up her left hand.

"Do you?"

"I asked you first."

"Fair enough," Abby said with a nod. "Honestly, when Laura first told me about her plans, I was a bit concerned that she might be rushing things, but later after she had bought you that ring, I went home and spent the night thinking about you…and about her."

"And?"

"Well, unless I'm mistaken, we all know that you most likely have years of therapy ahead of you. Agreed?"

"Yeah," Toni answered quietly.

"And I also think it's safe to say that we all know that some of your…your *issues* may never be completely resolved. Also true?"

"Yes."

"Laura doesn't care."

"What?"

"Laura doesn't care if she has to hold your hand when you walk into a store. She doesn't care if she has to order your meals, or keep a paper sack in every handbag she owns. It simply doesn't matter to her. She doesn't see your issues as problems, Toni, she just sees them for what they are, part of what makes you—*you*. I'm not saying she isn't happy when you take a step in the right direction, but if you never took another one, if this were as good as you could get, Laura wouldn't love you any less."

"So Laura's ready, but what about me?"

"Oh, you're more than ready."

"How do you figure that?"

"Because you've already come to terms with the fact that you have years of therapy ahead of you and that some problems may never be solved, but you and I both know you'll never give up trying, and we both know why."

"Laura."

Abby smiled. "I've never met two people more in love than you and Laura. You're both committed to each other, and you're both going into this with your eyes wide open. Neither of you are naïve enough to believe your life together will be perfect, but since you're both more stubborn than the day is long, I have no doubt that you'll make it work." Noticing a hint of concern on Toni's face, Abby asked softly, "Toni, do you love her?"

"More than I can say."

"Do you want to spend the rest of your life with her?"
"And then some."
"Then there's your answer. Stop worrying about your problems. Stop stressing over flawlessness, and just be happy that you've found what so many of us are looking for, and most likely may never find."
"What's that?"
"Your soulmate."

***

She straightened her blazer for the fourth time and ran her fingers through her hair for the third. The bell over the door announced the next customer, and perking up, she quickly smiled toward the sound, and then sighed at the sight of strangers coming into the pub. Silently admonishing herself for her adolescent anxiousness, Eleanor took another sip of her wine and tried to relax. It didn't work.

It had been over thirty years since she had visited this pub, but it was the first place that came to mind when she made the phone call. Years before, it had been their regular stop. A place to unwind and catch up with friends, they'd spend evenings surrounded by the comfort of familiar neon, laughing and drinking the night away before returning to the warmth of their home...and their bed.

As Eleanor remembered youthful nights filled with passion that wouldn't end until dawn she felt a hint of awareness settle between her legs, and with a snort, she shook her head. She was as hopelessly in love now as she had been over three decades before, and there was absolutely nothing she could do about it.

"Hiya, Ellie."

She breathed in deeply before lifting her eyes to meet his, and instantly their smiles grew wide. For a few seconds, neither could look away, until finally, Eleanor found her voice. "Hello, William. I'm glad you could make it."

"The apocalypse couldn't keep me away," he said, leaning down to place a soft kiss on her cheek. "You're looking as beautiful as ever."

"And you're still telling tall tales," she said, gesturing for him to sit.

Sliding into the booth, he motioned for the waitress, and after ordering a drink, he looked at the woman sitting across from him. It didn't matter that the auburn tresses which once had reached her waist in shimmering waves had been replaced by a short, layered bob, or that a few more laugh lines had been added by the passage of time. As far as Bill MacLeod was concerned, Eleanor was still the most beautiful woman he had ever laid eyes on.

His thoughts were interrupted when the waitress returned with his Scotch, and after quickly taking a sip, he said, "I was really glad you suggested this, Ellie."

"Oh?"

"Yes, actually...um...I was thinking about calling you."

"Is that so?"

"I know we see each other at Nancy's occasionally, but there's always so much going on over there. It's hard to have a conversation when all those children are running about."

"Yes, they do get quite noisy at times, don't they?"

"Was Laura like that?"

Smiling, Eleanor took a sip of wine. "Children make noise, Bill. It's a fact of life, and Laura made her fair share when she was that age. She'd have tantrums when she didn't get her way and scream her head off when a balloon I told her to hold on to was let go, but it's just something you learn to deal with."

"I never did."

"You never tried."

Bill's mood turned somber. Staring at the drink in his hand, almost a minute passed before he brought it to his lips to take a sip. Setting the glass on the table, he lifted his eyes to meet Eleanor's. "I should have."

Eleanor cocked her head to the side and looked more closely at the man who used to share her bed. His sandy hair was still as wavy as ever, and his skin was just as tan, but the emerald of his eyes seemed somehow brighter. And in that green of greens, Eleanor thought she saw a hint of something she never thought she'd see again.

"Are you okay?" she asked.

"Yes. Why?"

"I mean your health. You're not dying of some dreaded disease, are you?"

Bill laughed heartily. "No, still as healthy as ever, I'm afraid, except for the occasional twinge in my back. Why do you ask?"

"Because I think you just admitted that you regret walking away from us."

"I do," he said, hanging his head. "I should have been there for you both...taken care of you."

"You did your part."

"Paying for Laura's education is not what I'm talking about."

"You paid for a hell of a lot more than that, and we both know it. How that girl ever believed I could afford all those gifts is beyond me, and when you had that car delivered on her eighteenth birthday, I almost died."

"Yeah, but it's still just money, Ellie. I should have been there to teach her how to ride a bike. I should have been there when she skinned her knees and...and when she started dating. I should have been the one standing at the door, threatening every boy who walked inside."

Refusing to allow her amusement to show, Eleanor said, "Yes, well I don't think you need to worry about *that* any longer."

"No, I suppose not," Bill said. Emptying what remained in his glass, he motioned for the waitress to bring another round.

Between the wine and the proximity of William MacLeod, the pub seemed much warmer than when she had first walked inside. Removing her blazer, Eleanor placed it aside. "That's actually the reason I called you. Something has happened, and I think you need to know—"

"Happened? Has something happened to Laura? Is she all right?"

"Relax, William, she's fine. Actually, she's more than fine."

"More than fine?"

"She's in love...and engaged."

"Engaged?" William said as his whole face spread into a smile. "When did this happen?"

"A few days ago."

"Wait. Why are *you* telling me this? I know Laura doesn't think of me as her father, but I would have thought that this kind of announcement...well, that...that she'd—"

"She doesn't know I'm telling you."

William's smile faded as his eyebrows became one. "Ellie, what's going on? What's wrong?"

"There's nothing wrong, William, but I fear that Laura may need more than just me in her corner in the coming days, and I'm hoping that you love our daughter as much as I think you do."

"It seems I love her more every day," he said quietly.

Reaching across the table, Eleanor touched his hand, praying that the fair-minded man who had divorced her so many years before was still the man sitting across from her.

"William, our Laura is in love…with a woman."

CHAPTER FORTY

"How did this happen?"
"It happened like it always does. Two people meet, fall in love—"
"But a woman?"
"Yes, a woman."
"Have you met her?"
"Of course I have."
Leaning back into the booth, Bill MacLeod picked up his Scotch and drank it down. Raking his fingers through his hair, he waited until the burn of the alcohol subsided before asking, "And you're all right with this?"
"Yes, actually, I am."
"A lot of parents wouldn't be."
"Does that include you?"
Hanging his head, Bill stared at the table top. "All I've ever wanted was for Laura to be happy, but—"
"William, she is happy."
"But a woman?"
"Since when did you become a homophobe?"
Bill jerked up his head. "I am no such thing!"
"Could have surprised me."
"Jesus Christ, Ellie, this is a lot to take in. You of all people know I've never been prejudiced against gays or anyone else. If Laura

is...well, if she's gay, then so be it, but I need a bloody minute to wrap my head around it. All right?"

"I'll give you all the time you need," Eleanor said. Picking up her glass, she took a sip and waited.

A few minutes passed, and as Eleanor was about to order another glass of Chardonnay, Bill broke the silence. "And she's truly happy?"

"William, she positively glows when she's with Toni."

"Toni? That's her name?"

"Yes. Toni Vaughn."

Thinking for a moment, Bill said, "That's a strong name. A good name."

Smiling, Eleanor squeezed his hand. "I know there's a lot of water under the blasted bridge where you and Laura are concerned, but I do hope that one day our daughter realizes how much you love her."

"I doubt she'll ever give me that much time, Ellie, but as long as she's happy, I'm happy. If she needs someone else in her corner, you can count me in."

"Good," she said. Noticing that the noise level in the pub was continuing to rise as afternoon patrons ordered up their lager, Eleanor glanced at her watch. "William, do you have any plans for dinner?"

"No. Why?"

"Well, there's more I need to tell you, but this place is getting a little too loud. I thought we might grab a bite somewhere, if that's okay with you?"

"I'd love to," William said as he got to his feet. Holding out his hand, as their fingers meshed, he said, "Lead the way."

***

"I think I need a bigger car."

Placing the last bag of gifts in the back seat, Toni shut the door and walked around to stand with Laura at the rear of the car. Looking at the overfilled boot, she shook her head. "I think you need to learn how to pack less."

After giving Toni the evil eye, Laura turned back to the pile of suitcases. Grabbing a bag, she said, "I suppose I should just repack a few of these."

"Oh, no you don't. You start doing that, and we'll never get out of here. Now, stand back and let me see what I can do."

Standing off to the side, Laura watched as Toni shoved the cases right and left, and with a heavy push, she slammed the lid of the boot.

Smiling at her accomplishment, Toni looked over at Laura. "I recommend we don't open this until Scotland or the bloody thing will projectile vomit all over the motorway."

Playfully slapping Toni's arm, Laura set the alarm on the car and then followed her partner back into the house. Catching up with Toni in the kitchen, they both read over the list on the counter. Crossing off a few more items, Toni said, "Okay, we need to water the plants, turn down the heat, check all the doors and windows, grab the coffee flask, and then we should be good to go."

"Okay, I'll check upstairs. You do down," Laura said, running up the stairs.

Quickly roaming from room to room, Toni did as asked, and satisfied that everything was locked and bolted, she trotted up the stairs, almost colliding with Laura as she exited the bedroom.

"Oh, sorry. You forget something?" Laura asked.

"Yes, I did," Toni answered, pulling Laura into her arms. Lowering her face, Toni kissed Laura full on the lips.

Coming up for air after a few minutes later, Laura asked, "What was that for?"

"Consider it a bookmark."

"Excuse me?"

"So, in two weeks when we return, I'll remember where I left off," Toni said with a grin.

Tilting her head, Laura said, "What do you mean?"

"Well, I'm not going to make love to you in your mother's house."

"Why not?"

"Laura, be real. It's your *mother's* home, and I doubt she wants to hear her daughter screaming out instructions in the middle of the night."

"I do not scream."

"Yes, you very well do, and you know it."

Thinking for a moment, Laura said, "I can be quiet."

"Since when?"

"I've just never had a reason to. That's all."

"Laura, I love you and you know I love being with you, but it's not going to happen. I know you've said your mum is okay with our relationship, but I have no intention of flaunting it, or…or making her uncomfortable."

"And what about what I want?"

"Darling, it's only for two weeks."

Pressing her lips together so as not to laugh, Laura grabbed Toni's hand and led her into the bedroom. Kicking off her shoes, she turned around and commanded, "Fuck me."

"Excuse me?"

"You heard."

"Laura, the car is packed. The windows are locked and…and…and this is ridiculous," Toni said, watching as Laura stepped out of her jeans.

"If I can remain quiet, not scream, as you put it, then we make love in Scotland. If I make a sound, *one* bloody sound, I won't touch you or try to do anything to change your mind."

Toni thought she was prepared to argue more, but when Laura tossed her sweater aside, revealing a bra of red lace, Toni's brown eyes turned black with desire.

Aware she now had Toni's full attention Laura took a step in her direction. "Sweetheart, there's no way you're not going to take me up on this, and we both know it. Now, where do you want me? The bed, the floor, or right here where I stand?"

***

Standing in the doorway, he watched in silence as she busied herself at the counter. Dressed only in his shirt, she looked as she did decades before, and his heart skipped a beat.

"Did you find them?" she asked, noticing him standing a few feet away.

"Sorry, Ellie. I looked everywhere."

"Shit," Eleanor said, looking around the room.

"Don't worry. They'll show up." Noticing that Eleanor seemed to be distracted, Bill asked, "What's wrong?"

"What? Oh…oh, nothing, I'm just trying to think of what I need to do before they get here."

"Well, I already tidied the lounge and bedroom, so cross that off your list."

Raising an eyebrow, Eleanor asked, "When did you become so domestic?"

"Times change, Ellie."

"Speaking of time, you had better get out of here so I can get ready."

"I would, except someone is wearing my shirt."

Quickly looking down, Eleanor sighed. "Sorry. Bad habit, I guess."

As far as William was concerned, it was the best habit, and one he was thankful hadn't changed. Without saying a word, he followed Eleanor down the hallway to her bedroom, all the while staring at her bottom.

"I'm afraid it's a bit wrinkled," she said, quickly unbuttoning the Oxford.

"So am I," Bill said with a grin.

Snickering, Eleanor looked in his direction. Although approaching his fifty-sixth birthday, the years spent at sea had kept his body lean and muscled, and while the blond hair covering his chest had begun to turn gray, he was still as handsome as he had been on their wedding day. Aware of the moistness forming between her legs, Eleanor lowered her eyes, and seeing the bulge in his trousers, she happily sighed. Watching as he took a step in her direction, she said, "William, we don't have time for this."

"I know," he said. Pushing the shirt from her body, he lowered his head and covered a taut nipple with his mouth.

Cheerfully resigned to the fact they were about to make love again, Eleanor moved to the bed. Lying across the duvet, she watched as he stepped out of his trousers.

"William..." she said as she opened her legs.

"Yes, sweetheart?"

"We really do need to make this fast."

Pulling Eleanor to the edge of the bed, Bill smirked. "Let's hope they're running late."

***

"I hope you're satisfied," Toni said in a huff.

Glancing at her passenger, Laura smiled. "More than satisfied, actually."

"We're going to be late!"

"Only about an hour. No worries." Hearing Toni huff again, Laura laughed. "You *really* don't like losing a bet, do you?"

"It wasn't a bet, and you didn't play fair!"

"I most certainly did."

"Oh, no, you didn't. Between all the shopping, wrapping and packing, we haven't made love since Sunday night, and you know perfectly well how I get when it's been that long."

"This coming from a woman who thought she could do without for two weeks," Laura said, shaking her head. "Honestly, Toni, what in the world were you thinking?"

"I was trying to be considerate."

"To whom?"

"To your mother, of course."

"Sweetheart, my mother knows we're having sex."

"You told her!"

"Of course."

"What!"

"Toni, what the hell has gotten into you? You were sitting right next to me when I called her and told her about our engagement. Did you honestly believe that she thought our relationship was platonic?"

"Oh…um…no, I suppose not."

"You're *really* nervous, aren't you?"

"I'm trying not to be, but I haven't yet been able to master *calm*."

"You'll be fine. We've been there before, and you like my mum. Don't you?"

"Yeah…yeah, I do. She's great."

"That, she is."

"Why didn't she ever get married again? I mean, she's attractive and smart. I would have thought some bloke would have snatched her up by now."

"I think she prefers being single."

"Really?"

"She's dated a few men over the years, but none of them stayed around for very long. She's never said, but I think she just didn't want to get hurt again."

"You're talking about when your dad walked out."

"Yeah."

"Speaking of your father, I'm assuming I'm going to meet him this trip?"

"Apparently, you are, although it wasn't my idea."

"What do you mean?"

"I wasn't going to make any extra effort, but Mum believes he has the right to meet you before the rest of the family, so she texted me this morning to tell me she invited him over for dinner tonight."

When Toni didn't respond, Laura looked over, and seeing that she had paled by at least one shade, Laura reached over and squeezed her knee. "It'll be okay, Toni. If you get uncomfortable, I'll ask him to leave."

"It's not him I'm worried about."

"No?"

"I just realized that I've been so wrapped up in worrying about meeting your family, I totally forgot the fact that even if they don't have an issue with me...they may have an issue with *us*."

***

Standing in front of the mirror, she moved a few errant strands of hair off her forehead and chuckled at her reflection. A quick shower had erased the scent of sex, but it had done little to erase her rosy cheeks, and it had absolutely no effect on the smile gracing her face.

When they had left the pub, Eleanor's first thought had been to find a quiet restaurant where they could enjoy a meal while she spoke of Toni Vaughn, but as they looked up and down the street, a thought came into her head...and out of her mouth.

An hour later, they returned to her house, and over plates filled with Italian take-away, Eleanor explained the enigma who was now their daughter's fiancée. At first, hearing that the woman had spent time in prison, the hairs on William's neck stood on end. Clenching his fists, it was all he could do to control his temper, and seeing his green eyes darken, just as Laura's did whenever she got angry, Eleanor reached over and squeezed his hand. In a voice soft and filled with love, she began to tell him all she knew about the woman who held their daughter's heart in her hand.

There was no one William trusted more than Eleanor, and over the next hour or so as she spoke of the damaged woman who loved his daughter, he felt his heart begin to open. Eleanor talked of the woman's strengths and frailties, of her intelligence and humor, but most of all she spoke of Toni's love for Laura. By the time their bellies were filled and their wineglasses were empty, William and Eleanor were in agreement. Their daughter had fallen in love with an amazing woman.

After dinner, banished from the kitchen while Eleanor made some coffee, Bill returned to the lounge and looked at the photographs around the room. Walking to the mantle, he touched the silver frame which held a picture of a baby wrapped in a blanket, and his eyes filled with tears. He had missed so much.

For three decades, he had sailed the seas, feeling the sun on his skin and the taste of salt in his mouth. It was the life he had chosen, but as the years slipped by, he realized he had chosen poorly. He had brought women to his bed when the need was great, but they had never heated his blood with just a look, nor made him groan with satisfaction from just one kiss.

Sniffling back a tear, he turned as Eleanor walked into the room, and gazing at one another, both lost the ability to speak. It had been years since they had been alone. Years since they could talk without family or friends getting in the way and up until now, it was what they both wanted. Divorce may have ended their marriage, but nothing could erase their love.

With her hair shimmering in the softly lit room, Eleanor looked as she did so many years before. Feeling his body react to the beauty of the woman he loved, William held his breath and tried to memorize the moment.

Outside the cottage, winds whipped and temperatures continued to fall, but inside the house, it was warm and still. The tick-tock of the clock on the mantle seemed to slow as Eleanor gazed at the man she loved. Silently admonishing herself for the pangs of want settling in her core, she tried to find her voice, but it was gone. Swept away by the desire she saw in his eyes and the scent of his cologne in the air, Eleanor could do nothing but return his look, and when he took a half-step toward her, her breath caught in her throat.

"Ellie..." he said, stopping abruptly when his voice cracked like a schoolboy's. Clearing his throat, he started again. "Look, Ellie, I know that I made...I made a tremendous mistake by walking away from you and Laura, but I want you to know...no...I *need* you to know that I've never, ever stopped loving you both. I know you'll never forgive me for what I did back then, and...um...I can't ask you to, but if there's a chance, any chance at all that you and I...that we...oh, damn it all to hell," Bill growled, shoving his hands in the pockets of his trousers.

Eleanor's heart was racing and her palms were sweaty, but a smile was lurking just below the surface. Standing her ground, she refused to move until he said the words she needed to hear...even if it took all night.

Annoyed at his boyish fumbling, Bill wrinkled his brow. "You could help me out here, you know?"

"Not on your life," Eleanor said softly, allowing the corners of her mouth to move upwards just a tad.

Rubbing his chin, Bill stared at her for a moment before the words finally tumbled out. "Damn it, Ellie, I love you. I always have and I always will, and I've been a fucking bloody fool! I know I wasted a hell of a lot of years traipsing all over this world looking for something I thought I wanted, but I forgot to look here," he said, tapping his finger against his chest. "I forgot to look in my heart. I forgot that it only beats when I'm around you. I forgot that waking up beside you is the only way I want my day to start, and falling asleep in your arms is the only way I want it to end. I forgot how I loved to watch you wear my clothes after a night...after a night that turned into a day, and how we used to eat burnt dinners because...because we hungered for something else. Eleanor, I know that I've made mistakes. God knows I've made mistakes, but I don't want to make any more. I love you, Ellie, and I will until the day I die."

No longer able to hide her smile, Eleanor glanced at the clock on the mantle. "I expect them tomorrow around six." Seeing the confused look on William's face, she walked over and gazed into the green eyes that held her soul. "I know we're older, and one of us is apparently *much* wiser, but I fear unless we set an alarm, we may very well give our daughter more of an education than I think she needs."

Tears sprung to his eyes, and within seconds, they were in each other's arms. At first, their lips touched in slow, short kisses filled with uncertainty, but when Eleanor began to taste what she never thought she'd taste again, she deepened the kiss, and William answered in kind. She sighed at the solidness of his form as he held her tightly, and when his hands cupped her arse, pressing her even harder against his body, she smiled into the kiss.

Neither noticed the time as it ticked slowly by, for lost in the emotion called love, they stood in the lounge and kissed and kissed...and kissed some more. Finally, they parted, and no words were spoken as Eleanor led him to the bedroom. After lighting a few candles, she turned to the man she loved. "Say it again."

"I love you."

"Promise me that you'll never hurt me like that again."

No longer able to stop the emotion, tears cascaded down William's face, and in a ragged whisper he said, "I would sooner die a thousand deaths than to ever...*ever* hurt you again. I promise you, Eleanor, as God is my witness, I will spend the rest of my days loving you like no other man could."

CHAPTER FORTY-ONE

"Sorry we're late," Laura said, walking into the house. "There were some spots on the road that still had snow on them."

"No worries, sweetheart. You're here now and that's all that matters," Eleanor said as she pulled her daughter into a hug. "Oh, I'm so glad you decided to take me up on my offer."

"So are we," Laura said, looking over her shoulder at Toni, who seemed intent on staring at the floor.

Pulling out of Laura's arms, Eleanor walked over, and tilting her head to catch Toni's eye, she said, "I hear congratulations are in order." Seeing Toni grin, without thinking, Eleanor gave her a hug, but when she felt the woman stiffen, instead of letting go, she held on tight. Pausing for a moment, Eleanor whispered, "Your mother was a fool to let you go, but I never will. I have two daughters now, and I love them both."

Laura had no idea what her mother had whispered in Toni's ear, but when she saw Toni warmly return the hug, Laura's eyes glistened with emotion.

The embrace ended and the two women parted. For a moment their eyes met and then Eleanor watched as Toni's expression turned blank as she tilted her head to one side. "What's wrong, dear?" Eleanor asked.

GIVE ME A REASON

Confused and more than slightly amused at the thought that had just run through her head, Toni said, "Oh...um...nothing. You just...you just reminded me of Laura for a moment. That's all."

"Must be the lighting. They say those new bulbs do wonders," Eleanor said with a laugh. "But enough about me. I've been patient long enough. How about you show me that ring my daughter gave you?"

"Oh...oh, of course," Toni said, pulling off her gloves.

Smiling at the sight of the diamond on the woman's hand, Eleanor said, "It's beautiful, Toni. Oh, Laura, it's absolutely stunning. I've honestly never seen a more gorgeous ring."

"Well, you might want to rethink that," Laura said.

"What? Why would you say such a thing?" Eleanor asked, turning around.

"Because Toni decided that I needed one, too."

Quickly glancing back at Toni, Eleanor murmured, "Good girl," under her breath and then rushed to her daughter's side.

Laura's face turned radiant as she pulled off her brown suede gloves, her inner glow becoming brighter as she watched her mother's eyes bulge.

Trying to stay with the style Laura had chosen for her, Toni also purchased an emerald-cut diamond in a yellow-gold band, but while the cuts were identical, the band around Laura's finger held not only the large center stone, but channel-set into the shoulders were six smaller diamonds.

"Oh my," Eleanor said in a breath. Quickly glancing at her daughter, Eleanor turned and looked at Toni. "Oh my."

***

Looking up from the cutting board as Laura came into the kitchen, Eleanor asked, "All settled in?"

"Yes, and thanks for putting us in the same room."

"Why wouldn't I? I'm assuming Toni's gotten over her issues with being touched, at least by you, that is."

Seeing Laura's face flush scarlet, Eleanor laughed. "Oh, it does a mother's heart good to see she can still embarrass her child on occasion." Noticing the smile on Laura's face seemed to disappear a bit too quickly, Eleanor asked, "What's wrong, dear?"

"Mum, I know that you're okay with my relationship with Toni, but what happens if the rest of the family isn't?"

"What do you mean?"

"I don't want your Christmas ruined because of us."

"The only way my Christmas could be ruined would be if you and Toni weren't here to celebrate it with me."

"But—"

"No buts, Laura. I don't give a damn what the rest of the family thinks about it!"

"Does that include Bill?"

"I've already told your father."

"What? I thought that's why you invited him over here tonight."

"Well, I thought I should warn him—"

"Warn him!"

Startled by Laura's tone, Eleanor looked up and then immediately scowled. "Poor choice of words."

"Was it?"

"Calm your feathers, Laura. What I was trying to say was that I thought I should *inform* your father of Toni's...well, her idiosyncrasies, so he didn't walk in here and attempt to shake her hand or, God forbid, try to give her a hug."

Laura's anger disappeared in an instant. "I'm sorry. I wasn't thinking about that."

"Well, I assumed you probably had your hands full with Toni and getting ready for this visit, so I thought the least I could do is take care of your father."

"And did you?"

Images not meant to share with one's daughter filled Eleanor's mind, and as her cheeks began to burn she quickly turned toward the sink without saying a word.

"Mum? Are you okay?"

Pretending not to hear over the running water, several seconds passed before Eleanor turned off the taps.

"Mum?"

"I'm sorry. What?" Eleanor said, turning around.

"You said you talked to Bill. I was just trying to find out what his reaction was."

"Oh, well, as you might expect, he was somewhat surprised, and when he found out Toni had spent some time in prison, he was...well, let's just say he was concerned. But after I told him some of the particulars, he came to the same conclusion that I did. As long as you're happy, he's happy."

Laura narrowed her eyes as she stared back at her mother. "Really?"

"You seem surprised."

"I am."

"Why? Did you assume because of what he did all those years ago that he was some sort of…I don't know, monster?"

"He walked out on you."

"He walked out on *us*, but it wasn't because he didn't love us, Laura. He was just young and stupid."

"Why do you always defend him?"

"Why do you always defend me?" Toni asked, walking into the room.

"Hiya, sweetheart," Laura chirped. "Doing better?"

Eleanor let out a sigh, noticing that Toni appeared pale and on edge. "Oh my and here I thought you were comfortable around me."

"You're not the reason I'm nervous."

"Meeting William then? Laura's father."

"Meeting anyone actually, but I'll admit being around men is harder," Toni said.

"Mum, maybe you should call him. Tell him—"

"No, Laura," Toni said, taking a step in her direction. "This isn't just any man we're talking about. He's your father, and we should meet."

"I know, sweetheart, but we just got here, and if you need more time—"

"You can't protect me from the world. Remember?" Toni said, placing her hands on Laura's shoulders. "We both know I'm going to have issues. It's unavoidable, but your mum did a good thing by inviting him here tonight."

"Yeah?"

"Yes. That way I only have to worry about one new person instead of a group. I do better that way. You know that."

"Yes, I do."

"Then it's settled," Toni said, placing a light kiss on Laura's forehead. "But make sure you've got Abby on speed dial, just in case."

The ringing of the doorbell caused all three women to jump, and as Eleanor headed toward the entry, Laura glanced at Toni one more time. "You ready for this?"

"Ready," Toni said, taking Laura's hand. "I just hope he is."

When Eleanor opened the front door and saw William standing there, her face lit up. She leaned in for a kiss, but then jerked back when she remembered they weren't alone. Apologizing by way of a quick shrug, she ushered him inside, and even though they managed to keep their smiles under control, their eyes twinkled with a merriment that very well may have bested Santa Claus.

"Hello, William," Eleanor said softly. "Remember what I told you."

"Yes, dear," he whispered, placing a large bag on a nearby table. Removing his coat, he draped it over a chair, and as he picked up the bag, Laura came from the kitchen. Smiling, he went over and kissed her on the cheek. "Hello, Laura. I swear you're getting more beautiful every day."

Up until that moment, their meetings had been accidental and almost always wooden. One had never felt he had the right to expect more than cordial, and the other had never been willing to give anything but. So, slightly unsettled by her father's words and actions, it took a second before Laura said, "Um...hi, Bill. You're...you're looking well."

"Fit as a fiddle, as they say," he said, glancing over her shoulder.

The night before, Eleanor had done her best to describe the tall woman standing near the kitchen, but Bill quickly decided that her best apparently needed improvement. She had said Laura's partner was attractive, but the woman with black hair and soulful eyes was much more than that, and while Eleanor had told him that Toni was neither gruff nor butch, William hadn't believed her...but he did now.

"So, are you going to introduce us?" he asked, catching Laura's eye. "Or should I ask your mother to do me the honor?"

Laura flashed a dazzling smile, and then walking over, she took Toni's hand. Giving it a reassuring squeeze, she turned to her father. "Toni, this is my...my father, Bill MacLeod. Bill, this is my fiancée, Toni Vaughn."

Taking Eleanor's warning to heart, Bill didn't move an inch, and almost immediately, an awkward silence fell over the room. Realizing his lack of etiquette might be misinterpreted, Bill's face brightened with every ounce of charm he owned. "Pleased to meet you, Toni."

Toni stared back at the man for a moment. Just as Laura had described, he was tall, nearly Toni's height, and his face was tanned by years in the sun, but what Laura hadn't mentioned was that the gentleman standing with one hand in a pocket and the other holding a large paper sack was, in Toni's eyes, rather dashing. His wavy hair seemed to have a mind of its own, and even at a distance she could see that his eyes were a brilliant green. Matching the emerald in Laura's eyes, the color calmed her nerves, and slowly, she held out her hand. "It's a pleasure, Mr. MacLeod."

After one quick glance at Eleanor to silently get her approval, Bill pulled his hand out of his pocket and extended it to Toni. Tempering his normally firm grip, he was impressed when the one returned was confident and strong, and as they ended their greeting, he held out the bag he had been holding. "Well, I don't know about you, but I could do with a drink after that," he said, making light of the anxiousness that seemed to hang in the air. "How about you?"

Already flustered by the affection he had shown her seconds before, Laura was now dumbstruck. The man she believed meant nothing to her had just filled her heart with pride. In a few seconds, he had managed to break the ice, and with smiles on their faces, she watched as her partner and her parents went to the kitchen to pour themselves a drink. Scratching her head, Laura followed in silence, trying to make sense of the feelings that had just caused goose bumps to appear on her skin.

***

The rest of the evening moved smoothly, and conversation around the dinner table centered on the upcoming holiday. Eleanor talked about the decorating she wanted to do, and with groans and grins, they tried to plan their week, and when Bill volunteered his services, Eleanor was pleasantly surprised when both Toni and Laura agreed.

"Well, I don't know about you, but I think I need to rest a bit before we have dessert," Eleanor said, pushing out her chair. "How about I clean this up and we all relax for a few?"

"I'll help," Laura chimed in, grabbing her plate, but when Toni began to gather their glasses, Laura shooed her away. "We'll do it. Go get a smoke, and I'll make some coffee."

Enjoying the fact that her partner knew her so well, Toni went to fetch her jacket, and as she was walking to the back door, Eleanor said, "Oh, Toni. I had some work done out there. There's a new switch by the door. Turn it on when you go out."

Toni flipped the toggle and stepped outside to find that the gardens were now awash in low-voltage lighting.

The winter in Scotland had begun with a bang. With two weeks of frigid temperatures and more than an ample amount of snow, as Toni walked across the slate, she was thankful for the addition of the short border lamps. Casting their light over the patio, she could easily make out the shimmering patches of ice as she made her way to the bench. Pulling out her pack of cigarettes, she sat down and looked toward the garden.

Pathway lights had been placed alongside the stepping stones that led to the Japanese maple, and while the red leaves had long since blown away, she could still make out the branches, courtesy of a small spotlight placed at the base of the tree.

Hearing the door open, she turned and watched as Bill stepped outside.

Holding up his pipe, he asked, "Do you mind?"

"No...no, not at all," she said, unconsciously moving farther down the bench.

Standing by the door, Bill packed his pipe, and after fumbling for his lighter, he walked over and sat down. Blocking the breeze with his hand, he puffed on the stem until the tobacco caught fire. Within seconds, the air began to smell of earth and chocolate as the burley smoldered, and taking another puff, he pulled his coat closed. "It's a bit chilly out here tonight, isn't it?"

"Yes...yes, it is," Toni said, staring at the slate beneath her feet.

It felt odd to sit so close to a man and not feel fear, to not worry about the brass buckle on his belt or believe the words he spoke were untrue. They had only known each other for a few hours, but from the moment they met, it seemed to Toni that he was trying his best to make her feel comfortable. He hadn't offered his hand until she had offered hers. He hadn't tried to exclude her from conversations, or direct his attention only to his daughter or his ex-wife, nor had Toni wanted to be excluded. She found Bill charming and unassuming...just like his daughter.

"I hope you don't mind me volunteering to help you girls decorate."

"Um...no, that's fine."

"If you don't mind, I'd like to suggest we start on the outside tomorrow. If I know Eleanor, she'll probably have us hanging lights from the chimney, and they're calling for more snow in a few days. I don't want any of us standing on ladders in that kind of weather."

"I'm afraid all the ladder work will be up to you and me."

"Why's that?"

Pushing what remained of her cigarette into the dirt of a nearby planter, Toni said, "Laura's afraid of heights."

When Bill didn't respond, Toni looked in his direction, and watched as he slowly took a long pull on the pipe.

"I...I had no idea," Bill said softly as he turned to look at her.

Even in the shadows of the night, Toni could see the hurt in his eyes. He was a father who had a child he didn't know. He was clueless as to her favorite color or the type of music she liked. He had no idea if she enjoyed cooking or had a hobby, and the only thing he *thought* he knew was that one day she'd marry, start a family and give him grandchildren he'd probably never see, but even that was wrong...well, maybe just a bit.

"She's not very fond of spiders either," Toni said, hoping to provide him a bit more insight.

Giving Toni a quick glance, his frown eased just a bit. "Truth be known, neither am I."

It was enough to lighten the mood, and even though the night was frigid, neither seemed to want to leave the bench. Lighting another cigarette, Toni asked, "So, what time do you think we should get started tomorrow?"

"I can be here at any time. Earlier the better, as far as I'm concerned."

"Well, we might have a problem convincing Laura of that."

"Oh? Not an early riser?"

"If early is noon, then yes."

Letting out a laugh, Bill said, "It seems I have a lot to learn about her, don't I?"

"I think we all have things to learn."

"That's why I offered my services in the decorating department."

"It is?"

"Well, I'd like to get to know you both better before the family gathers, and I find you can learn a lot about a person whilst watching them untangle Christmas lights."

"Is that the only reason you volunteered?"

"What do you mean?"

"I just thought maybe you were trying to spend a bit more time with Eleanor, now that you're back together."

Having just taken a pull from his pipe, Bill began to choke on the smoke. After coughing and sputtering for several seconds, he glanced in Toni's direction. Seeing her smile, he returned the look. "You're perceptive, I'll give you that. Can I ask how you knew?"

"I spent a lot of years with nothing better to do than to watch people. When you came into the house, you couldn't take your eyes off her. It seemed to me that you both were trying hard to hide your smiles, and Eleanor had this...um...well, she had this look in her eye."

"A look? What kind of look?"

"Let's just say I've seen it in Laura's before."

"Did you tell Laura about this?"

"No. We haven't really had a chance to chat since you got here, and it's not my place to tell her, now is it?"

"No, I suppose not, but feel free to take the initiative," he said, chortling as he re-lit his pipe.

"You think she'll have a problem with it?"

"She hates me. Of course, she'll have a problem with it."

"I think you're wrong. I mean, from what she's told me, she doesn't really know you that well, and she's never used the word hate when she talks about you."

"Well, I know how she feels about you," Bill said, taking a puff on his pipe. "You can see it in her eyes and in her smile. She has a marvelous smile, don't you think?"

"Yes, she does," Toni said, eyeing the man to her right. "Can I make an observation?"

"Of course."

"It's clear to me that you love Laura, so why doesn't she know that?"

Taking a deep breath, he said, "Because I walked out on them. How do you forgive someone for that?"

"It seems Eleanor has."

"And I give thanks for that every day, but she and I have a history. We share memories filled with love and laughter. Laura doesn't have those memories. She was too young to remember...thank God."

Wrinkling her brow, Toni asked, "What do you mean, thank God?"

Pausing for a moment, Bill took a long pull on his pipe. As he slowly let the smoke escape, he thought about the woman to his left. Well aware of how difficult it was for her to trust anyone, while he had never told a soul about what had happened...trust goes both ways.

"Thirty years ago, I was a young and strapping lad who thought there was nothing I couldn't do. I worked hard and I played even harder, but then one day, Ellie told me she was pregnant and all of a sudden, nothing else mattered. I didn't care if I ever played another game of football or stepped foot on another boat."

"But I thought—"

Shaking his head, Bill said, "The happiest day of my life was the day Laura was born, but she was so bloody small. I was as strong as an ox and just about as clumsy, so it took Ellie days before she finally convinced me to hold Laura, and then I never wanted to let her go. Oh Christ, she was so soft, and she smelled...she smelled so new."

"Then why did you leave?"

As Bill remembered that day so many years before, tears welled in his eyes. Taking another pull on his pipe, he said, "When Laura was barely six months old, she got a wee cold. Eleanor needed to go into town to get some medicine, so I stayed home with the baby. A few minutes after Ellie left Laura began to cry and try as I might, I couldn't get her to stop. She just kept crying louder and louder, and gasping for air. It was positively awful. I felt like such a fool because I'd seen Ellie calm her so many times by simply carrying her around the house or rocking her in her arms, but when I tried it, it made matters worse. Christ, talk about frustrating! Anyway, having run out of ideas, I decided to just lie on the bed with her until Ellie got home, and within a few minutes, Laura stopped crying. I was so bloody proud of myself, because I accomplished what I thought was impossible. You know?"

"I can imagine."

"Well, after a short while, Laura fell asleep, and I got up to make a cup of tea. It was only a few seconds. A short walk to the kitchen...it was just across the way, and then I heard her scream. God, what an awful sound that was...what an awful, awful sound..." Bill's voice trailed off as he hung his head, and sliding down his face, his tears fell to the slate in silence.

Without giving it a second thought, Toni reached over and took his hand. Holding it gently, she gave it a squeeze as she waited quietly for him to continue.

Wiping the tears from his face, Bill shook his head. "She had fallen off the bed. She...she must have rolled over, and when I ran back into the room she was on the floor screaming so bloody loud...so bloody loud. Christ, I wanted to die. I got her to the bed and took off her outfit, this stupid little thing with all these snaps, but I couldn't even find a bruise. There wasn't a scratch or...or a bump...or anything, but it didn't matter."

"What do you mean?"

"I wasn't fit to be a parent. I was a clumsy oaf and I almost destroyed our child. How could I have faced Ellie if that had happened?" he said, raising his eyes to meet Toni's. "By the time Eleanor got home, Laura had stopped crying, but I couldn't bring myself to let her know what I had done. It was the last time I ever picked up Laura or stayed at home with her alone, and before she had turned one, I asked Eleanor for a divorce. It was the hardest thing I ever had to do in my entire life, but I loved them both too much to stay."

"Maybe it's time Laura found out the truth."

"What? Tell her that her father was a coward? I'm not sure that's a lovable trait."

Toni smiled, remembering all the times she had used that word to describe herself to Abby. Squeezing his hand again, when Bill looked up, she said, "I've called myself a coward more times than I can remember. I'm afraid of strangers and of places I've never been, and I'm not sure I'll ever completely grasp the concept of trust again." Still holding on to Bill's hand, she gave it a shake. "And touching someone...or having them touch me *usually* causes my heart to race, but Laura has looked past all of that. She's looked past the scars and all of my defects and sees what's underneath. I can't tell you if cowardice is a lovable trait or not, but I can tell you that your daughter doesn't base her opinion about someone just because they think themselves weak. I'm living proof of that."

"Toni, you're her partner. All I am is a stranger."

"William, your blood flows through her veins, and whether you were there to see her first steps or take her to school doesn't erase that fact. You gave up something precious and your reason for doing so was anything but cowardly. It's probably the most unselfish thing I've ever heard, and one of these days Laura needs to know the truth. Give her a reason to love you, and trust me...she will."

CHAPTER FORTY-TWO

Having already discussed the plans for decorating the night before, when William showed up the next morning, the women had already emptied the attic of all the boxes marked Xmas. Due to Laura's aversion to heights, Toni and Bill had agreed that they would do the exterior of the house, while Eleanor and Laura would begin inside. As the boxes were brought downstairs, the ones marked Inside had been put in the lounge, while the ones marked Outside had been placed in the front hall. When Bill walked into the house and noticed the stack by the front door significantly smaller than the one in the lounge, he glanced at Toni and winked. Unfortunately, his cheerfulness was short-lived.

Explaining she had purchased a few new things, Eleanor led them down the hall to her home office, and sliding open the pocket doors, she happily pointed to the stack of LED lights sitting on the floor. A short time later, bundled up and carrying insulated cups of coffee, Toni and Bill trudged out into the brightness of a chilly winter morning.

When Eleanor had decided to move from the city to the country, her goal had been to find a small cottage tucked somewhere off the beaten path. She wanted to enjoy quiet nights and star-lit skies without the noise of traffic or neighbors who played their music loud enough to rattle windows. She had spent several years searching through listings for homes situated around the cities in which she worked, and like so many other prospective buyers, many of her weekends had been spent at open houses, grimacing at the decorating tastes of others.

Discouraged and tired, she was driving away from yet another open house when she saw a *For Sale by Owner* sign on the side of the road. Peering through some overgrown weeds, she noticed a gravel driveway, and carefully maneuvering her car around the underbrush, she came upon a stone cottage covered in ivy. At first, sighing at the fact that it was almost twice as large as what she wanted, she, nonetheless, rapped on the door. Three hours later, she left holding a purchase agreement in her hand.

Built before World War II, the house had seen its share of conversions, both inside and out. While the stone façade for both the house and detached garage remained as it had been some eighty years before, the windows, doors and roof had all been upgraded only a few years before Eleanor moved in. After signing on the dotted line, her first order of business was to have all the ivy removed, and once a few spots of mortar were repaired, and the trim around the windows and doors received a fresh coat of paint, the old house didn't look so old...at least not on the outside.

Enlisting her daughter's help, over one very long weekend, they had worked at cleaning the house from top to bottom, and once the painters were finished the following week, Eleanor's not-so-little country cottage was quickly becoming a home.

In order to capture as much natural light as she could through the small, boxy windows set deep into the stone, all the walls and ceilings had been painted white, while colors to match the décor of the rooms had been chosen for the trim. The oak flooring, darkened by years of wear and varnish, had been stripped, sanded and re-coated and now its honey-color helped reflect the light streaming through the window panes.

Having seen her share of interior design horror stories in her many years as an estate agent, Eleanor's approach to decorating the lounge was simplistic and comfortable. Knowing that the focal point of the lounge would be the wall covered in stone holding one of the three fireplaces in the cottage, she purchased a broad-striped area rug with bands of tan and cream to cover the floor, the colors matching with the natural sandstone almost perfectly. The creamy hues repeated in the upholstery covering the sofa and chairs surrounding the hearth, and an over-sized burnt-orange ottoman acted as the coffee table, with the shade repeating in the throw pillows scattered on the sofa, as well as in the curtains surrounding the windows.

Careful not to go over the budget she had given herself, while Eleanor had sold most of her old furniture to make room for the new; several pieces in dark walnut were kept and now acted as accents in the room. Given the size of the lounge, her favorite reading chairs now sat opposing each other near the two windows on the front wall, and a tiny table on which to place her nightly cup of tea stood in between. Bookcases that had once stored her child's board games had been painted white and placed along the walls, with each shelf now holding pictures and mementos gathered through the years.

Returning from the kitchen with two cups of coffee in her hand, when Eleanor saw her daughter standing by one of the front windows, she grinned. "You know, if you keep checking on her, we'll never get anything accomplished."

"It's just that she's out of her element here," Laura said, turning away from the window. "And she has problems when it comes to strangers."

"I don't think I'd classify your father as a stranger. True, they only just met last night, but it seems to me that they're getting on rather well."

Eleanor was right. The night before, although hesitant at first to join in the conversation around the dinner table, as the evening wore on, Toni's anxieties seemed to fade. By the time the meal was over, she was easily conversing with both Eleanor and Bill, and when he had arrived at the house that morning, Toni greeted him with a handshake without batting an eye.

"Yeah, I guess," Laura said, glancing out the window again. "But he is a man…"

Rolling her eyes, Eleanor walked over and pulled Laura away from the window. "Laura, I know that Toni has certain issues when it comes to being around men, but this isn't just *any* man. This is your father. I know you don't know him very well, but I do, and they'll be fine. Now, stop worrying about what's going on outside and help me get this room in order. Okay?"

Looking around at the stacks of boxes scattered about, Laura said, "Okay. Let's get to work."

"That's my girl," Eleanor said, handing Laura a cup of coffee. "Now, have a sip of that while I go fetch the step stool."

A few minutes later, Eleanor returned, and seeing the amused look on Laura's face, she asked, "What's so funny?"

"Apparently, Bill isn't the only man you know," Laura said, holding out her hand.

Confused, it took Eleanor a few seconds to realize what her daughter was talking about. "Oh my," she said, taking the navy blue boxers from Laura. "Can I ask where you found these?"

"I was moving the magazine rack out of the way. They were behind it."

"I see," Eleanor said, crumpling the boxers in her hand. "Well, let me just put these in the laundry, shall I?"

Before Laura could say a word, her mother left the room, and immediately Laura's smile returned. At first, shocked to discover the undergarment, the more Laura thought about what it could mean, the happier she became. Through the years, her mother had dated a few men, but none had been around for long, and as far as Laura knew, none had ever visited her mother's bed...until now. Believing that Eleanor had finally found someone special, Laura was overjoyed, but she wasn't yet willing to share that information. After all the years of telling her mother about her love affairs, it was time to turn the tables...and the screws.

"So, care to explain?" Laura asked when Eleanor came back into the room.

"Explain what, dear?"

"Well, it's not every day that a daughter finds out that her mother is sleeping around," Laura said, quickly clamping her lips together to stop her smile from escaping.

"I most certainly am not!"

"Mother, there was a pair of boxers hanging off the back of the bloody magazine rack, for God's sake."

"That doesn't mean I've been sleeping around. It just means...it just means that I'm not as tidy as I used to be."

"So...what? You were doing laundry, and somehow they flew out of the basket and landed on the floor in the corner?"

"I don't think I like your tone. You're making this sound tawdry, and it's anything but."

"I don't know, Mum. Having men's underwear draped all over the lounge sounds a bit reckless if you ask me. I never knew you were that loose."

"Laura Margaret MacLeod, how *dare* you!"

Staring in shocked disbelief at her daughter, it wasn't until Laura crumpled to the floor in a fit of laughter that Eleanor understood that she was being played. Deciding to wait until Laura had herself under control, a few minutes later, Eleanor finally said, "It wasn't *that* funny."

Looking up, Laura wiped the tears from her face. "Oh, Mum, you should have seen your face."

Squatting by her daughter's side, Eleanor narrowed her eyes as she tried not to laugh. "I'm going to get you for that if it's the last thing I do."

"I'm sorry, but I couldn't help myself, and you were so...so *appalled*."

"You called me loose!"

Watching as her daughter dissolved into another fit of giggles, Eleanor waited a few seconds before asking, "You're okay with this then?"

"To tell you the truth, when I first found them I was...well, I was stunned. I mean, finding out that your mother is...is—"

"Getting some?" Eleanor said, humor shining in her eyes.

"Yes!" Laura said, jumping to her feet. "And why didn't you tell me sooner? I thought we didn't have any secrets."

"I wasn't sure how you'd take it, so I thought I'd wait a while. Get past the Christmas rush and all," Eleanor said, opening a box of decorations. Pulling out a length of green garland, she looked around the room. "How about we put this over the windows?"

Puzzled by the rapid change of subject, Laura took the garland, but her curiosity got the best of her before she reached the window. Turning around, she asked, "What's wrong?"

Looking up from a box of decorations, Eleanor said, "What do you mean, dear?"

"Mum, I wasn't born yesterday. Now, come on, out with it."

"I have no idea what you're talking about."

"Rubbish," Laura said, tossing the garland on a chair. "You're hiding something. Now, what is it? Is he married?"

"I won't even honor *that* with an answer, young lady."

"He is a *he*, isn't he?" Laura asked through a grin.

"I wouldn't have it any other way," Eleanor said, smiling back. "I'll leave the fairer sex to you. No offense."

"Okay, so who is he?"

Eleanor gazed at her daughter and quickly resigned herself to the fact Laura wasn't about to give up. Her chin was high. Her eyes were sparkling, and if anyone knew the breadth of Laura's stubborn streak, it was the woman who had raised her. Dogs with bones had nothing on Laura MacLeod. Inhaling slowly, Eleanor said, "It's your father."

"*What!*"

"It seems that we've decided to give it another go."

"Oh, you've *got* to be joking."

"No, I'm not."

Placing her hands on her hips, Laura said, "Have you forgotten that he walked out on you thirty years ago?"

"I haven't forgotten anything, Laura. Not one thing."

Sitting on the arm of the couch, Eleanor paused for a moment to get her thoughts in order. "A long time ago you asked me why I never dated. Do you remember?"

"Yes, of course."

"Well, I'm happy to say that it wasn't for the lack of invitations, but none of them held a candle to your father. It's just that simple. Their words weren't as sweet. Their cologne wasn't as familiar, and their touch wasn't his. Laura, I've loved your father for longer than you've been alive...and there's nothing I can do about it. You asked me if I remembered him walking out, and I can tell you the clothes he wore that day. I remember our first date, our first kiss, and when he told me he loved me for the very first time. I remember everything.

"I love him, Laura. I always have and I always will. I know you have ill feelings when it comes to your father, and rightfully so. All I'm asking is that you look at him the same way I look at Toni. He's the one that I want, Laura, so please be happy for me."

Eleanor had just put Laura where she, herself, had stood only a few months earlier. If Laura was to argue the point, to dispute her mother's choice of partner, then Laura would put her own beliefs ahead of her mother's. If she was to accept it, their relationship would remain strong and unwavering. There was no argument.

Going over, Laura knelt by her mother and took her hand. "If he makes you happy, Mum, then I'm happy. Just please don't expect me to call him Dad. Okay?"

"I wouldn't think of it, Laura," Eleanor said, smiling back at her daughter. "I wouldn't think of it."

***

"You knew?"

"No, not for sure. I just had a feeling."

"Why didn't you tell me?"

"I just told you, I wasn't sure."

"You could have mentioned it."

"What was I supposed to say?" Toni said, walking into the bathroom to brush her teeth. "I think your mother had a good shag today?"

"What!"

Poking her head out, Toni smiled. "When we walked in last night, she had this look in her eye, and it's the same one you get after we've...well, after we've had a good romp, shall I say."

"Oh, I can't believe this," Laura said, throwing herself on the bed. "My mother and...and *him*."

"He's not that bad, you know."

"I know. It's just...it's just weird. After everything he did, and after all these years, to think of them back together, it's just...*so* bizarre."

"Yeah, I guess it would be, but they both seem happy."

"That they do," Laura said as she placed her hands under her head. Staring at the ceiling, she thought about the day.

By early afternoon, the eaves of the cottage had been outlined in white icicle lights, and every shrub in the front garden had been draped in netted lighting. Silhouettes of deer wrapped in LED strands stood proudly under a tree, while angels with trumpets lined the driveway leading to the house. Gathering their empty boxes, Toni and Bill had trudged inside, and after being warmed by hot chocolate with just a splash of brandy, and a lunch of finger sandwiches, they joined Laura and her mother to finish what was left.

Having decided that they wouldn't get a tree until Sunday, one corner of the lounge was left untouched, but by late that afternoon the rest of the house was adorned in the colors and scents of the season.

The photographs and mementos lining the tops of the bookcases were rearranged to make room for candles smelling of pine and bayberry, and snow globes displaying tiny villages were placed lovingly alongside framed photographs of family and friends. Tall and stately nutcrackers stood guard on the window sills, and figurines of Santa Claus and angels greeted visitors in every room. The banister was draped in the same green garland as the windows, and white fairy lights were strung over the doorway, awaiting a sprig of mistletoe soon to be purchased.

A nativity scene which had been handed down through the family was placed atop the mantle, and Laura carefully arranged each figure exactly as her mother had shown her years before. Completing the decorations above the hearth, Eleanor placed two cast-iron stocking hangers to the left and right of the manger, but glancing at the stockings in her hand, she turned sad, mumbling that she had forgotten to buy another. Seconds later, her heart overflowed with love when Laura chimed in, "Don't you mean two?"

It was an afternoon filled with laughter and jokes, and as Laura watched and listened, she couldn't help but smile at the happiness she saw in both her parents' eyes.

Laura's thoughts returned to now, and glancing in Toni's direction, she remained quiet as she watched the woman get undressed. Doing her best to finish every meal put in front of her, Toni had finally managed to put on a few pounds. Even though her stomach was still flat and muscled, her hips had become soft and rounded. Secretly wincing at the stark white run-of-the-mill underwear Toni was wearing, Laura said, "We really need to get you some new things."

"What do you mean?" Toni asked, pulling on a pair of pajama bottoms.

"Aren't you the one that said white was boring?"

Smiling at the memory, Toni unfastened her bra, tossing it aside while she rummaged through a drawer for a T-shirt. Glancing in Laura's direction, as soon as she saw the look in her eyes, Toni said, "Don't even think about it."

"Think about what?" Laura asked, keeping her eyes fixed on Toni's naked breasts.

Quickly pulling a dark blue T-shirt over her head, Toni pushed the drawer closed. "You know exactly what I'm talking about."

"If I'm not mistaken, you *did* lose the bet," Laura said as she began unbuttoning her pajama top.

"Don't you dare," Toni scolded, striding over to fasten everything Laura had just unfastened. "It's only been two days, and you know how I feel about this. I don't want your mother hearing this bed squeak all night long."

"It won't take all night," Laura said, raising her eyes to meet Toni's. "Not unless you want it to."

Toni sat on the edge of the bed and laced her fingers through Laura's. "Can I just hold you tonight? Just hold you? Things are changing for me, Laura, and every day seems like something else new and wonderful is happening. I worked side-by-side with a man today—a *man*. I didn't feel the fear I thought I would, and even after he grabbed me—"

"He grabbed you!"

"I fell—"

"You fell!"

Placing her finger on Laura's lips, Toni said, "I slipped off the ladder, but your dad was there to catch me. At first, all I wanted to do was run, but then I saw his face, and my fear...my fear just went away. It was like...it was like taking the deepest breath you can and everything around you, the smells and the sounds, they just get inside of you and you know it's going to be okay."

Emotions began to rise to the surface, and as her eyes filled with tears, Toni said in ragged whisper, "I love you with all my heart, Laura, all of it, but tonight...tonight I just want to hold you in my arms and breathe you in. Can I do that? Will you let me do that...please?"

Laura pulled Toni into her arms. Covering them both with the quilt, she turned off the bedside lamp, and as they held each other close in the darkness...they breathed.

CHAPTER FORTY-THREE

The next morning the women returned to Stirling, and while Eleanor went in search of Christmas stockings and holders, Toni and Laura visited a few of the smaller stores to do a bit of last-minute shopping.

After paying for her purchase of two personalized Christmas stockings, Eleanor walked out of the store and opened her mobile, but before she could press the speed dial button, she heard someone call her name. Turning around, she scanned the crowd, and then saw Nancy and Peggy walking her way.

"Fancy meeting you here," Eleanor said as they approached.

"Of all people, Eleanor, I would have thought you'd have been done with your shopping months ago," Nancy said, leaning in for a quick kiss on the cheek.

"I thought I was, but I forgot a few things," Eleanor said, holding up the bag in her hand. Glancing at her niece, Eleanor's smile grew large at the sight of the woman's very swollen belly. "Hiya, Peggy," she said, pulling her into a hug. "I can't believe you still have four weeks to go!"

"Neither can I," the young woman jokingly moaned, rubbing her enormous baby bump.

"Ell, we were just going to grab a bite to eat. You interested?" Nancy asked, shifting one of her many bags to the other hand.

"Actually, I'm starving. Let me just call Laura to see if she'd like to join us."

"Laura? Laura's here already!" Nancy blurted. "Well, that's a shock. She always seems to be so busy, but I suppose when you don't have a husband and children to care for the world is your oyster, as they say."

Taking a deep breath, Eleanor held it until she smothered every cutting remark that came to mind. Thankfully, they died before she did. Forcing a smile to appear, she said, "Yes, I suppose, but Laura's decided to spend a few weeks up here this year. She actually arrived the other night with her partner."

"Her partner!" Nancy said, taking a half-step backward. "Oh, that's wonderful, Ellie! Maybe this means you'll finally get all those grandbabies you've always wanted."

Accustomed to Nancy's one-track mind, Eleanor glanced at Peggy, who in turn simply shook her head, silently apologizing for her mother's glib remark. Turning back to Nancy, Eleanor's eyes sparkled with mischief. "Let me just call them, shall I? I'm sure Laura can't wait for you to meet Toni."

***

Standing a short distance away from the entrance to the pub, Laura eyed the woman standing next to her. "You ready for this?"

"Let me just grab another smoke—"

"You've had two!"

Frowning, Toni pocketed the pack of cigarettes. "Sorry, just me being me...*again*."

"Look, I can call Mum back. Just because we said yes, doesn't mean we can't change our minds," Laura said, touching Toni on the sleeve. "You can meet them another day."

"That's just putting off the inevitable, isn't it?"

"Yes, but if you need a few more days—"

"I guess years aren't an option, huh?"

Taking Toni's hand, Laura gave it a squeeze. "Afraid not, sweetheart, but if you want to skip having lunch with them, that much I can do."

Laura was always *doing* for Toni. Always waiting, always helping, never pushing, and never putting her wants in front of Toni's, but Laura had wants, too. She had a family inside the pub waiting for her. Eager to see her, to chat and to laugh, but again, she was willing to walk away and all Toni had to do was ask. As Toni gazed back at Laura, everything Abby had taught her disappeared. "Do you love me?"

"More than I can put into words."

"And if I freak out in there?"

"You haven't done that in ages, sweetheart."

Squaring her shoulders, Toni nodded. "Okay. Let's go."

***

Nancy Shaw looked up from her menu just as her niece came into the bar, and noticing the person walking next to Laura, she let loose a loud guffaw. "Oh, Ellie, you really had me going for a moment, now didn't you?"

Confused, Eleanor looked up. Following Nancy's and Peggy's line of sight, she smiled when she saw Laura and Toni heading their way.

Sliding out of the booth, Eleanor hugged them both, and seeing the nervousness in Toni's eyes, she quickly slid back into the booth and motioned for Toni to follow. Holding Toni's hand under the table, she waited until Laura was seated to say, "Nancy and Peggy, this is Toni Vaughn, Laura's partner."

After quickly glancing at her cousin, Peggy smiled and held out her hand. "Nice to meet you, Toni."

Watching the exchange, Nancy's eyes traveled to Toni. With a penetrating stare, she scrutinized all she could see of her until it was her turn to extend her hand. Doing so, she said, "Yes, very nice to meet you."

"Thank you. Nice to meet you also," Toni said quietly.

Regarding the woman with a mixture of kindness and curiosity, Nancy couldn't pry her eyes away until the greeting had ended. Glancing in Laura's direction, she said, "Your mother didn't tell me you started your own business, Laura."

Tilting her head to the side for a second, Laura looked past Toni, and when she saw the amusement in her mother's eyes, the penny dropped. Giving Toni's knee a squeeze under the table, Laura said, "I didn't start a business, Nancy. Why would you think that?"

"Well, because she said you were here with your partner, but obviously, we've had a miscommunication."

Sitting quietly by her mother's side, Peggy Wallace studied the black-haired woman sitting opposite her for a few moments before glancing back at her cousin. Until the day Laura had left for university, Peggy and Laura had been inseparable. Born only four months apart, they had grown up in each other's shadow, and over the years, they had shared their dolls and their dreams. They had tittered over boys, blushed about firsts, and could even finish each other's sentences without batting an eye. So when Laura finally looked in her direction and their eyes met, Peggy simply tilted her head as if to ask *really* and grinning, Laura answered with a wink.

Lacing her fingers through Toni's in full view of everyone at the table, Laura said, "Actually, there wasn't any miscommunication, Nancy. Toni is my partner...as in significant other."

Nancy's eyes almost popped out of her head at the announcement, her mouth falling open seconds later to allow her to suck in all the air the room contained. Taking a quick gulp of her ale, she looked down her nose at Eleanor. "Well, I guess that means you'll never have those grandchildren you so desperately wanted, Eleanor. Feel free to visit mine whenever you feel the need."

"That won't be necessary," Toni said, looking up from the table. Locking her eyes on the woman who was wearing a turquoise and pink open-weave sweater, Toni said, "In this day and age, there are lots of ways to have children, and once Laura and I are married, we'll find the one that suits us best and use it...to our heart's content."

Although they tried not to show it, Laura and Eleanor were stunned when Toni spoke up. Packed tightly in on their side of the booth, they both could feel Toni's knees shaking under the table, and while her breathing appeared to be normal, her palms were sweating so badly they were both worried she was heading toward a panic attack...and as it turned out, she was.

The stores and streets had been crowded with last-minute shoppers, and having been shoved, jostled and touched more times than she could remember, before Toni ever stepped foot in the pub, her nerves had already been frayed. She had convinced herself that she could handle meeting these women, but doing it in a bar overflowing with people was not the place. It was noisy with patrons trying to talk over each other. The televisions were blaring, and sitting directly behind her in another booth were men smelling of ale and cigarettes. She was just about to excuse herself to go to the ladies' room when she had heard Nancy's haughty tone. It had set Toni's teeth on edge, and for a split-second, her fears had disappeared. Unfortunately, that second had long since gone.

Lowering her eyes, Toni leaned toward Laura and said quietly, "Slide out, Laura. I need the loo."

Laura had been staring back at her aunt, watching as the woman's face bloomed with embarrassment, but as soon as she heard the strain in Toni's voice, Laura looked at her partner. In an instant, she knew what was happening.

"Actually, so do I," Laura said, sliding out of the booth. Allowing Toni to pass, Laura said, "We'll be right back, Mum. Order us some wine, will you?"

***

"Breathe, sweetheart…just breathe."

I...I can't...I can't...I can't...breathe," Toni said as she gasped for air. "Can't...breathe...help...me..."

"Shit!" Laura said as she looked around the room for her handbag. Realizing she had left it in the booth, Laura's face went slack for a moment, but only for a moment. Returning her eyes to Toni, Laura spoke calmly and clearly, with not one ounce of worry in her tone. "Sweetheart, listen to my voice. I need you to breathe slowly, Toni. Just take nice easy—"

"Oh, my God, what's wrong?" Peggy said, seeing the two women huddled in the corner of the room. "Laura, what's wrong?"

"Don't ask questions, Peg. Just go get my handbag. I left it in the booth, and don't let them know about this. Okay?"

Without answering, Peggy waddled from the bathroom as fast as her pregnant body would allow. Getting to the booth, she quickly grabbed Laura's purse from the bench, and without batting an eye, she simply said, "Time of the month," and went back the way she came.

When Peggy returned to the ladies' room, she found Laura and Toni exactly where she had left them. Toni was still gasping for air, and Laura's faced was shrouded in worry. "What am I looking for?" she asked, holding up Laura's handbag.

Intent on trying to keep Toni calm, Laura didn't hear the door open and jumping, she cast a quick glance in Peggy's direction. "Oh, thank God, it's you. Look inside. There's a paper bag. I need it, Peggy. I need it now!"

Leaving Peggy to fumble through her over-filled handbag, Laura turned back to Toni. "Sweetheart, just keep listening to my voice. Okay? Remember what Abby told you. Concentrate on your breathing. Nice easy breaths...in and out—"

"I got it!" Peggy shouted, pulling the sack from Laura's handbag. Shaking it open, she said, "You keep talking to her. I've got this." Moving slowly so she wouldn't scare the panicked woman, Peggy placed the bag over Toni's mouth and nose.

For a split-second, Laura gawked at her cousin, but the sound of the paper bag crackling brought Laura's attention back to Toni. "That's it, sweetheart. Take some nice slow breaths just like Abby said. You know what to do. Just concentrate on my voice. You're safe, and we're here to help. Just focus on me, Toni. Forget about everything else. Just focus on me."

It took a while before Toni slowed her breathing enough for Peggy to feel comfortable removing the bag. Letting out a sigh of relief, she watched as Laura helped Toni slide slowly to the floor. "Is she okay?"

Brushing away the sweat-soaked strands of hair from Toni's forehead, Laura said, "Yeah, it's just going to take a few minutes."

"I take it that she's had these before?"

Looking up at her cousin, Laura said, "Yes, but she hasn't had one this bad for quite a while. Do you mind telling me how you knew what to do?"

As she walked over to the sink, Peggy said, "Did you forget my husband's a firefighter? Stephen's forever taking emergency services classes and I'm his study partner. You'd be amazed at what I've learned helping him cram for tests."

A minute later, Peggy returned to Laura's side, and handing her some damp towels, she said, "So if you ever break a leg, I'm your girl."

"Thanks, I'll remember that," Laura said, offering her cousin a weak smile.

"Maybe we should call a doctor."

"No, Toni doesn't like doctors," Laura said softly. "And besides, she's coming around now." Watching as Toni slowly opened her eyes, Laura whispered, "Hiya, sweetheart."

"I'm....I'm sorry, Laura. I'm...so sorry."

"Sshhh...don't apologize. You couldn't help it. It's okay."

"I fucked up, Laura. There were too many people today and I...I didn't give myself enough time to calm down before we came into the pub. I'm sorry. I'm really, really sorry."

"Relax, Toni. No worries. As long as you're okay, that's all that matters."

"I would have been all right if your aunt hadn't wound me up, but when she said that shit about grandchildren to your mum, I just...I just lost focus. Why did she have to say those things, Laura? Why?"

"Because she never thinks before she speaks," Peggy said. Seeing that Toni immediately cowered when she heard her voice, Peggy smiled and added, "Which is one of the reasons I now live in Falkirk."

"I'm...I'm sorry. I didn't know you were here," Toni said, looking up.

"No apologies necessary, Toni. I love my mother, but she can be a right pain in the arse sometimes."

It was enough to break the ice, and Toni relaxed against the tile wall. Running her fingers through her hair, she wiped the dampness on her trousers. "Christ, I'm soaking wet. I guess this one was bad, wasn't it?"

"Yeah, I'm afraid so, sweetheart, but if we use those hand dryers over there, no one will be the wiser. All right?"

"Okay, sure," Toni said as she struggled to stand.

"I'll guard the door," Peggy said, leaning her back against the only entrance to the room.

"Oh...um...no, that's okay, Peggy. I'll just lock it," Laura said.

"There isn't a lock, and we've been really lucky that no one's come in so far, so you had better hurry up," Peggy said, hitting her hand against the dryer push button.

Toni could see the concern on Laura's face, but she was too tired to argue or to worry about the other woman in the room. Pulling her sweat-soaked shirt over her head, she handed it to Laura and then leaned under the dryer to allow the warm air to wash over her.

Starting the second unit, Laura held Toni's shirt under the blower as she looked in her cousin's direction. Seeing the shocked expression etched on Peggy's face, Laura said firmly, "Peg, I trust what you see in this room, stays in this room. Yes?"

Prying her eyes away from the scars covering Toni's back, Peggy nodded. "Of course, Laura. Of course."

***

"Is she okay?" Eleanor asked, seeing Laura come in from the patio.

"She's fine. Just a bit annoyed that she lost control. That's all."

"Should I assume that Peggy knows what's going on now?"

"Well, she walked in on Toni having a full-blown panic attack, and she saw the scars—"

"What? How?"

"Toni was soaking wet after the attack, so we needed to dry her blouse, and Peggy had to stand guard at the door."

"Did she ask?"

"No, but I know she wanted to."

"Maybe you should tell her."

Yanking out a chair, Laura sat down. "Why should I have to? It's really none of her business."

"True, but you and Peg have always been so close, and she seemed quite tickled to find out that you and Toni were partners."

Smiling as she remembered her cousin's expression, Laura said, "Yeah, it didn't seem to faze her, did it?"

"No, but it shocked the shit out of your aunt," Eleanor said as she reached for a cookbook. "I never saw that shade of purple on a person's face before today. It really didn't go well with that God-awful cardigan she was wearing."

Laura chuckled softly as she gazed back at her mother. Nancy's sweater had been truly awful, but because of her mother, lunch at the pub was not.

After getting Toni sorted in the ladies' room, the three women had returned to the table, but before Laura could come up with an explanation for their delay, Peggy chimed in to say they had just been catching up and lost track of time. Doing as Laura had suggested, Eleanor had ordered them wine, and before Laura got settled in the booth, Toni had already managed to take a few sips to further steady her nerves. Fully aware that Nancy had not yet come to terms with Laura's relationship with Toni, Eleanor steered the conversation in Peggy's direction, and without missing a beat, Peggy took the lead. Talking about her children's antics and the upcoming birth of her third son, the rest of the meal was spent listening to amusing stories about Peggy's boys, and it wasn't long before both Eleanor and Nancy joined in with a few of their own.

"I love you, Mum."

Busy scanning recipes, Eleanor's head popped up. "What brought that on?"

"You were great today. I'm not sure many mums would be as accepting as you are."

"Laura, I love you and whether you believe it or not, so does your father. I think it's fair to say that we both adore Toni, but after today, perhaps we should rethink Christmas. Maybe it would be best if we just spend it here. Just the four of us. What do you think?"

Hearing the back door open, Laura held back saying anything until Toni had removed her coat. "Mum was wondering if we should change the plans for Christmas."

"Yeah? How?" Toni asked as she poured herself a glass of wine.

"She thought maybe you'd be more comfortable if we just had a small get-together here. Just you, me, Mum and Bill."

"Oh, I see."

"How'd you feel about that?"

"Honestly?"

"Of course."

Thinking for a moment, Toni took a sip of wine and knelt by Laura's chair. Smiling, she looked in Eleanor's direction and then back at Laura. "Give me a reason for changing our plans that doesn't have anything to do with protecting me, and I'll agree to it."

"Toni—"

"Laura, we've had this talk before. You can't keep trying to protect me—"

"But sweetheart—"

"Let me finish," Toni said, taking a seat at the table. "I started getting nervous after the fourth store, but I didn't tell you, and I didn't give myself enough time to regroup before we entered the pub. What Abby told me to do was working, but I didn't follow her instructions, and we both saw what happened, but I've learned my lesson, and it won't happen again. I know you're worried because there'll be a lot of people around on Christmas, but not all of them are strangers to me now, right?"

"I suppose."

"And I promise, if I start feeling stressed, I'll let you know or…or I'll go outside and grab a fag."

"They're predicting snow on Christmas."

Amused by Laura's pout, Toni said, "Well, then I'll make sure I wear my coat…just for you."

CHAPTER FORTY-FOUR

"I could stay like this forever."
"I figure in about twenty minutes you might get your wish."
"Whatcha mean?"
"Laura, I'm freezing my tits off out here."
"You're the one that wanted to come out for a smoke."
"Yes, but I didn't know that you were going to follow me and then insist on snuggling on this bench. I swear I think my arse is stuck to the iron."
"It's not that cold," Laura said, looking over her shoulder.
"You're only saying that because you've got your cute little bum in my lap. Whilst your posterior is nice and cozy, mine is becoming one with this bloody bench," Toni said, shifting her bottom on the metal.
"Seriously, Laura—"
"Please, just a few more minutes."
Toni sighed and wrapped her arms around Laura's waist. Resting her chin on Laura's shoulder, she looked at the smoke billowing from the house's chimney.
"What time's your dad bringing the tree?"
"Um...Mum said around five. Why?"
"No reason."
Again looking over her shoulder, Laura asked, "When was the last time you decorated a Christmas tree?"
"Probably when I was eleven or twelve."

"That can't be right."

"Why? Were you there?"

"No, but you said you didn't leave home until *after* university."

"True, but my parents liked to travel over Christmas, so normally they'd have the staff do all the decorating a few days before we were ready to go on holiday, and then it would all be gone by the time we got back."

"What about in your flat?"

"Laura, you saw my flat."

"No, not that one. The one where you lived before…before…"

"Everything went to shit?"

"Yes."

"Actually, I continued the Vaughn tradition, and as soon as Christmas break started, I'd get on a plane and spend my holiday touring ruins or…or walking on beaches. I did have one of those little ceramic trees back then. You know the ones with the tiny, colored ornaments, but one night it got…well, it got broken."

"How?"

"My girlfriend threw it at me."

Thinking for a moment, Laura asked, "Can I ask why?"

Smiling, Toni pulled her close. "She wanted long-term and I didn't, and when she gave me an ultimatum, I told her to have a nice life. Needless to say, it didn't go over too well."

"And how about now?"

"Stupid question, not worthy of an answer."

"Humor me."

"Ring finger, left hand. Need I say more?"

"Maybe," Laura said through a grin.

"How about…I love you."

"I love you, too."

"Good, and now that that's settled, can we *please* go inside? If we stay out here any longer, I won't defrost until spring."

"Wanna bet?"

***

Bill showed up with one freshly-cut Fraser fir just before five that evening. Following Eleanor's instructions, he chose neither the tallest nor the broadest tree in the field…or at least that's what he thought.

Taking into consideration the low ceiling in the lounge, he picked a tree slightly taller than six feet so when it was placed in the red metal stand, the top branch barely brushed the plaster. However, what the tree lacked in height it made up for in width and when Bill tried to push it back into the corner, he quickly discovered it had a bit more girth than he remembered.

"I swear, Ellie, it didn't look that big in the field," he said, standing in front of the wide-bodied tree. "Perhaps if you have some shears, I can trim it back a bit."

"Don't you dare," Eleanor said as she went over to stand next to him. "I love it. I absolutely love it."

"Are you sure? It does seem to own the room, if you know what I mean."

Stepping back, Eleanor surveyed the lounge. Seeing that the tree was far enough away from the hearth not to cause a fire hazard, she said, "It'll be fine, except I think we'll need more decorations. I didn't buy enough to cover this beauty."

"How about Toni and I run out and get some, and then we can pick up dinner on the way back?" Laura asked.

"Actually, that's a good idea, but you won't have to buy any decorations. There's more in the attic. If you two can go get dinner, your father and I can bring down the boxes."

"You game?" Laura asked, looking over at Toni.

"Sure, just let me get my coat."

***

"Shit!"

"Sorry, I forgot to tell you to watch your head," Eleanor called from the hallway. "You okay?"

"I'll heal," Bill said, flicking on the attic light. "Which boxes?"

"The ones with the big X on them...followed closely by M – A – S."

Peering down through the attic hatch, Bill said, "You know, I really thought I missed that smart-arse attitude of yours."

Smiling, Eleanor asked, "Changing your mind, are you?"

"Not a chance," Bill said as he turned around, promptly hitting his head against the next rafter. "Fuck!"

"Will you please be careful? I don't want you breaking anything."

"Don't worry, Ellie, I've got a hard head."

"I wasn't talking about your head. I was talking about my ornaments."

"Ha ha!"

Reaching up, Eleanor took the first of the three boxes, and by the time she managed to carry it downstairs, Bill was following with the other two.

"Be careful of your back."

"My back's fine, Ellie. You want these in the lounge?"

"Yes, by the tree. Do you want a beer?"

"You read my mind."

Disappearing into the kitchen, she opened a couple of bottles and was about to return to the lounge when Bill appeared in the doorway. Seeing the look in his eyes, she shook her head. "Sorry, sweetheart, but they won't be gone *that* long."

Bill took the bottles from her hands, and after setting them on the counter, he pulled her into his arms. "They'll be gone long enough."

***

"You know, I thought it was good idea that you wanted to learn the roads up here, but if you go any slower, we'll be late for Christmas," Laura said, watching the scenery slowly creep by her window.

"If you haven't noticed, there's snow on the ground."

"And if we were driving in that field over there, I'd be worried, but the roads have been dry for days."

"It's called being cautious."

Slowing even more so another car could pass, when she heard Laura's disgusted huff, Toni said, "Look, I'm just giving them some extra time."

"Who?"

"Your parents."

"My parents? What are you talking about? Time for what?"

Glancing to her left, Toni said, "You're the one that found the boxers. You figure it out."

"What are you—" Laura's mouth snapped shut. Scrunching up her face, she groaned, "Oh no, you don't...you don't think they're...they're—"

"We would be."

"Yeah, but...but...Toni, this is my *mother* we're talking about!"

"Yes, I know, and she's the same woman who had your father's underwear—"

"Okay! Okay! Okay!" Laura said, holding up her hands. "I get it, all right? Now, how about we just change the subject, shall we?"

"Does it bother you?"

"Talking about my mother shagging? Um…yeah!"

"Don't worry, Laura, they probably didn't have time to shag. Just a few healthy snogs, that's all."

"Toni! Enough!"

Laughing at Laura's horrified expression, Toni gave the car a bit more gas, and as the speedometer began to climb, she said, "Maybe you should call them on your mobile…just in case."

***

With their bellies full and coffee cups in hand, the foursome made their way to the lounge, and while Eleanor turned on the stereo, filling the house with the sounds of the season, Bill added another log to the fire. After unpacking the new sets of clear lights, Laura and Toni busied themselves at the tree, laughing more than once at the expletives coming from Eleanor and Bill as they worked to untangle the old multi-colored strands, and before too long, the tree was draped in a rainbow of color.

Ornaments were next, and the newly purchased decorations were slipped on hooks and hung from the branches, but as Eleanor had suspected, the two dozen shiny red baubles were simply not enough to cover the tree. Sitting cross-legged on the floor, she opened one of the old storage boxes and peeked inside.

Removing the tissue paper, Eleanor began pulling out the fragile ornaments that had been handed down through the years. Egg-shaped and shiny, the vintage reflector baubles were as pristine as the day they were purchased, and their surfaces still displayed designs of old amidst glitter applied over seventy years before. Carefully handing them up to Toni so a hanger could be attached, they were then passed to Laura, who lovingly hung them on the tree.

Lifting out a layer of cardboard, Eleanor smiled at the contents below. Removing a circle of plaster with a red ribbon threaded through the top, she handed it to Toni. "Laura and I made that when she was three."

At first, Toni didn't understand the emotion she saw in Eleanor's eyes, but when the disc spun on the ribbon, and she saw the imprint of a child's hand cast in the plaster, she grinned. "She was a small one, wasn't she, and apparently only had four fingers at the time," Toni said, examining the misprinted casting.

"What?" Laura said, grabbing the ornament from Toni's hand. "Mum, Toni's right. Where's my thumb?"

Laughing at her daughter's slack-jawed expression, Eleanor said, "You had hurt it a few days before we made that, and you absolutely refused to put it in the plaster. You were quite a hard-headed child, so I decided just to cast it like that. Now, I'm glad we did because I'll always remember you sitting at the table with this chubby-cheeked pout on your face. God, you were stubborn."

"Some things never change," Toni said under her breath.

"I heard that," Laura said, hanging the handprint ornament on a branch.

Eleanor returned to her discoveries, and pulling out a wad of tangled pipe cleaners, she said, "Laura found a package of her father's pipe cleaners in my desk. She was four, and she decided she was going to make every ornament for the tree that year." Holding up the tangled wad, Eleanor said, "Although I must say, this looks more like a pipe cleaner orgy now. Doesn't it?"

"Why don't we skip those," Laura said, walking over to look into the box. Reaching in, she pulled out a pale pink ornament and smiled. "I remember this."

Taking the sphere from Laura, Toni studied it for a moment and then scratched her head. "I have to admit that I've never seen a Christmas ornament decorated with bunnies before."

"That's because I made it," Eleanor said. "Laura was five and quite adamant about wanting a bunny for Christmas."

"A bunny?"

"Yes, a bunny. And like I said, she was quite unyielding, practically demanding that Santa bring her one."

"Demanding...imagine that," Toni said, eyeing her partner.

"Anyway, the last thing I needed was something else to take care of. I had my hands full with just her, so I went out to a local craft store and decided that I'd make her that ornament in hopes it would be enough."

"Was it?"

Eleanor shot a quick glance in Bill's direction and then looked back at Toni. "No, and eight months later we had *six* bunnies to take care of. Luckily for me, Laura lost interest, and I was able to give them to her school as pets. The last I heard they had to close that place, something about being overrun with bunnies."

"Ha ha," Laura said, hanging the ornament on the tree. "You make me sound like a terror."

"That's because you *were* a terror, my dear," Eleanor said, handing Toni a Styrofoam ball adorned with sequins. "Laura made that one in school. I think she was about six."

After giving the glittery jumble of sequins the once-over, Toni handed it to Laura. "Dreaming of being a disco queen, were you?"

"Funny," Laura said as she snatched it from Toni's hand and hung it on the tree. "Is there anything left in there that I didn't make, or are we going to travel down memory lane all night long?"

"A few, but these are the ones I really adore. I don't know what I was thinking, leaving them in the attic. They belong on our tree. They'll always belong on our tree," Eleanor said as she handed Toni some clothespin reindeer and angels. "Put those up there, Toni, will you please?"

"Yeah, sure," she said, turning to place them gently on the tree. "I agree with you, Eleanor. These are great."

"Yes, they are, but as Laura got older, making ornaments became secondary to buying them. So, I decided that we'd start a new tradition, and every year, I'd allow her to purchase one for the tree, anything she'd like, and it would be added to our collection," she said, handing Toni a bauble decorated with a ballerina. "She thought she wanted to be a dancer. She was eight."

"Interesting," Toni said, handing it to Laura. "You and your tutu, eh?"

With a sigh, Laura placed it on the tree. "Are we going to do this all night?"

Hearing a hint of annoyance in Laura's voice, Toni leaned over and whispered in her ear. "I love you, and I love what we're doing right now, and if you're a good girl, later on tonight, I'll love you even more."

"That's bribery," Laura said quietly.

"I prefer to think of it as..." Pausing, Toni chuckled to herself. "Yes, you're right. It's bribery."

Laughing, Laura turned and kissed her on the cheek. "I love you."

"I love you, too. Now, can we get back to discussing little Laura?"

"Yes," Laura said, playfully pushing Toni away. "Fine, tell your stories, show your pictures—"

"Oh, my God, I should get the scrapbooks!" Eleanor said.

"*No!*" Laura said, stomping her foot. "We're supposed to be decorating the tree tonight. If you pull those out, we'll never get finished."

Sending a wink in Toni's direction, Eleanor returned to the storage box, and over the next quarter hour she uncovered ornaments displaying fire trucks, dogs, starships and princesses, and they all found their way to the tree. Pulling the last one from the box, she handed it to Toni and then watched as confusion swept over her face as she stared at the dull black bauble in her hand.

"It was her goth year," Eleanor said flatly.

"Goth year?" Toni asked. Raising an eyebrow, she turned to stare at Laura. "*You* had a *goth* year?"

"No, I think it lasted about two weeks," Laura said, snatching the ornament from Toni's hand. "And I also wanted to dye my hair black and get my lip pierced, but Mum refused to allow it."

"Good woman," Bill chimed in, smiling at Eleanor as she opened the last box.

"These are more mementos than tree decorations, I'm afraid," Eleanor said as she pushed aside the crumpled tissue paper. "Oh, wait, here are a few more."

Pointing to a stack of papers tied in ribbon, Bill asked, "What are those?"

"Oh, they're some cards Laura drew when she was a child before buying became the norm."

"Can I see them?"

"Of course," Eleanor said, handing the stack to Bill.

Returning to the box, she uncovered a few more vintage ornaments, the last of which was a heavy crystal pendant with the words *First Christmas* engraved on the glass. Handing it to Laura, Eleanor said, "Your father gave me that...years and years ago. Please be careful with it."

"Sure, Mum," Laura said, glancing briefly at the leaded glass ornament before finding a strong branch to hold its weight.

After placing a few of the antique metal angels and sleighs that had been buried in the boxes around the room, they gathered the discarded tissue paper and straightened the lounge. About to close the storage box, Eleanor looked up to ask Bill for the cards, but the words died in her throat.

Pulling away the ribbon, he had in his hands memories shared by two. Folded paper decorated with crayons showed trees of red and dogs of blue, lopsided suns and crooked houses, and a family of three that soon became two as the tall stick figure standing next to the curly-headed one disappeared. Letters too difficult for a child of three or four to tackle were written every which way across the pages. Some were large and others were small and sometimes backward, but their message repeated in every card...*I love you, Mum*. Reading the words, Bill's eyes filled with tears, and as emotions rose in his throat, his hands began to shake.

"Why don't you girls go to the kitchen and put some biscuits on a plate?"

"In a minute, Mum, let me just finish—"

Laura stopped when Toni grabbed her arm and motioned toward the kitchen. Tilting her head, she was about to ask why, when she looked over to see her mother kneeling by Bill. It was more than obvious that the man was crying.

"What was that about?" Laura asked, once they reached the kitchen.

Glancing back into the lounge, as she watched Eleanor continue to comfort Bill, Toni whispered, "I think it's about a father realizing just how much he missed."

***

"I made us some tea," Toni said in a whisper, walking into the bedroom.

"Why are you whispering? My mother always reads before she goes to bed. She'll be awake for a few more hours, trust me."

"I have no doubt," Toni said with a crooked smile. "How was your bath?"

"It would have been better if you had joined me," Laura said, and then noticing Toni's expression, she added, "Why the silly grin?"

"Um…no reason," Toni said, putting the tea on the nightstand. Going to the dresser, she pulled out a clean pair of pajama bottoms and a T-shirt, and tossing them on the bed, began to get changed.

"Toni?"

"Yeah?"

"What are you hiding?"

"Nothing…see," Toni said, pulling her sweater over her head.

Although the sight of Toni wearing only a white bra and tight black jeans nudged Laura's libido, for a moment she pushed away the awareness between her legs and concentrated on the subject at hand.

"You're only flippant when you don't want me to know something. Now, what is it?"

"Laura, I seriously don't think—"

"Antoinette Vaughn, either you tell me—"

"Your mum isn't reading."

"What?"

"Your mum isn't reading."

"I heard what you said, but why does it matter what my mother is doing?"

"It doesn't. Good point!" Toni said. Turning on her heel, she disappeared into the bathroom and quickly shut the door.

A few minutes later, she returned to find Laura sitting cross-legged on the bed staring back at her.

"Toni?"

"Yeah."

"Did my…did Bill go home?"

"Um…no, apparently not."

"Is he in the lounge?"

"No, actually I…I didn't see him in there."

"Did you see him…anywhere?"

"Um…no. No, I didn't."

Scrunching up her face, Laura squeaked, "Did you hear him?"

"Actually…actually, I did."

With a groan, Laura fell back on the bed and covered her face with a pillow.

Laughing, Toni said, "You know, they *are* adults."

Pulling away the pillow, Laura said, "We've already had this discussion, and I know they're adults, but knowing that my…that Bill and my mother are downstairs right now probably…well, probably...well, you *know* what they're probably doing. It's just plain weird!"

Putting her jeans in the dresser, Toni said over her shoulder, "Well, you'd best get used to it, because by the sounds of it, they really enjoy doing it."

Hearing no response, Toni turned around just in time to get slammed in the face with a pillow. Picking it up, she climbed into bed with a smile on her face. "Sorry, but I just couldn't resist," she said, leaning in to kiss Laura on the cheek.

"I'm not sure which is worse, hearing all those stories about my decorating efforts when I was a child, or the fact that you're going to continue to remind me that my...that Bill and my mother are sleeping together."

"Don't forget about the scrapbooks," Toni said as she pulled Laura into her arms.

Relaxing into the warmth of the woman, Laura sighed and closed her eyes, but when Toni ran her tongue down her ear and begin to nibble on the lobe, Laura's eyes popped open. "What are you doing?"

"Grazing."

Smiling, Laura said, "Toni."

"Yeah?"

"This bedroom is right above my mother's."

"So?"

"They could hear us."

"You've already proven you can be quiet, and I want you."

"Sweetheart, I think maybe we should wait. Mum mentioned doing some shopping tomorrow so we'll have the house to ourselves."

Pulling back, Toni asked, "Are you serious?"

"I'm afraid so, sweetheart. Knowing they're down there doing what they're doing...well, it just kind of puts a damper on things for me."

"Shit," Toni said, falling back on her pillow.

"I'm sorry, but I think we should just get some sleep."

Staring at the ceiling, Toni took a long breath, exhaling slowly in hopes it would help convince her lower half to behave itself, but when it didn't work, she climbed out of bed. Placing a kiss on Laura's forehead, she said, "I'm not really that tired. Get some sleep. I'm going to go and read in the other room for a while. Okay?"

"Are you mad at me?"

"I'm not mad, Laura, I'm randy," Toni said, smiling as she straightened the quilt. "I'm just going to read for an hour or so and then I'll come to bed. I promise."

"Okay. Good night, sweetheart."

"Good night, darling."

***

An hour later, Toni looked up as Laura walked into the room. "Hey, I thought you were asleep."

"I dozed off for a few, but it's hard to sleep when you're not there."

"Sorry," Toni said, putting down her book. "I'll come to bed." Swinging her long legs off the bed, before she could stand, Laura came over and blocked her path.

"Not so fast, Miss Vaughn."

"Huh?"

"*This* bedroom is over the office."

Laura's words acted like a switch, and the sexual cravings Toni had managed to scold into silence returned instantly. Before she could blink, Laura kissed her, and open-mouthed and hungry, Toni answered in kind until their lips were swollen with passion. Although Toni had been the one who had admitted she was horny, Laura was coming in a close second, and wasting no time, she pulled the T-shirt from Toni's body and pushed her to the bed.

"Can you be quiet?" Laura asked, reaching for the waistband of Toni's pajamas.

"I promise. Oh, Laura...I promise."

Seconds later, Toni was naked, and wearing only her pajama top, Laura climbed onto the bed and smiled as Toni opened her legs. With the help of the light coming from the bedside lamp, Laura could see the glistening folds and sliding her hand lower, she murmured, "God, you're wet."

Biting her lip, Toni spread her legs even wider, and grasping fistfuls of sheets, she didn't make a sound when Laura pushed two fingers deep inside.

Laura had been the one who had remained mute the day they left for Scotland. Standing in their bedroom, she had refused to utter a sound as Toni sat between her legs, tonguing her to orgasm, but Toni was finding it hard to do the same. Pressing her lips together, she struggled to remain quiet as Laura stroked with skilled precision, but they both soon realized that Toni's silence wouldn't be the issue. When Toni began to match Laura's rhythm, the iron bed frame announced its age with an ear-splitting squeak that seemed to echo through the room.

"Shit," Laura whispered, placing her hand on Toni's belly to quiet her movement. "Sweetheart, I'm sorry, but you can't move. The bed...it's making too much noise."

Groaning her disapproval, Toni said, "Laura, I can be quiet, but for God's sake, you can't ask me not to move. That's...that's like asking me not to breathe."

Thinking for a moment, Laura pulled away and climbed off the bed. Seeing the frustration etched on Toni's face, Laura said quietly, "The floor, Toni. Get on the floor."

As soon as Toni stood, Laura pulled the duvet and pillows from the bed, and allowing them to puddle at their feet, she pushed Toni down into the softness.

Their lips met in a hungry kiss, and as her hand slipped between Toni's thighs once more, Laura whispered, "Now...where were we?"

CHAPTER FORTY-FIVE

"You're up early," Eleanor said, shuffling into the kitchen.

Looking up he smiled at the sleepy-eyed woman staring back at him. "Good morning to you, too."

"Whatcha doing?"

"I thought I'd make my girls some breakfast," Bill said, turning around and pulling Eleanor into his arms.

Their lips met in a slow good morning kiss, and then resting her head on his shoulder, she said, "I like that."

"What?"

"You calling us your girls."

"Good," he said, placing a kiss on her forehead.

Glancing at the clock on the wall, Eleanor said, "I'd best go wake them up."

"It's still early. Let them sleep."

"I would, except the ladies from church will be over tonight to pick up the biscuits I promised them, and we haven't begun to make them yet. Be right back."

A few minutes later, Eleanor stood in the hallway with a puzzled look on her face. She had knocked three times and called out their names twice, but having yet to receive a response she shrugged and opened their door. Seeing that the bed was empty, Eleanor was about to look out the window to see if Laura's car was gone, when she noticed the door leading to the other bedroom was open. Without thinking twice, she went over and looked inside. Seeing Laura and Toni asleep on the floor, Eleanor frowned and then crept back the way she came. Reaching the hallway, she closed the door and rapped loudly on the frame. "Laura! Toni! You awake?"

Eleanor patiently waited, knowing her pounding would have woken the dead and finally the door opened a crack. Seeing her daughter peeking through the opening, Eleanor said, "Sorry, I know it's early, but I wanted to let you know that your father is making us all breakfast. That is, if you're interested?"

"Oh...um...okay. Sounds good. We'll be down in a tick."

"Good, I'll let him know."

**

Standing at the sink washing the breakfast dishes, Eleanor asked, "Why didn't you tell me?"

"Tell you what?" Laura asked, stacking two more plates on the counter.

"That Toni had sleeping issues."

"What are you talking about?"

"If she needed a harder mattress or even a cot, I could have arranged it."

"Mum, what the hell are you talking about? Toni doesn't have any sleeping issues. She has the occasional nightmare, but that hasn't happened in a while."

"Then why were you two sleeping on the floor?"

Laura's mouth dropped open and staring at her mother, she asked hesitantly, "You were in our room?"

"This morning when I knocked and you didn't answer I let myself in and found you both on the floor in the other room. I just assumed—"

Eleanor lost her ability to speak when she saw Laura arch a single eyebrow, her eyes gleaming with humor as she stared back at her mother. Realizing her mistake, a blush to end all blushes crossed Eleanor's cheeks. Clearing her throat, she said, "I see. Well, I suppose I should reconsider entering your bedroom in the future without an invitation."

"Excellent idea," Laura said, kissing her mother on the cheek. "And I'm thinking I should do the same. Yes?"

A bit more color found its way to Eleanor's face. "I hope you don't mind, but it was rather late when we finished last night, and I didn't see the need for him to travel at that hour."

"Actually, I'm getting used to him being around, but it's still kinda weird knowing that you two are back together."

"From where I'm standing, it's kind of nice."

Seeing her mother's radiant smile, Laura said, "You really do love him, don't you?"

"With all my heart, Laura. With all my heart."

***

After receiving a whispered suggestion from Eleanor that he should bring back an overnight bag, Bill left just after breakfast to go to his apartment for a quick shower and a change of clothes, and two hours later he returned to a kitchen in shambles. Rolling up his sleeves, he began the task of washing all the bowls and measuring cups that had been piled by the sink during his absence, and amidst the sounds of laughter and the smell of vanilla, the morning faded into afternoon.

Standing at the sink, he listened to the women talk as they mixed and measured, and when expletives flowed from Toni's mouth when she forgot to use an oven mitt, he laughed heartily at her creative use of one particular word. His mouth watered at the smell of Scottish shortbread slowly baking in the oven, and his hand was slapped more than once when he tried to steal a freshly baked chocolate chip cookie off a tray. And as he waited for the next batter-covered bowl to be handed to him, Bill looked at the women in the room and smiled. In all of his life, there weren't many days burned into his memory...actually, up until today, there had only been three.

On the day of their wedding, Mother Nature had done her best to dampen the afternoon, but the spirits of a young man and woman on the threshold of starting a life together could not be washed away by raindrops and thunder. In a small church, atop a hill and surrounded by the greenery of the country they loved, they spoke their vows in front of family and friends. Wearing a Highland kilt, he had walked his bride, dressed in white, down an aisle covered in rose petals, and after carrying her over the threshold of their home that night, he made love to the woman who completed him...and created the one who would fill his heart with pride.

Nine months later, in the wee hours of a Friday morning he stood by a bed and marveled at the sight of his daughter. Swaddled in white cotton, with chubby cheeks and bright eyes, she stole his heart with her first coo. Tiny fisted hands reached up to him and when he held out a finger, and she took hold, it was like no other feeling in the world. He never thought he could feel humbled by just one touch, and he never thought it would happen again...but he had been wrong.

***

"Be careful."

"I'm fine."

"If you fall, Eleanor will have my head."

Smiling, Toni looked down at the ground. "If I fall, Eleanor will be the least of your worries."

"What do you mean?" Bill asked, shielding his eyes from the sun as he looked up at the woman on the ladder.

"You've obviously never seen Laura's temper."

"Have you ever seen Ellie's?" Bill asked.

"No, why?"

"Trust me, you don't want to," he said, snickering under his breath. "You going to be okay if I go finish up the shrubs?"

"Yep, only have a few more clips to go and then this part will be done. Go attack the hedges. I won't be far behind you."

Watching as Bill walked back to the front gardens, Toni returned to the task at hand with a smile on her face. He no longer felt like a stranger to her, and the anxieties that she had had the night before seemed to have disappeared. She liked him. He had an easiness about him. A relaxing, playful boyishness, and as they had covered the gardens in lights, she found herself laughing more than once as he mumbled four-letter words at the amount of decorations Eleanor had purchased. They chatted comfortably as they assembled silhouettes of deer and angels, while making fun of the other's inability to put Tab A into Slot C. The day was bright and crisp, and as she reached out to hook the next light into its clip, Toni breathed in the frosty air and smiled again.

Standing with a tangle of netted lights in his hand, Bill glanced in Toni's direction, frowning as she once again overextended her reach. It was something he had done more times than he could remember over the years, so holding back his comments, he was about to cover more shrubbery when he saw her slip. "Shit!" he said, tossing the lights aside as he bolted toward the ladder.

It took five long strides to get to her, but it seemed like an eternity as he ran across the gravel, and with every step he took, Bill prayed to God that he'd make it in time...and he did. Managing to wrap his arms around Toni before she collided with the stone-covered drive, they both fell to the ground with a thud. His back twinged at the impact, but he didn't care. Overcome with emotion at the near tragedy, he pulled her into a bear hug as he silently thanked God for his swiftness.

"Get your bloody hands off me!" Toni growled, struggling like a madwoman to get out of his arms. "*Let go of me!*"

For a split second, Bill didn't understand her terror-filled shrieks, but when Toni began kicking and punching to get away, he relaxed his hold and watched in shock as she scrambled across the driveway. Stunned and saddened, he didn't know what to do. Like an animal ready to attack, Toni remained crouched on the ground, glaring back at him as if daring him to move and Bill's heart broke at the expression on her face. She was terrified...absolutely terrified.

Eleanor had told him that Toni had been abused in prison. Over drinks and dinner, she had explained a few of Toni's fears and quirks, but it wasn't until that moment when Bill realized the depths of the woman's despair, and tears sprang to his eyes. Unconsciously, he shook his head, trying to say without words that she needn't fear him. That he would never hurt her, but how do you convince someone so frightened to trust?

Fearful that any sudden movement would cause more harm to the tormented woman, Bill cautiously got to his feet. Never allowing his eyes to leave hers, he prayed that she'd see the message they were sending. *Trust me. Please trust me. I won't hurt you.*

Enraged and ready to fight, Toni squatted on the ground with hands fisted as her enemy slowly got up, and when he stood tall, she tensed, preparing to strike out if he took one step closer. Trying to determine his next move, she looked him in the eye and in an instant, Toni's hellish nightmare ended.

He looked so sad...so hurt...and when she saw the tears rolling down Bill's face, she felt gutted. Like a deflated balloon, Toni sagged to her knees, embarrassed and ashamed. Finally able to hear the words of her heart over the deafening sounds of her terror, her gaze clouded with tears as the words kept repeating in her head. *He's not one of them. You can trust him. He's not one of them. You can trust him.*

Taking a ragged breath, she raised her eyes to meet his, and listening to her heart, she reached out her hand to him, praying he would take it…and he did.

Bill's heart grew large as he took two quick steps, and pulling Toni into his arms, they held each other close. They didn't need words. They didn't need explanations or apologies as she buried her head in his shoulder, and he buried his in hers.

He wasn't her father, but in his arms, she felt safe. A dozen men had given her a reason to fear, but this man had just given her a reason to trust and she knew she would never fear him again.

She wasn't his daughter, but the love he felt told him she was. Their souls had touched amidst gravel and fear, and a bond had been formed that would never be broken. He loved her. It was the simplest of truths, and he would protect her until the day God took him away.

Neither had a choice…all they had were reasons.

***

"William!"

Shaken from his thoughts, he looked at the woman who had called out his name. "Sorry, dear. What was that?"

"Where did you just go?" Eleanor asked, eyeing the man.

"Oh…um…just a bit of daydreaming. What did you need?"

"There are a few bags of tins in the office. Can you get them for us so we can get these biscuits packed up? The ladies will be here soon."

"Sure…sure," he said, tossing the towel on the counter as he walked out of the room. "Be right back."

Eleanor returned to the trays of shortbread, but hearing another "Shit!" fly from Toni's mouth, she looked up. "You didn't burn yourself again, did you?"

"No," Toni said, giving Laura a sideways glance. "Someone keeps swatting my hand away from the biscuits."

"That's because if you don't stop eating what we're making, we won't have any left to pack up," Laura said as she moved another baking sheet out of Toni's reach.

"It's better than the way I used to be, isn't it?"

Curious, Eleanor looked up from what she was doing. "Can I ask what that means?"

"Oh...um...I had a few problems...um...actually..."

Seeing Toni struggle for the words, Laura spoke up. "Toni used to ration what she ate. Something she had to do in prison, but she's getting better. It doesn't happen that often anymore, and when it does, we work through it."

"Oh, I see," Eleanor said quietly. "Well, then perhaps we should make a few more batches so we have plenty. How's that?"

"Works for me," Bill chimed in as he returned to the kitchen carrying a pile of tins. Placing them on the table, he added, "And my vote is for more shortbread."

"And who said you had a vote?" Eleanor asked with a twinkle in her eye.

"Ouch."

Enjoying the playful exchange, Toni glanced in Laura's direction and grinned when she saw the expression on Laura's face. Although adamant that she didn't think of Bill as her father, the look in Laura's eyes said just the opposite. They were smiling and bright, and filled with the love of a daughter for her father...whether she cared to admit it or not.

"I forgot about your sweet tooth," Eleanor said, opening a tin. "I'd best hide the chocolates, I'm thinking."

"Just don't hide them in the bedroom, unless you've forgotten what I'm like on a sugar high," Bill quipped, totally forgetting he was in mixed company.

Having returned to her work, when the room grew silent, Toni looked up and promptly bit her lip to stop herself from laughing. The faces of the three members of the MacLeod family now glowed with a brilliant shade of strawberry.

***

Alone on the patio, Toni pulled her coat tightly around her as she took a drag of her cigarette and gazed up at the evening sky. The sun's brilliance had long since been lost over the horizon, but a thousand stars and a phosphorescent moon illuminated the blackness of the night. With the temperatures dropping throughout the day, she wasn't surprised when she saw snowflakes begin to fall. Drifting to earth in a silent ballet, they floated and twirled their way to her, and she smiled as she watched them melt on her skin. It was quiet and peaceful, and with only the occasional rustle of dried leaves in the gardens to keep her company, when the back door suddenly opened, Toni nearly jumped off the bench.

"Sorry, didn't mean to scare you," Laura said, closing the door behind her. "I thought you might want something to drink."

Handing Toni a mug, Laura sat next to her, snuggling close against the chill of the night. "Mum said it was a perfect night for hot chocolate, and seeing the snow I'd have to agree."

"Me, too," Toni said, taking a hesitant sip of the steaming cocoa. Wrapping her arm around Laura's waist, she pulled her closer.

Giggling, Laura asked, "Are you trying to stay warm or looking for a good time?"

"A bit of both, I think."

Each got quiet as they watched the snow continue to fall, until after a few minutes, Toni said, "I'd like to have a garden like this someday."

"We can, if you'd like."

"Yeah?"

"Sure, but we probably need to find a place to live before we start talking about landscaping."

"Oh, Christ, I forgot about that."

"Well I haven't, and when we get back home, we need to start looking, don't you think?"

"I suppose."

"What's that about?" Laura asked, pointing to the frown on Toni's face.

"I know you're going to want me to go with you, but I'm not sure I'll be able to manage walking into strange houses."

"You're second guessing me again."

"Sorry, I just don't want you to do all the legwork."

"I won't. Sweetheart, once I tell the estate agent what we're looking for, she'll do most of the work. Plus, they all use the Internet now, so once we see something online we like, then I'll call and arrange a time for us to see it together. Okay?"

Smiling, Toni placed a quick kiss on Laura's cheek. "So, where do you want to live?"

"Wherever you feel the most comfortable."

"I like it here."

"That would be one hell of a commute."

"No, I mean, I like being away from the city. I like being able to sit outside and hear birds sing instead of traffic noise."

"Okay, we'll try to find a place away from all the hustle and bustle. How's that?"

"That works."

"Big house or small?"

"That depends on whether you were serious about having that horde of children you were talking about."

Pausing for a moment to think, Laura said, "I think large would be a good idea."

"I'd like to get an older one though. Something...something we can fix up together. Something that has some character."

"Okay, but I'll be honest with you. I've never really been into home repair."

"Neither have I, but it will give me something to do when you're waddling around with a swollen belly...for years and years and years."

Even though Toni's words were playful, the message she was sending was clear. Laura's eyes turned glassy as she gazed back at the woman, and then with a sigh, she leaned in for a kiss. The night was cold, but Toni's lips were warm and welcoming, and feeling no need to rush, a dozen light kisses were given until the tip of Laura's tongue touched Toni's lips. A pleasure-filled moan rose from Toni's throat as their kiss deepened, and when they finally came up for air, their breath steamed and swirled around their heads before fading into the darkness.

"I love you," Laura whispered softly.

"I love you back."

"You're amazing."

"Kiss that good, was it?"

Grinning, Laura said, "Yes, it was, but that's not what I'm talking about."

"No?"

"You surprised me today."

"How so?"

"When the ladies from the church stopped by. You weren't nervous at all, were you?"

"No, actually I wasn't."

"Can I ask why?"

"I think it's like Abby said," Toni answered, lighting a cigarette. "Make things familiar and they're not as scary. I know where the doors are in this house and where things are kept. I know that our room is right up the stairs and the patio is out the back door, and I know that your mum and dad are good people. It's not every day a parent learns their child is gay. And even though they both said it was okay, saying it and showing it are two different things, but they've done just that. They aren't put off when I touch your hand or kiss your cheek. It truly is okay, and because of it, because of how they've reacted, or better yet, how they *haven't* reacted, they've given me a reason to trust them and to know they'll protect me."

"Well, if they won't, I will."

"I know you will."

Gazing at the woman whose black hair was now dusted with white, Laura reached up and brushed away a few snowflakes. "Toni?"

"Yeah?"

"Kiss me again."

"My pleasure," Toni said, quickly tossing her cigarette in the snow.

***

"What are you doing standing in the dark?" Eleanor asked, walking into the kitchen.

"Come here," Bill whispered.

Raising her eyebrow, Eleanor went over and stood in front of Bill, and following his line of sight, she looked out on to the patio. Seeing their daughter locked in an embrace with Toni, she said quietly, "I believe this is called voyeurism."

"I think it's called watching young love. Honestly, Ellie, have you ever seen two people more in love than those two?" he asked, wrapping his arms around her waist.

"Yes, I think I have," Eleanor said, giving him a quick glance.

"I said *young* love," Bill quipped, resting his chin on her shoulder.

With a snort, Eleanor nodded. "Point taken."

"You know what I find amazing?" he said softly, watching as his daughter brushed snow from Toni's hair.

"What's that?"

"You had such an issue with Laura wanting to dye her hair or pierce her lip when she was sixteen, yet when she comes home and tells you she's in love with a woman it's simply not a problem. Don't you find that odd?"

"Not really."

"No?"

Leaning against his chest, Eleanor smiled when she saw the two women on the patio, once again locked in a heated embrace. "Those things would have taken away our daughter's beauty. Toni adds to it. Laura stands taller when she's around Toni. Have you noticed? She positively beams when the woman walks into a room or makes a joke. It's like...it's like they complete each other. What *I* find amazing is that when Toni gets scared, Laura can calm her with just one touch, and when Laura gets fired up, like the other night when we were making fun of her decorations, Toni can calm her down with just one whisper."

"You have any idea of how proud I am of you?"

"Me? What did I do?"

"You turned that little girl of ours into one hell of a woman, one hell of a human being for that matter. You made her strong and smart, and caring and beautiful. Christ, Ellie...she's perfect."

"I'd like to think you had something to do with that."

"Hardly! I wasn't around. Remember? The only thing she got from me is a few gifts she doesn't even know I gave her."

"You're wrong," Eleanor said, turning in his arms. "She has your smile, and the green in her eyes comes from you. She has your intelligence and your sense of humor, and God help us all, William, she has your temper, too. She's the best of both of us. Yes, I raised a child alone, but every time I looked at Laura, I saw you, and with that much love in my heart, how could I possibly go wrong?"

CHAPTER FORTY-SIX

"What's wrong?" Laura asked, seeing the puzzled look on her mother's face.

"That was Nancy on the phone. It seems that she's decided to have afternoon tea Thursday, and we're invited."

"That's kind of odd, don't you think?"

"What's odd about an afternoon tea?" Toni asked, glancing up from her book.

"It's not the tea so much as the time of the year," Laura said. "She normally holds them only in the spring or summer, and they're always formal. Fancy clothes, cucumber sandwiches, white gloves…she goes all-out."

"I didn't bring any white gloves," Toni said through a grin.

"Neither did I."

"Well, it appears that we don't have to worry about that," Eleanor said, returning to her spot on the couch. "Apparently, she feels horrid about the remarks she made when we had lunch the other day, and she'd like to make it up to us."

"But we'll see her on Saturday," Laura said.

"Yes, I know, but she thought it might be better if the family got to meet Toni without all the commotion that goes on over there on Christmas day. She's already called the girls, and they have the time, and she made it clear that it wasn't going to be anything formal. Just a small family gathering over some tea and scones."

"Long way to go for scones, if you ask me," Bill grumbled, tossing a magazine aside. "Well, I hope you ladies enjoy yourselves."

"You're invited, too."

"Doesn't mean I have to go, now does it?" he said, crossing his arms across his chest.

"You will if you know what's good for you," Eleanor said, giving his knee a squeeze.

Their eyes met, and before Eleanor had a chance to blink, Bill's face became etched with cheerful surrender. "Yes, dear...as you wish."

"What do you think?" Laura asked, turning to Toni. "She lives about an hour and half away, and we'll see her at Christmas, so if you want to skip it, that's fine with me."

Thinking for a moment, Toni leaned back into the sofa. "No, if it's all right with everyone else, I'd like to go. It might help take the edge off."

"The edge?" Bill asked.

Laura opened her mouth to speak, but Toni quieted her by touching her on the arm. "I'm at my worst when I'm somewhere I've never been, and even though Laura hasn't said anything, I know she's a bit worried about Christmas."

"Toni—"

"Darling, it's okay. You and I both know that it's one thing to put me in a house that's unfamiliar, but add to that the fact I'm going to be amongst virtual strangers, we could be asking for trouble, and we both know it. I, for one, don't want what happened in the pub to happen again at Christmas. If we go up a few days early, I can meet your cousins and get the lay of the land, so to speak. I think it would definitely help."

"Good, then it's settled," Bill said, relaxing into the sofa. "We'll visit on Thursday and enjoy a nice day without all those children running about."

"William!"

"What? Oh, come on, Ellie, that little Myles needs a good thrashing, if you ask me. Always running all over the place yelling *mine, mine, mine*. It truly is obnoxious!"

"He's three."

"Well, if they don't start disciplining him, I'll doubt he'll see four."

"He's not that bad."

"He's not that good, either."

"He's a child."

"Laura was never like that."

"How would you know? You weren't there, remember!" Laura blurted, glaring in Bill's direction. "What makes you think you have the right to judge a child's behavior? You gave that up when you decided that catching fish was more important than being a father. Stop insinuating that you knew me back then, Bill, because you didn't...and you still don't!"

A deafening silence fell over the room, and scowling, Eleanor shook her head. "Laura, please—"

"No, Ellie, she's right. I wasn't around," Bill said quietly, all the while returning Laura's angry stare with one of his own. "But I do know your mother, Laura. She would have never allowed you to act so rudely. I fear you must have learned *that* all on your own." Getting to his feet, Bill headed toward the kitchen. "I'm going out for some air."

Watching as he left the room, Eleanor sighed as she glared at her daughter. "I thought you were going to try to get along with him?"

"I was. I am, but it just...it just came out. I'm sorry."

"I'm not the one you need to apologize to," Eleanor said as she got to her feet and headed toward her bedroom. "Toni, do me a favor? When William comes back inside, tell him where I am. Will you please?"

Anger flickered in Toni's eyes as she glanced at Laura. "Sure, I'll let him know."

"Shit," Laura said, flinching when the bedroom door closed with a bang.

"He didn't deserve that," Toni said through clenched teeth.

"I was only stating the truth."

"No, you were ramming it down his throat. There's a difference."

"I'm sorry, but I was sitting there listening to him talk about raising a child and I just wanted to remind him—"

"But you don't have to. Don't you get that?" Toni said as she stood up. "Laura, that man doesn't need to be reminded of what he did because it looks him square in the eye every bloody day!"

"What the hell are you talking about?"

"Darling, look around you. This house is filled with photographs of you, but none of them include him. He sees a picture of a little girl in pigtails with a missing front tooth, but he never had the chance to play tooth fairy for her. He sees her dressed for a dance, standing next to a young man in an ill-fitting suit, and he wonders if *that* boy was the one. He sees you standing on the steps of your university with diploma in hand, but he can't remember the day or the smile you had when they called you up on that stage, because he wasn't there. The other night, he sat where you are right now and cried his eyes out as he read the Christmas cards you made for your mum, all the while wishing that one of them had been addressed to him. Laura, you don't have to remind him that he fucked up. Trust me, he knows!"

"Then why can't he tell me that?"

"Would it make a difference? Would words really be enough for you, because they aren't for me."

"What do you mean?"

"Just because someone tells me to trust them doesn't mean I can, or I will. I need a reason. You *know* that, and Bill knows that you need more than words in order to have a reason to forgive him, so he's doing the only thing he can do. He's giving you time to get to know him and hopefully to love him." Taking Laura's hand, Toni said, "Laura, you've given me so many reasons to trust and to love, but you also taught me something that I don't think even you realize."

"What's that?"

"Don't live in the past so much that it blinds you from the future."

Letting out a ragged breath, Laura said softly, "What do I do?"

"Go tell your *father* that you're sorry."

***

Laura was standing at the counter when he walked in the door and looking up, she asked quietly, "I was just making some tea. Would you like some?"

Bill took off his coat and tossed it on a chair. "No, I think I'll have something stronger if it's all the same to you."

Before he could take a step, Laura pulled two glasses from a cabinet and poured a splash of Scotch in each. Picking up one, she offered the other to her father.

"Thanks," he said quietly, taking the drink. Unable to make eye contact, Bill sat down at the table, bowing his head and staring blankly at the glass in his hand.

"I want to apologize for what I said earlier," Laura said, looking over at the man slouching in his chair. "You were right. It was rude and uncalled for."

"That's okay. We both know I deserved it," Bill said. Taking a sip of his drink, he paused and then raised his eyes. "I can't go back in time and change what I did, Laura."

"I know."

"I'm not expecting you...I'm not expecting you to ever look at me like you do your mother. She's your parent, and I never was, but I hope you'll be able to accept the fact that I'm here now, and I'm staying. I love your mother, and even though I'm sure you don't believe it, I love you, too, and I plan to spend the rest of my life proving it to both of you...as well as to your charming partner." Seeing his daughter's face light up, Bill added, "She's marvelous, Laura."

"Thanks," she said, walking over to sit at the table. "She likes you, too, which actually surprised me."

"Do you really think me that horrid?"

"No...no," Laura said, placing her hand on his arm. "That's not what I mean."

If Laura was still speaking, Bill didn't notice. Mesmerized by his daughter's touch, he stared at her hand on his arm and remembered tiny fingers reaching out to him so many years before. How could so many years have passed, yet her touch still feel the same? Brought back to his senses by the chimes from the mantle clock, he took a hasty sip of his drink before raising his eyes to meet hers. "I'm sorry...you were saying it wasn't what you meant?"

"No, it wasn't," Laura said, shaking her head. "Driving up here, all I could think of was all the things that could possibly rattle Toni. I knew that she'd be okay here in this house, but when it came to meeting the family and meeting you, I wasn't so sure."

"I'm not that awful, you know?"

Leaning back in her chair, Laura said, "Christ, you're as bad as Toni. She's forever trying to put words in my mouth, and she's horrible at it. Apparently, so are you."

"Oh...right. Well, perhaps I should let you finish then."

"Good idea," Laura said with a chuckle. "Like I was saying, she's at her worst when she's around strangers, and especially men, but around you, she's fine. A bit hesitant at first, but now it's like...I don't know, like she's known you for years and trusts you completely."

Thinking back to Toni's fall from the ladder, Bill said softly, "That's because she knows I'll never give her a reason not to."

***

Hearing the door open, Toni looked up from her book. Smiling as Laura walked into the room, she watched as she placed two cups of tea on the night stand. "So, did you get a chance to talk to your dad?"

"Yeah, when he came inside," Laura answered, kicking off her shoes and heading into the bathroom. "I apologized and told him that I'd try to curtail comments like that in the future."

Toni sat cross-legged on the bed watching Laura through the crack in the door. She was all too familiar with Laura's nightly routine of removing makeup, washing her face, brushing her hair twenty times and then cleaning her teeth, and Toni found herself looking forward to a lifetime of it.

When Laura finally emerged, she saw Toni's giddy expression and jerked back her head. "What's that look for?"

"I just like the way we are. That's all."

"What do you mean?" Laura asked, stepping out of her jeans.

"It's nice. Watching you get ready for bed...taking off your clothes. It makes me smile."

"I can see that, but that smile usually leads to other things, and I don't know that my back can handle another night on the floor."

"Is that your polite way of telling me to get my hormones under control?"

"Maybe," Laura said, removing her bra and quickly pulling on her pajamas. "But if you're lucky, they can run free and wild tomorrow."

"Why's that?"

"Da...um...Bill and Mum have a few things to get in Stirling tomorrow, and he asked if we wanted to come along, but I told him no."

"No? Laura, I told you this morning that I wanted to go out one more time."

"I know you did, but we can do that on Wednesday."

"What's the difference?"

Sauntering over, Laura pushed Toni to the mattress. Quickly straddling her, she placed a light kiss on Toni's lips. "The difference is that *tomorrow*, we'll have the house to *ourselves*."

***

The bed squeaked from their movements, but neither paid attention to the noise. With Eleanor and Bill out of the house, they were free to make love without the constraints of silence...and they were making good use of their time.

Before Bill's SUV disappeared down the driveway, Toni found herself being pulled up the stairs, and while she laughed at Laura's eagerness to get her alone, when she saw the heat in the woman's eyes, Toni's amusement turned into something else.

After closing the door to their bedroom, she took Laura to orgasm pressed against it, and minutes later, Toni found herself being stripped of her clothes and taken to climax as she stood in the middle of the room. Out of breath and covered in sweat, they ended up on the bed, lying naked on the sheets as their bodies slowly cooled.

A short time later, passions flared again. Climbing atop her lover, Toni groped and tweaked the breasts offered her while Laura ground herself into Toni's wetness until she begged Toni to take the lead...and take it, she did. Rolling Laura to the mattress, Toni lapped at her juices until Laura couldn't bear it any longer, and when the moans of her climax finally quieted, Laura gave back to Toni what she had been given, two times over.

"Do you think your parents will be suspicious when neither of us can move later tonight?"

Grinning, Laura looked at her exhausted, albeit happy, partner. "We'll get our second wind."

"I already had my second wind, and my third, come to think of it. Don't know if I've got any left."

Seeing that Toni's nipples were once again erect, Laura smiled and lightly touched the closest. "It appears that you do."

"Behave, woman! It's been hours since they left, and we both need a shower," Toni said, covering herself with the sheet.

"Is that an invitation?"

"Christ, you're horny!"

"Me?" Laura asked innocently.

"You're the one who dragged me up here."

"I don't remember you saying no."

"I don't remember you giving me a chance to. You practically pounced on me."

"You pounced back."

Toni's cheeks bested a cherub's as her face lit up. "Yes, I guess I did, didn't I?"

"I'm thinking you're not missing the fact that we aren't shopping today, are you?"

"No, but we need to go out tomorrow. I want to get your dad something."

"You don't have to. I'm not."

"You're not?"

"Well, maybe a card."

"Wow, that's pretty harsh, don't you think? I mean, you could at least buy him a...a tie or something."

"He doesn't wear ties."

"Okay, then how about a box of chocolates?" Toni asked.

"Why are you trying to get me to get him something? I'm sure he doesn't expect anything."

"Then it would be a nice thing to do, wouldn't it? Surprise him. Show him you care."

"And if I don't?"

"You don't mean that."

"What makes you so sure?"

"Because I've seen the way you look at him when you think no one's watching. Like you're trying to convince yourself that what you're feeling is wrong, when it's not."

"What are you talking about?"

"Darling, it's okay to love him."

"Maybe I don't want to," Laura said in a whisper.

"Maybe you just need a bit more time to get used to the idea," Toni said softly.

Pushing away her emotions, Laura quickly kissed Toni on the cheek, and grabbing her robe, she climbed out of bed and went into the bathroom to fill the tub. Appearing in the doorway a few minutes later, she said, "The water's hot. Care to join me?"

"Do I have to keep my hands to myself?" Toni asked, tossing aside the sheets.

Laura did a slow slide with her eyes, and Toni's nudity had the desired effect. Deciding to turn the tables, Laura shrugged out of her robe. Watching as Toni's eyes drank her in, Laura said, "Absolutely...*not*."

A few minutes later the bathroom was aglow with the soft light of candles, and in a tub filled with steaming water, they sat together in silence. With Laura resting against her chest, Toni closed her eyes and soaked in the warmth of the water, listening to her partner's steady breathing and enjoying the feel of Laura lightly stroking her thigh.

Interrupting the quietude, Laura asked, "Have you ever made love in a bathtub?"

Toni's eyes flew open, and then ever so slowly a leer spread across her face. "Where did that come from?"

"Just wondering."

"Um...yes, I have. You?"

"Duane tried once, but it wasn't really any good. Too much water, I guess."

"That's because he didn't know what he was doing. Give me that soap," Toni said, grabbing a sea sponge from the ledge.

"I wasn't asking," Laura said quietly, reaching for the bottle of shower wash.

"Sure you were," Toni said, filling the sponge with water. Squeezing it lightly, she reached around with her other hand, and in front of Laura's eyes, poured an ample amount of soap into the pores of the soft sponge.

"That's a lot of soap."

"Shush," Toni said as she squeezed the sponge a few times to let it absorb the soap. "Now, just lie back and relax. This shan't take long."

"That's a bit cocky," Laura said through a smile as she settled against Toni's breasts.

Deciding not to argue the point, Toni ran the sponge over Laura's arms. Lowering her voice to a breathy whisper, she purred in Laura's ear, "You see, it's not about penetration, darling. It's about anticipation and want. It's about the feel of the soap on your skin and the smell of lavender and honey in the air. It's about...it's about love and desire, heat and steam..."

Laura quickly found herself lost in the feel of Toni's breath on her neck, and the way the woman was gently washing her arms with the sponge caused goose bumps to appear on her skin. Fighting to keep her eyes open, Laura held her breath when Toni brought the sponge toward her chest, but instead of allowing it to touch her skin, Toni squeezed it, and the foam fell in silence, covering Laura's breasts in a warm, soft coating of white.

"You doing okay?" Toni asked, noticing that Laura seemed to have stopped breathing.

"Yes...I'm...I'm fine."

Kissing Laura on the neck, Toni ran the sponge over her right breast, and as Laura inhaled at the feel, Toni's other hand snaked around and covered the left. Smiling as Laura arched her body, Toni continued to wash with one hand while she fondled with the other. Enjoying the fact that Laura's nipples were rock hard and as erect as she'd ever seen them, Toni continued her seductive commentary. "Don't get me wrong, darling. I love being inside you, but when you're in the water, it washes away all that lovely lubrication we produce, so we have to draw upon other things to get you there."

Dropping the sponge in the water, Toni cupped Laura's breasts in her hands, and after pinching the pointed tips once or twice, she breathed deep before sliding one hand down Laura's belly toward where they both wanted it to be.

A sexy growl escaped Laura's lips once Toni's hand settled between her legs, and resting her head on Toni's shoulder, Laura closed her eyes.

Painstakingly slowly, Toni ran her finger over Laura's sex, taking her time with each crevice while her other hand continued to torture Laura's nipple with every pinch. "Feel good?" she asked in a whisper.

"Don't you stop...don't you dare stop..."

"I have no intention of stopping, darling," Toni said as she began running her finger in circles around Laura's clit. "But I have every intention of making you come."

Having slowed her attack on Laura's left breast, when Laura grabbed Toni's hand and placed it there again, Toni grinned at the plea and answered its demand. Returning to the swollen nipple, she rolled it between her fingertips, pulling hard against the tip as Laura squirmed between her legs.

Toni's caresses remained slow and casual under the water. The bubbles in the tub were gradually fading away, and the water had begun to cool, but Toni was resolute in her goal. She hadn't once tried to enter Laura, but her ministrations were having their effect, and when Laura's breathing began to come in gasps, and her squirms turned frenzied, Toni smiled and began to rub her finger against Laura's clit as fast as she could.

"Oh...oh...*yessss*..."

Feeling the body rush, Laura frantically grabbed hold of Toni's thighs. Arching her spine as the climax claimed her, water lapped over the sides of the tub more than once as Laura bucked and quivered through the spasms. Stilling her hand, Toni waited until Laura relaxed back into the water, and picking up the sponge, Toni tenderly rinsed the remaining soap from Laura's body. "You still with me?" she asked in a whisper.

"'Til death do us part."

CHAPTER FORTY-SEVEN

As he stood on the patio having a smoke, Bill turned his eyes to the sky. Having listened to the weather forecasters the night before, the morning was eerily calm for the weather they were predicting. Patches of blue could still be seen, but in the distance, clouds were forming, and when a blast of frigid air found its way through his jacket, Bill emptied his pipe and stepped back inside the house.

Over breakfast they discussed their trip. Since Bill owned a four-wheel drive vehicle and had driven the roads leading to his sister's home dozens of times, whatever the weather, he assured them it wouldn't be an issue. They all agreed to make the journey, so later that morning they climbed into his Land Rover and headed north.

Although they had spent their formative years living in Falkirk, when Bill's sister had met and married Lawrence Shaw, she had moved to an area just outside Kinlochleven to live in the house where her husband had grown up. Large and spacious, but well off the beaten path, it was where Nancy had raised her children, entertained her friends and on one summer day, it was where she had been met at the door by a group of his friends to tell her Lawrence was gone.

Since that time, whenever Bill visited he would listen as she'd complain about the miles separating her from the children she loved so much, but moving away from a home that held so many memories was impossible. So instead, several times a year, she'd have a family gathering, insisting everyone attend, and everyone did. You just didn't say no to Nancy Shaw.

Less than an hour after they left Carron Bridge the snow began to fall, and the farther they drove, the quieter they all became. Far from shopping malls and urban sprawl, the road was nearly empty of vehicles, and those that were traveling were doing it slowly.

Having not heard a sound in quite a while from the women sitting in the back seat, Eleanor looked over her shoulder and noticed that Toni's eyes were closed. At first believing that the woman was asleep, her opinion changed when she saw how Toni was holding the book in her lap. White-knuckled, she had all but bent the paperback in half. Thinking for a moment, Eleanor reached around and tapped Laura on the leg.

Looking away from the window, Laura's eyes met her mother's. Following her gaze, when she saw the way Toni was grasping the book, Laura leaned over and asked, "Toni...sweetheart, are you all right?"

She had been trying her best to quiet the panic rising from within by putting to use the lessons Abby had taught her, but it wasn't working. The sound of the tires on the snow and the rocking motion of the vehicle had taken Toni back in time to a journey she had made in the back of a box van with tiny windows, metal seats and chains rattling against the steel.

Toni opened her mouth to speak and instantly lost the battle. Feeling as if she were suffocating, she leaned back in her seat and began gulping in air as fast as she could.

"Da...um...Bill, stop the car. Will you please?" Laura said, rushing to unbuckle her seat belt.

"What?" he asked, looking in the rearview mirror.

"William, stop the car," Eleanor implored, unfastening her seat belt in hurry. "Toni's having a problem."

That was all he needed to hear, and quickly looking for a safe place to stop, Bill pulled off the road into a small pile of snow. In an instant, Toni opened her door and stumbled out. Managing to take only a few steps before she fell to her knees, she tried to fill her lungs with air she didn't need. Seconds later, both Laura and Eleanor were at her side, doing their best to quiet her anxieties.

"Sweetheart, it's okay. I'm here. You're safe. Just breathe. Remember what Abby said, Toni. Just take slow, easy breaths. Remember...slow, easy breaths."

"Can I do anything?" Eleanor asked.

"Just talk to her, Mum. Just talk to her."

Kneeling by Toni's side, Eleanor rested her hand lightly on Toni's shoulder. "Toni, William and I are here. You're safe. Remember, we're just going to Nancy's house. No one's going to hurt you there."

Hearing the crunch of snow, both women looked up as Bill approached. Walking around them, he knelt in front of the woman still gasping for air. Holding out his hand, he said, "Toni, take my hand."

"That's not what she needs," Laura said, glowering at the man.

Tuning out his daughter's words, Bill said firmly, "Toni, take my hand, lass. You can do it."

His voice was strong and clear, and Toni remembered the afternoon when he had saved her from the fall off the ladder. His arms were safe, and his words were true. He was Laura's father, and he would protect her. He promised.

Opening her eyes, Toni slowed her breathing and looked up at him. Her embarrassment blazed across her face, but it was dismissed with a subtle shake of his head, so after taking another ragged breath, Toni placed her hand in his.

"That's my girl," he whispered.

Stunned, both Eleanor and Laura remained kneeling as they watched him pull Toni to her feet, and without giving it a second thought, he reached down and dusted the snow from her trousers. "Now, why don't you sit up front with me for a while? I spent a lot of years on the sea, and I've got lots of tall tales to tell. How'd you like to hear them?"

Managing to give him a weak smile, Toni said, "I'd...I'd like that if...if Eleanor doesn't mind."

"I wouldn't mind at all," Eleanor chimed in, getting to her feet.

"Good. Well, I don't know about you ladies, but I think it's colder than a witch's tit out here. Shall we?" Bill said, grinning as he offered Toni his arm.

Without saying a word, Toni allowed herself to be led to the SUV, and climbing in the front seat, she had her seatbelt buckled before Eleanor and Laura had a chance to take a step.

Open-mouthed, Laura rose to her feet. For so long she had been the only one Toni had trusted, so the slightest hint of loss washed over her as she watched Bill lead Toni to the Land Rover, and then just as quickly, the feeling disappeared. Toni wasn't her possession. She was the woman Laura loved, and although she was baffled as to how Toni could so easily be calmed by a man who Laura still considered a stranger, that was Laura's issue, not Toni's.

Seeing the puzzled look on her daughter's face, Eleanor asked, "You okay?"

"Yeah, I'm just trying to make sense of what just happened," Laura said, brushing the snow off her jeans.

"Well, if I had to guess, I'd say that Toni has discovered something about your father that you've yet to realize."

"Oh yeah? What's that?"

"Even with all the mistakes he's made, he's still a good man."

***

For the next hour, Bill rambled on about his tales of the sea while Laura and Eleanor sat quietly in the back seat occasionally laughing and rolling their eyes at his exaggerations. Everyone else in the car had noticed the amount of snow falling, but listening intently to Bill's stories, Toni's head had remained bowed. Looking up to release the tension in her neck, her eyes bulged when she saw drifts of whiteness covering the landscape. "When did it start to snow like this?"

Bill looked up and caught sight of Eleanor in the rearview mirror, and when he saw her appreciative nod, he replied with a wink. Glancing to his left, he said, "It started about an hour ago, Toni, but no worries, the house is just down this road."

Peering through the glass, Toni said, "I don't see a thing."

"That's because there isn't anything to see. Just a lot of hills, meadows, trees...and snow."

With the closest town over ten miles away, the dirt road on which they were traveling had never seen a snow plow. Keeping the tires in the tracks made by others, Bill slipped the Land Rover into the lowest gear and carefully maneuvered down the winding path. Fifteen minutes later, he pulled up to a Victorian villa outlined in Christmas lights.

Covered in sandstone, the house was impressive and stately. Four oversized windows on the second floor matched the four dormers that ran along the slate-covered roof, and wreaths, dusted with snow, hung over the glass. The lower floor held two windows, identical in size and decoration to those above and centered between them was an understated wooden door set back into the stone of the house.

Knowing that when they returned on Christmas Day, the back of Bill's SUV would be filled with casseroles, biscuits and snacks, they had brought along all the gifts purchased for the children. After filling their hands with bags, they trudged up the stone steps leading to the house, and stomping their feet to rid themselves of snow, they rang the bell.

Opening the door, a blast of icy wind caused Nancy to shiver, and stepping back into her home, she waved her arm for her guests to enter. "Oh, my, it's absolutely bitter! Get in here right now."

Single file, they walked into the warmth of the house and breathed in the aroma of bread, baked fresh that morning. As they rid themselves of their coats, Toni looked around the spacious entryway. Large enough to encompass a hallway leading to the back of the house, as well as an expansive stairway leading the way to the upper floors, it was, nonetheless, simple and homey, not at all like Toni had imagined it would be.

"Thank you all for coming," Nancy said as she took their coats and hung them in the cloak room. "I hope the trip wasn't too awful."

"It's a bloody blizzard," Bill groused, handing her his coat.

"Oh, it is not, Billy. I swear you've gotten soft in your old age."

"Sort of like your head?" he asked.

Laughing, she slapped him on the arm and then turned to face her other three guests. Seeing Toni standing off to the side, Nancy went over and gave her an all-encompassing hug. "I want to apologize for my words the other day, Toni. I was wrong, and well…well, I was shocked. Please forgive me. I meant no harm."

Feeling as if she were being embraced by a giant marshmallow with carrot-colored hair, Toni couldn't help but grin. Returning the hug, she said, "Of course. No harm done, Nancy."

"Good," she said, holding Toni at arm's length. "Now, Laura why don't you give Toni a tour of the house, and your parents and I will catch up, and feel free to put those pressies under the tree."

Nancy flounced down the long hallway leading to the kitchen with her hips swaying left and right like a ship at sea. Rolling their eyes in unison at the woman's animated swagger, Eleanor and Bill followed.

Waiting until the others were out of hearing range, Toni leaned down and whispered, "I never thought I'd be afraid of breasts, but I swear I thought I was going to be squished."

"I told you they were big," Laura said with a snigger.

"So," Toni began, looking around the entry. "Which way is the tree?"

"There are probably at least three. Which one would you like to see first?"

"Three?"

"Come on, I'll show you," Laura said, taking Toni's hand.

The entryway was subdued, lacking both color and elaborate decoration, but it didn't take long for Toni to realize that the rest of the house erupted in both.

The first room they came upon was a small sitting area just past the cloak room, and when Toni peered inside, her mouth dropped open. Red and blue tartan wallpaper covered the walls, and although ending a few feet before it reached the ceiling, the swath of white plaster remaining did little to mute the color explosion. Scarlet drapes reached to the oak-planked floor, the majority of which was covered in a vibrant paisley area rug that swirled with hues of blue, green, purple and red. A shiny black upright piano sat along one wall while a diminutive cherry desk stood in the corner of another, and in the center of the room, opposite a small fireplace, were two wingback chairs, the color of their upholstery matching that of a martini olive. Curling her lip at the decorating disaster, Toni was thankful the room was too small to hold a Christmas tree.

Walking down the hall past the stairs, Laura opened the door to the first of several bathrooms in the house, and Toni quickly began to see a pattern. The floor was tiled in maroon, blue, and gray, similar to the tartan wallpaper she had viewed moments before, and the walls were covered in shiny apple-red tile, grouted in white. The fixtures matched the grout in color, and if it hadn't been for the bright pink towels hanging from the rods, the room was doable...at least for a short visit.

As they approached the kitchen, on the wall opposite the bathroom was a set of pocket doors and sliding them into the wall,

Laura stepped back and motioned for Toni to enter. As she took a hesitant step, Toni smelled the scent of pine, and smiling, she walked into Nancy Shaw's library. The color scheme wasn't something Toni would have chosen, but the small Norfolk pine just inside the doorway eased the pain in her eyes...slightly.

The room was painted a bright turquoise, but the bulky wood moldings surrounding the ceiling, floor and doors were glossy white, and the effect made the room appear as if it had jumped off a page of a comic book. To the far left was a small stone fireplace flanked by two red leather chairs, and a sofa in the same material and shade sat against the wall opposite the doorway. At first confused by the lack of furniture in the rather spacious room, when Toni noticed that the bottom shelves of the walnut bookcases were filled with games, dolls and toys, she realized the library had been converted into a playroom. Glancing at the tree, her assumption was confirmed. Every branch was filled with handmade ornaments made of pipe cleaners, felt-covered Styrofoam balls and colored paper.

After placing the children's gifts under the tree, Laura and Toni headed back to the front of the house, but came to a stop when the front door opened. Toni smiled immediately when she saw a familiar face, but when a man, tall and broad-shouldered, followed Peggy inside, Toni's expression turned solemn. Grabbing Laura's hand, she remained mute as Laura led her to the people standing just inside the door.

"So, you made it, eh?" Laura said, eyeing her extremely pregnant cousin. "I thought in your condition, you'd stay close to home."

"In a few weeks, he's not going to let me go anywhere, so when Mum came up with this idea, I jumped at the chance to be without the kids for a day."

"Where are they?"

"Stephen's parents have them. We pick them up tonight." Leaning in, Peggy gave Laura a kiss on the cheek, and glancing over her cousin's shoulder, she smiled. "Hiya, Toni."

"Peggy, nice to see you again," Toni said, finding it impossible not to smile at the familiar greeting Laura had used so many times.

Pointing to the man standing next to her, Peggy said, "Toni, this is my husband, Stephen."

Peggy had taken it upon herself to let Stephen know that Laura's partner was nervous around strangers, so displaying the friendliest smile he owned, Stephen Wallace held out his hand. "Pleasure to meet you, Toni."

Thankful she had taken Abby's advice, Toni had prepared herself to meet the man Laura had described as tall and muscular, but when his sleeve tightened around his bulging bicep, she hesitated for a few seconds before managing to find her voice. Extending her hand to the blond, blue-eyed man, Toni said, "Likewise...um...nice to meet you, too."

The handshake came to an end, but when Toni relaxed her grip, Stephen didn't do the same. Her first instinct was to yank her hand away, but something in his eyes made her stop. Although she tensed as he leaned in closer, she held her ground and then heard him chuckle. "And I hear you put old Nancy in her place about you two having children. Good for you!"

"Stephen!" Peggy scolded, playfully slapping him on the arm. "I told you to behave."

"What? What did I say?" he asked. "Peg, you know I adore your mum, but she can be a bit opinionated at times, and when she's not, she's quoting chapter and verse from *The Weekly Sun.*"

"Oh, I forgot about that," Laura said with a groan. "But I don't see any around, so maybe she gave up reading it."

Peggy jerked back her head as she stared at her cousin. "Not on your life. She probably just stashed them away so we wouldn't make fun of her."

"Well, best go say hello and all that," Stephen said, taking his wife's hand. "You two joining us?"

"In a minute," Laura said.

Waiting until Peggy and Stephen were down the hall, Laura turned to Toni. "Sorry, I didn't know Stephen was going to be here today. Are you all right?"

"Yeah, but if you hadn't told me what he looked like, I would have definitely had a problem. Christ, he's like one big walking muscle."

"That he is," Laura said, nodding in agreement.

"But you know what?"

"What?"

"I'm doing okay."

"Are you?"

"I think I've finally convinced myself that where your family's concerned, there's nothing to fear."

"Well, you may want to reserve judgment until you see the lounge."

"It can't possibly be worse than what you've already shown me."

"You wanna bet?" Laura said as she ambled over and opened the doors leading into the lounge. Looking over her shoulder, she burst out laughing when Toni's jaw hit the floor.

It took only two strides for the entire room to come into view, but when it did, Toni was shell-shocked. Standing in the doorway, she tried to wrap her head around a room erupting in every shade of pink known to man, woman...and beast.

If the lounge had been decorated in muted pastels or soft earth tones, it would have been a warm and comfortable space, but with walls of medicinal pink and drapes of bright raspberry, comfortable it was *not*.

The two large sofas sitting opposite one another in front of the fireplace and the three high-backed chairs near the windows along the front wall were upholstered in matching material. However, the soft white background of the fabric had been lost behind a design of pink, violet and rose flowers woven into the cloth, all of which had brilliant blue-green stems pointing in every direction. The shag area rug was striped in bands of fuchsia and puce, and the pillows scattered about were in a shade of magenta so vibrant Toni found herself blinking to clear the spots from her eyes.

Something about the Christmas tree in the corner caught Toni's eye, and when she went over and looked closely at the baubles filling the boughs, she fought to suppress a laugh. Never believing that Christmas ornaments could come in so many shades of pink, as Toni stood in front of the Fraser fir, she made a mental note to never buy anything in the color of cerise.

***

Standing in the conservatory just off the kitchen, Laura watched through the window as Toni and Bill stood in the snow feeding their nicotine habits.

After ending their tour at the lounge, Laura and Toni returned to the kitchen where they found everyone gathered around the center island, nibbling on biscuits. Chatting about the weather and the plans for Christmas Day, it wasn't until Nancy began to talk about an article she had recently read in her favorite tabloid when everyone got the same idea.

Announcing he needed a smoke, Bill headed outside as fast as his feet would carry him, and giving Laura an apologetic shrug, Toni grabbed her coat and quickly followed suit. Volunteering to ready the hearth in the lounge for a fire, both Eleanor and Stephen also escaped the conversation, which left Laura and Peggy standing with frozen stares of interest as Nancy chattered on about unexplained disappearances and aliens. Finally, in need of the bathroom, Nancy sashayed up the hall, leaving both Peggy and Laura thankful that she had consumed so much tea.

"How's Toni doing?"

"She's okay," Laura said, watching as her cousin lowered her very pregnant body into one of the chairs at the kitchen table. "But how are you doing?"

"Me? I'm fine. After you've had two, you become accustomed to feeling fat."

"Well, you look great."

"Thanks. I feel great."

"So, are you planning to stop at three or are you going to round up to the next even number?" Laura asked as she sat down.

"I think we're going to try for a girl."

"You said that the last time."

"I know, but Stephen apparently wasn't listening," Peggy said, giggling as she rubbed her belly. Watching as her cousin's attention was again drawn to the patio, Peggy rolled her eyes. "Laura?"

"Yeah?" Laura said, turning back around.

"Why didn't you ever tell me you were gay? I mean, we used to tell each other everything."

"I didn't know I was."

"What?"

"It's true. Before I met Toni, women didn't interest me...at least not in that way, but then I fell in love with her. I was...I was as stunned as anyone, but in a way, I think love transcends everything else. It made the fact that she's a woman inconsequential, at least to me. I don't know if I'm gay or straight or somewhere in between, all I know is that I'm in love. She does it for me, Peggy. She truly, truly does."

"Well, you won't get an argument from me. I think she's beautiful, and as long as you two are happy that's all that really matters."

"What about Dot and Alice? How do you think they'll handle it?"

Thinking for a moment, Peggy said, "Alice won't care. She's pretty much like me when it comes to things like this. Live and let live and all of that, and Ron has never struck me as being homophobic, so I doubt that there will be any issue there. Dorothy, on the other hand, will undoubtedly be shocked, but being politically correct, she won't show it. If I know Dot, she'll toss playful innuendo in your direction in hopes she'll get answers without having to actually *ask* the questions she so desperately wants to ask. And as far as Bernard is concerned, as long as it doesn't get in the way of his career, he really won't care. He can't see it from his house, so therefore, it doesn't matter."

"Is he really becoming that...that—"

"Pompous?"

"Yes."

"Unfortunately, he is. You know I really don't understand why he ever became a doctor. He just doesn't seem to have that type of personality. If you ask me, he's much more suited for a desk job, and he's even getting a little administrative belly on him from all those business lunches."

"And the children?"

"Oh, Laura, the kids are much too young to understand, except maybe for Emma, but stop worrying. It'll be fine."

"I'm not the one worrying."

"Oh? Toni?"

"Yeah."

"This may be none of my business, but can I ask what happened to her? Why is she so nervous around people, and those scars on her back...how she'd get them?"

The room got quiet for a moment as Laura played with a loose thread on the tablecloth, and then raising her eyes to meet Peggy's, she said, "Toni was...she was put in prison for something she didn't do. She was there for four years, and the guards brutalized her. They beat her...lied to her...and very nearly destroyed her."

"Oh, dear God, how in the world did she ever cope?"

"I didn't," Toni said, taking off her coat.

Startled, both women looked up to find Bill and Toni standing just inside the back door. Taking Toni's coat from her hand, Bill offered a smile to the two women sitting at the table, before walking from the room.

"I didn't hear you come in," Laura said, getting her feet.

"I know. Filling Peggy in on all the gory details, were you?"

Seeing the gleam in Toni's eye, Laura placed a quick kiss on her cheek. "Not all of them, and your nose is cold."

"That's because it's freezing out there."

"Well, if you'd quit smoking, that wouldn't be a problem."

"One habit at a time, remember? I promise, as soon as I've beaten all the other issues, I'll work on my one with nicotine. All right?"

"Yes, sweetheart."

Sitting at the table, Peggy watched the exchange and smiled. Laura and Toni exuded happiness, and while she didn't know all of Toni's problems, Peggy knew her cousin, and that made her smile grow even wider.

"What are you grinning about?" Laura asked.

"What? Oh...um...nothing. I'm just really happy for both of you. I think you make a marvelous pair."

"Thanks," Laura said, sliding her arm around Toni's waist. "We do, too."

"I hate to break this up," Bill said, coming back into the room. "Nancy thought you'd want to come up front. Dorothy and Alice just pulled up."

"Okay, Da...um...Bill, we'll be right there."

Toni and Peggy locked eyes for a moment, both secretly amused by Laura's struggle not to call the man by his fatherly title. Pressing her lips together to hide her mirth, Peggy pushed herself out of her chair, and a minute later, all three were heading toward the lounge.

"I'm going to hit the loo," Toni said, stopping at the powder room.

"You okay?" Laura said, touching Toni on the arm.

Seeing the worry on Laura's face, Toni sighed. "Laura, I've been drinking tea and was just outside standing in the cold. I've got to pee. That's all." Moving her face to within an inch of Laura's, she added, "Would you like to watch?"

Toni's playfulness told Laura all she needed to know, and letting go of Toni's arm, she said, "Sorry, sweetheart. I'll meet you in the lounge."

After spending a moment watching Laura's hips sway as she walked up the hall, Toni went into the bathroom to empty her bladder, and as she washed her hands, she heard the doorbell ring. Looking into the mirror, she straightened a few windblown locks and then shut off the light.

Stepping into the hall, she grinned at the commotion by the front door as excited family members rushed to meet others walking into the house. Taking a deep breath, Toni continued toward the hubbub, but a second later, she stopped dead in her tracks when she heard a voice. A voice she knew. A voice she told herself years before...she would never, *ever* forget.

CHAPTER FORTY-EIGHT

Toni was paralyzed. Incapacitated by fear, she couldn't move. She couldn't breathe. Was this her imagination, or was it her nerves getting the better of her...again? Had she wound herself so tightly that even a hint of foul prison familiar became reality? Swallowing hard, she closed her eyes, and cocking her head to the side, she listened. A chorus of voices chattered in unison, but with intent, she pulled out the sopranos, separated the altos and concentrated on those low and masculine, and then she heard him again...and her hands turned into fists.

Terror-stricken, her eyes flew open. With the front hall a flurry of activity, it took several seconds before she finally saw him. A bit heavier perhaps, and a bit older, but there was no mistake...it *was* him.

Like a snake, the smells and sounds of Thornbridge wrapped themselves around her, and as Toni's nostrils filled with the acrid odor of death and damage, her ears were deafened by the sounds of barred doors clanging shut down the wing. In the blink of an eye, she was transported back to hell.

Having greeted everyone, Eleanor had stepped back into the doorway of the lounge, and noticing Toni standing in the hallway, she was about to motion for her to join them when she saw the woman's face. Distorted in fear, Toni's skin had gone white and lines of terror were etched into her forehead.

Keeping one eye on Toni, Eleanor reached over and tugged Laura's sleeve, and when her daughter turned around, Eleanor whispered, "There's something wrong with Toni."

Laura glanced down the hall at her partner. Believing it was just Toni's anxiety kicking in, Laura's cheerful expression remained for a few moments before it slowly melted away. The look on Toni's face spoke volumes, and Laura's heart skipped a beat. When she had visited Toni's flat for the very first time, she had seen the look of terror, but this was different. This was far worse.

"Toni?" Laura said softly, taking one step in her direction.

"No," Toni said, shaking her head.

"Toni...sweetheart."

"No," Toni said again, holding up her hand. "Stay away."

"Sweetheart, it's me. Laura."

"*Stay the fuck away from me!*" Toni shouted.

The decibel level of the room went to zero as everyone stopped talking and stared at the woman in the hallway. Most were confused, but Eleanor and Bill were not. Holding their breath, they prayed their daughter could help the woman who was crumbling in front of them.

Nervously, Laura chewed on her lip, her eyes locked on the woman whose face seemed to be getting paler by the second. Taking a hesitant step toward Toni, she said, "Toni, it's me, Laura. You can trust me. You know you can trust me." Reaching out to her, Laura said, "Take my hand, Toni. Come on, sweetheart. You can do it."

Toni looked at the hand extended to her and saw nothing but handcuffs. Shackles, shiny and bright, they would be clamped around her wrists and secured so tightly that the thump of her pulse would cause pain. *Never again.* She took a step backward. *Never again.*

"Toni, please...you're scaring me."

For an instant, Toni thought she knew the voice. The accent was sweet and soothing, and she found herself wanting to listen to it. She wanted to believe it...but then it was gone. Like an evil nymph, terror whispered in her ear and blocked out everything else. *Trust no one and you will survive. Trust anyone...and you will die.*

Glaring at the stranger, Toni shook her head, silently warning the woman not to take another step, and when Laura did, Toni spun around and bolted down the hallway. For a split-second, Laura stared in disbelief, but when she heard the sound of glass breaking, she made a mad dash toward the back of the house.

The temperature in the room had already begun to drop when Laura reached the kitchen, the winter storm whipping in through the open back door. Rushing over, she paled when she spotted blood on the broken panes of glass, and narrowing her eyes, she peered through the whiteness of the blizzard to see Toni charging through the trees to the meadows beyond.

There was no time to think. No time to concern herself with the snow or the wind or the cold, there was only time to react, and darting out of the house, Laura gave chase.

Mindless of the weather, Toni ran through the snow with only one thought in her mind...escape. The bastards would not get her again. She had made sure of it. She had trained for it. Years of running on a treadmill had given her strength and stamina, and gulping in icy air, she high-stepped it through drifts as she ran over frozen fields covered in white. More than once she stumbled and fell, but growling at her misstep, she pushed herself up and started again. Behind her, she could hear someone calling her name, pleading for her to stop, but Toni no longer recognized the voice. To her, it was one of them. One who would promise safety and then cause pain. *Never again*. She ran faster.

Try as she might, Laura could not gain any ground on the long-legged woman in front of her, but stubbornly, she pushed herself to keep running. Her hands were freezing and her face was chafed by the harsh, cold air, and even though her lungs screamed with every breath she took, Laura could not stop...she would *not* stop.

Falling headfirst into a deep drift, Laura wiped the snow from her face. "Get up, goddamn it," she grumbled, scrambling to her feet. Seeing that the distance between them was growing, Laura drew in as much air as her lungs would hold and forced herself to run again, but after only a few minutes, she knew she had lost the battle. Slowing to a jog, she tried her best to stay in Toni's footprints, and then something in the distance caught her attention...and her heart stopped.

Calling on every ounce of energy she had left, Laura broke into a run, but within seconds she fell again. Dissolving into tears, she pounded her fists in the snow, berating herself for being so weak. Again and again she struggled to rise, but her body refused to listen. Spent, her lungs burning and her limbs shaking, she looked toward the heavens and howled, *"Toni!"*

The wind swirled around Laura as she knelt in the snow. The sound of her ragged sobs and desperate gasps were muffled by the whiteness surrounding her, and for an instant, the world turned deathly quiet...but then she heard a noise. It was a thudding, breathing noise that seemed to grow louder by the second, and looking over her shoulder, Laura saw Stephen running toward her.

"Laura! Jesus! Are you all right," he said, falling to his knees by her side.

"Stephen! Oh, thank God! Stop her. Please, stop her! There's a bridge," Laura said, pointing across the field. "There's a bridge, Stephen. Oh, dear God....please....please, you've got to stop her. You've got to stop her!"

Following Laura's line of sight, Stephen saw the small bridge in the distance, and looking back at Laura for only a moment, he rose to his feet and took off running as fast as he could.

Between the physical demands of his job and those that he put on himself, Stephen Wallace had always kept himself in shape. Hours in the weight room at the station and long bicycle rides on the weekends afforded him not only muscle, but also discipline. When he set his mind to do something, it would be done, so when he noticed Toni had begun to slow, he knew she was running out of steam, and he was not. In a few minutes, she would be his...or so he thought.

Toni's body was no longer hers. She told it to step. She told it to run, and she told it to breathe, but frozen and stiff, her body refused to listen any longer...and then the earth ended.

Somersaulting down the hillside, Toni grunted as she tumbled over the uneven ground until her fall finally came to an end at a downed tree drifted over with snow. Sitting in the cold, her jaw dropped open as she gasped for air, but when she heard a man's voice behind her, she struggled to her feet once more. Commanding her body to obey, Toni ignored the pain and plodded through the snow. One step, two steps, three steps...*never again*. Four steps, five steps, six steps...*never again*.

Delirious, Toni smiled at the cadence as it repeated in her mind...and then suddenly, she was on fire. Her feet, ankles, calves and thighs burst into flames, and as she opened her mouth to scream at the pain, water rushed in to silence her.

Scrambling down the embankment, Stephen jumped through the broken ice into the inky pool below, and hissing as the frigid river sucked away his strength, he waved his arms through the water, trying to find her. Again and again he swooshed through the blackness, and when something soft brushed against his hand, he yelled to the heavens, "Yes!"

Grabbing Toni by her hair, he brought her to the surface, and struggling to keep her head above the water, he dragged her to the shore. Climbing out, he took hold of her arms and with one strong yank, he pulled her onto the snow-covered earth and fell to his knees. Rolling her over on her side, he let the water drain from her mouth, and then lowering his ear to her lips, he held his breath and waited...but there was no sound to be heard.

"No, you don't!" he barked. *"No, you bloody don't!"*

Tilting Toni's head back, Stephen took a deep breath, and squeezing her nose shut, he placed his mouth over hers. Forcing air into her lungs in two quick puffs, he listened for only a second before he began chest compressions. Less than thirty seconds later, he filled his lungs again, and giving her two more quick breaths, when Toni still didn't respond, he started the process all over again.

Stephen lost count as to how many breaths he had given her, but when he felt the rumble of a cough growing in her throat, he quickly pulled her to her side. Watching as the water emptied from her lungs, he sat back and smiled, mindless of the shivers that had taken control of his body.

"Toni!" Laura screamed as she stumbled down the hill. "Oh, dear God, no!"

"She's okay. She's okay," Stephen shouted back. "She's...she's alive."

Scrambling to Toni's side, Laura said, "Oh, Toni. Sweetheart, talk to me. Please talk to me."

When Toni didn't move, Laura looked to Stephen for help, and with frozen fingers, he felt for a pulse. "She's alive, Laura. Sh-sh-she's hypothermic. W-we all are. We need t-t-to get help. Can you make it b-b-back to the house?"

"I'm not leaving you here!"

"You've got to...got to tell B-Bernard what's happened. He'll know what to do."

"I am *not* leaving you two here!"

"D-d-damn it, Laura, listen! I'll follow. I-I-I promise, I'll follow. I-I-I won't let her die, but the f-f-faster one of us can get back there to tell them what's happened, the b-b-better her chances. Laura, she doesn't have a lot of time."

That was all Laura needed to hear. Quickly pressing her frozen lips against Toni's icy cheek, she said, "I love you" in a kiss and then sprinted up the hill.

***

"How's your back?" Eleanor asked.

Shaking his head in disgust, Bill continued to stare out the window. Seconds after Laura ran from the house he had tried to follow, but slipping on some ice on the patio, when he hit the slate, his back gave out. Defeated, he returned to the house, fixed the window with duct tape and cardboard, and then waited like all the rest.

"It's fine now."

"Don't be so hard on yourself."

"They've been gone too long, Ellie," he said, wrinkling his brow. "And none of them were dressed properly."

Taking his hand, Eleanor gave it a squeeze. "I know, sweetheart, but Laura is smart and Stephen is strong, and God will protect them all. I know he will."

After insisting that the rest of the family stay in the lounge, Nancy strode into the kitchen and shouted, "Now, what the hell is going on here?"

"Not now, Nancy," Bill said, peering out the window.

"Yes, *now*," she said, placing her hands on her hips. "This is *my* house and *my* afternoon tea. How dare you bring a crazy woman—"

"*Shut the fuck up!*" Bill yelled, spinning on his heel to glare at his sister. "You shut your mouth, woman. You don't know anything about Toni, and I am not going to allow you to call her names! When and *if* the time is right, you may find yourself privy to that information, but right now, I'm worried about my daughter, her fiancée and *your* son-in-law, so I think it best you shut your mouth and say a prayer...for *all* of them. Do I make myself clear?"

"I'm afraid prayers aren't all they're going to need," Bernard said, striding into the kitchen with Dorothy, Alice and Peggy in tow. "I've asked Ron to call emergency services and then start the fireplace in the library. Nancy, I need you to gather as many blankets as you can find and put them in there, too."

Rolling her eyes, Nancy said, "Bernard, don't be ridiculous. There's a perfectly good fire burning in the lounge. Why bother starting another when—"

"Because the lounge is too bloody large, that's why. We can close the doors to the library and make it warm quickly, so please stop asking questions and do what I say, and while you're at it, find them all some clothes."

"Oh, now you're just being silly," Nancy said, crossing her arms across her enormous bosom. "This isn't a department store. I don't have clothes to fit them."

"Bloody hell, woman!" he yelled, causing everyone in the room to jump. "Do as I ask...*now*!"

Splaying her fingers across her chest, Nancy stumbled back a step, and then mumbling to herself, she stomped from the room.

Letting out a long, heavy sigh, Bernard glanced at the other women in the room. "Peggy, are you doing okay?"

Grinning at her brother-in-law's concern, Peggy said, "I'm fine, Bernard. A bit worried, but Stephen's strong, and I know he'll bring them back."

"Good, that's what I want to hear," he said, running his fingers through his hair. "Okay, Dorothy, I need you to put on some water. Make it warm, but not hot, and Alice, do you know if your mum has any hot water bottles?"

"Yeah, she used to."

"Well, then be a love and go find them. Can you do that?"

"Of course. Right away," Alice said as she scurried out of the room.

"There's Laura!" Eleanor screamed, pointing out the window.

Mindless of the ache in his back, Bill rushed outside, careful to avoid the ice on the patio as he ran to his daughter's side. "Oh, my God, Laura. We were so worried."

People can do the unimaginable when fear and adrenaline mix, and after she had placed a kiss on Toni's frozen cheek, Laura raced across the snow-covered fields with energy she didn't know she had. Mindless of the ice coating her hair or the burn in her lungs, she hadn't slowed a step until she reached the house. Gasping for air, she bent over as she struggled to breathe and her knees buckled instantly.

Pain crossed Bill's face as he gathered Laura in his arms, but refusing to acknowledge the twinge in his back, he carried her to the house. Met at the door by Eleanor and Bernard, he was ushered inside, but after taking only a few steps, Laura came to her senses.

"Put m-me down!" Laura said, squirming in her father's arms. "Put me down!"

"Okay, sweetheart. Okay," Bill said, allowing Laura to stand. "There you go."

"We need...we need to g-g-get help," Laura said, panting for air. "We've g-g-got to g-g-get help!"

Bernard walked between them, narrowing his eyes as he looked at the woman shivering uncontrollably in front of him. "We need to get you warm. You're hypothermic."

"No!" Laura said, pushing him away. "Toni...Toni...Toni fell in the w-w-water. Stephen got her out, and he t-t-told me to come back here. He s-s-said you'd know....you'd know what to do."

"Jesus Christ," Bernard said, rubbing his chin. "That puts a wrench in things." Seeing Ron come back into the room, Bernard asked, "Did you get through to emergency services?"

"Yeah, but with the snow, they said it could take hours. Apparently, there have been a few accidents and some of the roads are closed."

"All right then, we'll do it ourselves," Bernard said, reaching into his pocket. Tossing his car keys to Ron, he said, "There's a black bag in the boot. Get it for me, and then find Nancy and tell her to put the blankets and clothes in the library."

"Got it, doc," Ron said, quickly jogging down the hall.

Bernard moved closer to Laura, but when she backed away from his touch, in a tone soft yet stern, he said, "Laura, you aren't going to be any good to Toni like this. I need you to listen to me and do what I ask. Okay?"

"No!" Laura said, putting her hands up to keep him at a distance. "Toni...y-y-you have to...you have to help her. Not me. Not me...only her. I'm...I'm...I'm okay."

"No, you're not," Eleanor said as she strode over and took Laura by the shoulders. "So, we're going to do whatever Bernard wants us to do. I'm not going to stand by and allow your stubbornness to reign supreme. Do you understand me? When Toni gets back, she's going to need you, so the sooner we get you warm and into some dry clothes, the better off she'll be when she returns. Do I make myself clear?"

Laura's cheeks were covered in frozen tears, and as the new ones began to fall, they traveled down the same tracks to her chin. Shivering, she looked up at Bernard. "Don't...don't you...don't you let her die!"

"I have no intention of allowing that to happen," he said softly. "Eleanor, take Laura into the library and get her out of those clothes. All of them."

"I-I-I can do it," Laura said, taking a step.

"No, you can't," Peggy said. Getting to her feet, she looked at Bernard. "Stephen's had training in this. I know what to do."

"Good girl. I'll leave her in your hands then."

Having just piled clothing and blankets on a chair in the library, when Nancy saw Peggy and Eleanor guiding Laura into the room, her heart fell. "Oh, dear God! What can I do?"

Warmed by her mother's concern, Peggy said, "You two get her shoes and socks off, and I'll start with the rest."

Shaking her head, Laura said, "I-I-I can do—"

"No, you can't," Peggy said firmly, looking Laura in the eye. "Lesson 101 when treating hypothermia is that you never allow the victim to help. Moving about causes the cold blood from your arms and legs to travel toward your heart...and that's bad. Now, stop making a fuss, Laura. It's not like we didn't used to take baths together."

***

Fifteen minutes later, Bernard slid open the doors to the library, and when he saw Laura lying under an assortment of throws and quilts, he smiled at Peggy. "Well done."

Going over to the swaddled woman, he asked, "How you feeling?"

"Better. Warmer. Any sign of Stephen?"

"Not yet, I'm afraid, but the man runs marathons, Laura. He'll be here," Bernard said, kneeling by her side. "Do you mind if I check you over?"

"No, but I'm fine."

Bernard's eyes twinkled as he looked back at his knowledgeable patient. "How about you let me be the judge of that?" he said, reaching for her hand.

After taking Laura's pulse and checking her fingers and toes for frostbite, he reached into his doctor's bag and pulled out a stethoscope. Placing it in his ears, as he reached under the blanket, he said, "This may be a bit cold."

Snorting, Laura gave him a weak smile and a few minutes later, Bernard got to his feet. "You're going to be just fine. Your heart is strong, your lungs are clear and there's no sign of frostbite."

"Can I get up?"

"You can even get dressed, but you stay in here where it's warm. All right?"

"She won't leave," Eleanor said, rummaging through the clothes Nancy had piled on the chair. "Trust me."

Outside the library, Bill paced up and down the hallway, so when the doors finally slid open, he was at Bernard's side like steel to a magnet. "Is Laura okay? Bernard, is my daughter all right?"

"She's fine, Bill, relax. She's warm and getting dressed."

"Thank God."

"Bill! Bernard! *I see Steve!*" Ron shouted from the kitchen.

Stephen had started out slow, plodding through the snow with Toni in his arms, but when he started to shiver, he forced himself to jog and when that wasn't fast enough, he forced himself to run. He knew they didn't have long. Between the frigid temperature and the fall in the river, the odds were against them, but Stephen wasn't a betting man, and he was most assuredly *not* a quitter.

Cradling Toni in his arms, he ran, he jogged, he walked, and then he ran again, all the while refusing to allow the pain in his body to win out. It didn't matter that their clothes were stiff and frozen. It didn't matter that ice covered their chins and noses from moisture frozen as it was exhaled. All that mattered was getting back to Nancy's and when he saw the lights from the house in the distance, he stopped for a moment to place a frozen kiss on Toni's head before filling his lungs with air and trudging toward the lights.

Racing to the kitchen, Bill was on Ron's heels as he ran out the back door, and sprinting past the younger man, he got to Stephen within seconds. Even though he was shocked at the man's sallow and ice-covered appearance, Bill's eyes were drawn to the lifeless body in Stephen's arms.

"Is she...oh God...is she..."

"No. No, she's...she's alive, but...but she stopped shivering a f-f-few minutes ago," Stephen said, placing Toni in Bill's outstretched arms. "Get...get her inside. Get her inside n-n-now."

The exchange proved difficult as Stephen's shirt and Toni's sweater had frozen together, but after a few hard tugs, the fabric released and Bill rushed to get her into the house. Anxiously waiting just inside the door, Bernard quickly placed his fingers on Toni's neck before Bill came to a stop. Letting out the breath he'd been holding, Bernard said, "She's alive. Let's get her into the library, shall we?"

They sat with bowed heads and joined hands, praying their loved ones would return safe and sound, and lost in their thoughts, when the library doors slid open with a bang, all three women practically jumped off the sofa.

Seeing her father carrying Toni into the room, Laura's heart stopped. "Toni!" she shouted. Getting to her feet, she rushed toward the man. "Toni!"

"Stay back, Laura," Bernard said, pushing her away. "She needs medical attention right now, not someone crying over her. I know you mean well, but let me help her first, and then she's all yours."

Disregarding what he said, Laura tried again to get close, but this time Eleanor and Peggy pulled her away.

"Laura, Bernard's right. You aren't what she needs right now," Eleanor said.

As the rest of the family escorted Stephen into the room, Bernard took charge in an instant. "All right. Bill, put Toni on the sofa, and Ron, get Stephen close to the fire, but not too close. Put him in that chair over there," Bernard said, pointing to the leather wing-back by the fireplace. "Nancy, I need you to warm up some towels. Dorothy, get me something warm for them to drink. No tea. No coffee...broth if Nancy has any. Alice, fill those bottles with warm water...not hot...warm. Eleanor, find some scissors, and Ron, call emergency services again. See if you can find out where they are."

While all the commotion was going on, Peggy walked over to stand next to her husband, and dusting some snow from his hair, she asked, "You doing okay?"

"Never b-b-better," Stephen said through chattering teeth. "You?"

Smiling, Peggy said, "I love you."

"I-I-I love...love you more."

"I found three pairs of scissors," Eleanor announced, rushing into the room.

"Good!" Bernard said, whipping around. "Peggy, we need to get your husband out of those clothes—"

"I can...I can..." Stephen said, trying to stand up.

"Stay right there, man! I don't want you to move unless I tell you to," Bernard said. "Bill, give her a hand. Cut everything off and put him on the floor. Close enough to the fire to get warm, but only warm. Do you understand?"

"Yes," Bill said, taking a pair of kitchen shears from Eleanor.

When Alice walked back into the room carrying three hot water bottles, Bernard quickly checked them to make sure the temperature was correct. "Perfect," he said, placing them on the coffee table. "Now, be a love and figure out a way to make more. We need at least four. Okay?"

"I'll find something," Alice said, rushing from the room.

"And pull those bloody doors shut," he shouted. Taking the scissors from Eleanor, he turned to Laura and handed her a pair. "You need to cut off her clothes. Everything needs to be removed. Don't pull or tug. Cut it off. No hard movement. She needs to stay as still as possible. Can you do that?"

Setting her jaw, Laura snatched the scissors from his hand. "Yes, I can."

"I'll help," Eleanor said, taking the other pair from Bernard. "Let's go."

By the time Bernard returned to Stephen, Bill had the man stripped of his clothing and lying under a blanket a few feet from the hearth. Checking Stephen's hands and feet, Bernard shouted, "Nancy! Where are those bloody towels?"

"I've got them right here," she said, running into the room. "Fresh out of the dryer."

"Bill, wrap those around his hands and feet. I'll get his head. Peggy, be a love and get those water bottles."

Glancing at his patient, Bernard asked, "How you doing, Steve?"

"Better. Not so c-c-cold."

"You'll be fine. I don't see any sign of frostbite, so we're just going to warm you up slowly. All right?"

"Yeah. Okay."

"Dorothy, I need that broth!" Bernard shouted over his shoulder.

Appearing in the doorway within seconds, Dorothy rushed over and handed him a cup. "Here you go."

Feeling the heat radiating through the china, Bernard flung the cup into the fireplace. "I said warm, woman, not hot! Are you trying to kill them? Pull your head out of your arse and do what I ask!"

Paying no attention to his mortified wife as she ran from the room, Bernard looked over at Laura and Eleanor. "How you ladies doing over there?"

"We're trying, but the fabric is frozen," Eleanor called back.

Laura was trying to remain calm as she struggled to force the scissors through the ice-laden cloth, but Toni had begun to shiver so violently that Laura found herself having to regroup after each tremble racked Toni's body. Feeling a hand on her shoulder, Laura looked up to see her father staring down at her.

"Stand back. I'll do it. I'm stronger." For a split-second their eyes met, and reaching out, Bill brushed a strand of hair from Laura's face. "Come on, lass. Let your father lend a hand."

Tears welled in Laura's eyes. Handing Bill the scissors, she said, "Please, just be careful with her. She...she doesn't like to be touched."

"I know, sweetheart. I'll be careful."

Behind them, Dorothy came back into the room with two more cups of broth. Walking over, she held her breath as Bernard took it from her hand.

He grinned at the warmth coming through the cup, and then in a whisper, he said, "I'm sorry. I shouldn't have yelled at you, but I haven't been in this type of situation for a very long time."

"No worries, sweetheart," Dorothy said with tears in her eyes. "Just make me proud."

Smiling, he handed Peggy one of the cups. "Have Stephen take some sips of this. Not too fast though. Can you do that?"

"Absolutely."

"Good girl," he said as he headed to the sofa.

Bill had made short work of Toni's clothing, and with Eleanor and Laura at his side, protecting Toni's privacy as best they could, by the time Bernard came over, Toni was naked and lying under several blankets, shivering uncontrollably. Grabbing his stethoscope, Bernard checked her heart and pulse before placing a digital thermometer in her ear. Waiting for the beep, he read the display, and then rubbing his chin, he sat back on his haunches.

"What's wrong?" Laura asked.

"She's colder than I thought she'd be."

"Well, then let's move her closer to the fireplace."

"No, we can't risk moving her now. It's too dangerous," Bernard said, looking up at Laura. "She's your partner, isn't she?"

"Yes."

"Then take off your clothes and get under the blankets with her. She needs to warm up and body heat's our best option."

Mindless of the fact that she was standing next to her father, and Stephen was lying on the floor behind her, Laura did not have to be told twice. As the men quickly looked away, she pushed her oversized sweatpants to the floor, pulled the shirt over her head and then slid under the covers.

"Christ, she's freezing," Laura said, rubbing her hand briskly over Toni's arm.

"Don't do that!" Bernard yelled, placing his hand over Laura's. "Any excessive movements can trigger a heart attack. Her blood is frigid, and her heart won't be able to handle it. Just lie alongside her and share your body heat. That's all I want you to do." Looking over his shoulder, Bernard said, "Eleanor, get that cup of broth over there. We need to try to get some into her, but just a few dribbles at a time, and Bill, go find Alice and see if—"

"I tripled up some plastic bags," Alice said, running into the room. "I have four, just like you asked."

Smiling at her ingenuity, Bernard took them, and as he turned back to Toni and Laura, he glanced up at Bill. "Um...Bill, we'll need a bit of privacy here."

"Oh. Oh, right...of course," Bill said, turning away. "Call me if you need me."

Returning to the matter at hand, Bernard looked at Laura. "I'm going to put these around her, so I'll need to lift the blankets for that. Okay?"

"You're the doctor."

"Finally realized that did you?" he asked, moving the covers to place one of the bags under Toni's neck. "I thought you believed I was more of a prat."

"I don't anymore."

After putting two of the bags under Toni's arms and another near her groin, Bernard tucked the blankets around them and then placed a multicolored duvet on top of that.

"What now?" Laura asked, shifting just a little.

"Well, it doesn't appear that she has any frostbite, but I'm going to wrap her hands and feet like we did for Stephen. Your mum is going to get a bit of that broth into both of you and…and then we wait."

"Couldn't we drive her to the hospital?"

"No, not like this. She's too cold. Even the movement of the car could be too much. Trust me, Laura. I know what I'm doing. Our best bet is just to let her warm up slowly, and she'll be fine. I promise."

CHAPTER FORTY-NINE

It was almost two hours before Bernard allowed Stephen to get dressed, and sitting by the fireplace in clothes once belonging to Lawrence Shaw, he waited in silence, praying Toni would be all right.

"Here, I brought you some tea. Bernard said you could have some now," Peggy said, handing her husband a cup.

"Thanks. Anything from emergency services?"

"No, Ron called again. The storm is slowing everything down, and he thinks that once they found out we had a doctor here, that pushed us to the bottom of the list."

"Speaking of doctors," Stephen said, gesturing toward the man walking into the room. "He really is one, isn't he?"

Looking behind her, Peggy grinned. "Yes, I think he is."

Bill had kept the fire blazing, so as soon as Bernard entered the overly heated room, he unbuttoned his red and green waistcoat and tossed it aside. Rolling up his sleeves, he walked over and knelt by the couch. "How are you two doing?"

Shifting slightly under the blankets, Laura said, "She seems better. She stopped shivering a while ago."

Quickly taking Toni's temperature, Bernard smiled as he read the display. "Well, this is looking much more promising."

Glancing over his shoulder, he said, "Eleanor, get your daughter some clothes, and Bill, why don't you go to the kitchen and get a bit more of that broth from Dorothy." Grabbing another blanket from the arm of the sofa, Bernard stood and held it up to block everyone's view. "All right, Laura. Out you go."

A few minutes later, once again dressed in the oversized pink and green jogging outfit Nancy had given her, Laura sat on the edge of the sofa as Bernard folded the blanket and tossed it aside. Opening his black satchel, he pulled out some bandages. "Okay, now it's time to look at that arm of hers."

"Her arm?"

In all the commotion, no one had noticed the dried blood covering Toni's left forearm, but when Bernard reached under the blankets and pulled it out, Laura blanched. "Oh, I forgot all about the glass."

"I saw it when Bill brought her in, but it was the least of my worries at the time," Bernard said, gingerly wiping away the dried blood with a swab. "It didn't appear that it was anything too deep, and by the looks of it now, I think after a quick wash and some bandaging, it'll be fine."

Watching as the man tenderly disinfected and wrapped Toni's arm, Laura said, "I'm sorry."

"Sorry? For what?"

"For ever thinking you weren't a real doctor."

"You're not the only one. Somewhere along the line, I lost track of what made me want to become one in the first place, but today it all came rushing back."

"I'm glad it did."

"Yeah, me too," he said, slipping Toni's arm under the blanket, and just as he did, she began to stretch and shift. Seeing Laura reach over to stop her, Bernard quickly said, "No, don't. If she has the strength to move, let her."

"Is she waking up?"

"No, I don't think so. Probably just stiff and sore, and trying to get comfortable, but since she's come back up to a normal temperature she might be getting a bit warm. Let's get one of these blankets off her," he said, removing one of the three still draped over Toni.

Toni quieted for a moment and then with a grunt, turned toward the rear of the sofa. For a second, Laura forgot where they were as she smiled at the familiar position of her lover, but when she heard the shocked gasps from everyone in the room, she quickly covered Toni's exposed back with the blanket.

"Christ, that's where I know her from," Bernard said under his breath.

Laura froze. Allowing the words to settle in her brain, she turned and glared at the thick-waisted doctor. "You *bastard*!" she screamed, launching herself off the sofa. "*You bloody fucking bastard*!"

Stunned, everyone in the room stared in disbelief as Laura lunged at Bernard. Slapping and punching the man, it took several moments before anyone could react. Rushing over, Bill wrapped Laura in a bear hug and yanked her away.

"Laura, what the hell are you doing?" Bill said, struggling to keep hold of her.

"He's the one! He worked there. You *bastard*! How could you stand by and let them do those things to her?" Laura shouted, fighting to free herself from her father's hold. "How could you? *How could you*!"

"Laura, you're mistaken," Bernard said, shaking his head. "It wasn't—"

"No, I'm not! I heard what you said when you saw her scars. You recognized them. You *son of a bitch*! You recognized them because you're the one who stitched them up *without* giving her anything to kill the pain. You sick *pig*!"

"Laura, you're wrong," Dorothy said, coming over to stand at Bernard's side.

"No, I'm not!"

"Yes, you are!" Dorothy shouted, grabbing Laura by the sleeve.

"Dori, let her go," Bernard said, placing his hand on her arm.

After glancing at her husband, Dorothy sighed and then did as he asked. Releasing her grip on Laura, she backed away.

For a moment, Bill thought Laura's fighting was over, but as soon as Bernard took a step in their direction, she began to struggle to escape again.

Holding up his hand, Bernard said, "Laura, please just listen to me for a moment. That's all I ask."

"You can go to *hell*!"

"Laura—"

"*Fuck* you, Bernard! *Fuck you*!"

"Woman, shut up and listen to me!" Bernard yelled, his face turning red as his temper flared. "Do you honestly think that I would have spent the last two hours trying to save her bloody life if I'd been responsible for what you're accusing me of? Do you? *Do you!*"

As he had hoped it would, his question took some of the wind out of Laura's sails, and seeing that she stopped trying to fight her way out of Bill's arms, Bernard reined in his temper as well. "I'm sorry. I didn't mean to shout, but will you please let me explain. Please?"

With a huff, Laura scowled at the man. "Go ahead. I'm listening."

"I've worked all over the UK. You know that. Early in my career, I worked in Carlisle and one day the hospital got a call requesting a triage team be sent to a prison a few hours away. Being the up-and-coming doctor, I volunteered and a short time later I found myself on a bus being taken to God knows where. Now, we all assumed there had been some sort of accident, but when we got to the prison, we were told there had been some incidents of abuse to the prisoners, and before they could be transported, the officials wanted us to examine them, treat them for any injuries, and categorize...or rather *document* our findings.

"Like all young doctors, I had spent a fair amount of my time on graveyard shifts in emergency, so I was accustomed to seeing all types of injuries, but nothing could have prepared me for what I saw that day."

Closing his eyes for a second, Bernard let out a sigh. "Christ, I think that was the longest day of my life. They just kept coming into the exam room, one after another, some defiant and some docile, but all were damaged in one way or another.

"She was the last one I saw," Bernard said quietly, looking over his shoulder at Toni. "I remember looking up from my clipboard as she shuffled into the room. They had all been given hospital gowns and slippers, but she didn't look like a patient. She didn't even look like a prisoner. She looked like a refugee."

"A refugee?" Laura asked in a ragged whisper.

"She was gaunt...terribly, terribly thin, and her head had been shaved. Through the stubble I could see a few white lines, scars left behind by past injuries, and I remember looking at my nurse in disbelief and seeing tears rolling down her face. We were professionals. We weren't supposed to show emotion, but my God, how could we not?

"She never once looked up...Toni, I mean. She didn't volunteer a single word, unless we asked her a question, so we proceeded with the exam...and that's when I discovered the scars on her back." Hanging his head, Bernard's voice became a whisper. "Christ, I still remember trying not to vomit. I was so appalled...so sickened by it all. I still am."

Bernard raised his eyes to meet Laura's. "I fear that today is all my fault. I'm sure she never looked directly at me that day, but she must have recognized my voice when I came into the house."

Laura regarded the man in front of her, replaying his story in her head. "So you're saying your voice...*just* your voice caused all of this to happen?"

"If you don't believe me, ask her when she wakes up. I wasn't one of her abusers, Laura. I swear to God, I wasn't."

The room was quiet except for the crackle of the fire. Those unaware of the tragedies and injustices in Toni's life had been enlightened and most felt as Bernard did the day he saw Toni's scars. Tears flowed freely, and heads shook in silence as innocents tried to wrap their heads around all things evil and dark.

***

Eleanor walked into the room carrying a tray of tea. After offering cups to Stephen, Peggy and Bill, she made her way to the sofa where her daughter sat on the edge, gazing at the woman covered in blankets.

"Here, take this," Eleanor said, handing Laura a cup.

"Thanks."

"How you doing?"

"I'm fine, Mum. I'm just worried about Toni."

"Bernard thinks she's going to be okay. He says there's no sign of frostbite or water in her lungs. Thank God."

"So is the family in shock?" Laura whispered.

"The family is worried about you, and about her."

"What happens when she wakes up, Mum? I couldn't calm her down before—"

"Well, we'll soon find out," Eleanor said softly, taking the cup from Laura's hand. "It appears she's coming to."

Hot and cocooned, Toni awoke slowly. Breathing in the smell of leather and cloth, she could hear someone whispering, and taking a deep breath, she rolled to her back and opened her eyes.

"Hiya, sweetheart," Laura said quietly, placing her hand on Toni's arm.

Toni's mouth was dry and her eyes refused to focus, but she offered the voice she knew so well a weak grin. "Hey."

"How you feeling?"

At first, Toni was confused by the question, but then she wasn't. Her vision still wouldn't clear and when she took a breath, her chest felt tight and sore. Aches in her back and legs announced themselves when she tried to move, so quieting, she blinked a few more times to clear the cobwebs. When Laura finally came into view, Toni groused, "What the hell are you wearing?"

Smiling, Laura looked down at the baggy pink and green outfit. "It belongs to Nancy."

"What happened to your clothes?"

Thankful Toni was still groggy, Laura said quietly, "Why don't we get you dressed, and then we'll talk?"

Blankly staring at Laura for a moment, Toni lifted the blanket and paled. "Where are my clothes? Laura, what the hell is going on?"

"First clothes, sweetheart, and then answers. I promise."

***

Having been ordered to stay in the warmth of the library, with Peggy by his side, Stephen remained near the fire as he sipped his tea. Bill leaned against the doorway as if protecting the occupants from intrusion, and Eleanor sat on the arm of the sofa, watching as her daughter handed Toni a cup of broth.

"What's this?"

"It's just broth. Drink it. It's good for you."

"I'd prefer coffee or tea, if it's all the same to you," Toni said, shoving the cup in Laura's direction.

Toni's confusion had given way to annoyance. She wanted her own clothes, but was given an oversized track suit in pink and black to wear. She wanted privacy, but instead was told to dress behind a blanket held up by Eleanor, and now wanting nothing more than a cup of coffee and a cigarette, she was handed lukewarm broth and told to drink it. Toni was sore, stiff, frustrated and getting angrier by the second.

"And what the fuck happened to my arm?" she blurted, pushing up the sleeve of the baggy top.

"Toni, calm down," Laura said quietly.

"I am calm. I just want some answers. That's all."

Before Laura could provide any, the library doors slid open and everyone's eyes were on Bernard as he stepped into the room.

"I thought I'd...I'd check on my patient," he said softly.

"Patient?" Toni asked, glaring at Laura. "What does he mean by patient, and who the hell is he anyway?"

Baffled, Laura looked at Bernard and then back at Toni. "That's Bernard, sweetheart. You remember me telling you about him? He's married to Dorothy."

Thinking for a moment, Toni said, "Oh, yeah...the doctor."

"That's right."

"Did he do this?" Toni said, motioning toward her bandaged arm.

"Yes, he did."

"What did I do? What happened to me? Laura, I'm confused," Toni said, running her fingers through her hair.

"Sweetheart, you...you got a bit worked up when Bernard walked into the house earlier."

"Worked up?"

"You panicked."

"Panicked?" Toni said, narrowing her eyes. "What do you mean panicked?"

"You...you recognized him and I guess it caused some sort of flashback to Thornbridge. You got scared and ran out of the house. I tried to catch you, but I couldn't, and then you fell into the river. If it weren't for Stephen..."

Toni's head jerked up as the pieces of the puzzle began to fall into place. A crowd of voices, but one was clear above all the others, and then there was cold and wind...and wet. She remembered hands, strong and masculine, yanking her away from the pain, and a mouth, warm and unfamiliar, pressed against hers, but then frost and ice lodged itself in her veins and she was engulfed by blackness. Inky and thick, the darkness swept over her, pulling her down and weighing on her like a coffin trying to close. She had felt it before. Dozens of times, lying alone in a cold and damp cell, death had stalked her, beckoning her with promises of warmth. *Relax in the arms of death and hurt no more.*

Unconscious, Toni's mind had roamed free, taking her back to times when she had smiled easily, riding horses through fields of heather and jumping fences withered and broken by age. Memories filled her mind like photographs, and in snapshot after snapshot, she saw her life...and then she saw her love. Auburn hair brushing against her skin like butterfly wings, a sexy laugh, a giggle, a blush...a promise. Toni had made a promise. Not yet sealed and stamped, but it was a promise nonetheless. *'Til death do us part.* Suddenly, the allure of warmth was no longer tempting. The devil and his disciples dressed in prison officer uniforms could all go straight to Hell, and when Stephen breathed in again...she breathed out.

Toni raised her eyes and stared at the man dressed in a wrinkled white shirt and brown trousers. She glanced at his belt of leather, fastened with a polished silver buckle, and then back at his face as she tried to place him in her Thornbridge memories, but he didn't belong there. "I don't remember you."

"Sweetheart, you never saw Bernard, but you heard him. That's what triggered all of this. It was his voice."

"What?"

"He was one of the doctors they called in when they closed Thornbridge. He was the one who examined you that day, so when you heard his voice, you—"

"Wait," Toni said, holding up her hand to quiet Laura. "Give me a minute."

Cocking her head to the side, Toni closed her eyes and waited while the last piece of the puzzle slipped into place. What had been muddled and clouded by near-death suddenly became crystal clear. Opening her eyes, she turned and looked at Laura. In a voice void of emotion, she said, "It wasn't him."

"What do you mean?"

"I don't know that man," Toni said, pointing at Bernard. "I've never seen him before."

"I know, Toni. You weren't listening—"

"Laura, it was the other one...Cameron."

Laura looked around the room and saw her confusion mirrored on the faces of her family. Turning back to Toni, she placed her hand on her arm. "Sweetheart, there isn't anyone here by that name. Maybe you just need a bit more rest."

"Stop trying to placate me!" Toni shouted, jumping off the sofa. "I'm not a bloody child!"

"I know you aren't," Laura said, getting to her feet. "But Toni, you've been through a lot today. You're just a little confused right now."

Exasperated, Toni turned her back on Laura and yanked up the baggy sweatshirt, exposing the myriad of hellish scars. "Do you honestly think I'd ever forget the face of the bastard that did this to me?" she screamed. *"Do you!"*

When Laura didn't answer, Toni lowered the shirt and turned around. For a moment, their eyes met, and seeing the doubt in Laura's, Toni set her jaw. *"He—is—wearing—the—fucking—belt!"*

He had watched and listened, and before the words had left her mouth, William MacLeod knew the truth. It wasn't hard to count to four, and knowing that three of the men in the house were currently standing in the library, he rushed out of the room.

Storming into the lounge, he saw Ron standing by the fireplace while Alice sat quietly in the chair by the front windows. Pointing in Ron's direction, he shouted at his niece, "What's his name?"

"I'm sorry. What?"

"I said…what is his name?"

"You know his name."

"His full name, Alice! What's his *full* bloody name?"

"Oh…um…it's Cameron Wesley Thomson. I thought you knew that."

CHAPTER FIFTY

Born Finlay Ranald Cameron in one of the most impoverished sections in all of Glasgow, he had grown up wearing tattered clothes and eating meals consisting of porridge and potatoes. A bastard in the truest meaning of the word, he was raised without a father, and even though his mother showed him all the love she could, more often than not, she showed love to others as well. They came and went from the tiny apartment he called home, simpering like fools when they had picked her up at the door, only to return her a few hours later with her clothes rumpled, her makeup smeared and her body smelling of sweat. He hated them...but he hated her more.

Playing in the streets and alleyways with children no better off than himself, he was relentlessly teased about his name. Even the destitute neighbors with toothless smiles cackled behind his back at the haughty handle he had been given, but the ridicule had made him strong, and genetics had made him handsome.

With wavy black hair and eyes the color of cinnamon, he used his boyish good looks and charm to his advantage. Using a wink and a smile, he'd beguile store owners out of biscuits, and whispers of *"Please, can you help me"* convinced teachers to spend their free time tutoring him. Day after day, he listened intently as they taught, but he didn't just study their lessons...he studied them. Their words were proper and their manners refined, so when his mother was off scrubbing the floors of office buildings, and his friends were outside playing football he stayed home with a book. Reading aloud, he practiced until he could pronounce each word without a hint of the dialect that proved him poor.

At night in the small, dingy flat, he listened as neighbors screamed and yelled foul words at their spouses and children, and he decided that was not going to be his life. He wouldn't haul rubbish or sweep roads, working for hours doing menial labor while being ordered about by a fat-bellied man with beard stubble and no education. Finlay Ranald Cameron wanted more...and *he* wanted to be boss.

Afforded only the most basic of educations, he realized that he'd never be the CEO of a Fortune 500 company, but when he saw an advertisement for prison officers, he knew he had found his niche. While he wouldn't rule thousands, or even hundreds, he would receive the respect he needed to feed his ego...and he *would* rule. So, once settled on a career and having conquered the accent he loathed, he began visiting a local gym to work his body until it was muscled and strong. He had a plan. He had a goal, and while he was sure he'd have the prisoner's respect by simply putting on the uniform, he wanted more. He wanted them to tremble at the sight of him.

Upon entering the prison service, he found himself assigned to a prison just outside of London, but the minimum-security penitentiary didn't house the prisoners he wanted to rule. Inmates convicted of insurance fraud and corporate crimes were not dangerous and hardened. They were portly and posh, and obediently followed all the rules as they waited for their sentences to end. So, keeping abreast of positions opening in other prisons throughout the United Kingdom, he applied for several, but his lack of experience hampered his acceptance until a job was listed for a prison in the north of England. Labeled as high security, his mouth watered as he read the job listing, and when he realized that it was a women's prison, he smiled and bared his pearly white teeth.

For years, he had hidden his hatred for women behind a demeanor worthy of a gentleman, and his portrayal had been flawless. Handsome and strong, he had never had a problem getting dates, and pretending to listen, care and sometimes even love, he had taken what he wanted from each and gave little, if anything, in return. To him, they were a means to an end. A vessel in which to empty his seed, and once that had been accomplished he had no further use for them. They were weak. They were stupid. He was not.

Although always careful, choosing only blondes or redheads to bring to his bed, more than once he crept away in the middle of the night, fearing his hatred for the gender was about to take control no matter what the color of their hair. Well aware of the punishment he would receive if he ever allowed the beast to escape, he learned to control his disdain. Visiting the gym once, twice or three times a week, he took his aggressions out on weighted bags until his hands were bruised and his muscles ached. It was the only way to release the animal inside and still keep his freedom...or so he thought.

He traveled twice to the prison hidden away in the north of England to be interviewed for the position. Answering questions about rules, regulations and punishments, he thought he had hidden his true self behind his charm like he always had, but he was wrong...and the governor was delighted. Six weeks later, Finlay Ranald Cameron walked across the gravel drive of a prison called Thornbridge, and upon entering the stone-walled penitentiary he breathed deep the smell of despair. It smelled marvelous.

***

With only a few years of experience in the prison system, he had expected to receive the graveyard shifts that so many loathed, but his first few months at Thornbridge were spent in the morning hours, awakening women from their beds and watching as they shuffled sleepily to the servery. It didn't take long for him to notice how some of the convicts seemed more damaged than they had the day before, and while he couldn't have cared less, his curiosity was piqued.

The days moved slowly for him, and just like he had in school, he watched the people around him. He knew which prisoners were the worst, and he tried his best to always be close when a fight would break out. He loved being able to pull them apart, mindless of the strength of his grip or the force of his actions. He knew he was leaving bruises behind, and it was all he could do to hide the stiffness between his legs.

Late one afternoon, close to when his shift was ending, a fight erupted in the courtyard. Women were screaming and cheering as two of the most violent tried to kill each other. Forgetting himself for only an instant, he unleashed the beast. Minutes later, the two women lay on the ground, bruised and bloodied. Standing in the snow, he looked at what he had done and paled, believing he had lost his job, but then another officer approached and patted him on the back. With a knowing smile, the man shook Finlay's hand, silently congratulating him on his graduation to the night shift.

A few days later, on a cold winter evening under a black sky dotted with stars, he trudged across the snow-covered drive leading into the prison to begin what he had thought would be eight hours of listening to the silence of a sleeping jail. He could not have been more wrong. He didn't know that the harsh realities of Thornbridge blossomed at night.

Under dim lighting, he walked with officers around the levels, wondering why they would snicker by a door or pause as if trying to decide something. Then, told to stand near the rail, he watched as they unlocked a cell, woke the woman inside and proceeded to beat her. They didn't have a reason. They didn't need one...and neither did he.

Three cells were unlocked and three times he watched, but when they opened the final cell that night, they smiled at him and motioned for him to enter. It was his turn.

His shaft grew rigid as he stepped inside, and removing his thin black belt, he kicked the bunk to make sure she was awake before lashing it across her back. She was one of the crazies. A demented woman with blonde wispy hair and a wild look in her eye, and she cried out when the belt marked her skin. In a cockney, nasally voice that caused his lip to curl, she pleaded for him to stop, but what she wanted didn't matter.

A short time later, as the other officers returned to the lounge for coffee and a smoke, laughing whole-heartedly at what they had done, he trotted quickly to the restroom. Standing in a stall under flickering fluorescents, he groaned as he held himself in his hand and released into the stained porcelain toilet. He had never felt so alive.

***

Answering with a quick and definitive "Yes" when asked if he wanted to work only the night shift, during the day he spent his time searching for the perfect belt. It had to be wide and thick, able to withstand the force of his blows and the buckle...the buckle had to be strong and sharp. Spending his afternoons visiting nearby towns and villages, he finally found a shop that suited his needs. Tucked down an alleyway, behind a weather-beaten wooden door was Servitude, a shop for those who enjoyed a rougher lifestyle with obedience being the forefront. When he walked inside and smelled the leather, his mouth watered. He scrutinized dozens of belts until he found what he desired, and then he spoke to the artisan...and together they designed the buckle.

One week later, he returned to pick up his treasure. The gap-toothed craftsman crooked his arthritic finger and ushered him into the back room, and smiling a smile filled with stained teeth, he placed his creation in Finlay's hands. It was as he had ordered. Larger than a business card, rectangular and brass, the edges were rounded and smoothed while the hook on the back was long and filed sharp, but he was puzzled by the weight, and his bewilderment showed on his face.

Noticing his client's confusion, the artisan took the belt and revealed its true glory. Bending the buckle away from the leather strap, he pushed in the center and easily slipped out the false back which he reversed and slid into place. Now, instead of one hook, there were three. Small and deadly, like the poisoned hatred that pulsed in Finlay's veins, two more curves of steel had been welded to the plate to the right and left of the center sharp. Staring at the hooks, he smirked as he imagined the pain they would inflict.

He used it sparingly at first, noticing that the damage from even the simplest of strikes wreaked havoc on their skin, but the feeling it gave him was beyond anything he could have dreamed. With it in his hand, he felt like a god, and more times than not when he left the prison in the early morning hours, he would be hard and erect and in need of something more.

Traveling for miles, he visited the towns where he knew he could find whores eager to open their legs, and he would take them again and again and again. Slamming into them with a fury fueled by thoughts of screams and blood, he would feed the beast until it was satisfied, and then he returned to his flat where he would sleep away the day...dreaming about the night.

***

He had seen her a hundred times. Tall and slender with jet black hair, she reminded him of the mother he abhorred, and he thirsted for her like no other. He yearned to beat her until she screamed, but the senior officers were the ones who chose which cells to open at night, and they kept her all to themselves. He would stand just outside the door, listening as their belts and boots hit her skin, and while his peers could bring her to cries, muffled by the pillow on which she buried her head, he knew he could do better. With his belt, he could bring her to shrill shrieks and screams that would echo through the halls for hours.

His attraction for the gaunt prisoner with sunken eyes and a learned past was well known, and the other officers dangled the possibility of him visiting her cell for months, so when his birthday arrived, they gave him a present. Led to the block, to the cells buried deep in the bowels of the prison, they handed him a key, and while they stood in the corridor and listened...he did what he knew he could do.

Entering the dark concrete hole, he left the door open enough so that light streamed in, and waiting until she awoke, he pulled the belt from his trousers and fixed the buckle properly. The first strike grazed off her shoulder, and his manhood came to life when he heard her yelp in pain, but when the next got snagged on her clothing, he took two quick steps and began grabbing at the tatters she wore. He was brutal and unyielding as he tore away the fabric, exposing her body to his eyes, but her nudity wasn't what he needed. He needed her pain...so he picked up the belt and started again.

Her arm stopped the next strike from landing, but undaunted he swung again and again until she was too weak to fight back. Watching as she turned her back on him, he licked his lips and then struck her with a force that sent her to the wall. Grasping at the rocks, she screamed for the very first time. His trousers tightened at the blood-curdling shriek, and lashing out again, he watched as her back began to flow blood like a river. It poured from her skin, covering her arse and legs in crimson that seemed almost black in the light, but the beast needed more...so he hit her again.

It was her howls of agony that finally brought them into the cell, and seeing what he had done, they pulled him away and closed the battered steel door to lock her inside. Admonishing him for going too far, they told him to leave for the night, and he eagerly agreed. Barely able to make it to his car before ejaculating in his trousers, he drove to a place he normally only visited in the early morning hours. Finding a dark-haired whore, he pulled her into an alley, paid her a few quid and then punished her with his staff, but it wasn't enough for the beast. Feeling like a magnificent being that held all the power of the world in his hands, he opened his wallet again and pointed down the alley, and eagerly the prostitute followed. A few hours later, shadowed by the darkness of the night, he walked to his car, and the few people still on the street never noticed the stains on his clothes.

After what happened on the block, he was never allowed to visit her again. The death of a prisoner could easily have been hidden, but they all enjoyed her a little too much to allow that to happen. So, while his colleagues entered her cell on occasion in the middle of the night, he would visit others, and while she would cry, his would scream.

One year faded into the next, but he didn't notice. He didn't care. He had the life he always wanted. Administering pain during the night, ridding his body of need during the morning and sleeping on sheets, bleached and white during the afternoon became routine. And on weekends, he would satisfy his needs by reading bondage magazines and surfing the Internet for sites filled with black-haired beauties. He knew the beast would never be tamed, but controlling it had become easier; however, on one crisp day, his life...his paradise...crumbled around him.

***

It happened a few minutes before his shift was to end, and like locusts, they swarmed Thornbridge. Shouting their titles and their orders, they shoved prison officers as if they were the inmates, and stunned, he watched as his friends turned into blubbering fools. Screaming their innocence, they were handcuffed and hauled away, so when it became his turn, he did just the opposite. Standing tall, and catching the eye of the man in charge, as the shiny shackles were clamped around his wrists, he suggested that perhaps they could strike a deal...and they did.

For hours, he sat in one of the rooms used for prisoner's adjudications and grassed on his fellow officers. Names and times, dates and details were given without blinking an eye, and in exchange, they gave him his freedom. He handed them back a badge displaying the name he abhorred, and they gave him a new one to hide behind. The men and women he had worked with for four years would spend the next several years of their lives behind bars, but he would not. He would walk free and start a new life as Cameron Wesley Thomson.

Returning to Scotland, he took a job as a laborer with a construction company, and having never been afraid of hard work, it wasn't long before he was promoted to crew leader and then to foreman. The physical labor took its toll on the beast and many a day he returned home too tired to even open a magazine, but when the urge returned, so did his habits. He would spend hours surfing the Internet for photographs and videos of bondage and brutality until his body craved release, and then he would leave his flat in search of a whore to satisfy his need, but it wasn't long before his desires outweighed his income. While most were cheap enough, the first didn't always quench his thirst and he would have to prowl the streets for another or answer to the beast. Hunger would turn to anger if not fed properly...this much he knew.

One night he decided to try his luck at a neighborhood pub in hopes of persuading a woman to give him what he normally paid for, and after priming himself with a few hours of porn, he walked down the street to the bar. Noticing a woman sitting alone in the corner he went over and turned on the charm. Flashing his best smile, a minute later he was sitting at her side and ordering another round of ale.

Alice Burns was not what most would consider a raving beauty, but she wasn't unattractive either. Fair-skinned and freckled, she was a bit on the plain side, but just a bit, and after a short conversation, he felt himself at ease with her. She seemed innocent enough. Hardly worldly, therefore, hardly smart, and after learning she had just gone through a nasty divorce, he was ready to pull out all the stops until she told him about her daughter. His plan was for a lover, not a family, so when he left the pub that night, he had no intention of calling the number he had asked for, but a few weeks later he changed his mind.

After visiting several pubs in the area and browsing the selection of single women, he decided that a plain woman with a child seemed safer. What better way to appear normal than strolling through town with her on his arm, and the child, if he had his way, he'd deal with as little as possible. He thought his strategy was perfect, except one night he made a mistake.

Spending his usual pre-date time viewing videos, he ran across one that turned his blood so hot he knew he needed to release the beast before he met Alice that night or his plan would be ruined. Jumping into his car, he sped to the next town and looked for his victim. Spying a hooker on a street corner, he could hardly contain his excitement. She was perfect. Tall and slender with hair the color of onyx, he opened his billfold and invited her into his car. Driving to an abandoned building, they walked inside and made the deal, but little did she know she was making a deal with the devil.

Two hours later as the sun slipped behind the horizon, he drove back to his apartment and showered the smell and blood off his skin. With the images still fresh and fertile in his mind, there was no more need for videos before picking up Alice promptly at eight, and after dinner, they returned to his place like they had done so many times before.

They had been lovers for weeks, and while he was normally gentle and attentive to her needs, that night was all about him. Voracious, he took Alice on the sofa and then on the bed, and after a short rest, he started again. But in his zeal, in his zest to control, to consume and to own, he forgot one very important thing...and six weeks later, Alice told him she was pregnant.

His reaction surprised even him, for he had never considered having children, but to ask her to abort the pregnancy left a foul taste in his mouth. This was his child. This was his immortality. This was *his* creation.

So, over a period of two years, he built a new life, complete with a wife and a child. He had the best of everything...again. When he felt the urge, when he felt the beast fighting to escape, he would visit towns far away and do what he needed to do to survive. He never raised a hand to his wife or to the children, but when a dark-haired whore caught his eye...she was never so lucky.

CHAPTER FIFTY-ONE

He turned and glared at the man standing near the hearth. With the images of the scars on Toni's back still fresh in his mind, William MacLeod's blood ran cold. "You bastard!"

Ron didn't move. He didn't even blink. Staring into the fire, he didn't acknowledge the other man's presence until Bill shouted again, and this time everyone in the house heard his voice.

"*I'm talking to you!*"

Slowly turning around, Ron said, "What are you going on about?"

"You worked there, didn't you?"

"Worked where, Bill? Honestly man, have you been hitting the Scotch, or did you get frostbite on your brain running around in the snow?"

"I'm stone cold sober, and you...you're a *son of a bitch.*"

Tensing at the words, Ron could feel the beast begin to awaken. Setting his jaw, he growled, "Watch yourself, Bill. I don't like being called names I don't deserve."

"What are you going to do? Whip me with your belt?"

"What the *hell* are you talking about?"

Giving the man a subtle sneer, Bill shook his head. "Oh, so we're going to play it that way, are we? So now I suppose you're going to deny working at Thornbridge."

"I work for Ross Construction, Bill. I've never worked for a company called Thornbridge."

"It wasn't a company. It was a prison."

"I've never worked in a prison."

"Liar."

Standing tall, Ron's chest swelled as a knowing grin crossed his face. "Call them up. Ask them."

Bill looked at the cordless handset sitting on the table and then back at Ron. "You know I can't. They closed the place years ago."

The corners of Ron's mouth turned upward. "Pity. I guess you'll just have to believe me then, now won't you?"

Bill stared back at the arrogant man. Cocking his head to the side, he considered what next to do and then his eyes drifted to the phone. Picking it up, he handed it to Alice. "Do me a favor, dear. Call emergency services and see where they are."

"Put the phone down, Alice," Ron barked. "I called them less than an hour ago and there's no need to keep bothering them."

Staring at the phone in her hand, Alice looked at her uncle and then at her husband. "Maybe I should call—"

"I said put the bloody phone *down!*"

Aware of the tension building in the room, Bill looked at his niece. "Perhaps it would be best if you go join your sisters for a while. Give Ron and me a chance to sort this all out."

"She stays here!" Ron shouted.

"No, she doesn't," Bernard said from the doorway. Keeping one eye on Ron, he walked over and offered Alice his hand. "Come on, love. I'll fix you a spot of tea."

Ron had never laid a hand on Alice in anger, but more than once she had seen his rage, and it had terrified her. Pausing only for a second, she took Bernard's hand, and allowed herself to be led out of the room.

His wife's defiance fueled his anger, and glaring at Bill, Ron said, "I don't know who the hell you think I am—"

"I think you're an arse, Cameron. I think you're a vile, filthy monster who gets off on beating women."

"And *you're* a daft *prick!*"

"Am I?"

"Yes!"

Neither man knew much about the other. Having only met at family functions, their conversations had always been polite but brief, so Ron had no idea that William MacLeod was a thinking man. A man who pondered and then reacted, and right now, Ron was the subject under Bill's microscope. It was easy for Bill to see the sweat glistening on the man's upper lip, and that his face had reddened more than one shade in only a few short minutes, but it wasn't until Bill saw the veins in Ron's neck bulge, that he realized that Ron wasn't just angry. He was enraged, and deep down, Bill smiled.

Bringing his eyes up to meet Cameron's, Bill said, "Fine, then take off your belt."

"Why?"

"Because Toni says—"

"Toni? Toni!" Ron yelled, waving his arms in the air. "Are you telling me this is about that lunatic in there?"

"She's hardly crazy."

"Well, she's hardly sane, now is she, or do you know lots of women who take off running through the snow like she did. Christ, she almost killed herself *and* Steve. If you ask me, someone should lock her up and throw away the fucking key."

"I think it would better suit the world if you were the one locked up."

"Old man, I've had enough of this!" Ron said, heading toward the doorway.

Quickly blocking his path, Bill said, "Not so fast."

"Bill, seriously, that woman in there is delusional. She's wrong, I tell you. She's wrong!"

"Then you won't mind taking off your belt."

"Yes, actually I do," Ron said, looking down his nose at Bill. "I don't need to prove myself to you or to anyone."

"I'm afraid you do," Bernard said as he appeared in the doorway. Holding up the phone in his hand, he said, "I took it upon myself to call emergency services. I spoke to two different supervisors, and they checked their logs. No calls came from this number today."

Looking Bernard square in the eyes, Ron shrugged. "They made a mistake."

"Jesus Christ, Ron!" Bernard said, tossing the phone on a chair. "What the hell were you thinking? They could have died!"

"I'm telling you—"

"There's a simple way of proving us wrong, Cameron," Bill said, getting in between the two men. "Take off your belt...*now!*"

Ron's eyes turned to slits as he stared back at Bill, but arrogant and confident, he hid his rage behind a forced smile. "Fine, and then I expect an apology from all of you, especially that crazy bitch in the other room." Pulling the belt from his trousers, he placed it in Bill's hand. "There you go, old man. Satisfied?"

Surprised by the weight of it, Bill focused on the buckle as he turned it over, expecting to see evidence that would prove him right, but instead, there was nothing except a single hook protruding from the edge. The buckle was scratched and worn, but as he inspected it this way and that, he couldn't see anything that would have made the triple marks on Toni's back.

Rubbing his chin, he paused and then turned his attention to the belt itself. It was broad and bulky in his hand, and as he ran his fingers over the leather, he stopped when he noticed steel grommets wedged in the belt holes. Flipping over the buckle again, Bill ran his finger across the hook, his breath catching in his throat when the barb cut him like a razor.

After putting the tip of his finger in his mouth to clear away the blood, Bill studied the small gouge the hook had made. Looking up at Ron, he said, "It's a bit sharp, don't you think?"

"It came that way," Ron said, holding out his hand. "Now give it back."

Once again, Bill put his finger to his mouth, letting his tongue run over the cut on his fingertip as he tried to unravel the mystery. After a few moments, he said, "Bernard, keep him company for a minute, will you?"

Leaning against the door frame, Bernard crossed his arms. "It would be *my* pleasure."

The doors to the library slid open, and all eyes were on Bill as he walked over to the sofa and knelt in front of Toni and Laura. "Ron says you're wrong," he said quietly, looking at Toni.

"I'm not wrong," Toni said, shaking her head. "I'm not."

"I don't think you are, lass, but I need your help," he said as he brought the belt from behind his back.

"Christ!" Toni screamed, jumping to her feet. "Get that away from me! Get that fucking thing away from me!"

Laura got to her feet in an instant, and standing by Toni's side, she glared at her father. "What the hell do you think you're doing?" she shouted. "Get that out of here!"

"I would, but if this is the belt—"

"*It is*! Goddamn it, why don't you believe me?" Toni yelled as tears filled her eyes.

"I do, Toni. I do...but I can't see anything to prove it. It's just a normal belt with a normal buckle."

"That's not right," Toni said, wiping the tears from her face. "That's what he used. It sliced me like a knife!"

"I can't see how, lass" Bill whispered. "I honestly can't see how."

Everyone in the room was focused on her, and in their eyes, Toni saw doubt and pity staring back at her. They thought she was crazy and for a split-second so did she...but only for a second.

It had been the one memory that had been the most difficult to block from her thoughts, but closing her eyes, Toni willed herself back to a night in a dimly lit cell, remembering every detail, every smell...and every sound.

Opening her eyes, she looked down at Bill. "He did something to it. Just before...just before he started, he did something to it. I remember there was a sound...a scraping sound...."

Bill's brow furrowed as he flipped the buckle over again, and getting up, he went to the fireplace and held it close to the light. Feeling a tap on his shoulder, he looked up and his eyes met Stephen's.

"Do you mind?" Stephen said, holding out his hand.

"Of course not," Bill said, handing him the belt.

As a firefighter, there were times when Stephen had ridden in an ambulance holding the hand of one of his colleagues injured in the line of work, and he had always been amazed at how compact and neat the vehicles were. Everything had a place. A cubby-hole or a shelf designed specifically to hold one particular item, so with the flip of a switch or a turn of a lever what was needed was freed in an instant. Looking at the belt in his hand, Stephen flipped over the buckle and examined the back.

Seeing it covered by a steel plate, Stephen's brow wrinkled. Why would a brass buckle need steel to back it up? Pausing for a moment, he bent the buckle away from the leather and looked at the edge. Spying two small v-shaped openings, he glanced at Bill for a second, and then he pressed his thumbs against the buckle's back.

Toni's head popped up as a shiver ran down her spine, the familiar click, a sound she hoped she'd never hear again. Grabbing Laura's hand, Toni held on tight.

Nancy and her daughters crept closer, and as they held their breath, their eyes darted back and forth from the buckle in Stephen's hand, to Bill and then to Toni. In a room warmed by a crackling fire, no one moved and no one breathed.

Stephen Wallace risked his life every day. Walking into buildings engulfed in flames or scrambling across rooftops to cut openings for the fire to escape, dozens of times he had felt fear...a slight inkling that danger was near. As he looked at the plate in his hand, the same feeling washed over him. Holding his breath, he flipped it over and a collective gasp filled the room as everyone saw the two razor-sharp hooks welded on the back. Shaking his head at the brutality, Stephen slipped the plate back into the buckle, and as it snapped into place, Laura began to cry. It was the most evil thing she had ever seen.

In an instant, Bill bolted from the room. Reaching the lounge, he slowed not a step as he charged the man wearing a smirk.

"You *son of a bitch!*" he shouted as their bodies collided, landing on the carpet with a thud. "How could you do that?" he screamed as he drove his fist into Ron's face. "*What kind of monster are you?*"

Bill managed to get several good blows in before Ron got the upper hand. Twenty years younger and with muscles that still bulged, with one shove, he pushed Bill to his back, and while Bill's punches were hard, Ron's were brutal.

In stunned silence, the family remained in the library for a few moments, but when Eleanor realized Bill had stopped shouting she ran up the hallway. Entering the lounge just in time to see Bill's face turn bloody, she screamed at the top of her lungs, "*Somebody stop him!* Oh, dear God...please...please, *someone stop him!*"

First to the chest and then to the face, Ron's fists hit their targets with destructive precision, but as he pulled Bill up by the front of his shirt to land another punishing blow, someone grabbed him by the collar and pulled him back.

In a flash, Ron jumped to his feet. Twisting away from Stephen's hold, Ron landed a solid punch to Stephen's jaw. Staggered, Stephen shook off the cobwebs and grabbed Ron in a bear hug, and together they fell to the floor. Wrestling on a carpet now speckled with blood,

Stephen could feel his energy begin to dwindle as he tried in desperation to block the flurry of punches being thrown his way.

Ron was relentless. The beast was now free. Feasting on the pain it was causing, it was quickly becoming ravenous. Commanding him not to stop, *never* to stop, as each blow landed and more blood was spilled, it begged Ron for more. It needed more...and Ron was going to give it all it wanted, but as he was about to land the next brutal jab, he was grabbed from behind.

Bernard tried his best to pull Ron away, but he was no match for the beast and within seconds, he was knocked out cold by a powerful uppercut that sent him slumping to the floor. Without missing a beat, Ron turned back around and zeroed in on Stephen again.

Finally managing to get to his feet, Bill reacted instantly. Scrambling over a sofa, he threw himself on top of Ron, breaking his hold on Stephen, but the ex-prison officer was just too strong. Fueled by adrenalin and hatred, it only took a few moments before Bill, once again, was on the receiving end of Ron's brutality.

One by one, the other women in the house joined Eleanor at the doorway. Looking on in horror as the fight continued, it wasn't until Ron began beating Bill again when something inside of Laura gave way. Mindless of Ron's obvious strength, she rushed into the room and jumped on top of the man pummeling her father.

"Get off my father, you bastard!" she screamed, beating on Ron's back with her fists. "Let him go. You're killing him! Goddamn it...*let go of him!*"

Releasing his grip on Bill's shirt, he turned to Laura, and with one shove, Ron sent her flying into the sofa. He came to his feet with a sneer, and as Laura climbed off the couch, she returned Ron's steely glare with one of her own. Never believing he would be stupid enough to strike her, Laura said, "I'd think twice before you try to hit me, Ron. That wouldn't sit too well with the police."

"*Fuck* the police," he snarled as he drew back his arm, and with all his strength, back-handed Laura across the face.

The force sent Laura over the back of the sofa and with a yelp, she landed on the floor. Stunned, she fought back the tears welling in her eyes. Her face felt like it was on fire, and she was petrified. She could hear the shouts from the other women as they pleaded for Ron to stop, but by their screams, Laura knew Ron had no intention of stopping. She tried twice to get to her feet, but the room was still spinning around her, so all she could do was wait...and pray.

It had been several weeks since he had beaten a woman, and when he walked behind the sofa and saw the terror in Laura's eyes...he grew hard. He looked around the room for a moment and the beast was happy with what it saw. Three men had tried to stop him, but they had failed, and were now lying bruised and bloodied on the floor like ragdolls tossed from a shelf. Behind him, he could hear the pleading cries of the women, and it was all he could do not to laugh in their faces. They were so weak. They were so pathetic. They were so stupid.

Laura had told her to stay in the library, and slipping into the role of obedient prisoner, Toni had done just that. Sitting on the sofa, her knees shook as she listened to the muffled voices coming through the doors. She had no idea what was happening, and the longer she waited, the more worried she became. Why hadn't anyone returned to get her? Had they called the police? Was Cameron gone?

Finding a sliver of courage, Toni got to her feet. Sidestepping the belt still lying in the middle of the floor, she went to the doors and opened them a crack just in time to hear Laura's cry of pain. In the blink of an eye, Toni's fear disappeared and rage took its place.

Towering over Laura, Cameron licked his lips in anticipation and waited. This was the part he liked the most. When they cowered in fear and pleaded for their lives with tears rolling down their cheeks. It proved them weak, but Laura wasn't like his other victims. While he could see her fear, he also could see her defiance.

Laura stiffened her posture as she stared back at Cameron. Her heart was hammering against her ribs and she could feel the pulse in her neck throbbing as blood rushed through her system, and as she held her chin high, she stole a quick glance at her surroundings. Blocked by furniture and the man standing in front of her, Laura's only option was to crawl backward toward the tree. Keeping her eyes fixed on her assailant, she managed to move only a few inches before she felt the branches touch her hair. She had run out of room.

With a sneer, Cameron reached for his belt, but when he felt the empty belt loops, he paused. Tilting his head, he had a decision to make. Would she feel his fists or his feet? Glancing down, when he saw the steel-toed work boots peeking out from under his jeans, a smile smeared its way across his face.

Following his eyes, Laura gasped when she saw the heavy boots he was wearing. Like a poker tell, the look on his face said it all, so she was ready when he swung his foot toward her head. Raising her arm to block the kick, Laura cried out as the boot connected with her forearm and sent lightning bolts of pain radiating up her arm. Holding it against her chest, she tried to push herself under the tree, but blocked by branches and presents, there was nowhere to go. Watching in terror as he lifted his foot for another strike, Laura turned her face away. There was nothing else to do.

***

They had shouted. They had pleaded and they had wept. They were no match for the monster who had beaten their husbands and they knew it, but a mother protects her young...no matter what. When Ron raised his boot to her daughter, Eleanor fought her way out of Nancy's arms, but before she could take a step, Toni pushed her aside as she ran past.

Fearless, Toni rushed into the lounge, but when she saw the battered men lying on the floor, her courage began to fade, and when she caught sight of Cameron, it all but disappeared. Her heart began to race, pounding in her ears like a freight train bearing down on her and for a split-second, Toni wanted to run...and then she saw Laura. Halfway under the Christmas tree and cradling her arm, Toni could see the pain etched in Laura's face. She was hurt...and *he* was the one who had hurt her.

Fixated on Laura, Cameron had no idea that Toni was standing behind him, but as he swung his leg at Laura's head for the second time, his momentum was stopped by a pain so intense it caused him to howl. Grabbing his jaw, he held it for a moment before pulling his hand away to find it covered in blood. Confused, he spun around and found Toni standing behind him with his belt in her hand, and the look on her face said it all. He would never be considered handsome again.

The hooks had buried themselves in his chin and when Toni pulled the belt away for another strike, they sliced him from chin to ear...and the result was ghastly. Just like it had done to her back, the two smaller barbs had sliced him cleanly, but the center one caused a gash so deep that part of his cheek now hung in a flap. Bringing his hand to his face again, the blood ran through his fingers and down his arm, and glaring at Toni, he took a step toward her and snarled, "You *bitch!*"

Toni raised the belt, preparing to strike him again, and Cameron froze in place. It became a standoff as each glared at the other, daring a move to be made. Toni could hear the moans and the whimpers of those injured and of those worried, but she kept her eyes solely on her target and waited.

She was terrified, but she refused to show it. A few feet in front of her was the man who had once tried to kill her, and as she looked into his eyes, she saw that the monster was still very much alive. Pure hatred stared back at her. A malignancy so evil that the hairs on her neck stood on end and the thought of even taking a breath seemed impossible, but when she glanced down for a second and saw Laura still lying on the floor, Toni's backbone straightened. Raising her eyes, she glared at Cameron as she called out, "Laura, are you okay?"

Practically lying under the Christmas tree, the only thing Laura could see was Cameron's back, so when she heard Toni's voice, it took a few seconds for her to answer. "Yeah...yeah...I'm okay, Toni," Laura said, sliding out from under the boughs. "I'm fine."

His stomach began to churn as his life's blood dripped down his throat, and slowly picking up a nearby throw pillow, Cameron pressed it against what was left of his cheek. "So, Vaughn, I suppose you think this makes us even?"

There had been plenty of time in Thornbridge for Toni to think about revenge. She had often wondered if it would taste as sweet as her thoughts had made it out to be, but standing there and seeing the damage that only one strike had caused, the taste was anything but sweet. Would the shedding of more of his blood bring back what she had lost? If she caused him more pain, would it lessen hers? Would vengeance erase her scars or simply add more? Mentally, Toni shook her head. Enough was enough.

Slowly she stepped backward, making sure each foot was sound before she moved the other, never once taking her eyes off Cameron. Pieces of broken lamps crunched under her feet and pillows were kicked aside until the path she created was wide and clear. Nodding toward the front door, she said, "Get out."

Narrowing his eyes, he looked toward the door and then back at the belt in her hand. "I'm not that stupid. I walk past, and you get another shot."

"By the looks of what's left of your face, if you don't, you're going to bleed to death, and I doubt anyone here will really give a shit if that happens," Toni said, tightening her grip on the belt. "So, it's your choice. Take your chances trying to find someone to put your face back together or stay where you are, and we'll all watch you die. It really doesn't matter to me, because if there's one thing I learned in Thornbridge...it was how to kill time."

CHAPTER FIFTY-TWO

Holding the blood-soaked pillow hard against his face, Cameron's eyes remained locked on Toni, and as he weighed his options, he spit a thick wad of crimson saliva onto the carpet. Another minute passed before he took a cautious step toward the hallway, and every eye in the room followed him as he headed for the door. Stopping for a moment, he gestured for Alice to follow, but when he saw her take one step closer to her mother, Cameron snorted in disgust. Yanking the door open, he staggered out into the night.

Nancy ran to the door, and as soon as she threw the bolt, Toni dropped the belt and rushed to Laura's side. Helping her as she got to her feet, Toni asked, "Darling, are you all right? What did he do? Did he hurt you?"

"Yeah, but I don't think anything's broken," Laura answered, pulling up the sleeve of her sweater. Looking at the bruise already forming on her arm, she slowly bent her arm and flexed her wrist. "It's not broken...just sore."

"What about this?" Toni asked, running her finger gingerly down the bruise on Laura's cheek.

"That's sore, too," Laura said with a quick smile.

"Dear God, if anything had happened to you—"

"Sweetheart, I'm fine, really," Laura said, touching Toni on the sleeve. For a second, they were lost in each other's eyes, but when

Laura heard the voices in the lounge grow loud, she blurted, "Toni, my family! My dad!"

Toni ran to the center of the room with Laura following closely behind, and coming to a dead stop, they both surveyed the damage.

The room was in shambles. Neatly placed furniture had been upended, and lamps with delicate shades lay broken on the floor. Puddles of blood stained the carpet, and the flowered upholstery once displaying only shades of pink, now had sprays of red added to the mix, but the furnishings were secondary to the people scattered about the room.

They both breathed a sigh of relief when they saw Stephen sitting up and holding Peggy's hand while Bernard tended to the man's injuries, but then Laura heard someone crying, and she looked toward the hearth. Seeing her father lying on the floor with her mother hovering over him, Laura's heart stopped.

"Dad?" she said in a whisper. Grabbing Toni's hand, they both listened as Eleanor wept over her husband.

"William...sweetheart, talk to me. Please William...please say something," Eleanor begged.

"Ellie..." William said softly.

"Yes, sweetheart?"

"I can't breathe."

"What? Oh, no, William, is it your heart?"

"No," he said, opening his eyes. "You're stealing all my air."

Dumbfounded, Eleanor stared back at the man. Seeing the grin on his face, she sat back on her haunches. "I will get you for that if it's the last thing I do."

Chuckling, Bill struggled to sit up. "Sorry, couldn't resist."

"How you doing, Bill?" Bernard asked, crawling over to check on his next patient.

"I'm okay. Bruised, but not broken as they say."

"I'll be the judge of that," Bernard said, eyeing the bruises on Bill's face. "Eleanor, Dorothy...can I ask you to please get us some water and ice. The sooner we get some icepacks on these men, the sooner this swelling will go down."

"Of course, right away," they answered in unison.

With Eleanor no longer blocking his line of sight, when Bill saw his sister with the phone in her hand, he yelled across the room, "Nancy, what are you doing?"

"I'm calling the police."

"Put the phone down."

"I most certainly will not," she stated as she hit the first number.

Pushing Bernard's hand away from his face, Bill shouted, "Nancy, put the fucking phone down...*now*!"

The room went silent as all eyes turned to Bill, and seeing that he had his sister's full attention, he said, "I threw the first punch. You call the police, and all that bastard has to do is claim self-defense and the only ones going to jail will be us. That includes Toni, and I, for one, think she's been through enough. Now, please do us all a favor and put the phone down. Okay?"

"Yes...yes, of course," Nancy said, placing the receiver on the table. Looking across the room at Toni, she said, "I'm sorry. I-I wasn't thinking. I'll just go help Eleanor with the ice."

"That means we can't call emergency services either," Bernard said as he poked and prodded Bill's ribs. "They see this mess and they'll call the police for sure."

"Is Stephen...*ouch*...is Stephen okay?" Bill asked.

"Yes, there's nothing broken as far as I can tell, but I really think you both need some x-rays just to make sure."

"Same problem...*ouch*...damn it, Bernard," Bill said, flinching as Bernard touched another tender spot. "We walk into emergency looking like this, and they'll ask too many questions."

Standing near enough to hear the conversation, Toni's eyes traveled from Laura and then to Bernard. "If they need help, call for it. Don't worry about me."

"Sweetheart, no one's calling anyone. It's too risky," Laura said, grabbing Toni's hand, the movement causing pain to radiate up her arm.

Seeing Laura wince, Toni called out, "Um...Bernard...can you please take a look at Laura. She's hurt."

"Oh, will you please stop worrying about me. It's just sore," Laura said.

"Let me see," Bernard said, walking over to them.

With a huff, Laura pushed up her sleeve. "It's just a bruise."

Viewing the damage, he asked, "Does it hurt to move it?"

"It aches, but that's all," Laura said, carefully flexing her arm. "I'm fine. Really, I am."

"Well, it doesn't appear to be broken, but you should probably get an x-ray."

"Then it's settled," Toni said, looking at the doctor. "Call emergency and get them here. I'll take my chances."

"Toni—" Laura began.

"We'll go to different hospitals," Stephen shouted. "We can just tell them we were in a pub fight. This time of the year, it happens all the time."

"Stephen's right," Bill chimed in. "If he goes to one up here, and I wait until we're closer to home, there won't be a problem. No one will ever know."

Toni stood there listening as those she didn't even know tried to protect her. Strangers who knew so little yet cared so much was something she wasn't prepared for and the emotions she had kept at bay since stepping into the lounge began to show. Her eyes filled with tears as she looked around the room.

Battered husbands with bloodied faces claimed they were fine, while wives who knew better tried not to show their concern. A doctor's wife, who had arrived earlier that day wearing cashmere and cologne, no longer seemed to care that her hair was a mess, and her makeup was smeared. Somewhere along the way, an earring had been lost, and the bracelets that had once jingled and jangled on her wrist had been removed. Now, sitting on the floor, she tenderly held a bag of ice to her brother-in-law's face as his pregnant wife looked on, and talking in whispers, the three exchanged grins filled with love.

A woman with sadness in her eyes stood alone in the corner. Framed by errant strands of brown hair, her face looked younger than her years, but the girlish freckles could not hide her grief as she watched victims receive care...but she was a victim, too. A casualty of the truth, she looked as pummeled as those sitting on the floor, but while they were offering words of comfort to each other, she remained penitent and silent.

Two who were not strangers to Toni sat near the fireplace, and she watched as Eleanor washed the blood from William's knuckles and raised his hand to her lips to gently kiss away the pain. He was the one who had come to her defense. Throwing down a gauntlet, he hadn't cared about age or strength or ability. He cared only about her. A few days earlier, after she had fallen from a ladder, he had held her in his arms and without words, assured her he would protect her, and he had kept that promise without blinking an eye. There was once a time when Toni believed no man would ever make his way into her heart, but as she took an unsteady breath, she knew she had been wrong. One had...and he would remain there forever.

Toni's eyes followed the owner of the house when she came back into the room. Disheveled like the rest, while her clothing was still flamboyant, her effervescent nature had disappeared.

Nancy Shaw was a woman who had once only judged on looks and appearance, but the reality that monsters can hide behind handsomeness had just slapped her in the face. Boastfully proud of her family, to all that would listen, she had always painted a portrait of bliss and beauty, but standing there now she saw the truth. Physical features didn't matter. Scars were just marks and grandchildren were gifts not to be flaunted, and all of a sudden she felt so small and so stupid. Looking around, she grimaced at the furnishings that once seemed so important. The upholstery that had taken weeks to find, the custom-fitted drapes in the perfect shade of raspberry, and the lamps with their silk shades trimmed in gold brocade had all been ruined in an instant, and she found herself smiling because she didn't care. Things were just things, easily replaced...but families were precious.

She was still proud, and her heart grew larger with the feeling, but it wasn't because her family was handsome or beautiful. It wasn't because they were learned or rich. It was because they stood up for someone unable to stand for herself, and none of them, not one, had concerned themselves with anything but Toni's well-being. Yes, Nancy was proud...but this time it was for all the *right* reasons.

Glancing toward Alice, Nancy sighed. She had tried earlier to console her, only to be shooed away, but Nancy Shaw didn't take no for an answer, especially not from one of her children. Going over, she stood in front of her daughter and opened her arms. Alice slowly shook her head again, silently pleading that her mother leave her be, but Nancy didn't listen. Pulling her daughter into a hug she offered the comfort only a mother could, and although Alice tried to fight it, once in her mother's embrace, the floodgates opened...and her healing began.

"Toni, are you all right?"

Slowly turning around, Toni looked into Laura's eyes. Lost in the pools of green staring back at her, Toni thought about Laura's question. Was she all right?

It had always been her greatest fear, and it had gnawed at her psyche since the day she had left Thornbridge. If ever she was given the opportunity to pay back what had been done to her, would she become the murderer she had been convicted of being? As Toni thought about her answer, a smile came to her face.

She had never imagined she would run in fear, but that's what she had done, and afterward, when she finally did have the chance, when the advantage was hers to give back what had been done to her, she couldn't do it. She didn't want to. She didn't *need* to. Her reasons didn't matter any longer, and she wasn't about to lose her freedom because of him. Retribution wasn't worth the price, and suddenly she realized that she *was* all right. She *was* okay. Not perfect...far from perfect...but she wasn't a murderer. She wasn't evil waiting to happen. She was just a person with a few bad years. A woman with a few quirks, but most of all she was a survivor who finally figured out how to survive. It's easier to cope with life when you realize that you're not a monster...you're just human, and you have all the frailties to prove it.

As she waited for Toni to answer, Laura stood by her side looking up at her in amazement. After all that had happened, Laura had expected to see fear or hesitancy, some small sliver of panic, but instead she saw a smile. Confused, Laura touched Toni on the hand. "Sweetheart, are you okay?"

Toni's smile grew a wee bit larger as she gazed back at Laura. "Yeah...yeah, I think I am."

***

"Is Dad asleep?" Laura asked, seeing her mother quietly close the bedroom door.

"Yes, it didn't take long," Eleanor said, going over to join Laura on the sofa. "How about Toni?"

"I helped her with a bath and then got her into bed. She was exhausted."

"I wish she would have gone to emergency with your father. I know Bernard said her lungs sounded clear, but—"

"Mum, I couldn't bear to force the issue, not after all she went through today. He said he'd check on her Saturday, and until then we'll just keep an eye on her. Okay?"

"Speaking of Saturday, I hope you didn't mind that I offered to have Christmas dinner here. Between the memories of today and the state of Nancy's lounge, I thought we'd all be a bit more comfortable."

"No, of course not, but I was a little surprised everyone agreed so quickly. After everything that's happened—"

"That's exactly why they agreed, Laura."

"What do you mean?"

"I think this year we all have a reason to be extra grateful for the family we have. Don't you? We came together today. We put aside our petty differences and our opinions, and acted as one. It's what a family does. Today opened our eyes as to just how much we care for one another, and when you realize that, you don't want that feeling to end. I think we're all looking forward to the chaos of Christmas. To the laughs and the memories, to the endless jokes about your ornaments and to the questions that I'm sure your cousins are dying to ask. After pain comes healing, and I think that Christmas...*this* Christmas...will give us all a chance to heal a bit and to love each other even more."

"I never thought about it that way."

"That's not all you didn't think about."

"Huh?"

"You do realize that you called your father *Dad* earlier. Don't you?" Eleanor asked with a grin.

"Did I?" Laura said, looking away.

"Oh, Laura, you're such a dreadful liar."

Turning to face her mother, Laura sighed. "I've been daft, haven't I?"

"You had your reasons."

"No, all I had was a chip on my shoulder, for as long as I can remember."

"Well, apparently it fell off today."

"Yeah, it did," Laura said, wiping away a tear. Sniffling back another, she said, "When I saw Ron beating him up...I don't know, something inside just...just let loose. All of sudden, he wasn't just an acquaintance. He wasn't just this man that I saw a few times a year.

He was my dad, and he was defending the woman I love. He wouldn't have done that if he...if he didn't...if he didn't *care* for me."

Reaching over, Eleanor took Laura's hand. "He *loves* you, Laura, and you, my darling daughter, love him, so please stop trying to avoid the word."

"Was it wrong for me to hate him for what he did?"

"No, because what he did *was* wrong."

"Why didn't he ever tell me that he cared about me? I mean, we've seen each other almost every year, but he never said a word. He never tried...he never tried to make a connection with me."

"Have you ever wanted to ask for something, but believed you didn't have the right to?"

Thinking for a moment, Laura said, "Yeah, I suppose."

"I'm not saying that it's a good reason, but by the time your father figured out what a fool he'd been, you were already old enough to make it perfectly clear you didn't want anything to do with him. Why ask the question if you're sure of the answer?"

"He wasted a lot of time."

"You'll get no argument from me on that one."

"How do I tell him, Mum? How do I tell him that I love him?"

"I think you'll figure it out."

***

She looked up from the table as her daughter walked into the kitchen, and taking off her reading glasses, she asked, "What are you doing up at this hour?"

"I couldn't sleep. It's hard to find a comfortable position when you're the size of a chalet," Peggy said, waddling to the stove.

"Yes, I remember," Nancy said with a giggle. "Would you like me to make you some tea?"

"No, I've got it," Peggy said, filling the kettle. "Are there any of those biscuits left?"

Getting to her feet, Nancy smiled as she pointed to the table. "You sit and I'll get you something."

"Mum—"

"Peggy...sit!"

With one hand pressed against her lower back, Peggy slowly made it to the table, and sliding into a chair, she snickered seeing the stack of old issues of *The Weekly Sun* piled on the table. "Honestly, Mum, you really need to stop reading this rubbish."

"It's not rubbish," Nancy called back as she plated some biscuits.

Glancing at one of the headlines, Peggy said, "No, and I suppose aliens landing in Edinburgh last week is God's honest truth?"

Laughing, Nancy walked over and sat down, placing the food and the tea on the table. "Okay, well that bit was rubbish, but there are some good stories in there, too."

"I suppose."

"Thank you for agreeing to stay the night. I would have been worried sick if you had tried to make it home tonight."

"Well, Stephen was in no shape to drive and his parents were more than happy to keep the boys for the night. They'll no doubt be spoiled rotten by the morning," Peggy said. Seeing her mother frown, Peggy quickly added, "No worries, Mum. You'll get plenty of time to spoil them at Christmas."

Nancy beamed, and looking at her daughter, she asked, "How are you holding up? Is the baby okay?"

"He's fine, Mum," Peggy said, rubbing her belly. "He's been kicking and moving about like he's trying to rearrange something in there."

"I was worried. What with everything that went on today. You're so far along—"

"I'm not that lucky," Peggy said with a laugh. "He's got a few more weeks of cooking before it's time for him to appear, and he knows it. Besides, you keep forgetting what my husband does for a living. If I got stressed out every time I thought Stephen was in danger, I'd be a basket case."

"Well, you are my strongest daughter. I'll give you that."

"Speaking of daughters, I heard you talking to Dot on the phone earlier. How's Alice holding up?"

"She's doing okay. Emma was apparently a bit curious about why they were going to stay with Bernard and Dorothy, but Cora's much too young. Luckily, I think with Christmas being only a few days away, it will help everyone forget about what happened...at least for a little while."

Watching as her mother rearranged the tabloids, Peggy asked, "How about you? How are you doing?"

"Considering that two people almost died today, my lounge is in shambles, and my son-in-law apparently is a shit of massive proportions, I'm doing rather well."

"Yeah?"

"I had a brandy a little while ago. It took the edge off," Nancy said, tittering to herself as she picked up her reading glasses. Noticing that Peggy was getting up, she asked, "Are you all right?"

"Yes, I just have to pee *again*. Be right back."

Turning back to the newspapers, Nancy picked up the next in the stack and slowly began to scan the pages. Muttering as she dismissed article after article, by the time Peggy came back, Nancy had her nose buried so deep in a tabloid, she didn't even notice her daughter was there.

Gathering her plate and cup, Peggy placed them in the sink. "I think I'll try to get some sleep. You should, too." Reaching the doorway, Peggy stopped. "Mum, did you hear me?"

Startled, Nancy looked up. "I'm...I'm sorry, dear. Did you say something?"

"Yeah, I'm going to bed. Do you need anything before I go up?"

Looking at the newspaper in her hand, Nancy said, "Yes. Do me a favor, Peggy, and hand me the phone."

"Mum, it's after midnight. Who could you possibly need to call at this hour?"

Tossing her glasses on the table, Nancy leaned back in her chair. "The police."

CHAPTER FIFTY-THREE

Lying under the heavy quilt, Laura breathed in the warmth, and snuggling deeper into her cave made of soft linen, she waited for sleep to take her again. She didn't know what time it was, and she didn't care. She just wanted the aches, pains, and memories from the day before to disappear, at least for a little while longer, and they would have if she hadn't heard a groan. Her eyes flew open. Squinting at the bright morning sun streaming through the windows, she tossed back the quilt and found the bed empty. Toni was gone.

Laura's thoughts returned to the old Toni, the damaged Toni, the Toni who had contemplated death when life had become too difficult, and with her heart pounding in her chest, Laura was about to call out when she saw the light under the bathroom door. Hearing yet another loud grunt of pain, she scrambled out of bed and ran to investigate. Pushing the door open, she rushed inside.

Sitting on the toilet, Toni jumped a few inches when the door flew open. Scrunching up her face at the aches the movement had caused, she yelled, "What the *fuck*, Laura!"

"Toni, what are you...what are you doing?"

"What does it *look* like I'm doing," she answered in disgust.

"But I heard a...I heard a groan."

"That's because I got down okay, but when I tried to stand up, it hurt like a bugger."

Laura's first instinct was to laugh, but it was quickly replaced by sympathy for a woman who had gone through so much the day before. In years to come, she would joke about this moment, but now was not the time. "Do you want some help?"

Finally finding a bit of amusement in her situation, Toni grinned. "Please, if you don't mind. I'd hate to have you call emergency just to get me off the bloody toilet."

A few minutes later, with pajama bottoms no longer gathered around her ankles, Toni stood at the vanity while Laura used the facilities behind her.

"I can't believe how sore I am," Toni said as she washed her hands. "I feel like I've been hit by a lorry."

"Between your run and the fall in the water, I'm not surprised."

"Even my hair hurts."

Smiling to herself, Laura flushed the toilet and then went over and looked up at her confused partner. "That's because Stephen pulled you out of the water by your hair."

"What? He decided to go caveman?"

"It was the only way he could get you to shore. You were dead...dead...weight..." Laura's face scrunched up as her emotions rose to the surface. Tears filled her eyes, and placing her hand over her mouth, she began to weep.

"Hey. Hey, what's this?" Toni asked, cupping Laura's chin in her hand. "Darling, what's wrong?"

"You...you weren't breathing. Oh, Toni...you almost died."

Toni wrapped her arms around Laura and held her close. "Darling, it's okay," she whispered. "I'm alive, Laura. I'm bloody sore, but I'm alive. So please, please don't cry."

Sniffling, Laura took a deep breath and stepped back. Wiping a tear away, she said, "I love you so much. Do you know that?"

"Well, you did just lift me off the toilet, so I'm fairly certain that love was involved, unless you have a perversion I'm not aware of. Do you?"

"Actually, I do have one."

"Oh, yeah?" Toni said, leaning her head to the side.

"It seems I have a fetish called Toni Vaughn."

Toni's eyes creased at the corners, and for a second, all her aches and pains faded away. "I guess that means you won't have a problem helping your fetish get dressed then, huh?"

"You sure you don't want to stay in bed today?"

"No, I'm hungry, and I think the more I move about, the less sore I'll be."

Placing a quick kiss on Toni's lips, Laura said, "Okay. Let's go find you some clothes."

Following Laura into the bedroom, Toni sat on the edge of the bed while Laura got dressed.

"Be with you in a second," Laura said as she pulled on her jeans.

Seeing Laura's pained expression as she struggled into the tight denim, Toni asked, "Is your arm bothering you?"

"We've already discussed this. It's bruised, not broken," Laura said as she pulled up the zip. "And before you ask, because I *know* you will, the bruise on my cheek doesn't even hurt."

"I'm sorry he hit you."

"I know you are, sweetheart, but it's over. Let's just forget it. Okay?" Laura said, stepping into her boots. Opening the dresser, she pulled out a pair of red flannel pajamas. "How about these?"

"I'm not wearing those!"

"Why? I thought they were your favorite."

"Laura, I can't stay in my pajamas all day."

"Why not?"

"Because...because...because I'm not sick. That's why!"

"This coming from a woman who couldn't get off the toilet a few minutes ago."

"I'm sore, not sick."

"Fine," Laura said. Reaching into the drawer, she pulled out a sweater. "Put it on."

"I need a bra."

"Oh, even better," Laura said, opening another drawer to find one of Toni's white bras. Tossing it on the bed, Laura said, "There you go."

Totally forgetting that her body was one big ache, Toni reached for the brassiere and winced. "*Fuck.*"

"You okay?"

"You did that on purpose."

"Yes, I did," Laura said, folding her arms across her chest. "Now, do you need another demonstration, or have I won this argument?"

***

"How old are you?"

Looking up from the cookbook she was reading, Toni answered, "Thirty-four. Why?"

"Just wondering," Bill said.

"How old are you?"

"Fifty-five, but today I feel like I'm a hundred."

"I know what you mean," Toni said, letting out a long breath as she settled back into the sofa. Resting the cookbook on her lap, she looked in his direction. With the help of ice packs, the swelling around his eyes had disappeared, but the bruises that had begun to form the night before had now blossomed into blue-black splotches that covered his cheeks and chin. "Do you feel as bad as you look?"

"Oh, thanks!"

"Sorry," Toni said with a laugh. "Didn't mean that the way it came out."

Smiling back at her, he said, "Actually I don't. I'm just stiff and sore...like I'm atrophying."

"Yeah, me, too," she said, stretching her arms above her head.

"I hope you don't mind me saying this, but after all that's happened, you seem to be coping rather well."

"Laura said the same thing to me last night."

"Can I ask what your answer was?"

Pausing for only a moment, Toni told Bill what she had confessed to Laura the night before. Her biggest fear was that murder lurked in her heart, but she had been wrong, and that knowledge in its own way, had set her free. For a few minutes, the words flowed easily as if she was telling a story, but when she looked up and saw his battered face, the memories of the night came rushing back.

In terror, she had run from the man she had known as Cameron. In anger, she had proven him evil, and with determination, she had managed to stand her ground when all around her were bleeding and injured. Through it all, she had never allowed one tear to fall...until now.

It was impossible to stop. Bowing her head, she turned as if to hide from him, but he had heard the emotion in her voice, and grunting at the pain in his muscles, Bill moved from chair to sofa. Wrapping an arm around her as she wept, when she turned and buried her head in his shoulder, he held her close and said not a word. None were needed.

***

"Here, drink this," he said, handing her a glass.
"What is it?"
"Ten-year-old single malt."
"Bill, it's eleven o'clock in the morning."
"So?"
Taking the glass from his hand, she said, "The last person who served me alcohol this early was my shrink."
"Now *there's* a doctor I want to meet," he said with a laugh as he gingerly sat back down.
"Sorry about earlier."
"Never apologize for being human, Toni. After all that you've been through in the past twenty-four hours, I think it definitely called for a good cry, or perhaps two."
Watching as Bill sipped his drink, Toni asked, "Should you be drinking that? I thought Eleanor said the doctors gave you something for pain."
"They did, but I much prefer numbing myself with alcohol rather than using drugs."
"Alcohol is a drug."
"True, but it's much tastier than those pills in the bedroom."
Taking a sip, Toni smiled at the sweet toffee flavor of the single malt. "This is good."
"I told you...much better than those nasty pills, and it has the same effect. I haven't met a Scotch yet that can't relax my muscles," Bill said, chuckling to himself.
"You should slow down or you're going to get pissed."
Bill's smile disappeared. "And that would be a problem why exactly?"
"Are you angry?"
"Maybe just a little."
"At me?"
"What? No, no, no, of course I'm not angry with you, Toni. Don't be absurd."
"Then with whom...or what?"

"Mortality."

"Sorry?"

"Mortality. Twenty years ago, I would have knocked that bastard through the walls of that bloody house, but last night I couldn't even hold my own for more than a few minutes. It's a hard lesson to learn when all of sudden you realize you're old."

"You're hardly old."

"Well, I'm hardly young."

Eyeing the man, Toni's eyes crinkled at the corners. "So, you wallow in self-pity often, do you?"

Bill opened his mouth to argue and then just as quickly it closed. Shaking his head, he said, "I was, wasn't I?"

"Just a bit, but it's quite understandable looking the way you do."

"Oi!"

Toni let out a laugh, and exchanging grins, in unison they leaned back into the softness of the sofa.

"I haven't been pissed in years. How about you?" Bill asked, staring at the liquor in his glass.

Thinking for a moment, Toni said, "Christ, I can't remember the last time. At least...I don't know, maybe eight or nine years ago. Why?"

"Care to give it a go?"

"Are you suggesting that we get drunk?"

"Yes, actually, I am."

"I don't think that's a good idea."

"Give me one good reason why it isn't."

***

"What the hell is this?" Laura asked, walking into the kitchen to find the table overflowing with wrapping paper, bows and ribbon.

Looking up, Bill said, "We were bored, so we decided to finish our wrapping. Do you need a hand with the packages?"

Believing their sluggish expressions were due to exhaustion, Laura shook her head. "By the time either of you manage to get them inside, it'll be tomorrow," she said, heading back out the door for another trip. "Be right back."

"Are we going to be in trouble?" he asked, looking in Toni's direction.

"You are."

"Me? What about you?"

"I've got *issues*, remember?" Toni said with a lopsided grin. "I've had a *very* stressful week. Wouldn't want to push me over the edge again, now would she?"

"Oh, now that's just not fair."

"What's not fair?" Laura asked, returning with more bags.

"Your partner here has decided that she's not in trouble, but I am, simply because *she's* had a stressful week," Bill said, rolling his eyes.

Something in the tone of her father's voice caused Laura to turn around, and spying the open bottle of whisky on the table, she blurted, "Have you been drinking?"

"Maybe a bit, but I can assure you it's for a *very* good reason," Toni said, gulping what was left in her glass.

"What's going on?" Eleanor asked, carrying the last of the packages into the kitchen.

"They're pissed."

"What?" Eleanor said, quickly glancing at the two sitting at the table. "You're drunk?"

"For medicinal purposes only, my dear. No worries," Bill said as he reached for the bottle.

"Oh, no, you don't," Laura said, grabbing it out of his hands.

"Oi! Give that back."

"What the hell are you thinking? Mum said the doctors gave you something for the pain."

"I didn't take it. I decided I wanted Scotch more than I wanted a pill," Bill said, reaching for the bottle. "Now be a good girl and give your father back his booze."

"I'll do no such thing," Laura said, placing the bottle on the counter. "And exactly what, Miss Vaughn, is your *very good reason* for getting drunk at one o'clock in the afternoon?"

"Muscle relaxer."

"Excuse me?"

"Muscle relaxer," Toni said with a titter as she winked at Bill.

"I heard you the first time, but I'm not sure I understand."

"Laura, Laura, Laura...where have you been?" Toni began, waving her hands in the air. "Alcohol makes a person relax, and when a person is relaxed, so are their muscles. So you see, by being relaxed—"

"Don't you mean drunk?"

"Point taken," Toni said, holding up one finger. "By being *slightly* inebriated, my body no longer hurts."

"That's because you numbed it with alcohol."

"Exactly!"

Laura's mouth opened, but she couldn't think of anything to say. Looking at her mother for guidance, Eleanor simply shrugged in return.

Quite entertained by the situation, Eleanor said, "I think we'd be wise to get them into bed."

"Sorry, Eleanor, you're a babe, but I only have eyes for Laura."

"Toni!" Laura yelled.

"What? What did I say?"

Walking over, Laura glared down at her partner. "Can you stand?"

"Yep."

When Toni made no move to get up, Laura rolled her eyes. "*Will* you stand?"

"I'll do anything for you, darling," Toni said as she climbed out of the chair. "Now, whatcha have in mind?"

Laughing as she wrapped her arm around Toni's waist, Laura said, "How about I take you upstairs so you can sleep it off."

"Are you going to sleep with me?"

"No, I'm going to come down and put all these groceries away so we can start fixing some things for tomorrow."

"When the Scotch wears off, my muscles are going to hurt again."

"Then I'll run you a bath."

"Will you join me then?" Toni asked, wiggling her eyebrows. "You know...like we did last week?"

There was absolutely nothing Laura could do to hide the swath of scarlet blazing across her face, so she didn't even try. With a shake of her head, she guided Toni to the door, and looking over her shoulder at her mother, she said, "Good luck. Somehow, I think you're going to need it, too."

"From where I'm standing, I think *you're* going to need a whip and a chair," Eleanor said with a laugh.

Thankful Toni was wearing pajamas, when they got to the bedroom, Laura managed to turn down the bed and get Toni into it without too much difficulty. Arranging the quilt around her drunken partner, Laura sat on the bed and looked at the woman she loved.

"What are you looking at?" Toni asked in a whisper.

"You."

"Got a spot on my face?"

Lightly touching a patch of red on Toni's cheek, Laura said, "No, just some wind burn."

"You mad at me?"

"No."

"Don't be mad at Bill. It wasn't his fault."

"I'm not mad at anyone, Toni."

"You sure?"

"Positive," Laura said with a grin.

"I love you."

"I love you, too."

"Kiss me."

With a sigh, Laura leaned in for a kiss and when the first one ended, the next began. Tenderly, their lips met again and again, and breathing deep, Toni threaded her fingers through Laura's hair, and when the tip of her tongue touched Laura's lips, Laura couldn't refuse. Tongues began to explore, and smiles were born in their hearts and cores as they spoke their love without words. Finally, feeling Toni's hands begin to travel south, Laura pulled away. "*You* need to get some sleep."

"I'm not that drunk, you know?"

"I know, but you *are* tired."

"I don't want to sleep away the day."

"I'll wake you in a couple of hours. How's that?"

"Promise?"

"Yes," Laura said, watching as Toni's eyes grew heavy.

"I love you."

"You already said that," Laura whispered.

"It's worth repeating."

***

Skipping down the stairs, when Laura saw her mother coming from the bedroom rearranging her blouse, a hearty laugh escaped. "It seems I wasn't the only one needing a whip and a chair."

"Yes, well, I forgot your father was an octopus in a past life," Eleanor said, following Laura to the kitchen. "But he should be asleep for most of the afternoon."

"I promised Toni I'd wake her in a few hours," Laura said, looking at the groceries piled on the counter. "So, where do you want to start?"

"Well, the chicken, beef and bacon need to marinate overnight for the soup, so I'll start with that. How about you chop up the vegetables for the stuffing? Can you handle that?"

Hearing a note of sarcasm in her mother's voice, Laura said, "You say it as if I don't know my way around the kitchen."

"Oh, you know your way. As long as it comes out of box or a can, you're good to go."

"Ha ha. I'll have you know that I made chicken soup from scratch, and Toni thought it was delicious."

"Chicken soup? Was someone sick?"

"Yes, Toni had the flu."

"That explains it then. She must have been out of her mind with fever," Eleanor said under her breath.

"I heard that."

Smiling, Eleanor went about preparing the meats for the soup. A few minutes passed while both busied themselves with the tasks at hand, until Eleanor asked, "So, what are your plans? You've never said."

"What do you mean?" Laura asked, looking up from the cutting board.

"Well, you're engaged. Any thought of where or *when* you'll get married?"

"Actually, we really haven't talked about it. We have to find a house first and—"

"A house?"

"Oh, yeah. I'm selling mine."

"What? Why?"

"When Toni moved in she was my lodger, and in a way she still feels like that at times. Like she doesn't have the right to voice her opinion because—"

"It's your house and not hers?"

"Yes, and with all her insecurities, this is probably going to be the easiest one to fix."

"So any thoughts as to where you'll move?" Eleanor asked, reaching into a cabinet for a pot.

"Toni likes it up here."

Seeing her mother's head pop up like a children's toy, Laura smiled. "Sorry, Mum. I love you, but our jobs are in London."

"They don't have to be," Eleanor said in a voice syrupy sweet.

"Yes, they most certainly do...at least for now."

Regarding her daughter through narrowed eyes, Eleanor asked, "Are you trying to give me hope with that statement, young lady?"

"No, more like trying to get you off my back," Laura mumbled. A second later, Laura laughed as she dodged a stalk of celery, thankful that her mother's aim had never been true.

***

Toni drew a long, slow breath as she rolled to her side. Casually placing her arm around Laura's middle, she spooned against her and sighed.

"Hiya," Laura whispered.

"I thought you were supposed to be in the kitchen baking a pie or something," Toni mumbled into Laura's neck.

"I was, up until about forty minutes ago. Mum and I decided to take a break, so I came up for a short kip."

"Why didn't you wake me?"

"Exactly what purpose would that serve?"

"The usual purpose," Toni said, placing a kiss on the back of Laura's neck.

A slow smile grew on Laura's face. "You are in no shape for that, Toni, and we both know it."

"True, but haven't you heard that it's better to give than to receive?" Toni asked, sliding her hand under Laura's T-shirt.

Laura couldn't help but moan when Toni's hand covered her breast. While a thin layer of fabric lay between Toni's palm and her skin, Laura knew that if she didn't act fast, Toni's skillful fingers would find their way under her bra. The only problem was...Laura didn't want to act fast.

Hearing no argument, Toni moved a bit closer and slipping her fingers under the spandex, she smiled when she felt the erect nipple. Caressing it gently, she listened as Laura's breathing grew louder, but with no need to rush, she continued to softly rub and tweak the tip until it was hard and surrounded by pebbles of pink.

Laura closed her eyes and luxuriated in the sensual massage, and when Toni's hand finally began to creep lower, all Laura could do was purr in anticipation.

Easily opening the snap of Laura's jeans, Toni pulled the zip down ever so slowly, taking great pleasure in the lackadaisical tempo she was setting. Hearing a contented sigh slip from Laura's lips when the zipper finally reached its end, Toni pushed her hand under the denim, and Laura sighed again. Toni's fingers traveled over the silk of Laura's knickers, and when Laura shifted just a bit, Toni slipped her hand between Laura's legs.

"Oh," Laura said in a whisper as Toni rubbed her through the silk. "Oh...yes."

Toni continued to tease Laura through the fabric. Gently wiggling her finger over the rapidly thickening folds, it didn't take long before Laura's passion soaked through the material.

With a low, sultry growl, Toni moved her hand under the silk, and before she reached the patch of brown curls, Laura raised one knee and offered herself to her partner.

Laura was dripping with desire, and Toni's fingers easily moved through the swollen petals, pressing and tweaking, rubbing and wiggling, until Laura began to pant. Short, ragged gasps signaled her need, and the sound caused Toni's own juices to flow freely. Waiting only for a moment, Toni pushed her finger inside of Laura.

Knowing they weren't alone in the house, Laura bit down on her lip to prevent the sounds of ecstasy from escaping as Toni entered her. Craving all Toni could give her Laura grabbed Toni's wrist and encouraged her to go deep...and to go hard.

At first, Toni didn't heed Laura's request, but then slowly she began to increase the force and depth of her strokes. Unable to move for fear the bed would squeak, Laura could do nothing but lie there in silence as Toni took her to orgasm. Again and again, Toni tormented Laura with skillful probing until finally, Laura felt the contractions begin. Knowing she wouldn't be able to stop her cries of pleasure from escaping, Laura buried her face in the goose down pillow as the climax swept over her.

Moving away enough to allow the heat between their bodies to escape, Toni listened in silence as Laura's breathing slowly returned to normal. Smiling, she asked, "Are you still alive?"

A gurgle of laughter slipped from Laura's lips as she turned in Toni's arms. Studying her face for a moment, she said, "You are the most beautiful woman in the world."

"Second most beautiful."

"What say we call it a tie?"

CHAPTER FIFTY-FOUR

"Absolutely not."
"But it's tradition."
"I don't bloody care!"
Coming into the kitchen with Toni one step behind, Laura asked, "What the hell is going on?"
"Your father wants to get a branch from the rowan, and I told him no," Eleanor said, crossing her arms.
"Oh," Laura said quietly.
"Hello? I'm new here. Could someone explain what this is all about?" Toni asked.
"Sorry, sweetheart," Laura said. "It's a Scottish tradition to burn a small branch from a rowan at Christmas. It's supposed to clear away any bad feelings like jealousy or mistrust between family, friends and neighbors."
"That sounds like a great tradition to me. So what's the problem? Aren't there any rowans around?"
"Yes, there are," Bill said, pointing out the window. "Past the maple, there are at least four or five—"
"And I had them all trimmed this past spring!" Eleanor said, glaring at the man. "William, you can't reach the branches without a ladder, and I'm not having you traipse out there in the snow carrying a bloody ladder. Now stop acting like—"
"I'll do it," Toni said.

"Toni...no," Laura said, touching her arm. "You're still sore—"

"Please, Laura. It's a tradition, and after everything that's happened, having a bit more luck on our side sounds like a good idea to me. Don't you think?"

"I suppose—"

"Good," Toni said with a quick nod. "Now, where's the ladder? Oh, and I suppose I'll need a saw."

"I'll show you where they are," Bill chimed in as he began to head for the hallway.

"William!" Eleanor shouted, stopping the man in his tracks.

Slowly, Bill turned around, and with all the boyish charm he could muster, he said, "Yes, dear?"

Eleanor knew she had lost the argument as soon as she saw the playful look on Bill's face. "Just please do me a favor and don't hurt yourself. Okay?"

Smiling, Bill strutted over and kissed her quickly on the cheek. "Wouldn't think of it, love." Turning to look at Toni, he said, "Now, let me just get my coat, and we'll be off."

Watching them disappear into the hall, Eleanor said, "Laura?"

"Yeah, Mum?"

"I don't know about you, but I have this feeling we're going to have to keep those two separated."

**

"I feel like I could sit here until spring," Bill said, relaxing into the sofa.

"You shouldn't have had that last slice," Eleanor said, nudging the empty pizza box on the ottoman with her foot.

"I'm not full...just content. I can't think of a better way to spend Christmas Eve than with you three lovely ladies."

The smile on Laura's face matched that of her mother's and Toni's, and gathering the paper plates and discarded napkins, she headed to the kitchen. "Coffee, tea...or something stronger?" she said over her shoulder.

Three voices became one in an instant. "Stronger!"

Snickering, Laura tossed out the rubbish, and then opening a cabinet, she perused her mother's wine selection.

"Dry and red is my choice," Toni said as she came into the kitchen and placed the empty pizza boxes on the counter.

"I know what you like."

"Yes, you do," Toni whispered, wrapping her arms around Laura's waist.

"What's gotten into you?"

"What do you mean?"

"You've been quite...um...*attentive* today."

"Am I not always?"

"Yes, but after everything that's happened, I expected you to be a little...a little less—"

"Horny?"

"Yes!" Laura said with a laugh. "Don't get me wrong, I don't mind. I was just wondering why?"

"Honestly?"

"Yes, please."

"I'm alive."

"What?"

"I'm alive, and I feel good," Toni said with a shrug. "I don't know how else to explain it, but sitting out there, chatting and laughing as we all sat around eating pizza...it just felt so right. So...so normal and comfortable."

Turning in Toni's arms, Laura looked up at the woman. "It sounds to me like you're happy."

"I am," Toni said as she leaned in for a kiss.

The kiss was slow and soft, and it would have lasted much longer if Bill hadn't shouted from the lounge, "Oi! Where's our drinks?"

Amused by the interruption, they separated and while Toni uncorked a bottle of Pinot Noir, Laura grabbed the glasses, and together they returned to the lounge.

"It's about time," Bill said, sitting on the floor by the tree.

"Where's Mum?" Laura asked, handing him a glass.

"Using the loo."

"Why are you sitting on the floor?"

"Your mother and I were talking while you were *snogging* in the kitchen, and we thought it might be a good idea to open our presents tonight. Tomorrow is going to be chaotic around here, what with all the children and the food, but of course, if you'd rather wait..."

"No, we can, that is as long Toni doesn't mind."

"I've been wondering for days what's in that large one," Toni said, pointing to a coat-sized box wrapped in foil. "Give it here, Bill."

"No, no, no," Laura said quickly, scrambling to intercept the package before it got to Toni's hands. "This one needs to wait, sweetheart."

"They're all going to wait," Eleanor said, coming back into the room carrying some shopping bags. "At least until we take care of a few more things."

"Like what?"

Smiling, Eleanor pulled a box of votive candles from one of the bags and handed them to Laura.

"I can't believe I forgot," Laura said as her mother handed her a lighter.

"Quite understandable, sweetheart," Eleanor said. "Why don't you and Toni do the honors?"

"All right," Laura said, reaching out to take Toni's hand. "Come on."

When they reached the hallway, Toni pulled Laura to a stop. "What's going on?"

"Tonight is Christmas Eve."

"I know that."

"But in Scotland, it's also called Oidche Choinnle."

"Say what?" Toni said, jerking back her head at the Gaelic flowing easily from Laura's mouth.

Grinning, Laura said, "It means Night of Candles."

"Okay?"

"You remember how I said that Mum likes to go all-out for Christmas?"

"How could I forget? I'm the one who was hanging lights from the rafters."

"Well, it's her favorite time of the year because she loves all the Scottish traditions, and one of them is to put candles in the windows on Christmas Eve to light the way for the Holy Family. And legend has it that shopkeepers used to give out Yule candles to strangers to help guide their way and keep them safe, so tomorrow when everyone gets here, we'll give the rest to them."

"Really?" Toni asked softly.

"Yeah."

Smiling at the sentiment, Toni said, "Where do we start?"

"Upstairs. Let's go," Laura said, trotting up the stairs.

When they returned to the lounge a few minutes later, Toni was surprised to see both Eleanor and Bill removing their coats. Noticing that the crisscrossed stack of wood near the hearth had grown taller by a few rows, she asked, "Okay, so what's this all about, or did someone forget to pay the power bill?"

"*This* is more superstition than anything else," Laura said, putting the remaining candles on the bookcase. "It's said if you keep a fire going on Christmas Eve, the sprites roaming around outside won't get down the chimney to wreak their havoc."

"The *sprites*?"

"I said it was a superstition."

Glancing at the stack of wood again, Toni said, "So, wait. Are you saying someone stays up all night to make sure it doesn't go out?"

"I'll stoke it before we retire and then get up around three to check on it," Bill chimed in. "After all, we wouldn't want any sprites ruining our day, now would we?"

"Heaven forbid," Toni said, smiling back at the man whose eyes were filled with whimsy. "So, Bill, tell me, exactly what *does* a sprite look like?"

Placing his finger on his lips, he thought for a moment. "Well, to tell you the truth, Toni, I've never really seen one, but I'm told they're a bit like an elf...only with teeth."

"Sounds scary."

"Yes, indeed. I've also heard that most have red hair, green eyes and are about this high," Bill said, holding his hand a few feet off the ground as he glanced at Laura. "And they have one hell of a temper."

"My hair is auburn. I'm taller than that, and Mum was right!" Laura said, playfully bumping her hip into Toni's. "We seriously need to keep you two separated."

"What are they up to now?" Eleanor asked, coming out of the bedroom carrying what appeared to be more Christmas decorations.

"Just working on their comedy routine, I think," Laura said with a laugh. "What's all that?"

"The new stockings. In all the commotion, I forgot to put them up," Eleanor said, setting the two cast-iron hangers on the mantle. Placing the stocking on the hooks, she stood back and admired the embroidered names of *Toni* and *William* stitched across the white bands. "That's much better." Turning around, she handed a small package to Toni. "Hang that up. Will you sweetheart?"

Glancing at the package, Toni pulled the mistletoe from the cellophane. "Now, *this* is a tradition I know about," she said. Walking over, she hung it from the garland draped over the doorway, and then turning on her heel, she crooked her finger at Laura. "Come here and be my first victim."

Laughing, Laura sauntered over to Toni and looked up at the sprig above their heads. "Just to let you know, in Scotland mistletoe is supposed to bring luck and ward off evil spirits."

"Is that so?"

"Yes."

"And…um…it's got nothing to do with a kiss?"

"Some people think it does."

"Laura?"

"Yes?"

"I'm one of those people," Toni said as she pulled Laura into her arms and placed a chaste kiss on her lips.

"If you two keep snogging, we'll never get to the presents!" Bill shouted as he topped off their wine glasses.

Grinning, Laura and Toni walked over and sat on the floor near the fireplace, each taking a glass as it was offered.

"So, now that all the traditions are out of the way…" Toni said, reaching for the large foil-wrapped package.

"Not so fast," Eleanor said. Taking the rowan branch from the top of the wood pile, she placed it in Laura's hands. After one quick glance at William, Eleanor leaned in close to her daughter. "Put it in the flames, Laura. Clear away the bad feelings and make room for the good."

With an infinitesimal nod, Laura smiled as she took the branch, and crawling over, she placed it in the hearth.

"*Now* the traditions are over," Eleanor said, sitting on the sofa. "So which package first?"

"This one," Toni said, grabbing for the large box again.

"No, not that one, Toni. Really…it needs to wait," Laura said, reaching for the box.

"Why?"

It was a simple question, but one not easily answered with her parents sitting only a few feet away. Thinking quickly, the corners of Laura's mouth turned up just a hair. "Because *they* aren't white."

Toni tilted her head to the side. Staring at Laura, she replayed the words in her mind and when the answer came, Toni's eyes bulged. "Oh!" she said, shoving the box into Laura's outstretched hands. "Oh...well...um...perhaps Laura is right on this one. Maybe I should wait until...um...until later to open it."

Bill's eyes darted from Toni to Laura, and then back at Eleanor. Shaking his head, he said under his breath, "I'm not going to ask."

"Neither am I," Eleanor whispered in return. "Neither am I."

***

Kisses were given and looks of love were exchanged as they opened their presents of clothing and books, and as the fire crackled in the hearth and wine was sipped, love filled the room.

When Toni and Laura had returned to Stirling earlier in the week to finish their shopping, Toni insisted they go to Barleys. After spending a better part of a morning decorating the outside of Eleanor's house with Bill by her side, Toni knew what she wanted to get the man. So, strolling over to their selection of gloves, she perused the rack until she found the perfect pair of fur-lined leather worthy of the man who had become her friend.

Even though Laura was determined to buy her father only a card for Christmas, while she was waiting patiently for Toni to decide on the gloves, she noticed a display of woven scarves. Going over, she ran her finger over the soft Scottish cashmere and debated. Convincing herself that her decision was only because of the Christmas music spewing from the overhead speakers, she pulled out one displaying the MacLeod tartan and then walked with Toni to the register.

Toni watched as Bill carefully opened the gift from his daughter, the smile on his face matching the one she had worn the day Laura had bought the scarf.

"Oh, Laura, it's marvelous," Bill said, fingering the cloth. "Thank you so much."

"You're welcome, Bill," Laura said softly.

"And these gloves, Toni. How very thoughtful of you."

"I'm glad you like them, Bill," Toni said.

"Well, it seems we made short work of that," Eleanor said, laughing at the emptiness under the tree.

"Actually, I have a few more," Bill said, getting to his feet. "Be right back."

Disappearing into the bedroom, he emerged a minute later carrying a shopping bag. Returning to his place on the sofa, he reached into the bag and pulled out a small box wrapped in red foil. Handing it to Eleanor, he said, "This is for you."

"But you already gave me the sweater...and this cookbook."

"Just open it, Ellie."

Pursing her lips, Eleanor sighed and pulled apart the ribbon. Tearing away the wrapping, she held her breath as she opened the ring box.

"I hope you don't mind, but I took the liberty of looking through your jewelry box to find them. I had them cleaned and polished in hopes...in hopes that you'll wear them again," he said, pointing to the rings he had given her over thirty years before. "Of course, if you want new ones, I can—"

"Don't you dare," Eleanor scolded as tears appeared in her eyes. "These are the only rings I ever want from you."

"Does that mean yes?"

Pausing for a moment, she looked at her daughter. Seeing the happiness in Laura's eyes, Eleanor smiled back at William. "Yes."

"*Woohoo!*" Bill shouted, pulling Eleanor into his arms.

Before she knew what was happening, Eleanor found herself locked in a passionate kiss, and momentarily she forgot where she was, but as the kiss began to deepen, she came to her senses. Freeing herself from Bill's embrace, she said, "William, sweetheart, we have guests."

"Oh...oh...of course," he said, quickly glancing at Toni and Laura. "Sorry, I guess I got a bit excited."

"No problem, Bill," Toni said, smiling as she picked up the empty wine bottle. "But I think this calls for some more wine. I'm going to go grab another bottle and get a quick fag. Be right back."

"Not yet," Bill said, reaching into the bag by his side. Handing Toni a small box, he said, "This is for you."

"But you got me the—"

"Why is it that all the women in this house believe themselves only deserving of one gift, eh? Now, don't argue with me, Toni. Just open the present."

With Laura looking over her shoulder, Toni did as asked. Tearing away the silver paper, she discovered a small blue jewelry box, and opening the lid, she peered inside at the gold and silver necklace it contained.

Moving from the sofa, Bill knelt on the floor in front of her as she gazed at the gift. "The gold part is the Trinity Knot, also known as the Celtic love knot. The silver design behind it is a thistle, our national flower. Legend has it that when the Vikings were about to attack a Scottish castle, one stepped on a thorny thistle, and his cry of pain alerted the Scots inside of his existence, thus saving the castle." When Toni raised her eyes to meet his, Bill said, "It protected the Scottish, and my hopes are that it will protect you, lass. That it will act as a talisman, so that smile you wear so well will continue to shine."

Toni's eyes filled with tears, and removing the necklace from the box, she placed it in his hand. "Will you?"

Bill's chest swelled with pride and his face glowed with a light that came from his heart. "I'd be honored." Getting to his feet, he walked around the sofa, and after fastening the silver clasp, he leaned down and placed a light kiss on the top of Toni's head. "May it protect you for forever and a day."

Returning to the bag, Bill pulled out the remaining present. Handing it to Laura, he said, "Last...but certainly not least."

Knowing better than to argue the gift, Laura smiled politely as she quickly unwrapped the present, and when she saw a delicate gold dress watch, her eyes opened wide.

"We both know that it's impossible for me to go back in time and right the wrongs I've made," Bill said quietly. "What I hope is that over the coming years, you'll allow me the time to try. The time to...to show you just how much I truly love you and how proud I am to say you're my daughter. I'm sure you don't think I have a right to feel that way, but I can't help it...I do."

Laura listened to his words, and staring at the watch she could feel tears forming. Raising her eyes, she was about to tell him that she loved him, when an idea popped into her head. Quickly regrouping, Laura said, "It's beautiful, Bill. Thank you for your sentiments, and...um...well, all I can say is that we'll see what happens. Okay?"

***

"We'll see what *happens*!"

"Sshhh, they'll hear you."

"I don't bloody care," Toni barked, closing the bedroom door. "Your father poured his heart out to you down there, and all you could think of saying is *we'll see what happens*?"

Single-minded, Laura ignored Toni's rant as she headed to the other bedroom, and by the time Toni caught up with her, Laura had opened almost every drawer in the room.

Staring in disbelief at the mayhem Laura had caused in only a few seconds, Toni said, "What the *hell* are you doing?"

"Looking for something."

"I can see that, but whatever it is, it can wait."

"No, it can't."

"Yes, it can," Toni said, grabbing Laura's arm. "Laura, you need to go down and talk to him."

"Tomorrow."

"No! Today...tonight...right *now*!"

"Toni, relax."

"I will not relax until you give me one bloody reason why you just treated him like that. He loves you, Laura, and we both know you love him."

"I do," Laura said, pulling her arm from Toni's grasp. "Now seriously, sweetheart, I really need to find something."

Stunned by Laura's admission of love, for a moment Toni just stood there with her mouth open. Watching as Laura continued to turn the room upside down, Toni's annoyance returned, and rolling her eyes, she stomped back to their bedroom.

"Found them!"

Hearing Laura's announcement, Toni's curiosity won out, and going back into the other room, she found Laura sitting on the bed. Seeing what she had finally found, it only took a moment for Toni to understand.

"So...what do you think?" Laura asked, looking up.

"I think it's the most brilliant bloody idea you've ever had."

CHAPTER FIFTY-FIVE

Hearing the first chirp of her alarm, Toni quickly reached over, quieted the clock and turned on the bedside lamp.

"Oh, that's just rude," Laura muttered as she snuggled closer. "Turn it off."

Smiling at her sleepy partner's pouting tone, Toni whispered, "And a Merry Christmas to you."

Without opening her eyes, Laura nuzzled her face into Toni's neck. "Merry Christmas, sweetheart. Now, let's go back to sleep."

"Last night, you said you wanted to get up early. Remember?"

Instantly, Laura was awake. "Shit! What time is it?"

"Relax, it's just after five. We have plenty of time."

Scrambling out of bed, Laura ran to the bathroom and before Toni could rub the sleep out of her eyes, Laura came rushing back out. "Are you going to help me?"

With a snort, Toni climbed out of bed. "Can I use the loo first?"

"Yes, but make it quick."

A few minutes later, they crept down the stairs. Doing their best to be quiet, it seemed the floorboards were conspiring against them, and with every step they took, the old oak squeaked under their feet. Tiptoeing over to Eleanor's bedroom, Toni listened for signs of life and then gave Laura a thumbs-up. Standing guard at the door in case anyone awoke, Toni watched as Laura ran to and fro, completing the task she had started the night before.

"What do you think?" Laura whispered.

Looking around the lounge, Toni grinned. "I think we should go back to bed. Come on."

Tiptoeing up the stairs, they returned to their bedroom, and after quietly latching the door, Toni let out a big yawn before climbing under the quilt. Waiting until Laura snuggled up against her, Toni reached for the lamp and said, "The way I see it, we still have at least two more hours of sleep coming to us."

Nestling close, Laura draped her leg over Toni's. "So I guess that means you're tired."

"Are you saying I shouldn't be?" Toni asked, giving Laura a sideways glance.

"It depends."

"On what?"

"Well, I thought maybe we could start our own tradition," Laura said, placing her hand on Toni's breast. "But it all depends on how sore you are because I wouldn't want to...*hurt* you."

Chuckling to herself, Toni pulled her hand away from the lamp, and within seconds, Laura was straddling her hips. Looking up at her lustful partner, Toni whispered, "Laura?"

"Yeah?"

"Hurt me...but do it quietly."

Smiling, Laura leaned in for a kiss, and as their lips met, the world stood still. Aches and pains were dissolved by love and need, and as fingers meshed, bodies molded, and Christmas morning was lost in the passion of two becoming one.

The squeaky bed frame made not a sound for their movements were slow and tender as fingers found flesh, and as clothing was discarded, smiles were born. Curves and swells were fondled and tasted, and kisses turned intoxicating as tongues, warm and moist, simply could not get enough.

With no need to rush, their rhythm was calculated and sensual, and when breathing eventually turned ragged and skin glistened with sweat, their eyes locked. Their carnal waltz was nearing its end as both could feel the quivers deep inside begin to build, and welcoming the inevitable, Toni sat up and Laura wrapped her legs around her waist. Each buried her face into the other's shoulder, and in silence, they gave themselves to it. The softest of moans slipped from their lips, and shuddering in each other's arms, they held on tight until the last spasm of rapture had passed.

Slowly, they parted, and after placing a feathery kiss on Laura's lips, Toni laid back and Laura quickly cuddled in alongside her. After covering their nakedness with the quilt, Toni whispered, "I'm really starting to like all these traditions of yours."

"Good to know," Laura murmured as she snuggled in even closer.

Leaning over, Toni flicked off the lamp and then kissed Laura on the top of her head. "Merry Christmas, darling."

"Merry Christmas, sweetheart."

***

"Merry Christmas," Bill said, waking Eleanor with a kiss.

Smiling, she breathed in his scent. "Merry Christmas, sweetheart. What time is it?"

"Half-seven, so if you want to make it to nine o'clock service, you'd best get up."

Giving him a quick kiss on the lips, Eleanor climbed out of bed and grabbed her robe. "I'll go brew some coffee if you want to shower first."

"We could shower together."

"Not if we want to make service on time. Now get moving. I'll make sure Laura's awake."

Shuffling out of the bedroom, Eleanor made her way through the darkened lounge, and flicking on the kitchen light, went about making a pot of coffee. Filling two mugs, she slowly made her way back to the bedroom, but halfway through the lounge, something caught her eye. Turning on a table lamp, she blinked to clear the spots...and then nearly dropped the coffee.

"Oh my," she whispered. Placing the mugs on a nearby table, Eleanor sat on the arm of the sofa as she looked around the room. After several minutes, she managed to stop her tears, and drying her eyes, she picked up the coffee and headed back to the bedroom.

"There you are," Bill said, stepping into his trousers. "I thought you got lost."

"Sorry, I got distracted," Eleanor said quietly.

"You okay?"

"I'm wonderful, but I forgot to wake up the girls. Care to go up and rap on their door?"

"Sure, no problem," Bill said as he fastened the last button on his shirt.

Taking his coffee, he kissed her quickly on the cheek before he left the room, and counting to ten, Eleanor took a deep breath and quietly followed him. As she expected, he hadn't made it far.

Standing only a few feet from the bedroom door, Bill had stopped in his tracks near a table displaying the first of many handmade Christmas cards…all of which were addressed to him.

Walking over to the nearest, he paused for only a moment before picking it up, and in an instant, his eyes filled with tears. Drawn in crayon on the front was a stick figure family of three standing under a disproportionate, blue Christmas tree. Smiling softly at the childish artwork, he held his breath as he opened the card. Inside, in letters sloppily written as if by a child, he read the words, *"Merry Christmas, Daddy."*

"Oh, Christ," he said, covering his mouth as tears rolled down his face. "Oh…dear…God."

Noticing Bill beginning to sway, Eleanor rushed over, and putting her arm around him, guided him to a chair. "I think you had better sit down for a minute."

"Did you know?" he asked.

"I had no idea," she said, sitting on the arm of the chair. "That's why it took me so long to get back to the bedroom. If I had walked in crying my eyes out, you wouldn't have been surprised."

Reaching out, he took another from the table. Similar to the first, it showed another family of three, but this time, instead of standing under a Christmas tree, they were surrounded by bunnies wearing red and green bows. Chuckling at the humor, he opened the card expecting to see more levity, but when he read the words *"I love you, Dad,"* written on the inside, he began to cry even harder.

Wrapping her arm around his shoulders, Eleanor pulled him close, and knowing no words were needed, she remained silent. Hearing a floorboard creak, she looked up to see Laura standing in the doorway, and smiling at her daughter, Eleanor mouthed the words "I love you" before returning her attention to William. Watching as he traced a misshapen bunny with his finger, she said, "I'd have to say she was never much of an artist."

Shaking his head, he sniffled back a tear. "It's the most beautiful card I've ever seen."

"I'm glad you like it, Dad."

Hearing the endearment he never thought he would hear, Bill wept openly. Looking up, he saw his daughter standing across the room, and taking a deep, ragged breath, he stood on shaky legs. It took only seconds to reach her, but when he did, Bill suddenly had no idea what to do.

Sensing his hesitation, Laura opened her arms. "Merry Christmas, Dad."

Bill fell into Laura's arms and held on tight. "Oh, Laura, I love you so much. I'm so sorry for what I did. I'm so sorry for walking away. Oh dear God, I love you so much. I love you so much."

Toni stood on the stairs, looking on with tears in her eyes. The night before, sitting on the edge of the bed, she had watched Laura draw trees of blue and orange and stick-figured people with curly hair and smiling faces. She had looked on with amusement while Laura, determined to make the cards appear as if written by a child, used her left hand to draw most, and when Toni read the sentiments inside, she cried, for Laura had finally spoken the words of her heart.

Catching Eleanor's eye, Toni motioned toward the kitchen, and with a nod, Eleanor quietly walked past the two people still hugging under the mistletoe.

As Toni headed to the coffeepot, Eleanor wiped a tear from her cheek. "Did you have anything to do with this?"

"No, it was Laura's idea. She spent half the night writing them...one for every year he missed," Toni said, pouring herself some coffee. "Do you want a cup?"

"Actually, if it's all the same to you, what I'd really like is a hug. That is, if you don't mind."

Toni put aside the coffee, and walking over, she wrapped her arms around Eleanor. "I don't mind at all, Eleanor. I don't mind at all."

***

Hearing the back door open, Toni smiled at Bill as he made his way to the bench, and unlike the first time they had met outside for a smoke, this time he didn't ask before sitting down next to her.

"They're going to start talking if we keep meeting like this," he said, pulling his pipe from his pocket.

"Sorry, Bill, you're not my flavor."

Grinning, he said, "Thanks for coming to morning service with us."

"You're welcome."

"You did rather well for it being so crowded."

"What did you think I'd do? Run, screaming in terror?"

"Wasn't sure," he said with a shrug. "But those blue-haired old ladies scare the shit out of me."

Throwing back her head, Toni burst out laughing. Taking a few moments to get herself under control, she said, "Thanks, I needed that."

"What do you mean?"

"Just a bit nervous about today. That's all."

"Oh? Can I ask why? It's not like you haven't met them all before, and if you're worried about Alice, don't be. She won't be here."

"What? Why?"

"Dorothy called this morning while you and Laura were getting ready for church. Alice decided that it was best that she spend the day alone with her girls, so they had their Christmas celebration last night. Emma, her oldest, is apparently asking a lot of questions and this will give Alice more time to talk to her without all of us being around."

"Shit," Toni said under her breath.

"Don't."

"Don't what?"

"Don't you dare blame yourself for her not being here today."

"Well, if it weren't for me—"

"If it weren't for you, none of us would know what kind of man Ron is, and Alice *and* her children would still be living with the son of a bitch. *You're* the reason they're not. *You're* the reason they're safe."

Toni flinched, her eyebrows drawing together as Bill's words nestled into the crevices of her mind, and then Laura's favorite phrase popped into her head. *Give me a reason.*

How many times had Toni asked herself why? How many times had she looked for the reason? Sitting alone in her cell, covered in bruises and blood, she had talked to God. She had asked him so many times—why? Why her? If she had made a left in her life, instead of a right, would things have been different? Would a no instead of a yes have changed her path so drastically that Alice and her children would have eventually felt the sting of Cameron's belt? Was this the reason Toni had been looking for, or only another question that would never be answered? Is there really a reason for everything?

"Are you okay, Toni?"

"Huh?"

"You have an odd look on your face."

"Oh, sorry...just thinking about something."

"Should I ask?"

With a snort, Toni shook her head. "Not unless you want to be confused."

"Hey, you two, Dorothy and Bernard just pulled up," Eleanor called from the back door.

"We're coming," Bill said, tapping what remained of the tobacco in his pipe into an empty planter. Offering his hand to Toni, he said, "Come on, time to greet the family."

Taking the last drag of her cigarette, Toni flicked it into the planter and took his hand. "I've got nothing to fear, right?"

"That depends," Bill said, looking her in the eye as she stood up.

"On what?"

"On whether they brought Myles or left him at home."

***

By the time Bill and Toni reached the front hall, Laura was busy hanging up Dorothy's coat while Eleanor carried bags filled with gifts into the lounge.

"Merry Christmas, Dot," Bill said, giving his niece a kiss on the cheek.

"Merry Christmas, Bill," she said, returning his affection. "Merry Christmas, Toni."

"Hi," Toni said, and then running her fingers through her hair, she sighed. "Um...I mean, Merry Christmas."

Sensing the woman's nervousness, Dorothy held out her hand and smiled. "With all that went on the other day, I don't believe we were ever properly introduced. Dorothy Montgomery-Smythe."

Pausing for only a moment, Toni shook the woman's hand. "Toni Vaughn."

Suddenly, the front door banged open and a little boy with curly red hair ran inside. Two steps behind was Bernard, and offering everyone a very quick "Merry Christmas," he continued to chase his son into the lounge.

"I'm afraid that's Myles," Dorothy said with a snicker as she picked up the infant carrier by her leg. "And this is Neville."

"And I'm going to snatch him away from you right now, if that's all right," Eleanor said returning to the group gathered by the door.

"Be my guest, Eleanor, but I warn you, he may be wet."

"I'll take my chances," she said, taking the carrier from Dorothy's hand. "We'll be in the lounge if you need us."

"Right, well, he's playing with my phone, so that should keep him quiet for a few minutes," Bernard said, coming back into the front hall. Placing his coat in Laura's outstretched hand, he smiled at Toni. "And how are you doing today?"

"I'm okay."

"Any problems breathing? Any coughing?"

"No, I feel fine."

Cocking his head to the side, he glanced at Laura for a moment, and when she nodded, he let out a breath. "Well, that's good to hear. You're a very lucky woman, Toni."

"Yes, I am," Toni said, taking a step in his direction. "I...I didn't get a chance to thank you for all you did the other day. I'm still a bit fuzzy on what actually happened, but Laura tells me you're one of the reasons I'm standing here today." Holding out her hand, Toni said, "And I just wanted to say thank you."

Bernard's face brightened to almost a blinding intensity as he took her hand. "You are very welcome, Toni. Very, very welcome." As the handshake ended, he noticed the bandage peeking out from under the sleeve of her shirt, and ever so gently, he touched the gauze. "I'd like to take a look at that today, if you don't mind."

"Stop being so grabby, Bernard. We have all day for that," Dorothy said with a wave of her hand. "I don't know about either of you, but I could use a cup of coffee. Kitchen's through here, isn't it?" Not waiting for an answer, she sashayed past everyone and disappeared through the doorway.

Smiling at his wife's overt attempt at haughtiness, Bernard shook his head. "I'd better go check on Myles."

"I think I'll join you," Bill chimed in as he headed into the lounge. "The way these two are talking, I seriously need to start getting used to being around children."

"Laura, could you come here for a moment?" Eleanor called from the lounge.

"Sure," Laura said. Stopping at Toni's side, she touched her hand. "You going to be okay if I leave you alone?"

"I'm fine. Go see what your mum wants. I'm going to get some more coffee."

"All right, sweetheart. Call me if you need me."

Dorothy was just filling a cup when Toni came into the kitchen, and offering it to Toni, she said, "I'm sorry about Bernard going all doctor on you. He truly does mean well. As a matter of fact, between you and me, ever since the other night he's been a changed man."

"How so?" Toni asked, taking the coffee.

"It's been a long time since he's actually had to *practice* medicine, but after what happened the other day...well, let's just say I wouldn't be surprised if before too long he turns in his executive office for a white coat and a stethoscope."

For the first time, Toni noticed Dorothy's appearance. Clothes designed by men with hyphenated names had been replaced by a casual dark green sweater over straight-legged jeans. Her red hair, that two days earlier had been piled high atop her head, was now hanging down her back in a ponytail, and instead of a dozen bracelets of gold jangling on her wrist, only one small gold chain could be seen.

"How come I think that you're okay with that?" Toni asked.

"Probably, because I am," she said, taking a sip of coffee. "Don't get me wrong. I always enjoyed going to all the conferences and parties, but after the other day, I started thinking about a few things. I've decided that being a good mother is more important than being on the cover of society magazines. I have no idea what made Ron the way he is, but I'm going to make sure that *my* boys grow up knowing right from wrong. I have no doubt that poor Myles is going to have a problem learning that he no longer rules the household, but I think I have enough time to correct the mistakes I've made with him."

"Is he really that—"

Toni was interrupted by the three-year-old boy racing through the kitchen. Circling the center island, he ran between her legs and then his mother's, all the while giggling and laughing as he held his father's mobile in his hand.

"Myles, give me back my phone," Bernard demanded, running into the kitchen.

"I thought you said he could play with it," Dorothy said, watching with amusement as her son darted past his father and ran through the house.

"I forgot to lock the bloody keypad, and I'm fairly certain he just called someone in Japan!" Bernard said before quickly running after his son.

Both women laughed at the man's predicament, and as Dorothy refilled her coffee cup, Toni walked to the cooker and checked on the soup that had been simmering all morning.

Leaning against the counter, Dorothy studied the woman for a minute. "So, Peggy tells me that you and Laura plan to have children. Yes?"

Looking up, Toni smiled. "Yes, Laura wants children."

"And how about you?"

"I want what Laura wants. I actually never thought about having kids before...um...when I was younger, and honestly, I don't know the first thing about raising a child, but I'm willing to learn."

"Well, I should warn you that when we were growing up, Laura always said she wanted to have a house full of kids. Back then, I think the magic number was six."

Toni raised her eyes to Dorothy's for only a second, but it was enough to make Dorothy erupt into laughter. "Oh, you poor woman."

Tickled by the woman's reaction, Toni said, "Well, between you and me, I'm hoping she'll come to her senses."

"And if she doesn't?"

"Then I guess we'll have six," Toni said without missing a beat. "Whatever Laura wants, whatever I can give her...I will."

"Then how about giving me a kiss?" Laura asked from the doorway.

Instantly, Toni's face split into a grin, and placing the lid back on the soup, she casually strolled over and kissed Laura tenderly on the lips.

Rolling her eyes at the sight of the two women embracing, Dorothy said, "I've accepted the fact that you're gay, Laura, but could you keep the snogging sessions to a minimum until I've had at least another two or three cups of coffee?"

***

"Thanks for helping me make dessert," Laura said, closing the refrigerator door. "We tried to get everything done yesterday, but we ran out of time."

"No worries," Dorothy said, tidying the counter. "A Christmas without Crannachan just wouldn't be Christmas."

"I totally agree."

"It's a shame Alice won't be here. It's her favorite."

Laura frowned, and after pausing for a moment, she asked, "Dot, how's she doing?"

"She's actually doing okay, all things considered."

"Has she heard from Ron?"

"No, not so much as a peep, and if he does try to contact her, we'll know it."

"Why?"

"Because she had her mobile disconnected, and we've moved her into our guest house. Since our property is gated, Ron would have to go through us to see her...and we won't allow that to happen. She's absolutely terrified of him, Laura, and since she can't even go back to work because he could find her there, this gives her a place to call her own and as much time as she needs to get things sorted without having to worry about money or bills."

"Oh, shit! I never even thought about her job. Dot, if there's anything I can do. If there's anything she needs—"

"Laura, relax. You're acting like you're somehow responsible for this and you're not," Dorothy said, placing her hands on her hips. "We all love Alice and she's not going to want for anything. I guarantee it. It's just going to take some time."

"Yeah, I suppose, but she should be here. I just feel bad that—"

"Trust me, Laura. She's where she wants to be today, and if she found out that you were moping about, she'd feel dreadful. Now please, let's just enjoy the day because that's what Alice would want us to do. All right?"

Thinking for a minute, Laura said, "Okay, but do you think she'd mind if we called her later?"

"I was planning on it," Dorothy said as she picked up her coffee cup. Seeing the dregs that remained, she glanced at her watch and then back at her cousin. "You know, Laura...it's almost noon."

Laura looked at the coffee pot and then at the bottles of wine lined up on the counter. "Red or white?"

"White, I think. It's still early," Dorothy said, pouring what remained of her coffee in the sink.

A few minutes later, with glasses of Chardonnay in hand, they sat at the kitchen table. Sipping her wine, Dorothy watched as Laura's eyes drifted to the woman sitting outside on the patio smoking a cigarette.

"So, when exactly did you decide to take a walk on the wild side?" Dorothy asked, breaking the silence.

"Sorry?"

Pointing out the window, Dorothy said, "I seem to remember that you used to like them a bit more...well, masculine, shall we say."

"Things change, I guess," Laura said with a shrug.

"You go from straight to gay and all you can say is *things change*?"

"I fell in love with her, Dot. I didn't plan it, it just happened, but I'm happy. Actually, I'm beyond happy."

"I can see that," Dorothy said. Noticing the ring on Laura's finger, she said, "And that's quite a marvelous ring you've got there. Congratulations, by the way. Peggy told me."

"Thanks."

"I hope we'll be invited."

"Of course, but don't expect anything lavish. It's going to be a small wedding."

"You used to want a big one."

"True, but I also used to want a man."

"Good point," Dorothy said, clinking her glass against Laura's before she took a sip. Glancing out the window at the woman sitting on the bench, Dorothy said, "Can I ask you something?"

"Sure."

"Toni's been through hell, hasn't she?"

"Yeah, she has," Laura said softly.

"Well, you know Bernard knows a lot of doctors—"

"Thanks, but she's already seeing a doctor. My friend, Abby, is a psychologist."

"I was actually talking about plastic surgery. It could help cover up some of those scars on her back." Seeing Laura's eyes widen, Dorothy said, "I saw them the other day. Everyone did."

"Oh, I forgot about that," Laura said, slouching in her chair.

Again, Dorothy's eyes were drawn to Toni. She looked so normal...so intact, like the only weight on her shoulders was from the jacket she wore, but Dorothy had heard the story, and she had seen the scars. A vision of the buckle flashed through her mind, and squeezing her eyes shut for a second, she willed it away. "I can't begin to imagine how she survived that," she said in a whisper.

The smallest of smiles appeared on Laura's face. "She's a lot stronger than she appears at times...and quite stubborn."

Knowing her cousin all too well, Dorothy let out a laugh. "Oh, I'd love to be a fly on the wall of *your* house when you two get into a row."

Before Laura could speak, the back door opened and Toni came inside. Seeing the two women sitting at the table, she grinned. "Let me guess. Swapping recipes?"

"No, we were talking about you if you must know," Laura said, getting to her feet to give Toni a quick peck on the cheek.

"An intriguing subject, am I?" Toni asked, looking at Dorothy.

Pressing her tongue against the inside of her cheek, a devilish look came into Dorothy's eyes. "Well, we haven't had time to get to the really juicy parts, so I'll have to get back to you on that one."

***

Less than an hour later, Nancy, Peggy, Stephen and their two sons, Paul and Gavin, arrived. Unlike their out-of-control cousin, Myles, the two little boys stood quietly at their parents' sides as all the introductions were made. Politely giving small kisses and hugs to everyone, when their father suggested that they play in the lounge, they eagerly took his hand as he led the way.

Waiting in the doorway, Peggy watched as Stephen and the boys began assembling a new train set, and then catching the eyes of her sister and cousin, she gestured toward the kitchen. A few minutes later, the three women sat around the kitchen table enjoying a few minutes of quiet time.

As Dorothy refilled her wine, she glanced at Laura and unable to contain herself any longer, she blurted, "So...what's it like?"

Laura's cheeks heated immediately. Looking back and forth between her two cousins, their smiles said it all. "Please tell me you're not asking for details," Laura groaned.

"Well, I'd ask you to draw us a picture, but after seeing your attempt at artwork on those cards in the lounge, I doubt that would help," Dorothy said, sending a wink in her sister's direction.

"Dorothy, stop, you're embarrassing her," Peggy said, trying to hold back her grin. "Besides, from what Laura has told me, Toni's been gay a lot longer than her. If Laura doesn't want to share, perhaps Toni will. I mean, she probably knows lots of...um...*things*. Don't you think?"

The memory of Toni's lesson in the bathtub came rushing back, and sitting up straight, Laura blurted, "Oh, no, you don't."

Dorothy quickly glanced at her sister and winked. "Hit a nerve, did we, Laura?"

"You two need to behave. I've never asked you to give me any intimate details about your partners."

"Our partners were men. Yours is a woman, and that's new and different, and...*interesting*," Dorothy said, leaning closer.

"What's interesting?" Toni asked as she came into the kitchen.

"Nothing, sweetheart," Laura said quickly. "Nothing at all."

Dismissing Laura with a wave of her hand, Dorothy said, "We were just asking Laura what it was like to be with you, and she won't tell us."

For a moment, Toni's eyebrows knitted, but when she saw the playful looks on the faces of Laura's cousins, she held back her smile and sauntered over to the table.

"Let me guess. You want to know the secrets of lesbian love," she said in the most provocative tone she could muster. Resting her hands on Laura's shoulders, she looked at the two very eager women sitting at the table, and placing a soft kiss on the top of Laura's head, Toni purred, "Darling, tell them whatever you wish. I'm sure they'd be more than interested in knowing about bathtubs and soap...and the like."

Laura had neglected to use one word when describing her cousins to Toni...and that word was tenacious. Watching as her partner nonchalantly strolled back to the counter to refill her wine, Laura thought about the implications of Toni's statement, and her cheeks darkened to their deepest. Refusing to look in her cousins' direction, Laura kept her eyes on Toni, hoping and praying that she would come to her rescue, but when Laura saw the smirk Toni was wearing, she slouched in her chair. She was a goner.

After corking the bottle, Toni looked up, and it was all she could do not to burst out laughing. Three slack-jawed faces were staring back at her, one of which was now the darkest shade of red imaginable. Meandering over to the table, she placed another light kiss on Laura's head, winked at Dorothy and Peggy and then left the room without saying a word.

Seconds later, Dorothy and Peggy turned to Laura and spoke as one. "Bathtubs?"

Entering the lounge, Toni smiled at the life it held. Three little boys were stretched out on the floor near the Christmas tree, playing with their trains and toys as they chattered away. Bernard and Bill relaxed on the sofa sipping their whisky while Neville slept between them, and Eleanor and Nancy sat near the front windows, tittering at the children's antics.

Near the fireplace stood Stephen, and watching as he tended to the fire, Toni set her jaw, filled her lungs and strode across the room.

They had exchanged greetings an hour earlier when he had arrived, so when Stephen turned around to find Toni standing behind him, he grinned. "Hey there."

Wincing at the sight of the bruises on his face, she asked, "How you doing?"

"Me? I'm fine," Stephen said, rubbing his bruised jaw. "This will be gone in a few days and then all we'll have left is the memory."

"Well, I don't remember much, but I do know you saved my life. I'm...I'm not sure how I'll ever be able to repay you for that, but...but I want to thank you for doing it."

"You're welcome," Stephen said, holding out his hand.

Toni paused for a moment as she stared at his outstretched hand, and then raising her eyes, she said, "I've got problems."

Smiling, Stephen shrugged. "Don't we all."

"A lot of them have to do with men."

"Understandable. Some of us are pains in the arse."

Grinning, Toni said, "You're not."

"I'm not so sure about that. After all, you really don't know me that well."

"I think I know all I need to know."

"Yeah?"

Toni's eyes locked on Stephen's, and taking a step closer, she wrapped her arms around him. Kissing him lightly on the cheek, she whispered, "I know I wouldn't be alive if it weren't for you. I know you risked your own life to save mine, and I know...I know that the only reason you had for doing what you did was because it's who you are...and I thank God for that."

"Not switching sides, are you?" Peggy asked, waddling into the lounge.

With a laugh, Toni released her hold on Stephen, and blinking back her tears, she looked in Peggy's direction. "Wouldn't think of it."

Peggy shuffled over, her face a wee bit rosier than it had been earlier and her eyes sparkling with humor. "After what Laura just told me, I don't blame you."

***

Gifts were exchanged and snacks were nibbled, and when the snow began to fall again, children and adults alike, scrambled for their boots and mittens.

Walking into the lounge, Nancy smiled at the disarray of Christmas. Bows were scattered here and there, and bits of ribbon littered the floor. Wads of wrapping paper having not yet met their demise in the hearth had been crammed into boxes, and toys assembled by frazzled fathers, waited for their owners to return.

"Here you go, sweetheart," Nancy said, handing Peggy a cup of tea. "Are the boys still outside?"

Amused that her mother had grouped the young and old under one heading, Peggy chuckled. "Yes, but I'm not sure who was more excited about building a snowman, Stephen, Bill or the kids."

"Don't forget about Bernard. He seemed to have a bit of pep in his step also."

"I think that had something to do with the fact that Myles can't run very fast in the snow."

"Yes, you're probably right," Nancy said with laugh.

Breathing in deep the aroma of turkey wafting through the house, Peggy said, "Dinner smells delicious."

"Yes, it does," Nancy said quietly.

"Do they need any help?"

"No, between Eleanor, Laura, Toni and Dorothy, they've got it all under control. Trust me."

Staring at her mother for a moment, Peggy leaned a little closer. "You know you need to tell them."

"Yes, but I don't need to tell them today."

"You were amazing yesterday," Peggy said softly.

"Was I?"

"Yes. When they demanded to question everyone, and you picked up the phone and called the Chief Constable, I thought I was going to die."

"Gordon was your father's best friend, and after being married to a policeman for so many years, I know their procedures. I wasn't pressing charges against Ron for the damage to my home. All I was doing was providing them with possible evidence, and until they get the test results and find Ron, this is all speculative anyway. There was no need to bring anyone else into this yet, and Gordon agreed. This isn't about what Ron did to Toni. It's about what that bastard did to all those poor women. So, if the blood evidence on the belt ties Ron to the victims, everything else is moot."

"I hope so for Toni's sake."

"Me, too, sweetheart," Nancy said with a nod. "Me, too."

***

Late in the afternoon, they feasted on Christmas dinner, and while there was barely elbow room around the table, no one seemed to care. Over the years, Bill had spent many a Christmas dinner at his sister's house, watching as his brother-in-law or his nieces' husbands had served the Christmas turkey, so when Eleanor put the carving set in his hand, Bill couldn't contain his smile. Proudly, he placed thick slices on plates as Eleanor spooned on piles of stuffing and passed around homemade cranberry relish. Glasses were filled and refilled with wines of both red and white as laughter filled the room, and the sounds of a family rejoicing in their new-found love for one another grew loud as they spoke of Christmases long since gone.

After one quick glance at Eleanor, Bill stood up and tapped his knife on a glass. "I'd like to propose a toast."

The room went quiet, and while everyone reached for their goblets, Bill sorted out his thoughts. Looking around the table, his eyes stopped when they met Eleanor's, and clearing his throat, he said, "I stand amongst you a man enlightened. Never in my dreams had I allowed myself to believe that I'd ever have my Eleanor's love again, but I do...and I thank God for it. She has forgiven me for my blunders, my youthful arrogance, and most of all, for my stupidity." Raising his glass, he said, "To the woman I love with all my heart, my dearest, Eleanor."

Taking a sip, he waited until everybody else did the same, and then gazing at his daughter, he said, "To my Laura..." Stopping abruptly, Bill hung his head as he tried to choke back his tears. "Okay, this one is going to be a bit tougher, I think," he murmured.

No one moved or said a word, but around the table, eyes grew moist.

Taking a deep breath, Bill looked up and gazed at the woman sitting at the other end of the table. "To my daughter, Laura," he said, holding up his glass. "It's so hard for me to believe that I had anything to do with your being in this world, because in my eyes, you are perfect...and I am most assuredly not. You are more than any father could ever hope for, and I love you with all my heart. I thank you for allowing me to become your father again, and I promise to never give you a reason to regret it."

Bill smiled softly as his daughter wiped away a tear, and after taking a sip of wine, his eyes shifted to the woman flanked by Eleanor and Laura.

"Now we come to you, lass," he said, his voice betraying him as it dropped into a shaky whisper. "As a man, I think myself strong, but I am weak compared to you. And not to speak out of turn, but I'm sure we all wonder how you survived...and I'm sure we all thank God it wasn't us.

"At times, we complain about our lives, about our hard days at work or at home, but we have no idea what *hard* is...do we? Well, at least we didn't until we met you.

"You've given us all a reason to cherish those we love. You've given us all a reason to complain a wee bit less about life's troubles, and you've given us all a reason to raise our glasses to you...and to thank God for bringing you into our lives."

Raising his glass, in a tear-filled breath, Bill said, "To Toni...for giving us a reason."

EPILOGUE

Six months later, standing near a boulder atop a hill overlooking a field of heather, they were married.

One, in simple black trousers with a peasant shirt of white waited nervously for her bride to arrive. Fidgeting with the sleeves of her blouse, it wasn't until Toni saw the steely glare of her best man that she stilled and waited like all the others for Laura to appear.

He had been the man who had saved her life, and now he protected in his hand bands of gold that would be exchanged in only a few minutes. Giving Toni a quick wink, Stephen looked to the family and friends seated in white folding chairs a few feet away. Locking eyes with his wife, he mouthed the words "I love you" and then glanced at their infant son, Anthony, cradled in her arms. The child began to whimper as if on cue, and Stephen rolled his eyes, chuckling under his breath as he turned back to the woman standing next to him. Seeing the look in Toni's eyes, Stephen followed her gaze, and he couldn't stop himself from uttering, "Wow."

Wearing a flowing white dress and holding a bouquet of roses and thistle close to her bosom, arm-in-arm with her father, Laura slowly made her way up the hill. In her shoe was a sixpence, put there by her father as was the Scottish tradition, and over her shoulder was a sash of MacLeod tartan. She kept her eyes on Toni, never once looking to make sure her footing was sound, and without one stumble, Laura came to a stop a few feet away from the woman she loved.

Bill gazed at his daughter for a moment before leaning over to kiss her on the cheek. Breathing deep, he took Laura's hand and placed it in Toni's. "I give to you my daughter's hand, and she gives to you her heart." Taking the sash from Laura, he said, "These are our colors...our tartan, and now, they are yours."

Draping it over Toni's shoulder, Bill placed a soft kiss on her cheek, and taking a ragged breath, he stepped back.

They had agreed upon a simple service, and after the pastor had spoken his words, it was time for them to speak their own. Smiling softly at the nervousness she saw in Toni's eyes, Laura gave her hand a squeeze, silently asking permission to go against plan and speak first, and seeing Toni nod, Laura took a ring from Stephen's open hand and placed it on Toni's finger.

"With this ring, I pledge to you my love...forever and always. I promise to be your wife, your lover and your friend. I promise to be there for you in sickness and in health, through steps forward and backward, through nerves and nightmares, through insecurities and fears. I will never falter in my love for you, for you complete me, Antoinette...and you are the reason I breathe."

Toni blinked back her tears as Laura slipped the ring on her finger. She knew her knees were trembling badly, and even though she had practiced a hundred times the words she wanted to say, when Toni looked into Laura's eyes, her mind went blank.

Toni took a deep breath and quickly followed it by another as her heart began to race, but when she glanced at the wedding ring on her finger, her anxieties disappeared. Even though most of the words still escaped her, she smiled at Stephen, and when he opened his hand, Toni plucked the ring from his palm. Slipping it on Laura's finger, she said, "With this ring, I give you my love, my heart and my soul...for as long as we both shall live. I promise to be your wife, your lover, your friend, and the mother to your children no matter how many you decide we should have." Toni paused for a moment, and offering Laura a weak grin, she said, "I had a lot of things I wanted to say here today, but it seems that I've forgotten most of them."

"That's okay, sweet—"

"Darling...I'm not through," Toni said softly.

Laura blushed as a titter of amusement rolled through the guests like a wave. Biting her lip, she silently apologized to her soon-to-be wife with a roll of her eyes.

GIVE ME A REASON

After giving Laura's hand a reassuring squeeze, Toni said, "No one really knows the reasons why things happen, but if I were asked to go back and repeat my past, I would do it in a heartbeat because it led me here to you. Like I said, I've forgotten most of what I wanted to say, but there's one thing I need you to know. A few months ago, I lay dead in the snow...and *you* are the reason I came back."

Tears flowed freely from family and friends alike as the two women kissed. Although protocol dictated that their first kiss be chaste, Laura couldn't resist taking it one step further. When they finally came up for air, they were greeted by loud whistles and applause, and joining hands, they walked toward their guests, both wearing smiles that bested the brilliance of the sun.

***

Running his finger down his face, he traced the scars again. It was now a habit for they were a reminder of his one mistake. He had been so careful, or so he thought, but a heavyset woman with a penchant for bright colors and tabloid newspapers had been his undoing, and he was now paying the price.

Preferring to draw the attention of their readers to economy woes, politicians caught with their pants down and the latest celebrity to overdose on drugs, most publishers had buried the articles about murdered prostitutes in the bowels of their newspapers. Crimes against the dregs of society, as far as they were concerned, were a waste of good ink...but the editors of *The Weekly Sun* felt differently.

Built on sensationalism and gossip, their pages were filled with out-of-focus photographs of celebrities at their worst, reports of aliens, and articles about unsolved mysteries, both new and old. The murders of prostitutes were still not worthy of headlines, but the gory details of the crimes had been enough to warrant a column or two not far from the front page. With their no-holds-barred approach and a plethora of anonymous tipsters, even though photographs of the corpses were never released, their writers had managed with mere words to keep more than one reader from falling asleep at night. From the horrific conditions of the bodies, to the way the murder weapon had left three almost identical marks across the skin of the victims, no detail, no matter how horrid, had been left out. Quotes from experts stating that the victims appeared to have been brutally raped before and after their demise had been printed in bold and italics, and it was suggested to the women who worked the streets in and around Glasgow that they dye their hair blonde...for he liked it dark.

When the first body was found, swollen and misshapen in an abandoned building, the police had labeled it a random killing. Four months later, the skeletal remains of another woman were discovered in a deserted warehouse, and the same conclusion was reached. Unnamed, unclaimed and unidentifiable, both had been buried in pauper's graves on the edge of town, but when Jane Doe number three turned up, the police realized the killings were not random...they were serial.

A small task force was formed to work the case, but all the murders had taken place in sections of the city where people made it a habit of looking the other way. With no witnesses or clues, other than the strange, triple-track wounds on the victims' bodies, after months of investigation the police reached a dead end. But a few days before Christmas, in the wee hours of the morning, a call came into the London Road police station in Glasgow from a woman stating she knew the identity of the man *The Weekly Sun* had labeled "The Red Light Slasher."

Believing that the woman had consumed a bit too much Christmas cheer, at first the police simply jotted down a few notes. Ever so politely, they smiled into the phone and listened to her story, but when she made mention of a belt, its buckle fashioned with three prongs on the back...the police stopped smiling.

Undaunted by the weather, even though it took the two Detective Inspectors nearly four hours to travel to Nancy Shaw's home, it was time well spent. Lying on the floor in her lounge was a weapon covered in the blood of a man who more than once had left his DNA on a brutalized victim.

It took nearly two weeks to find him, but when they did, he wasn't what they had expected. Courteous and polite, Cameron went with them willingly. He was smart enough to know the beast could not be seen, so keeping it hidden behind compliance and a gentlemanly air, he moved through the months of remand, trial and imprisonment with not so much as a harsh word entered into his file.

It was the way it had to be. He was smart. Bide his time and conduct himself properly and his sentence could be reduced, and so far time had been on his side. There had been ten, but only four had been discovered before the ravages of exposure and rodents had erased the scars of a buckle and the semen of a monster.

Sentenced to life, all believed he would live out his days behind stone and steel, listening to men bellow about their aches, their pains and their victims, but he had other plans. Yes, he would spend years behind bars, but that would give him the time he needed to control the beast...and to think about her.

Black hair and eyes of cinnamon were not easily forgotten, and if he had his way, he would see those eyes again.

The End

ABOUT THE AUTHOR

Lyn Gardner began her career writing fan fiction. In 2009, she sat down and wrote a story with no expectations other than to entertain. Three years later, at the insistence of her readers, and after listening to their praise as well as their prods, she published her first book - Ice.

Now a multi-published author, Lyn lives in the sunny state of Florida where she enjoys playing a round of golf every now and then...that is, when her muse isn't whispering in her ear.

You can find out more about the author by visiting her website or her blog, or feel free to follow her on Twitter or Facebook...and by all means, say hello if you'd like.

Blog: www.lyngardner.blogspot.com
Website: www.lyngardner.net
Facebook: https://www.facebook.com/#!/lyn.gardner.587
Twitter: @LynGardner227

Other Works by Lyn Gardner

Ice

Mistletoe

Made in the USA
San Bernardino, CA
22 August 2015